SURPRISED BY BEAUTY

Surprised by Beauty

A Listener's Guide to the Recovery of Modern Music

~

REVISED AND EXPANDED EDITION

By Robert R. Reilly
with Jens F. Laurson

Foreword by Ted Libbey

IGNATIUS PRESS   SAN FRANCISCO

Para Blanca, la verdadera música

[In] sound itself, there is a readiness to be ordered by the spirit, and this is seen at its most sublime in music.

— Max Picard

Contents

I. THE COMPOSERS

II. TALKING WITH THE COMPOSERS

Foreword to the First Edition

Shortly before the turn of the last century, in an essay titled "Criticism", the great American writer Henry James penned a few lines that go to the very crux of what it means to be a critic and to write about the arts. "The critical sense is so far from frequent," he wrote, "that it is absolutely rare, and the possession of the cluster of qualities that minister to it is one of the highest distinctions. . . . In this light one sees the critic as the real helper of the artist, a torch-bearing outrider, the interpreter, the brother."

"Absolutely rare"—with those two words James drove home the point, as valid now as it was then, that real criticism is profound and penetrating, an art in itself; that it requires vision, a keen mind, vast experience, and a wealth of knowledge, along with an understanding of the artistic enterprise and a sense of the sublime. It's dispiriting that so little of what is written about the arts today actually measures up to this standard and that so few of those who write about the arts have torches capable of lighting the way. Among those few, Robert Reilly certainly stands out. Indeed, in many ways he epitomizes the kind of critic James was writing about. Yet I wonder what James himself would have thought of the 20th century, of which he witnessed only the first 15 years. In particular, I wonder what James would have made of a century in which, for quite a few creators, art ceased to be what he said it should be: a search for "hard latent value". In so many ways, 20th-century art—and music stands right up there at the head of the parade—was a search for systems and procedures whose purpose was precisely to relieve the artist of any obligation to be concerned with value. And it was a contrived search at that.

Much of it was about poking holes in the past—or as one rather notable European stage director put it a few years ago, about jamming "spokes into the wheel to test the quality of the material". Because the 20th century was a time of political and social chaos, of personal alienation and suffering, many 20th-century artists (and critics) reasoned that contemporary art, in order to be valuable, had to somehow reflect that. Art had to be ugly because life was ugly. Indeed, it was the artist's duty not to create the illusion of a clean reality but to show how polluted reality is and thus to provide an opportunity for purification.

In a society shot through with vulgarity and loudness, music should be vulgar and loud, or at the very least, it should lack beauty.

One can sympathize with this view up to a point. Of course composers and other artists should be free to jam spokes in the wheel. Indeed, there are times when they must do so, as Beethoven did. The arts are one of our best protections against dogmatism of any stripe and a powerful weapon against complacency. But showing us how rotten reality is and how twisted we are, is not their sole purpose. Nor can it be said that the pursuit of complexity for its own sake is a valid aim. Unfortunately, that seems to be what much 20th-century art was about. Process became synonymous with progress, and a vast array of methodologies—artificially contrived systems and procedures based on mechanical or mathematical concepts—took the place of straightforward communication.

Music, by its very nature, was an easy victim of this trend toward reductionism. But some composers resisted, and it is their work that is the subject of this book. In the pages that follow, Robert Reilly redraws the map of modern music. He shows that during the 20th century—in the midst of what in so many ways was a meltdown of Western culture —there were composers who stood firm and wrote music that was bold and original yet also rooted in the emotions, music that was not only interesting but moving and beautiful. Again and again, what it took to write music like that was courage—the courage of an outrider to hold a torch against the darkness and light the way for others. It is the same kind of courage often needed to stick by one's faith in today's world.

The true artist of any era must seek to give pleasure, to create things expressive of beauty and truth. As we know, the truth can sometimes be troubling. It can also be powerful, dramatic, moving, consoling, and celebratory. This concept of the artist's mission was what guided Mozart and Michelangelo. And in their hands artistic expression became, in effect, praise of creation and of the Creator. As this book makes clear, the best music of the 20th century also, in spite of the odds, succeeded in doing that. It developed our capacity for feeling, deepened our compassion, and furthered our quest for and understanding of what Aristotle called "the perfect end of life". In short, it drew us closer not to mere "reality" but to God.

—TED LIBBEY
Author of *The NPR Guide to Building
a Classical CD Collection*

Preface to the Second Edition

Contemporary music, by which I mean music of the 20th and 21st centuries, has been my preoccupation. When discussions began about the possible content of the first edition of *Surprised by Beauty* (2002), it turned out that the majority of my columns for *Crisis* magazine from the previous ten years had been about this era. This was not the product of any design on my part but simply reflected my desire to understand what was going on around me. More than 14 years later, there is even more to try to understand.

What I had heard, in part, was lots of noise, and I was intrigued as to how it had gotten itself passed off as music. In an interview with British music critic Martin Anderson, German composer Claus Ogerman said, "Look back at Donaueschingen (the German Mecca of the avant-garde), where they've been playing modern music since 1923 or '24—they've premiered 2,000 compositions there, of which none has left any mark. It's as if you had a factory producing things that weren't working." The remark is more amusing than accurate, but I have been fascinated as to why almost an entire century devoted itself to producing music that doesn't work and even more curious about the relatively unknown music written during that same period that does work. Let's call it, as does one music professor, "the *other* 20th century".

I wondered how the composers of beauty had sustained themselves during a period of such confusion and downright hostility. That was the subject of my book, and it is now, thankfully, an old story. The younger generations of composers, who had had enough of the enforced sterility of mandatory dodecaphony (also known as 12-tone technique, the composition method devised by composer Arnold Schoenberg), and they decisively rebelled against and repelled the forces of noise. Even if you are a music lover—like many I know—you probably have not come all the way out of the bunker into which you retreated to survive the 20th-century assault of noise. But it's okay: The war is over. You can come out now. The army of noise emptied its lungs screaming its loudest and then whimpered away.

Today's composers have returned to tonality, melody, and gorgeous harmonies. Beginning in the last several decades of the 20th century, in fact, there has been a musical renaissance both in this country and in

Europe. In a small way, this book brings attention to it. Throughout, it explores the nature of the crisis through which modern music passed and the sources of its recovery.

In the 1980s, the *New York Times* Arts and Leisure section featured a headline that propounded the following artistic dilemma: "Beauty or the Pain of Truth?" The question was obviously loaded, but it is worth examining for what it reveals about the cultural pathology of our recent past. There is an implied syllogism in the title that runs something like this: truth is painful; beauty is not painful; therefore, beauty is not true. This line of thought invites the ultimate conclusion that truth is ugly. But ugliness is the aesthetic analogue to evil. Is truth evil, then, or is evil true? Some such supposition must have inspired the proliferation of ugliness in the arts of the 20th century. Ugliness became a norm. In music, you can hear it in the wailing and screeching of a multitude of compositions that embrace the agony of the 20th century by making listeners suffer. Why? The hackneyed answer is the "horror" through which we have lived; we must express this horror. Yet composers did not write atonal, cacophonous music after the plague wiped out nearly half of Europe. Have we suffered worse? The answer is yes. The Black Death did not produce ugly music because the people who lived through it did not lose their faith.

The single clearest crisis of the 20th century was the loss of faith. Noise—and its acceptance as music—was the product of the resulting spiritual confusion and, in its turn, became the further cause of its spread. Likewise, the recovery of modern music, the theme to which this book is dedicated, stems from a spiritual recovery that is made explicitly clear by the composers to whom I spoke in the interviews collected in the last part of this book. I also try to spell out the nature of the crisis and its solution in the two essays that serve as bookends to the chapters on individual composers. It is not my contention that all of these composers underwent and recovered from the central crisis of which I speak, but they all lived and worked within its broader context. Many of them simply soldiered on, writing beautiful music as it has always been understood. For this, they suffered ridicule and neglect. I believe their rehabilitation will change the reputation of modern music. There are many such composers, too many to include in this small guide, though it now contains 40 more than in the first edition, along with mention of many new recordings that have come out over the past decade.

In any case, as the reader shall see, it is the spirit of music that has concerned me most. In my efforts to discern it, I have discovered many treasures. The purpose of this book is to share them, to entice you to hear them—because beauty is contagious. In his book, *Bach: Music in the Castle of Heaven*, English conductor John Eliot Gardiner writes that experiencing Bach's masterpieces "is a way of fully realizing the scale and scope of what it is to be human". The reader may be surprised by the number of modern compositions for which this is also true. We try to describe them as best we can while acknowledging the truth of what Monsieur de Sainte-Colombe (ca. 1640–1700) purportedly said: "Music exists to say things that words cannot."

The first edition of *Surprised by Beauty* (2002) contained a selection of columns and interviews originally published in *Crisis* magazine. With the assistance of the brilliant young music critic Jens Laurson, this new edition doubles the size of the original book. *Crisis* columns published over the subsequent decade have been added. The first edition chapters have been revised with updated discographies. In some cases they have been substantially expanded to roughly twice their size, for example, the chapters on John Adams, Steven Gerber, Lowell Liebermann, George Rochberg, Dimitri Shostakovich, Ralph Vaughan Williams, Mieczysław Weinberg, and others. New chapters have been specifically written for this book. They include: (from Robert Reilly) Alfredo Casella, Kenneth Fuchs, Hans Gál, Jennifer Higdon, John Kinsella, David Matthews, George Tsontakis, and Karl Weigl; (and from Jens Laurson) Walter Braunfels, Erich Wolfgang Korngold, Ahmed Saygun, Eric Zeisl and Franz Mittler. All of the composers were chosen for their contributions to the maintenance and/or recovery of beauty in music.

An accompanying website for *Surprised by Beauty* has been set up at www.SurprisedByBeauty.org. This includes continuously updated Recommended Recordings sections for each chapter with convenient links and further essays of the authors on beauty in modern music.

I have many people to thank. Jens Laurson and I have worked together on music since we first met in 2003. What began as discussions over the first edition of this book turned into his own burgeoning career as a music critic both in the United States and Europe. A self-described musical omnivore, he could read notes before he could read letters. However, letters about music are his forte; he writes with spirit, panache, and great insight, obviously animated by love. It has been a great pleasure to share and to discuss our musical discoveries together, as only two music fanatics can. He has been my editor at the online journal *Ionarts* for countless concert and opera reviews over the past decade. It is only fair play that I now have had the opportunity to edit him. He should not be blamed for the things I write, though I would like to take credit for what he has written. It is a delight to welcome him to this volume as a contributing author and to thank him for doing so.

I am especially grateful for the generous support of the Earhart Foundation, its president Ingrid A. Gregg, its secretary and director of program Montgomery Brown, and its board of directors in granting me a research fellowship for the development of this new edition. Deal Hudson, former publisher and editor of *Crisis* magazine, is the person who first approached me with the idea for this book. His friendship, persistence, and support have been invaluable. Ted Libbey, one of the foremost music critics in America, has been my mentor, advisor, and editor in a number of music publications, including the late, lamented *High Fidelity*, *Schwann/Opus*, and *Musical America*. He has been at my side through most of my writings, and I am most grateful for his guidance. And the members of my own family have suffered through many years of deadlines, their ears aching from the many extra hours of music that they have had to endure (though some of which I hope they have enjoyed).

I owe special thanks to the following people: Martin Anderson at Toccata Classics; Klaus Heymann at Naxos; Paul Tai at New World Records; Melissa Kermani at Albany Music Distributors; and the staff at Harmonia Mundi. Without the help of all of these people, this book would not be possible. Jens F. Laurson is grateful to Jim Allison, Ben Finane, and Tim Page.

We are both grateful to Ignatius Press, especially to the ever-patient and highly skilled senior editor Vivian Dudro and to John O'Rourke (Loyola Graphics) for his heroically meticulous proofreading and corrections.

Is Music Sacred?

As the most immaterial art, music is often thought to be the most spiritual. By its nature, is music sacred? If so, what is sacred about it? These might seem strange questions to ask in a secular age, but the presumption that there is something special about music pervades even our culture.

Consider the poster I once spied on the side of a Washington Metrobus that advertised the benefits of the D.C. Youth Orchestra Program. It announced that the happy children shown with their instruments "are playing their way to a bright future". Why should that be? Does playing music make you a better person? A review of a performance of Shostakovich's piano music said that his Prelude in C Major "immediately takes us into the pure, sane world that betokens the composer's escape from mundaneness into the higher reality of music". What is "higher" about the reality of music, and how does the composer reach this reality?

To answer these questions, one must journey back to ancient Greece, to the first writings about music and reflections on its meaning. According to tradition, the harmonic structure of music was discovered by Pythagoras about the fifth century B.C. Pythagoras experimented with a stretched piece of cord. He found a fascinating array of proportional intervals between tones, mathematical relationships that inhere in the very structure of musical sounds. When plucked, the cord sounded a certain note. When halved in length and plucked again, the cord sounded a higher note completely consonant with the first. In fact, it was the same note at a higher pitch. Pythagoras had discovered the 2:1 ratio of the octave. Further experiments plucking the string two-thirds of its original length produced a perfect fifth in the ratio of 3:2. When a three-quarters length of cord was plucked, a perfect fourth was sounded in the ratio of 4:3, and so forth. These sounds were all consonant and extremely pleasing to the ear. The significance that Pythagoras attributed to this discovery cannot be overestimated.

Pythagoras thought that number was the key to the universe. When he found that harmonic music is expressed in exact numerical ratios of whole numbers, he concluded that music was the ordering principle of the world. The fact that music was denominated in exact numerical ratios demonstrated to him the intelligibility of reality and the existence of a reasoning intelligence behind it. He wondered about the relationship of these ratios to the larger world. (The Greek word for ratio is *logos*, which also means "word" or "reason".) He construed that the harmonious sounds that men could make, either with their instruments or their singing, were an approximation of a larger harmony that existed in the universe, also expressed by numbers, which was exemplified in "the music of the spheres". As Aristotle explained in *Metaphysics*, the Pythagoreans "supposed the elements of numbers to be the elements of all things, and the whole heaven to be a musical scale and a number". This was meant literally. The heavenly spheres and their rotations through the sky produced tones at various levels, and in concert these tones made a harmonious sound that man's music, at its best, could replicate.

This discovery was fraught with ethical significance. By participating in heavenly harmony, music could induce spiritual harmony in the soul. Following Pythagoras, Plato taught that "rhythm and harmony find their way into the inward places of the soul, on which they mightily fasten, imparting grace, and making the soul of him who is rightly educated graceful." In the *Republic*, Plato showed the political import of music's power by invoking Damon of Athens as his musical authority. Damon said that he would rather control the modes of music in a city than its laws, because the modes of music have a more decisive effect on the formation of the character of citizens. The ancient Greeks were also wary of music's power because they understood that musical discord could distort the spirit, just as musical concord could properly dispose it. In the *Republic*, Plato warned, "There could be no greater detriment to the morals of a community than a gradual perversion of chaste and modest music."

This idea of "the music of the spheres" runs through the history of Western civilization with an extraordinary consistency, even up to the 20th century. At first, it was meant literally; later, poetically. Music was seen as almost more a discovery than a creation, because it relied on preexisting principles of order in nature for its operation. It would be instructive to look at the reiteration of this teaching in the writings of several major thinkers to appreciate its enduring significance and also the radical nature of the challenge to it in our own time. For a good part of the 20th century, music was decidedly not seen as sacred. The magnitude of this rupture can only be grasped against the background of the preceding millennia.

In the first century B.C., Cicero spelled out Plato's teaching in the last chapter of his *De re publica* (*On the Commonwealth*). In "Scipio's Dream", Cicero's Scipio Africanus asks the question: "What is that great and pleasing sound?" The answer: "That is the concord of tones separated by unequal but nevertheless carefully proportional intervals, caused by the rapid motion of the spheres themselves. The high and low tones blended together provide different harmonies." Cicero explains in great detail the various movements of the spheres and which tones they produce, ending with "the other eight spheres, two of which move at the same speed, [producing] seven tones. This number being, one might say, the key to the universe. Skilled men imitating this harmony on stringed instruments and in singing have gained for themselves a return to this region, as have those who have cultivated their exceptional abilities to search for divine truths." Cicero explicitly presents the case that the right kind of music is divine and can "return" man to a paradise lost. It is a form of communion with divine truth.

In the late second century A.D., St. Clement of Alexandria baptized the classical Greek understanding of music in his *Exhortation to the Greeks*. Using Old Testament imagery from the psalms, St. Clement said that there is a "New Song" far superior to the Orphic myths of the pagans. The New Song is Christ, Logos himself: "[I]t is this [New Song] that composed the entire creation into melodious order, and tuned into concert the discord of the elements, that the whole universe may be in harmony with it." It is Christ who "arranged in harmonious order this great world, yes, and the little world of man, body and soul together; and on this many-voiced instrument he makes music to God and sings to [the accompaniment of] the human instrument." By appropriating the classical view, St. Clement was able to show that music participated in the divine by praising God and partaking in the harmonious order of which he was the composer. But music's goal became even higher because Christ is higher. With Christianity the divine region becomes both transcendent and personal because Logos is Christ. The new goal of music is to make the *transcendent* perceptible. The transcendent was a notion alien to the ancient world, which held the gods to be within the cosmos.

The early sixth century had two especially distinguished Roman proponents of the classical view of music, both of whom served at various times in high offices to the Ostrogoth king Theodoric. Cassiodorus was secretary to Theodoric. He wrote a massive work called *Institutiones*, which echoes Plato's teaching on the ethical content of music, as well as Pythagoras' on the power of numbers. Cassiodorus taught that "music indeed is the knowledge of apt modulation. If we live virtuously, we are constantly proved to be under its discipline, but when we sin, we are without music."

Boethius served as consul to Theodoric in 510. He wrote *Principles of Music*, a book that had enormous influence through the Middle Ages and beyond. Boethius said,

> Music is related not only to speculation, but to morality as well, for nothing is more consistent with human nature than to be soothed by sweet modes and disturbed by their opposites. Thus we can begin to understand the apt doctrine of Plato, which holds that the whole of the universe is united by a musical concord. For when we compare that which is coherently and harmoniously joined together within our own being with that which is coherently and harmoniously joined together in sound—that is, that which gives us pleasure—so we come to recognize that we ourselves are united according to the same principle of similarity.

In his *Etymologiarum* (ca. 633), St. Isidore of Seville stated, "Thus without music no discipline can be perfect, for there is nothing without it. The very universe . . . is held together by a certain harmony of sounds, and the heavens themselves are made to revolve by the modulation of harmony."

It is not really necessary to cite further examples after Boethius because *Principles of Music* was so influential that it held sway as the standard music theory text at Oxford until 1856. Until the 20th century, it was generally accepted that music approximates a heavenly concord, that it should attempt to make the transcendent perceptible and, in so doing, exercise a formative ethical impact on those who listen to it.

Even in the 20th century, this notion was not entirely lost. Three short examples should suffice. Ferruccio Busoni said, "Our Tonal System is nothing more than a set of signs. An ingenious device to grasp somewhat of the eternal harmony." Jean Sibelius, anything but an orthodox Christian, hearkened back to St. Clement when he wrote, "The essence of man's being is his striving after God. It [the composition of music] is brought to life by means of the logos, the divine in art. That is the only thing that has significance." Igor Stravinsky proclaimed, "The profound meaning of music and its essential aim is to promote a communion, a union of man with his fellowman and with the Supreme Being."

However, the hieratic role of music was lost for most of the 20th century because the belief on which it was based was lost. Philosophical propositions have a very direct and profound impact on composers and the kind of music they produce. John Adams, one of the most popular American composers today, said that he had "learned in college that tonality died somewhere around the time that Nietzsche's God died, and I believed it." The connection between the two is quite compelling. At the same time God disappears, so does the intelligible order in creation. A world without God is literally *unnatural*. If there is no God, there is no Nature, that is, the normal and ideal character of reality. Stripped of its normative power, reality no longer serves as a reflection of its Creator. If you lose the Logos of St. Clement, you also lose the ratio (or, logos) of Pythagoras. The death of God is as much a problem for music as it is for philosophy. Tonality,[1] as the preexisting principle of order in the world of sound, goes the same way as the objective moral order.

The impact of nihilism on the arts of the 20th century was succinctly explained by the late English conductor Colin Davis:

> Have you read *The Sleepwalkers* by Herman Broch? In it, Broch analyzes the disintegration of Western values from the Middle Ages onward. After man abandoned the idea that his nature was in part divine, the logical mind assumed control and began to try to deduce the first principles of man's nature through rational analysis. The arts followed a similar course: each art turned in upon itself, and reduced itself further and further by logical analysis until today they have all just about analyzed themselves out of existence.

If there is no preexisting, intelligible order to apprehend, if there is no "music of the spheres" to approximate, what, then, is music supposed to express? If external order does not exist, then music collapses in on itself and degenerates into an obsession with techniques. Any ordering of things, musical or otherwise, becomes purely arbitrary.

Music's self-destruction became inevitable once it undermined its own foundation. In the 1920s, Arnold Schoenberg decisively steered

---

[1] Tonality is meant in an expansive sense to include all non-atonal music.

music down a path from which it seemed it might never return. After taking morbid romanticism about as far as it physically could go, in a magnificent two-hour composition for a Malherian megaorchestra and chorus called *Gurrelieder*, he turned against his first love with an almost pathological vengeance through his "emancipated" dissonance. Dissonance, of course, had been used in music before—but for the purpose of dramatizing disorder or conveying anxiety. Haydn, for example, used dissonance to great dramatic effect to portray chaos in *The Creation*. Many composers used dissonance expressively to portray combat, storms, and so on, but it was never a *norm* until Schoenberg.

This revolution was presented as historically necessary due to the supposed exhaustion of the tonal resources of Western music. It was as if one could run out of tonal music as one might run out of fossil fuel. But as Ernest Bacon once pointed out, Mozart never used two harmonies in a row that other composers had not used long before him, yet his works do not suffer from "exhaustion", but are preternaturally fresh. The real problem, as indicated above, is quite different.

Schoenberg unleashed the forces of disintegration in music through his denial of tonality. He contended that tonality does not exist in Nature as the very property of sound itself, as Pythagoras claimed, but was simply an arbitrary construct of man, a convention. This assertion was not the result of a new scientific discovery about acoustics; it was a product of Schoenberg's desire to demote the metaphysical status of Nature. He was irritated that "tonality does not serve, [but rather] must be served." He preferred to command. As he said, "I can provide rules for almost anything." If tonality is merely a matter of human convention to which man has become habituated, then it is something from which he can be weaned. Schoenberg's whole system is really an attempt in music to prove this philosophical proposition.

Schoenberg took the 12 equal semitones from the chromatic scale and commanded that music be written in such a way that each of these 12 semitones be used before any one of them is repeated. If one of the semitones is repeated before all 11 others are sounded, it might create an anchor for the ear, which could then recognize what was going on in the music harmonically. The 12-tone system guarantees the listener's disorientation. All tones become "equal" in the sense that they have no discernible relationship to one another. Once a complete row is presented, it can be subjected to any variety of manipulations and permutations. Schoenberg said that he could substitute a "system" for Nature and that the systematization of atonality in a row would unify music as tonality had in the past: "The method of composing with 12 tones purports reinstatement of the effects formally furnished by the structural functions of harmony."

Schoenberg proposed to erase the distinction between tonality and atonality by immersing man in atonal music until, through habituation, it became the new convention. Then discords would be heard as concords. As he wrote, "The emancipation of dissonance is at present accomplished and 12-tone music in the near future will no longer be rejected because of discords." Of his achievement, Schoenberg said, "I am conscious of having removed all traces of a past aesthetic." This is nowhere truer than when he declared himself "cured of the delusion that the artist's aim is to create beauty". This statement represents a total rupture with Western musical tradition and is terrifying in its implications when one considers what is at stake in beauty. Simone Weil wrote, "We love the beauty of the world because we sense behind it the presence of something akin to that wisdom we should like to possess to slake our thirst for good." If beauty is gone, so too must be the presence behind it.

The loss of tonality was also devastating at the practical level of composition because tonality is the key structure of music. Tonality is what allows music to express movement away from or toward a state of tension or relaxation, a sense of motion through a series of crises and conflicts, which can then come to resolution. In a way, atonality is not devastating because it removes consonance (which, try as it may, it can never achieve entirely); it is harmful to the drama of music because it gets rid of the dissonance that allows resolution in the first place. It is the language of irresolution. Without tonality, music loses harmony and melody. Its structural force collapses. Gutting music of tonality, as Schoenberg did, is like removing grapes from wine. You can go through all the motions of making wine without grapes, but there will be no wine at the end of the process. Similarly, if you deliberately and systematically remove all audible tone relationships from music, you can go through the process of composition, but the end product will not be comprehensible as music. You will not even be able to remember it. As British composer Nicholas Maw (1935–2009) said, "The problem for me was that serialism rejected whole areas of musical experience. I later realized the difficulty was that it's an invented language that deals only with the moment as it passes. There is neither long-term nor short-term memory. You could even say that the memory is suppressed." This is not a change in technique; it is the replacement of art by an ideology of organized noise.

As English composer David Matthews (b. 1943) wrote, "The loss of accessible, singable melody in the music of Schoenberg and his successors was a devastating blow to music's comprehensibility." Erich Wolfgang Korngold's son, Ernst, related an amusing episode in which Schoenberg was trying to demonstrate to his father the merits of his serial system—in this case, that if you wrote a series of notes and then reversed the series, the theme remained the same. Ernst recounts, "Schoenberg took out a pencil and held it up and said, 'Erich, what is this in my hand?' And my father said, 'It's obvious; it's a pencil.' Schoenberg turned it upside down with the eraser at the bottom and said, 'Now what is it?' And my father replied, 'It's still a pencil—but now you can't write with it!' "

Schoenberg's disciples, however, applauded the emancipation of dissonance in serial music—"Adherence is strict, often burdensome, but it's salvation", proclaimed Anton Webern—but soon they preferred to follow the logic of the centrifugal forces that he had unleashed. Pierre Boulez thought that it was not enough to systematize dissonance in 12-tone rows. If you have a system, why not systematize everything? He applied the same principle of the tone row to pitch, duration, tone production, intensity, and timbre—every element of music. In 1952, Boulez announced, "Every musician who has not felt—we do not say understood but felt—the necessity of the serial language is useless." He also proclaimed, "Once the past has been gotten out of the way, one need think only of oneself." Here is the narcissistic antithesis of the classical view of music, the whole point of which was to lift a person up into something larger than himself. American composer Philip Glass, speaking of the Paris music scene under Boulez in the 1960s, said that it was "a wasteland, dominated by these maniacs, these creeps who were trying to make everyone write this crazy, creepy music".

Some of Schoenberg's disciples saw that 12-tone music is no less a convention than tonality. Unlike Boulez, they asked, quite logically: If you're going to emancipate dissonance, why organize it? Why even have 12-tone themes? Why bother with pitch at all? Edgard Varèse rejected the 12-tone system as arbitrary and restrictive. He searched for the "bomb that would explode the musical world and allow all sounds to come rushing into it through the resulting breach". When he exploded it in his piece *Hyperprism*, Olin Downes, a famous New York music critic, called it "a catastrophe in a boiler factory". Still Varèse did not carry the inner logic of the "emancipation of dissonance" through to its logical conclusion. His noise was formulated; it was organized. There were indications in the score as to exactly when the boiler should explode. What was needed, according to composers such as John Cage, was to have absolutely no organization and to strive for the nonmental. Cage created noise through chance operations by rolling dice. He drew notes according to the irregularities in the composition paper. He sliced up tape recordings, jumbled them up, pieced them together again, and then played them as "music". His point was metaphysically, if not musically, potent: there is no fixed Nature to music. Disfigurement is the means to discredit Nature systematically by destroying form.

In the past several decades, there has been an extraordinary recovery from the damage that was inflicted by those who institutionalized the ideas of Schoenberg and his disciples. Almost without exception, this recovery has been undertaken by composers who were completely immersed in Schoenberg's system but who rebelled and returned to tonal music. George Rochberg was the dean of the 12-tone school of composition in the United States and the first to turn against it from within its own ranks. In 1964, Rochberg was thrown into a crisis by the death of his 20-year-old son. He came out of it saying, "I could not continue writing so-called serial music. It was finished, hollow, meaningless." He found that serialism "made it virtually impossible to express serenity, tranquility, wit, energy". In his Third String Quartet, Rochberg recovered the world of tonality. The quartet was accompanied by a manifesto in which he said:

> The pursuit of art is much more than achieving technical mastery of means or even a personal style; it is a spiritual journey toward the transcendence of art and of the artist's ego. In my time of turning, I have had to abandon the notion of originality in which the personal style of the artist and his ego are the supreme values; the pursuit of the one idea, uni-dimensional work and gesture, which seems to have dominated the aesthetics of art in the 20th century; and the received idea that it is necessary to divorce oneself from the past. . . . In these ways, I am turning away from what I consider the cultural pathology of my own time toward what can only be called a possibility: that music can be renewed by regaining contact with the tradition and means of the past, to re-emerge as a spiritual force with re-activated

powers or structure; and, as I see it, these things are only possible with tonality.

Since 1964, the possibility that Rochberg foresaw has become a reality. There is not space to enumerate the many composers of whom this is true (though many are included in later chapters), but one is worth mentioning as symptomatic of the broad recovery and the reasons for it. The before-mentioned John Adams rejected his college lessons on Nietzsche's "death of God" and the loss of tonality because, like Pythagoras, he "found that tonality was not just a stylistic phenomenon that came and went, but that it is really a natural acoustic phenomenon". In repudiation of Schoenberg, Adams went on to write a stunning symphony titled *Harmonielehre* (*Theory of Harmony*—riffing Schoenberg's influential treatise of the same name) that powerfully reconnects with the great Western musical tradition. In this work, he wrote, "There is a sense of using key as a structural and psychological tool in building my work."

Even more importantly, Adams explained, "The other shade of meaning in the title has to do with harmony in the larger sense, in the sense of spiritual and psychological harmony." Adams' description of his symphony is explicitly in terms of spiritual health and sickness. He explains that "the entire [second] movement is a musical scenario about impotence and spiritual sickness. . . . [I]t has to do with an existence without grace. And then in the third movement, grace appears for no reason at all. . . . That's the way grace is, the unmerited bestowal of blessing on man. The whole piece is a kind of allegory about that quest for grace." It is clear from Adams that the recovery of tonality and key structure is as closely related to spiritual recovery as its loss was related to spiritual loss. As one of Rochberg's former students, the late American composer Stephen Albert, put it, "It is a matter of trying to find beauty in art again, for art is about our desire for spiritual connection."

Cicero spoke of music as enabling us to "return" to the divine region, implying a place once lost to man. Contemporary British composer John Tavener agrees: "My goal is to recover one simple memory from which all art derives. The constant memory of the paradise from which we have fallen leads to the paradise which was promised to the repentant thief." Tavener, Adams, Rochberg, Albert, and many composers like them have restored music to its role of recollecting paradise and bringing us ever closer to the New Song that shall resound throughout eternity. If you listen closely, you can hear strains of it now.

I

THE COMPOSERS

John Adams: The Search for a Larger Harmony

The central fact of history is the Nativity. It poses the singularly important question: Who is Christ? Few ages would seem further removed from a concern over the answer than our own. However, America's most popular composer, John Adams (b. 1947), has written an opera/oratorio on the subject titled *El Niño* or, as it was called at its Paris premiere, *La Nativité*. Adams has composed several highly successful operas based on contemporary events—*Nixon in China*, *The Death of Klinghoffer*, and most recently, though less successfully, *Dr. Atomic*—as well as many orchestral and vocal scores, but nothing in his background would have led one to expect that he would turn to religious subject matter. That he did is in and of itself a significant cultural barometer.

Since my first exposure to his music, I have been intrigued by Adams because he is a member of a generation of composers that was indoctrinated in Schoenberg's ideology of systematized atonality and then found his way out of it. His way was at first minimalist, but he soon turned to richer forms of expression.

Adams reported that he had learned to believe in college that "tonality died somewhere around the time that Nietzsche's God died." His recovery involved a shock of some kind: "When you make a dogmatic decision like that early in your life, it takes some kind of powerful experience to undo it." Adams ultimately rejected his college lessons on Nietzsche's "death of God" and the loss of tonality because he found that "tonality was not just a stylistic phenomenon that came and went, but that it is really a natural acoustic phenomenon." Therefore, said Adams, "I've never truly felt like a vanguard personality. My attitude toward creation is one of incorporating in my compositions everything I've learned and experienced of the past. I've never received any powerful creative energy from the idea of turning my back on the past. . . . There is a sense of the past in it."

Because of the prominent role he has played in the recovery of contemporary music, I have always been curious about the spiritual resources Adams was drawing on in his life and work. Is it Christianity or some kind of New Age spirituality? *El Niño* gives only a partial answer. Adams said he was surprised that he wanted to write a *Messiah* because of his "somewhat checkered religious background". This impulse seems to have come not simply from a love of Handel but from his own amazement at the miracle of birth as he experienced it when his daughter was born in 1984: "There were four people in the room, and then there were five." This metaphysical jolt bore fruit in *El Niño*: "Telling the story of birth, not necessarily the birth of Jesus, but just the archetypical experience of a woman giving birth—through the words of women—became the generating idea behind *El Niño*." Adams' first title for the work was *How Could This Happen?*, from a 16th-century German Advent antiphon.

There was another idea, he said: "I envy people with strong religious beliefs. Mine is shaky and unformed. I don't know what I'm saying, and one reason for writing *El Niño* was to find out." With the help of director Peter Sellars, Adams selected texts from a variety of sources, one-third of them in Spanish or Latin. He used the Bible and the works of Hildegard von Bingen; Sor Juana Inés de la Cruz, a 17th-century Mexican mystic; and several poets. Adams' musical resources include a soprano, a mezzo-soprano, a baritone, a chorus, and an orchestra.

Adams begins his exploration in a surprisingly conventional way, using the beautiful, anonymous medieval English poem "I Sing of a Maiden", followed by a section from a Wakefield mystery play on the Annunciation. He then intersperses the first of several startling poems from the 20th-century Latin American poetess Rosario Castellanos, this one titled "The Annunciation". Her poems are electrifying and bold explorations of what Mary might have felt as she anticipated and then experienced Christ's birth. (If for no other reason, I would be grateful to this work for introducing me to her poetry.) The libretto then turns to the Gospel of Luke for the Visitation and the Magnificat. This first part of the oratorio is very effective and quite moving, especially in its DVD version, where one can see the tears in soprano Dawn Upshaw's eyes during the Annunciation.

Unfortunately, three of the next four numbers are drawn from the Gnostic Gospels. In literary and doctrinal terms, they stick out like sore thumbs, serving at least to confirm one's faith in the Holy Spirit's critical powers. Joseph, who speaks not a word in the canonical Gospels, is quite voluble here, complaining bitterly about Mary's pregnancy. Mary is also loquacious. Extensive use of the Gospel of Pseudo-Matthew is made in the second part of *El Niño*, confusing the fabulous with the miraculous in the story of Christ's life. The texts are absurd. Why did

Adams and Sellars feel compelled to use them? Perhaps for their poetic charm. However, it reveals that they approach canonical Gospels and pseudo-Gospels alike, as if both were enriching myths à la Joseph Campbell.

What is the larger truth to which these myths point? In an interview on the DVD, Sellars says, "When you speak of these spiritual subjects, they can never be reduced. More is happening than you can possibly take in because the story is immense and happening on multiple levels always." So far, so good. But then he opines, "There is no one point of view about Mary. It's the opposite. The nature of truth is not that it belongs to this person or that person. The truth hovers in the middle."

Clearly, neither Sellars nor Adams accepts Christian revelation on its own terms. They use it to try to sanctify every woman's motherhood with Mary's motherhood. Ultimately, this does not work because, in the process, they lose the source of that sanctification: Mary's motherhood is demoted because it is no longer distinct. As the jacket cover to the DVD says, the story of Jesus is told "through the image of modern-day Marys". This perspective is particularly clear in the film Sellars made to accompany the oratorio, as seen on the DVD.

Yet all is not lost. Despite the confusion, a sense of the sacred permeates *El Niño*, if only because Adams has such a profound appreciation for the mystery at the foundation of existence. This grasp of mystery lends great beauty, charm, and power to various parts of this work. Especially captivating are the vocal settings of the Spanish poems and Hildegard von Bingen's "O Quam Preciosa". The portrayal of the three kings and the presentation of the gifts is enchanting.

The CD and DVD releases of *El Niño* share the same marvelous soloists, countertenors, chorus, and Deutsches-Symphonie Orchester Berlin, under Kent Nagano. If this piece fails to convince, it is not because of the performance. Soprano Upshaw, mezzo Lorraine Hunt Lieberson, and baritone Willard White are superb. The DVD is both a richer and more confusing experience, largely because of Sellars' film, which portrays Mary as a young Latino woman, complete with face jewelry, driving around southern California with her boyfriend. However, his choreography for the soloists and chorus on stage is compelling.

"The most important thing is the humanity of the message, the depth of the emotional experience," Adams declares in the *El Niño* DVD interview, "and perhaps that can work its way into a moral change on the part of the listener. But I don't try to convert my audience." Ultimately, *El Niño* is not a contemporary affirmation of faith but an affirmation of contemporary faith.

How Could This Happen? Adams asked in his original title. He fails to answer this question. But, of course, no one could. The real question is: What happened? Who is Christ? Despite his search, it seems clear that Adams still does not quite know what he believes about all this. He does, though, capture and convey a genuine astonishment at creation and the astounding mystery of birth. The beauties in this work show Adams to be a composer with a major gift who is reaching with his heart for something not yet within his grasp. Who can predict what is next for this man who knows that grace can appear "for no reason at all"?

In 2003, Adams tried to extend his spiritual reach to a most difficult subject—the terrorist attack on the World Trade Center. *On the Transmigration of Souls* was written to commemorate the victims of 9/11. *Transmigration*, performed by New York Choral Artists, the Brooklyn Youth Chorus, and the New York Philharmonic, under Lorin Maazel, picked up Grammy Awards for Classical Album (Nonesuch 79816-2), Orchestral Performance, and Classical Contemporary Composition. It also won the Pulitzer Prize in 2003.

I have always looked forward to listening to a new Adams work. I am on his side. His *Harmonielehre* was a breakthrough composition in the early 1980s that heroically declared the recovery of tonality, with all the resources of music triumphantly restored. At the very beginning of this work we hear, not a pulse, but a pounding succession of E-minor chords that seems to announce, almost angrily, that the last barrier to recovery is down. Adams said of his opening, "Yes, the chords are, in a sense, exorcistic." It is an exorcism of the hermetic, the sterile, the reductive, the destructive. Adams did a great deal to sweep aside the sterile academicism of American serialism in such beautiful works as *The Wound-Dresser*, a poignant setting of Walt Whitman's poetry from the Civil War. I wish for Adams to succeed because I sense that he is always trying to move in the right direction.

To memorialize 9/11 is a tough assignment for any composer. Adams' title in *Transmigration* reminded me of a line from Christopher Marlowe's *Doctor Faustus*, in which Faustus, faced with impeding damnation, laments, "Ah, metempsychosis, were that true, this soul should fly from me and I be changed into some brutish beast." Faustus preferred reincarnation as an escape from Mephistopheles and judgment. As Fr. James Schall has said, reincarnation is a this-worldly substitute for resurrection. What, I wondered, could the concept of transmigration bring to the awful events of 9/11? Unfortunately, despite all the praise and prizes, the answer is not enough.

I cringe to call Adams' work politically correct because I have no doubt of his sincerity. It is the critics whom I doubt. What could they have been thinking to elevate this work to the status it now enjoys? My first guess is that it is because it is "inclusive". All kinds of people died on 9/11 from all kinds of religions and perhaps some from none. There is nothing in *Transmigration* that could possibly offend any of them doctrinally. That is its problem.

Transmigration opens with the rustle of tape-recorded street sounds from New York City. Then, a boy deadpans the word "missing" some 30 times, as other voices begin a litany of the dead, repeating names and brief descriptions. A children's choir sings in the upper registers in the background; then adults join in, singing, "We miss you; we all love you" over and over, along with texts taken from the missing-persons signs posted at Ground Zero. A trumpet intones Charles Ives' tune from the *Unanswered Question*. Spoken phrases, like fragments floating in the debris of sounds, interlace each other, creating a kind of counterpoint with the instruments and choir. Adams weaves an interesting tapestry out of this that is undeniably touching.

Two-thirds of the way through its 25-minute duration, the music builds to a huge climax with enormous sea-swells of Sibelian bass strings and brass, under scurrying strings in the upper registers, that erupts into choral shouts of "light" and "love". This is followed by a long decrescendo during which the recitation of names and phrases resumes. Then, more street sounds.

When I first listened to the CD of *Transmigration*, I was moved. For a time, I worked in the Pentagon, not far from one site of 9/11. At the very point where the plane slammed into the building taking 184 lives, there is now a chapel in which Mass is said every weekday. I remember the column of smoke as I drove in that morning, and phone calls to friends near the Twin Towers in New York. To hear some of the names recited, to listen to fragments of cell phone conversations, and to lines from the missing-persons posters near the World Trade Center is quite enough to bring it back and make your heart ache for the families that grieved then and are still grieving now. Yet, the second time I listened, I felt nothing. The shock had worn off and, musically, it was not interesting enough to sustain repeated listening.

In *Transmigration*, one is left simply with the sadness of the thing— the sense of loss, and the wish for there to be more, without there really being a way for there to be more. Adams said, "Transmigration means the movement from one place to another or the transition from one state of being to another." Yes, they have changed. They are dead. They are gone. But to where? And what for? Metempsychosis doesn't cut it. I would rather have these questions answered within a religious tradition that I do not share than left with Ives' *Unanswered Question* because, I suspect, those answers in alien faiths will come far closer to meeting human needs than exclamations of "light" and "love".

One can hear Adams' spirit straining against the slavery of death, wishing to break its bonds through the exercise of memory and love. But wishing does not make it so. Yearning may, however, at least point you in the right direction; open you to the possibility of the transcendent. And the transcendent has a text far more compelling than Adams' libretto. That text is the Requiem. Death by terrorism reminds us of the terror of death. Resurrection reminds us of the victory over death. I recently overheard one mother telling another how to tell her very young children that their grandfather was dying. "Don't talk about death without talking about heaven", she counseled. I want to hear that in music. In *Transmigration*, unfortunately I don't.

I have kept waiting for Adams to do it again—by which I mean something as dramatically significant as his *Harmonielehre* or as beautiful as *The Wound-Dresser*. I suppose that is why I felt disappointed with his release on Nonesuch (79857-2), which rather pretentiously places two works, *The Dharma at Big Sur* and *My Father Knew Charles Ives*, on two CDs, though they would easily fit on one.

Charles Ives (1874–1954) is surely the single most overrated American composer, and I am not attracted by the conceit that Adams' father knew him. In the first movement of the Ives piece, Adams' evocation of him borders on cliché as it includes an imitation of two bands passing each other and the cacophony they produce—a signature experience in Ives' life that led to his embrace of and delight in dissonance. Yes, I know it can be fun but, please, it is time to move on. This is not to say that some of Adams' pastiche in this work is not fun; it is.

The *Big Sur* piece is a concerto for electric violin and orchestra, the second movement of which is a tribute to breakthrough minimalist composer Terry Riley. Some of the sonorities are quite beautiful, but to me, the keening sound made by the electric violin can come close to irritating and, worse, near to kitsch when it becomes syrupy, which it occasionally does here. I do not think there is enough spine in this work to keep it from being high-level mood music, although Adams achieves some real grip in the thrilling, almost overwhelming climax. If only the rest of the work deserved it. (Adams' Violin Concerto from 1993 is the stronger work.) In a music shop once (when there were such things), I found classical music in a bin labeled "Classical and New Age". I am sorry to say that is where *Big Sur* belongs.

A Naxos CD brings Adams' complete piano music together, with pianist Ralph van Raat, in beautiful, spirited performances. Even at his most minimalist, Adams knew how to create lovely, even exhilarating music, as his early *Phrygian Gates* demonstrates. The much later *Hallelujah Junction* (1996) shows that he has never quite shaken his minimalist roots or stopped aiming at the ecstatic.

Whatever reservations I may have expressed about some of Adams' work, no one interested in understanding the recovery of modern music can do without listening to *Harmonielehre*, and everyone who does will be the richer for it.

Recommended Recordings

El Niño, Kent Nagano, Deutsches Symphonie-Orchester Berlin, with Dawn Upshaw, Lorraine Hunt Lieberson, Willard White, Nonesuch 79634 (two CDs)

El Niño, Arthaus Musik DVD Video 100 22032

Harmonielehre, Short Ride in a Fast Machine, Michael Tilson Thomas, San Francisco Symphony, SFS Media 53

Fearful Symmetries; The Wound-Dresser, John Adams, Orchestra of St. Luke's, Nonesuch 79218

On the Transmigration of Souls, Lorin Maazel, New York Philharmonic, Nonesuch 79816

Concerto for Violin, Robert McDuffie, Christoph Eschenbach, Houston SO, Telarc 80494

Complete Piano Music, Ralph van Raat, Naxos 8.559285

Stephen Albert: Aiming at Epiphany

At the turn of the New Year in 1993, as I was paging my way through the newspaper, I happened to glance at the obituaries. The paper almost fell from my hands when I saw the name of friend and composer Stephen Albert, dead at 51, cut down in an auto accident on December 27, 1992. Steve and I had just had one of our marathon phone conversations barely a week before his death, and he was as full of enthusiasm as ever. He urgently invited me to Baltimore to hear Yo-Yo Ma premiere his new Cello Concerto and insisted I finally make the trip to Cape Cod to spend a long weekend with his family. It was inconceivable to me that this dear man, so full of life, love, and passion, was gone. As far as the loss to the world of music was concerned, the *Washington Post* put it well: Steve's death "deprived American music of one of its most luminous talents".

Appropriately enough, Steve and I first met on the telephone. I was writing a piece on the current state of American music that included interviews with some of the neotonal composers who had rejected Schoenberg's 12-tone system of atonality. My calling card with Steve was a very favorable review I had written for *Musical America* of his gorgeously lyrical *Flower of the Mountain* and the dramatic *Into Eclipse*, recorded by Nonesuch (9 79153-2). He remembered the review, so we were off to a good start. I was soon astounded by his frankness and willingness to speak about the spiritual disease afflicting the arts and our times.

Contrary to the romantic image of the artist as something akin to an idiot savant, possessed by the divine afflatus, who knows not what he does, most composers are very articulate and literate—and respond very particularly to philosophical claims and metaphysical propositions. Steve Albert was one of these. In our many hours of conversation, on the phone and during visits, half the time was spent discussing God— who he is, how we know him, whether he can be reached, and how crazy the current world is in light of his Being. The conversations were almost Dostoyevskian, except there was no madness in them; they were illumined by Steve's passion, thirst, and drive for truth.

Steve rebelled against the highly esoteric, dehumanized "cult of the new" that dominated much of the American musical scene. As such, he felt "out of step with the establishment". About his studies he told me, "Starting back in the early 60s, I felt I was fleeing from a cultural funeral. People didn't see the caskets yet, but I saw them. The only honest thing was not to be a part of it—to resist it. Once you bought the cultural Bolshevism of the time, you were down the mindless trail of the avant-garde. Twenty-five years down the line I suspect that one will look back with mystification as to how people took the 50s to the 70s seriously except as some kind of sociological aberration."

What particularly provoked Steve about 12-tone music was its implied premise, as he said, that "the past has no meaning. What was going on was the massive denial of memory. No one can *remember* a 12-tone row. The very method obliterates memory's function in art." Steve sensed the possible recovery of music that would "reach out and touch an audience once again", as his music so successfully does. (It will be no surprise that he was a student of George Rochberg.) To achieve this, he thought it necessary to reconnect with and "to re-examine ideas and practices that were part of a 600-year continuum" of musical tradition. Steve believed that "the continuum still moves through our soul as a subterranean river flows faithfully and silently beneath the parched desert." That silent river broke into beautiful song in his lyrical and highly expressive works.

Steve's music has been called neoromantic because of his return to tonality and long-lined melody. He rejected what he described as both "the unrelieved dissonance of serialism and the unrelieved consonance of minimalism". He said that he was searching for a new synthesis and for "memorable ideas that seem timeless". In a 1990 interview with the *Baltimore Sun*, Steve explained:

> I felt that music had reached an impasse. The only real masterpieces after World War II had been by Shostakovich. The only place most new music was going was over a cliff into an abyss, and the so-called conservative alternative seemed to be mired in stasis. The only way out of it, it seemed to me, was to go back to where music had been shortly after the turn of the century. Eschewing the music of Schoenberg, Webern and Berg, I became interested in composers like de Falla, Sibelius and early Stravinsky. I wanted a complexity of texture that bears repeated hearings and I wanted at the same time to have a surface accessibility.

The most prominent influences on Steve's music can be easily heard: Strauss, Stravinsky, and Sibelius. That may seem an odd admixture, but Steve assimilated them into his unique sound world, which can be heard in a number of his recorded works. Among them are a rich setting of Molly Bloom's words from James Joyce's *Ulysses*, titled *Flower of the Mountain* (which Albert told me was inspired by Strauss' *Four Last Songs* and by Mahler); his Pulitzer Prize–winning symphony *RiverRun*, which was the major piece of American music Mstislav Rostropovich brought with him on his famous return to Russia with the National Symphony Orchestra; a violin concerto, *In Concordiam*; and his Concerto for Cello and Orchestra, a very powerful and moving piece written for cellist Yo-Yo Ma, recorded by Sony with David Zinman and the Baltimore Symphony Orchestra.

Steve's stylistic signature is so pronounced that, after listening to several of his works, I could identify a composition as his within the first few bars in a blind listening session. He used the piano as an orchestral instrument in a unique way. He creates a powerful sense of undertow with the rippling bass notes and sounds the alarm with trills in the upper registers. His string writing is very rich. In all, his music is very effective in creating an air of expectancy—as if some revelation is at hand. He had a tendency to rework his materials from composition to composition, but without exhausting them—as if within them he would finally bring forth a final epiphany. The very tension in that effort provides some of the expressive power in his work.

Steve thought his 1990 Cello Concerto his best composition, and it shows him at the top of his powers. We used to argue over the merits of various composers, and he was not pleased with my weakness for Benjamin Britten's operas or for the symphonies of Carl Nielsen, which, he said, did not have any good tunes. I would retaliate by trying to sing or hum one, which I'm sure only weakened my case. Regardless, Steve's concerto displays his superb melodic gift. It contains one of his finest and longest themes, utterly haunting and completely memorable. It is stated for the first time at the beginning of the piece by the cello alone, in a declamatory fashion. After an orchestral interjection, the cello restates the theme—this time in an achingly lyrical and tender way, with Sibelian string undercurrents. Steve told me that this theme was unconsciously inspired by the falcon motif in Strauss' opera *Die Frau ohne Schatten*. I cannot hear any direct similarities, maybe a faint echo in an accompanying figure, but perhaps that's where the divine afflatus comes in. Yo-Yo Ma premiered this piece with the same artists on the Sony recording, so this CD should be considered definitive. However, Steve sent me a concert tape of the premiere. In it, I detect more passion and engagement than I do on this recording. The Sony performance is more subdued and reflective. The work can bear that interpretation, but it does not have the same overwhelming impact. In both performances, Yo-Yo Ma's artistry is breathtaking. It is a complete mystery to me as to why this gorgeous concerto has not become a regular repertoire piece.

When the accident occurred, Steve had just finished the short score of his Symphony No. 2, which had been commissioned by the New York Philharmonic. This work, as orchestrated so capably by composer Sebastian Currier, received its world premiere recording by the Russian Philharmonic Orchestra, under Paul Polivnick. It is accompanied by Symphony No. 1: *RiverRun*, for which Steve won the Pulitzer Prize in 1985.

These symphonies, like Steve's other music, fulfill his demand that music have a sense of "moving from points of artificially induced conflict to a sense of settling—of moving to an epiphany—tension and resolution". Of his endeavor, Steve said, "It is a matter of trying to find beauty in art again" because "art is about our desire for spiritual connection." In tribute to Steve's achievements, music critic Theodore Libbey once said, "It's what the art is in touch with that is important. It is no longer appealing for artists to dwell upon the chaotic, the painful, the ugly—which we have been told are the principal realities of our time. Stephen Albert was reaching for something beyond that—toward the transcendent."

Recommended Recordings

Symphony No. 1: *RiverRun*; *To Wake the Dead*, Christopher Kendall, Twentieth Century Consort, Lucy Shelton, Delos 1016

Symphonies 1 & 2, Paul Polivnick, Russian PO, Naxos 8.559257

In Concordiam; *Tree Stone*, Gerard Schwarz, Seattle Symphony, New York Chamber Symphony, Naxos 8.559708

Concerto for Cello and Orchestra ("The New York Album"), David Zinman, Baltimore SO, with Yo-Yo Ma, Sony 57961

George Antheil: Bad Boy Made Good

I am torn between writing about American composer George Antheil's life and writing about his music. Each contains such wild improbabilities that one cannot help but be intrigued and amused by the delightful eccentricities of both. I wonder if the connection between the two might not be crime—of both the literal and the musical sort.

Take, for instance, Antheil's introduction to music as a very young child, living with his parents across the street from the New Jersey State Penitentiary in Trenton, where he was born in 1900. A pair of old maids moved into the house next door and began pounding away on the piano in shifts day and night. When they finally stopped, it was discovered that the noise had been a cover for a tunneling operation to the prison, which led to one of the most sensational jailbreaks in New Jersey's history. This bizarre occurrence was the source of Antheil's initial love of a certain kind of piano playing and music. As early as 1921, he announced his desire to become "noted and notorious . . . as a new ultramodern pianist composer". He went on to scandalize the music world with violent piano compositions such as *Sonata Sauvage*, *The Death of Machines*, and the *Airplane Sonata* that caused riots in several European cities.

Like an inhabitant of the institution across from his childhood home, Antheil seemed to enjoy the danger of near escapes. The riots that his music provoked led him to obtain a pistol. "A real one!" he gleefully recounted. "I bought a small .32 automatic, for which I had a silken holster made to fit under my arm. Thereafter I would publicly produce my ugly little automatic, in approved American gangster fashion, and place it on the piano in full view before each recital. I never had anymore trouble until the Nazis." How can you not like a man like this?

Well, perhaps by listening to his music—especially if you are not fond of incessantly pounding rhythms and unresolved dissonances. The strident tendency in Antheil's music reached its apogee in his most infamous piece, *Ballet mécanique*, which rocked the Parisian music world in 1926 with another riot. Naxos has released a new recording of this "classic", along with others of his works, performed by the Philadelphia

Virtuosi Chamber Orchestra, under Daniel Spalding. Antheil threw airplane propellers, electric buzzers, percussion, and sirens into this cacophonous exercise in pure rhythm. (Anyone who has sat through an evening of Japanese drumming would understand the experience and its visceral thrill.) The futurists, Dadaists, and other ultramodernists fell into raptures, and the rest were appalled. As a result, Antheil was a made man, an enfant terrible, or, as he called himself in the title of his highly amusing autobiography, the *Bad Boy of Music*. He stood shoulder to shoulder in Paris with his friends Ezra Pound, Picasso, James Joyce, Fernand Leger, and the rest of the avant-garde. As Pound wrote, he was "the first American or American-born musician to be taken seriously". At the same time, Aaron Copland said that Antheil possessed "the greatest gift of any young American now writing".

However, Antheil's fame came at a price. The New York premiere of his ballet turned into a fiasco due to the power of the large airplane propellers that blew the front-row patrons from their seats. Not even the American avant-garde was amused. Antheil was written off as a charlatan. He retreated first to Europe and then to Hollywood, where he wrote a distinguished group of film scores, including *The Plainsman*, *Spectre of the Rose*, *Knock on Any Door*, and *The Pride and the Passion*. His reputation as a serious classical artist dwindled to that of a one-work composer. He came to regret this deeply. In 1945 he reflected, "It is terrible when I think that [with the *Ballet mécanique*] I am still included in the chapter on young American composers. Because of this, the *Ballet mécanique* has become for me what the C-sharp Prélude must have been for Rachmaninoff—to put it plainly, my nightmare." Also, Antheil claimed that the work was misunderstood: "I had no idea of copying a machine directly down into music, so to speak. My idea, rather, was to warn the age in which I was living of the simultaneous beauty and danger of its own unconscious mechanistic philosophy, aesthetic." His later music proves the authenticity of this remark.

In fact, after 1926, Antheil turned away from his early radical experiments because, musically speaking, he had to. *Ballet mécanique* is as far as one can go in its direction. Adding another propeller or two leads nowhere. So Antheil followed his idol, Stravinsky, into neoclassicism that produced works such as Symphony for Five Instruments and Concert for Chamber Orchestra. After his move to Hollywood in 1935, Antheil underwent another major reevaluation. He delved into the classics—Beethoven, Mahler, and Sibelius ("I discovered, for instance, that Sibelius was not so bad after all. How effete my tastes had become in Paris.'')—and concluded that "no young artist starts the world all over again for himself but merely continues . . . the heritage of the past, pushing if possible on a little further." Antheil's path in this direction was provided by other Russian models, particularly Shostakovich and Prokofiev. On them he based his new orchestral works, including his last three symphonies.

The financial difficulties Antheil had to endure because of his notoriety turned him to a number of curious nonmusical pursuits that link him again with the crime theme. In 1930, T. S. Eliot edited and published Antheil's crime novel, *Death in the Dark*, about the murder of a concert agent. Antheil became an expert in the field of endocrinology as it relates to criminal behavior. He was consulted by a number of police departments and won an honorary life membership in the Paris police force for his study of glandular disturbances in criminals. He published *Every Man His Own Detective*, intriguingly subtitled, *X Marks the Gland Where the Criminal Is Found*.

In other writing pursuits, Antheil produced *The Shape of the War to Come*, published in June 1939, in which he predicted the events of World War II with astonishing precision. He missed Pearl Harbor by only a month. The editor of the *Los Angeles Daily News* was sufficiently impressed to make him the paper's war correspondent. Other wartime activities included designing a radio-controlled torpedo with actress Hedy Lamarr, with whom he shared the patent. He also syndicated a column of advice to the lovelorn, "Boy Advises Girl". Some claim Antheil inspired Nathanael West's novel *Miss Lonely Hearts*.

Because Antheil's life is so interesting, I have left less room for detailed notes on his symphonies. There is no doubt that they rely heavily on their Russian models (one critic suggested that instead of calling Antheil an American Shostakovich, Shostakovich ought to be called a Russian Antheil). Thanks to the CPO and Naxos labels, the now-emerging secret is that during his time of relative obscurity, Antheil wrote a good deal of very fine music. The six symphonies, except for the Second and the original (apparently very different) version of the Fifth, are now all available. American conductor Hugh Wolff and the Frankfurt Radio Orchestra on CPO are a good and obvious choice, although Naxos has released an excellent CD offering Symphonies 4 and 6, with *McKonkey's Ferry*, played by the National Symphony Orchestra of Ukraine, under Theodore Kuchar.

The CPO label gives us three CDs with Symphonies 1 and 6, with *Archipelago* (if you love high jinks in music, listen to this cross between George Gershwin and Xavier Cugat); Symphonies 4 and 5; and Symphony No. 3, with overtures, all brilliantly played by Hugh Wolff and his Frankfurt forces. The amusing thing about the Symphony No. 3, subtitled *American*, is that the America it portrays alternates between Coplandesque Americana and visits from the continent. Shostakovich shows up regularly. Mahler visits in the Andante. And in one of the strangest interpolations I have heard in music, Antheil drops a development section from Sibelius' Fifth Symphony into the third movement. You will not be bored by this or the three overtures and the ballet *Capital of the World*, which are included. In brief, this is good, high-spirited, and imaginative music, though not great by its own points of reference —Stravinsky, Prokofiev, and Shostakovich. These works bear out the verdict of the American composer and critic Virgil Thomson that "the bad boy became a good boy." By this, he meant that Antheil's later works entered the mainstream of music with their melodic richness, orchestral virtuosity, and classical forms.

Naxos has the *Ballet mécanique* with Daniel Spalding conducting the Philadelphia Virtuosi Chamber Orchestra in the reduced 1953 version of four pianos and percussion—a terrific disc not the least because it also includes the First Serenade for Strings, the Poulencish Symphony for Five Instruments (bassoon, flute, trombone, trumpet, and viola), and the Concerto for Chamber Orchestra.

Although composed the same year as the *Ballet mécanique* (1926), there is nothing at all shocking in the Piano Concerto No. 2 or for that matter in *Dreams*, or in the Serenade No. 2. The three works are also performed by the Philadelphia Virtuosi Chamber Orchestra, under Daniel Spalding, with pianist Guy Livingston, on a New World Records CD. The ballet *Dreams* is steeped in Stravinsky, but for all of its derivativeness, it is a lot of fun, has a marvelous sense of play, and evokes a kind of circus atmosphere, though it is about a ballerina's dreams. Antheil is fully in command of a number of musical idioms (waltz, march, polka, folk song, etc.) and mixes them with aplomb. Playful high spirits infect the other works, as well. The Piano Concerto mixes Bach with its Stravinsky, and gives a good simulation of Bohuslav Martinů's neobaroque music in its last movement.

Add the complete string quartets (three numbered quartets and two smaller works, on Other Minds Records), the Piano Concertos (No. 1

from 1922 and No. 2 from 1926, on CPO), and all the important short solo piano pieces (coupled with Conlon Nancarrow works, played by the excellent Herbert Henck, recorded for ECM), and you have the basics well covered. If you enjoy the rambunctious, boisterous, and brilliant, give this bad boy a second chance. We all deserve one, and you won't regret it.

Recommended Recordings

Symphonies 1 & 6 and *Archipelago*, Hugh Wolff, Frankfurt RSO, CPO 999 604

Symphonies 4 & 5 and *Decatur at Algiers*, Hugh Wolff, Frankfurt RSO, CPO 999 706

Symphony No. 3; *Tom Sawyer*; *Capital of the World*, Hugh Wolff, Frankfurt RSO, CPO 777 040

Symphonies 4 & 6 and *McKonkey's Ferry*, Theodore Kuchar, Ukrainian NSO, Naxos 8.559033

Ballet mécanique, Serenade for String Orchestra No. 1; Symphony for Five Instruments; and Concert for Chamber Orchestra, Daniel Spalding, Philadelphia Virtuosi Chamber Orchestra, Naxos 8.559060

Ballet mécanique, Maurice Peress, New Palais Royale Orchestra & Percussion Ensemble, Mendelssohn String Quartet, Nimbus 2567

Dreams; Piano Concerto No. 2; Serenade No. 2, Daniel Spalding, Philadelphia Virtuosi Chamber Orchestra, New World Records 80647

Piano Concertos 1 & 2, Eiji Oue, North German RSO, Markus Becker, CPO 777 109-2

Sonatas for Violin & Piano, Mark Fewer, John Novacek, Azica 71263

Piano Music, Herbert Henck, Conlon Nancarrow, ECM 465829

Complete String Quartets, Del Sol String Quartet, Other Minds Records, 1008 or Mondriaan String Quartet, Etcetera KTC 1093

~

Richard Arnell: Sheer Musical Vitality

I have been very curious about the attention given to British composer Richard Arnell (1917–2009) by the Dutton label. It has released his seven symphonies (the last of which was completed from sketches by Martin Yates), five of his six string quartets, other chamber music, ballet music, and piano and violin concertos. That is quite a commitment to a hitherto unknown. Is this, I wondered, another neglected talent on the artistic level of Edmund Rubbra or William Alwyn, whose well-deserved revivals have preceded Dutton's attention to Arnell? I began by exploring the mammoth, more-than-hour-long Symphony No. 3, written in 1944–1945. My initial impression was of repeated runs at heaving a heavy object into the air, getting it partially aloft, wobbling a bit under its enormous weight, but never relaxing the muscles in the upward lift. The very scale of this work creates a sense of expectancy, as if a great proclamation is about to be made. I was confirmed in my opinion when I read the CD booklet, which quoted Alwyn's comment that "the composer rarely relaxes the earnestness of his thought or the strength of his muscles." Also, Rubbra weighed in: "Obviously a work that because of its sheer musical vitality should be performed."

What does it sound like? I hear a little influence from Shostakovich (perhaps a smidgen in the Presto movement), to whom the booklet suggests it might owe something. It has an inimitably English sound but definitely not from the pastoral school. And I do not think it is beholden to Vaughan Williams. It is most reminiscent of William Walton's great Symphony No. 1, especially in the Andante and Allegro movements. It is as highly charged and also as distinctly Sibelian in places. It is not as thematically tight as Walton and has a more cinematic flavor. Regardless, it is a magnificent, even extravagant achievement. It does produce the promised major statement with an almost Elgarian nobility. As it is dedicated "to the political courage of the British people" during World War II, this is as it should be. The more I listen to this symphony, the higher my opinion of it climbs, leaving me staggered that it went unperformed for some 50 years. How wonderful the composer was still alive to enjoy this belated recognition, delivered in such a stirring performance by the Royal Scottish National Orchestra, under Martin Yates.

Having finally grasped the ambitious idiom in which he worked, I went on to devour the other Dutton recordings, also with Yates' Royal Scottish National Orchestra. Arnell's time has finally come. Now I can only wonder how works of this magnificence and of such noble striving could have been overlooked for so long, particularly in Great Britain, where they are given to doting on even their third-rate composers. Arnell is decidedly first-rate. How hard this neglect must have been for the composer, most likely overlooked in the post–World War II era because he eschewed the avant-garde and wrote unabashedly tonal music. Also, the American composer and critic Virgil Thomson remarked that Arnell's work conveyed "an emotional reality that we are not accustomed to associate with the British composer". Was his intensity too over-the-top for his compatriots? One would not think so after the ferociousness of Vaughan Williams' Fourth Symphony. Or had the time for Elgarian nobility passed, destroyed in the blitz? In any case, fellow composer Patrick Jonathan gave a poignant portrait of the price Arnell paid. He said that Arnell kept a blanket draped over the bookshelves where he stored his works in his study because he could not bear to look at them "just sitting there, and not being played". Now we know what we were missing. Composer and conductor Warren Cohen, who has premiered many of Arnell's works in the United States, said, "It was my discovery of Arnell's music that was a critical part of the development of my theory of the vagaries of fame, and how loosely connected to quality is the fame of the composer."

Arnell's First Symphony presages all that was to come in an already accomplished way. His Sixth Symphony, which accompanies it, is more coiled, compressed, and explosive, like a late Havergal Brian work, though less jagged and angular. The Second Symphony is paired with a huge and hugely enjoyable Piano Concerto. In Symphonies 3, 4, and 5, Arnell seems to be working with variations of the same basic themes —similar thematic material keeps resurfacing at climactic moments. It is music of enormous tumult. There is always an underlying excitement and the sense of reaching for and finally achieving something magisterial. He could build over huge spans. There are moments of almost Bruckner-like magnificence and, occasionally, terraced dynamics that are also reminiscent of Bruckner.

The beginnings of both Nos. 4 and 5 are tremendously exciting. No. 5's first movement has a reach for the ecstatic that is reminiscent of Edmund Rubbra's great symphonic works. Only after great striving does it reach a state of exultation. The Andante in No. 5 sounds as if it is from one of the brilliant orchestral interludes in Benjamin Britten's opera *Peter Grimes*. Arnell's facility with orchestral colors reminds me of his and Britten's American friend Bernard Herrmann, the great film composer who championed Arnell's work in the United States. In fact, there are moments of cinematic extravagance in Arnell's music that make me want to hear his film scores, of which he composed some 30. British conductor Thomas Beecham called Arnell "one of the best orchestrators since Berlioz". One also detects the influences of Prokofiev, a slight bit of Shostakovich, and a hint of Martinů. Aside from Rubbra and Britten, the other major British influence on Arnell was, as mentioned, William Walton.

The earnestness of Arnell's symphonies may leave the impression that he was without humor. His ballets *The Great Detective* and *The Angels* prove otherwise. They are delectable, somewhat puckish works that show how easily lovely melodies flowed from Arnell when that is what he wanted to produce. It is here that one hears the light touch from some of Prokofiev's delectable ballet music.

Dutton also offers a recording of Arnell's Violin Concerto in One Movement. The concerto is everything his dramatic, ecstatic symphonies led me to believe it would be, and it comes with two other treats, violin concertos by Thomas Pitfield and Guirne Creith. Violinist Lorraine McAslan gives impassioned performances, especially of the gorgeous unaccompanied cadenzas in the Arnell work. She also captures the gentle lyricism in the Pitfield concerto. Martin Yates and the Royal Scottish National Orchestra make this a very attractive offering for anyone interested in tonal 20th-century violin works. As for Arnell's string quartets, music critic Hans Keller said the Fifth Quartet was "one of the great unknown string quartets of the 20th century". Conductor Warren Cohen declared that the Lento movement of the Third Quartet "is simply one of the most beautiful six minutes of music I have ever heard".

This cycle of practically unknown symphonies and other orchestral works and chamber music prove the 20th century to have been far more musically interesting and rich than many may have thought. If works like these, which have a genuine claim to greatness, are only just now surfacing, what still may lie beneath? One cannot possibly praise the Dutton label and the forces it employed too highly for having removed the blanket from over these treasures and for offering them to us in such resplendent performances and recordings.

Recommended Recordings

Symphonies 1 & 6, Martin Yates, BBC Scottish SO, Dutton CDLX 7217

Symphony No. 2 & Piano Concerto No. 2, Martin Yates, Royal Scottish NO, David Owen Norris, Dutton CDLX 7184

Symphony No. 3 & *The New Age* Overture, Martin Yates, Royal Scottish NO, Dutton 7161

Symphonies 4 & 5, Martin Yates, Royal Scottish NO Dutton 7194

Violin Concerto in One Movement (plus Guirne Creith & Thomas Pitfield Concertos), Martin Yates, Royal Scottish NO, Lorraine McAslan, Dutton 7221

The Great Detective; *The Angels*, Martin Yates, BBC Concert Orchestra, Dutton 7208

String Quartets 1–5, Tippett String Quartet, Dutton 7268

The Unnumbered Symphonies, Martin Yates, Royal Scottish NO, Dutton 7299

~

Malcolm Arnold: English Enigma

The staid English sense of manners and propriety has always been counterpoised by a compensating eccentricity. The English do not tolerate peculiarity; they take pride in it. Once during a visit to a London club, I was quite accidentally thrown together for an evening with a marquis from one of fair Albion's most famous families. He wore no socks, laughed like a hyena, and in his back pocket, sported a huge red bandanna that he frequently flourished when taking copious quantities of snuff. The next morning, one of the club butlers sidled up to me and said, "Oh, sir, I see you were with the marquis last night." "Yes, Henry", I replied. "Well," the butler confided, "that's the real thing!"

One would think that this prideful indulgence would extend to those who hear a different drummer in the world of music. But such has not always been the case with English composer Sir Malcolm Arnold, who certainly is the real thing. With all the recorded care the British have lavished on their 20th-century composers, why have they neglected Arnold for so long? Perhaps because he is too atypical, even for the British. His music tweaks; he is the closest the British have come to Francis Poulenc, the marvelously mischievous French composer. Also, critics seemed perplexed by Arnold's extraordinary knack for popular tunes, somewhat akin to that of the late Morton Gould in this country. Both composers suffered for their popularity with the "unwashed". Additionally, in certain of his later symphonies, Arnold reveals an acerbic and violent side that stands in juxtaposition to his customary lyrical warmth and jocularity. People have come to accept the giant orchestral raspberries in Shostakovich's symphonies but not yet, apparently, in Arnold's.

Arnold's neglect was keenly felt by some of his compatriots—especially professional musicians who knew a master was in their midst. In 1990, I received a letter from the celebrated British cellist Julian Lloyd Webber. He wrote: "Arnold has had a very poor deal in this country—the symphonies are virtually never programmed—it is rather a national disgrace. (How many movements like the slow movement of the Second [Symphony] are there around nowadays?)" Happily, this "national disgrace" has been remedied with three concurrent traversals of Arnold's nine symphonies by the Chandos, Conifer, and Naxos

49

labels. The results of all three ventures are outstanding. (The Conifer has been deleted, reissued on Decca, and moved out of print again. But the Conifer prints are available on-demand and easy to find used.) These releases join a growing number of other recent recordings of Arnold's many concertos, overtures, dance suites, chamber music, and film scores. Arnold's time has come at last and, happily, Arnold, who died a month before his 85th birthday in 2006, lived to see it.

Arnold was born in 1921 in Northampton, a musically fecund town that also produced composers Edmund Rubbra and William Alwyn. Arnold showed early promise by steadfastly refusing to go to school. Educated at home by an aunt, he later did a stint at the Royal College of Music, from which he once bolted and had to be begged back by its director, composer George Dyson. Arnold learned the orchestra from the inside, which tells in his amazingly deft and highly transparent orchestrations. He became principal trumpet in the London Philharmonic Orchestra at the ripe age of 21. He at first refused military service during World War II but then later volunteered. He was relieved from duty after shooting himself in the foot. He returned to the London Philharmonic but, after winning the Mendelssohn Scholarship in 1948, left to devote himself to composition and conducting.

Arnold's style of writing tonal, tuneful, and very entertaining music was officially frowned upon. Critics found it unseemly that a 20th-century composer would write in a classical divertimento style in an age of angst and ugliness. For example, instead of producing a *Quartet for the End of Time* (Olivier Messiaen) during World War II, Arnold composed mellifluous serenades. As British critic Donald Mitchell once wrote, "The very emphasis on the melodic dimension in Arnold's art itself gives rise to suspicions that . . . we are succumbing to the blandishments of the popular, while the composer is somehow abandoning the pedestal of high art and is wanting in seriousness." As if to confirm this diagnosis, Arnold turned to film scores to support himself. He wrote more than 100, including the Oscar-winning *The Bridge on the River Kwai* (dashed off in 15 days). The film income left him free to write his "serious" music, some of which was deliberately silly. In collaboration with musical humorist Gerard Hoffnung, he produced such works as *Grand, Grand Overture*, which includes parts for three vacuum cleaners and a floor polisher, and *Grand Concerto Gastronomique*, scored for eater, waiter, food, and orchestra (what, no claret?). Even on these high jinks, Arnold lavished melodies that would leave most composers green with envy.

Arnold's main body of work also contains a good deal of humor. He is such a complete master of both classical and popular idioms that he can play freely with them. And play he does, weaving them in and out of each other with a dizzying dexterity that leaves the listener exhilarated by the high spirits of the thing. Staccato jazz rhythms, Caribbean marimba bands, and march music mix with what at times sound like hilarious send-ups of Mahler, Shostakovich, and Sibelius. In fact, Arnold admits all three composers are major influences on him. He adds Berlioz for reasons that could well describe his own music. Of Berlioz, Arnold said: "His compositions always strike me as so fresh. . . . If he can express his ideas by a melody only he does so, and if it is a melody based on tonic and dominant harmonies (which would have been considered by some as 'old-fashioned' in his day) he is not afraid to do so." Neither is Arnold, who deploys his wonderfully memorable tunes with such abandon, not only in his more popular pieces but also in his sometimes very serious symphonies.

Arnold accomplishes all this with what seems to be a cheeky breeziness. It is quicksilver music—one moment it sparkles, the next it brays. Some listeners misinterpret Arnold's extraordinary fluency as facileness. But Arnold makes what he does look easy in the spirit of the famous dictum *Ars est celare artem* (True art conceals art). A closer inspection reveals the hand of a master craftsman. In its sheer sound, Arnold's music gleams. Though there is no mistaking Arnold for anything other than a 20th-century composer, the strong element of fancy in his music owes much to the spirit of the late 18th century. Like the classical composers, Arnold has a fine sense of scale, which enables him to create effective dramas within whatever forms he chooses, be they the limited ones of chamber music or the more expansive ones of the symphony. In either case, Arnold can turn from wit to wistfulness within a few bars, and he can be both haunting and puckish almost simultaneously. Arnold also hails from an earlier era in his belief that music "is a social act of communication among people, a gesture of friendship". This is musicians' music, not in some esoteric way but in the sense that it is first of all a joy for musicians to play and therefore, not surprisingly, for us to hear.

It is mainly Arnold's puckish side that is showcased in three Helios CDs devoted to his chamber music. While the pranks, as well as the range of expression, that he can pull off with a full orchestra are missing, one can only marvel at the level of invention and wit manifest in many of these miniatures—including a goodly number for solo instruments. Sonatinas for solo instruments are rather exposed forms in which to write, and one had better have something fairly amusing or important to say to sustain them. Arnold proves himself a master with unfailing ingenuity, sparkle, and spice.

While much of the music on these discs is written in a divertimento style, all is not high spirits and hilarity. Certain pieces have a Shostakovich-like melancholy and intensity, in particular the Piano Trio, op. 54. For the most part, however, novel treatments of delectable melodies abound, sometimes in highly unusual instrumental combinations, dictated by the fact that those were the instruments that Arnold's friends played. For example, the Trio for Flute, Viola, and Bassoon, op. 6, is a Mozartian delight of ease, transparency, and grace. It was written in 1942 for the diversion of friends in the London Philharmonic, and it shows not a whit of war strain. The Divertimento for Flute, Oboe, and Clarinet, op. 37, is another lesson from Arnold to those who think we may live in too cruel a time to sustain the divertimento form at its highest level. The breezy, nostalgic Oboe Quartet, op. 61, is in the same league.

Naxos has a recording of Malcolm Arnold's delightful Concerto for Two Pianos, Concerto for Piano Duet and Strings, *Fantasy on a Theme of John Field*, and *Overture: Beckus the Dandipratt*. I cannot think of more agreeable listening. In one movement or even moment, the music is piercingly lovely (the first concerto's exquisite Andante con moto), in the next raucous; the priceless element of fancy and play in this most mercurial music is pervasive. It is a riot of humor and whimsy, with interjections of sudden, wild drama.

Of the nine symphonies, the First, Second, and Fifth are perhaps the most immediately engaging. The first two especially are full of breezy optimism and joie de vivre. After the Fifth, the symphonies take on a darker and more somber cast, yet even they have unexpected moments of sprightliness. Arnold will interrupt a Shostakovich-like onslaught with a wistful melody that seems to arrive from another world. What is it doing there? Is it, as Donald Mitchell suggests, a product of Arnold's "unique recovery of innocent lyricism"? Or is Arnold being deliberately corny? One would have to think so from a composer so in command of his resources and idioms. Arnold explains that "in times of great emotion we speak in clichés." In any case, these stylistic discrepancies set up a unique kind of tension in these works. Critic Hans Keller has tried to unlock their enigmatic meaning: "Arnold's profundity usually manifests itself in pseudo-shallowness, which is his historical inversion of pseudo-profundity." Any music that could give rise to such a sentence must be worth listening to.

After his Eighth Symphony, Arnold suffered a breakdown and underwent an excruciating five-year period of suffering. His Ninth Symphony reflects Arnold's experience of "having been through hell", but is also, according to him, "an amalgam of all my knowledge of humanity". The first three movements seem indistinguishable from his typical works. The last movement, as long in duration as the first three put together, is an amazingly spare, bleak procession through despair, yet still there is in it a beautiful Malherian melody. Arnold has written some extraordinary adagios—in the Second and Fifth symphonies particularly—but nothing to compare to the elemental grief and resignation he has achieved here. Yet despair, however real, does not have the last word. At the very end, when all seems lost in sorrow, a D-major chord lights up the landscape. "You get to the last D-major chord," Arnold said of the finale, "and you know . . . you've won through." Arnold won through, and I am sure that his legacy will extend well beyond his wish "to be remembered as a man who wrote tuneful music".

Recommended Recordings

Dances (English, Scottish, Cornish, Irish, and Welsh), London Philharmonic, Sir Malcolm Arnold, Lyrita 201 or Queensland SO, Andrew Penny, Naxos 8.553526

Symphonies 1 & 2, NSO Ireland, Andrew Penny, Naxos 8.553406

Symphonies 3 & 4, London SO, Richard Hickox, Chandos 9290

Symphonies 5 & 6, London SO, Richard Hickox, Chandos 9385

Symphony No. 9, NSO Ireland, Andrew Penny, Naxos 8.553540

Film Music (including *The Bridge on the River Kwai*), London SO, Richard Hickox, Chandos 9100.

Concertos: Two Violins, Clarinet, Flute, Horn (No. 2), Mark Stephenson, London Musici, Lyn Fletcher, Kenneth Sillito, Michael Collins, Karen Jones, Richard Watkins, Conifer Classics 74321-15004 (available as an ArkivCD)

Chamber Music, vol. 1, Helios CDH 55071; vol. 2, CDH 55072; vol. 3, CDH 55073. I recommend them in reverse order.

Cello Concerto; Symphony for Strings; Fantasy for Recorder and String Quartet, Naxos 8572640

Ballet Music, Rumon Gamba, BBC PO, Chandos 10550

Concerto for Two Pianos; Concerto for Piano Duet and Strings, Esa Heikkilä, Ulster Orchestra, Phillip Dyson, Kevin Sargent, Naxos 8570531

String Quartets 1 & 2, Malcolm Arnold, Maggini Quartet, Naxos 8557762

~

Samuel Barber and His "School": American Beauty

Despite Hollywood's attempts to portray our lives as empty and ugly in movies like *American Beauty*, there is such a thing as beauty in America. A thread of beautiful music runs through the nation's entire history. Yet I would challenge you to name a single living American composer. If you can, it is probably John Adams, he of *Nixon in China* and *Harmonielehre* fame (all of it deserved). I don't blame you if you can't name any others. Even if you are a music lover—like many I know—you probably have not come all the way out of the bunker into which you retreated to survive the assault of noise that commenced in the 20th century.

In any case, the evidence for American beauty is abundant. The Naxos label has been engaged in an extensive survey of American music in a series called American Classics, in which you will find some of the big names of American music—Samuel Barber, Paul Creston, Aaron Copland, David Diamond, Roy Harris, Walter Piston, William Schuman—as well as some of the lesser ones, in impeccable performances. One need only hear the release featuring the lovely Piano Trios 1 and 2 by Arthur Foote (1853–1937) to know that our beauty was originally imported, like almost everything else, from Europe. In the 20th century, however, those European threads were woven into an American musical tapestry of unique design. As with so many American things, strength, directness of expression, an openhearted yearning, and an element of naïveté characterize the musical patterns that emerged.

Naxos has also undertaken a traversal of the music by a 20th-century exemplar of American beauty, composer Samuel Barber (1910–1981). Barber knew that beauty is a kind of food for the soul that makes it only hungrier. That is why the abundance of it in his music pierces through to something beyond itself and easily brings the listener to tears. Barber's best-known work is his *Adagio for Strings*, an orchestral arrangement of the second movement of his String Quartet. There is hardly a more familiar or more moving piece of American music.

I once heard *Adagio* in the living room of Russell Kirk, father of the American intellectual conservative movement, in faraway Mecosta, Michigan, performed by a local quintet of female musicians (the cello part was doubled). At first, I simply resigned myself to hearing a musical warhorse played by provincials. But then I was overwhelmed, even shaken, by the intensity of the beauty evident in a very heartfelt performance. I will never forget the experience. In fact, I cannot forget most of Barber's music, and I never tire of making its reacquaintance.

Naxos has offered several CDs of essential Barber. The first contains his two symphonies and his brilliant *The School for Scandal Overture*, which catapulted him into the limelight in his early 20s. The second contains two less familiar but equally worthy works—the Cello Concerto and the *Medea Ballet Suite*—plus the omnipresent *Adagio for Strings*. All are more than ably performed by the Royal Scottish National Orchestra, under Marin Alsop, with cellist Wendy Warner. The idiom of this music may be late-romantic, but it is unburdened by the kind of Germanic heaviness that sank this kind of music on the Continent.

Barber gave romanticism a fresh start with his melodic and orchestral genius. For this, he became the composer the avant-garde loved to hate. He was the last thing they wanted—a musician who breathed new life into a language they had declared dead, if not forbidden. Though Barber suffered personally from unremitting critical denigration, he was rewarded by enormous popularity with the concert-going public. The reason the public never abandoned Barber can be heard in one of his most popular works, the Violin Concerto, performed by the young Hilary Hahn—in one of her first recordings for Sony—with the St. Paul Chamber Orchestra, under Hugh Wolff. This work is certainly an American classic and was one of the most performed concertos of the 20th century. It is a stirring, passionate piece, with bravura passages for the soloist that were clearly written not simply for show but in service to a higher cause.

Its disc-mate is a work by composer and double-bassist Edgar Meyer (b. 1956), written for Hahn. This is a sweet and ingratiating piece with a languid, mesmerizing beauty that, at the very end, slips into Americana. Nonetheless, it inspired me to search out Meyer's Quintet for String Quartet and Double Bass on the Deutsche Grammophon label. While several of its movements are also highly rewarding, others lapse into a folk-fiddle hoedown that left me feeling as though I had been mugged by a bluegrass crossover composer, which, in fact, is what Meyer is. He is good enough, however, that I hope he crosses over more completely into classical music.

Naxos' fifth installment in the Barber cycle features the Second and Third of his three dramatic Essays for Orchestra, *Toccata Festiva*, and, most importantly, the radiant *Knoxville: Summer of 1915*. Barber said *Knoxville* was written to capture "a child's feelings of loneliness, wonder, and lack of identity in that marginal world between twilight and sleep". It does more than that. Commissioned in 1947, *Knoxville* is a setting of a text by James Agee that served as a prelude to his heartbreaking unfinished novel, *A Death in the Family*. Here a child speaks of the simple sights and sounds of an evening with his family on the lawn before going to bed. Out of this, Barber created a sublime masterpiece that captures the poignancy of the transitory, and the aching, universal experience of "lack of identity". After praying for his family, the child speaks of them as "those [who] receive me, who quietly treat me, as one familiar and well-beloved in that home; but will not, oh, will not, not now, not ever; but will not ever tell me who I am."

No, of course they will not, cannot, because your identity is hidden in your Creator, who will show you to yourself when he meets you. If you can listen to this music and Agee's words without tears streaming down your face, you have not listened closely enough. Soprano Karina Gauvin soars in vocal glory to the extraordinarily beautiful accompaniment of the Royal Scottish National Orchestra, under Marin Alsop.

The Chandos label has also enriched the catalogue of Barber recordings by compiling all three Essays for Orchestra on one disc, along with excerpts from his opera *Vanessa*, *Music for a Scene from Shelley*, and *Medea's Meditation and Dance of Vengeance*. These were originally issued separately as disc-mates for Neeme Järvi's recordings of other American music with the Detroit Symphony Orchestra. It made great sense to bring them together on one CD.

While Barber faced derision, he did not have to deal with complete obscurity. As the whole of the 20th century has slowly come into view after the demise of the 12-tone school, the extent of the damage from its half-century hegemony keeps popping up in the form of revived, heretofore neglected music from that era. Otherwise, how can one account for the fact that Vittorio Giannini's full-blown, romantic Piano Concerto and his Symphony No. 4 each received only their second performances for the purposes of a Naxos recording? They were debuted in, respectively, 1937 and 1960. Anyone who loves Rachmaninoff will be swept away by the big-boned, gorgeously melodic Piano Concerto, dashingly played by Gabriela Imreh, with the Bournemouth Symphony Orchestra under Daniel Spalding.

Giannini's Fourth Symphony leaves youthful romanticism aside for music that is more tautly and closely argued, though just as, if not even more, compelling than the piano work. Giannini said that he was motivated by "an unrelenting quest for the beautiful, with the humble hope that I may be privileged to achieve this goal, if only for one precious moment and share this moment with my listeners". He certainly achieved more than "one precious moment" in the second movement, Sostenuto e calmo; it has to be one of the most beautiful, stirring movements in the American symphonic repertoire. As Giannini said, "If you want to be an artist you must realize that you must build and live in an interior world of Beauty and dedication to your art and service to God." Listen to Giannini's Sostenuto to hear what this means in sound. How could this possibly be only the second performance of something this wonderful?

Conductor Daniel Spalding moves the British Bournemouth Symphony Orchestra to play as if to the American manner born. The first chair players in oboe, clarinet, horn, and violin all deserve huzzahs. Booklet notes are by the finest critic of American music, Walter Simmons. This release is a huge gift at a budget price.

It is also for allowing us to hear the "non-classic" American composers (in the sense of their even greater obscurity) that we should be particularly grateful to Naxos. Some of these are older folks like Paul Fetler (b. 1920), who were simply overlooked in the din caused by the army of noise. The Ann Arbor Symphony Orchestra, under Arie Lipsky, gives Fetler the first recording dedicated solely to his music. From what I hear on this disc, it is way overdue. The CD begins with *Three Poems by Walt Whitman*. I abhor music with narration, which is what this is, but the quality of Fetler's settings is so brilliant that I endured Thomas Blaske's readings. I was enraptured by the evocative nocturnal tone poem Fetler was developing in the first poem for nearly three minutes before the narration began. The impressionistic music is so beautiful that I wish Fetler had set these texts as songs instead. The Capriccio that follows is a delightful piece full of, in Fetler's words, "whimsy and playfulness". It reminds me of Prokofiev in his lighter vein. The major work on this CD is the Violin Concerto No. 2, with violinist Aaron Berofsky. This full-throated, highly lyrical music, composed in 1980, is directly in the lineage of Barber's Violin Concerto. This may be old-fashioned music, but it is so enchanting that it vindicates Fetler's statement that "what was modern is modern no more. All the issues vanish, only expression remains." The Ann Arbor performances were recorded live, with completely silent audiences who obviously were as taken with this music as you will be.

James Aikman (b. 1959) has written a violin concerto subtitled *Lines in Motion*. Its opening ostinato is repeated a few too many times in the opening minute and a half, but the work is soon rescued by a highly lyrical and rhapsodic violin line that is extraordinarily long. It sets up a deeply felt yearning against the somewhat mechanical ostinato. This segues into a very stirring "Quasi una fantasia", which is the heart of the work. It, too, achieves a Barber-like beauty. Music like this is a nail in the heart of the avant-garde. The concerto is followed by the exquisite *Ania's Song: A Pavane for String Orchestra* and a Concerto for Saxophone and Orchestra. This CD is another winner in the Naxos American Classics series, and is done to perfection by the St. Petersburg State Symphony Orchestra, under Vladimir Lande, with the excellent violinist Charles Weatherbee.

One can hardly say that John Corigliano (b. 1938) has been overlooked. He is one of the most celebrated contemporary American composers. He had a big hit with his film score to *The Red Violin*, later utilizing the music in a number of forms. Perhaps the most successful is the *Red Violin Chaconne*, which he turned into a full-blown violin concerto, *The Red Violin*, in 2003. It is a big-boned piece that, like the Fetler and the Aikman, harkens back to Barber. I particularly enjoyed Corigliano's remark that the liberty of first writing this highly romantic music for film allowed him to bypass his "censor button". He knows how to write a great melody, and he has one in the opening movement, which he calls "a passionate romantic essay". This theme ties together the whole concerto, which was written, as Corigliano said, " 'in the great tradition' kind of concerto" in memory of his violinist father, who was the concert master of the New York Philharmonic. The sizable concerto is accompanied by the fantastic time machine *Phantasmagoria*: Suite from *The Ghosts of Versailles* (2000), Corigliano's hit opera written for the Metropolitan Opera. Violinist Michael Ludwig is dazzling in the concerto, and JoAnn Falletta and the Buffalo Philharmonic Orchestra play with requisite passion and care throughout.

Conductor Falletta, this time with the London Symphony Orchestra, brings us the startlingly gracious music of Jack Gallagher (b. 1947). The works on this new American Classics CD fit exactly the description of American music at the head of this chapter. Do you want optimistic exuberance? Go to the *Diversions Overture* that begins the program. Poignancy? The liltingly lovely Berceuse. Music does not get much lovelier than this. Vivacity? The Sinfonietta for Strings demonstrates how Americans can continue the great British tradition of such string works (think Britten). The Pavane movement in this piece goes as directly to the heart as does the Berceuse. It begins like one of Vaughan Williams' great string works. The Symphony in One Movement: *Threnody* pretty much has it all, including some stabbing chords at the end that could have come out of Bernard Herrmann's great score for *Psycho*. I highly recommend this CD for the shell-shocked. You will think you have been cheated that you have not heard it before.

Other labels, like Koch, also entered the lists on behalf of American beauty. Like some of the above, Ian Krouse (b. 1956) seems to have picked up the violin where Samuel Barber set it down. His Rhapsody for Violin and Orchestra is passionate music in which the thirst for beauty is intense. He deploys an achingly lovely melody in the form of a huge arch. This is a gorgeous, dramatic piece that shows that Barber's school of music is still very much alive today. It is accompanied by his *Cuando se abre en la mañana*, a rhapsodic song for soprano and guitar, and two chamber works, *Thamar y Amnón* and *Tientos*.

As one might deduce from the titles of his works, Krouse, who lives in Maryland, has developed a strong predilection for Spanish things (as have I, being married to a Spaniard). His ravishing song, which sets words written by Federico García Lorca, one of the great Spanish writers and artists of the 20th century, to music, is completely convincing in the Spanish style in which he has written it. In fact, it is masterly, as are the two equally accomplished chamber works, all written in the 1990s. Listening to a CD like this, from a composer of whom I had never previously heard, is a wake-up call.

Dominick Argento (b. 1927) is known primarily as a composer of operas and song cycles. He has spent most of his career in Minneapolis, where he has been a professor of composition and opera history. He is an American treasure and, like most American treasures, neglected. In 1987, he composed a stunning Te Deum. Virgin Classics released a superb recording that inexplicably disappeared after a few years in the catalogue. That omission has since been rectified by the RCM label, which issued a new recording with the Los Angeles Master Chorale and Sinfonia Orchestra, under Paul Salamunovich, paired with Maurice Duruflé's *Messe "Cum jubilo".* At first, I thought this rendition was a bit too reverential compared with the vigor of the Virgin performance. But after all, this *is* reverential music, though large portions of it burst with life and joy.

The more I listen, the more convinced I am of Argento's own endorsement of this interpretation, which he calls "an act of love" that "penetrates to the very heart of the work". Argento interpolates anonymous Middle English texts between the Latin sections of the Te Deum. The effect, as well as the musical idiom Argento uses, is redolent of Benjamin Britten's best works. This may not be liturgical music in the strictest sense, but those who tell me that nothing of note has been composed since the Second Vatican Council need to listen to this vibrant work.

Reference Recordings has given us a CD of some of Argento's orchestral works and suites from two of his operas, *The Voyage of Edgar Allen Poe* and *The Dream of Valentino.* Both the performances by the Minnesota Orchestra, under Eiji Oue, and the recording quality are of demonstration caliber. The CD shows both Argento's sense of humor, with an accordion tango in the *Valentino* music, and his exquisite sense of orchestration, with more delicate pieces such as *Valse triste* and *Reverie: Reflections on a Hymn Tune.* Argento has spent many summers in Florence, and its bell towers make their presence delightfully felt in much of his music, particularly in *A Ring of Time,* a piece based on the four seasons. Bells and chimes resound throughout.

Another Reference Recording offers Argento's *Casa Guidi,* a glorious orchestral song setting of texts from Elizabeth Barrett Browning's letters to her sister from Florence, gorgeously sung by Frederica Von Stade. It is about as drop-dead beautiful as vocal music gets, enveloped in luminous orchestration. If Richard Strauss had been an American, he might have written something like this, without at all sounding like himself. Two entrancing orchestral works accompany this, the playful Capriccio for Clarinet and Orchestra and *In Praise of Music: Seven Songs for Orchestra.*

What do all these American works have in common? They all have great melodies. These composers all want to communicate with you through their music. Samuel Barber and his "school" add to the abundant evidence that the thread of beauty in American music remains unbroken. I know you have had a rough time—so have I, especially since I did not go into the bunker during the full-frontal assault. But I am out here to give the "all clear" signal. Open your ears and give these American Classics the chance they deserve.

Recommended Recordings

Arthur Foote

Piano Trios 1 & 2, Naxos 8.559039

Francesca da Rimini, Four Character Pieces, Suite in E Major, Gerard Schwarz, Seattle SO, Naxos 8.559365

Samuel Barber

Complete Orchestral Works, Marin Alsop, Royal Scottish National Orchestra et al., Naxos 8.506021 (6 CDs), or individually below:

Symphonies 1 & 2, *The School for Scandal Overture*, and First Essay for Orchestra, Naxos 8.559088

Knoxville: Summer of 1915; Second and Third Essays for Orchestra; *Toccata Festiva*, Naxos 8.559134

Cello Concerto; *Medea Ballet Suite*; and *Adagio for Strings*, Marin Alsop, Royal Scottish National Orchestra, Wendy Warner, Naxos 8.559088

Violin Concerto (plus Edgar Meyer Violin Concerto), Hugh Wolff, St. Paul Chamber Orchestra, Hilary Hahn, Sony Classical 89029

Three Essays for Orchestra; Excerpts from *Vanessa*; *Music for a Scene from Shelley*; and *Medea's Meditation and Dance of Vengeance*, Neeme Järvi, Detroit SO, Chandos 9908

Vittorio Giannini

Piano Concerto, Symphony No. 4, Daniel Spalding, Bournemouth SO, Gabriela Imreh, Naxos 8.559352

Paul Fetler

Violin Concerto No. 2: *Three Poems by Walt Whitman*; Capriccio, Ann Arbor SO, Arie Lipsky, Aaron Berofsky et al., Naxos 8.559606

James Aikman

Violin Concerto: *Lines in Motion*; *Ania's Song*; and Concerto for Saxophone and Orchestra, Vladimir Lande, St. Petersburg State SO, Charles Wetherbee, Taimur Sullivan, Naxos 8.559720

John Corigliano

Violin Concerto, *The Red Violin*; *Phantasmagoria*; Suite from *The Ghosts of Versailles*, JoAnn Falletta, Buffalo PO, Michael Ludwig, Naxos 8.559671

Jack Gallagher

Diversions Overture; Berceuse; Sinfonietta for Strings; *Symphony in One Movement: Threnody*, JoAnn Falletta, London SO, Naxos 8.559652

Ian Krouse

Rhapsody for Violin and Orchestra; *Cuando se abre en la mañana*, *Thamar y Amnón*, and *Tientos*, James Sedares, New Zealand SO et al., Koch 7482 (OOP)

Dominick Argento

Te Deum (plus Duruflé *Messe "Cum jubilo"*), Paul Salamunovich, Los Angeles Master Chorale, RCM 12002

Valentino Dances and Orchestral Works, Reference Recordings RR-91

Casa Guidi, Frederica Von Stade, Eiji Oue, Minnesota Orchestra, Reference Recordings 100

Evensong: Of Love and Angels, Lewis, Futral, Reed, Cathedral Choral Society, Gothic Records 49269

~

Walter Braunfels: Beauty and Eternal Order

Jens F. Laurson

It's a shame that those artists who were banned by the Nazis have remained in obscurity. Just imagine how these artists must have felt —those that survived—when they had hoped to be performed after 1945, after years of darkness, only to find out that their music was no longer wanted. How it must have been for Braunfels, after those years of inner emigration. What a disaster for him. What a story! Because his music is so good, I'd do it anyway, even without the story. But in the combination of his personal history and the quality of his work, Braunfels is really an obligation for me.

Conductor Manfred Honeck had just finished leading the Stuttgart State Orchestra in Walter Braunfels' Great Mass, and talked excitedly, passionately about the composer in a tiny backstage room of the Stuttgart *Liederhalle*. It was the first performance of the Mass since its premiere in 1927 under Hermann Abendroth and the crowning part of Honeck's three-year focus on Braunfels during his time in Stuttgart. The work had never been lost; it's unquestionably a work of considerable importance, ample beauty, and great profundity. To hone in on the reason why it took until April 2010 to get a modern-day performance is to unearth the story of all those early 20th-century composers whose music died twice: once when the Nazis declared their music *Entartete Kunst*, "Degenerate Art". And then again when postwar Europe experienced an aesthetic paradigm shift.

The paradigm shift never actually happened in listening habits (people went on, happily, listening to Bach and Beethoven and Richard Strauss), but the caesura was meaningful for all contemporary music, which had a more difficult time getting funded and played if it didn't adhere to the new avant-garde standards that the arbiters of taste— critics, program directors in radio stations, professors—deemed untainted. The various schools of tonal music—in fact any form of romantic music and nearly the whole prewar aesthetic—had come into disrepute in the West and in Germany in particular. A lot of music that might have eked out a place in the repertoire was never given the chance to impress audiences to become part of the musical vernacular.

The once ill-boding term "Degenerate Art" used to ban and prosecute artists that did not fit the Third Reich's narrow aesthetic prescriptions has been reclaimed, at last, flipped around, and is now a tag of honor that helps many of the doubly ignored composers to some highly overdue exposure.

Walter Braunfels (1882–1954), son of a granddaughter of composer Louis Spohr, is a prime example for this, and his biography is unusual only in that he did not emigrate and that he survived. Briefly sidetracked by a stint of law and economics at university, he was nudged back to music by a performance of *Tristan und Isolde*, and he continued to pursue his musical education to become a pianist and to study composition with the now equally unknown, but similarly splendid, Munich composer Ludwig Thuille and the famous Wagner-conductor Felix Mottl.

Between the wars, Braunfels was the second most performed opera composer in Germany after Richard Strauss. His first successes came before World War I, including his opera *Princess Brambilla*. But he came to even wider notice for his sacred music—most notably his Te Deum —which was inspired by his conversion to Catholicism, which happened after Braunfels returned home, wounded late in the Great War. His opera *The Birds*, based on Aristophanes, premiered in 1920 and had 50 performances in Munich in its first two years alone. The great musicologist and Mozart biographer Alfred Einstein wrote, "I do not believe such a complete work of art has ever before been performed on the German operatic stage. There is an imperative at work here which calls for comparison with Wagner's *Meistersinger* and Pfitzner's *Palestrina*." All that need be added is that anyone who enjoys the lyrical operas of Richard Strauss is in for a major treat.

But Braunfels' career came to an abrupt end when the Nazis took power. His father, Ludwig Braunfels, had been baptized into Protestantism as an infant by his converted Jewish father in 1838. So Walter—despite the family's early conversion or his considerable artistic status—was a "Half-Jew", or "First Degree Mischling", according to the Nuremberg Race Laws. That would have been enough reason for his career—even life—to be in peril, but Braunfels also had the effrontery to reject the Nazis when they approached him to write their party anthem. His music was banned, and Braunfels dismissed from his post as director of the Cologne Academy of Music, which he had cofounded. Braunfels, unwilling to leave Germany, went into inner exile and worked secretly in his house on Lake Constance.

During that time he wrote an opera based on Paul Claudel's mystery play, *L'Annonce faite à Marie*—an opera of concentrated radiance and luminosity. One can only wonder at the faith burning in the heart of a man who could write a work about divine forgiveness as he lived under an ideology of hatred. He was animated, he said, by "the possibility of creating a musical mystery play which makes visible the knowledge of the greatest possible beauty and eternal order". In the next to last scene, when the Gospel Christmas narrative is sung, Braunfels came very close to his goal. *Verkündigung (Annunciation)* was set to a German translation, since Claudel would not give his permission for a French version by a German composer.

After the war, performances of Braunfels' music were few and far between, although he was briefly reinstated as the head of the refounded Cologne Conservatory. Even now there are just a handful of recordings of his music. Back in his dressing room in Stuttgart, Honeck mused on why the Great Mass took so long to be performed:

> Yes, it sat there, bid its time, unrecognized for its greatness, underestimated, and perhaps a couple times someone got as far as the second page, saw what lineup it required, and quietly put it back. "We can't sell that, it's a whole evening's worth of music, it would need a special occasion." And I suppose that special occasion never came up. Even anniversaries of his birth—his hundredth in 1982—or his death— fiftieth in 2004—weren't considered, which is too bad. But if a work is good, its time will come. And the time *has* come. And it really *was* about time.

He continued with increasingly effusive enthusiasm:

> I mean, in a way it's a shame that after 80 years we are only now, finally, giving the second performance of this Great Mass. . . . He takes the word first, and then he composes around it. The word is first with Braunfels, always. You feel it all the time. Even in the Agnus Dei: "Dona nobis pacem . . ." To end a piece with a boys' choir is really unbelievable. What is the reason to end a piece with the boys' choir? The innocence of children, the idea of peace carried forward by children. . . . With Braunfels, it's never about himself.

While the Great Mass isn't a liturgical work—in any case it wasn't intended for a church service—it also isn't, minor similarities with Verdi apart, a secular Requiem either. It speaks directly from a sincere spiritual urge; it is far removed from being absolute music in the mere guise of a Mass. "The works addressed a *need* of my father", said Braunfels' octogenarian son after the performance, greatly moved finally to hear the work he remembered well from listening to the singers' rehearsals at home while hiding beneath the grand piano.

Honeck became a Braunfels devotee when he was to conduct Braunfels' opera *Jeanne d'Arc: Scenes from the Life of St. Joan*, which Braunfels composed during the war. "That was my first encounter with Braunfels and I was a little hesitant at first and asked for a score. But the deeper I went into the score, and the more I got to know this music, the more I was convinced. And I was even more moved when I heard his story, which touched me a lot."

From Honeck's recording with the Swedish Radio Orchestra, I discovered just how beautiful an opera *Jeanne d'Arc* is. But what I really noticed only during a performance of *Jeanne d'Arc* at the 2013 Salzburg Festival was how uncommonly good the libretto is—perhaps the best opera libretto I've encountered. The way Braunfels managed to put it together from the original French and Latin 15th-century trial documents makes this distant, far-removed story palpable, indeed riveting, for a 21st-century audience. Every character is three-dimensional; the text is alive, realistic, and natural, taken straight out of life.

For all the helpful (or helpless) comparisons to his contemporaneous opera colleagues: Richard Strauss (easily dismissed for their very different musical accent), or Paul Hindemith (who hasn't Braunfels' touch for melody and easygoing charm), or Hans Pfitzner (whose talent in referencing earlier musical styles rings a bell in Braunfels' work), Braunfels' music is unique. It envelops the ears like a sea—in a unique style that could be called late-romantic—but really offers an aural window onto a music that might have been (and actually *was* for its brief period), had World War II and its subsequent aesthetic realignment never happened.

Braunfels' hand at drama and his careful consideration of the text betray the opera composer, not only in the Great Mass, but also in the Te Deum. While preparing for *Jeanne d'Arc*, Honeck wanted to get his hands on every available piece. When he hit upon the Te Deum, he knew he had struck gold.

It's a *great* Te Deum; I love Bruckner's Te Deum, and I saw Braunfels' in that line. And in some ways it's perhaps an even greater piece. I was really amazed, so I performed it in Stockholm and we recorded it, because at the time there wasn't a CD of it available. Since then the Profil-Hänssler label has found, cleaned up, and released an old recording of it with Günter Wand which I must say is wonderful, too. You feel the spirit in the interpretation. And not only do you have the Bruckner connection here, but Günter Wand was also a student of Walter Braunfels in Cologne.

This magnificent piece, in the great tradition of the Te Deums by Berlioz and Bruckner, is so glorious and exhilarating that it is enough to make one rethink one's whole attitude toward the Weimar Republic. If a work of this kind had been possible at that time, maybe the horror show that followed was not as inevitable as many think.

It might take several spins to grasp the Te Deum in either recording —especially to those who find the Bruckner Te Deum a little elusive. The Pittsburgh audience and chorus, however, were quick on the up-take: When Honeck performed just the massive 20-minute first move-ment, he was amazed with the reaction of the people to Braunfels' mu-sic. "The choir, they fell in love with that movement. Of course, it's a very romantic movement; it's a *Lohengrin*-moment in music. . . . But it *is* great", he hastened to add, as if the *Lohengrin* reference had cast that into doubt. I don't hear a clear *Lohengrin* reference in the Te Deum until the third movement (about three minutes in), but instead I hear Braunfels' own densely beautiful romantic music in the first movement, along with a few moments reminiscent of other composers, notably a brief Carl Orff bit toward the end.

Walter Braunfels has another conductor-champion in Ulf Schirmer, head of the Leipzig Opera and the Munich Radio Orchestra. With the latter, he performed many of Braunfels' secular works, among them his four cantatas—one each for Advent, Christmas, the Passion, and Easter. When the Easter Cantata from 1944 finally saw the light of day 70 years later, Schirmer suggested that this would be the last world premiere of a significant work by Braunfels, whose catalogue seems largely discovered and performed—at last, if not yet well recorded. Consonant, dramatic, excited, the work climaxes in an extended Hal-lelujah run-up before ending with a doxology.

Recordings of these cantatas were made and, one hopes, will be is-sued in due time. Premiered in 1920, *Fantastic Appearances of a Theme by Hector Berlioz* (perhaps more efficiently referred to as his "Berlioz Overture") is a set of variations on Mephistopheles' "Song of the Flea" from *The Damnation of Faust*. It is a wild tour de force, a phantasmagoric piece every bit as orchestrally brilliant as the best of Richard Strauss and completely worthy of its source in Berlioz. CD reviewer David Hurwitz likened the work to Richard Strauss' *Don Quixote*—on LSD.

In 2010, RCA released a disc with the world premiere recording of the Braunfels Sextet, coupled with Adolf Busch's delightful work for the same constellation of musicians. Written in 1945, the 40-minute Quintet in F-sharp Minor (and sounding about half as long) is a work steeped in melancholy, with an almost Schubertian poignancy to it, and it cuts through the heart. It sits at the far end of the Beethoven-Wagner-Pfitzner trajectory, chromatic-romantic, sweeping-yet-dense, without a hint of academicism. However, the fourth movement, Finale-Rondo, beginning dolefully, slips into a Janáček-style dance that lifts the spirits and dispels the gloom. The ARC musicians (Artists of the Royal Conservatory, Toronto) do a marvelous job bringing these works fully to life, a service they have provided in their equally outstanding releases of Mieczysław Weinberg and Julius Röntgen works. This is not to be missed by chamber music aficionados. Braunfels also penned two quartets, substantive works of somber beauty whose lineage clearly goes back to Schubert and which are equally worth exploring.

Recommended Recordings

The discography of Walter Braunfels' work is still dismal but, as the example of Weinberg shows us, that can change quickly—it will have to, and it will. There simply is too much great music out there, and many fine musicians tired of the same-old repertoire will find their way to it. Meanwhile, the curious listener has to make do with what little there is, most of which is thankfully of superb standards. If you are unsure about his music, start with the *Phantastical Appearances*, then the String Quintet. You should be hooked by then and go down either the secular or operatic route first, according to personal preference.

Jeanne d'Arc, Manfred Honeck, Swedish RSO & Choir, Eric Ericson Chamber Choir, Juliane Banse et al., Decca 4099953. A terrific opera in a wonderful recording from Swedish Radio that Decca issued, but unfortunately not worldwide, and for now only available as a European import. The arts team at Decca put Lady Godiva on the cover, which is momentarily confusing (and tasteless), but it's all Joan of Arc on the inside.

Die Vögel (*The Birds*) Lothar Zagrosek, Deutsches Symphonie Orchester Berlin, Berlin Radio Chorus, Helen Kwon, Endrik Wottrich et al., Decca 448679

Or: James Conlon, Los Angeles Opera, Darko Tresnjak (director), Désirée Rancatore, Brandon Jovanovich et al., Arthaus Musik DVD 101529 or Bluray 101530. The choice here really is one of seeing or just hearing an opera; mine is hearing. As for the seeing, the Los Angeles Opera staging looks like a high school production that might intend to be naïve, but ends up naff—from the non-existent acting and pedestrian ballet section to the corny makeup and costumes. Musically, Conlon's Los Angeles performance, like Zagrosek's, is first rate, except for the poor German of more than half his cast.

Verkündigung, Ulf Schirmer, Munich RSO, BR Klassik 900311. Or: Dennis Russell Davies, Cologne SO, EMI/Warner 555104. The second-ever recording of Walter Braunfels' *Annunciation* is a stupendous performance of the Braunfels-devoted Ulf Schirmer and his Munich Orchestra. Juliane Banse, as in *Jeanne d'Arc*, is a boon to the composer and heads a splendid cast.

Great Mass, Manfred Honeck, Stuttgart State Orchestra & Opera Chorus, Decca 1130211. Or: Peter Weigle, Konzerthaus Orchestra Berlin, Berlin Philharmonic Chorus et al., Capriccio C5267. It would be silly to suggest that the performance Honeck conducted and happily convinced Decca to publish on CD could not be bettered. The soloists, for one, did not all excel. But their performance was spirited and committed throughout. And on CD, perhaps because of edits, it sounds even cleaner than my memory of the performance would have had it.

Te Deum, Manfred Honeck, Gitta-Maria Sjöberg, Lars-Erik Jonsson, Swedish Radio Orchestra & Chorus, Orfeo 679071. Or: Günter Wand, Leonie Rysanek, Helmut Melchert, Cologne RSO, Gürzenich Choir, Profil 026002 (also on: Acanta 233670). Honeck is gracious—and right—to mention the Günter Wand recording, because even the 1952 sound can't hamper the emotional quality of his performance. While Honeck's grasp and Orfeo's crisp sound make it the obvious first choice, Wand is the disciple's pick.

Phantastical Appearances of a Theme by Hector Berlioz, Günter Wand, West German RSO, Profil 026004. Or: Dennis Russell Davies, Vienna RSO, CPO 999882.

The *Phantastical Appearances* was recorded in 2001 by Dennis Russell Davies, who is to be praised for a sumptuous performance. However, Gunter Wand adds a touch of greatness to it in his 1953 recording, which, in good monaural sound with the Cologne RSO, is more bracing and exciting. This might be the recording to listen to. But, just to make it more difficult, Dennis Russell Davies throws in Braunfels' substantial, very beautiful Serenade for Chamber Orchestra, which tilts the scales back toward Davies.

String Quintet (plus Adolf Busch, String Sextet), ARC Ensemble, RCA 764490. This is not to be missed by lovers of chamber music.

String Quartets 1 & 2, Auryn String Quartet, CPO 999406. The String Quartets, substantive works of somber beauty, are out of print in CD format right now, but are available used, as downloads and streams.

Concerto for Organ, Boys Choir, and Orchestra; Toccata, Adagio and Fugue for organ; *Symphonic Variations on an old French Folksong*, Iveta Apkalna (organ), Munich Symphony, Tölz Boys' Choir, Hansjörg Albrecht (conductor, organ), Oehms 411. Wilhelm Furtwängler conducted the premiere of this Catholic concerto, written for the organist and cantor of the St. Thomas Choir of Leipzig, Günther Ramin.

With its chorales, it follows stylistically the Great Mass and the Te Deum; the bold and dramatic gestures of the first movement put it in the proximity of heavy German romantics à la Max Reger and Josef Rheinberger before it starts to wax lyrically, leading to the chorale "Welcome Mother of God, house of God, Purest Light". The *Symphonic Variations* are lush late-romanticism much like the *Berlioz Variations*. In the late Toccata, Adagio and Fugue, Braunfels pares down his vocabulary to the essential.

Complete Songs, Marlis Petersen, Konrad Jarnot, Eric Schneider, Capriccio C5251

∼

Frank Bridge: A Bridge Too Far?

There are certain one-work composers whose renown, however un-
fairly, seldom extends beyond a single composition. Take English composer Gustav Holst, who lived to rue the popularity of *The Planets*,
which eclipsed his many jewel-like compositions. His countryman and
contemporary Frank Bridge (1879–1941) seems to have suffered a similar fate, though in his case as a three-work composer. In the mid-
1970s, the EMI/Warner label issued a stunning recording of Bridge's
The Sea, *Summer*, and *Enter Spring*, gorgeous tone poems of the first
rank, beautifully performed by the Royal Liverpool Philharmonic, under Sir Charles Groves. This recording, now available on a midprice
CD, is a classic. The New Zealand Symphony Orchestra, under James
Judd, offers a newer, energetic performance of these three on the budget Naxos label. Beyond these popular works, little was known, except that Bridge was Benjamin Britten's teacher. Britten memorialized
Bridge in his popular *Variations on a Theme by Frank Bridge*.

Thanks to the Chandos label, this abbreviated version of Bridge has
changed. Chandos has issued seven CDs in its complete traversal of
Bridge's orchestral music, each one containing a recording premiere and
featuring the superb BBC National Orchestra of Wales, under Richard
Hickox. A fascinating picture emerges of a composer who sometimes
left his audience somewhat confused over what to expect from him.
Was Bridge a British pastoralist, a romantic, a salon composer, or a
modernist? A partial yes to each of these seemingly mutually incom-
patible designations may provide clue as to why Bridge's work was
neglected for so long. No one thing seems to have been consistently
true of him except for the high level of his craft.

The heart of the consternation over Bridge is that, after the First
World War, he jumped ship and, in the words of the *Musical Times*
in 1930, "made common cause with the advocates of modernity and
put technical interest before aesthetic pleasure". In other words, he
succumbed to Arnold Schoenberg's Second Viennese School of organized atonality. Anyone wishing to illustrate this thesis might turn to
the budget Naxos CD containing Bridge's First and Third Quartets,
compellingly played by the Maggini Quartet. The 20 years separating

these two works contain a rude journey from the world of Schubert and Dvořák to that of Alban Berg and Béla Bartók. However, this puts the matter way too simply. The Chandos CDs and other releases show a far more complicated picture of a composer who may have varied his style but who never lost his essentially rhapsodic and somewhat melancholic nature. And despite the scenario of his "progressive" evolution proffered by many critics, Bridge proved perfectly capable of returning to his earlier tonal style when it suited his purposes. Listen, for example, to the sweetly simple *The Christmas Rose* from 1929 or to his last work, *Rebus*. Bridge was neither doctrinaire nor driven by Schoenberg's revolutionary ideology. Only in England, which was largely immune to the dodecaphonic plague, could he have been considered a revolutionary.

In Bridge's musical pedigree may lay the seeds of some of the confusion. His principal teacher at the Royal College of Music, Charles Stanford, was in thrall to Brahms. From Stanford, Bridge learned a German craft and discipline that would stand him in good stead in terms of the formal construction of his many rhapsodies and fantasies. Bridge's early music seems more continental European than English. In harmonic warmth and melodiousness, Dvořák comes to mind, as does even Tchaikovsky in *Mid of the Night*. The sumptuous, absolutely gorgeous String Sextet in E Flat (1912) could easily pass as a work from the twilight of the First Viennese School with Alexander Zemlinsky, early Arnold Schoenberg, and Franz Schmidt, though without the hint of decay from over-ripeness that is in their music. The Hyperion label, featuring the Raphael Ensemble, offers a new, indispensable recording of this work that also displays Bridge's considerable melodic gift. It is especially effective in capturing the Schubertian poignancy of the second movement. Do not miss it.

Bridge may have had a formal grounding in German structure, but his sensibilities were French. The influence of impressionism from Debussy and Ravel is highly audible in the great sense of refinement in even Bridge's most vigorous works and very direct in pieces like the *Two Intermezzi from "Threads"* and the delightful *Vignettes de danse*, composed as late as 1938. Coincidentally, Bridge wrote *The Sea*, described by Britten as "a riot of melodic and harmonic richness", at the same hotel in Eastbourne in which Debussy put the finishing touches on *La Mer*.

Despite French and German influences, Bridge was not immune to his native soil and first flourished during the bucolic period in British music at the beginning of the 20th century. Derisively called "the cowpat" school, this vein of light romantic music, steeped in pastoral reverie, was once described to American composer Aaron Copland as like "looking at a cow over a fence". "Yes," responded Copland, "and the cow is looking back." Bridge may have participated in the pastoral school, but with a vigor that belied any bovine disposition. His magnificent evocations of nature have an elemental aspect to them, most especially in *The Sea* and *Enter Spring*, which is overwhelmingly powerful. These tone poems easily sweep away any contemporaneous British works of the same sort. If Delius' music seems too flimsy or diaphanous, and Bax' too glutinous, Bridge's works have just the right measure. Nothing quite like them was heard until Britten's *Four Sea Interludes from Peter Grimes*, which, in its turn, was clearly inspired by Bridge.

Nonetheless, one wonders about Bridge's partial conversion to atonality after the First World War, especially in the later chamber pieces and in *Oration* (1930), a cello concerto, and *Phantasm* (1931), a piano concerto—although these are not as forbidding as it may sound. Many critics have used the war, in which Bridge lost close friends, and Bridge's pacifism to explain his conversion. However, one writer intriguingly suggested that it was not so much the war, as it was Bridge's dawning realization that his marriage was infertile that drove him into a more hermetic means of expression. I have always wondered what impelled composers in this direction. One inadequate explanation is the search for new resources. This new language for Bridge, however, seems both to express a deep hurt, whatever its source, and to hide it. It is as if there is a wound that he cannot afford to show openly. It is interesting that he stopped writing songs and choral music after 1925 —as if he ceased singing. His more tonally conflicted kind of music, sometimes despite itself, seems ineluctably to express disillusionment and anger. Hear, for instance, the pained, halting steps in the laments of the third movement of the Piano Trio No. 2. Bridge obviously knew the expressive content of this sad language and how to employ it to great effect.

Every time I think I have Bridge properly categorized, he slips away. Bridge proves elusive because he was an ambidextrous composer. Not only could he switch between distinct styles, he could also almost simultaneously deal with quite contradictory content. Right in the middle of the swaggering exuberance of *Enter Spring*, Bridge broke off to compose the touching lament for Ophelia, *There Is a Willow aslant a Brook* (1927)—two pieces at the opposite ends of the emotional spectrum. Bridge did too many different things well. That makes him confusing but also uniquely rewarding, as the Chandos CDs reveal.

Beginners with Bridge should start with either of the inexpensive renditions of the big trio of tone poems on EMI/Warner (still my first choice) or Naxos. If they strike your fancy, explore further into the varied world of this intriguing man with the Chandos series, which contains such major additions as the *Dance Rhapsody*, and with the various chamber work releases.

Recommended Recordings

The Sea; Summer; Enter Spring, Sir Charles Groves, Royal Liverpool PO, EMI/Warner 5 66855 or James Judd, New Zealand SO, Naxos 8.557167

String Sextet; Quintet; *Lament*, Raphael Ensemble, Hyperion 67426

String Quartets 1 & 3, Maggini String Quartet, Naxos 8.557133

String Quartets 2 & 4; *Phantasy Piano Quartet*, Maggini String Quartet, Naxos 8.557283

Isabella; Enter Spring; Mid of Night; Two Poems, Richard Hickox, BBC NO Wales, Chandos 9950

The Sea; Dance Poem; Dance Rhapsody; Norse Legend, Richard Hickox, BBC NO Wales, Chandos 10012

Phantasm; Summer; Vignettes de danse; There Is a Willow, Richard Hickox, BBC NO Wales, Chandos 10112

A Prayer; Oration; Rebus; Lament; Allegro moderato, Richard Hickox, BBC NO Wales, Chandos 10188

Suite; Valse Intermezzo; Two Intermezzi; The Hag, Richard Hickox, BBC NO Wales, Chandos 10246

(Richard Hickox' Bridge is also available as a 6-CD Collector's Edition, Chandos 10729)

Phantasy Quartet; Phantasie Trio in C Minor; Piano Trio No. 2, Dartington Piano Trio, Helios 55063

∽

Benjamin Britten: The British Neo-Renaissance

Benjamin Britten (1913–1976) may be the figure of his generation in the pantheon of the English neo-Renaissance whose music will be heard two centuries from now. He was the first English composer since Purcell, two and a half centuries his predecessor, to compose masterpieces in so many genres—theatrical, operatic, vocal, orchestral, chamber, and choral. Britten consciously emulated Purcell. He composed his famous *The Young Person's Guide to the Orchestra* as variations and a fugue on a theme from Purcell's *Abdelazar*. When asked by a critic where he had learned to set English poetry to music, Britten replied, "Purcell." Also, Britten's Second String Quartet was composed in commemoration of the 250th anniversary of Purcell's death.

Though influenced by Purcell, Britten's music is not self-consciously English. It does not spring from the English folk song movement of Vaughan Williams and Holst, nor is the tug of the 19th century felt in it. In Britten, it is almost as if English music had matured to the point that it no longer had to worry about its national identity.

At the same time, Britten shared in the basic conservatism of his predecessors. His music is not only tonal but sometimes diatonic. There is nothing new in his harmonic idiom (but neither was there in Mozart's). His technique may not be original, but his inspiration is fresh. The level of his invention is so high and that of his craft so accomplished that his works can stand on their own without having to be seen or justified as "progressive" leaps into some avant-garde future. English critic R.T. Beck summed up Britten's achievement this way: "The originality is not that of a Schoenberg or a Stravinsky, but something quite individual, the rediscovery of expressive and poetic beauties in a language long since thought to be dead, that of tonality and the triad."

With the production of his operatic masterpiece *Peter Grimes* in 1945, Britten did for English opera what Elgar had done for the English symphony. It was the first English opera in more than two centuries to take and hold the world stage. It is a very powerful, haunting drama— stark, somber, harrowing, and heartrending. Against the background of the harshness of the sea, a tragedy of almost Greek proportions is worked out as the larger-than-life but flawed character of Peter Grimes is driven to destruction.

I date my acquaintance with the opera to the early 1970s, when I had the privilege of twice seeing Jon Vickers perform the title role at the Metropolitan Opera. His performance provided one of the greatest theatrical/dramatic/operatic experiences that I have ever had. This was for two reasons. *Peter Grimes* is great art, and it was given a great performance. What are the standards for this judgment? In a 1981 interview, Vickers gave them himself. He said, "Great art wrestles with the timeless, it wrestles with the universal, and at every point deals with the ever-present argument of what constitutes the fundamental moral law." *Peter Grimes* does this. Of his aim as an artist, Vickers said, "I try to touch the fundamental essences of the struggle of existence that are timeless and universal, so that I can reach through the proscenium arch and sort of gather the audience into my arms and bring them into the stage and say, 'You feel these things with me; you feel these emotions with me. You put yourself into these situations and when you go out of here and you wrestle with those thoughts and emotions, you might go out of here a better person.'" He did that to me, and I will never forget it. You can hear him do it in the 1978 recording he made with Colin Davis and the Royal Opera House Chorus and Orchestra on an inexpensive Decca re-issue of the Philips original.

A key moment in *Peter Grimes* is in the solo near the end of act 1, when Grimes sings of the Great Bear and Pleiades, and asks, "Who can turn skies back and begin again?" The drama of the opera is in answering this question. Is there any recovery from the consequences of the accident that killed Grimes' young apprentice at sea and left Grimes under a cloud of suspicion? Or will he be consumed by fate? Is his fate his insurmountable character flaw? Or is this about all of us who wish we could begin again because of something we did or something that happened to us? All of this is gathered up in this heartbreaking solo. Vickers caught this shattering moment and insight into the human condition in an unforgettable way.

It is Grimes' relationship with Ellen Orford that gives suspense and tension to these questions. She is his only source of hope. Can her love turn skies back, so that Grimes can begin again? Her warmth is effectively contrasted to the surrounding coldness. Grimes' a cappella soliloquy in which he goes mad at the end is one of the most psychologically gripping scenes in opera and a brilliant demonstration of Britten's economy of means and dramatic simplicity in producing devastatingly powerful effects.

That brilliant economy and simplicity were exhibited repeatedly in

Britten's series of chamber operas and church parables. He saw opera on the grand scale as too expensive to be practical, though he produced several more, including *Billy Budd* and *Gloriana*. Although neither achieved the popularity of *Peter Grimes*, *Billy Budd* is a work of close to comparable stature and its reputation has grown over the years. His brilliant opera *A Midsummer Night's Dream*, as magical a setting of Shakespeare as has ever been done in any medium, is almost in a category by itself. The smaller-scale works include the comedy *Albert Herring*, *The Turn of the Screw*, and the *The Rape of Lucretia*. Though the events of *Lucretia* are set in 500 B.C. Rome, Britten places the problem of evil in a Christian context by having the women in a chorus at the end ask: "Is it all?" To which the men respond that it is not: Christ "bears our sin and does not fall. . . . In his passion is our hope." The ending was considered quite controversial. Britten observed, "I've discovered that being simple and considering things spiritual of importance produces violent reactions."

This side of Britten is also heard in his parables for church performance (*Curlew River*, *The Burning Fiery Furnace*, and *The Prodigal*) and his religious works for children such as *St. Nicolas* and the enchanting *Noye's Fludde*, to say nothing of the utterly charming *Ceremony of Carols* for boys choir. In such works, the deceptive simplicity, the novelty of effect achieved with so few means, and the purity of purpose come through with startling mastery. Beck assigns the success of the ingenious church parables to "a striking combination of elements derived from Gregorian chant, primitive polyphonic techniques and eastern sophistication". None of these may be new, but their synthesis in an expressive unity is.

On a much larger scale, Britten achieved a tremendous success with his *War Requiem*, written for the opening of the rebuilt Coventry Cathedral in 1962. His use of the Latin Mass for the Dead and the war poetry of Wilfred Owen combined to make one of the 20th century's choral masterpieces. He was as successful in a lighter vein with the rambunctious, joyous, rollicking *Spring Symphony*, with choral sections based on excerpts of English poetry from the 16th to the 20th centuries. I cannot imagine a more exuberant celebration of the restorative power of nature.

The breadth of Britten's genius also encompasses ballet, with his delightful, full-length fairytale *The Prince of the Pagodas*; many song settings, such as *The Holy Sonnets of John Donne*; and chamber music. His achievement can be measured by his own standard. He said, "I write music for human beings—directly and deliberately. . . . I want my music to be of use to people, to please them, to 'enhance their lives' (to use Berenson's phrase)." On receiving the first Aspen Award, in 1964, Britten put it in almost the same words: "It is a good thing to please people, even if only for today. That is what we should aim at—pleasing people today as seriously as we can, and letting the future look after itself." To have done this in the 20th century, a time of destructive ideologies whose aim was not to "please" man—but to remake him by force—was a rare accomplishment.

Britten's singular accomplishment was summed up by English critic John Deathridge:

> Britten's knack of turning the skies back to the music of the past, without the irony of Stravinsky or the greyness of Hindemith, has had a wide resonance. There is no question that he has composed much that is new; but a consistent feature of his work, the significance of which has been ignored by many critics, is his ability to re-create references from the past with which his listeners can find some emotional identification. With allusions from Gregorian chant to middle-period Stravinsky, he has created in his music a sympathetic framework for a public which has rejected the 'nonsense' of contemporary music in favour of an identification with the past which is closer than ever before.

Recommended Recordings

Britten recorded a great deal of his music for London/Decca. One can turn with confidence to any of these, including the *War Requiem*. I will not list them here, but I particularly recommend his recording of *A Midsummer Night's Dream* (London 425 663, OOP but currently available as part of the Britten Operas II box on Decca 475 6029).

Not with Britten conducting:

Peter Grimes, Sir Colin Davis, Jon Vickers, Heather Harper, et al., Royal Opera House Covent Garden, Decca 478 2669 (formerly on Philips)

Spring Symphony (plus *Four Sea Interludes*), André Previn, Dame Janet Baker, Robert Tear, Sheila Armstrong, London Symphony Orchestra, EMI/Warner 64736 (OOP)

Spring Symphony (plus *Welcome Ode* & Psalm 150), Richard Hickox, London SO, Chandos 10782

The Prince of the Pagodas, Oliver Knussen, London Sinfonietta, Virgin Classics 91103 (OOP, reissued on EMI/Warner 49829, where it was coupled with Bartók's *Miraculous Mandarin*, and already out of print again)

War Requiem, Mariss Jansons, Christian Gerhaher, Mark Padmore, Emily Magee et al., Bavarian RSO and Chorus, BR Klassik 900120

Violin Concerto (also includes Mieczysław Weinberg's Violin Concerto), Mihkel Kütson, Linus Roth, German SO Berlin, Challenge 72627

Canticles, Julius Drake, Ian Bostridge, Christopher Maltman et al. Virgin/Erato 5 45525 (OOP)

∼

John Cage: Apostle of Noise

The 20th century is unique in its promulgation of noise. I do not mean industrial racket, the sounds of traffic, or the incessant hum of frost-free refrigerators. I mean the presentation of random noise as art. Never before has an artist asked an audience to come to a prearranged place at an appointed time to be assaulted by sheer noise. This is unique both on the artist's part, that he would dare to ask, and on the audience's, that it would respond and consider such an experience worth having.

Yet such was the case with the career of John Cage (1912–1992), the apostle of noise. Typical of Cage were compositions whose notes were based on the irregularities in the composition paper he used or selected by tossing dice or from charts derived from the Chinese *I-Ching*. Those were his more conventional works. Other compositions included the simultaneous twirling of the knobs of 12 radios; the sounds from records playing on unsynchronized variable-speed turntables; or the sounds produced by tape recordings of music that had been sliced up and randomly reassembled. He could be methodically maniacal. As Jens Laurson said of Cage's *Freeman Etudes*, "No note can be connected to any other note to make a melody or a form, by the composer's own design, reducing the performer to an assembler of random sound objects."

Cage was one of the progenitors of the "happenings" that were fashionable in the 1970s. He presented concerts of kitchen sounds and sounds of the human body amplified through loudspeakers. Perhaps Cage's most notorious work was his *4'33"*, during which the performer silently sits with his instrument for that exact period of time, then rises and leaves the stage. The music is whatever extraneous noises the audience hears in the silence the performer has created. In his book *Silence* Cage announced: "Here we are. Let us say Yes to our presence together in Chaos."

Was Cage a mountebank? What was the purpose of all this? Precisely to make the point that there is no purpose, or to express what Cage called a "purposeful purposelessness", the aim of which was to emancipate people from the tyranny of meaning. The extent of his success can be judged by the verdict rendered in the prestigious *New Grove Dictionary of Music*, which says Cage "has had a greater impact on

world music than any other American composer of the 20th century".
Also, the *New York Times* considers him "one of the most influential
composers of our time".

Cage certainly had an impishly attractive side to him, and his out-
rages had a liberating influence on a number of composers. They used
his anarchism as an excuse to escape from the stultifying confines of
Arnold Schoenberg's 12-tone system, which dominated the music scene
at the time. But Cage was not just tweaking noses. He was in earnest,
and his earnestness was based on a view of reality with a very clear
provenance. Cage himself acknowledged three principal gurus: French
composer Eric Satie, Henry David Thoreau, and Buckminster Fuller
—three relative lightweights who could not among them account for
Cage's radical thinking. The prevalent influence on Cage seems to have
been Jean Jacques Rousseau, though he goes unmentioned in Cage's
many obiter dicta. Cage's similarities with Rousseau are too uncanny
to have been accidental.

With his noise, Cage worked out musically the full implications of
Rousseau's non-teleological view of nature. Cage did for music what
Rousseau did for philosophy. (If this essay is beginning to sound theoretical, it is because Cage is largely a theoretical composer.) Perhaps
the most profoundly anti-Aristotelian philosopher of the 18th century,
Rousseau turned Aristotle's notion of Nature on its head. Aristotle said
Nature defined not only what man is but what he should be. Rousseau
countered that there is no Nature that is an end—a telos—only a nature that is a beginning: man's end is his beginning. There is nothing
he ought to become, no moral imperative. There is no purpose in man
or Nature; existence is therefore bereft of any rational principle. Contra Aristotle, Rousseau asserted that man was not by Nature a social,
political animal endowed with reason. What man has become is the
result not of Nature but of accident. The society resulting from that
accident has corrupted man.

According to Rousseau, man was originally isolated in the state of
nature, where the pure "sentiment of his own existence" was such that
"one suffices to oneself, like God." Yet this self-satisfied god was asocial and prerational. Only by accident did man come into association
with others. Somehow, this accident ignited his reason. And through
his association with others, man lost his self-sufficient "sentiment of his
own existence". He became alienated. He began to live in the esteem
of others instead of in his own self-esteem.

Rousseau knew that the prerational, asocial state of nature was lost forever, but thought that an all-powerful state could ameliorate the situation of alienated man. The state could restore a simulacrum of that original well-being by removing all of man's subsidiary social relationships. By destroying man's familial, social, and political ties, the state could make each individual totally dependent on the state and independent of each other. The state is the vehicle for bringing people together so that they can be apart: a sort of radical individualism under state sponsorship.

It is necessary to pay this much attention to Rousseau because Cage shares his denigration of reason, the same notion of alienation, and a similar solution to it. In both men, the primacy of the accidental eliminates Nature as a normative guide and becomes the foundation for man's total freedom. Like Rousseau's man in the state of nature, Cage said, "I strive toward the nonmental." His quest was to "provide a music free from one's memory and imagination". Life itself is very fine "once one gets one's mind and one's desires out of the way and lets it act of its own accord".

But what is its own accord? Of music, Cage said, "The requiring that many parts be played in a particular togetherness is not an accurate representation of how things are" in nature, because in nature there is no order. In other words, life's accord is that there is no accord. As a result, Cage desired "a society where you can do anything at all". He warned that one has "to be as careful as possible not to form any ideas about what each person should or should not do". He was "committed to letting everything happen, to making everything that happens acceptable".

At the Stony Point experimental arts community where he spent his summers, Cage observed that each summer's sabbatical produced numerous divorces. He therefore concluded, "All the couples who come to the community and stay there end up separating. In reality, our community is a community for separation." Rousseau could not have stated his ideal better. Nor could Cage have made the same point in his art more clearly. For instance, in his long collaboration with choreographer Merce Cunningham, Cage wrote ballet scores completely unconnected to and independent of Cunningham's choreography. The orchestra and dancers rehearsed separately and appeared together for the first time at the premiere performance. The dancers' movements have nothing to do with the music. The audience is left to make of these random juxtapositions what it will. There is no shared experience —except of disconnectedness. The dancers, musicians, and audience have all come together in order to be apart.

According to Cage, the realization of the disconnectedness of things creates opportunities for wholeness. "I said that since the sounds were sounds this gave people hearing them the chance to be people, centered within themselves where they actually are, not off artificially in the distance as they are accustomed to be, trying to figure out what is being said by some artist by means of sounds." Here, in his own way, Cage captures Rousseau's notion of alienation. People are alienated from themselves because they are living in others. Cage's noise can help them let go of false notions of order, to "let sounds be themselves, rather than vehicles for man-made theories", and to return within themselves to the sentiment of their own existence. Cage said, "Our intention is to affirm this life, not bring order out of chaos or to suggest improvements in creation, but simply to wake up to the very life we're living, which is so excellent."

That sounds appealing, even humble, and helps to explain Cage's appeal. In fact, Cage repeatedly insisted on the integrity of external reality, which exists without our permission. It is a good point to make and, as far as it goes, protects us from solipsists of every stripe. Man violates this integrity by projecting meanings upon external reality that are not there. This, of course, is the distortion of reality at the heart of every modern ideology. For Cage, however, it is the inference of meaning itself that is the distorting imposition. This is the real problem with letting "sounds be themselves" and letting other things be as they are, because it begs the question, "What are they?" What is the significance of reality's integrity if it is not intelligible, if there is not a rational principle animating it? If the rest of creation is not intelligible, are we? Where does "leaving things as they are" leave us?

From the traditional Western perspective, it leaves us completely adrift. The Greco-Judeo-Christian conviction is that nature bespeaks an intelligibility that derives from a transcendent source. Speaking from the heart of that tradition, St. Paul said in Romans 1:20, "Ever since the creation of the world his invisible nature, namely, his eternal power and deity, has been clearly perceived in the things that have been made." By denigrating reason and denying creation's intelligibility, Rousseau and Cage severed this link to the Creator. Cage's espousal of noise is the logically apt result of this. Noise is incapable of pointing beyond itself because it is unintelligible. Noise is the black hole of the sound world. It sucks everything into itself. If reality is unintelligible, then noise is its perfect reflection.

This does not mean there is not a form of spirituality in Cage. There is, but it is spiritual nihilism. Some of it may derive from Cage's fascination with Zen Buddhism; Cage's cure for egotism is not humility but the elimination of the ego. But Zen Buddhism does not lead to Cage's ultimate destination. He was led there by Rousseau, whose conception of man's autonomy spawned first the French Revolution and then, through his notion of alienation, Marxism. It should therefore come as no surprise that Cage developed a revolutionary political program. Cage realized that his "work has stopped being purely musical. . . . I mix musical needs with social needs." Noise, he discovered, can be used to destroy power: "I want to destroy it [power]. When I really began making music, I mean, composing 'seriously', it was to involve myself in noise, because noises escape power, that is, the laws of counterpoint and harmony." Noise's property as a political dissolvent enhanced Cage's appreciation of rock music: "In rock, the traditions are drowned in sound. Everything becomes confused—it's wonderful!"

Cage was fooling himself if he thought he was destroying power; he was destroying order. Destroying order creates an opportunity for a certain type of power to ascend. What sort of power that might be became clear from Cage's infatuation with Mao Tse-tung's totalitarianism. In the early 1980s, Cage said, "The Maoist model managed to free a quarter of humanity: that gives cause for thought. Today, without hesitation, I would say, for the moment, Maoism is our greatest reason for optimism."

Antithetical to Cage's view, Swiss writer Max Picard observed that in "sound itself, there is a readiness to be ordered by the spirit and this is seen at its most sublime in music". As we have seen, Cage's denial that sounds have any disposition to be ordered by the spirit led him away from far more than music. It may be unfashionable to go from the *I-Ching* to the New Testament, but a few refreshing lines of clarity from 1 Corinthians provide the needed antidote to Cage: "If even lifeless instruments, such as the flute or the harp, do not give distinct notes, how will any one know what is played? . . . [B]ut if I do not know the meaning of the language, I shall be a foreigner to the speaker and the speaker a foreigner to me. . . . I would rather speak five words with my mind, in order to instruct others, than ten thousand words in a tongue" (14: 7, 11, 19).

Recommended Recordings

It might seem strange to recommend anything after this chapter, but there are sides to every serious artist, however contrary to one's own views, that are worth considering. Musically, the most adventurous readers of this book might look into John Cage's String Quartet in Four Parts. In this strictest and most classical of musical forms, Cage is at his least disorderly and creates a lightly electrifying, tender atmosphere. Also, his early, downright melodic ballet, *The Seasons*, is worth a listen. The main recommendation is a beautiful film by Allan Miller and Paul Smaczny about Cage, which proves to be insightful, felt, never hagiographic, and worthwhile regardless of how one likes or ignores Cage's output. Finally there is an album by David Greilsammer that pairs and contrasts sonatas of Domenico Scarlatti with a few of Cage's sonatas and interludes for piano that Cage prepared with bolts and screws and anything else he found in his drawers. The works have in common that they are short, that their composers weren't concerned with the structures of their time, that they're playful and thoughtful. In close proximity, Bach-contemporary Scarlatti seems more original while Cage's exotic, percussive sounds seem somewhat more conventional. The result is either enervating or a cheeky aural delight.

String Quartet in Four Parts, *Four*, Arditti Quartet, mode 27

The Seasons (plus *Seventy-Four*; Concerto for Prepared Piano; Suite for Toy Piano), Dennis Russell Davies, American Composers Orchestra, Margaret Leng Tan, ECM New Series 1696

John Cage: Journeys in Sound, Allan Miller and Paul Smaczny, Accentus DVD/ Blu-ray 20246

Domenico Scarlatti & John Cage, *Sonatas and Interludes*, David Greilsammer, Sony 8888376402

Alfredo Casella: Italian "Logical Discursiveness"

Ever so slowly, we have been getting a more complete picture of Italian orchestral music as it emerged from under the complete domination of opera in the 19th and first half of the 20th centuries. This expanded view began with the Naxos label's traversal of Gian Francesco Malipiero's eleven magical symphonies. Malipiero (1883–1973) also devoted himself to resurrecting pre–19th-century Italian music, which he would occasionally repackage into suites such as *Gabrielana*, based on the music of Gabrieli; and *Madrigali*, orchestral arrangements of vocal works by Monteverdi. Malipiero's exact contemporary, Alfredo Casella (1883–1947), did the same thing with his *Scarlattiana*, a delightful, vivacious setting of themes from Antonio Scarlatti's sonatas, and *Paganiniana*, obviously after the works of Niccolò Paganini. Together, Malipiero and Casella were largely responsible for the revival of Antonio Vivaldi's works. Were these simply exercises in nostalgia? I think they constituted a charm offensive by these composers (and also by Ottorino Respighi, who did the same kind of thing)—a gentle way of reminding the Italian music-loving public that Italian music had a pretty proud history once, not just Italian opera.

Casella, however, did himself no favors by expressing his frustration with the tyranny of opera by attacking Italy's operatic sacred cow, Giuseppe Verdi. In a 1913 article, he claimed that Verdi was nothing more than a "businessman" who had succeeded by "exploiting political opportunities" and "pandering to the crudest, basest bourgeois taste". Since that "crude" taste would be the one shared by most Italians, this was not a good public relations move on Casella's part.

To rub salt in the wounds, Casella also spearheaded the introduction of contemporary music through the creation of the Società Nazionale di Musica (later renamed Società Italiana di Musica Moderna) in 1917. His dogged advocacy of contemporary European music and its clear influences on his work helped earn him the accusation of being too "international", rather than Italian, in style. He also proved to be politically maladroit, to put it mildly. After extensive stays conducting and concertizing in the United States, Casella chose to return to Italy at the time of Mussolini's rise. He was an Il Duce enthusiast (as were most Italian composers) who naïvely never seemed to realize the full implications of Fascism. Casella was not an anti-Semite; his wife was Jewish, and Mario Castelnuovo-Tedesco (1895–1968), an Italian Jewish composer, was a good friend. In any case, Casella's once-substantial reputation evaporated after World War II, just as did Malipiero's, when the avant-garde took over. Casella was remembered more as a pianist, conductor (including of the Boston Pops), and teacher (the great film composer Nino Rota was one of his students), than as a composer. *Scarlattiana* was about the only composition that survived his eclipse.

Within the past decade and a half this has begun to change. According to the ArkivMusic site, there are more than two score recordings of his works currently available. What we can now hear is highly variegated, a musical smörgåsbord. First, Casella enthusiastically embraced late romanticism à la Mahler and early Schoenberg, impressionism à la Debussy and Ravel, and then briefly flirted with avant-garde expressionism, before taking up neoclassicism in mostly neobaroque forms, with strong influences from Stravinsky. In other words, prepare for variety. You can witness these influences in various stages of digestion as if you were viewing Casella's musical intestines through an X-ray. They are that clear. If you ever wished to be a musical diagnostician, here is your chance: "Suffering from a bit of Ravel here; a clump of undigested Stravinsky there; he's hiccupping some Mahler now; whoops, there goes Sibelius."

When he recovered from his romantic phase, the now neoclassical Casella sometimes let baroque forms get more out of him than he was able to get out of them. Like Bohuslav Martinů, who also heavily favored baroque forms in many of his compositions, Casella could occasionally lapse into sewing machine music, with some pile-driving, chugging ostinatos. However, when the digestion process was complete and all of these influences and forms became Casella, he produced some very special, highly distinctive works out of them. In any case, observing the development of this process is both instructive and highly entertaining.

The Naxos and Chandos labels have led the revival of Casella's major orchestral works. The big news is the appearance of Casella's Three Symphonies from both labels. These works allow us to witness the composer's evolution from the bombast of late romanticism to a lean, but no less melodious, neoclassicism. The first two symphonies are late romanticism at its overblown, cataclysmic best. Casella studied in France, but I hear the steppes of Russia here, in all their gloom and doom, via Rimsky Korsakov, Mussorgsky and even Tchaikovsky (though Casella specifically mentioned Borodin as an influence), especially in the second movement of the First Symphony. Casella was gifted with great themes, and he knew how to milk them for all they are worth. He liked the theme to the Adagio of the First Symphony so much that he used it again in the Adagio of the Second. It is so gorgeous that you will not mind. Francesco La Vecchia and the Orchestra Sinfonica di Roma give an excellent world-premiere performance recording of Symphony No. 1 on Naxos. Gianandrea Noseda and the BBC Philharmonic offer a tauter interpretation—one that clips more than six minutes off the Roman timing—with superb sound on Chandos.

The Second Symphony is even better. Simply add Mahler (whose Seventh Symphony Casella transcribed for piano, four hands) to the Tchaikovsky equation, with a brief visit from Wagner's Valkyries, who go riding in the middle of the first movement. *Gramophone* magazine's reviewer went into high dudgeon over this work, declaring that he was not for a moment persuaded by "its hyped-up bombast and soft-centered pseudo-eloquence". What's more, it prefigures "the worst kind of movie music bathos, though even Cecil B. de Mille might have balked at having his more sentimental images so relentlessly underlined". Yes, it is *that* good. As we all deserve a good wallow now and then, I recommend the Second for the purpose. As musical melodrama, it is so over the top that it almost transcends itself.

Of the two recordings, I prefer the Chandos version with the BBC Philharmonic, under Noseda, to the Naxos release, because it has even more swagger, grip, and panache, plus superb sonics, from which the music particularly benefits. It is paired with *Scarlattiana*. Naxos' Roman forces take more than five minutes longer with the Second, but add a great companion piece, the haunting *A notte alta* for piano and orchestra, which displays some of the impressionist influences Casella fell under in his Paris years.

The Symphony No. 3 comes from another sound world (written 30 years after the Second)—a neoclassical one, with shades of Shostakovich and Stravinsky. Gone are all the excesses that the *Gramophone* reviewer deplored. However, the melodies remain. It could otherwise pass as a product of mainstream American symphonism of the mid-20th century. In fact, it was commissioned by the Chicago Symphony

Orchestra for its 50th anniversary and was a huge hit at its premiere. The only mystery is why it has taken this long to revive. The Third Symphony has received the most attention of any of the Casella works with three recordings on offer. The first entry was CPO's, paired with *Italia*, a colorful, engaging evocation of Sicily and Naples, with some rousing reprises of *Funiculì, funiculà* (cribbed from Luigi Denza). The West German Radio Symphony Orchestra Cologne, under conductor Alun Francis, puts its heart into both works, which CPO captures in excellent sound. La Vecchia and his Roman forces give a similarly attractive reading with almost identical timings on Naxos. Noseda drives the music harder with an exciting sense of grip without losing any detail. Occasionally, however, although the timing difference with Francis and La Vecchia is only three minutes, he sounds a bit rushed. La Vecchia's and Francis' slightly more spacious treatments have their advantages. If you can buy only one Casella CD, a recording of the Third Symphony may be the one to have, but then you would miss the fun of his stylistic journey through the romantic thickets to an open clearing.

Choosing between the two traversals, Noseda captures the greatest excitement and has the advantage of the spectacular recordings by the Chandos engineers. Heard on his own terms, however, La Vecchia has a great deal to offer in the greater breadth of his readings, and the Naxos sound is fine. Naxos also has a considerable price advantage.

Written two years earlier (1937) than the Third Symphony, the Concerto for Orchestra is comparable in its quality, with the same welcome breeziness to its sweeping melodies. Indeed, Casella called it "undoubtedly my most complete achievement in the field of orchestral music and the attainment of a stylistic and formal goal I had been aiming at ever since *Italia*". It likewise was written for an orchestra's 50th anniversary celebration—in this case, the Amsterdam Concertgebouw, directed by Casella's good friend Willem Mengelberg. There are two available recordings from the same contestants in the symphonic traversal. Noseda's performance of the Concerto on Chandos clips more than five minutes off La Vecchia's time on Naxos. It is jittery but exciting. Noseda's urgency imparts a joyful exuberance, as contrasted with La Vecchia's mellow serenity. From the large divergence in timings, one would expect an apparent slackness in La Vecchia's interpretation, but such is not the case, except in the slightly sleepy Passacaglia. In this movement Noseda's fleet interpretation is superior. There is, however, generally no lack of drama in La Vecchia's well-balanced reading. Both performances capture the celebratory air.

Another Naxos release offers Casella's rhythmically driven, highly energetic, but melodically lyrical Cello Concerto, accompanied by the sheerly delightful *Scarlattiana* for piano and orchestra. While this budget CD has some stiff competition from the more expensive Chandos releases, it also contains the world-premiere recording of the magical *Notte di maggio* (A Night in May) for voice and orchestra, deliciously drenched in atmospheric mystery. Casella predicted, "You'll love the poetic effect", and indeed I do. Call it Italian impressionism (Casella was a friend of Debussy). The same forces, the Orchestra Sinfonica di Roma, under conductor Francesco La Vecchia, used in Naxos' traversal of the symphonies, deliver the goods here in very compelling performances. Cellist Andrea Noferini gives a tour de force rendition in the Cello Concerto. These three works from 1913 (*Notte*), 1926 (*Scarlattiana*), and 1935 (the Cello Concerto) are different stylistically but highly attractive in their own ways, thanks to Casella's chameleon talents and melodic gift.

The early Suite in C Major from 1909–1910 is a very robust and entertaining work. While listening, one can play "name that composer". Mahler predominates in the first movement. There is Sibelius at the beginning of the third movement, Bourrée, but then it segues into Korngold, and then to Mahler. The kaleidoscope of influences comes in such a rush that one barely gets a handle on one, when another comes along. Casella puts the mishmash of influences together so unabashedly and enthusiastically that it is unfailingly entertaining. This is music with gusto.

The Partita is a neobaroque confection with a sprightly piano part, full of delight and fancy. It's not very hard to understand why this festive charmer was apparently very popular in the Europe of its day. In the finale, Casella employs a traditional tarantella from southern Italy that he was accused of filching. However, it sticks out so recognizably that he can't have intended its use surreptitiously. It's all part of the fun.

Introduzione, aria e toccata is another work of Casella's maturity in which the neobaroque forms do not dominate the material but seem completely natural to it. It is immediately appealing. Casella was justifiably proud of this composition. He said it was "a new advance in the monumental baroque style; the triptych is a unified work, animated by a single spirit and dynamic will", with its first movement achieving "a free but nonetheless solidly organic form—the fundamentally Italian form of which our great composers of the 17th and 18th centuries were

masters, and which I shall provisionally call 'logical discursiveness'."
The second movement, Aria, is very lovely, dreamlike, almost like an
Italian Samuel Barber.

From today's aural perspective, it is hard to believe that any of
Casella's music was thought to be radically modern in its time, but
we can get a sense of how it produced this reaction by listening to the
17-minute *Elegia eroica* (1916), available on either Chandos or Naxos,
composed "in memory of a [nameless] soldier killed in the war". It
effectively expresses distress, sorrow, and shock—so much so that the
audience at the premiere was shocked by its dissonant language. There
is no soft-soaping or glorifying war for Casella in his depiction of a
"tempest of death". Even today, this is not an easy listen. Casella also
treated the subject of World War I in his *War Pages*, which provides five
snapshots: *Advance of German Heavy Artillery*, which is very redolent of
Arthur Honegger's depiction of the steam locomotive in *Pacific 231*,
though written five years earlier; *Before the Ruins of Rheims Cathedral*;
Cossack Cavalry Charge; *In Alsace: Wooden Crosses*; and *In the Adriatic:
Italian Cruisers Carrying Armaments*. Giacomo Puccini was one of the
admirers of this highly colorful musical portraiture, which Casella had
subtitled *Musical Films*.

Even in his early phase, when he was ingesting the influences of
other composers, Casella's music is unfailingly imaginative. However,
in his fully mature period, he achieved a balance of form and substance
—finally getting more out of baroque forms than they got out of him
—that led to some highly original works expressing the "logical discursiveness" he so admired. Sometimes it can be hard to figure out
how some of these compositions work exactly, but that scarcely im-
pedes the great enjoyment they provide. Whatever Casella did, he did
it wholeheartedly. His music embraces you; it is hard not to embrace
it back.

Recommended Recordings

Symphony No. 1; *Elegia eroica*; Symphonic Fragments from *Le Couvent sur
l'eau*, op. 19, Gianandrea Noseda, BBC PO, Chandos 10880

Symphony No. 1; Concerto for Piano, Timpani, Percussion and Strings, Francesco La Vecchia, Rome SO, Naxos 8.572413

Symphony No. 2; *A notte alta*, Francesco La Vecchia, Rome SO, Sun Hee You,
Naxos 8.572414

Symphony No. 2; *Scarlattiana*, Gianandrea Noseda, BBC PO, Martin Roscoe, Chandos 10605

Symphony No. 3; *Italia*; *Introduzione, corale e marcia*, Gianandrea Noseda, BBC PO, Chandos 10768

Symphony No. 3, *Italia*, Alun Francis, Cologne West German RSO, CPO 777 265

Symphony No. 3; *Elegia eroica*, Francesco La Vecchia, Rome SO, Naxos 8.572415

Notte di maggio; Cello Concerto; *Scarlattiana*, Francesco La Vecchia, Rome SO, Naxos 8.572416

Concerto for Orchestra; Suite in C Major; *Pagine di guerra*, Francesco La Vecchia, Rome SO, Naxos 8.573004

Concerto for Orchestra; *A notte alta*; *La donna serpente* Symphonic Fragments, Gianandrea Noseda, BBC PO, Chandos 10712

Introduzione, aria e toccata; Partita; *La donna serpente*, Francesco La Vecchia, Rome SO, Naxos 8.573005

Violin Concerto, et al., Vaclav Smetácek, André Gertler, Prague SO, Supraphon 3904. Supraphon has resurrected the 1971 recording that pairs Casella's beguiling Violin Concerto with Malipiero's equally entrancing Violin Concerto.

∼

Maurice Duruflé: A Requiem to Die For

Requiems are for the living. They shape our attitude toward death. What should we expect? Peace and serenity or terror and judgment? Heaven or hell? It depends on the composer.

In their Requiems, Hector Berlioz and Giuseppe Verdi frighten us with rafter-shaking, apocalyptic visions of the Dies Irae. Just as composing symphonies became a problem after Beethoven, writing Requiems after Berlioz and Verdi posed similar challenges. They are impossible to top eschatologically.

In his far more pacific portrayal, French composer Maurice Duruflé, like his teacher Gabriel Fauré, decided not even to try to depict the end of the world. Duruflé consoles and comforts us, not only by deleting the Dies Irae altogether from his Requiem, but by depicting death as the joyous entry into an eternity of rest. The agony is over; be not afraid. Given my druthers, I would die with Duruflé.

His Requiem from 1947 originated in a suite of organ pieces based on plainsong from the Mass for the Dead. When he received a commission from Durand Publishers, he expanded them into the Requiem. The Requiem is listed as op. 9, which would normally indicate that it is an early work. In his lifetime, however, the meticulous Duruflé was to publish only a dozen works, mostly for organ. The Requiem is the chef d'oeuvre of his maturity.

To distinguish Duruflé's Requiem from those of Verdi and Berlioz is not to say that it is devoid of drama but rather to place it within the tradition in which Duruflé was working. The scale of his conception may have been constrained by the plainchant on which the piece is based, but the work gains in richness from its use. Add to plainchant the sensuous harmonies of Debussy and Ravel, which Duruflé had learned so well, and you have a mesmerizing combination, simultaneously modern and archaic. As Duruflé wrote, "In general, I have attempted to penetrate to the essence of Gregorian style and have tried to reconcile, as far as possible, the very flexible Gregorian rhythms as established by the Benedictines of Solesmes with the exigencies of modern notation." For its time, however, Duruflé's work was considered reactionary. Recall that this man was a fellow student and friend of avant-garde composer Olivier Messiaen, yet Duruflé's work could easily have been written at the time of Fauré's Requiem, 50 years earlier.

Duruflé's Requiem opens very dreamily. Gentle orchestral undulations underlie the smoothly flowing plainchant of the Introit. The requested peace has already been granted. The Kyrie confirms this. It doesn't so much ask for mercy as celebrate it. Finally, in the Offertorium, one glimpses the inferno from which the soul has been saved. Dissonances depict the punishments of hell, but even the request for deliverance from them is almost triumphant. Then St. Michael arrives almost as sleep might, in a moment of hushed lyricism, to lead the soul into heavenly light. The Sanctus begins with another repeated rippling figure in the orchestra, closely related to that of the Introit, which gives one the impression of being carried forward on gentle waves. The Sanctus slowly builds to a triple-forte climax at "Hosanna in excelsis", then subsides peacefully back into the rippling *moto perpetuo* with which it began. The Pie Jesu is a very poignant, gentle supplication, the point of repose at the heart of the work. The Agnus Dei restores a sense of motion and confidence that the "requiem sempiternam" has been granted. Lux Aeterna evokes what the eternal rest might be like.

In short, Duruflé's Requiem is dramatic but not apocalyptic, sweet but not confectionery. It benefits from the most attractive features of the French aesthetic: lightness of touch; refinement; delicacy. Duruflé succeeded in his desire to avoid the excessive settings of his predecessors and produced one of the most beautifully lyrical, comforting liturgical works of the 20th century.

Duruflé fashioned three versions of the Requiem to meet the practical necessities of church performance: one for full orchestra, one for chamber orchestra, and a bare-bones version for organ and cello. All, of course, include chorus. He left as optional whether certain parts of the text were to be taken by soloists or a full choir. His own thoughts leave little doubt as to which of the three versions he least preferred: "The reduction for solo organ (and choir) may prove inadequate in certain parts of the Requiem where the expressive timbre of the strings is needed."

His opinion is vindicated by a Hyperion release of the solo organ and cello version performed by the Westminster Cathedral Choir led by James O'Donnell. It is Duruflé Lite. It is almost like a piano reduction of a Beethoven symphony. It does not do the work justice. Arguments over the sense of intimacy gained lose when compared with the orchestral loss. After all, Duruflé, an organist, would not have bothered composing for full orchestra if he thought the queen of instruments could convey his meaning. Specialists may well be drawn to this recording, but even a specialist might be put off by a lack of drama in O'Donnell's conception.

One should look elsewhere. The interim chamber orchestra version is admirably presented on an earlier Hyperion release with the English Chamber Orchestra and the Corydon Singers, directed by Matthew Best. This recording conveys much of the Requiem's impact, but Best's excellent soloists are most expressive. Thomas Allen shows how powerful and moving the baritone part can be sung over the solo organ and, then, the naked strings in "Domine Jesu Christe". It is chilling and effective. Nonetheless, the glory and sensuousness of the full orchestral version immediately beguile the listener in a performance from the late 1980s, featuring the late Robert Shaw and the Atlanta Symphony Orchestra and Chorus in a superb, grandiose performance on Telarc. Listen to this recording next to the Hyperion, and you will find it hard to believe it is the same work. The choral perfection at which Shaw aims is well suited to a liturgical work of this nature. Perfection, or at least the illusion of perfection, creates a sense of distance—precisely the quality required by a reflective work of this kind that becomes, ironically, all the more moving for it. Its pristine beauty shines forth. Shaw's orchestra is equally impressive. The balance between chorus and orchestra could hardly be better. This is simply one of the most beautiful choral recordings I have ever heard, and it has the added advantage of being paired with a lovely performance of Fauré's Requiem.

Recommended Recordings

Requiem (chamber version); *Four Motets*, Matthew Best, English Chamber Orchestra, Soloists, Corydon Singers, Hyperion 66191 (Also released as Hyperion 67070 with the Fauré Requiem instead of the *Four Motets*). Or: Bill Grayston Ives, English Sinfonia, Soloists, Magdalen College Choir Oxford, Harmonia Mundi 807480 (plus *Four Motets*, *Messe "Cum jubilo"*).

Requiem (Orchestral Version); plus Fauré, Requiem, Robert Shaw, Soloists, Atlanta SO & Chorus, Telarc 80135

~

Edward Elgar: The Dream of a "Better Land"

Edward Elgar (1857–1934) was the greatest Catholic composer at the turn of the 19th century and the greatest English composer since Purcell some 200 years earlier. After the two-century musical hiatus, Sleeping Beauty in the form of Elgar awoke to dazzle the world with a blaze of passionate gorgeousness. Like the founder of anything, Elgar did not seem to come from anywhere. He is not the sum of his antecedents. His formal education ended at age 15, after which he became a free-lance musician. He was distinctly lower class. Yet, he single-handedly reestablished English music on the world stage. Though he wrote his share of typical salon music, Elgar's great works, saturated with a powerful sense of longing, convey an overwhelming emotional surge that must have shaken the Victorians (or Edwardians) of his day. Englishmen were not supposed to be this expressive.

If Elgar was a mystery in terms of his antecedents, the creation of music was equally a mystery to him. Elgar was improvising at the piano one day when his wife happened to interrupt and point out a melody he had just created that would have otherwise passed unnoticed in the flow of his improvisation. This accident struck Elgar as a creative mystery or enigma. He went on to compose his set of *Enigma Variations* (1896) on the theme his wife had caught. This orchestral tour de force, along with his orchestral song cycle *Sea Pictures*, did much to establish his reputation. After 10 years of work, Elgar produced his First Symphony in 1908. Hans Richter, the conductor of its premiere, heralded the work as a masterpiece. The public agreed, and it was given an astounding 100 performances in its first year. The Violin Concerto and then his Symphony No. 2 of 1911 followed, and an autumnal Cello Concerto of 1919 closed out his most productive period.

The principal impression left by these extraordinary works is a unique combination of passion, nobility, and grandeur swathed in a rich sunset glow. Elgar marked a number of movements in his scores *nobilmente*, a favorite word he may well have coined, that denotes the spirit of his music along with its emotional depth. Those familiar only with his *Pomp and Circumstance* marches, who think Elgar was simply an Edwardian ceremonial celebrator of empire or a Victorian sentimentalist, have yet to probe the enigma of the genius who set the foundation of British music for the 20th century.

There was far more to Elgar than that. Elgar's mother, Ann, was a convert to Catholicism and, despite her husband's objections, raised her children in the faith. Among the things she used to read them as youngsters was a poem called "The Better Land", which spoke of a place of no sorrow or tears. This place was "beyond the tomb".

Elgar never forgot. Death was never far from his mature works. But unlike some of the neurasthenic composers at work at the same time, his preoccupation with death was not morose and sickly. It expressed itself indirectly in an orchestral style that was extremely rich and conveyed a sense of ripeness, or even overripeness, and autumnal glow. It was a noble summing-up. What could follow such a sense of radiant fulfillment but a farewell? That farewell was death itself, not as a nihilistic ending but as a passage to eternal life. This valedictory quality gives Elgar's music a powerful poignancy, which some critics misinterpret as nostalgia for the fading glory of the British Empire. It is far more than that; it is music pointing to a "Better Land", which is why we still listen to it and are moved.

At the heart of Elgar's output is a work that makes explicit this implicit theme of death. It was written in 1900, after the highly successful *Enigma Variations* and before the First Symphony. It is *The Dream of Gerontius*, one of the most extraordinary choral works ever written. It is also a stunning affirmation of Catholic faith. Upon hearing Sir John Barbirolli conduct it in 1958 at the Castel Gandolfo, Pope Pius XII, himself only days from dying, said, "My son, that is a sublime masterpiece."

When Elgar married in 1889, the priest of St. George's in Worcester, where Elgar had served as organist, gave him as a wedding present a copy of "The Dream of Gerontius", a long mystical poem written in 1865 by John Henry Cardinal Newman. This poem had some currency in Anglican England, not only because of Newman's fame, but because a copy of it, with General Charles "Chinese" Gordon's underlining and notations, was found near Gordon's body after his heroic death in Khartoum. Copies of Gordon's annotated text circulated widely in England, and one found its way into Elgar's possession. The poem depicts the agonizing death of Gerontius, his experience of the afterlife, and his passage to the seat of judgment, escorted by his guardian angel. After judgment, his soul departs for purgatory.

Elgar heavily edited the original poem, which has seven sections. He largely retained the first section portraying the deathbed scene, while the remaining six dealing with the afterlife were telescoped into a second part just twice the length of the earthly opening. This new emphasis gave greater weight to the drama of Gerontius' death. Newman's poem is startlingly literal, visionary but didactic. The psychology of a dying man is convincingly captured, but Gerontius' recitation of certain Catholic doctrines on his deathbed is dramatically awkward. Equally awkward are the metaphysical observations Gerontius makes in the afterlife such as, "I am not self-moving." Also, some of the language is stilted. It is a measure of Elgar's melodic gift that he could make the following sound mellifluous: "They sing of approaching agony Which thou so eagerly didst question of." Nonetheless, despite its shortcomings, the poem compellingly presents the greatest drama human beings face and the one they fear the most.

Elgar put flesh and blood, even in its incorporeal parts, on Newman's creation of Gerontius and made him live, die, and live again. The 10-minute orchestral prelude is in itself a close-to-overwhelming experience in which Elgar presents the themes that will appear throughout the hour-and-a-half piece in leitmotiv fashion.

A pulsing, clock-like ticking figure measures the dying man's last moments. Then, the hammer blows of approaching death sound. The very moment of death (*novissima hora est*) is depicted with music of breathtaking serenity. The demons' cacophony is captured with the brilliance of Berlioz. The angel sings with pure rapture. With shades of Wagner and Brahms, but very much in his own voice, Elgar transports his listeners as close to the "Better Land" as one can come without going there.

Nothing could be more ambitious than what Elgar undertook or appear more easily ridiculous (a man's soul singing with its guardian angel?). Elgar felt very exposed. Exactly how exposed is clear from the bitterness he expressed at the inadequately prepared and badly bungled premiere at the Birmingham Musical Festival in 1900. After the performance, he wrote: "Providence denies me a decent hearing of my work: so I submit—I always said God was against art and I still believe it. . . . I have allowed my heart to open once—it is now shut against every religious feeling and every soft, gentle impulse for ever."

When a later performance of *Gerontius* was presented properly prepared, the work's value was immediately recognized by a broad public.

Elgar recovered and went on to open his heart in many other masterpieces, including two oratorios based on the New Testament: *The Kingdom* and *The Apostles*.

The totally Catholic character of *Gerontius* did not escape attention. Sir Charles Stanford was alleged to have remarked to Elgar, "My boy, it stinks of incense." For this reason, there were protests that *Gerontius* was unsuitable for performance in Anglican cathedrals. For a performance at Worcester Cathedral, the clergy insisted on deleting Roman Catholicisms from the text. In his review, the *Pall Mall* critic wrote: "A Roman Catholic priest of known wit, who was present this morning at the performance, suggested that instead of omitting the words 'In purgatory', the difficulty might have been better solved by simply putting 'Fried souls'."

Elgar was very clear about how he wished *Gerontius* to be performed: passionately (as is also evident from the excerpts he recorded in 1927). During one rehearsal, he entreated the tenors to sing the Kyrie, marked *pianissimo*, with "more tears in the voices" as if "they were assisting at the death of a friend." He thought of *Gerontius* more in the Italian opera tradition than as a staid English oratorio. After Elgar, *Gerontius* found its ideal interpreter in Sir John Barbirolli, who gave definitive performances of many of Elgar's masterpieces. In preparing for one performance of *Gerontius*, Barbirolli could have been speaking for Elgar when he scolded the tenors and basses in the Demons' Chorus: "You're not bank clerks on a Sunday outing, you're souls sizzling in hell." Himself a Catholic, Barbirolli believed that only a choir of Catholics could fully understand the transcendent vision Elgar and Newman tried to communicate. The very fact that he thought so is an indication of how deeply he understood and sympathized with this work. In his 1965 recording, he conveyed this vision with the greatest urgency, eloquence, and a surging vitality. Of this recording, Barbirolli said: "I wanted to leave it as a kind of testament of my faith." It features the Hallé Orchestra and is distinguished by a totally convincing performance from tenor Richard Lewis as Gerontius and the sublime singing of mezzo-soprano Janet Baker as the angel.

If you have ever had to keep watch at the deathbed of someone close to you, you may have difficulty keeping your composure listening to this piece. Your reaction may be Elgar's own as he conducted *Gerontius* in 1902, shortly after his mother's death: he wept. But as Cardinal Newman writes at the end of "Gerontius", "Farewell, but not for ever! . . . I will come and wake thee on the morrow."

Recommended Recordings

The Dream of Gerontius, Sir John Barbirolli, the Hallé Orchestra, Janet Baker, Richard Lewis, Kim Borg, EMI/Warner 91973 (plus *The Music Makers* under Adrian Boult), and EMI/Warner 73579. Or: Sir Adrian Boult, London PO, Helen Watts, Nicolai Gedda, Robert Lloyd, EMI/Warner 66540 (plus *The Music Makers*).

Enigma Variations, Sir John Barbirolli, the Hallé Orchestra, EMI/Warner 7691 852

Cello Concerto: *Sea Pictures*, Sir John Barbirolli, London Symphony Orchestra, Jacqueline Du Pre (coupled with the incandescent *Sea Pictures*, in which Janet Baker is also the soloist in one of the great vocal recordings), EMI/Warner 56219

Symphony No. 1, Sir John Barbirolli, the Philharmonia Orchestra, EMI/Warner 7645112

Symphony No. 2, Sir John Barbirolli, the Hallé Orchestra, EMI/Warner 764 724

Violin Concerto; *Introduction and Allegro for Strings*, Vernon Handley, London PO, Nigel Kennedy, EMI/Warner 332872

∿

Einar Englund: Out of the Shadows

The Finnish CD label, Ondine, has recorded the first complete traversal of Einar Englund's seven symphonies, and the budget Naxos label has issued a magnificent recording of Englund's Second and Fifth Symphonies, along with his First Piano Concerto. The now available evidence reveals a major 20th century symphonist who was left in the shadows. Why was Englund (1916–1999) ignored and why is his work emerging only now? There are several intriguing reasons. The title of Englund's autobiography, *In the Shadow of Sibelius*, gives one of them. Jean Sibelius (1865–1957), the brightest star of the nationalist romantic movement in Scandinavia, so dominated the musical galaxy with his seven symphonies and many tone poems that lesser lights were hardly visible. For Finland, Sibelius created the same problem that existed in the German world after Beethoven. What was one supposed to do after that?

More of the same would simply not do because it could not be done as well, as the epigones of Sibelius discovered to their regret. Also, the world had substantially changed with the onslaught of the Second World War. Until Englund burst forth with his First Symphony in 1946, no one in Finland knew quite how to extend the symphonic form post-Sibelius. Englund had endured four years of the Second World War as a combatant, barely escaping with his life. He conveyed his and his country's experience in what is conventionally called a neo-classical musical language, but one that speaks with a ferocity and dissonant edge that is far from the nature idylls and frosty mountain peaks of Finnish romantic nationalism. Thus, his First Symphony (which actually contains echoes of Sibelius) became known as the "War Symphony". Not only did it speak to what Finland had endured in its heroic response to the brutal assault from the Soviet Union in 1939, but it gave a new, yet still tonal, vocabulary to the war generation in which it could continue to speak. Here was a work, quickly followed by an even finer Symphony No. 2, that did not sound like Sibelius, but that magnificently succeeded on its own grounds. The vivid contrast of Englund's music to Sibelius' brought him to immediate prominence.

Ironically, that celebrity is another reason for Englund's obscurity.

By the late 1950s, the 12-tone avant-garde, spawned by Arnold Schoenberg, had swept through Scandinavia with a vengeance, leaving Englund
as practically the only prominent composer not embracing it. With masterful understatement, he called systematized atonality "wearying",
and chose silence to compromise. "In the light of my strict musical
education," he said, "the new trends were like a mockery of the composer as a serious artist. As a result, there was nothing left for me to
do but bide my time, waiting for a more propitious moment." The
wait was almost 15 years, punctuated by only one major and several
minor works. The 10 years preceding his Third Symphony in 1971
were of complete compositional silence. A hiatus of that length can
end almost any reputation, especially when the avant-garde is in charge
of reputations. To remove any doubt that his silence was a reactionary
indictment of the avant-garde, Englund continued to defend the values
he cherished through his position as a music critic and as a professor
at the Helsinki Academy.

When the grip of the 12-note disciples loosened, an unrepentant Englund came roaring back with a defiant, bold Third Symphony, as if to
say, "See!" He went on to produce the main body of his symphonic
work in the last two decades of his life. He also composed a number
of concertos for piano, clarinet, and violin; incidental music; chamber
music; and choral works. Throughout, he stuck to the same basic language he had developed before his protracted silence. Englund's music
remained tonal and his forms traditional, attributes which usually mean
music that is easily accessible.

Englund's works, however, possess a toughness and an integrity that
demand a great deal of attention before they yield their considerable
treasures. His message is not an easy one, no more than were the experiences he endured, which included, besides the war, the loss of two
children and his first wife. His music can be tumultuous, searing, occasionally caustic, but often very reflective in a touching, nostalgic way.
His lyricism is most often latent; he does not wear beautiful melodies
on his sleeves. There is a lively sense of propulsion generated by rhythmic vivacity and a tonal architecture that, no matter how storm-tossed
the dissonances, always points to the home port. His musical themes
can at first appear unremarkable, but they prove to be very durable
and, on repeated acquaintance, unforgettable. Englund was a master
craftsman in this respect. As he said, "I play through my material hundreds of times to test it for its fatigue point. Only if the musical idea

retains its original freshness despite wear is it worth keeping." To my surprise, some of Englund's themes that more or less passed me by the first few times I now cannot get out of my mind.

The musical influences on Englund are obvious. In an interview in 1963, he admitted Stravinsky and Bartók as the two composers who had influenced him most, but there are others just as apparent. Shortly after the war, Englund made a trip to Russia, where he was exposed to the works of Shostakovich and Prokofiev.

It is especially the former who can be heard in many of the symphonies, especially the martial war works, such as Nos. 1 and 5. The opening slow movement of the Fourth Symphony, written "to the memory of a great composer" (probably Shostakovich), comes close to the finest, most heart-rending slow movements in Shostakovich's symphonies. In my first encounter with Symphony No. 2, subtitled *Blackbird* for its flute theme, I wrote down, "Malcolm Arnold, Harald Sæverud (in the wind writing), Sibelius, and Bohuslav Martinů" as a few of the influences that suggested themselves. Few critics have remarked upon what seems a clear influence from the great Danish composer Carl Nielsen. Englund makes prominent use of brass and timpani in much the same threatening way that Nielsen employed it, especially in Nielsen's Fourth Symphony, *Inextinguishable*. For instance, in Englund's Fifth, the shrieking woodwinds attempt to flee the pounding timpani and brass that threaten to crush the life out of them. The forces of life are never so triumphant in Englund as they are at the end of Nielsen's Fourth Symphony, but the conclusion to his Third Symphony comes close in its exuberance, as does the finale of No. 1, which Englund described as "the joyous shout of a young man who survived the war".

Also in temperament, Englund's music is closer to Nielsen's in the sense that it is a reflection not so much of the forces of nature, as of human experience and man's reaction to the forces of antilife. Despite all this, Englund's music does not sound derivative. He is in charge of these influences, not subservient to them.

A good place to start an exploration of Englund's work is with the Naxos CD, because it contains my two favorite symphonies, 2 and 4, along with the sprightly, percussive First Piano Concerto. The performances by the Turku Philharmonic, under Jorma Panula, are marvelous. In these works one hears Englund's preoccupation with time and memory. In the Tempus fugit movement of the Fourth, there is an intriguing ticktock ostinato figure. This is not the only work in which Englund replicates the sound of clocks. One might then proceed to Ondine's release of the Cello Concerto, coupled with the Sixth Symphony, for an example of Englund's more reflective side. The very finely wrought Cello Concerto is strangely reminiscent of Samuel Barber's music. Englund's piece is deeply ruminative, with a veiled poignancy and touching lyricism. One has the sense of listening in on something private. Here, too, the performances are superb.

The text from Heraclitus that Englund uses in the choral portions of his Sixth Symphony says that "the road up and down are one and the same." Time and its ravages may be one of Englund's concerns, but it does not panic him. He observes their grim workings with stoicism and a certain detachment, which accounts for the classical balance and clarity of his music. I doubt if the whole body of his work will be included in the classics of the 20th century, but I believe more than several works will endure. Englund's own test was to see if they would wear well, and they do, whether the road is going up or down.

Recommended Recordings

Symphonies 2 & 4; Piano Concerto No. 1, Jorma Panula, Turku PO, Naxos 8.553758

Cello Concerto; Symphony No. 6 (*Aphorisms*), Eri Klas, Tampere PO, Ondine 951

Symphonies 1 & 2, Peeter Lilje, Estonian State SO, Ondine 751

Symphonies 4 & 5: *The Great Wall of China*, Eri Klas, Tampere PO, Ondine 961-2

Symphonies 3 & 7, Ari Rasilainen, Tampere PO, Ondine 833

~

Gerald Finzi: Intimations of Immortality

British composer Gerald Finzi (1901–1956) was a self-professed agnostic. But like Ralph Vaughan Williams, Finzi seems to have been that special breed of believing agnostic who could write sublime, religiously inspired music.

How could this be? In my own experience with agnostics, I have found that they are often particularly close to God—intimate enough to hold a personal grudge. Often, it has to do with a misunderstanding as to who he really is or what he has done. Frequently, their objections to God concern things to which God himself objects, like the suffering of children or death.

This latter subject is one with which Finzi had intimate familiarity as a young child, and it might be the key to his dilemma. When Finzi was seven, his father died. By the time he was 17, Finzi's three elder brothers had died, as well as his beloved music teacher, Ernest Farrar, who was killed at the front in World War I. What was Finzi to make of this? Thomas Traherne, the 17th-century metaphysical poet from whom Finzi took the text of one of his greatest compositions, wrote, "It is not our parents' loins, so much as our parents' lives, that enthralls and blinds us." Was it his absent father, the very lack of a parent's life, that made Finzi angry with the Father or at least blinded him to his existence?

Finzi's frequent encounters with death easily explain his attraction to the poetry and the pessimism of Thomas Hardy, another English agnostic, many of whose poems Finzi set to music. During the latter part of his relatively short life, Finzi lived under the death sentence of Hodgkin's disease, which carried him off at age 55. It's only natural that he should have been fixated on the transitory nature of things. It's harder to explain Finzi's love for the works of 17th-century English metaphysical poets and his penchant for setting explicitly religious texts. What was the source of hope for this pessimist?

The answer comes from Finzi's profound appreciation for and immersion in the beauty of nature. Haunted by death and inflamed by nature's beauty, where could Finzi go to deal with the dichotomy between the two? Ineluctably, he turned to traditional Christian texts.

He wrote a Magnificat; *In Terra Pax*; *For St. Cecilia*; *Lo, the Full, Final Sacrifice*; and other such religious works. What creates the tension in Finzi's works is the intense experience of beauty juxtaposed with the looming presence of death. Beauty and death do not comfortably co-exist. Beauty signals a certain message that death denies. That is the conundrum of human existence that Finzi's music so movingly captures with a kind of melancholy grandeur.

Finzi is the composer of beginnings and endings, of birth and death. The two musical bookends of his work in a thematic, if not a chronological, sense are his two masterpieces, *Dies Natalis*, op. 8, and *Intimations of Immortality*, op. 29. In *Dies Natalis*, Finzi set the text of Thomas Traherne's poem of that name for tenor and orchestra. The work depicts a newborn child's first sensations of the world. *Dies Natalis* is suffused with such a sense of pure innocence, seemingly free of original sin, that it could easily double as a Christmas Nativity. Who but Christ could exult, as in one of the composition's climaxes, "How Divine am I!"? In fact, the composition was inspired by Botticelli's painting *Mystic Nativity* in the National Gallery of Art and by the carved angels in March Church.

Yet the work is otherwise vague enough in its references that it could also stand for the unsoiled character of every newborn on whom the marks of mortality and the consciousness of sin have yet to be visited. The unsullied joy, the sense of wonder, and the celebration of creation are conveyed with a spontaneity and rapture that are breathtaking. As Finzi recalled in 1939, "There is a great resemblance between the static and the ecstatic. I discovered this one day when I was standing in March Church looking up at the double hammer-beam roof and the row of carved angels—which gave the feeling of a Botticelli Nativity and were static from very ecstasy." All of Finzi's slow movements have this same sense of still rapture and an Elgarian nobility. But even this glorious song of the newborn ends diminuendo, as if in a premonition of the sadness ahead.

That sadness is fully expressed in *Intimations of Immortality*, a setting of William Wordsworth's poem (absent two stanzas), for tenor, chorus, and orchestra. This, perhaps, is an even greater work than *Dies Natalis* because it directly addresses the conflict between beauty and death and thus reaches greater depths. Wordsworth's poem is one of the supreme reflections on the transience of things. Finzi matched the text with his most sublime music.

Some of the climaxes in the introduction, which celebrate the beauty and the joy of life, are reminiscent of the momentous, frightening claps of thunder in Sir Edward Elgar's *The Dream of Gerontius*, when the soul of Gerontius comes into the presence of God. The similarity of language cannot have been accidental. In other words, beauty was Finzi's window onto God, his meeting place with him. As such, it's filled with exaltation, awe, and even fear. The threatened loss of this beauty, which comes with the approach of death through age, provides the heartbreaking poignancy that runs throughout the piece. As the Wordsworth text says, "Nothing can bring back the hour / Of splendour in the grass, of glory in the flower." Yet, the very loss of beauty somehow presages its recovery.

As the texts he set demonstrate, Finzi held the Platonic view that we come from the divine, are soiled by this world, and "forget" our origins. He humorously remarked on this in one of his Crees Lectures in 1953: "We all know that a dead poet lives in many a live stockbroker. Many of these people, before they fade into the light of common day, have had an intuitive glimpse which neither age, nor experience, nor knowledge, can ever give them."

In our experience of beauty, Finzi thought, we "recollect" and gain a dim intimation of our immortality. In fact, this is exactly how Finzi describes the process of his creative work and the nature of its rewards: "The essence of art is order, completion and fulfillment. Something is created out of nothing, order out of chaos; and as we succeed in shaping our intractable material into coherence and form, a relief comes to the mind (akin to the relief experienced at the remembrance of some forgotten thing)."

While the content of Finzi's music is that "forgotten thing", its style is inimitably English in character and expression. Steeped in Elgar, Finzi may not seem so original in his language, but he uses it to perfection. His more contemporary influences include his older friend Vaughan Williams, who championed his works; Gustav Holst; and William Walton. Finzi was able to express an exquisite sensitivity without becoming precious. As his other works show, he could also flex considerable orchestral muscle. Listen, for example, to his superb cello and clarinet concertos.

The magnificent Cello Concerto was Finzi's last work, and it shows him operating at his full powers. This is a passionate work that seems to be searching the darkness that Finzi knew would soon enfold him. He began work on it after he learned of the incurable illness that would prematurely end his life. As powerfully disturbing as the opening Allegro is, the very touching Andante quieto shows that Finzi could still recollect the gentle pastoralism that was his hallmark. Naxos' recording also has the *Eclogue* for piano and strings and *Grand Fantasia and Toccata*. The beautiful performance by the Northern Sinfonia, under Howard Griffiths, with cellist Tim Hugh, makes this bargain disc a steal.

We need no longer fear the passing of things, the passing of ourselves, into the dust from which we came. We were given an everlasting gift, the Conqueror of sin and death. Finzi's works are suffused with deep intimations of this wonderful, breathtaking truth. As Traherne's words say in Finzi's *Dies Natalis*, "From God above / Being sent, the Gift doth me enflame / to praise his Name." Agnostic or not, this is what Finzi did. Listen, and weep for joy.

Recommended Recordings

Dies Natalis (with Britten, Serenade, Nocturne), Jacqueline Shave, Britten Sinfonia, Mark Padmore, Harmonia Mundi 807552. Or: David Hill, Bournemouth SO, James Gilchrist, Naxos 8.570417 (plus *Farewell to Arms, Two Sonnets*).

Intimations of Immortality; *Grand Fantasia and Toccata*, Richard Hickox, Royal Liverpool PO, Philip Langridge, Philip Fowke, EMI/Warner 64720 (OOP, ArkivCD). Or: David Hill, Bournemouth SO & Chorus, James Gilchrist, Naxos 8.557863 (without the *Grand Fantasia* but including *For St. Cecilia*).

Intimations of Immortality and *Dies Natalis*, Matthew Best, Corydon Singers & Orchestra, Hyperion 66876. This is the only label with both works on one CD in slightly less expressive performances than the EMI/Warner releases.

A Centenary Collection: Clarinet Concerto; *Love's Labour's Lost*; *Eclogue*, William Boughton, English String Orchestra, Martin Jones, Alan Hacker, Nimbus NI 5665. A wonderful CD released in 2001 for the centennial of Finzi's birth.

Clarinet Concerto; *Five Bagatelles*; *A Severn Rhapsody*, Howard Griffiths, Northern Sinfonia, Robert Plane, Lesley Hatfield, Naxos 8.553566

Violin Concerto; *In Years Defaced*; Prelude; Romance, Richard Hickox, City of London Sinfonia, John Mark Ainsley, Tasmin Little, Chandos 9888. The first complete recording of the Violin Concerto for confirmed Finzi aficionados. Re-issued with the terrific Cello Concerto (with Vernon Handley and Raphael Wallfisch) on Chandos 10425.

Cello Concerto; *Grand Fantasia and Toccata*; *Eclogue*, Howard Griffiths, Northern Sinfonia, Timothy Hugh, Peter Donohoe, Naxos 8.555766

Kenneth Fuchs: American Rhapsody

When commiserating with those concerned over our declining culture, I, a natural pessimist, am nonetheless moved to say, "But you
must know that there is a renaissance in American Classical music."
"What do you mean?" they ask, puzzled. "Well," I respond, "I mean
Ken Fuchs, among others." Why him? I will let composer Richard
Danielpour describe Fuchs (b. 1956) to you: "A composer who is able
to evoke joy, tenderness, humor, wildness, and a sense of the tragic
coherently within the same work does many of us a great service: he
reminds those of us who love music why we continue to embrace it
as an integral part of our lives."

Fuchs is an exemplar of the recovery of American music. His music rejoices. And he speaks eloquently of his experiences through the
period of recovery. He wrote to me:

> It is amazing to see now, from the vantage of over 25 years, what was
> actually happening. We really were at the beginning of a movement.
> The whole generation before that was so musically dry and barren and
> acrid and arid. Thank God people had the courage of their convictions
> to write music invested with feeling and emotion! . . . I remember all
> too well, as a student at Juilliard in the late 70s and early 80s, what that
> felt like. Even during those years, well after the shift had started, it was
> a very steep climb out of a trench. The Juilliard composition faculty
> at the time consisted of Babbitt, Carter, Diamond, Persichetti, and
> Sessions. Quite a group. Although none of them really ever pushed
> their own styles as dogma, it took a *lot* of courage in that heady en-
> vironment to write truthful music in a style that would eventually
> become part of "the new romanticism."

My first exposure to Fuchs' music was *An American Place* (for orchestra), written to express the "brash optimism of the American spirit".
This it does in a very appealing, in fact exhilarating, musical outburst,
which Fuchs builds toward John Adams–like chugging ostinatos and
beautiful, soaring melodies. In the liner notes, Fuchs says that "the
score reflects the palette of musical sounds that have developed in the
United States during the last hundred years . . . and is intended to
suggest the rich body of music created by the American symphonists

who have come before me and from whom I continue to take inspiration."

Fuchs is obviously trying to write in a popular style and he succeeds without being cloying. Also on this Naxos release is Fuchs' *Eventide*, a concerto for English horn, harp, percussion, and string orchestra. It is another immediately appealing work: enchanting, exquisitely fine, and gorgeously melodic. In *Out of the Dark*, Fuchs shows that he can write dissonant, thorny music to reflect upon his favorite Helen Frankenthaler paintings. However, by the third movement, *Summer Banner*, he returns to his gracious, mellifluous style. This is all beautifully played by the London Symphony Orchestra under JoAnn Falletta.

Another Naxos CD, again featuring the London Symphony Orchestra, or its members, under conductor JoAnn Falletta, provides an expanding picture of Fuchs' talents. The CD begins with *United Artists*, a scintillating tribute to the London Symphony Orchestra, which Fuchs came to admire during its recording of his first Naxos CD. *United Artists* is a five-minute fanfare that has something of the vivacious demeanor of Leonard Bernstein's *Overture to Candide* or of one of Malcolm Arnold's spirited confections. This is an excellent public celebration that lets the orchestra strut its stuff.

Quiet in the Land is as interior a piece as *United Artists* is an exterior one in orientation and spirit. As the composer writes in the liner notes, "I wondered how quiet the spirit of our land might be." This mixed quintet for strings and winds moves into Samuel Barber/Aaron Copland territory with its mellifluous melody and gentle, rippling beauty. Fuchs calls it "a sonic ode to the expansive landscapes and immense arching sky of the great Midwestern Plains". As a Midwesterner, I can attest that this scenery evokes a deep sense of yearning and expectation. Fuchs captures these feelings with real poignancy. This 12-minute piece is a reflective gem.

The next two pieces, *Fire, Ice, and Summer Bronze*, for brass quintet, and *Autumn Rhythm*, for wind quintet, derive their inspiration from paintings by, respectively, Helen Frankenthaler and Jackson Pollock. I have never cared for the works of these artists, but if Fuchs can draw this kind of inspiration from them, I had better take another look, or at least try to see them through his music.

The thing that continually impresses is the level of refinement in the writing. This man does not have to shout to make himself heard. As I have noticed in his work before, there is a sense of ease in his music. By this I do not mean easiness, but a calm confidence in what he is doing and in the quality of his material. He is endowed with a major melodic gift. Also, he is not afraid to take the time to let things develop with a sense of natural growth. In *Autumn Rhythm*, he captures some of the insouciant breeziness that only a master like Malcolm Arnold could achieve in his wind writing. This is another exquisite gem.

The longest and last composition on the CD is *Canticle to the Sun*, a concerto for French horn and orchestra (2005). This work catches the kind of Celtic magic and orchestral glitter that I used to hear in the work of the late Welsh composer William Mathias. Fuchs makes a gloriously long-lined melody for the French horn out of the hymn tune to "All Creatures of Our God and King". This outwardly celebratory, declamatory work is infused with inner joy. Listen to it, or to any of these works, and you will know what Fuchs means when he says, "I make no apologies for writing from the heart." No apologies needed; this is the vindication.

The third Naxos CD of Fuchs' orchestral works is also brilliantly played by the London Symphony Orchestra, under Falletta. Like Aaron Copland, Fuchs has a way of capturing the stirrings of the human heart and the yearnings of the soul in highly spirited, soaring music. His works carry within themselves an inimitably American sense of expectancy, of horizons glimpsed and striven for, and, finally, of boldly announced arrivals. He achieves all this within the conventional means of tonality. Orchestrally, he employs a sparkling kind of American impressionism, though I also hear a dash of Benjamin Britten's *Sea Interludes* in *Atlantic Riband*. *American Rhapsody* is, according to Fuchs, a romance for violin and orchestra. It has a Samuel Barber–like melodic appeal and orchestral lushness to it. If I wanted an English reference point for its upward spiraling solo violin line, I would choose Vaughan Williams' *Lark Ascending*. Violinist Michael Ludwig plays with both elegance and exquisite feeling. So does violist Paul Silverthorne in the lovely *Divinum Mysterium*, a one-movement concerto for viola and orchestra inspired by a Protestant hymn tune. This is unfailingly appealing and immediately accessible music.

After I wrote an enthusiastic review of Fuchs' *An American Place*, he contacted me and suggested I listen to his chamber music on a stunningly good Albany Records CD of String Quartets 2, 3, and 4. I am glad he did; these are among the best pieces of American chamber music I have encountered. Fuchs writes with a Janáček-like wildness, employs at times a piercing intimacy of a highly lyrical nature, and has a haunting Bernard Herrmann–like quality to some of his themes and mysterious ostinatos. It is hard to imagine a better or more gripping performance than this one by the American String Quartet.

His latest chamber music release also comes from Naxos and includes *Falling Canons* (Christopher O'Riley, piano), *Falling Trio* (Trio21), and String Quartet No. 5: *American* (Delray String Quartet). The *Falling* pieces are offshoots of a previous work, *Falling Man*, written for baritone and orchestra in the aftermath of September 11, 2001, with a text based on a fragment from Don DeLillo's novel *Falling Man*. Naxos has released this composition with other of Fuchs' works for voice and orchestra, such as *Movie House* (Seven Poems by John Updike for Baritone Voice and Chamber Ensemble) and *Songs of Innocence and of Experience* (Four Poems by William Blake for Baritone and Chamber Ensemble).

Falling Canons is a very concentrated, rigorous work that develops its theme, a cascading downward piano motif, in seven canons until, as Fuchs says, "All seven pitches of the scale are represented in a descending fashion." This is the starkest music I have heard from Fuchs. When a composer pares himself down to strict essentials for this kind of contrapuntal writing, one sees what he is made of. He can't hide behind the orchestration. Fuchs shows his spine. This work reminds me of Shostakovich's Preludes and Fugues, which, of course, are, in turn, strongly redolent of Bach. That is a very distinguished pedigree, and Fuchs' marvelous contrapuntal writing is fully up to the challenge. Fuchs does not shy from exploring the darker side of things, but he does so in a way that would have been familiar to Bach or Mozart.

The Fifth Quartet, according to the composer, "is alternately lyrical and playful, sometimes brusque and muscular, at times elegiac, and it is meant to suggest the resilience and brash optimism of the American spirit." It has a subdued, sweet beginning with a gorgeous theme. At about three minutes in, it starts dancing—almost a little hoedown, but the sheer loveliness of it keeps things mellow. One almost wonders if it will dissolve in its own beauty—this glittering, luminous sound. The second movement contains an insinuating, insistent, almost obsessive theme that is passed from instrument to instrument—done pizzicato on the cello—with a doleful melody cast across it that fails to subdue this nervous Scherzo. The third movement starts with a pained utterance in several chords. Then Fuchs returns to the exquisite opening theme but casts it more darkly and somberly. Now the violin begins a sad little dance, which stops, then starts again. It is a bit like some of Shostakovich's Jewish-inspired quartet writing. The dance dissolves, and the obsessive melody from the Scherzo reappears, followed by a moving lament. Everything that has happened so far in this Quartet seems to be gathered up in this movement, including motivic elements of the *Falling Man* theme. Its wildness and sense of immediacy once again recall Janáček. The closing Allegro begins exuberantly. The spirited double fugue of the last movement is a thrilling tour de force of counterpoint and melody. It banishes the preceding sadness. This is jubilant music that fulfills Fuchs' purpose of affirmation. The Fifth is one of the finest quartets of the past several decades—*American* or otherwise.

Falling Trio uses the same principal theme for a one-movement work that, like *Falling Canons*, has seven "fantasy variations". Also like *Falling Canons*, it has a mesmerizing quality. At about four minutes in, a countertheme to the doleful *Falling* refrain begins to sing in the violin, with the piano playing a rippling ostinato under it. After some harsh piano attacks, it does so again at about 10 minutes. The two themes struggle and finally meld together. As one would expect, the resources of a trio flesh out the treatment in a rich and at times highly romantic way. There is some tough stuff and sadness in this ultimately very touching and finally consolatory work. It has an impressive range of expression for a 13-minute composition and further displays Fuchs' ingenuity in exploiting every potential aspect of his *Falling Man* theme without any feeling of artificiality.

There is little in contemporary music that is as directly expressive as the music of Kenneth Fuchs. It goes right to the heart and stays there. If you think America's song has already been sung, you need to listen to him.

Recommended Recordings

An American Place; Eventide; Out of the Dark, JoAnn Falletta, London SO, Thomas Stacy, Timothy Jones, Naxos 8.559224

United Artists; Quiet in the Land; Fire, Ice, and Summer Bronze; Autumn Rhythm; Canticle to the Sun, JoAnn Falletta, London SO, Timothy Jones, Naxos CD 8.559335

Atlantic Riband; American Rhapsody; Divinum Mysterium, JoAnn Falletta, London SO, Michael Ludwig, Paul Silverthorne, Naxos 8.559723

String Quartets 2, 3, 4, American String Quartet, Albany 480

Falling Canons; String Quartet No. 5; *Falling Trio*, Christopher O'Riley, Delray String Quartet, Naxos 8.559733

Hans Gál: Unbroken

Austrian Jewish composer Hans Gál (1890–1987) fled the Nazis from Mainz, Germany, where he was director of the Music Academy, in 1933, and then from his native Vienna in 1938, at the time of the Anschluss. After a period of internment on the Isle of Man (his internment diary from 1940, *Music behind Barbed Wire*, is available from Toccata Press), he eventually moved to Scotland, where he became an Edinburgh University professor of music, teaching music theory, counterpoint, and composition. Before his exile, Gál was a composer of note in the German-speaking world, where his operas, orchestral works, and chamber music had achieved a significant level of popularity. The Nazis suppressed his works, which were practically unknown in his adopted country. Musically speaking, he had been eclipsed. However, throughout this long period (his last listed composition is a *Moment Musical* for treble recorder, composed at age 96), Gál continued to compose, apparently unconcerned by the lack of any prospect that his work would be performed. As the saying goes, he was writing for the desk. He died at the ripe old age of 97.

That might have been the end of the story. Who would've known? In his last year, Gál said, "This rupture in my life, it cannot be made up for. In my case, Hitler really succeeded!" It seemed so—until recently. It was not only Hitler who guaranteed Gál's obscurity. As was the case with other composers embargoed by the Nazis, such as Günter Raphael and Walter Braunfels, the ascendancy of the avant-garde after World War II sidelined any prospect for the revival of his music. It was too passé. However, glimmers of interest began to be shown, spurred on by Gál's grandchildren and curious musicians.

Now, some 30 years after his death, there are a score of recordings of his music available, and we can find out what was in his desk. It is a remarkable, even mind-boggling discovery. It is almost archaeological in its significance. It is as if civilization had not really been almost fatally disrupted, but had kept on in the study of this man who quietly refused to bend to barbarism. This is music for those who thought the world had ended, and who can now discover that it didn't. The great tradition of Western music from the 18th century on continued in this man, quietly but surely. Despite the catastrophes, Gál remained remarkably steadfast. He said, "The rupture that entered my life in 1933 only influenced the circumstances of my life, not my oeuvre itself, which continued on its course unchecked." Indeed, it did, remarkably so. What if you simply refused to accede to the prevailing political and musical trends of your time? The answer is: Hans Gál.

Needless to say, it wasn't easy. In a 1971 interview reproduced in the *Hans Gál Society Newsletter*, Gál said, "In 1933 . . . everything was over for me: with the Nazi takeover I was radically eliminated, as a Jew. My operas disappeared from the stage, my music from the platform and from the catalogues of my publishers." Gál's music was driven underground. "A new chapter had begun," he remarked, "and not a nice one, I can assure you. To build up a new existence at near 50 is no joke." However, what is extraordinarily surprising is that Gál's uprooting did not sever him from the source of his inspiration—as happened with so many expatriate composers. Away from their native soil, they withered. With Gál, you cannot tell from his music that he ever left—not even 50 years later.

What does the music of this remarkable man sound like? Michael Haas, the author of *Forbidden Music*, made this illuminating remark: "If Schoenberg's contemporaries Franz Schreker and Alexander Zemlinsky demonstrated that progressive Viennese composers writing tonal music could coexist with the Second Viennese School [Schoenberg, Berg and Webern], Hans Gál represented the more startling view that the First Viennese School [Haydn, Mozart, Beethoven, and Schubert] still had quite a bit of life left to it." And, one might add, it still had something to say in terms of grace, beauty, and balance. Unlike the works of Zemlinsky or Schreker, Gál's do not suffer from a sense of overripeness or imminent decay. Nor do they signal a world about to end. In 1921, music critic Paul Stefan observed that "the Lieder, choruses and especially the various genres of chamber music that I have heard show him, rich in form and partial to melody, to be quite clearly following in the footsteps of Johannes Brahms."

Of his near contemporaries, Gál sounds most like Franz Schmidt (1874–1939) and, a bit less so, like Richard Strauss (1864–1949), without the latter's exaggerated opulence. Gál explained his admiration for Schmidt to British music critic Martin Anderson: "Schmidt was one of the most completely natural musicians I have ever met, an extremely gifted man and very capable indeed." Schmidt had moved to Vienna to study with Anton Bruckner in 1890, the year Gál was born. In turn, in 1919, Gál assumed the position once held by Bruckner at the University of Vienna. Not only are Schmidt's four symphonies finally available today, but so are Gál's.

There is something expert about Gál's music without a hint of pedantry. If it did not sound too self-congratulatory, I would say that Gál is a composer for the connoisseur. I mean this in the sense that the fineness of what he does can easily be overlooked. It is music of technical sophistication and emotional restraint. It does not command your attention. You have to give it. His music in no way forces itself upon you; it has a sense of privacy. It is very inviting, but you have to walk through the door. Otherwise, it is written in *echt* Viennese style of the pre–12-tone variety and without a whiff of decadence. It is very much part of a *living* tradition.

Gál never felt the need or the desire to change his style throughout his long and productive career. This is not to say that he did not modify his musical language—listen, for example, to the quite different harmonic vocabulary used in the Second Quartet after the First—depending on his expressive needs. In a 1971 interview, Gál explained, "Developing my musical language organically, I have saved myself the trouble of tumbling from one 'ism' to another by never accepting any. . . . Expressing myself musically I had always the feeling of speaking my native language." That natural musicality is exactly what is conveyed in his works. A former student recalled that Gál dismissed some semi-improvised modern works by saying, "In the music where there are no wrong notes, it follows there can be no right notes either." This is exactly the problem with a great deal of the music that drowned Gál's out. All I hear in him are *right* notes. They give clear evidence that the line to the great tradition in music was, in fact, not broken, either by the depredations of the Second World War or by Arnold Schoenberg. Here preserved intact are the senses of structure, balance, and proportion, not as if in aspic, but living, breathing.

It is worth hearing Gál directly express his idea of balance (sometime in the mid-1920s): "Impressionism—that giving of oneself to the moment at the expense of form—is as foreign to me, even in opera, as pathos, the exaggeration of expression, or the mechanistic-playful as a shutting-off of expression. Opposition to false pathos led to impressionism and opposition to that led to the mechanistic-objective; I believe that all three are in the wrong, since the nature of all true art always comes down to a balance between form and expression."

The Avie label has given us all four symphonies, in splendid performances and recordings—two of them even twice. There are those of Thomas Zehetmair (Nos. 1 and 2) with the Northern Sinfonia and all four with Kenneth Woods and the Orchestra of the Swan. Zehetmair matched his Gál symphonies with those of Schubert (Nos. 6 and 9, respectively); Woods matched his with those of Schumann's four symphonies. I prefer to have my Gál all in one place, which is happily available on the subsequent set of the four Woods recordings that came about thanks to Kickstarter crowd financing. But I understand the point the conductors were making by matching his music with Schubert or Schumann. They are placing Gál in the lineage to which he belongs and of which he is so obviously a continuation. It is not mere hype to title the CD paired with Schubert *Kindred Spirits*. The Viennese world of Schubert is still present in Gál. In fact what Gál said of Schubert in comparison with Beethoven applies to the spirit of his own music: "That Schubert, in all innocence, set against Beethoven's epic and heroic ideal his own, directly opposed view of life, a quiet serenity unclouded by the stresses of will, was his greatest, but never fully appreciated deed." The pairing with Schubert's Sixth Symphony makes even more sense when one realizes that Gál's First was awarded the Columbia Broadcasting Schubert Centenary Prize in 1928. Gál's First Symphony begins with a long-lined theme in the strings, repeated in the winds. It is fresh and engaging, charmingly balletic in places, with some of the effervescence of Prokofiev, though without a Russian sound. In fact, it has a touch of musical chinoiserie.

In some ways, the most remarkable of the four symphonies is Gál's Symphony No. 2, composed in Edinburgh between 1942 and 1943. Its British premiere came in March 1950. It seems never to have been performed again until this recording. The Second begins with an attractive theme in the strings that is then picked up by the winds, which pass it back and forth, until the brass and timpani enter in a more aggressive version of it. But then it melts into a lovingly gentle theme. One notes immediately how thematically well developed and coherent this music is. It is also extraordinary in its gentleness and reflective nature. According to Kenneth Woods' booklet notes, Gál considered calling the extraordinary 15-minute Adagio both "Elegy" and "Dirge", but emphasized that it is "really more consolation than funeral music".

It is, in fact, music from a lost world (with shades of Franz Schmidt) that speaks with such grace that one almost gasps at the magnitude of the loss. Didn't Gál know, one is tempted to ask, that everything had fallen apart? Indeed, he did. The year before he completed this work his sister and his aunt had committed suicide to avoid deportation to Auschwitz, and while he was composing it, his youngest son took his own life under the strain. Things fell apart, but Gál did not fall apart inside. What spiritual resources the man had to keep this equilibrium is not remarked upon, but it is one of the most remarkable things about him and his music. He more than kept his balance; he maintained an inner coherence. Clearly, this was a man at peace with himself.

How did he do it? For that, you must listen to the music. There is something innocent, almost preternatural, about it. This is not to say that the music is untroubled. The trouble, however, does not shatter the music as in so many modern compositions, but is dealt with in *musical* terms. What do I mean by that? As in Mozart or Haydn, horror never horrifies. The music never shrieks or leaves you disoriented. In fact orientation seems to be its whole purpose.

The Second symphony exists in two recordings, both on Avie. Woods' performance is exquisite. It is only about a minute and a half longer than Zehetmair's very fine interpretation, but it tells in moments of ravishing beauty for which Woods was willing to give some extra attention. If you are only getting one Gál Symphony, get this one.

The Third Symphony, which opens with such a gentle, lovely theme on the oboe, then the flute, before the horns zone in more assertively, has simply to be one of the most graceful modern symphonies. There is a haunting Viennese waltz lilting through parts of it. How can any-thing this lovely—try to resist the gorgeous Andante—not have been performed in 55 years, until this superb recording by Kenneth Woods and the Orchestra of the Swan?

Symphony No. 4: *Sinfonia concertante* is very genial, almost a confec-tion, light-hearted, very mellow, with echoes of Strauss and Schmidt. If Gál characterized Schubert as of "quiet serenity unclouded by stresses of will", one could easily apply the same remark to the Fourth. Gál said, "This work is akin to a concerto grosso, combining a symphonic structure with the brilliant display and competitive spirit of four soloists who act both as a group and as individuals, emulating each other." The soloists are violin, cello, flute, and clarinet. With the Scherzo, Gál ex-plicitly refers to the commedia dell'arte characters of Harlequin and Columbine.

Woods and the Northern Sinfonia offer an immensely attractive CD

of Gál's concertante works for violin, with Annette-Barbara Vogel as
the soloist. The opening Fantasia movement of the Violin Concerto,
composed at the height of Gál's success in Germany in 1932, has an
instantly memorable theme, long-lined and lyrical. Three minutes in,
you might think Vaughan Williams had a hand in it. Well before he
crossed the channel, Gál was sounding like an English pastoralist. This
is the first orchestral work of Gál's that I encountered, and it raised him
even higher in my estimation. The second movement, marked Arioso,
is just as beautiful and runs into the concluding, lively Rondo.

Vogel's playing is a labor of love, as is the dedicated performance
of the Northern Sinfonia under Woods. It is a measure of the damage
the Nazis did that this work was not heard after 1933 until 2004. It
is, I suppose, easy it imagine how music this lovely and civilized was
first suppressed and then overlooked in the ideological age of the 20th
century. How wonderful that Avie has revived it. The concertino is
just as delicious as the concerto, and the *Triptych* shows that Gál never
lost his bearings. There is also an equally fine recording of the Violin
Concerto on the Gramola label (98921), with violinist Thomas Al-
bertus Imberger and the Israel Chamber Orchestra, which offers a bit
more of an old-Viennese flavor.

The warmth and beauty of Gál's Cello Concerto from 1944 reminds
me of Othmar Schoeck's Cello Concerto, written only three years later.
It has a similar sumptuousness and autumnal feel to it, but also a lyrical
delicacy. Gál seems to have loved the oboe and writes for it beautifully.
There are frequent exchanges between the winds and the cello. This is
one of his more softly romantic works, infused with gorgeous melody.

There is something particularly special about Gál's chamber music.
He told Martin Anderson: "During many, many years in this country
during the latest 20 or 25 years of my life as a composer, I mainly wrote
chamber music. It was because of the intimacy and the feeling of being perfectly in balance with myself. I can't express it in any different
way." Elsewhere, he said, "Chamber music, as the most intimate form
of expression, is the realm to which the musician repeatedly returns in
order to retain the link with the essence of things."

The Avie label has released a CD with Gál's Two Violin Sonatas
and the Suite for Violin and Piano (AV 2182), written between 1920
and 1935. It and the other works on this CD have immediate appeal,
especially as delivered by violinist Annette-Barbara Vogel and pianist
Juhani Lagerspetz. Gál's grandson described the op. 17 Sonata as "pos-

sibly one of Gál's most outwardly-expressive chamber works". This remark should be understood within the context of Gál's being essentially an inwardly expressive composer.

On two CDs, the Meridian label offers the complete Gál Quartets, played by the Edinburgh Quartet, starting with the extremely fine Quartets 1 and 4, and the exquisite *Improvisation, Variations and Finale on a Theme by Mozart*. In 1929, critic Erwin Kroll hailed the First Quartet as "one of the few creations of recent date which really breathe something of the spirit of Schubert. This quartet is Schubertian in its blissful major-minor tonality, its melodic richness, its piquant rhythms and dance-like exhilaration." One might also add Dvořák for the sheer melodiousness of it. This music in no way forces itself upon you; it has a sense of privacy. Its fineness is unobtrusive. It has seldom left my CD player and is especially close to me in the quiet night hours.

The liner notes for volume 2 (Quartets 2 and 3, with 5 *Intermezzi*) have it exactly right in saying that Gál's world "is civilized and exists for those who have the patience to listen attentively". It is unobtrusive. Its beauties are subtle, finely wrought and exquisite in detail. This is contemplative, gentle music. Not many composers in 1969 wrote works like Quartet No. 3. The youthful *Intermezzi* from 1914 are sheer delight with the Edinburgh Quartet. I also enjoy the Camerata CD of Gál's Piano Trios, which display his signature refinement. Bending and twisting with summery delight, the Trio in G Major makes no bones about Schubert and Brahms as its musical idol—no doubt radical in 1949, its time of composition. It is a measure of the 20th century's brutality that music such as this could have been neglected.

Available on an Avie CD of Gál's String Trios, the *Serenade in D* is sheer delight, graceful, spirited, and slyly humorous. The charming second movement, Cantabile: Adagio, has to be one of the loveliest things that Gál wrote. He said, "The most perfect and most transparent form of polyphony is three voices; for that reason I have always had a special liking for the trio as the noblest medium of polyphony." His special affection for the form shines through this *Serenade* and its accompanying Trio, which is of a darker mood. Conductor Woods joins the Ensemble Epomeo as a cellist in these touching performances.

Gál's music sustains a world that has passed, or that perhaps never fully existed, through the sheer act of the creative imagination. Socrates said he lived according to a city in speech that was higher than his actual city of Athens. He declared: "In heaven there is laid up a pattern of it [the ideal city] methinks, which he who desires may behold, and beholding may set his own house in order. But whether such a one exists, or ever will exist in fact, does not matter; for he will live after the manner of that city, having nothing to do with any other." Likewise, Gál lived according to a higher city in music. I think that is why he was imperturbable through the worst of times, and why he never lost his bearings, as did so many of his contemporaries. That is why he could say he was perfectly in balance with himself.

Aristotle said that one does not know if a man has had a good life until he has had a good death. In the days before his own death from cancer at the age of 97, this is how Gál behaved according to his wife Hannah: "He could no longer eat, and became weaker from day to day. Nevertheless, every day he came down on the stair-lift, fully dressed, and stayed in his room until it was time to go to bed, reading, listening to music." Since he could no longer consume food and knew that he was dying, his conduct, even from these few details, is revealing. That he insisted on maintaining full dress reminds me of Confucius' dictum that "outward form leads to inward grace." Having heard this kind of composure in his music, it does not surprise me to learn of composure in the man. It appears that he spent his final hours in contemplation of and reflection upon the highest things in the music and the literature that he had served, and that had served him, so well throughout his long life. It sounds very much like a philosopher's death—in the image of Socrates. Gál did not drink the hemlock. Cancer gave it to him. However, his response seems similar. He accepted it within the broader perspective of these higher things. There, one can't help but think, went a noble soul.

Contrary to what Gál thought, in his case Hitler did not succeed. It is Gál who succeeded—unbroken. The catastrophic rupture in his life *is* being made up for. The dimensions of his success are partially revealed in these superb releases. May there be many more such revelations, especially in terms of his operas and other works, such as the cantata *De Profundis*.

Recommended Recordings

Symphony No. 1 (with Schubert's Sixth Symphony), Thomas Zehetmair, Northern Sinfonia, Avie 2224

Symphony No. 2 (with Schubert's Ninth Symphony), Thomas Zehetmair, Northern Sinfonia, Avie 2224

Symphonies 1–4, Kenneth Woods, Orchestra of the Swan, Avie 2232

Cello Concerto (plus Elgar Cello Concerto), Claudio Cruz, Northern Sinfonia, Antonio Meneses, Avie 2237

Violin Concerto; Violin Concertino; *Triptych for Orchestra*, Kenneth Woods, Northern Sinfonia, Annette-Barbara Vogel, Avie 2146

Violin Concerto; Violin Sonata, Roberto Paternostro, Israel Chamber Orchestra, Thomas Irnberger, Evgeni Sinaiski, Gramola 98921

Quartets 1–4, Edinburgh String Quartet, Meridian 84557

Two Violin Sonatas; Suite for Violin and Piano, Annette-Barbara Vogel, Juhani Lagerspetz, Avie 2182

Piano Trios; Variations on a Popular Viennese Tune, Karin Adam, Doris Adam, Christoph Stradner, Camerata 28149

Piano Trio (plus Goldmark & Zemlinsky Piano Trios), Thomas Irnberger, Evgeni Sinaiski, Attila Cernitori, Gramola SACD 98933

String Trios (plus Hans Krasá Works for String Trio), Ensemble Epomeo, Avie 2259

Music for Cello, Alfia Nakipbekova, Jakob Fichert, Toccata Classics 0043

The Complete Works for Solo Piano, Leon McCawley, Avie 2064

The Complete Piano Duos, Goldstone and Clemmow, Divine Art 25098

Steven Gerber:
"The Integrity of the Musical Material"

In an interview with the *21st Century Music* journal, composer Steven Gerber (1948–2015) said, "One thing that I've been curious to notice, and that I have mixed feelings about, is that at least with my recent music, the people who seem to respond to it the most seem to be people who are not big fans of contemporary music. And they tend to be people like me who are skeptical of most contemporary music." He added, "I like music that is very expressive, very out front emotionally, and I hope that mine is, and yet technically I think it is extremely restrained."

This statement should allay the anxieties of jilted concertgoers and music lovers who have been unpleasantly jolted by cacophonous attacks from the avant-garde world of sound. Far more consoling and pleasing to the suspicious victims of these assaults, however, are the works of this composer, by whom I was so impressed that I sought and made his acquaintance. By beginning in this way, though, I do not mean to suggest that Gerber's music simply serves as an aural antidote to an ear ache or that he in any way writes down to those distressed souls who cannot endure a full dose of musical modernity. What he has achieved is so much more and stands very much on its own.

The first two CDs of Gerber's music appeared simultaneously in the early 2000s, one on the Koch label and the other on Chandos. The Koch release featured Gerber's Violin Concerto, Cello Concerto (1994), and *Serenade for String Orchestra* (1990). The Chandos CD presented Gerber's Symphony No. 1, Viola Concerto, Triple Overture, and *Dirge and Awakening*, all of them composed during the 1990s, except for the symphony, which was completed in 1989. For those who appreciate contemporary music that maintains its link with the tonal tradition, these works were a major discovery. The discovery was all the more surprising when one considers that Gerber trained under Milton Babbitt, one of the high priests of Schoenberg's "coterie of 12-notery", as it was called by British composer Robert Simpson. In the 1980s, Gerber abandoned 12-tone music and began working in a tonal (if at times dissonant) idiom.

Gerber's Symphony No. 1 immediately brings to mind Shostakovich in its searing intensity, its gravity, and the nagging insistence of its motifs. "I suppose it was influenced by the fact that I'd been listening to and studying a lot of Shostakovich", said Gerber. After listening to this work and the others on the Chandos CD, I was not surprised to learn that Gerber was for a time the most frequently performed living American composer in Russia. The Viola Concerto and *Dirge and Awakening* also tap into the darker areas of the soul in a gripping, moving way. Do not be discouraged by this description. The agony that Gerber expresses is musically compelling. My only reservation is that in certain sections of the symphony, I find the means of development slightly ponderous. The background seems too much in the foreground—a tendency that Gerber rightly ascribes to minimalism, which, he says, "sounds to me like accompaniment with the melody omitted".

Gerber, however, never omits the melody. In fact, the music on the Koch disc confirms him as a composer with a major melodic gift. His violin and cello concertos and his *Serenade* may exude a very Russian seriousness of purpose, but they *sound* American. There is a great breadth to them and a touching lyricism, especially in the slow movements. Gerber's passionate Violin Concerto, composed in 1993, sounds as if he had picked up the violin where Samuel Barber laid it down. The Lento movement is ravishingly beautiful. The shades of Shostakovich are gone. In their stead, I hear the direct lineage to Barber, maybe a hint of Randall Thomson, and playful allusions to Sibelius (especially in the first movement of the Cello Concerto) and the English pastoral tradition (especially in *Serenade*). The two concertos are classical in their construction: theme, countertheme, development (variation), recapitulation, and resolution. Yes, the sonata form is alive and well. This music is satisfying to listen to and easy to follow. While that may sound condescending, it is intended as a tribute to a masterly composer who was bold enough and confident enough in his materials to write transparently.

Early in the millennium, after I wrote reviews of these two CDs, Gerber began a conversation with me—I was the director of the Voice of America at the time—that ended with my asking him to compose a *Fanfare for the Voice of America* on its 60th anniversary, with the word

"America" spelled out in its musical equivalents. The piece was duly premiered and broadcast worldwide, and most of it was then incorporated into his Second Symphony. The *Fanfare* (reorchestrated) was also used in *Music in Dark Times*, which the San Francisco Symphony premiered under conductor Vladimir Ashkenazy in 2009.

I was also impressed by how very good Gerber's music sounds when I had the opportunity to hear his Symphony No. 1 in Washington, D.C., performed by the Washington Metropolitan Philharmonic, conducted by Ulysses S. James on February 17, 2008. Gerber's work is so transparently scored and fluently written that it depends on a good deal of orchestral virtuosity for its impact. (It was very well performed by the Russian Philharmonic Orchestra, under Thomas Sanderling, in the Chandos recording.) Sometimes, when it might seem that there is not much going on in the music, Gerber is showing us the sheer beauty of the sonority he has created. He has a kind of elemental respect for the purity of sounds in the spirit of Max Picard or, in terms of contemporary composers, perhaps Arvo Pärt, though Gerber is no minimalist. The Philharmonic let us experience Gerber's wonderful ear for string sonorities. This semiprofessional orchestra was able to achieve a fine sheen in its playing. It also captured the sense of looming danger and what Gerber himself called the "spookiness" in the middle section of the symphony. In an after-concert talk, Gerber admitted to "Copland and Shostakovich influences, and, yes, Britten too". I would add a dash of Prokofiev. I should mention that Gerber won the Philharmonic's composition competition in 2007 for his Symphony No. 2, as a result of which it was played by the Philharmonic later in 2008.

All of which brings us to the Arabesque Recordings CD of Gerber's superb Clarinet Concerto (2000–2002), *Spirituals for String Orchestra* (1999–2001) and the *Serenade Concertante* (1998). When I first listened to the CD, I told Steve that the concerto reminded me of Aaron Copland's great Clarinet Concerto. He responded, "Copland is far and away my favorite American composer, and I am well aware of his influence on me, so I appreciate your comment all the more for that." He added, "I love the Copland Concerto too, and I'm sure all that harp and strings at the beginning of my piece is what reminded you of it."

The languorous opening theme also struck me as Coplandesque, with more than a soupçon of Ravel, who could also capture this kind of magical dreaminess in his music. Perky interchanges with the other winds and harp follow, accompanied by chordal interjections from the strings, which then lead toward a dazzling clarinet solo, played with great sensitivity by Jon Manasse, for whom the concerto was written. Toward the end of the movement, Gerber returns to the meltingly lovely opening theme.

The second movement has that moody element of spookiness mentioned in the First Symphony. The sense of unease and sadness becomes agitated before subsiding into a softer kind of melancholy. After a short clarinet solo, the music slowly builds again in a gathering sense of foreboding, brilliantly built, until the threat dissipates, if not disappears, when an ascending motive of three notes (two up, one down), first sounds in the high strings against the vertiginous scalar descents of the clarinet, and is then repeated by members of each section of the orchestra, with the last note held in valedictory fashion by brass and then strings.

It is an extraordinary, inspired maneuver, one reminiscent of Copland at his best. Gerber takes the doleful theme and transmutes it momentarily into something that shines through the gloom. The composer explained to me how it works: "These three notes are the same as the first three notes of both the passacaglia and the fugue in that movement, only the first note is an octave lower this time, so instead of going down a minor second and then down a major third, this motive goes up a major seventh and then down a major third. The motive in this form can first be heard as a countersubject in the fugue, first by the bassoon after the English horn has entered, then in the English horn, etc." It is a breathtaking moment and an illustration of the tremendous refinement with which Gerber wrote. The spooky theme returns in the clarinet, supported by strings, but then the concerto closes by returning to the gorgeous, dreamy opening of the first movement. This concerto is a major addition to the repertory.

In the *Spirituals*, ten pieces based on black spirituals, Gerber gives us some achingly beautiful string music, touched with a sweet melancholia. The string writing here and in the *Serenade Concertante* is solidly in the Gould, Diamond, Copland vein, and adds to it beautifully. There is graciousness to all of it, with a delicious dreaminess in places. These should become repertory pieces. The St. Petersburg State Academic Symphony, under conductor Vladimir Lande, plays these works movingly.

I should add that I have had the chance to listen to a performance recording of Gerber's *Two Lyric Pieces for Violin and Orchestra* (2005). Like the Violin Concerto, it too brings to mind Samuel Barber in its luminous, heartfelt beauty. One hopes for a commercial recording.

Gerber's Naxos CD of chamber music—Piano Trio, Duo, Elegy, and *Notturno*—is a fascinating traversal of this composer's stylistic journey, as it contains works spanning the period from 1968 to 2001. It serves as a miniature musical autobiography. I would first direct listeners who are unfamiliar with Gerber's music to his orchestral works, such as the Symphony No. 1, the wonderful Clarinet Concerto, or the cello and violin concertos on Koch, because they are major works.

The Naxos CD contains shorter compositions and includes some real gems, for example, the exquisite *Three Pieces for Two Violins* and the *Gershwiniana for Three Violins*. In fact, almost all of the nine pieces here are jewels. They are works from the inner world of the human spirit. As such, they are highly contemplative and concentrated, and sometimes spare, but no less achingly beautiful for that. It was no surprise when Gerber said that one of them had its origins as a study.

The early pieces, according to Gerber, show the influences of Bartók and Elliott Carter. He moved away from that chromatic style to what is now popularly called neoromanticism. Consistently, these works show that Gerber had never been afraid of writing highly exposed melodic lines. He dared simplicity and achieved a kind of precious stillness that makes all the more intriguing and significant the development of his material from out of the center of silence. This CD is an invaluable supplement for the Gerber fan and a highly attractive proposition for anyone attracted to the chamber instrument combinations Gerber employed. The performances are first rate.

When I asked Gerber what his expressive aims were, he answered:

> I think one of the things that always attracted me most to music is the fact that it is not verbal—you know, I'm sure, the famous quote from Mendelssohn that the emotions in music can't be put into words not because they are too vague but because they are too specific. While I certainly hope my music is emotional and emotionally satisfying I don't often put into words what I am trying to express and don't really aim for anything more specific than the fulfillment, as best as I can, of what Yehudi Wyner called "the integrity of the musical material".

Elsewhere, Gerber said, "More and more people . . . have been telling me how spare my music seems. I'm aware of this, and I think it stems from my dislike of the over-complexity of so much 20th-century music and from my love of simplicity and directness. I'd rather risk overdoing things in that way, and in clarity, then risk the opposite, opaqueness and over-complication."

In sum, what we have here is music that is simply beautiful and, as such, expresses its own message directly from the integrity of its materials.

Recommended Recordings

Symphony No. 1; Viola Concerto; Triple Overture; *Dirge and Awakening*, Chandos 9831

Violin Concerto; Cello Concerto; *Serenade for String Orchestra*, Koch 7501

Clarinet Concerto; *Spirituals for String Orchestra*; *Serenade Concertante*, Arabesque Recordings CD Z6803

Piano Trio; Duo; Elegy; *Notturno*, Naxos 8.559618

String Quartets 4–6; Fantasy, Fugue, & Chaconne for Viloa and Cello, Amernet String Quartet, Albany 1570

～

Morton Gould: Maestro of Americana

Albany Records' CD of Morton Gould's music, including his Pulitzer Prize winner from 1995, *StringMusic*, has sold more than 3,000 copies—best-seller status in the classical music world. This issue was preceded by a tribute album at the time of Gould's death in 1996, featuring some of Gould's Americana and his popular *American Symphonette No. 2*. In the liner notes to the tribute CD, Peter Kermani, the co-owner of Albany Records, claims that Gould was a great American composer. "Now as we come to the end of this glorious age of dissonance we call 20th Century Music," he writes, "it is my belief more than ever that the music of Morton Gould will endure because he knew America. He felt it in his bones—its humor and patriotism, its rhythm and pulse." To help prove the point, Albany has retained in its catalogue a two-CD set of older recordings of seven Gould compositions spanning four decades of his work, such as the Concerto for Viola and Orchestra, *Soundings*, and *Symphony of Spirituals*. Kermani's praise may be exaggerated, but he and Albany Records have performed a singular service to American music by making so many of Gould's works available.

Kermani was right to stress that Gould's music is inimitably American. Gould (1913–1996) was particularly adept at drawing on and displaying the richness of American musical idioms—all of them. His ability to assimilate jazz, blues, pop, boogie-woogie, big band, honky-tonk, hymns, hoedown, and folk gave his music an irresistible American tang. And by offering familiar tunes in serious concert treatments, Gould drew attention to how good basic American materials were. His orchestral settings of hymns, "The Star-Spangled Banner", various popular dances, and folk songs were done out of a deep respect and love for these materials. For his treatments, Gould deservedly earned the reputation as a master orchestrator.

However, Americana can be a dangerous business, often amounting to little more than banal exploitation of patriotism and the popularity of others. But Gould did not need folk tunes or hymns as a compositional crutch. In his many other works, he showed that he could just as easily write melodies that could pass for the original thing. For example, his *Spirituals* (1941) for string, choir, and orchestra succeeded—without quoting actual hymns—at evoking the overall mood of American spirituals.

Gould also wrote a considerable body of work outside the popular vein of Americana, including a number of concertos and three symphonies. His more abstract works, however, were all clearly abstractions *from* something. They never lost their reference points. As Gould said, "I have always been and still am stimulated by the vernacular, by the sound of spirituals, jazz, etc. . . . I would imagine that although I might venture into more complicated abstractions, there is always present, in one form or another, at least the residue of these influences." Along with the vernacular, one detects in Gould's more serious works the influences of some of the major composers of his day: Aaron Copland primarily, but also Shostakovich, Stravinsky, and Poulenc.

Gould covered the musical map in a career that began as a child prodigy. He sat down at the piano and began improvising at the age of four. His understandably startled father recalled, "How and when Morton learned music is a mystery." Little Morton composed and published his first work at age six—a piano waltz called *Just Six*, a title that displays Gould's typically impish humor. His formal musical education included a year at the Institute of Musical Art when he was eight and, later, composition study at New York University. Gould had to drop out of high school to help support his family during the Depression. He played piano in vaudeville, movie theaters, and jazz bands. He also toured colleges and conservatories, where he exhibited his extraordinary skill at improvisation. The audience would throw him a musical phrase out of which he would then immediately construct a fugue.

Gould first became famous conducting, composing, and making arrangements on weekly radio programs. By 1943, he was nationally known as the musical director of the *Cresta Blanca Carnival* and *The Chrysler Hour* on the CBS radio network. It was in his radio days that Gould composed his very popular *American* and *Latin-American Symphonettes*—so titled, Gould explained, because it was the era of the "dinette and kitchenette". Gould went on to compose ballets (*Fall River Legend* and *Interplay*), Broadway shows (*Billion Dollar Baby*), and film scores (*Windjammer* and *Holocaust*).

Gould's music shows his extraordinary grasp of musical form but also his gift for brilliant orchestration, a subject he was never able to study formally. Perhaps his lack of formal training left him free to develop his native feel for textures, rhythms, and sounds so idiosyncratically

American. As a result, his music, though conventional in terms of tonality and structure, always sounds fresh. It is also enlivened by Gould's love of syncopations and polyrhythms. Such was Gould's mastery that he was basically at play in the field of American music, and his sense of enjoyment and fun unfailingly communicates itself.

The double-CD set from Albany starts with *Housewarming* and *Flourishes and Galop*, two short works from the early 1980s. They were both written for the opening of new symphony halls and convey a lively sense of occasion and spirit—clearly music for beginning something. *Housewarming* especially expresses a jubilant musical consecration. The 1944 Viola Concerto shows a darker side to Gould's lyricism that sounds at times Hungarian. This lovely, rhapsodic piece lay neglected for four decades until Robert Glazer revived it with the Louisville Orchestra.

Columbia, another commissioned piece for an opening—this one for the Merriweather Post Pavilion in Columbia, Maryland—plays on the themes from "Hail Columbia" and "Columbia, the Gem of the Ocean". This rousing music is a brilliant example of Gould's ingenuity at using popular American melodies without descending to the level of the banal. *American Symphonette No. 2* is a fun, jazzy suite from 1939, the middle movement of which, Pavane, may be Gould's single most popular piece of music.

Symphony of Spirituals is an American bicentennial commission that hearkens back to Gould's earlier success with *Spirituals* from 1941. It is a substantial piece, lasting more than 20 minutes. It does not utilize any actual spirituals but, in four abstract movements—"Hallelujah", "Blues", "Rag", and "Shout"—gives Gould's highly idiosyncratic, kaleidoscopic impression of spirituals—both black and white—employing fugues, toccatas, and dance rhythms. *Soundings* is in the same serious vein. The most abstract and impressionistic of any of these works (or perhaps expressionist, as Gould calls it), it explores the thematic material of its two movements, "Threnodies" and "Paeans", in unconventional and arresting ways. *Soundings* of these depths belie those who would dismiss Gould as merely an entertainer.

RCA deserved a gold star in 1984 for bringing out one of the very best Gould CDs, featuring two magical works, *Burchfield Gallery*, from 1979, and *Apple Waltzes*, from 1983, both performed by the American Symphony Orchestra, under Gould's baton. *Burchfield Gallery* has been described by one critic as a cross between Vivaldi's *Four Seasons* and Mussorgsky's *Pictures at an Exhibition* (very light on the Mussorgsky, I would say). It is a set of musical impressions of Charles E. Burchfield's nature paintings, celebrating the seasons. Gould said that his "musical celebration" or "lyrical paean" evokes the "vibrant lights and shadows, constant motion, and dancing rhythms" of Burchfield's canvases. It also captures the crepuscular murmuring and twittering of the fantastical birds and creatures Burchfield depicts. The result is sheer delight. *Apple Waltzes* was written for use in a longer ballet and was Gould's personal tribute to the late George Balanchine, who was to have choreographed it. The seven short waltzes, in varying tempos, are simply delicious. Unfortunately, RCA deleted this CD, but it is available again as an ArkivCD.

Albany's album, *A Tribute*, contains *American Ballads*, *Spirituals for Strings*, and *American Symphonette No. 2*. It will rouse the most jaded listener to toe-tapping. I first resisted listening to the settings of such familiar fare as "America the Beautiful" and "Were You There?" but became entranced at the brilliance and exuberance of Gould's settings, in wonderful performances by the London Philharmonic, conducted by Kenneth Klein.

Another Albany release is especially interesting. It displays the other side of Gould in three works without any explicit American references. Gould's *Showpiece for Orchestra* (1954) was written to display the orchestra's instruments for a Columbia Records demonstration disc. It is a highly enjoyable suite of seven short movements that are not in any obvious way demonstrating anything other than the lovely charms of the music. I particularly fell for the gorgeous *Serenade*. The Piano Concerto (1938) shows a tougher "bad boy" side to Gould, with its tone clusters, hard-driving rhythms, and anxious moodiness. But it proves that Gould could take the advanced compositional techniques of his time and turn them to good musical purpose. It is an impressive piece. The first movement contains what sounds like an obvious tribute to Stravinsky. Hilariously, during a rehearsal of the Concerto by pianist Randall Hodgkinson, who so capably plays it on this recording, Gould remarked, "That guy Stravinsky's been stealing from me ever since I was a kid."

StringMusic is a lyrical work that finally won Gould the coveted Pulitzer Prize in 1995. A deceptively simple piece in five movements, *StringMusic* begins with an affecting melody, which the string sections echo back and forth to each other. As Gould said, "The effect is like a responsory service." The relatively subdued mood of the opening movement is broken by a tango, which lightens up the atmosphere but also, surprisingly, has its sweet and delicate moments. The longest movement is a dirge, striking in its spareness, that shows how much Gould learned from Shostakovich, who, of course, in turn learned from Mahler. You have to be a master to write in this sort of naked style. This is my kind of minimalism. The short Ballad that follows is poignant, openhearted, and gorgeously melodic, bringing Mahler's music even closer to mind, especially the Adagietto from the Fifth Symphony. The closing movement crackles with energy and concludes with a loud pizzicato snap. The work is brilliantly executed by the Albany Symphony Orchestra, conducted by David Alan Miller. The recording is superb.

Albany provides another CD of American music, containing premiere recordings of Gould's Symphony No. 3 and Roy Harris' Symphony No. 2, again performed by the Albany Symphony Orchestra under Miller. Curiously, both composers abandoned their progeny, and it took Miller's efforts to shape up the original scores for presentation here. It was worth the effort. Gould's Third shows how serious he could be in the symphonic genre. One of its most striking aspects is how obviously influenced he was by Harris' work, which is why it makes such a logical disc mate. The Super Audio CD has spectacular sound.

On Gould's completely fun side is his *Cowboy Rhapsody*. Anyone who loves Aaron Copland's *Rodeo* will also love this Gould romp, which uses some of the same melodies. No one could put together a confection of Western tunes the way Gould does here and have it melt your heart and delight your ears, no matter how many times you may have heard this medley. This is especially so when it receives such spirited playing by the Sinfonia Varsovia, under Ian Hobson, on an Albany CD. It is accompanied by Roy Harris' Symphony No. 11, Cecil Effinger's Little Symphony No. 1, and Douglas Moore's Symphony No. 2.

Typically, the angst crowd did not consider Gould's work difficult enough to take seriously, and his music was dismissed with the deadly word "derivative". In any case, Gould outlived his detractors and became an elder statesman of American music, though the perky vivacity of his later compositions belies the title. In the works from the late 1970s to the end of his life, one is struck by the feeling that this is not the music of an old man but of an incredibly fertile musical intelligence bursting with energy, imagination, and melody. As for his works' popularity, Gould made no excuses. He had a reason for writing music that was accessible. "I've always felt", he said in a 1953 interview, "that music should be a normal part of the experience that surrounds people." Toward the end of his life, Gould recalled, "I wanted to share my music with others. Communication was always terribly important to me." If the continuing popularity of his music and the response to these recordings are any indication, Morton Gould accomplished his mission.

Recommended Recordings

Burchfield Gallery; *Apple Waltzes*, RCA Victor Red Seal (arkivmusic.com)

Showpiece; Concerto for Piano; *StringMusic*, Albany Symphony Orchestra, David Alan Miller, Albany Records 300

American Ballads; *Spirituals for String Orchestra and Harp*, London Philharmonic Orchestra, Kenneth Klein, Albany Records 202

American Symphonette No. 2; *American Salute*; *Housewarming*; *American Symphonette No. 2*; *Symphony of Spirituals*; *Flourishes and Galop*; Concerto for Viola; *Columbia* (Broadsides for Orchestra); *Soundings*, Louisville Orchestra, Lawrence Leighton Smith and Morton Gould, Albany Records 13

Symphony No. 3 (with Harris Symphony No. 2), Albany Troy 515

Cowboy Rhapsody; Roy Harris' Symphony No. 11; Cecil Effinger's Little Symphony No. 1; and Douglas Moore's Symphony No. 2, Albany Troy 1042

~

Roy Harris: Singing to America

Roy Harris was born in a log cabin in Lincoln County, Oklahoma, on Lincoln's birthday, February 12, 1898. If that does not sound American enough, his music certainly does. Roy Harris sang America's song as few composers have. I am not referring to his orchestrations of popular American folk songs, his treatment of ballads such as "When Johnny Comes Marching Home", or his other Americana. Far more ambitious, Harris sought to capture the deeper soul and the character of America on a musical canvas that could encompass its vastness, excitement, and yearning. Here is how he put it:

> The moods which seem particularly American to me are the noisy ribaldry, the sadness, a groping earnestness which amounts to suppliance toward those deepest spiritual yearnings within ourselves; there is little grace or mellowness in our midst; that will probably come after we have passed the high noon of our growth as a people.

For Harris, one milestone on that path of growth was Lincoln and the Civil War. Lincoln epitomized for him America's greatness, and he celebrated it in several symphonies and choral compositions. Harris said, "Lincoln was the personification of a human ideal, an ideal for freedom, which had to be fought, bled for, and lived for." Harris' musical programs speak explicitly of epic struggle, striving, suffering, deep longing, and hope. Their heroic affirmations are hard-won.

Without ever condescending to his audience, Harris succeeded in developing a musical language with broad appeal that spoke in an inimitably American way. As musicologist and conductor Nicolas Slonimsky wrote, "He has a natural gift for the melodic line, and his melodies are in some uncanny way reflective of the American scene without being literal quotations." Cab drivers and baseball managers, as well as his musical peers, wrote Harris fan mail about how much his music meant to them. He was rewarded with enormous popularity during the prime of his career. A 1935 nationwide radio poll and a 1937 Scribner's survey rated Harris the premiere American composer.

Starting in the late '60s, however, his reputation began to fade and his music faced obscurity. The reasons are many, but works with meaning were unwelcome in a cynical time that purveyed music as a series of arbitrary sonic manipulations. Noble portrayals of the American spirit became politically incorrect.

After this long period of neglect, Harris' centennial in 1998 finally spurred some attention, beginning with some half-dozen CDs from the enterprising Albany Records label, making it possible to hear glimpses of his unique genius. Several other companies offered one Harris work each on CDs with other composers' pieces. Still, these were meager rations when the scope of his work is considered.

By the time of his death in 1979, Harris had produced more than 200 compositions, including 13 symphonies. Until fairly recently, few of them were available on recordings. Today, there are more than 40 CDs of Harris' music available, although there are still a number of gaps. There are no currently available recordings of the First, Tenth, Twelfth, and Thirteenth Symphonies. By far Harris' most famous composition is his Symphony No. 3, called by conductor Serge Koussevitzky "the greatest orchestral work yet written by an American". The astute composer and critic Virgil Thomson concurred in that opinion as late as 1970, remarking that this symphony "remains to this day America's most convincing product in that form". The Third has achieved classic status and remains deeply impressive in Leonard Bernstein's first recording with the New York Philharmonic in 1961.

This one-movement work exemplifies Harris' organic feel for huge musical structures composed of soaring arches of melody (much like those of Sibelius), vivid counterpoint, and chorale. It is marked in five sections: "Tragic", "Lyric", "Pastoral", "Fugue", and "Dramatic-Tragic". It starts with a chant-like melody in the basses that has a profoundly moving liturgical feel to it, a kind of *American Gothic* or Ansel Adams in sound. Bernstein chose to rerecord the Third with the New York Philharmonic in a live performance for Deutsche Grammophon in 1987. The epic sense of build and excitement is somewhat superior in his older version, but the newer one has better sound and is coupled with an excellent performance of William Schuman's Third Symphony.

The popularity of Harris' Third Symphony threatened to saddle him with a reputation as a one-work composer. Without Albany Records and the Naxos label, one could have only wondered what his other symphonies sounded like and take on faith the critical verdict that, soon after the Third, Harris lapsed into self-imitation. The single most powerful argument against that opinion is found on Albany's world premiere recording of Harris' Symphony No. 6: *Gettysburg Address*, now seconded by one on Naxos. The magnificent Sixth alone gives the lie to the one-work bum rap. This is a powerful, visionary work commemorating the fallen from the Civil War. It communicates Harris' signature sense of longing and openness, achieving a kind of prairie majesty that is inimitably American.

How is it that music of this majesty, breadth, and sweep, music of such deeply ruminative power and ecstatic exuberance, could have been neglected for so long? In Lincoln's Gettysburg Address, Harris said that he found "a classic expression of that great cycle which always attends any progress in the intellectual or spiritual growth of people". Each of the symphony's four movements carries a citation from Lincoln's text: "Awakening", "Conflict", "Dedication", and "Affirmation". The work is not literally programmatic, and those who wince at Aaron Copland's *Lincoln Portrait* need have no fear here of banal musical illustrations. Listen to how this music builds inexorably and opens up such breathtaking landscapes. The yearning and expectancy of the first movement are magically conveyed, and there are few things in American music as moving and achingly beautiful as the first half of the "Dedication" movement, before it begins to meander a bit.

Harris' movements often follow the same basic structure of building a huge, wandering chorale that finally finds a melody it embraces, exultantly lifts up, and releases in a mighty, crushing climax. For example, "Affirmation" closes with a shattering finale in brass and timpani. With its sheets of string sound, brass declamations, and long-lined melodies, Harris' orchestral language is unique and distinctly American. Few American composers have attempted to paint on such a broad canvas and, if this symphony is not perfect, it nonetheless contains some sublime music. An attempt at greatness at this level is far more interesting than a perfectly executed, less ambitious work. The performance by Keith Clark and the Pacific Symphony Orchestra is inspired, revelatory even. The sound of this 1981 digital recording has a stunning dynamic range, with electrifying brass and timpani. The CD also includes works of Samuel Barber and Aaron Copland.

American conductor Marin Alsop takes on Harris' two wartime symphonies from 1942 and 1944, Nos. 5 and 6, with the Bournemouth Symphony Orchestra on a Naxos release. The Fifth is another stirring work, relayed by radio to American troops around the world during

World War II (Harris was the head of music for the Office of War Information), and it needs no apologies and is no less stirring today. The Fifth was found by many to be a worthy successor to the magnificent Third. The Naxos recording is very fine and detailed, revealing more of this music than the prior recordings on the Albany and Louisville labels. Alsop takes a bit more time in the Sixth than did Keith Clark in his galvanizing version, but what little she may sacrifice in vitality, she gains in clarity. It is wonderful to see Harris finally getting this kind of recognition.

Harris' Second Symphony, found on the Albany release already remarked upon in the Morton Gould chapter, is a work of premonitions. One hears themes he developed in his later works. It is wonderful to have this performance to help complete the picture of this idiosyncratic genius. All in all, this is a brilliantly executed, inspired pairing.

In its invaluable American Archives Series, Albany has resurrected the first recording of Symphony No. 7, made in 1955 by the Philadelphia Orchestra, under the baton of Eugene Ormandy (accompanied on the CD by Walter Piston's Symphony No. 4 and William Schuman's Symphony No. 6). Harris heavily revised this work over several years and then made further changes after hearing this recording. It has many marvelous moments, but in its first half, the music seems to drift aimlessly over the leisurely strumming of the double basses. Eventually, it develops a more energetic sense of direction. It is time to hear this symphony in its final version in a modern recording. For a brief period, we could do that with the Koch recording by the New Zealand Symphony Orchestra, which unfortunately has been deleted. However, now we can listen to it thanks to Naxos, which has issued the Seventh, along with Symphony No. 9 and *Epilogue to Profiles in Courage—J. F. K.*, with the National Symphony Orchestra of Ukraine under Theodore Kuchar. About the Seventh, Harris said, "The work was conceived as a dynamic form within an interrupted time span of 20 minutes. In one sense it is a dance symphony; in another sense it is a study in harmonic and melodic rhythmic variations." *Musical America* greeted this work with the exclamation: "The Seventh is one big song!"

Albany Records also used to carry another Harris premiere, the Concerto for Violin and Orchestra (1949), a one-movement work neglected for 35 years, but that recording has now reverted to the First Edition label from which it initially came. The Concerto is entirely winning in its prairie lyricism, melodic beauty, variation development, and dancing finale. An exuberant introduction gives way to the solemnity and sadness of the long-spanned main theme in the violin, which, in alternation with the orchestra, becomes first ruminative and then fanciful in a folk-fiddle kind of way. The violin is then called back by the orchestra to the more serious matters of the main theme, on which it touchingly rhapsodizes. After a demanding cadenza, the brass and basses reassert the solemnity of the main theme, while the soloist and tutti violins play a clever counterpoint over it. The effect is beguiling. While less monumental and visionary than his symphonies, this concerto shows an equally winsome side to Harris' genius.

The Albany CD had also contained two prime Harris symphonies: a 1978 recording of Harris' Symphony 1933 (No. 1), conducted by Jorge Mester, and a 1965 recording of Symphony No. 5, led by Robert Whitney. Harris wrote the following description of his stirring First Symphony, which was the first American symphony to be recorded commercially: "In the first movement I have tried to capture the mood of adventure and physical exuberance; in the second, of the pathos which seems to underlie all human existence; in the third, the will to power and action." Alas, the First Edition repackaging of the Violin Concerto and the Fifth Symphony dropped the First in favor of *Kentucky Spring*, and it is now unavailable. Nonetheless, this CD is mandatory for the Violin Concerto.

While I love Harris' Violin Concerto, I knew nothing about his highly original Concerto for Two Pianos and Orchestra, and had never heard of the Kleos Classics label that released it, along with two works in the same genre by Arthur Benjamin and Pierre Max Dubois. The latter two works are fun and entertaining, but the Harris work is a major piece filled with his signature sense of longing, openness, and a prairie majesty. This rambunctious, exhilarating work was not performed until more than a half century after its 1946 composition. Harris fans will be grateful to pianists Joshua Pierce and Dorothy Jonas and the Slovak Radio Symphony Orchestra, under Kirk Trevor, for opening this particular window one of our great composers.

Three substantial Harris chamber works are available on a Koch recording, featuring the Third Angle New Music ensemble from Portland. All of Harris' music seems hymn-like, impelled by yearning, mourning, and celebration. He found "suppliance toward those deepest spiritual yearnings within ourselves" to be typical of the American character and that is what we hear expressed in the intense Quintet for Piano and Strings, the Violin Sonata, and String Quartet No. 3, a moving homage to Bach. As the quartet and quintet are otherwise unavailable, these fine performances are indispensable for Harris devotees or anyone wondering about the source of his influence.

Another Albany treat features Harris' complete piano works and his Sonata for Violin and Piano, performed by pianist Richard Zimdars and violinist Alexander Ross. Here is a mix of Americana, miniatures, and some of Harris' earlier French-influenced works (he studied with Nadia Boulanger), among which is the Sonata for Piano, op. 1. Much of what is on this CD is minor Harris. By far the strongest work is the substantial Sonata for Violin and Piano from 1942. It makes one eager to hear Harris' other chamber music. The other chamber work currently available is the *Three Variations on a Theme* (String Quartet No. 2), a very attractive, amiable work written in 1933 that has an unmistakable American flavor to it. It can be found on a New World Records collection of American String Quartets.

Finally, Albany gives us a broad selection of Harris' superb choral music. The 1947 Mass, for men's chorus and organ, originally commissioned by St. Patrick's Cathedral in New York, is a vigorous, virile piece with medieval plainchant and Renaissance polyphony transmuted into Harris' particular idiom. The polyphonic Gloria is particularly striking. Harris shows how beautifully he could write for women's voices in his a cappella work, "I Hear America Singing", a wordless vocalise on "ah" and "oh". Harris wrote that "Walt Whitman was the great singer of democracy", and he turns to that poet for the texts to half the works on this CD. All are splendidly sung by the Robert Wesleyan College Chorale under conductor Robert Shewan.

As unique a voice as Roy Harris was, he was imbued with tradition and repulsed by the self-referential music of modernism. He said, "It really is an attitude of supreme egoism wherein the individual assumes a *summum bonum* of all wisdom and beneficence in his own self. One generation is not long enough for man to become wise; and so we have suffered greatly in losing the wisdom of tradition." Roy Harris is now part of that tradition. In recovering his legacy, we may find some of that lost wisdom.

Recommended Recordings

Symphony No. 3 (with *Diamond*; Symphony No. 4; Thompson, Symphony No. 2), Leonard Bernstein, New York Philharmonic, Sony 60594

Symphony No. 3, Leonard Bernstein, New York Philharmonic, DG 419780. The epic sense of build and excitement is superior in Bernstein's older version, but this has better sound and is coupled with a fine performance of William Schuman's Third Symphony.

Symphony No. 6 (*Gettysburg Address*), Keith Clark, Pacific SO, Albany Troy 064

Symphonies 5 & 6, Naxos 8.559609

Concerto for Violin and Orchestra, Symphony No. 5, Leighton Smith, Louisville Orchestra, First Edition 5. Violinist Gregory Fulkerson, who gave this work its first performance in 1984, is superb in this 1985 recording, ably abetted by the Louisville Orchestra, conducted by Lawrence Leighton Smith.

Symphony No. 7, Eugene Ormandy, Philadelphia Orchestra, Albany Troy 256. The CD also includes Walter Piston's Symphony No. 4 and William Schuman's Symphony No. 6.

Symphonies 7 & 9; *Epilogue to Profiles in Courage—J. F. K.*, Naxos 8.559050

Concerto for Two Pianos and Orchestra, Kleos Classics KL 5129

Quintet for Piano and Strings; Violin Sonata; and String Quartet No. 3, Koch KIC CD 7515

Sonata for Violin and Piano, Richard Zimdars, Alexander Ross, Albany Troy 105

Three Variations on a Theme (String Quartet No. 2), Emerson String Quartet, New World Records 80453

Bernard Herrmann and Nino Rota:
Film Music and Beyond

"Movie music!" is the exclamation of recognition that newcomers often make upon first hearing classical music. They seem as delighted with this discovery as was Molière's bourgeois gentleman when he realized he had been speaking prose all his life. One tries not to wince noticeably when explaining to the neophyte that William Tell rode long before the Lone Ranger galloped along to Rossini's overture or that the Wagner's Valkyries stormed through the skies well in advance of the helicopter assault in *Apocalypse Now.*

Yet the newcomer's reaction makes sense. The infant movie industry first appropriated classical music for the sound tracks of silent films and then began commissioning original music from established European classical composers, whose arrival in Hollywood usually came courtesy of the Nazis. One has only to think of Erich Wolfgang Korngold or Miklós Rózsa. For a good part of its history, movie music was, in a sense, classical music.

Film scores, therefore, provide the point of entry to the world of classical music for many young people whose exposure to the movies invariably comes well before a trip to Carnegie Hall. In my own case, it was *War and Peace,* with a brilliant score by Italian composer Nino Rota, which led to my first LP acquisition. Even as a young grade-schooler, I was entranced by the delicious waltz Rota wrote for the great ballroom scene in which Prince Andrei (Mel Ferrer) decides he must marry Natasha (Audrey Hepburn), and I was thrilled by the martial music for the Battle of Borodino. I wanted the album as a memento of the movie, but some of the music was also good enough to listen to on its own. Had I known enough, I would not have been surprised by this. Rota had a substantial career apart from his many film scores, including *The Godfather, Romeo and Juliet,* and all of Fellini's movies, as a classical opera and concert composer. Only in recent decades have many of his concert works been made available on CD.

My early experience, however, did not lead to a lifetime of collecting film scores, and I am mystified by those who do. In fact, I can count on one hand the few I have purchased. I thought Elmer Bernstein's evocation of the world of childhood was magical in *To Kill a Mockingbird*, and his great Western film score for *The Magnificent Seven* has been issued by MGM RCD 10741. I loved the Straussian richness of John Williams' score to *Dracula*, and I was haunted by the trumpet solo over the plains of Libya in *Patton*. I also was entranced by George Auric's score to one of my favorite films, Jean Cocteau's *Beauty and the Beast* (now available on an excellent Marco Polo CD 8.223765). That's about it, and I confess I only listened to these albums a few times.

The problem with movie music as music is that it is necessarily subordinate to the movie and is supposed to operate somewhat subliminally. It is an art of illustration. A composer friend of mine once waltzed into a film studio and demanded that the producers make a movie according to his score. While this worked for Prokofiev collaborating with Sergei Eisenstein, he was unceremoniously shown the door and told never to return. Why, then, listen to film scores apart from the films for which they were written? As one of the greatest film composers, Bernard Herrmann, said, film scores provide either musical scenery or an emotional counterpart of the drama. One may wish to bask in the musical scenery, but the appeal is limited for the simple reason that movie music does not usually develop. There is little there to hold the attention once an attractive theme has been repeated several times or the novelty of an orchestral effect has worn off.

I do not mean to denigrate the art of film scoring, for I greatly admire its supreme practitioners, such as Bernard Herrmann (1911–1976) and Nino Rota (1911–1979). But my exposure to their film music usually leads me to seek out their concert works to see what they can do when not constrained by a script. For instance, I recently saw *The Ghost and Mrs. Muir* for the first time since childhood and was beguiled by Herrmann's haunting expression of bittersweet yearning. The theme he used sounded familiar, and I found a variation of it in his exquisite Clarinet Quintet: *Souvenirs de voyage*, in which he captures the kind of aching lyricism that was his hallmark. (The performance by clarinetist David Shifrin on the Delos label expresses this perfectly.) As I began listening to more of his film scores, I was struck by how much of the music was based on ingenious variations of the principal theme in the Quintet, including *North by Northwest*, *Marnie*, *Fahrenheit 451*, and *Vertigo*.

I never tire of hearing this wistful theme because it is so perfectly expresses the mysterious heartache that romance often awakens but can never fully satisfy. By using it in all its various guises, Herrmann was able to cast a spell over entire films and psychologically capture the audience in so complete a way that his music can hardly be called incidental. For this reason, he is one of the few film composers whose scores I enjoy listening to in their entirety, rather than as suites of high-lights. Thanks to Marco Polo, this is now possible with *Garden of Evil* (8.223841) and *Jane Eyre* (8.223535); and thanks to Arista, *Taxi Driver*, Herrmann's last and unusually jazzy score, is available (07822-19005). Herrmann was also expert at conveying a delicious sense of disorientation in the Hitchcock films in which so much of the drama depends on the characters' inability to distinguish between reality and unreality. The single most stunning recording of a Herrmann Hitchcock score is the Varese Sarabande CD of the compete score of *Vertigo*, with Joel McNeely conducting the Royal Scottish National Orchestra. An older (though early digital) recording from 1980 that is still worth hearing features the score for *North by Northwest*, with Laurie Johnson and the London Studio Symphony Orchestra (Varese Sarabande 47205).

This achingly nostalgic theme also appears in the new Naxos label release (8.570186) of Herrmann's score to *The Snows of Kilimanjaro*. It is introduced on the oboe in the lovely Nocturne. It reappears as a variation in the following "Memory Waltz". The Adagietto, the "Letter", and the "Farewell" are all saturated with the theme. Herrmann's use of it is obsessive (and obsession was the theme of many of the films he scored, especially for Hitchcock) but never tiresome, because the music goes to something so deep in the human soul concerning loss and yearning that I am always nearly overwhelmed by its powerful undertow. Thus I treasure this release with the Moscow Symphony Orchestra conducted by William Stromberg. With it is the equally fine score to *5 Fingers*, a superb spy movie with James Mason.

Strains of this melody can also be heard in an excellent new Chandos CD with Herrmann's score to *Hangover Square*, a deliciously done film-noirish movie about a deranged composer. It contains the highly romantic *Concerto Macabre*, which the insane musician plays as a house burns down around him at the climatic finish. It does not get much better than that, except this release also contains the more famous score to Orson Welles' *Citizen Kane*, complete with the faux opera aria from the fictitious work, *Salammbo*. The recording and performances by the BBC Philharmonic under Rumon Gamba, are smashingly good.

It helped that Herrmann was also a brilliant orchestrator. Herrmann left behind the extravagant Viennese lushness of Wolfgang Korngold's film treatments and favored a more economical use of the orchestra. Perhaps the most famous example of this is the score for *Psycho*, written for strings only. Yet when called for, Herrmann could also whip up a wonderfully Wagnerian delirium, as in the Tristanesque *scene d'amour* in *Vertigo*. His wizardry with a wide assortment of instruments can be heard in the more exotic films he scored, such as *The Seventh Voyage of Sinbad*, *Journey to the Center of the Earth*, and *The Day the Earth Stood Still* (available on various London midpriced CDs, conducted by the composer). These scores are fun to listen to for their brilliant orchestral effects, but understandably do not hint at the psychological depths of Herrmann's other music.

Along with the Quintet, Herrmann has other concert works well worth exploring. His Symphony No. 1 is a highly accomplished, very exciting work that deserves wider currency. It can be heard on Koch, with the Phoenix Symphony under James Sedares. (Alas, Herrmann's own recording on the Unicorn-Kanchana label is no longer available.) The idiom may be neoromantic, but it has a crisp freshness and is completely free of the almost obligatory Americana that came with most works of this kind at the time (1941). Herrmann's one string quartet, *Echoes*, from 1964, precedes the Clarinet Quintet but is equally attractive and comes from the same world of nostalgia and yearning, albeit with a more pervasive sense of sadness. Its themes will be familiar from a number of movies, including *Psycho*.

Herrmann's opera, *Wuthering Heights*, is a very gripping work, at turns stark and ecstatic, bleak and passionate. While Herrmann did not live to see an opera house performance, he conducted a convincing recording with the Pro Arte Orchestra and various soloists on Unicorn-Kanchana (UKCD2050/51/52), which unfortunately appears to have been deleted.

Nino Rota shared with Herrmann an expressive directness, seeming simplicity of means, and total mastery of craft. Suites of his film music can be heard on several collections, with Riccardo Muti, a Rota student and grateful champion, conducting on Sony CDs. One contains a ballet suite drawn from *La strada*, a suite of dances from *Il gattopardo* (*The Leopard*), which proves that Rota's wonderful waltz from *War and Peace* was not an exception, and an excellent concert work, Concerto for Strings (Sony SK 66279). Recent releases have focused on Rota's symphonic and chamber works, a number of which have never been available before now. BIS has issued Rota's first two symphonies, performed by the Norrköping Symphony Orchestra, under Ole Kristian Ruud. These youthful works overflow with melody and grateful harmonies. One may not claim greatness for them, but they are immediately likable and endearing. Rota himself was not in the least worried about the stature of his work and preempted any condescension toward it by saying, "Look, when they tell me that in my works I am only concerned with bringing a little bit of nostalgia and a lot of good humor and optimism, I think that this is how I would like to be remembered: with a little bit of nostalgia, a lot of optimism and good humor." Rota studied with Alfredo Casella and Ildebrando Pizzetti, but I hear an even more pronounced influence in his symphonies from another member of the *generazione dell'Ottanta*, Gian Francesco Malipiero. In addition, the end of the First Symphony comes very close to quoting the utterly magical finale of Richard Strauss' opera *Daphne*.

An enchanting BIS recording of Rota's chamber music, recorded live at the Lockenhaus Festival, presents his Nonet; Trio for Flute, Violin, and Piano; and other chamber works. Many of these exhibit Rota's neoclassic side, perhaps developed during his long friendship with Stravinsky. The melodies are still gorgeous, but the rhythms are spikier and the textures take on a Gallic clarity. The music, however, never displays the acerbic edge of many of its neoclassical contemporaries and is an unalloyed delight to listen to.

The French connection comes to mind again in listening to Rota's piano concertos. Here it is the impish spirit of Francis Poulenc that adds spice and levity to the Rachmaninoff-inspired melodic swells that roll so impressively through each movement. Two concertos received their premiere recordings on Chandos, with pianist Massimo Palumbo and the I Virtuosi Italiani under Marco Boni. The first movement of the E-minor Concerto, "Piccolo mondo antico", begins with a meltingly lovely, dreamy theme that recurs in various guises. The work is a pianistic showpiece that starts out like an Italian Rachmaninoff then moves through a slow movement of clouded joy and longing smiles that sounds more like Ravel than anything else and ends with a flashy bang. The Concerto in C Major starts with a delightful, delicate, faux-18th-century melody that Rota has great fun playing with. Both works provide a great deal of sheer enjoyment.

In Rota's popular *Concerto soirée* for piano and orchestra (1961), the level of Poulencian whimsy and insouciance rises to new heights in one of the most delightful, high-spirited musical romps of the past 60 years. There is finally an excellent modern recording of this work on Arts Music, with pianist Benedetto Lupo and the Orchestra Sinfonica Siciliana under Massimo de Bernart. It is accompanied by the *Sinfonia on a Love Song*, from 1947, which is comparable in its beauty to the two earlier symphonies. Both works demonstrate how music flowed from Rota's classical compositions into his film scores: from the *Concerto soirée* to *La strada* and *Otto e mezzo* (*8-1/2*); and from the Sinfonia to *The Crystal Mountain* and *Il gattopardo*.

In its laudable series of Nino Rota's orchestral works, the Chandos label issued the premiere recording of his Harp Concerto. This CD also contains his Concertos for Bassoon and Trombone, and *Castel del Monte*: Ballad for Horn and Orchestra, beautifully played by various soloists and I Virtuosi Italiani under Marzio Conti. The reason you have not heard these compositions before is that they were meant to be enjoyed, and that used to be forbidden. Now eat of the fruit.

Herrmann and Rota prove that the best movie music invites further listening to the works of its creators. If you are impressed by a film score, there is a good chance you will find lurking behind it a classical composer with an even richer cache of concert works, usually neglected because of his greater fame composing for movies.

Recommended Recordings

Bernard Herrmann

Symphony No. 1, James Sedares, Phoenix Symphony, Koch International 3-7135 (out of print but available used and as downloads)

Souvenirs de Voyage for Clarinet Quintet (with works by Quincy Porter, Charles Ives, and David Diamond), Chamber Music Northwest, Delos 3088. Or: Tippett String Quartet, Julian Bliss, Signum UK 234 (includes Herrmann's *Echoes* and the *Psycho Suite for Strings*).

Vertigo, Joel McNeely, Royal Scottish National Orchestra, Varèse Sarabande 5600 (OOP)

Hangover Square; *Citizen Kane*, Rumon Gamba, BBC PO, Chandos 10577

Music for Alfred Hitchcock, John Mauceri, Danish National SO, Toccata Classics 241 (with works by Franz Waxman, Dimitri Tiomkin et al.)

Nino Rota

Symphonies 1 & 2, Ole Kristian Ruud, Norrköping SO, BIS 970, or Marzio Conti, Filarmonica '900, Chandos 10546

Symphony No. 3; *Divertimento concertante*; *Concerto soirée*, Gianandrea Noseda, Filarmonica '900, Chandos 10669

Chamber Music: Nonet; Cantilena; Trio for Flute, Violin and Piano et al., Kremerata Musica, Hagen Quartet et al., BIS 870

Piano Concertos, Hannu Lintu, Janne Mertanen, Tampere PO, Alba 310

Cello Concertos; *Il gattopardo*, Dirk Kaftan, Friedrich Kleinhapl, Augsburg PO, Ars Production SACD 381052

Concertos for Bassoon; Harp; Horn; Trombone, Marzio Conti, I Virtuosi Italiani, Chandos 9954

Sinfonia sopra una canzone d'amore; *Concerto soirée*, Massimo de Bernart, Benedetto Lupo, Sicilian SO, Arts Music 47596

Jennifer Higdon: A Musical Lark

Jennifer Higdon (b. 1962) is one of those remarkable creatures, like Libby Larsen (see her chapter, p. 192), who seems perfectly at ease with the wonder of musical sounds within a tradition that for her is unbroken. In a *Fanfare* magazine interview, she spoke of her experience of judging a recent competition of young composers. She said, "I've looked at 78 applicants. I think only one or two of the scores were atonal, which is amazing—all the rest of the works were tonal." As she said elsewhere, "There's a lot more melody being written. I think composers want the music to communicate more." She is one of them. This is the revolution, or counterrevolution, to which I have been trying to point. It has produced a sea change.

A late starter who taught herself to play the flute at age 15, Higdon wrote her first composition at 21. She earned a master's and doctorate in composition from the University of Pennsylvania, a bachelor of music in flute performance from Bowling Green State University, and an artist diploma from the Curtis Institute of Music in Philadelphia. To these academic qualifications, she has added a bundle of prizes, including the 2010 Pulitzer Prize in Music for her Violin Concerto and the 2009 Grammy Award for Best Contemporary Classical Composition for her Percussion Concerto.

Speaking of her own musical favorites, Higdon said, "John Adams is one composer I really admire; [Aaron] Copland and [Samuel] Barber are others." As these are among the most immediately appealing American composers, it should be no surprise to hear Higdon say, "You don't need to know a thing about classical music to understand my music. It's very straightforward and very American-sounding." By which she means, "It has an American type of energy and active rhythms. It really moves along at a fair clip." Indeed it does, though she is also capable of expressing moments of great repose.

Higdon's works on two Telarc CDs give evidence of her success. A collection of American works on Telarc's *Rainbow Body*, titled after Christopher Theofanidis' composition of the same name, includes Higdon's work, *blue cathedral*, a luscious, dreamy tone poem, composed as a memorial to her brother. Telarc has also devoted a complete CD to Higdon's works, Concerto for Orchestra and *City Scape*, a musical portrait of Atlanta, that give a fuller idea of the scope of her talent. The concerto is a musical romp with a high energy level that deftly exploits orchestral color to the fullest. Higdon definitely tips her hat in Bartók's direction, as one would have to in a composition of this name, with the scurrying strings in the opening part of the first movement. However, the feature that caught me most by surprise is the audible influence of Finnish composer Einojuhani Rautavaara in the concerto's sweeping climaxes. Higdon's string writing in the second movement is simply superb and is reminiscent of the best of Benjamin Britten and Michael Tippett in this genre. I also wonder if she has not heard the magical works of Welsh composer William Mathias. This is bold, imaginative music, made all the more exciting by the fact that it is completely conventional. Into these works, and into *blue cathedral*, Robert Spano and the Atlanta Symphony Orchestra breathe vibrant life.

Higdon's prize-winning Violin Concerto is a scintillating, engaging work with crystalline orchestration, including knitting needles on crotales (wonderful-sounding antique cymbals) and glockenspiel. The music skitters and percolates, punctuated by sound effects. These are not the bleeps and blurbs of the avant-garde; they all fit in rhythmically and usually coalesce gradually into a line or melody. The violin, gorgeously played by the concerto's dedicatee, Hilary Hahn, introduces a long-lined melody with gentle instrumental apostrophes sounding around it like musical lightning bugs. There's a lot of violin chattering with different groups in the orchestra with an occasional whacking from orchestral tutti outbursts that sound like angry George Gershwin. The lovely Chaconni movement is the most American sounding, open-hearted and open prairie-like. I was not surprised to read one critic mention the music of Roy Harris in connection with it. Aside from whatever American influences, I can't help but note the occasional wave of Rautavaara-like string sound wafting through the piece (all to its advantage). Anyone who enjoys the violin concertos by Roy Harris or Stephen Albert will enjoy this. It is paired with the Tchaikovsky Violin Concerto. The Royal Liverpool Philharmonic Orchestra under Vasily Petrenko plays all in.

I am even more taken by Higdon's chamber music. On a Naxos release with the Cyprus String Quartet, her Piano Trio, *Voices*, and *Impressions*—the latter two for string quartet—sound like they are spilling out from a source of irrepressible energy. The tremendous excitement often overflows itself. The "Fiery Red" movement of the Piano Trio is music with its finger in a light socket. It is exhilarating and exhausting. Higdon uses descriptive subtitles for each movement of these works, an indication of her highly coloristic writing. The sheer sounds she creates are entrancing and harmonically fresh. The music is not only highly evocative and energetic, but can be mesmerizing in its lyrical stillness. The "Grace" movement from *Voices* marvelously depicts "the quiet presence that exists in a being's soul". The "Quiet Art" movement of *Impressions* is equally beguiling. Higdon's salute to Debussy and Ravel in this four-movement work is exquisitely beautiful. I find this adventurous music irresistible.

Another CD of her chamber music, from Koch, titled *Summer Shimmers*, confirms that favorable impression, especially its opening piece, a piano sextet called *Zaka*. The energy is mixed with occasional wistfulness. It is the latter quality that Higdon captures in her *Summer Showers*, a piano sextet with winds and horn, which is one of those hazy, deliciously lazy evocations of summer, with a strong nostalgic pull. *Autumn Reflections* is in the same reflective mood. The flute was Higdon's first instrument, and there are two solo flute pieces, *Song* and *rapid.fire*, which demonstrate her love for it and the fact that her music does not need to be busy to make an impression. All of this music is immediately appealing, which comports with Higdon's declaration that "it is important that music communicates."

The Naxos CD of Higdon's Early Chamber Works certainly communicates, with help of the Serafin String Quartet, in world premiere recordings of her *Sky Quartet* (1998/2003), the Sonata for Viola and Piano (1990), *Dark Wood* for bassoon, violin and cello, the String Trio (1988), and the string quartet treatment *Amazing Grace* (1998/2003). The first movement of the quartet, titled "Sky Rising", is typical Higdon—exciting rhythms, snappy syncopation, pizzicato strings, and rising melody that then soars and swoops. The second captures the rapture of the blueness of the sky in an unmistakably open, American idiom.

The Bridge label shows Higdon pursuing her avian interests in a quartet titled, *An Exaltation of Larks*, played appropriately enough by the Lark Quartet. It is another quintessentially American work of open-hearted yearning and spirited beauty reflected in "birds flying and singing wildly". Her Piano Quintet (piano left-hand) is, if anything, even more delightful, starting with the first movement's exhilarating "Racing through Stars". Higdon has a flair for the descriptive, hilariously so in the third movement, "I Saw the Electric Insects Coming", as wonderful an evocation of insects swarming as I have ever heard— a kind of musical onomatopoeia. "Summer Shimmers across the Glass of Green Ponds" conveys a touching delicacy. Along with its energy, this music possesses irresistible elements of whimsy and wistfulness. Pianist Gary Graffman and the members of the Lark Quartet fully enfranchise this music.

Were I to express any reservation regarding Higdon's music, it might be this—and I felt it most strongly when I heard the Washington, D.C., premiere of her Piano Concerto, with the National Symphony Orchestra. The hyperactivity can sometimes make it difficult to follow. I have sometimes thought that the rhythmic excitement makes the music seem about to jump out of itself. There is, of course, a very playful element in this. Busy is not bad. Bohuslav Martinů was busy. But there is such a thing as being too busy. Like Martinů's music, hers occasionally threatens to run into itself. However, that's part of the excitement. In any case, no matter how percussive the music occasionally gets or how distractingly exotic the orchestration can become, the beating heart of an American romantic is never too far below the highly active, attractive surface of Higdon's music—which helps to explain why she is one of the most frequently performed living American composers.

Recommended Recordings

blue cathedral et al., Robert Spano, Atlanta SO, Telarc 80596

City Scape; Concerto for Orchestra, Robert Spano, Atlanta SO, Telarc 80620

Violin Concerto, et al., Vasily Petrenko, Royal Liverpool Philharmonic, Hilary Hahn, DG 14698-02

Sky Quartet; *Amazing Grace*; Viola Sonata; *Dark Wood*; String Trio, Serafin String Quartet, Eric Stomberg, Lawrence Stomberg, Charles Abramovic, Naxos 8.559752

An Exaltation of Larks; *Scenes from the Poet's Dreams*; *Light Refracted*, Lark Quartet, Gary Graffman, Bridge 9379

Piano Trio; *Voices*; *Impressions*, Cypress String Quartet, Adam Neiman, Naxos 8.559298

Summer Shimmers; *Zaka*; *Autumn Reflections*; *Song*; *Dash*; *rapid.fire*, Lark Chamber Artists, Koch 7738

Vagn Holmboe: The Music of Metaphysics

Some years ago in the *New York Times*, critic Richard Taruskin spoke of Danish composer Vagn Holmboe (1909–1996) as "possibly the greatest living traditional symphonist". I wish I had written that. In fact, I had intended to, but it was too late. Holmboe died in 1996. However, I believe that Holmboe's music will secure him a place as the finest Danish symphonist since Carl Nielsen and as one of the great European composers of the 20th century. This has become increasingly clear now that so much of his work is available on CD. The BIS label has issued a complete set of Holmboe's symphonies, played by the Aarhus Symphony Orchestra under conductor Owain Arwel Hughes. The Dacapo label has released complete traversals of Holmboe's string quartets, played by the Kontra Quartet, and his chamber concerti, played by the Danish Radio Sinfonietta under Hannu Koivula.

You may not have not heard of Vagn Holmboe (pronounced "vaughan HOLM-bow-a"). That's because his music was, as Taruskin notes, "traditional". Someone forgot to tell Holmboe that tonality was exhausted and the symphony dead. After his studies at the Royal Danish Music Conservatory (which he entered with the recommendation of Carl Nielsen) and with composer Ernst Toch in Berlin, Holmboe went on to compose 13 symphonies, 20 string quartets, 13 chamber concertos, various concertos, 14 motets, and several operas. He was still at work at the age of 86 when he passed away on September 1, 1996.

Of all the attributes that could be assigned to Holmboe, the one that suggests itself most strongly is integrity. The man seemed incapable of writing a note that was not honest. There is nothing gratuitous or superficial. His work exhibits a combination of toughness, lyricism, and rhythmic vitality. It is rooted and real, though the source of that reality may be somewhat unfamiliar. It reflects nature but not in a pastoral way; this is not a musical evocation of bird song or sunsets. Neither is it nature as the 19th century understood nature—principally as a landscape on which to project one's own emotions. Holmboe's impulse was to move outward and upward. His music reveals the constellations in their swirling orbits, cosmic forces, a universe of tremendous complexity but also of coherence.

Holmboe's music is visionary but not revolutionary. The strongest influence is Carl Nielsen. Anyone who loves Nielsen's music should be drawn to Holmboe's. From Nielsen, Holmboe drew the orchestral means to generate cataclysmic power, including Nielsen's devastating tympanic eruptions. Holmboe also learned from Nielsen how to intertwine delicately rich woodwind lines of great contrapuntal beauty. Otherwise, one hears traces of Shostakovich, Stravinsky, and Sibelius. In spirit, Holmboe seems situated somewhere between Sibelius' total absorption into nature and Nielsen's fierce humanism. He shares Sibelius' otherworldliness but blends it with Nielsen's passion for the "inextinguishable" forces of life.

The first five of Holmboe's 13 symphonies are more conventional than his later works but no less fine. They fit in with other tonal and neoclassical works of the period. The Second, Third, and Fifth are particularly good. The only symphony I am not totally convinced by is the Fourth, subtitled *Sinfonia Sacra*. I find the stridency of parts of this wartime work grating and the echoes of Carl Orff in the choral sections tiresome. Holmboe did a much better job commemorating the war years with his moving sinfonia, *In Memoriam*, written after the Eighth Symphony (and once titled as the Ninth Symphony). By the time of the Sixth Symphony, Holmboe had found his unique voice, though it was through a process of evolution rather than radical change. The Sixth through the Thirteenth are extraordinary works that belong in the canon of the 20th century's best. The Eighth Symphony, *Sinfonia Boreale*, is especially noteworthy. I first heard this tumultuous, heaven-storming piece on a Turnabout recording more than 30 years ago and was stunned that such a masterpiece had not swept the world before it. Written in Holmboe's old age, the last three symphonies show no diminution in his visionary powers, though they employ lighter textures.

Holmboe found his unique voice through a technique he called metamorphosis. According to Holmboe, "Metamorphosis is based on a process of development that transforms one matter into another, without it losing its identity." Holmboe explained that contrasts, however strong they may be, are always made of the same basic material and are complementary rather than dualistic. This kind of development, he said, "must be characterized by the strictest logic, so that each strand in the process of change stands out clearly as an inevitable necessity, pointing in ever-increasing measure toward the final change". As inevitable as the transformations may seem after hearing them, they never sound predictable as they are developing. Most importantly, metamorphosis "has a goal; it brings order to the process and enables it to create a pattern of the same perfection and balance as, for example, a classical sonata." Holmboe's metamorphosis is something like the Beethovenian method of arguing short motives; a few hammered chords can generate the thematic material for the whole work. In this way, the thematic material defines its own development.

Holmboe's technique also has a larger significance. In one of the BIS liner notes, composer Karl Aage Rasmussen observes that Holmboe's metamorphosis has striking similarities to the constructive principles used by Arnold Schoenberg, the father of 12-tone music. However, Rasmussen says, "Schoenberg found his arguments in history while Holmboe's come from nature." The difference is decisive since the distinction is metaphysical. And music is essentially the "sound" of metaphysics, as it is always based on the composer's conception of what constitutes reality. The argument from history leads to creation ex nihilo, not so much in imitation of God as a replacement for him —the Nietzschean will to power. Schoenberg's systemized dissonance eviscerated the world of nature and resulted in noise. The argument from nature leads to creation in cooperation with the Creator and to a larger harmony. Rasmussen spells out exactly the theological implications of Holmboe's approach: "The voice of nature is heard . . . both as an inner impulse and as spokesman for a higher order. Certainty of this order is the stimulus of music, and to re-create it and mirror it is the highest goal. For this, faith is required, faith in meaning and context or, in Holmboe's own words, 'Cosmos does not develop from chaos without a prior vision of cosmos.'" Holmboe's words could come straight from one of St. Thomas Aquinas' proofs for the existence of God. The remark reveals both the composer's metaphysical grounding and his breathtaking artistic reach. This man was not simply reaching for the stars but for the constellations in which they move—and beyond. Holmboe strove to show us the cosmos, to play for us the music of the spheres.

Holmboe's music is quite accessible but requires a great deal of concentration because it is highly contrapuntal. Its rich counterpoint reflects creation's complexity. The simultaneity of unrelated strands of music in so much modern music (as in the works of Charles Ives and John Cage) is no great accomplishment; relating these strands is. As Holmboe said, music has the power to enrich man "only when the music itself is a cosmos of coordinated powers, when it speaks to both feeling and thought, when chaos does exist, but [is] always overcome".

In other words, chaos is not the problem; chaos is easy. Cosmos is the problem. Showing the coherence in its complexity is the greatest intellectual and artistic challenge, because great artists must share in the divine "prior vision of cosmos" that makes the cosmos possible. As Holmboe wrote, "In its purest form, [music] can be regarded as the expression of a perfect unity and conjures up a feeling of cosmic cohesion." This feeling of cohesion can be, he said, a "spiritual shock" for modern man.

Holmboe's contrapuntal fabric is fascinating. From disparate strands, the composer seems to be stitching together the cosmic and the sublunary, the human and the divine. One moment his music seems to be tracing some celestial movement, the next it is magically transformed into a child's tune. Holmboe employs what sound like musical pinwheels—musical motifs that whirl around in their own orbits. As expressions of human passion, these swirling arabesques might seem obsessive. Used to portray human endeavor, they would sound mindlessly motoric; used to depict nature, they are stellar. Danish lyricist Paul la Cour caught this aspect of Holmboe's music when describing the Eighth Symphony. Holmboe's great polyphonic passages, he said, seem to be "closely related to the majestic monotony of nature". It is no surprise that Holmboe spoke of true musical art as a microcosm, "like the structure of atoms, or the galaxies of the universe". The two are interchangeable in their revelation of natural order. Holmboe moves from cosmos to microcosm and back again with ease. Listen, for instance, to the opening of Chamber Concerto No. 9 or the first five minutes of Chamber Concerto No. 7: Are these tunes from a calliope or a solar system?

In its great polyphonic complexity, his music is almost inexhaustibly interesting. Because of its thematic unity, the music is easy to follow, but one never gets the sense of having exhausted its riches. Each listening supplies fresh revelations.

Holmboe's 13 chamber concertos, from the Marco Polo Dacapo label, show a lighter, less turbulent, very beguiling side of Holmboe. For the newcomer to Holmboe's music, the chamber concertos make a good introduction. All of his stylistic traits are present, but these works are less intimidating than the magnificent, highly-charged symphonies, of which there are also 13. In any case, these beautiful works are indispensable for gaining a more complete picture of the greatest Danish composer since Nielsen.

A Dacapo disc brings us three world premiere recordings of concertos that bookend Vagn Holmboe's career. The forceful Allegro moderato of the 1992 Viola Concerto has the timpanist so pound away that it would do Nielsen's Fourth Symphony proud. Focused yet lavishly folk-inspired, it is bound to be acknowledged as one of the great Viola Concertos. The 1929 Concerto for Orchestra, brash and dark, is the finest neoclassicism, asserting its youthful quality with confidence and severity. The 1979 Second Violin Concerto is a stellar firecracker, prompting thoughts of Mendelssohn here, Enescu there. The persuasiveness of these works reflects on the ability and verve of the performers—the Norrköping Symphony Orchestra, under Dima Slobodeniouk (conductor), with Erik Heide (violin), Lars Anders Tomter (viola)—making this an ideally accessible and rewarding Holmboe entry-point.

Holmboe's richly contrapuntal thinking also naturally lent itself to the string quartet, and it is no wonder that he composed 20 of them. His cycle easily stands beside the great achievements of Shostakovich and Robert Simpson. There are many treasures in this music, though I am almost inclined to call them "hidden" because Holmboe's style is so reserved. The quartets are perhaps Holmboe's most difficult music to appreciate at first hearing. They display little surface charm, are very tightly argued, and require repeated acquaintance to reveal their very considerable treasures. He described his style as "controlled ecstasy".

The most recent CDs in the series, volumes 6 and 7, contain the last five quartets, four of which are based on the times of day, and a fragment of String Quartet No. 21, on which Holmboe was working when he died in 1996 in his native Denmark. These last five quartets, like the others, are concentrated and require concentrated listening. There may be no blinding epiphanies in this music, but as in the works of his model, Haydn, these quartets maintain a steady, indeed extraordinary level of craftsmanship and inspiration. Patient listening, which should begin with the earlier, more lyrical quartets, reveals a musical intelligence of the highest order. Anyone who appreciates Bartók's or Shostakovich's quartets should have little trouble with them.

There is also a Dacapo CD that contains five short chamber works that have heretofore been unrecorded: *Primavera* for flute, violin, cello, and piano; *Gioco* for violin, viola, and cello; Sonata for flute solo; *Ballata* for violin, viola, cello, and piano; and Quartet for flute and violin, viola and cello, all played by the Ensemble MidtVest. This CD is a revelatory introduction to the broad range of his music. The playfulness of *Primavera* is a nice contrast to the seriousness of *Ballata*. These are not simply shavings from the Master's bench, but are works which each stand as an integral jewel. This will be a mandatory purchase for Holmboe fans.

Altogether, Holmboe's work demonstrates that the music of the spheres is above us, beyond us, but also within us.

Recommended Recordings

The best way to start is with the complete symphonies. If that's too much at once, try Symphonies 8 and 9 or Symphonies 6 and 7. I would not want to miss any of the gems in the chamber concerti series, either. It makes sense to follow the string quartets in their order of issue.

Complete Symphonies 1–13, Sinfonia, and *In Memoriam*, Owain Arwel Hughes, Aarhus SO, BIS 843-846

Symphonies 8 & 9, BIS 618

Symphonies 6 & 7, BIS 573

Chamber Concertos: Nos. 1–3, Nos. 4–6, and Nos. 7–9, Marco Polo 8.224038, 8.224063, and 8.224086.

Viola Concerto; Concerto for Orchestra; Concerto for Violin No.2, Dima Slobodeniouk, Norrköping SO, Erik Heide, Lars Anders Tomter, Dacapo SACD 6.220599

Chamber Music I: *Primavera*; *Gioco*, et al., Ensemble MidtVest, Dacapo 8.226073

Chamber Music II: Eco; *Aspects*; Sonata for Solo Cello; Sextet; et al., Ensemble MidtVest, Dacapo 8.226074

Complete String Quartets, the Kontra Quartet, Dacapo 8.207001

Chamber Symphonies, John Storgårds, Lapland Chamber Orchestra, Dacapo SACD 6.220621

Sinfonias I–IV, Hannu Koivula, Danish Radio Sinfonietta, Dacapo 8.226017–18

Toccata Press, the book-publishing arm of Toccata Classics, published *Experiencing Music: A Composer's Notes*, an invaluable book of Vagn Holmboe's writings about music in which he discusses the nature of music, from the point of view of the composer, the performer, and the listener.

~

Leoš Janáček: Czech Passion

It took a half century after the death of Czech composer Leoš Janáček (1854–1928) for his music to emerge before a worldwide audience. Much of the credit for its current esteem goes to the advocacy of the late Sir Charles Mackerras, the British conductor who studied in Czechoslovakia and returned bearing treasures. His superb opera and orchestral recordings from the late 1970s and the 1980s elevated Janáček from a parochial specialty to international stardom. Such long neglect would have meant permanent obscurity for music of less conviction and fire.

Like Béla Bartók after him, Janáček began with 19th-century romanticism but then abandoned it for folk-inflected music of national consciousness. He modeled his music on the speech patterns of the Czech language. This hardly seems a recipe for international acclaim, and during his lifetime, his success, though great, was limited to his homeland. Yet his music has immediate appeal and tremendous impact, because he wrote with such compelling vision. Janáček said, "I penetrate because there is truth in my work; truth to its very limit. Truth does not exclude beauty, on the contrary, there should be truth as well as beauty, and more and more. Life, mainly. Always eternal youth. Life is young. It is spring. I am not afraid of living; I like it terribly." One can feel that life pulsing in every bar of his music.

Janáček tried to express the inexpressible, not in some ethereal or abstract way but, like Dostoyevsky, with tremendous human passion as if his life depended on it. As did Mozart in his own way, Janáček anthropomorphized the orchestra. The instruments become human voices. In Mozart they sing; in Janáček, they speak—or try to, for what they attempt to express is beyond human language.

This desperate sense of yearning gives Janáček's music special poignancy and power. It is expressed not in any form of technical innovation, for his music is tonal throughout, but in certain stylistic features: for instance, in the extremes of instrumental ranges, highly charged dance rhythms, and short, punchy themes. Verging on hysteria and seemingly spontaneous, Janáček's music nonetheless maintains a tight inner logic; it communicates with an elliptical economy of means that leaves one puzzled as to how it works musically. In dizzyingly quick turns, the music can be ferocious, with a barbaric energy, then achingly lyrical, and then wildly jubilant. Even when festive, it is so wildly festive that one can feel an underlying longing that no earthly happiness can fulfill. With Janáček, there is no gentle tapping on the gates of heaven, no being wafted into paradise on swells of perfumed ecstasy. Heaven is the object of human passion. Janáček will take it by storm and, if necessary, break down its gates to get in.

One can hear this unquenchable yearning at its most intense in his late masterpieces, especially the *Glagolitic Mass*, the *Sinfonietta* from 1926, the two String Quartets, and the late operas. The galvanic *Glagolitic Mass* is in Old Church Slavonic, the liturgical language used by Sts. Cyril and Methodius when they converted Moravia in 863. Janáček wrote on the title page, "God is gone up with a shout." He said, "I depict in it, to a certain extent, the legend which says that when Christ was hanged on the cross, the heaven was torn asunder. Well, I am making it both roar and lightning." The result is a volcanic masterpiece, one of the greatest choral works of the 20th century. The faith it expresses, however, is somewhat unconventional. Janáček was peeved when a critic wrote that *Glagolitic Mass* indicated that Janáček had become an Orthodox believer in his old age. Janáček replied: "I am not an old man, and I am not a believer—until I see for myself." Yet, at the same time, he said, "I wanted to portray the nation's faith not on a religious basis but on a strong moral one which calls God to witness."

The *Sinfonietta* is a secular equivalent to the *Mass* in its wildness, orchestral brilliance, use of punchy motifs, and dramatic abbreviation. Its finale is one of the blazing glories of 20th-century music. In recordings it is usually paired with the colorful and almost equally brilliant *Taras Bulba*. Sir Charles Mackerras is a good recommendation for these works, as he is for all the operas. But the Czech conductor Karel Ančerl brought a special visionary intensity to his performances of these three pieces with the Czech Philharmonic in Supraphon recordings from the early 1960s. His *Glagolitic Mass* won the 1964 Grand Prix del'Academie Charles Cros. Supraphon has reissued these recordings in various CD formats, usually at midprice. They are indispensable.

Janáček was as eccentric in his choice of opera subjects as his music is original. Like Dostoyevsky, he believed dramatic extremes are more likely to reveal the fundamental truths of the human heart. His predilection for bizarre subjects was seen as early as 1897 in his cantata *Amarus*. This work is based on a poem about an illegitimate child sequestered in a monastery, whose adolescent heart is fatally stirred by the loss he feels upon seeing, for the first time, two lovers embrace. He then expires upon his mother's grave. *Káťa Kabanová* is about adultery and suicide. *Jenůfa* concerns jealousy and infanticide. The *Makropulos Case* is about the despair of a woman who, having found eternal youth, seemingly could not die, and her relief in finally doing so after 300 years. *The Cunning Little Vixen* was inspired by a cartoon strip depicting the adventures of a vixen, in both human society and the forest. *From the House of the Dead* is based on Dostoyevsky's novel of the same name.

The Cunning Little Vixen, the most charming of Janáček's operas, intermingles animal and human in novel fashion. While distinct, the two interact within nature, which enfolds them both within cyclical currents of loss and renewal. The love duet between the fox and the vixen is as dramatic and sensuous as anything opera has to offer. The music is neither cute nor syrupy; it is filled with delights and great energy (e.g., the vixen's wedding and the ballet of the fox cubs). In the last scene the gamekeeper reflects in a long, autumnal monologue on the mysteries and the magic of nature, which he knows is overtaking him as well. We are left with old age in spring, a mixture of sweetness and pain. Janáček called this opera "a merry piece with a sad end". The end so moved him that he asked for it to be played at his funeral. So, on August 15, 1928, over his open coffin in the Old Brno Augustinian Monastery, a singer intoned the gamekeeper's epilogue: "People will bow their heads and will understand that heavenly bliss has passed by all around them."

With *From the House of the Dead*, we enter the gloom of a czarist prison camp. But the gloom is not overwhelming. In fact, this opera is exhilarating, with a compactly powerful and moving score. Straining for the inexpressible reaches of the spirit, it almost shouts to God. On the title page of this opera, Janáček inscribed, "In every creature a spark of God." During its composition, he said: "I'm finishing perhaps my greatest work—this latest [and last] opera. I feel so excited as if my blood wanted to gush out." That's evident in the music. This is a work of extremes, veering between desperation and hysterical joy. It is exhausting but not enervating, and there are lyrical respites. It is one of the most original, powerful works in the world of opera.

Jenůfa is especially gripping because, as Jens Laurson posits, it is a treatise on Choice and Consequence. In a way, it is *the* "abortion" opera in which bad choices and character flaws lead to an outcome in which even the best (or seemingly best) choice is a horrible one. The piercing irony (nay, tragedy) that the sanest person, the one with the most steadfast moral compass, is the very person that ultimately commits the most heinous crime—is at the heart of this. A deeply caring, insightful, world-wise woman goes terribly wrong in her attempt to do right. This is searing material.

Orchestral suites have been drawn from these operas, and one of the most attractive renditions of them is by conductor José Serebrier and the Czech State Philharmonic on a two-CD package from Reference Recordings. One of the CDs also contains the *Sinfonietta*; *Taras Bulba*; and the *Lachian Dances*. The sound is stunningly good. I was all the more surprised at how idiomatic the performances were when Serebrier told me that he had not been intimately acquainted with Janáček's music before undertaking these recordings.

Another work of Janáček's maturity that is typical of his penchant for the bizarre is his symphonic poem, *The Danube*. It is based on two poems depicting desperate women drowning themselves. Janáček did not finish the score but left the orchestrated sketches for four movements, the third of which includes a vocalization for soprano. A Naxos CD offers a completed version that displays the formidable merits of this work. The CD also includes the incidental music to *Schluk und Jau*, a play by Gerhardt Hauptmann. The music does not sound incidental at all. It was written in 1928, the year of Janáček's death, a time when the composer was at the height of his powers. The two movements presented here, Andante and Allegretto, are vintage Janáček that can stand next to the *Sinfonietta* in their power and appeal. The Allegretto is especially noteworthy. It is an amazing piece of music that packs more into its short duration than most symphonies and builds to an exhilarating ending.

For those who know only the Janáček of blazing horns, thundering timpani, and crying voices, his piano oeuvre will come as a surprise, with its intimacy and modest scale. The intensity, though, emerges in a style that is as close to impressionism as Janáček ever came. This is not a cool impressionism; nature is not being impersonally evoked in shimmering *reflections d'eau*. Rather, it is haunting, nocturnal music of moving simplicity and directness, deeply expressive of human feelings. Rudolf Firkušný, a pupil of Janáček, was deservedly famous for his beautiful interpretations of Janáček's piano music. The Piano Works / Solo Piano, Concertino, and Capriccio performed by him are available on a two-CD set from Deutsche Grammophon, with Rafael Kubelik and the Bavarian Symphony Orchestra in Concertino and Capriccio. I have heard no pianist who makes the solo piano works "speak" more intensely than the brilliant Ivan Moravec. Unfortunately, his sublime performances on the Nonesuch label from 1983 were deleted. If you can find the old LP or cassette, grab it.

Both of Janáček's string quartets are masterpieces. They evoke, in Janáček's words, "exaltation, passionate declarations of love, anxiety, indomitable yearnings". They are among the most nakedly emotional works ever written. Of the Second Quartet, *Intimate Letters*, Janáček said the music is "like a piece of living flesh. I don't think I ever shall be able to write anything deeper and more truthful." He didn't. It was his last work. He was dead within the year of its completion.

If there is divine madness in music, this is it.

Recommended Recordings

Glagolitic Mass (and *Taras Bulba*), Karel Ančerl, Czech PO, Supraphon 3667 (Karel Ančerl Gold Edition, vol. 7)

The standard for the *Glagolitic Mass* is Janáček's revised edition. The reconstructed original version, however, contains the wilder, more complex rhythmical structures Janáček had initially written and is well worth hearing once one has fallen in love with the Ančerl recording. Marek Janowski (Pentatone 5186388) and Mackerras (Chandos 9310, Supraphon DVD 7009) are good choices for the original version that can sound hectic to ears firmly used to the more even time signatures of the version Janáček modified to appease the performers.

Sinfonietta (also includes Martinů's *Frescoes of Piero della Francesca* and *Parables for Orchestra*), Karel Ančerl, Czech PO, Supraphon 3684 (*Karel Ančerl Gold Edition*, vol. 24)

String Quartets No. 1 Kreutzer & 2 Intimate Letters (also includes Erwin Schulhoff's *String Quartet No.1*), Talich Quartet, La Dolce Volta 256

The outstanding 1962 Grand Prix du Disc–winning performances by the Janáček Quartet are out of print, but are available as downloads from Amazon, for example. The Talich Quartet performances are superbly moving, too, and have thankfully been re-issued on the extraordinarily fine La Dolce Volta label. There are almost 50 versions of the two quartets from every string quartet worth its salt. Two modern recordings are worth singling out: The Mandelring String Quartet's gentle, lyrical performances are special and they also add the original version of the *Intimate Letters* where Janáček, perhaps with greater symbolical than musical consequences, substituted a viola d'amore for the viola. (Audite 92545) The other is the no-holds-barred performances of the Pavel Haas Quartet, who couple these quartets, on two separate discs, with the equally worthy quartets of the quartet's namesake, Pavel Haas. (Supraphon 3877 & 3922)

Káťa Kabanová, Charles Mackerras, Vienna Philharmonic, Elisabeth Söderström, Peter Dvorsky et al., Decca 475 7518

Jenůfa, Charles Mackerras, Vienna Philharmonic, Elisabeth Söderström, Peter Dvorsky, Lucia Popp et al., Decca 475 8227

From the House of the Dead, Charles Mackerras, Vienna Philharmonic, Dalibor Jedlicka, Jiří Zahradnícek, Ivo Zidec et al., Decca 475 5790

The Cunning Little Vixen, Charles Mackerras, Vienna Philharmonic, Lucia Popp, Eva Randová, Dalibor Jedlicka et al., Decca 475 8670

The Makropulos Affair, Charles Mackerras, Vienna Philharmonic, Elisabeth Söderström, Peter Dvorsky et al., Decca 478 1711

These five operas are gathered in a budget 9-CD Decca box (475 6872), alas, without libretti.

Opera Suites; *Sinfonietta*; *Taras Bulba*; *Lachian Dances*, José Serebrier Czech State PO, Reference Recordings 2103

On an Overgrown Path; Sonata; Concertino; *Capriccio*, Rafael Kubelik, Bavarian RSO, Rudolf Firkušný, DG 449 7642

The Danube (fragment); *Schluck and Jau, Moravian Dances*; Suite op. 3, Libor Pešek, Bratislava Slovak State PO, Naxos 8.555245

DVDs:

The Makropulos Affair, Esa-Pekka Salonen, Vienna Philharmonic, Angela Denoke et al., directed by Christoph Marthaler, C Major DVD 709508 / Blu-ray 709604

This *Věc Makropulos* from the 2011 Salzburg Festival catches the Vienna Philharmonic at its rare best and Salonen allows for great sweep and drama and sometimes ferocious energy.

The Cunning Little Vixen, Václav Neumann, Berlin Philharmonic, Ruth Schob-Lipka, Rudolf Asmus, et al., directed by Walter Felsenstein, Arthaus Musik DVD 101297. Staged by Walter Felsenstein in the tradition of the famed Czech stop-motion animation, and it's cute beyond belief. The 1956 black and white film version suffers from less than ideal sound and picture quality but the enchanting poetry and perfectly bearable lightness of this "performance" —quite like Max Reinhart's 1938 *Midsummer Night's Dream*—invariably casts its spell on the viewer.

∼

John Kinsella: Irish Liberation

When British music critic and founder of Toccata Classics, Martin Anderson, first directed my attention to Irish composer John Kinsella (b. 1932) and the CD release of his Sixth and Seventh Symphonies on the Irish label RTÉ lyric fm, I was only vaguely aware of him. I saw a blurb by BBC Radio 3, proclaiming Kinsella "the most significant Irish symphonist since [Charles Villiers] Stanford". Since I had never been inspired to listen to a Stanford symphony more than once (though I found much to admire in his Requiem and Stabat Mater), this did not lead me to expect much. What were the odds that Kinsella would turn out to be a major symphonist, even though he has 11 such works to his name? Well, the praise turns out to have been a considerable understatement. Here is a composer punching in the heavy-weight class (though there is nothing pugnacious about his music). The works on the disc pack a wallop. They immediately led me to obtain the other recording of his symphonic works available at that time, a Marco Polo CD containing Symphonies 3 and 4, made back in 1996.

It struck me that the quality of these four works was such that the fact that all the symphonies were not available in recordings constituted some kind of scandal—since partially rectified by issues of the Fifth and Tenth Symphonies on Toccata Classics and the Ninth on the ICO label. In general, I would say that Kinsella offers a potent combination of the influences of Bruckner and Sibelius, melded into his own distinctive voice, which bursts forth in volcanic eruptions of brass and timpani, deployed and layered in so effectively that they scale the heights of expression. The acknowledgment of Sibelius is explicit in the Seventh, about which Kinsella wrote, "It would be true to say that this work was written with a keen awareness of Sibelius' Seventh Symphony." This is in the way of homage rather than imitation. The same is true of the Bruckner influence, evident in Kinsella's ability to build symphonic moments of overpowering mass and uplift. He wrote, "Parts of my Third Symphony visit Bruckner's sound world. . . . The work is entitled 'Joie de vivre' but it is about the joy of 'Being alive' rather than the standard interpretation of that phrase." Dedicated to his parents, "part one is the masculine section," he writes, "part two is the feminine", and *he* is the coda.

The brilliance of his highly imaginative, fantastical orchestration did not lead me to think of Stanford, but of Berlioz. That impression was vindicated when I found Kinsella stating, " 'Generally speaking, my style is very bold, but it has not the slightest tendency to subvert any of the constituent elements of art. The prevailing characteristics of my music are passionate expression, intense ardour, rhythmical animation and unexpected turns.' Quotation: Berlioz. Aspiration: mine." To which can only be added: Aspiration achieved. This is viscerally thrilling music, thoroughly engaging, rhythmically propulsive, and essentially lyrical. By emphasizing the massive, electrifying deployments of brass and timpani, which achieve a magnificence that is rare in contemporary music, I do not mean to slight Kinsella's equally effective evocations of stillness and joy. The performances by the RTÉ National Symphony Orchestra must have warmed the composer's heart. By all means (and you can find it on the Internet), obtain a copy of this RTÉ lyric fm CD, so that you can hear what I am talking about. Then track down a copy of the Marco Polo CD.

I gained another impression from a first-chair musician from a major orchestra to whom I introduced these works. He wrote to me: "The Kinsella symphonies are really excellent! I knew nothing of this composer but I would be thrilled to perform these. He certainly loved the bassoon, I must say. He's to the bassoon what Mahler was to the trumpet. Even within familiar tonal language, he strikes me as quite unique in the colors and feelings he achieves. That's hard to do standing on the shoulders of so many greats that came before." That is a good measure of Kinsella's achievement. He stands on the shoulders of giants, and then he adds something inimitably his own.

This might not have happened. According to Irish writer and composer Séamas de Barra, Kinsella was very attracted to the European avant-garde in his early days and embraced the serial method of composition. Apparently, he later came to sense a lack of inner conviction in much of what he heard from this school. After completing his Third String Quartet, he was thrown into a stylistic quandary that silenced him for a year and a half. When he came out of it, according to de Barra, Kinsella wished "to reclaim from the 12-tone series the structuring force of tonal attraction". When I asked Kinsella by way of correspondence what took him out of the serial school, he answered, "With regard to serialism I can say, looking back now, that it was a means to an end. Having been suffocated by studies in harmony, etc. —oh! Paul Hindemith, where were you then?—I resorted to serial ways like most composers of the time. It was strangely liberating. Not necessarily for what it was, but what it freed me from. The rest was a process of freeing myself, in turn, from strict serialism and arriving at a language which allowed me to say (sing?) my bit." In his 50s, he began to write symphonies that demonstrate his superb ability to do exactly that. He hasn't stopped since. Looking back, Kinsella writes, "The malign influences of the early 20th Century are recognized for what they truly are. I feel myself it's more about dark forces, sometimes showing up clearly in individuals, rather than systems as such. These are, after all, only tools to be used. But it's when these are twisted into dogmas and imposed on people that the damage can be done."

More of the still and contemplative side of Kinsella is available on a CD from the Irish Chamber Orchestra on its own ICO label. The CD, titled *Hommage: John Kinsella*, offers some wonderful string music: Symphony No. 9; *Hommage à Clarence*; *Nocturne for Cello and String Orchestra*; *Elegy for Strings*; and *Prelude and Toccata for String Orchestra*. I wondered how Kinsella, shorn of his virtuoso abilities for orchestration, would fare with strings alone. The answer is: quite as well as did Benjamin Britten, Gustav Holst, or Frank Bridge in their string works. The Ninth Symphony is actually quite spirited, with an infectious rhythmic vivacity and highly transparent writing that plays off both Johann Cruger's and J. S. Bach's versions of the hymn tune *Jesu meine Freude*. The Presto impetuoso movement is pure exhilaration. The still part comes in the deeply ruminative Largo, which is almost Arvo Pärt–like in its approach to the very edge of silence. This is followed by a highly animated Allegro and capped off with a sprinting Vivace. *Hommage* begins with Sibelian murmuring in a string ostinato, with an exquisitely tender lament in the solo violin. It is a tribute to fallen violinist friend. *Nocturne for Cello and String Orchestra* is Kinsella's equivalent to Samuel Barber's *Adagio for Strings*. It is ravishingly beautiful. *Elegy for Strings* is the moving slow movement of the Ninth Symphony recast as a free-standing work. This well-played but hard-to-find CD is worth the search (see below in Recommend Recordings).

The most recent symphonic release pairs the Fifth and the Tenth on Toccata Classics. Symphony No. 5: *The 1916 Poets*, written in 1992, is a bit of a hybrid that includes parts for speaker and baritone. It sets poems by three Irish poets, Joseph Mary Plunkett, Thomas MacDonagh, and Patrick (Pádraig) Pearse, all of whom were involved in Irish revolutionary politics. They were executed for their part in the 1916 Easter Uprising. This work, however, is not political. It goes much deeper. I am congenitally averse to symphonic music with narration (for instance, as much as I like Aaron Copland's music, I refuse to listen to his *Lincoln Portrait* again), so I approached this work with some trepidation. However, the brilliance of its orchestration and the dramatic lyricism of its themes captured my attention and then, with repeated acquaintance, my affection.

The poetic texts begin with a striking image from Plunkett of "the Reaper, the dead Christ upon his cross of wood". The Reaper is the reaped, a profoundly ironic mystery ("one must die that many live") to which the work will return at the very end. The next poems are life-affirming—a father's wishes for his infant son (a kind of counterpart to William Butler Yeats' poem "A Prayer for My Daughter"), though curiously the propulsive music is more apprehensive, even ominous, than celebratory in character, and a paean to a spring flower, the crocus. It soon becomes clear that these affirmations are there only to accentuate the contrast with the unmitigated harshness of the mordant reflections on the transience of beauty and the brutality of death in the following poems, which are introduced by a close to three-minute orchestral tone poem. These bitter reflections are then subsumed, if not relieved, at the very end by the mortality of Christ himself. The world is shot through with the devastation of death, which achieves its supreme expression in the dead Christ. The last poem, also by Plunkett, says, "His crown of thorns is twined with every thorn, His cross is every tree", upon which the climax of the last movement, indeed of the whole work, is reached, followed by a nearly three-minute orchestral dénouement. The framing perspective of the work looks unflinchingly on the Cross (not the Resurrection) as the source of hope. Death is universal, but Christ's death portends more because his Cross participates in all death, thereby redeeming the loss. Together, poems and music seem to be a not-so-sublimated *cri de coeur*: "*I* am on cross", to which the answer comes, "Look, so is *he*." This profound mystery is what this very striking music and poetry touch upon. As dramatic as it is, I think the experience of its drama is intended to incite reflection upon these deepest mysteries. I will be returning to it for that reason.

The musical settings are so effective that they have become for me inseparable from the words. In fact, "settings" may be the wrong word, as the words of the poems seem to grow out of the music as much as the music out of the words—except in the case of the narration where the music is more clearly illustrative. Speaker Bill Golding modulates his voice to the music so well that it becomes another instrument.

Baritone Gerard O' Connor sings ardently but his vibrato occasionally compromises his diction. The RTÉ National Symphony Orchestra, under Colman Pearce, gives a very stirring performance.

Symphony No. 10 (2010), played by the Irish Chamber Orchestra, under conductor Gábor Takács-Nagy, is a more conventional symphony composed for a classical-sized orchestra. Dolefully, slowly, the solo clarinet presents the principal theme, which quickly changes character when what seems like its distant variation is taken up by pizzicato strings in a highly vivacious, syncopated rhythm. It's as if an animated child had picked up the theme from the clarinet and decided to dance to it. In fact, it's hard to sit still listening to this music. The timpani and winds accentuate the punchy rhythm, followed by the brass which ramps things up even further. To call the music enlivening is an understatement.

The highly intriguing second movement, Largo-Andante, begins exactly as the first with the clarinet solo that then is joined by oboe, bassoon, and strings, this time non-pizzicato. The long-lined string theme is traded back and forth with the brass and winds in some highly atmospheric music. It seems to be trying to reach a kind of sad, valedictory repose, announced by a plaintive horn solo, but is overcome by a more tumultuous grief that reaches a climax and then, exhausted, lapses into silence—out of which the clarinet theme again emerges in another attempt at repose. This movement contains some slashing string chords out of Bernard Herrmann and some other string writing as close to Shostakovich as Kinsella comes. It is haunting.

The highly energetic last movement has a Janáček-like (from the *Sinfonietta*) peroration, with gurgling winds, brass calls, and thundering timpani answering each other, speaking with telegraphic intensity in kaleidoscopic colors, surging with excitement right up to a false ending—at which a giocoso bassoon then seems to have some fun. Things unwind with the return of the starting measures of the opening theme on the clarinet, which are then laid to rest by staccato strings playing *pianissimo* over a gentle drum roll.

It's stunning that a near-octogenarian composer would write music of this intensity. In the CD jacket notes, Kinsella says that the performance "was one of the most fulfilling experiences of my musical life". One can easily hear why.

Now we await the recently completed Eleventh Symphony which, the composer informed me, "is in three movements with an approximate duration of 30' and in a style similar to Symphony No. 10. Again,

I use a classical orchestra with just one flute but with the addition of a trombone and a glockenspiel—sounds that will have a resonance for Sibelius symphony lovers." One hopes that the Irish Chamber Orchestra will undertake its performance and recording.

On a difficult to find CD, Urtext Digital Classics offers Kinsella's Cello Concerto, written for cellist Carlos Prieto in 2000, accompanied by Shostakovich's Cello Concerto No. 1 and Celso Garrido-Lecca's Cello Concerto, with the Xalapa Symphony Orchestra, under Luis Herrera de la Fuente. Kinsella's 25-minute virtuoso work is almost like one giant cadenza, with an incredibly long-lined and very memorable melody for the cello, fabulously framed with his imaginative orchestration. But clearly the cello is the star here. Why isn't this work in the repertory? It begs for a major league recording.

Toccata Classics is promising more Kinsella. I am looking forward to String Quartets 3, 4, and 5, as well as *Synthesis*, with the Vanbrugh Quartet, forthcoming on TOCC 0229. The aforementioned Séamas de Barra has written a major book, *John Kinsella, Irish Symphonist*, which will soon be published by Toccata Press.

Does Ireland know what a treasure it has in this man's music? It should tell the world.

Recommended Recordings

Symphony No. 6; Symphony No. 7; Prelude and Toccata; *Cúchulain and Ferdia: Duel at the Ford*, National Chamber Choir of Ireland (Symphony No. 7), RTÉ NSO/Proinnsías Ó Duinn, Gavin Maloney, RTÉ lyric fm CD134

Symphonies 3 and 4, Proinnsías Ó Duinn, NSO Ireland, Marco Polo 8.223766

Symphony No. 9; *Hommage a Clarence*; *Nocturne* for Cello and String Orchestra; *Elegy for Strings*; and Prelude and Toccata for String Orchestra, Andrew Gourlay, Irish Chamber Orchestra (available from the Irish Chamber Orchestra's website and as MP3s on iTunes and Amazon.)

Symphony No. 5: *The 1916 Poets*, Gerard O' Connor (baritone), Bill Golding (speaker), Colman Pearce, RTÉ NSO; Symphony No. 10, Gábor Takács-Nagy, Irish Chamber Orchestra, Toccata Classics TOCC 0242

Cello Concerto; et al, Carlos Prieto, Xalapa SO, under Luis Herrera de la Fuente, Urtext Digital Classics JBCC 083

∽

Charles Koechlin: Aural Alchemist

In the latter half of the 19th century, German music so dominated the European continent that the French were left wondering what could be distinctively theirs, aside from French insouciance, wit, and whimsy. As mentioned in the chapter on Albert Roussel, France could not compete in the symphony (Beethoven, Brahms, Bruckner, etc.), and Wagner had swamped the opera world. Eric Satie (1866–1925) came to the rescue. As Satie wrote, "I explained to Debussy that a Frenchman had to free himself from the Wagnerian adventure, which wasn't the answer to our national aspirations. I also pointed out that I was in no way anti-Wagnerian, but that we should have a music of our own—if possible, without any sauerkraut." Satie's ingenious solution was for French music to imitate French painting. Why not look to "the means that Claude Monet, Cézanne, Toulouse-Lautrec and others had made known? Why could we not transpose these means into music?"

The fruit of Satie's suggestion is the brilliant impressionist music exemplified by the works of Claude Debussy (1862–1918), Maurice Ravel (1875–1937), and Albert Roussel (1869–1937). This music is French in its sheer refinement of sound, its transparency, and most of all, its preference for evocative imagination over more formal concerns. A single colorful chord can be left suspended in the ether, unresolved in an overall harmonic scheme, if it creates the right impression. One can daub with notes as Seurat daubed with bright pigments on a canvas. This is an art of allusion and depiction.

One of the most interesting members of the impressionist generation was perhaps its least known, Charles Koechlin (1867–1950), who was born in Paris only five years after Debussy, but who outlived him by more than 30 years. Koechlin came late to music, after illness waylaid his military engineering career. He discovered in his courses with fellow student Maurice Ravel that "sometimes a single bar by an ingenious colleague is enough to open the door to enchanted gardens." Koechlin stepped through that door and became a sorcerer of the first order. French composer Darius Milhaud (1892–1974) called him a "magician", and conductor Heinz Holliger an "alchemist of sound".

It is thanks to Holliger and the Hänssler Classic label that we can now fall under Koechlin's spell. Hänssler has undertaken a major effort to bring Koechlin's neglected works to light. It is a huge challenge since there are 226 opus numbers in Koechlin's catalogue, and many contain scores of works (e.g., there are no less than 96 pieces for solo flute based on Anatole France's *La Révolte des Anges*). Hänssler has made an excellent beginning with six CDs of vocal works with orchestra, other major orchestral works (featuring the superb Radio Symphony Orchestra of Stuttgart), and very charming chamber compositions with flute. Most of these are world premiere recordings. When you listen to this music, you will wonder: How can this be? How, for instance, can an impressionist nocturne as gorgeous as *Vers la voûte étoilée* (Toward the Vault of the Stars), composed in 1933, have not been performed until 1989? How many masterpieces are still lying around in Koechlin's desk drawers?

As a late starter, Koechlin did not gain full confidence in his orchestral abilities until 1900, but he excelled to the point that he orchestrated works for Debussy (*Khamma*) and Fauré (*Chanson de Mélisande*). His future promise can be heard in the Hänssler two-CD collection of his Vocal Works with Orchestra (Hänssler), composed during the 1890s. But the word "promise" sounds patronizing when applied to these magnificent, fully mature compositions. Harkening back to Berlioz and Gounod, pointing forward in his use of wild, coloristic effects, Koechlin could, whenever he wished, bathe his music in the impressionistic glories of Debussy and Ravel or give it the delicacy of Fauré (with whom he studied) and then toughen it up with some Roussel-like grinding rhythms. All these resources are brought to bear for expressive use in the texts Koechlin sets. Two particularly affecting ones are the *Trois mélodies*, op. 17, and the *Chant funèbre à la mémoire des jeunes femmes défuntes*, op. 37. The latter employs the text of the Requiem in a spell-binding 21-minute setting.

How good was he compared to his impressionist confreres? Simply listen to the *Études antiques*, op. 46, on the second disc of the Vocal Works release, to sample the level of enchantment. The *Trois poèmes*, op. 18 are an example of this same high art with voice and orchestra. But after 1900, Koechlin moved on to paint on huge orchestral canvases in a language uniquely his own. In his massive orchestral tone poems, the music is splashed on in what may seem haphazard ways. In general, Koechlin's music meets musician Federico Mondelci's description that "the language is extremely refined, with the modal harmony painting a melancholy landscape. Counterpoint is widely used. . . . Koechlin wrote with great freedom. His use of atonality, tonality, and modality creates a unique atmosphere, often dreamy, naïve, and timeless." The music can often seem to drift—not aimlessly—but as in a dream, with an extremely spacious sense of time. Koechlin is not afraid to keep the music barely above the level of audibility, as if it were a haze settling upon you, or to engage in raucous outbursts of Mahlerian proportions. As much as he felt that a composer should free himself of "schools, traditions, and dogmas", he also believed that "one of the most dreadful diseases of our day is the desire to be modern."

Perhaps the defining composition of his career is *The Jungle Book*, a series of enormous symphonic poems written over a period of 40 years, inspired by Rudyard Kipling. There is nothing quite like this more than 80-minute piece—intoxicating evocations of spring, the atonal chattering of the monkeys, banality and ecstasy conjoined. Much of it is gorgeous, but when Koechlin reaches for the outer limits of harmony, the music can be quite grating, purposively so. There is a complete recording of *The Jungle Book* on RCA, a nearly complete one on Marco Polo, and one of its main movements, *La Course de printemps*, op. 95, on Hänssler, is coupled with *Le Buisson ardent*, an impassioned evocation of rebirth.

Literature was not Koechlin's only inspiration. He fell in love with the movies. The most famous orchestral incarnation of the infatuation was the *Seven Stars Symphony*, in which he depicted Douglas Fairbanks, Lilian Harvey, Greta Garbo, Clara Bow, Marlene Dietrich, Emil Jannings, and Charlie Chaplin. These enchanting tone poems, free from Hollywood clichés, are also on the out-of-print RCA recording, but more economically available on EMI/Warner Classics. Koechlin was so entranced by a flattered but somewhat alarmed Harvey, the British-German actress, that he wrote more than 100 *hommages* to her. In memory of Jean Harlow, there is the *Épitaphe de Jean Harlow: Romance for Flute, Saxophone, and Piano*.

Le Docteur Fabricius, Koechlin's last main composition, is paired with *Vers la voûte étoilée*, on another stunning Hänssler release. *Le Docteur* was written to a scenario by Koechlin's uncle about the indifference of nature to man and man's ultimate transcendence of it. It is a strange, wonderful piece. Injustice is appropriately portrayed by an atonal fugue. Contemplation of the night sky brings calm, followed by consolation, and then ecstatic joy, made all the more special by the marvelously loopy sound of the ondes Martenot, one of Koechlin's favorite instruments. Though some of this strange music may sound old-fashioned for 1949, it also seems to presage the still stranger music of Olivier Messiaen that was soon to follow.

Koechlin's photographic hobby may provide some insights into his unique and complex style. He took pictures with a device called a Verascope, which produced an early version of 3-D when developed on glass plates and viewed through a stereoscope. Koechlin took his Verascope everywhere and produced some 3,000 photos. Two intriguing examples decorate the jacket cover of the *L'abbaye* release from the Skarbo label (a Gothic ruin) and an inside page of the Hänssler release of *Les Heures persanes*, op. 65 (Arab riders going through an arch in Fez, Morocco). His photographic interests reveal Koechlin's propensity to attempt to reveal multiple dimensions of reality at the same time.

Is there a 3-D aspect to Koechlin's music? Sometimes, it sounds as if there is—simply because of the music's extraordinary richness and complexity. In fact, some of Koechlin's works can sound like the aural equivalent of a Verascope photo without the stereoscope to see it through. This is because of his employment of techniques that are polytonal—using more than one tonal center or key alongside, and sometimes against, another—polyrhythmic, and even polystylistic. This can get confusing. It can produce a huge sonic welter, a veritable jungle of sound. However, because of it, it is all the more breathtaking when all of a sudden, stereoscopically, things are snapped into focus, resolving themselves in a magnificent, arching melody.

Why was Koechlin's music not popular? Perhaps it was his attitude to the music of his time. Of one of his works, he said, "It is situated at the antipodes of our present life (factories and sporting matches) and of current music aesthetics (dynamism and 'constructivism')." Also, as he said of Mowgli at the end of *La Course de printemps*, he "lingers rather apprehensive at his glimpse into the mystery of creatures and things. Thus the work concludes with a sort of question mark." There is always a question mark in mystery; that is why it is mysterious. If you prefer a strong resolution to things, Koechlin may not be your man.

About *Vers la voûte étoilée*, Koechlin said, "My dream has remained the same from the very beginning, a dream of imaginary far horizons —of the infinite, the mysteries of the night, and triumphant bursts of light." If you would like to listen to this dream, take ample time, and try these superb Hänssler Classic CDs.

On a smaller scale are Charles Koechlin's works for chamber ensembles, offered on a Timpani CD, which informs us that two of these pieces, the *Sonate à 7* for flute, oboe, harpsichord, and strings and the two sonatinas for oboe d'amore or soprano saxophone and chamber orchestra, are world premiere recordings. These little, quiet jewels are offered for refreshment and contemplation by the Initium and Contraste ensembles in a recording that makes it sound as if they are playing in your living room. The accompanying Septet for Winds and *Paysages et marines* for ensemble offer little soufflés in sound. There is genuine delight in this modestly scaled music. If you already know the chamber music of Ravel and Debussy, Koechlin should be your next stop.

Hänssler also offers some of Koechlin's chamber music with flute, which fortunately does not duplicate any of the works on the Timpani CD. It contains the marvelously fluent Divertissement for Two Flutes and Alto Flute/Clarinet; *Suite en quatuor* for Flute, Viola, Violin, and Piano; and the Trio for Flute/Oboe, Clarinet, and Bassoon in G Major, among others. This disc demonstrates what a superbly talented miniaturist Koechlin was.

Somehow, I missed the first two Hännsler Classic issues of the works for piano, but volume 3 (*des horizons lointain*) inspires me to catch up. Much of the music could be located somewhere between Eric Satie and Debussy and Ravel. But Koechlin has his own particular genius. Pianist Michael Korstick deploys liquid, subtle playing that is perfect for this music. The dreamy delights here are irresistible. Try the Andante con moto, and you will see what I mean.

We also have available Koechlin's String Quartets 1 and 2, performed by the Ardeo Quartet on the Ar Re-Se label. Anyone who loves French musical impressionism (think of the Ravel String Quartet), especially when imbued with warmth and nostalgic yearning, will love these works. The First Quartet has become a favorite. In the first movement, Koechlin goes from bittersweet heartache to the ecstatic. The Andante has a kind of lazy sorrow to it, and the Finale sparkles with Mozartian vivacity. The Second Quartet begins with one of Koechlin's experiments. He tries to see how close he can pare things down and approach stasis without losing our interest. He succeeds in this haunting work. Bravo, or I should say brava, to the four ladies comprising the Ardeo Quartet.

My most recent discovery is Koechlin's half-hour, very touching Sonata for Viola and Piano, op. 53, on a CD with similar works by

Charles Tournemire and Pierre de Breville, on the ATMA Classique label. Koechlin did not just deal with aural ephemera, and this work shows the depths of feeling he could express in what seems to be a lament for World War I, during which he worked as a nurse.

All this seems barely to scratch the surface of the treasures in this alchemist's chest. By all means, step through "the door to enchanted gardens" and begin listening.

Recommended Recordings

Vocal Works with Orchestra, Juliane Banse, Heinz Holliger, Southwest German RSO Stuttgart et al., Hänssler CD 93.159

Le Docteur Fabricius; *Vers la voûte étoilée*, Heinz Holliger, Southwest German RSO, Hänssler CD 93.106

Seven Stars Symphony, Alexander Myrat, Monte Carlo PO, EMI/Warner 64369 (OOP, available used an as an Arkiv CDR)

Le Buisson ardent; *La Course de printemps*, Heinz Holliger, Southwest German RSO, Hänssler CD 93.045

The Jungle Book, David Zinman, Iris Vermillion, Johan Botha et al., RSO Berlin, RCA Victor Red Seal 61955 (OOP, available used and as an Arkiv CDR)

Works for Chamber Ensembles, Ensemble Contraste; Initium, Timpani 1193

Chamber Music with Flute, Tatjana Ruhland, Yaara Tal et al., Hänssler CD 93.157

Piano Works, vol. 3, Michael Korstick, Hänssler 93.261

String Quartets 1 and 2, Ardeo Quartet, Ar Re-Se label 20063

String Quartet No. 3; Piano Quintet op. 80, Antigone Quartet, Ar Re-Se 20091

Sonata for Viola and Piano (also includes viola sonatas by Charles Tournemire and Pierre de Bréville), Steven Dann, James Parker, ATMA Classique 2519

1914: Quintet for Piano and Strings, op. 42 (also includes Louis Vierne's Violin Sonata and Twelve Préludes, op. 38), Tamara Atschba, Louise Chisson et al., Gramola 99040

Erich Wolfgang Korngold: Rejected Wunderkind

Jens F. Laurson

The music of Erich Wolfgang Korngold (1897–1967) has enjoyed a major renaissance over the last three decades. He is no longer the neglected, unknown master, the hidden Wunderkind of 20th-century classical music. The point is proven by the pleasant fact that his entire œuvre is available on commercial recordings—from more than 20 different versions of the Violin Concerto on CD (Jascha Heifetz, Itzhak Perlman, Gil Shaham, Anne-Sophie Mutter, Renaud Capuçon, Arabella Steinbacher, to name just some of the more prominent and better accounts), all the way to a proud rendition of "The Goose-liver at the Durschnitz-residency", an insouciant song for baritone that Dietrich Henschel has recorded.

Your Korngold 101 knowledge can be encapsulated thus: precocious teen and Wunderkind who composed too-beautiful music to be taken seriously at a time when modernism swept the cultural stage; composer of highly successful film music in his years in Hollywood—and consequently snubbed by the "real classical music" elite. That's good enough for a start—but as with any subject, increasing proximity and familiarity make matters more complicated and interesting.

The story of Erich Wolfgang, who composed his most advanced and tonally daring music as a teenager, is also the story of his father, Julius Leopold Korngold (1860–1945). As chief music critic for the *Neue Freie Presse* and successor to the (in)famous Eduard Hanslick, Julius Korngold was the most influential music critic of his time. He commanded not just the most important music criticism position in Vienna, when concert reviews were front-page material, he was the arbiter of what was good and bad. In essence he was the pope of musical taste. Julius' word carried weight. So much weight, indeed, that his word could make artistic life in Vienna near-impossible for anyone who aroused his fervent ire. In that sense, Julius Korngold—an ardent fan of Mahler and a cantankerous opponent of atonal modernism—not only shaped the musical life of Vienna but also that of Berlin, where many fled who could not get a leg on the ground in hostile Vienna.

He must have had musical ambitions for his son (little Erich was given his middle name in honor of Mozart, which considering his father's middle name and the path that Erich should take, has a prescient quality), but even he could not have begun to suspect just how talented his son would turn out to be. The elder Korngold didn't trust his potential bias at first and sought the opinion of 40 leading critics everywhere *but* in Vienna to judge his 11-year-old son's ballet piano score to *The Snowman*. The response ranged from baffled enthusiasm to bewilderment and outright disbelief that a child should have been able to write this advanced music.

One critic in Budapest was so enthused that he went public with his finding—and before long (against the will of Papa Korngold), *The Snowman* was given a big premiere in a gala performance honoring the emperor's name day on October 4, 1910. Erich Wolfgang Korngold's career as a composer was spectacularly launched at the age of 14.

Not the least to escape temporarily his unbearably overbearing father, Korngold went to Hollywood for one season. There Max Reinhardt, his collaborator on many Strauss-operetta projects, persuaded Korngold to work with him on Warner Brother's 1935 *Midsummer Night's Dream*. Once Hollywood had taken notice of Korngold—at his arrival by far the most talented musician to work in film—his future options looked bright when he *had* to leave Vienna: this time not to escape his father's influence but Hitler's reach. Julius, first reluctant to leave his homeland, joined Erich and his wife, Luzi, at the last possible moment.

Korngold's career in film took off as he revolutionized the trade and established standards still valid today. This resulted in memorable scores to classics such as *Sea Hawk*, *Captain Blood*, and *Robin Hood*, as well as the less classic *Kings Row*, which was the breakthrough hit for the 40th president of the United States—and its music was played at both Reagan inaugurations. *Anthony Adverse* (1936) and *Robin Hood* (1938) won Korngold two Academy Awards; *Captain Blood* (1935) and *Sea Hawk* (1940) got him two more nominations.

The work for which Korngold was long kept in the memory of concertgoers, when he was otherwise least appreciated, is the reasonably well known, if no longer often performed, opera *Die tote Stadt* (1920). Apart from being a repertory staple in the past, its primary claim to fame is the duet-cum-soprano aria "Mariettas' Lied", a greatest hit that you can find performed by a whole assortment of great sopranos, past and present, on YouTube.

But Korngold's possibly greatest, certainly biggest, opera is *Das Wunder der Heliane* (1927). With its polytonal harmony it's a more taxing and demanding opera than *Die tote Stadt*. More ambitious than sweet, it is a more satisfying and deeper work. It was given 45 performances between the two opera houses in Hamburg and Vienna alone, and it was immediately embroiled in the culture war. At the time, young Korngold was pitched (not the least by his father) against more modern composers. *Heliane* was compared to Janáček's *Káťa Kabanová* (1922), Schoenberg's *Erwartung* (1924), Berg's *Wozzek* (1925), Hindemith's *Cardillac* (1926), Stravinsky's *Oedipus Rex* (1927), and especially Ernst Krenek's *Jonny spielt auf* (1927). The contemporary and greater success of Krenek's *Jonny spielt auf* obscures our view of this battle, but the two operas were pitched against each other as unequal equals. The monopolist Austrian tobacco manufacturer figured he could make some money off the controversy that dominated the cultural scene from Berlin to Vienna and promptly issued two cigarette brands: an unfiltered cigarette, rough and strong, made from American tobacco, named Jonny, and cigarettes with perfumed Egyptian tobacco, colored filters, and housed in a fancy hard pack, named Heliane. Economics mirroring art, the Jonny brand still exists, Heliane does not.

Compared to Franz Schreker's sublime *Die Gezeichneten* or Debussy's *Pelléas et Mélisande*—operas from 1902 and 1911, respectively—the harmonically less daring style of *Heliane* might make it seem charmingly outdated for its time, but nonetheless wonderful for that. More French, but also similar, is the 1907 opera *Ariane et Barbe-bleue* by Paul Dukas (of *The Sorcerer's Apprentice* fame). The similarity with the latter is not too surprising: Korngold, coy or blunt, said he had copied from no other opera as much as Dukas' *Ariane*. You can also hear some similarities to Richard Strauss' *Die Frau ohne Schatten* (1919) and *Die ägyptische Helena* (1928).

Derided by the modernists and championed by conservative elements, *Das Wunder der Heliane* was soon thereafter considered Degenerate Art and banned by the Nazis. But *Heliane* not only suffered from musico-political controversies, it also was hampered by a modest libretto and odd story. Not speaking German is no disadvantage to the enjoyment of this opera. *Heliane* offers a rich score, thick with eroticism, busy and shrill at times, luscious and elegant elsewhere . . . and three hours of that.

When Korngold died on November 29 in 1957, Louis Kaufman,

among others, performed at the memorial concert at Schoenberg Hall, University of California. Kaufman played violin in many of Korngold's movies but was also the first violinist to record Vivaldi's *Four Seasons*. The divisions between film and "proper classical" music were permeable back then, at least in the United States. Not back home in Austria, however. After a heart attack in 1945, Korngold returned to Austria in 1947 and met with jealousy. On his first trip, he was not even allowed to enter his former family home in Vienna. There were a few personal honors and occasional high-profile performances, but no sustained interest or appreciation in the composer who had so unforgivingly been stained by Hollywood and popularity. Eventually the Korngolds sold their house, which they had by then successfully reclaimed, and moved back to the United States—fully aware that Austria was not going to be a welcoming home again. However, Austria has slowly but steadily become more hospitable to his music, because the beauty of it is too great to be denied in perpetuity, by the Viennese or lovers of beauty anywhere.

Recommended Recordings

Violin Concerto, op. 35; *Much Ado about Nothing*, op. 11 (plus Barber Violin Concerto), Gil Shaham (violin), André Previn (piano, conductor), London SO, DG 439886. Two great romantic violin concertos are played with utmost mastery and beauty and a very soft touch. Unlike his later recording with Anne-Sophie Mutter, André Previn neither plays up the film music aspect (much to the performance's benefit), nor does Shaham self-consciously struggle against its Hollywood-ring.

Violin Concerto, op. 35; *Much Ado about Nothing*, op. 11; Suite, op. 23; *Helen's Song*, Benjamin Schmid, David Frühwirth (violins), Henri Sigfridsson (piano) et al., Seiji Ozawa (conductor), Vienna Philharmonic, Oehms OC537. Benjamin Schmid's live performance of the concerto at the 2004 Salzburg Festival under Seiji Ozawa with the Vienna Philharmonic is lively and leaves no punch unthrown in the finale.

Das Wunder der Heliane, Berlin RSO, John Mauceri (conductor), Decca 829402

Symphony in F Sharp, Philadelphia Orchestra, Franz Welser-Möst (conductor), EMI/Warner 86101. Curiously the Symphony—dedicated to F. D. Roosevelt—was broadcast before it was premiered in concert. Rudolf Kempe and the Munich Philharmonic did the latter, from which comes the first recording. Despite a few cut bars, it is the rawest and most exciting reading.

Piano Concerto for the Left Hand (plus Joseph Marx Piano Concerto), Marc-André Hamelin (piano), BBC Scottish Orchestra, Osmo Vänskä, Hyperion 66990. There really is no recording to challenge Hamelin's account. If the Violin Concerto could be thought of as Korngold's *Rosenkavalier*, the Piano Concerto would be his *Salome* (Gary Graffman).

Cello Concerto (plus Ernest Bloch *Schelomo*, Berthold Goldschmidt Cello Concerto) Julian Steckel (cello), Rheinische Philharmonie SO (Koblenz), Daniel Raiskin (conductor), Cavi Music 8553223. Marvelously played and programmed, this combines three concertos that all belong in this book. Korngold culled and expanded the Cello Concerto from a sequence he wrote for the Bette Davis film *Deception*. For a bit of American music trivia: Korngold's Cello Concerto was premiered by the Hollywood String Quartet's Eleanor Slatkin—while she was pregnant with Leonard Slatkin's little brother, Fred Zlotkin. The two brothers have even recorded the work—for a freebie disc that came with the *BBC Music Magazine* many moons ago.

Sextet, op. 10 (plus Schoenberg, *Verklärte Nacht*), Raphael Ensemble, Hyperion 66425, Helios 55466. Two of the most wonderful chamber works from that period from composers who would go into such different directions, musically, if not geographically.

Sextet, op. 10; Piano Quintet, op. 15, Camerata Freden, Tacet 198. Camerata Freden brings a tenacity to these works that makes both more interesting listening, but maybe less inviting by eschewing superficial beauty for depth.

Suite for Piano Left Hand and Strings, op. 23; (plus Franz Schmidt, Left Hand Piano Quintet), Leon Fleisher (piano), Yo-Yo Ma (cello), Jamie Laredo, Joseph Silverstein, (violins), Sony 48253. The all-star cast—central among them Fleisher, a pianist who understood what being limited to the left hand meant like no other since commissioning pianist Paul Wittgenstein—tends to these rarely performed works with great care and passion.

String Quartets 1–3; Piano Quintet, op. 15, Aron Quartett, Henri Sigfridsson (piano), CPO 777436

String Quartet No. 2, op. 26 (plus Pavel Haas String Quartet No. 2, Joseph Haydn, Quartet, op. 64 5 "The Lark"), Adamas Quartett, Gramola 99011. Perhaps the Korngold quartet should have been programmed first, because the more radical Haas quartet does rather steal the limelight.

Die tote Stadt, Soloists, Royal Stockholm Opera Orchestra, Leif Segerstam (conductor), Naxos 8.660060. This or the 1975 recording under Erich Leinsdorf (RCA Victor Gold Seal 7767) is a fine choice for this standard work in the canon of romantic opera. The Naxos recording makes for a surprisingly tenacious, evenly cast, and marvelously conducted challenger to Leinsdorf's classic set.

Sursum Corda; Sinfonietta, BBC PO, Matthias Bamert (conductor), Chandos 10432. These are two early symphonic works and they are tremendous achievements, rivaling the symphony for bristling romanticism.

The Sea Hawk and other excerpts, National Philharmonic Orchestra/Charles Gerhardt, RCA Victor Gold Seal 7890. This magnificent recording with Gerhardt could be difficult to find but worth seeking out. (ArkivMusic offers it as an ArkivCD.) If you want to hear the very complete music of *Sea Hawk*, go with William Stromberg's very fine recent Naxos recording.

Complete Piano Sonatas, Michael Schäfer (piano), Profil Hänssler 4083. The teenage work that is the Second Sonata combines Viennese fin de siècle and intellectualism in ways one would think impossible coming from a boy of 13.

∼

László Lajtha: Music from a Secret Room

The Cold War was so cold that it took more than 10 years after its end for some forbidden composers' works to be thawed out for a general hearing. It was only then that music by Hungarian composer László Lajtha (1892–1963) at last emerged from the deep freeze in which the Hungarian Communist regime had placed it.

In 1947, when Lajtha (pronounced "loy-tah") returned to Hungary after a year's work in London on the film score of T. S. Eliot's *Murder in the Cathedral*, the Communists confiscated his passport and stripped him of all his official positions. He was designated a "political resistance fighter". He had been the director of music for Hungarian Radio and the director of the Museum of Ethnography and the National Conservatory. Not only had Lajtha been contaminated by foreign contacts, his sons had emigrated to England and America (a capital crime), making him additionally suspect. His sons were branded "dissidents" who could not safely return to Hungary. Lajtha himself was harassed and shadowed by the security services, and his friends dared to visit him only in secret.

Despite this, Lajtha was awarded the prestigious Kossuth Prize in 1951, not for his suppressed compositions but for his research into Hungarian folk music. His friends had to persuade him to accept the prize, lest he be found in open defiance of the authorities. Though nearly destitute himself, he gave away all the prize money to the poor. After 14 years of internal exile, the year before his death in 1963, Lajtha was allowed out of Hungary for one trip. Never able to see his two American granddaughters, he communicated with them in little piano pieces that he dedicated to them.

What is perhaps most extraordinary about Lajtha's music from this period is that it is not a reflection of the circumstances in which it was written. Anyone who saw Eastern Europe under Communism knows how drab and gray it was. Much of the music it produced was either a harsh, hermetic reflection of this oppression or a banal celebration of the proletariat written for the commissars. Lajtha's music is neither of these: It is free. Even in internal exile, he maintained his creative independence and integrity. How did he do this? In 1950, he wrote to one of his sons: "Just as in the town I have a room that is mine and only mine, so I have in my soul a secret room of my own. It has nothing to do with reality, yet it is more real." In his extraordinary religious music, Lajtha revealed the ultimate source of that reality, especially in his *Mass in a Time of Tribulation* and Magnificat.

Lajtha's biographical facts would be of little more than historical interest if he were not a major composer. In the popular mind, only two great Hungarian composers inhabited the 20th century: Zoltán Kodály (1882–1967) and Béla Bartók (1881–1945). Now we can say there was a third. The proof of this is at hand.

The Marco Polo label issued seven CDs of Lajtha's orchestral music (available as CD-Rs or MP3 from Amazon), including all nine symphonies, and one CD of his piano music. The Hungaroton label released four CDs containing a good deal of Lajtha's chamber and choral music and four others of the complete string quartets.

Only ten years younger than his two famous fellow composers, Lajtha shared with Kodály and Bartók their love for and research into Hungarian folk music. He accompanied them on collecting expeditions and made many of his own. His music springs from the same folk ethos as theirs and is as much a reaction against the prevailing avant-garde atonality of the time. Yet Lajtha departed significantly from his senior colleagues in several ways. Unlike them, he rejected the German influence prevalent at the Budapest Academy of Music where he studied. Lajtha did not care for Wagner or for German music after Schubert in general. This included Arnold Schoenberg's innovations, which Lajtha found restrictive and pedantic. Rather, he turned toward France for his inspiration, particularly to his hero, Debussy.

Between 1911 and 1913, he spent half his time in Paris, where he studied with Vincent d'Indy. His French sensibilities were so pronounced that Bartók teased Lajtha by calling him "the Latin". The French returned the favor by publishing Lajtha's music (Alphonse Leduc in Paris) and awarding him membership in the Académie des Beaux-Arts, the only other Hungarian composer to be so honored besides Franz Liszt.

Lajtha's other departure was his choice of the symphonic form, which was virtually untouched by Kodály and Bartók except for youthful experiments. Lajtha's nine symphonies stand unchallenged as an absolutely unique contribution to Hungarian music of the 20th century. The key to appreciating Lajtha's symphonies is not to expect them to develop in the typical German way. Perhaps that explains *Gramo-*

phone magazine's puzzlement at Lajtha's Symphony No. 7. Its reviewer complained, "There are plenty of ideas, but none of them develops with much conviction: time and again I found myself raising a hand to welcome a promising thematic or dramatic fragment, only to hear it whittle away in the wake of something new." That is exactly what Lajtha intended: a chainlike succession of ideas that, when developed at all, usually proceed in variation form.

Lajtha's symphonies are kaleidoscopic and fanciful, often charged with dance rhythms, and full of folk-like melodies and a profound sense of underlying mystery. Instead of the German symphonic model, think more of the 20th-century symphonies of Malipiero, Milhaud, or Martinů and add a dash of Janáček for a gypsy-like wildness. As with Malipiero's music, it is often hard to distinguish the differences between Lajtha's symphonies and his suites. Lajtha's works also share some similarities with Malcolm Arnold's nine symphonies, particularly their amount of burlesque and parody.

The entry in *The New Grove Dictionary of Music* says that "the influence of Magyar folk music is less obvious in his works than in those of Bartók and Kodály." Yet on first acquaintance, the uniquely Hungarian flavor of Lajtha's melodies is the most striking feature of his music. One is also immediately impressed by the highly colorful orchestration, luminously set forth with impressionist clarity. The content may be Hungarian, but the sensibility is French. Harp, saxophone, wood blocks, xylophone, and percussion frequently add spice to the swirling strings. Bartók's influence is especially felt in Lajtha's shimmering evocations of a mysterious twilight world similar to that found in Bartók's famous "night music". It is no wonder that Bartók admired his younger friend for doing the same thing so well—indeed, as well as Bartók himself, although with a more Gallic flavor.

Nonetheless, Lajtha's sound world is identifiably distinct. After immersing myself in his music, I could easily identify a piece of his I had never heard before within a few measures. While his music could almost survive on its exotic orchestral atmospherics alone, Lajtha also possessed a major melodic gift and a high level of craftsmanship. He said, "In all works of art the quality of craftsmanship is a decisive factor of evaluation." In this respect, Lajtha clearly measured up to the standards of Kodály and Bartók. Marco Polo's traversal of the symphonies is accompanied by some of Lajtha's other orchestral works: three suites from ballets; a huge set of *Variations for Orchestra* taken from the music for *Murder in the Cathedral*; and several other pieces, including the ballet Capriccio. The mood varies considerably from a kind of light and brilliant divertissement in the suites and some of the symphonies to the more harrowing and troubling disturbances of the other, usually odd-numbered symphonies, such as No. 7: *Revolution Symphony*, which evokes the tragedy of the Hungarian uprising in 1956. Yet none of the works is monochromatic. The variety within any of them can be absolutely wild, at one moment haunting, the next whimsical, then nostalgic, then brash. Lajtha can do this and make it seem completely natural. He was able to step in and out of an eerie dreamlike state with ease.

The symphonies to which I have returned most often are the middle ones, Nos. 3 through 6, which may provide the best introduction to Lajtha. However, all the symphonies are highly accomplished products of Lajtha's maturity. He was already 44 years old when he produced his highly charged First. Symphony No. 4, subtitled *Spring*, is a breezy and attractive score with a mini–violin concerto in the first movement and highly evocative gypsy-like melodies. The second movement is redolent of Janáček; the third, of Malcolm Arnold. A soul mate to Symphony No. 4, No. 6 is also breezy in its opening movement, followed by another utterly enchanting piece of "night music", which is almost Mendelssohnian in its magical charm. This music is wonderfully mysterious in its crepuscular murmurings. The upper string registers are gently brushed to sound like cicadas, the high flutes twitter-like birds, and other burbling sounds enchant the ear. Lajtha's Third Symphony, drawing again from his music for *Murder in the Cathedral*, is more somber but gravely beautiful. No. 5 is a beguiling lament, suffused with yearning for a lost, mysterious world.

Lajtha's chamber works, which first put him on the musical map, constitute the most clearly French-influenced part of his oeuvre. In 1929, he won the Coolidge Prize for his Third String Quartet. Anyone who thrills to the chamber works of Ravel and Roussel for similar ensembles will be entranced by Lajtha's Harp Quintet No. 2; his Trio for Harp, Flute, and Cello; and his Trio for Flute, Cello, and Harp contained on two Hungaroton CDs. Equally beguiling are the ravishing songs set in Lajtha's *Trois Nocturnes* for soprano, flute, harp, and string quartet. The workmanship is dazzling, the inspiration high. Except for the intrusion of Hungarian melodies in these pieces, anyone would swear they were French born and bred.

Only after all his symphonies had been released was a complete traversal of Lajtha's 10-string quartets undertaken by the excellent Auer String Quartet, and then made available by the Hungaroton Classic label. String Quartets 6, 8, and 10, are beguilingly played. These are quartets for those who have trouble digesting the quartets of Béla Bartók. In several movements, Lajtha even goes back to the *quatuor brillant* model from the first half of the 19th century (e.g., Louis Spohr), a miniconcerto for the first violin, with the other instruments playing an accompanying role. String Quartet No. 10 is subtitled *Transylvanian Suite in Three Parts*. Of the second movement, Lajtha said that the instruments "create the likeness of an immaterial, intangible misty image of a dream flickering past our eyes on fairy legs, pianissimo all the way". One hears in Lajtha a Mendelssohnian fleetness, French refinement, and Hungarian folk melodies. This is music of enchantment with an entrancing level of fancy. In turns touching and exhilarating, this is some of the most accessible quartet writing of the 20th century and remains one of its hidden treasures.

Lajtha's music for string trio, Serenade, op. 9, and *Soirs Transylvains*, op. 41, again display his signature French clarity, Hungarian melodies, and Haydn-like composure. The music is marvelously played by members of the eponymous Lajtha Quartet on a Hungaroton Classic release. These two half-hour works never flag in their level of invention, wit, and innate musicality. As its title tells us, the second of the two works is more completely immersed in the Hungarian musical ethos and the crepuscular magic that were Lajtha's specialty. I defy you to resist its charms and not be drawn by it to his other works.

Lajtha also excelled in choral music. The religious works presented on two other Hungaroton CDs demonstrate a sublime command of the voice to express a deep faith. Lajtha's *Missa in Diebus Tribulationis* was composed in 1950, a very difficult year for him and also the year in which the Communist regime suppressed the monasteries in Hungary. The Mass conveys a sense of mourning and loss but also of solace and even joy. Obviously, Lajtha had no hope of having the work performed; it came from the workbench in his "secret room". According to his widow, it was, for Lajtha, "an escape into a more beautiful, spotless world".

This is a Mass of both exquisite refinement and moving simplicity. Its origins are steeped in Gregorian chant and French harmonies. The orchestration is luminously transparent, and the melodies are gorgeous.

After starting each movement with Gregorian chant, Lajtha begins to elongate and transform the vocal lines, setting them forth monophonically and then intertwining them polyphonically. The full orchestra is used sparingly and to powerful effect, as in the peroration at the end of the Gloria. However dolorous, this is finally a work of soothing beauty. Gregorian chant is also the touchstone for Lajtha's Magnificat and his *Three Hymns for the Holy Virgin*, both works from the mid-1950s for choir and organ. Lajtha saw his Magnificat as the antithesis to "the stridency, the trumpeting, the Baroque majesty of the fortes in the Magnificat of Bach and other masters". This was, Lajtha said, "the hymn of a half-girlish voice sung on the shores of Lake Gennesaret". What he wished to express in this seraphic music was "gentleness, grace, beauty, tenderness, humility". It was, he wrote, "as if the soul, the happy, young, maternal soul, were bursting out and rippling in soft waves over the whole world". Except for the aggressive organ interludes, this is what Lajtha achieved in this sweet music, written with his feather-light French touch. How warm must have been this secret room of his to produce such clear but gentle illumination.

Recommended Recordings

The Symphonies 1–9 and accompanying orchestral works on Marco Polo are performed by the Pécs Symphony Orchestra, under Nicolás Pasquet. Though a provincial ensemble, the Pécs players seem to have this music in their blood and give gripping performances. It is a pity that Marco Polo seems to have deleted them (physical copies, anyway) from the catalog, but they are available as CD-Rs from Amazon. I suggest exploring them in the following order:

Symphonies 3 and 4; Suite No. 2, Marco Polo 8.223671

Symphonies 5 and 6; *Lysistrata* Overture, Marco Polo 8.223672

Symphony No. 1; *In Memoriam*; *Suite pour Orchestre*, Marco Polo 8.223670

Symphony No. 2; Variations for Orchestra, Marco Polo 8.223669

Symphony No. 7; Suite No. 3; *Hortobagy*, Marco Polo 8.223667

Symphonies 8 and 9, Marco Polo 8.223673

Capriccio (ballet), Marco Polo 8.223668

The Hungarian Chamber Musicians on the Hungaroton releases give exquisite performances of the following:

Marionettes; *Trois Nocturnes*; Harp Quintet No. 2, Hungaroton 31776

Trio for Harp, Flute, and Cello; Trio for Flute, Cello, and Harp; Two Pieces for Flute Solo; *Sonate en concert* for Flute and Piano, Hungaroton 31647. The Auer Quartet's four volumes of the string quartets (and the string trios) and indeed all the Lajtha releases on Hungaroton seem to hurdle toward being out of print, too. Snap them up as you can; if you are a young aspiring string quartet, add them to your repertoire!

Quartets 1, 3, 4, Hungaroton 32542

Quartet No. 2; Piano Quintet, Hungaroton 32545

Quartets 5, 7, 9, Hungaroton 32543

Quartets 6, 8, 10, Hungaroton 32544

String Trios: *Serenade*; *Soirs Transylvains*, Hungaroton 31979. Of the two choral releases on Hungaroton, the Mass is indispensable. Both are performed exquisitely. The Mass is from a live performance.

Missa in Diebus Tribulationis (includes Leó Weiner's *Romance* and György Ránki's *Lament of Jesus*), Kálmán Záborszky, Szent István Király SO & Chorus, Hungaroton 31833

Magnificat; *Three Hymns for the Holy Virgin*; Four Madrigals; String Quartet No. 10, Györ Girl's Choir, Chamber Choir of the Liszt Academy, Tátrai Quartet, Hungaroton 31453

∿

Libby Larsen: The Natural Sound of Music

As I have long asserted, the symphony is not dead, did not die, and is alive and well, even here in America. I submit as evidence the works of Libby Larsen (b. 1950), as engaging a living composer as we have today. Larsen feels that many modern symphonies are "vacuous", which attests to her critical faculties, yet she remains loyal to the form. That loyalty is displayed on three Koch CDs, containing three of her five symphonies. Larsen is not tied strictly to the form, as several of these works could pass for suites or concertos for orchestra. However, the point remains that here is an artist working within traditional forms with traditional means in a fresh manner.

Hailing from Minnesota, Larsen seems to have been somehow immunized by the Midwest from the didactic, ideological struggles that enervated the works of so many coastal composers. She is one of those extraordinary souls who simply writes music, without having felt the obligation to interiorize the crisis of 20th-century music that nearly drove it to its grave. Not having suffered from serialism, she has not had to work her way therapeutically through minimalism as a recovery from it. That means there is something natural about her music. It does not mean that her work is not challenging. It is, but because of the fecundity of her imagination and her vibrancy of expression. When Larsen says "I believe we still have things to say in the symphony", she should be understood within her perspective that the composer's task is "to communicate something about being alive through music". Her works are as bracing an affirmation of life as I have heard in contemporary music.

For instance, I was completely taken in by my first exposure to her work, Symphony: *Water Music* (1984) that shows her deep affinity for nature. "I know that nature speaks to me all the time as I compose", Larsen said in an interview. *Water Music* was written as a salute to Handel's work of the same name on the 300th anniversary of its composition. If this is Handel in the United States, he arrived here via Debussy and has been thoroughly Americanized. This is an exhilarating piece of music that seems to tumble out of itself. It contains a welter of orchestral color and rhythmic snap, with swirling melodic fragments floating upon its flowing surface. *Water Music* is alive, pulsing, demanding to be heard in its sense of urgency. It has a wildly improvisational air, as if the music is being made up as it is being played. It does not seem to have formal characteristics on first hearing. You get the sense you are in for the ride of your life and you had better hang on and see what happens next.

In other words, this is not meditative music. It is music recreating an experience that you can later meditate on. I wrote these words before reading Larsen's statement that "I want to give the listener not the sound of the bird so much as the feeling of flying, not the footsteps on the mountain so such as the sense of climbing." In *Water Music*, as in so many of her other works, she succeeds, in this case with the movements "Fresh Breeze", "Hot, Still", "Wafting", and "Gale".

Though not a symphony, Larsen's tone poem, *Deep Summer Music*, reinforces the merits found in *Water Music*. As her subtitles to *Water Music* indicate, Larsen does not shy away from explicitly describing the pictorial aspects of her work. In fact, she says, "I visualize as I compose." Remarking upon the "sweep of the horizon and depth of color" of the Midwestern plains, she states that "the glory of this phenomenon is particularly evident at harvest time, in the deep summer, when acres of ripened wheat, sunflower, corn, rye and oats blaze with color. In the deep summer, winds create wave after wave of harvest ripeness which, when beheld by the human eye, creates a kind of emotional peace, and awe." Not only does she convey this marvel of nature's abundance, but she specifically places the human observer of it as the solo trumpet, personified as "the presence of the individual amidst the vastness of the landscape". This gorgeous piece also exhibits more of Larsen's lyrical gift in beautiful long-lined melodies.

Melody also sustains Larsen's superbly crafted Symphony No. 4: *String Symphony* (1998), in which she forgoes the richer palette of full orchestra—something in which she usually revels, with bells, chimes, and marimbas. Larsen believes that highly-charged rhythms and percussion instruments are the singular contributions of 20th-century music. This understanding is emphasized in a good deal of her work. Here, however, she seems to take respite in modal harmonies, an almost English kind of pastoralism, and gentle, almost dreamy melodies. Perhaps the *String Symphony* is a reaction to the percussiveness of some of her other music. Here she shows that, for all the motivic fragmentation she favors in her more impressionistic efforts, she too can write the long melodic lines required of truly symphonic works.

Interestingly, the second movement, "Beauty Alone", sounds as if it is based on a variation of a Dies Irae motif. The last movement plays with this same theme but more within Larsen's typical rhythmic preoccupations. In fact, it is called "Ferocious Rhythm", though there is nothing particularly ferocious about it. Just as Benjamin Britten's salutary influence can be heard in the music of Larsen's teacher, Dominick Argento (listen to his stunning Te Deum to see what I mean), so too does the *String Symphony* show traces of Britten's brilliant string writing. This marvelous piece can stand next to the string works of Britten, Tippett, Rorem, and Diamond as a sterling example of its genre.

Larsen's *Lyric Symphony* seems to be ironically titled because it is far less lyrical than the *String Symphony* and does not really bear resemblance to Alexander Zemlinsky's similarly titled work, a gorgeously overripe representation of music. What it does share from the era of the early 20th century are highly chromatic harmonies that bear out Larsen's statement that her "style is not recognized in the consistent use of a harmonic language." In the liner notes to the CD, composer Russell Platt writes that "harmonically the whole thing sounds like Gershwin queerly tainted by Berg." This is a darker-hued work with the sense of disorientation and anxiety that heavily chromatic harmonies can convey. I do love how, partway into the first movement, Larsen temporarily dispels the anxiety with a huge upswelling in the deep brass that sounds like something out of Lester Trimble's great Symphony No. 3.

Parts of this work, especially the second movement, invite the question of how far Larsen can go on her harmonic and rhythmic strengths alone. In the "Quiet" movement, the answer is pretty far. She achieves an intriguing impression of stasis. Yet one is always waiting to see when, or if, she is going to resolve things in a full-blown melody. She usually does, and the expectation she sets up is part of the dramatic suspense that keeps one riveted. However, this does not always work. In the last part of the *Lyric Symphony*, Larsen seems to rely too much on punchy, percussive rhythms. They become fatiguing. However, if Larsen's rambunctiousness occasionally gets the better of her, I say: Oh, *felix culpa*! Look at what her sense of adventure has accomplished.

I have only briefly mentioned Larsen's educational pedigree—principally that she studied with one of the relatively unsung heroes of Amer-

ican music, Dominick Argento. An equally decisive impact seems to
have been Sister Colette, one of the St. Joseph nuns at Christ the
King School in Minneapolis. Larsen writes that "Sister Colette was
extraordinary in the kinds of repertoire she gave me. I played very
unusual repertoire—Mozart, Bartók, Stravinsky, Japanese music and
boogie right away. That variety was very important in introducing so
many different musical sounds and colors to me." Larsen's easy mastery of musical idioms reminds me of Peter Schickele. Equally important, in the pre–Vatican II era in which Larsen's grade school studies
took place, the students of Christ the King learned to read and to sing
Gregorian chant, starting in the first grade. Thus, says Larsen, "I became fascinated with rhythm through a natural grounding in Chant."
She laments the loss of this resource, and so should we. Maybe that is
where the natural sound of Larsen's music comes from.

Recommended Recordings

Symphony: *Water Music* (1984); Overture: *Parachute Dancing* (1983); *Ring of Fire*; Symphony No. 3: *Lyric* (1995), Joel Revzen, London SO, Koch 7370

Symphony No. 4, *String Symphony* (1998); *Songs of Light and Love* (1998); *Songs from Letters* (1999), Joel Revzen, Scottish CO, Koch 7481

Deep Summer Music (1983); Solo Symphony (1999); Marimba Concerto: *After Hampton* (1992), Maria Alsop, Colorado SO, Koch 7520

∼

Morten Lauridsen: *Shining Night*

Morten Lauridsen, the most frequently performed American choral composer, received the 2007 National Medal of Arts—the highest award given to artists by the United States government—"for his composition of radiant choral works combining musical beauty, power, and spiritual depth". In 2012, he came to Washington, D.C., for the local premiere of the documentary film *Shining Night*, which Michael Stillwater had made about him. The title comes from the text of the James Agee poem "Sure on This Shining Night", which Lauridsen exquisitely set for chorus and piano. What I saw—and heard—left me deeply moved.

I already knew that Lauridsen was articulate because I had interviewed him by phone some years before about the stunningly beautiful Hyperion CD of his *Lux Aeterna*; *Ubi Caritas et Amor*; and other choral works. When he wrote this piece in 1997, Lauridsen was facing his mother's impending death. He told me, "I purposely chose those texts that had the recurring symbol of light." *Lux Aeterna* is not a liturgical work, strictly speaking, but it is sacred in sound because beauty of this sort is sacramental. In style, Lauridsen was inspired by Renaissance master Josquin des Prez. He not only draws upon Renaissance forms, he remains true to them, albeit with some modern harmonies. "I did try to create a very beautiful piece", he said. "We try to get to that point beyond words." He has done so in a work whose serenity and tenderness bring to mind the spirit of Maurice Duruflé's equally consoling Requiem.

Also on this CD is an exquisitely beautiful and moving *Ave Maria*. I have seldom encountered anything so suffused with love for Mary. When I asked Lauridsen, a Protestant, about this, he responded, "I don't have to belong to the Catholic Church to be in love with Mary." Sometime later, Lauridsen sent me the original manuscript sketch of the opening measures of *Ave Maria*, because the composer knew how much I love the work. The preciousness of this gift goes without saying. There is another recording of this and *Lux Aeterna*, on the RCM label (1970s), with the 60-voice Los Angeles Master Chorale, under Paul Salamunovich. The acoustic is too reverberant to hear all the details in the *Ave Maria*, but the *Lux* is performed with special ardor.

In the *Wall Street Journal*, Lauridsen explained what he was trying to achieve in his sublime choral work *O Magnum Mysterium*, also contained on the Hyperion and RCM CDs. "In composing music to these inspirational words about Christ's birth and the veneration of the Virgin Mary," he said, "I sought to impart . . . a transforming spiritual experience within what I call 'a quiet song of profound inner joy'. I wanted this piece to resonate immediately and deeply into the core of the listener, to *illumine* through sound." St. Augustine said, *Cantare amantis est*, "To sing is characteristic of the one who loves", or in Josef Pieper's translation, "Only the lover sings." If you want to *hear* what St. Augustine meant, you should listen to this radiant music.

You also might—no, must—see *Shining Night*. At the Washington premiere, I had the pleasure of meeting the filmmaker, Michael Stillwater. In every great work of art, there is stillness at its center. Stillwater captures this in the breathtaking natural beauty of the Northwest, where Lauridsen keeps a home on Waldron Island, and in Lauridsen's music, and he shows us the relationship between the two. Lauridsen says, "Life is a mystery. There is something bigger than us out there. And how do we tap into that? You go down deep, and this island especially provides me the opportunity to get there." The marvel of Stillwater's film is that he lets us take this journey with Lauridsen.

Lauridsen is an articulate but not loquacious man. When he has nothing to say, he remains silent. Stillwater's camera does not shy away from this. It remains still with him. It is not an empty stillness. The silence, in fact, is as expressive as the speech. There are lovely moments of introspection and peace captured here. There are also wonderful scenes, away from Waldron, of the music being performed by various groups here and in Europe.

After the premiere, Stillwater asked me if we could get together and discuss Morten's music. He came to my home with his camera. We walked into the forest across the street and, for a supplement to the documentary, he asked me to comment on film about Lauridsen's compositions. This was a real privilege to serve the beauty I had seen and heard. Here is what I said:

Morten Lauridsen as a composer is aiming at the highest goal of art, which is to make the transcendent perceptible. That is communicated so movingly in his music, and one immediately senses a stillness in the man. One already knows the stillness from his music and, in Michael Stillwater's extraordinary film, that stillness is exquisitely captured in the beauty of the surroundings of his music and in the man himself. His music is worthy of the preceding silence because it knows that the silence is not a form of emptiness, but that it is gestational. It's full. And when one is immersed in it, you create basically the sound of that silence. That is when music is at its most beautiful, and when it touches upon the permanent things, when it touches upon eternity, and that is what he has achieved in his remarkable music.

There is another feature about his music. It deals with profound loss, and we know from what he himself has said that *Lux Aeterna* was written as his mother was dying. Now, what Morten has been able to do is not simply experience loss as a terrible, terrible emptiness. He puts it in context of the meaning of the loss—that life, though it passes, is redeemable: that, in fact, it finally isn't a loss. And that is why there is a trail in his music, both in the forms and the languages he employs, going back to Renaissance and medieval music that is traditional, but also with some modern harmonies. So nothing is lost in his music itself, which is, in part, about the recovery from loss and what the true meaning of the loss is in that context of redemption. So this is also music very expressive of a very profound and deep faith. I don't think he could touch upon eternity in the way he does, I don't think he could make the transcendent perceptible in the way he does, without that ground of faith in him. And it speaks to people, not in any sectarian way, though he is using some Latin texts—it just goes right to the soul.

Lauridsen also has a secular side, on exhibit on a Hyperion CD, which contains his *Mid-Winter Songs* (Robert Graves), *Les Chansons des roses* (Rainer Maria Rilke), and *Nocturnes*, along with a few shorter religious pieces. In these secular works, Lauridsen writes spirited, dramatic music, tinged with the influence of Benjamin Britten's brilliant choral music and song settings. Things simply do not get lovelier than the last two songs of *Les Chansons*—"La rose complète" and "Dirait-on"—except perhaps on the less secular side, with the exquisite Ave, Dulcissima Maria, which is redolent of Lauridsen's sublime Ave Maria. Polyphony sings brilliantly with the Britten Sinfonia, under Stephen Layton. I know the composer was thrilled with this performance, because he told me so from London. You will be, too.

Lauridsen and his music (and Stillwater's film) remind me of Igor Stravinsky's remark that "the stained glass artist of Chartres had few colors, and the stained glass artists of today have hundreds of colors, but no Chartres. Not enlarged resources then, but men and what they believe." Of course you need skill as a composer and a filmmaker (though, startlingly, given its level of accomplishment, this is Stillwater's first film). You need to master your craft, but what you believe is decisive. Who would imagine that in the Los Angeles of today, where Lauridsen teaches, someone would have the faith to paint in the colors of Chartres, or that an American filmmaker would have sensitivity to capture those colors on film? As Lauridsen, says, "There are too many things out there that are away from goodness. We need to focus on those things that ennoble us, that enrich us." If you are open to this kind of beauty, here it is.

Recommended Recordings

Lux aeterna; *Ubi Caritas et Amor*; *Ave Maria*; *O magnum mysterium*; Madrigali, Stephen Layton, Polyphony, Hyperion 67449

Lux aeterna; *Les Chansons des roses*; *Ave Maria*; *Mid-Winter Songs*; *O Magnum Mysterium*, Paul Salamunovich, Los Angeles Master Chorale, RCM 19705

Nocturnes; *Mid-Winter Songs*; *Ave, Dulcissima Maria* et al., Stephen Layton, Polyphony, Hyperion 67580

Sure on This Shining Night; *Canticle: O Vos Omnes*, Nocturnes et al., Mark Singleton, Voce Chamber Artists, CDBaby 29719

Shining Night: A Portrait of Composer Morten Lauridsen, Michael Stillwater, Hänssler DVD 98046

∽

Jonathan Leshnoff: Reinvigorating Past Forms

What I admire about the Naxos American Classics series is that it is not all classics. It is not only restorative, returning great but neglected works to us by past American masters, but exploratory. Naxos is not afraid to gamble on younger, relatively unknown American composers. Who, for instance, is Jonathan Leshnoff (b. 1973), to whose music Naxos has already dedicated three releases? I became intensely interested in the answer to this question after repeated hearings of his Violin Concerto; *Distant Reflections*; and String Quartet No. 1.

I was impressed by Leshnoff's vivid imagination and sophisticated ear for sonorities and the soaring lyricism and passion of his music. These works have immediate appeal, but the attraction strengthens with further acquaintance because the music has an underlying introspective character of real depth. The *Baltimore Sun* (February 11, 2006) suggested that, despite his originality, Leshnoff "seems to be channeling, say, Samuel Barber" in the Violin Concerto. I saw, or rather heard, the point but more in respect to the "Autumn" movement of the String Quartet, which is reminiscent of Barber in his meltingly lovely Adagio, and perhaps to the mesmerizing *Distant Reflections*, a 10-minute piece for off-stage string quartet, on-stage violinist, pianist, and strings. But what struck me in the Violin Concerto was what sounded like the clear and laudable influence of the music of my late friend Stephen Albert, one of the champions of the return of tonality and melody in American music. The very beginning of the piece sounds like a quintessential Albert declamatory moment in both its theme and orchestration.

The impression was so strong that I decided to pursue it. By e-mail, I found Leshnoff at Towson University in Maryland, where he is a professor of music. He also serves as composer-in-residence with the Baltimore Chamber Orchestra. He was delighted by my query, and a series of interesting exchanges ensued. He said:

> Albert's influence is very present in my music. I met him when he came to guest lecture at Peabody when I was a freshman there (1992). Immediately, I was taken by his music. He died the next year. Since then, I have studied and analyzed many of his works and have tried to

reconstruct his harmonic theories. I have annotated scores of Albert's major works in my office, and I can go on for hours about "things" I find him doing. If I were to describe my direct relation to Albert, it would be in the realm of his harmonic ideas. I think I am constructing a harmonic language that is distinct, but I credit Albert as my inspiration and launching point.

It is quite extraordinary that the impact of Albert's music could be so profound on someone who did not have the opportunity to study with him. Leshnoff is self-taught in Albert.

I sent Leshnoff some things I had written about modern music and about Albert's teacher George Rochberg. I spoke of the seminal breakthrough these composers made in releasing the stranglehold of Schoenberg's dodecaphony and of the courage that it took. Leshnoff responded, "Though Rochberg paved the way, it still gets lonely and every once in a while I need to be around 'friends'. Reading what you write, it seems that Rochberg, Albert, you and I are all of the same ilk—though it was the former who made it possible for me to be me without the pain they went through swimming upstream." I found that remark very touching and a wonderful tribute to what Rochberg and Albert, both heroes to me, made possible for others. In 2013, Leshnoff told *Fanfare* magazine, "I don't feel that newness in composition has to be experimental. It doesn't have to be a process of abandonment, which it has been in past decades. I believe that there is creativity and newness in reinvigorating the age-old beloved techniques of counterpoint, harmony, line, form, and orchestration." Speaking of Bach, he wondered, "How someone could be so consigned to rules but so absolutely and utterly creative? That's the battle cry of reinvigorating the past forms." In addition to which, he said, "I have to write after my heart."

Back to the Violin Concerto, what we hear in the Naxos CD is a 2007 revision of Leshnoff's original 2005 work. Completely new is the fifth movement, Elegy, which is deeply affecting and exquisitely beautiful. So is the second movement, marked "Slow". I remember David Diamond, another great American composer whom Leshnoff calls to mind, saying that "you must develop the long line in your music, try to write very long melodies. . . . There must be radiant melody and urgency of rhythmic impulse." Here is where Leshnoff excels. It is hard to think of a recent work that can compare to the length of his melodic lines in this concerto, or to their radiant beauty. He is also, like Albert, rhythmically and sonically alive. These long lines are set within glimmering orchestration. His use of the piano in its lower registers to function as a kind of musical undercurrent reminds me of Albert, as does his opening brass declamation in the first movement.

I did not read the CD liner notes until after listening to the Concerto several times. I am glad that I did not. Part of Leshnoff's inspiration for this work comes from a World War II tragedy—the awareness of which it might be best not to have in mind if you want to experience the music without the freight of any outside association. That said, violinist Charles Wetherbee plays as if for his life in a very exciting and deeply touching performance, ably supported by the Baltimore Chamber Orchestra under conductor Markand Thakar.

The String Quartet No. 1 is very attractively and imaginatively divided among the four seasons. I have already remarked upon the Barber-like beauty of the "Autumn" movement. This is a very engaging work, which receives a fine performance from the Carpe Diem String Quartet.

The second Naxos CD of Leshnoff's music contains his First Symphony; Double Concerto for Violin, Viola, and Orchestra and *Rush*, an orchestral opener, conducted by Michael Stern and the IRIS Orchestra. Leshnoff's works especially feature the yearning, nostalgia, and striving in American music, exquisitely expressed with gorgeous melodic lines. In his new CD, he intertwines two such lines in the Double Concerto for Violin, Viola, and Orchestra. The viola and violin partner and play off each other in this shimmering, radiant music. I detect the influence of Albert's works also in this piece, along with an almost Bernard Herrmann–like emotional undertow. It is the undertow effect that adds such poignancy to the upward striving of the soloists. Like his superb Violin Concerto, the Double Concerto should become a repertory item.

It is joined by Symphony No. 1: *Forgotten Chants and Refrains*, which enticingly explores the past using some quotes from 17th-century Jewish composer Salomon Rossi, excerpts from a Guillaume Dufay Mass, and Gregorian chant. As you might imagine from these sources, the symphony at times has a liturgical feel to it. It also has what sounds like a variation from the Requiem theme. In all, it is a reflective, though at times lively piece. The themes the trombones play may be from Gregorian chant, but they sound like something out of the exotic world of Alan Hovhaness.

The third Naxos release contains chamber music. Leshnoff's String Quartet No. 2, subtitled *Edelman*, is a lovely little work (only 13 minutes long) meant to portray a couple in honor of their 50th wedding anniversary. The first movement opens with a descending motif rippling through the four instruments from violin down to the cello, then picked up individually and varied. The theme, it turns out, is based on a chant Dr. Edelman sings on Sabbath evenings. The descending theme is counterpoised with an equally attractive ascending one. The second movement portrays Mrs. Edelman with a flowing, tender melody. The third movement is rhythmically energetic and jubilant in spirit. *Seven Glances at a Mirage* is an intriguing set of variations for violin, clarinet and piano. Though tightly organized around a main theme, this 12-minute piece contains a great deal of variety provided by Leshnoff's thorough exploitation of the properties of each of the three instruments. In style, it is the least romantic of the pieces on this CD. *Cosmic Variations on a Haunted Theme* is a mesmerizing set of nine variations on two themes for piano trio. Leshnoff knows how to use silence and the sparseness of a single instrument set against it to express a mysterious stillness. He can also get explosions of energy from the three massed instruments—once again, providing a broad range of expression.

Leshnoff has also composed choral music, including *Requiem for the Fallen*, "a piece dedicated to civilian and military lives lost in recent wars". He finished a Flute Concerto for the Philadelphia Orchestra in 2011. He now has to his credit four string quartets, two oratorios, seven concerti, trios, a string sextet, and numerous solo and chamber works. Current projects include a second symphony, a guitar concerto, and a clarinet concerto.

Leshnoff said to me, "I'm far from a Stephen Albert." I am not so sure. From what I have heard so far, the distance is not all that great. Plus, he has no need to be another Albert. What he has obviously caught from him is passion, brilliant orchestral colors, long-lined melodies, complete accessibility, and a deeply expressive romantic vein. But Leshnoff is his own man in *what* he is expressing, and that is as openheartedly and as touchingly conveyed as music can. This young composer has already created a substantial body of work and, if past is prelude, has a great future in front of him.

Recommended Recordings

Violin Concerto; *Distant Reflections*; String Quartet No. 1, Markand Thakar, Charles Wetherbee, Baltimore CO, Carpe Diem String Quartet, Naxos 8.559398

Symphony No. 1; Double Concerto; *Rush*, Michael Stern, IRIS Orchestra, et al., Naxos 8.559670

String Quartet No. 2; *Seven Glances at a Mirage*; *Cosmic Variations on a Haunted Theme . . . without a chance*, Carpe Diem String Quartet, Naxos 8.559721

∿

Lowell Liebermann et al.: Keeping America Real

Many people view America as the new Rome. Americans are builders and organizers, practical people who, when in need of culture, borrow from Europe—just as Rome borrowed from Greece. Of course, there is truth in this comparison, but it has its limits. It is precisely the practical nature of the American people that insulated the United States from the ideological ravages of Europe and made the continuation of art possible here.

In the 20th century, Europe largely destroyed its culture, which is why so many of its artists and intellectuals fled to America. When philosopher Eric Voegelin left Nazi Germany in 1938, he was in a state of despair over the fate of the West. In the United States, however, he saw that the practicality of the American people was rooted in experience, in an acceptance of reality that was not filtered through ideological lenses. He took hope. In American music, we can hear what he saw. In terms of music, this meant the retention of melody, harmony, and rhythm in the works of some of our major composers.

Though for one painful generation many composers abandoned these essential elements, American music recovered from the loss more quickly than did European music. Despite its temporary allure, the ideology of Arnold Schoenberg, which was supposed to ensure the supremacy of German music for another 100 years, passed through America's bloodstream without inflicting permanent damage because it was alien to our practical nature.

From the beginning, America's sense of realism immunized a number of American composers against Schoenberg's ideology. Samuel Barber and certain others who never forsook music as a medium for beauty left a living legacy that is now being cultivated by our contemporaries. This is abundantly clear in releases of recent American music by Lowell Liebermann (b. 1961) and others.

An uninhibited generosity of spirit characterizes Liebermann's music. In his Symphony No. 2, available on a Delos CD, he displays a talent for soaring melody that takes one's breath away. Unlike some others, he did not have to find his way back to tonality. He was firmly rooted in it by his studies at Juilliard with David Diamond, perhaps America's greatest symphonist.

Stylistically, the work is situated somewhere between Vaughan Williams' First Symphony and a Mahler symphony, with some Berlioz added for good measure. The fact that the score of this work could have been recovered from a 75-year-old time capsule will either delight or puzzle you. Why, you may wonder, did this young man write in such a reactionary style? I can only answer that the work does not display any signs of being self-consciously reactionary. It appears to be the product of real conviction. The proof is that it achieves a sweeping grandeur that is hard to resist.

Liebermann's Second Symphony is a choral work that invites comparison to Beethoven's Ninth. Liebermann plays with that allusion in the closing movement's choral fugue and the hammered chords that end the work. But it is not only the Walt Whitman text that he chooses to set that reminds one of Vaughan Williams' *Sea Symphony* (also set to a Whitman text), it is also the billowing surges of music that culminate in a rhapsodic invocation of natural wonder. (In both cases, I object only to the puerile pantheism of Whitman's poetry, which can be avoided by ignoring the words.)

The second movement is an orchestral march of the martial character favored by Mahler and Shostakovich, but without the former's neuroses or the latter's sarcasm. The third movement, Largo, returns to Liebermann's opening theme in a reflective, moving way before a joyous, choral finale brings the work to a magnificent conclusion. Whatever one makes of the atavistic tendencies in Liebermann's work, there is no denying its quality, extraordinary craft, and memorability.

The symphony is accompanied on the Delos disc by a very fine, gloriously melodic Flute Concerto, the musical touchstone for which is Prokofiev. After the first movement, which could have come out of Prokofiev's *Romeo and Juliet* ballet, Liebermann turns to a style more akin to his Second Symphony. Both works were recorded in live concerts given by the Dallas Symphony Orchestra under Andrew Litton. The audience is inaudible, but the excitement is not. The recording is spectacular.

There is a somewhat softer, more languid performance of the Flute Concerto by the flutist to whom it was dedicated, James Galway, who plays it mellifluously with the London Mozart Players conducted by Liebermann himself. This RCA Victor CD also features the almost even more attractive Concerto for Piccolo and Orchestra, in whose finale Liebermann, in a *jeu d'esprit*, quotes from Mozart's Symphony

No. 40, Beethoven's *Eroica*, Sousa's *The Stars and Stripes Forever*, and the Concerto for Flute, Harp, and Orchestra.

We also have an array of Liebermann's chamber music on several CDs from Albany Records, Koch, and Artek. The first contains Piano Trios 1 and 2, the Concerto for Violin, Piano, and String Quartet; and *Two Pieces for Violin and Viola*. Liebermann's more conservative idiom, which shows French influence along with Shostakovich's, is highly rhapsodic, gorgeously melodic, and dramatically charged. The appeal is undiminished by the fact that much of it could have been written a hundred years ago. Liebermann is clearly a romantic. There is poignancy both in his music and in the fact that he would continue to write works like this. I think that Stephen Hough, the pianist who plays Liebermann's Piano Concertos 1 and 2 so brilliantly on the Hyperion label, gets it exactly right when he writes, "Unlike the reactionary who looks backward *at* tradition, Liebermann looks forward *with* tradition, confidently employing modern techniques alongside materials of the past with a refreshing lack of self-consciousness or anxiety."

The Koch CD contains the Quintet for Piano, Clarinet and String Trio, Six Songs, and the Quintet for Piano and Strings. I find both a marvelous delicacy that is almost Mozartian in its refinement and an underlying energy in this highly lyrical music. Particularly irresistible are his slow movements—the Largo in the Clarinet Quintet and the Adagio in the Piano Quintet. Liebermann often deploys a long piano line of Schubert-like beauty with skittering strings under and around it; then the strings pick up the melody with a shimmering piano ostinato underneath. The question as to whether Liebermann's style is out-of-date simply vanishes with music of this quality. The performances are superb, enhanced by the glittering playing of pianist David Korevaar. The Trio Fedele plays Liebermann's Trios 1 and 2 for Flute, Cello, and Piano, along with the Sonata for Flute and Piano on the Artek CD. These works also possess a lucidity that is Mozartian but with a strong French flavor (Ravel).

Liebermann is not the only one keeping America real. There are others. The Centaur label has introduced the music of Charles Roland Berry (b. 1957), an American composer originally from Michigan, with his Symphony No. 3 and his Cello Concerto. On his web site, Berry puts forth an artistic credo that could be the manifesto of realism in American music:

To me, the audience should be the arbiter of artistic accomplishment. . . . They are the ones for whom my music is intended. I hope
to reach their ears by providing enough common ground between
what they already enjoy (the Masters of the Past) and what I need to
say. I choose not to write music in languages only understandable to
other composers. I feel free to use any musical elements which provide emotional impact and communicate effectively. I consider each
element with care: Form, Melody, Harmony, Orchestration, Rhythm,
Texture. I do my best to balance the elements against each other, so
that one element does not over-ride all the others. I like a good tune.
Lyrical lines, or lines with memorable rhythms, attract me.

They will attract you, too, in these very beautiful works, which have
a pervasive Dvořák-like emotional warmth. The appeal is immediate
in the singing, somewhat breezy character of the Cello Concerto, endowed with an American spirit of openness and optimism. The sweet,
lovely melodies clearly come straight from Berry's heart and will go
straight to yours. This is a man who does not care for modern schools
of composition. He writes it as he feels it. I cannot think of when I have
heard contemporary works of music that are as big-hearted as these.
Berry describes the prevailing mood of Symphony No. 3 as "calm and
optimistic", but it is also exuberant and permeated with joy.

A student of George Rochberg (see Rochberg chapter, p. 274 and
interview, p. 483), Stephen Jaffe (b. 1954) said:

Pieces like Rochberg's Third String Quartet and Crumb's *Ancient
Voices of Children* opened up lots of territory. It allowed for a composer
to speak in a way that was broad, where you could partake of different
kinds of experience from the total musical world we live in: some are
informal, down-to-earth, while some are intense and uplifting. . . .
I've tried to follow up after their revolution and speak a musical language that is broad, but I want to speak it eloquently [in a way that
is] cut of the same cloth.

So what has this allowed him to do? The answer is in Jaffe's Violin Concerto, offered on Bridge Records, and it is a knockout. The
sweetly lyrical opening line in the violin is assaulted by some orchestral
outbursts that challenge it. By rising to the occasion, the violin engages
the orchestra and gets it reluctantly to sing and dance along. This is a
highly imaginative, rhythmically alive, and finally ecstatic work. The
Odense Symphony Orchestra, under William Purvis, gives an exciting

performance, that is immeasurably helped by the extraordinary artistry of the great American violinist Gregory Fulkerson, who has done so much during his career to advance new American music.

Ellen Taaffe Zwilich (b. 1939) is a composer whom I have always tried to like. She has written a number of well-crafted symphonies and concertos that somehow do not remain in memory. I seldom revisit them. Not so her Violin Concerto (1998), which is a real American classic that should enter the regular repertory. Like her other works, it inhabits the traditional world of tonality, but seems imbued with a higher level of imagination and energy. I have listened a dozen times and will go back for more. Zwilich seamlessly integrates a line from Bach's great *Chaconne* for solo violin into a kind of blues riff in the wonderful, haunting second movement. I will not soon forget this very appealing work, performed on Naxos by violinist Pamela Frank, and the Saarbrücken Radio Symphony Orchestra under Michael Stern, in a stunning live recording.

French impressionism is alive and well in America today in the chamber music of Daniel Godfrey (b. 1949). His String Quartets 2 and 3, along with *Romanza* (from String Quartet No. 1), have real sensual warmth, with a touch of the sensibility of Schoenberg's *Transfigured Night* and of the ardent spiritual yearning of Pēteris Vasks. These very touching works are completely tonal and basically pick up from the point where music was derailed some four score years ago. Like most composers his age, Godfrey was raised with 12-tone music and dabbled in Webern. I would love to learn the story of his embrace of tonality, which is so complete and convincing that it sounds completely unselfconscious. It is remarkable that music like this is being written, recorded, and widely celebrated. The Cassatt String Quartet give deeply committed performances on this singular Koch Classics release. Koch also released a recording of seven compositions under the title *Wrinkled Moon*, played by members of the St. Paul Chamber Orchestra in various combinations, also including piano solo in *Festoons*. As I detected in his fine quartets, Godfrey is also a musical Francophile, all to good effect. Even when the source of his inspiration is Russian, as in the folk material in *From a Dream of Russia*, the accent remains French. This is finely jeweled, attractively subtle, reflective music.

Another enterprising American Classics CD from Naxos contains String Quartets 1, 5, and 6 by Benjamin Lees (1924–2010), rivetingly performed by the Cypress String Quartet. I do not know much about this man's music, which is why I am so deeply grateful to Naxos for the introduction. Now I want to know more. These are extraordinary, deeply thoughtful, intellectually intriguing, intense chamber works that so fit their medium that they seem quintessential. I am not at all surprised that Chamber Music America chose Quartet No. 5 as one of the 101 Great Ensemble Works. If you have made it past the Britten and Shostakovich quartets, here are works that will fully engage you. Lees does not offer sensuous surface appeal, but the depth is there. The latter two quartets were written in the 21st century. Obviously, Lees was working full steam ahead at the top of his game when he wrote them.

I also need to mention that Toccata Classics has released a CD of Lees' piano music, played with a combination of steel fingers and delicacy of touch by Mirian Conti. This music displays a high level of imagination and a sense of mischief. On a personal note, I was delighted to read that the second of the three *Odyssey* pieces played here was commissioned by the U.S. Information Agency in 1986. That happened to be from the Artistic Ambassadors Program, which, with its founder, pianist John Robilette, I helped begin in 1982. Although I left USIA in late 1983, how nice it is to see—or, rather, to hear—the exceptional fruit it bore.

Nothing could sound more American than Stephen Hartke's Clarinet Concerto. This jazzy, highly syncopated work is dominated by infectious rhythms. It is subtitled *Landscapes with Blues* and beautifully captures the spirit of the blues without musically condescending to it, a kind of 21st-century Gershwin. Hartke gives this and the other works on a new Naxos release finely grained textures that display an ear for subtle detail. This is a composer to watch. He must be very pleased by clarinetist Richard Stoltzman's fabulous performance, as well as by the IRIS Chamber Orchestra, under Michael Stern.

Daron Hagen (b. 1961) also has a very heartfelt quality in his Piano Trio No. 3: *Wayfaring Stranger* (2006), which is based on the hymn *Poor Wayfaring Stranger*. Until I read the Naxos program notes, I had not known that this work was written in memory of his brother. It is very touching and directly affecting. Anyone who thinks that modern American composers do not write music that, without condescending to any sloppy emotions, goes straight to the heart should listen to this work. The equally attractive Piano Trio No. 4: *Angel Band* (2007) is also based on a hymn and has a strong Appalachian feel to it. It, too, is very moving and, at times, ecstatic. The earlier two piano trios on this CD, Nos. 1 and 2, are more angular, acerbic, and modern sounding, at least in part, with less direct appeal, though filled with obvious promise. The Finisterra Trio delivers what sound like definitive performances. There is a real joy of discovery here.

Dan Welcher's String Quartets 1–3, also on a Naxos CD, are beautifully performed by the Cassatt String Quartet. These superb works reinforce my conviction that chamber music is thriving in the United States. Ken Fuchs, Daniel Godfrey, Jonathan Leshnoff, Steven Gerber, Paul Moravec, George Tsontakis, and Jennifer Higdon are other composers who immediately spring to mind, along with Lees and Welcher. Welcher's Third Quartet, subtitled *Cassatt*, was written for the eponymous quartet and inspired by Mary Cassatt's paintings. This music has a most welcome sense of playfulness, as in its references to Ravel and Falla in the first movement and in its treatment of the melody of the "Soldier's Chorus" from Gounod's Faust in the second. The meltingly lovely third movement, according to the composer, "is all about melody. . . . There is no angst, no choppy rhythms, just ever-unfolding melody and lush harmonies." It quotes from Debussy and, like Cassatt's paintings, is imbued with a French spirit. All three Welcher quartets are extremely well crafted. The Second, *Harbor Music*, shares in the impressionistic perspective of the Third. The First is cut from a different cloth; it is more angular and acerbic but never, even in its angry moments, off-putting.

The next steps for American music may not be entirely discernible from listening to these works, but it appears there is a future for keeping American beauty real.

Recommended Recordings

Lowell Liebermann

Symphony No. 2; Flute Concerto, Andrew Litton, Dallas SO, Delos 3256

James Galway plays Lowell Liebermann: Concerto for Piccolo and Orchestra; Concerto for Flute, Harp and Orchestra; Concerto for Flute and Orchestra, Lowell Liebermann, James Galway, London Mozart Players, RCA Victor Red Seal 63235

Piano Concertos 1 & 2, Lowell Liebermann, Stephen Hugh, BBC Scottish SO, Hyperion 66966

Piano Trios 1 & 2; Concerto for Violin, Piano and String Quartet; and *Two Pieces for Violin and Viola*, Ying String Quartet, et al., Albany 684

Quintet for Piano, Clarinet and String Trio; Six Songs; Quintet for Piano and Strings, David Karevaar, Jan Manasse, et al., Koch 7743

Trios 1 & 2 for Flute, Cello and Piano; Sonata for Flute and Piano, Trio Fedele, Artek 0034

Charles Roland Berry

Symphony No. 3 & Cello Concerto, Theodore Kuchar, Gabriel Faur, Janáček PO, Centaur 2898

Stephen Jaffe

Violin Concerto; Chamber Concerto, *Singing Figures*, Donald Palma, Gregory Fulkerson, Odense SO, Bridge 9141

Ellen Taaffe Zwilich

Violin Concerto; *Rituals*, Michael Stern, Pamela Frank, Saarbrücken RSO, IRIS CO, Naxos 8.559268

Daniel Godfrey

String Quartets 2 & 3; *Romanza*, Cassatt String Quartet, Koch 7573

Wrinkled Moon, Adrienne Kim et al., Koch 7679

Stephen Hartke

Clarinet Concerto, Michael Stern, Richard Stoltzman, IRIS CO, Naxos 8.559201

Benjamin Lees

String Quartets 1, 5, & 6, Cypress String Quartet, Naxos 8.559628

Toccata for Piano; Sonata Breve; *Odyssey*; *Ornamental Etudes* for Piano, Toccata Classics 0069

Daron Hagen

Piano Trio No. 3; *Wayfaring Stranger*; Piano Trio No. 4: *Angel Band*, Finisterra Trio, Naxos 8.559657

Dan Welcher

String Quartets 1−3, Cassatt String Quartet, Naxos 8.559384

Gian Francesco Malipiero: Beyond Italian Opera

Italian music is so synonymous with opera that most music lovers would be hard put to think of any Italian orchestral or chamber music from the last two centuries. The one exception may be the music of Ottorino Respighi, especially his highly colorful trilogy of tone poems: *Fountains of Rome*, *Pines of Rome*, and *Roman Festivals*. Respighi and a group of his contemporaries rebelled against the hegemony and conventions of *verismo* opera, the realist late-romantic opera of their time. These composers, all born around 1880, came to be known as the *generazione dell'Ottanta*. They turned to Italian preclassical instrumental and vocal music for inspiration. Their number included Ildebrando Pizzetti (1880–1968), Alfredo Casella (1883–1947), and Gian Francesco Malipiero (1882–1973).

Verismo opera was not their only problem. Italian instrumental music, after having been a leading influence from the Renaissance through the mid-18th century, was eclipsed by developments in the German-speaking world. From Haydn onward, the symphony, with its dramatic sonata-allegro form, reigned supreme. Rejecting this Austro-German domination, these Italian composers looked back as far as the 16th century to musical traditions in their own country, and to contemporary France and Russia where alternatives to German-style symphonic thinking had been explored by such composers as Claude Debussy and Igor Stravinsky.

Among the *generazione dell'Ottanta*, the most original and productive composer was Malipiero. He felt that verismo opera, "with its wallpaper scenery, [was] an ephemeral digression which could never thwart the musical revival of a country with a glorious past". As a musicologist, Malipiero did much to revive that past by editing the works of Monteverdi, Vivaldi, Lotti, and Marcello. As a composer, he produced such a profusion of instrumental and orchestral works as to almost make up for an entire century's omission. Of modern composers, very few, like Darius Milhaud and Heitor Villa-Lobos, rival him in sheer output. As in any large body of work, the quality varies. Nonetheless, Luigi Dallapiccola, the most noted Italian composer of the next generation, proclaimed that Malipiero, and not he, was the greatest Italian composer of his day. According to Dallapiccola, Malipiero was "the most important [musical] personality that Italy has had since the death of Verdi".

The great American composer David Diamond told me that during his many years in Italy the only sympathetic voice was that of Malipiero. Malipiero counseled him: "Don't you worry for one moment. Your day is coming. I waited a long time and my day has come and gone. You will have a great, great public one day." Malipiero was right about Diamond but wrong about himself. His day may have come and gone, but as with most composers of real worth, his day has dawned anew. Thanks to the enterprising Naxos label, all of Malipiero's symphonies have been recorded, and as Diamond said, "They are marvelous works." Malipiero's complete string quartets are also available in stunning performances by the Orpheus String Quartet originally on ASV, but now reissued on Brilliant Classics. My strong impression from having listened to the quartets is that, if Leoš Janáček had been an Italian educated by Claude Debussy, this is sort of what you would hear. Debussy's influence is especially evident in Malipiero's harmonic palette. Like Janáček, Malipiero seems to have made up the rules as he went along in a seemingly spontaneous, improvisatory manner that is directly communicative.

Music poured out of Malipiero. In 1912, impatient to get on with things, he entered five works, each under a different pseudonym, in a competition held by the Academy of St. Cecilia in Rome. He gained instant notoriety by winning four of the five prizes. In 1913, Malipiero traveled to Paris where a galvanizing encounter with Stravinsky's *The Rite of Spring* led him to renounce almost all of his early works and begin again. The experience woke him, he said, "from a long and dangerous lethargy". In Paris he also became acquainted with Casella, with whom he was to work closely in promoting new Italian music.

While *The Rite of Spring* left a powerful impression, what seemed to influence Malipiero even more was Stravinsky's neoclassical style, in which Stravinsky turned to composers such as Pergolesi in his delightful 1919 *Pulcinella Suite*. Malipiero did something similar with his *Vivaldiana*, Casella with his *Scarlattiana*, and Respighi with *The Birds* (using Rameau and Pasquini). In any case, Malipiero returned to Italy for good, freed from any formal constraints, and began composing in a style in which sheer fancy is the predominant element. He settled in Asolo, near Venice, and rarely ventured forth. Music flowed into old age. Malipiero continued to compose until he was 90.

Naxos has released world premiere recordings of several orchestral works in very fine performances by the Orchestra Sinfonica di Roma, under Francesco La Vecchia. These include its charming evocations of birds in the *Impressioni dal vero I–III* (Impressions from life) and two suites from his *Pause del silenzio* (Breaks in silence). Essentially, these are highly imaginative little tone poems.

There is a delicious languidness about this music. The level of sheer fancy is irresistible. Listen, for instance, to the "Dialogue of the Bells" at the beginning of the second *Impressioni*. This is one of the best Malipiero CDs out there and a great introduction to this magician's music.

On five CDs, the Naxos label provides Malipiero's ten numbered symphonies, as well as five unnumbered sinfonias with descriptive titles, all performed by the Moscow Symphony Orchestra conducted by the late Antonio de Almeida. Malipiero was not a symphonist in the traditional sense but a musical poet who arranged his inspirations in a series of suites. Malipiero believed that "the Italian symphony is a free kind of poem in several parts which follow one another capriciously, obeying only those mysterious laws that instinct recognizes." He viewed his role as that of a musical magician. He conjured an Arcadian world of cascading lyricism, pastoral reverie, bittersweet nostalgia, and, finally, elegy.

Essentially picturesque, his music presents a series of processionals, dances, fanfares, songs, and impressionist sketches delightfully knit together with kaleidoscopic abandon. Mixing the archaic with the modern, and modal harmonies with spicy dissonances, Malipiero's is a highly evocative language, unmistakably his own. Like Respighi, Malipiero loved the archaic, but unlike Respighi, he did not romanticize it in Technicolor. Eschewing voluptuousness, he preferred shimmering refinement to the blatant orchestral orgies of Respighi.

Of the five Naxos CDs, I will select a few highlights. I am grateful that Malipiero did not destroy all of his pre-Parisian works, because the *Sinfonia del mare* (1906) is a gem, all the more astonishing in that he wrote it unaware of Debussy's *La Mer*. It has one of the most magical beginnings: twilight murmurings in the strings and winds that give over to one of the most delicious melodies ever written. Equally fine is the beguiling *Sinfonie del silenzio e della morte* (1909–1910). The second movement will introduce you to the languid Arcadian reveries in which Malipiero seems to suspend time. Symphony No. 1, evoking the four seasons, begins in the same vein. The Symphony No. 2, subtitled

Elegiaca, beautifully expresses valedictory sentiments. The Symphony No. 3, subtitled *Delle campane*, starts buoyantly with festive chattering in the winds that is later undercut by more serious brass declamations and sighs in the bass strings. Melancholy eventually prevails.

The next movement, Andante, takes us back into the most beguiling kind of Arcadian dream. Here the tolling bells of the subtitle become clearer. The last movement, Lento, movingly portrays the bells, using the string basses and the lower registers of the piano, while a lament is played in the upper strings. The Symphony No. 4, titled *In Memoriam*, is dedicated to the memory of Natalie Koussevitzky. Its second movement, Lento funebre, is a brilliantly evocative funeral march. Imaginative touches abound in all of these works. This is musical beguilement and enchantment at the genius level.

After Symphony No. 7: *Delle canzone*, something changed. Malipiero drew a chromatic veil over his works as if to say, "Now you must look deeper to see their beauties; I will not show them to you as I did." The surface appeal is gone and the works become far more enigmatic, if not at times inaccessible. This process did not occur, at least not to the same extent, over the course of Malipiero's eight string quartets, which are very rewarding works. They do, however, become increasingly concise. Listening to the First, I was astounded that it was written before Janáček's First String Quartet, which employs an eerily similar language. Like Janáček's work, it is vibrant and pulsating with life. Malipiero remarked that he wanted to "get away from the atmosphere of chamber music and let us breathe the air of the streets and the countryside". These works, with their finesse, rhythmic precision, and passion, belong in any 20th-century chamber music collection.

The CPO label has given a gift of all of Malipiero's six fantastically colorful and often highly lyrical Piano Concertos on a two-CD set in gorgeous SACD sound and exquisite performances by the Saarbrücken Radio Symphony Orchestra, under Michele Carulli, with pianist Sandro Ivo Bartoli. Also, Supraphon has resurrected the 1971 recording of Malipiero's entrancing Violin Concerto, with André Gertler. It is accompanied by the equally beguiling Violin Concerto of Malipiero's soul mate, Alfredo Casella.

A highly imaginative Italian writer, Maurizio Carnelli, has suggested that the episodic nature of much of Malipiero's writing is expressive of a fractured view of life, a realization of life's senselessness. I don't think so. There is a difference between arbitrariness and the capriciousness that Malipiero extolled. The capricious is not senseless; it is playful. The capricious expresses a life-affirming and delightful confidence in what is. The arbitrary, on the other hand, is mistrustful of being and vindictive. The senseless becomes tyrannical and mordant. I do not hear this in Malipiero's work. If Malipiero's music is episodic, so is life. Life, after all, does not come in sonata-allegro form. Malipiero felt that life's moods could be better captured in sonic poetry. After listening to these treasures, who can refute him? Referring to the long series of *Dialoghi* for various instruments that he composed in the 1950s, Malipiero said that they were "born as if by magic". That is, indeed, how his best works sound.

Recommended Recordings

Vivaldiana: Sette invenzioni, et al., Peter Maag, Veneto PO, Marco Polo 8.223397

Impressioni dal vero I–III and *Pause del silenzio I–II*, Francesco La Vecchia, Rome SO, Naxos 8.572409

Symphonies 1 & 2; *Sinfonie del silenzio e della morte*, Antonio de Almeida, Moscow SO, Naxos 8.570879

Symphonies 3 & 4, *Sinfonia del mare*, Antonio de Almeida, Moscow SO, Naxos 8.570878

Symphonies 5, 6, 8, & 11, Antonio de Almeida, Moscow SO, Naxos 8.570880

Symphony No. 7; *Sinfonia in un tempo*; *Sinfonia per Antigenida*, Antonio de Almeida, Moscow SO, Naxos 8.570881

Six Piano Concertos, Michele Carulli, Sandro Ivo Bartoli, Saarbrücken RSO, CPO 777 287-2

Violin Concerto, (also includes Alfredo Casella, Violin Concerto) Václav Smetáček, André Gertler, Prague SO, Supraphon Archiv SU 3904-2

Eight Quartets, Orpheus String Quartet, Brilliant Classics 8550 (OOP)

L'Orfeide, Hermann Scherchen, Maggio Musicale Fiorentino Orchestra, Tahra 190–191 (OOP)

Frank Martin: Guide to the Liturgical Year

One of the best musical guides through the liturgical year is the son of a Swiss Calvinist minister, Frank Martin (1890–1974). Born in Geneva in 1890, Martin was encouraged by his parents to pursue a career in physics and mathematics. As a youngster, however, he exhibited a powerful inclination toward music. He began composing music at the age of nine. At 12, he was deeply moved by a performance of Bach's *St. Matthew Passion*. Bach's lasting influence was apparent from Martin's motto: "Bach today, yesterday and forever."

After meeting Swiss conductor Ernest Ansermet, Martin came under the influence of the works of Debussy and Ravel, which bore fruit in his beautiful Piano Quintet of 1919. That influence, however, was fleeting. Martin was far more decisively formed by his encounter with Schoenberg's serialism. He said, "I can truly say that at the same time I both fell under the influence of Schoenberg and rebelled against him with my whole musical being." Martin struggled to adapt Schoenberg's 12-tone technique to his own compositional needs, which required the retention of tonal harmonies. "In Schoenberg I found an iron straitjacket from which I took only what suited and allowed me to craft my own style of writing", he declared. Martin is primarily known for his success in this endeavor, with such brilliant works as the *Petite Symphonie Concertante*; Concerto for Seven Wind Instruments, Timpani, Percussion, and Strings; and his *Ballads* for various instruments.

My own admiration for Martin was limited to these and a few other works. Some of his music I found brittle. Martin's instrumental works were interesting, but seldom compelling. His superb craftsmanship, however, is never in doubt. It is when Martin moved from craft to conviction that the kind of gray aridity I occasionally found disappeared. I mean by this a religious conviction of the deepest sort. The famous cellist Pierre Fournier said Martin's creative genius was "nurtured by the silent meditation in his work and by the fervor of his faith". That faith animates moments of transfixing beauty in Martin's sacred music, when he seems to break through the limitations of his medium to reveal the holy.

It is the character of Martin's faith that defines him. "As the son of a minister, and as the son of a minister who has not renounced his faith," he said, "religion has affected me twice as strongly." Yet Martin's religion did not have a sectarian cast. Rather, he seems to have been a pre-Reformation Christian with Catholic tastes. In fact, after listening to his sacred works, one must go even further. Martin's religious sensibility, if not his musical style, was essentially medieval. In reflecting on the text of the Requiem, he wrote, "These pictures originating from the Middle Ages appealed directly to the depths of my soul." This seems also to have been true of the Mass; the Gospel narratives he set in his Passion, *Golgotha*; the *Maria-Triptychon*, consisting of the *Ave Maria, Magnificat,* and *Stabat Mater*; the *Monologues from Jedermann,* Hugo von Hofmannsthal's play after the medieval morality play *Everyman*; *In Terra Pax,* an oratorio with texts from Isaiah, Revelation, the Gospels, and the Our Father; and the oratorio *Le Mystère de la Nativité,* based on a French medieval mystery play, from which Martin also drew for his short oratorio *Pilate.* Even some of Martin's instrumental music is explicitly religious, as in his *Polyptyque* ("Six Images of the Passion of Christ") for violin and two string orchestras.

It is not only the subject matter, but the spirit in which he approached it that defines Martin as medieval. In an age when so many considered the artist the subject of his art, Martin thirsted for anonymity. In *Entretiens avec Jean-Claude Piguet* (1967), Martin recalled that he did not initially compose his sacred music with any intention that it should be performed. He described his Mass as "something between God and myself". Martin thought that ideally it should be premiered anonymously in a liturgy. Realizing that such an attempt would only draw more attention to its author, he kept his Mass in a drawer for 40 years.

In another way, however, Martin did achieve a kind of anonymity. While listening to his religious music, one never thinks of Martin. As well made as it is, the music is never clever in a way that would call attention to its maker. This is partly the result of Martin's superb craftsmanship; so well suited are the means that the end is reached without drawing attention to them. But more certainly, this is due to Martin's humility and deep reverence for his subject matter. For Martin, Christ's Passion was "the greatest of all subjects".

With Martin as our guide through the liturgical year, we should begin with his Mass because the Mass more or less carries the liturgical year within itself each day. In 1922, Martin began composing one of the sweetest, most gentle Masses of the 20th century, which has the intimacy of a personal confession of faith. It ranks with other 20th-century settings by Ralph Vaughan Williams, Francis Poulenc, and André Caplet. Martin was 32 when he began his Mass, finishing it four years later with the addition of the Agnus Dei. He then placed it in a drawer for the next four decades. "I did not want it to be performed," Martin said, "since I was afraid that I would be judged from a purely aesthetic viewpoint. . . . I felt then that an expression of religious feelings should remain secret and removed from public opinion."

Martin's only a cappella work, the Mass is written for double choir. With alternating homophonic, antiphonal, and polyphonic passages, the choirs express hushed reverence, wonder, and exultation with a clarity and luminosity rare in its century. Martin's private musical devotion bespeaks an already deep, personal relationship of a man on his knees before his Savior.

For the first of the two central events of the liturgical year, Christmas, Martin composed an oratorio in 1959. *Le Mystère de la Nativité* contains some of the most touching, faith-filled music I have heard. The character of this work calls to mind the carved wooden panels depicting biblical scenes found around the exterior of the apse and choir walls of many medieval cathedrals. It is as if these medieval bas-reliefs suddenly sprang to life musically, though in a 20th-century idiom. However, the idiom is not Martin's usual chromaticism. In *Le Mystère*, he said that he "used a very bare and entirely diatonic musical language for the celestial world". For the scenes in hell, an atonal language expresses the diabolical cacophony (though the devils are more redolent of Punch and Judy than Milton).

For his text, Martin drew from Arnoul Greban's *Le Mystère de la Passion*, written around 1450. Greban's Passion play consists of 35,000 verses, most of them in rhymed couplets. Martin extracted 12 scenes that neatly encapsulate salvation history up to the Presentation in the Temple. After a prologue in heaven, we are shown devils rejoicing in hell at the arrival of the first human souls; Adam and Eve in limbo, anxiously wondering, "When com'st Thou, sweetest Messiah?"; and then God sending Gabriel to Mary. The remaining scenes take us from the Annunciation to the Presentation. Both the text and the music have that special kind of innocence, intimacy, and sense of spiritual reality that only those with true faith possess. The setting of Gabriel's announcement to Mary is one great love song, as are Mary's first words to the newborn Jesus. Simeon's longing to see the Messiah could not be more beautifully and poignantly expressed or the celebration at Jesus' arrival in the Temple more joyously conveyed.

Le Mystère is a highly lyrical work of true radiance, a rare masterpiece of the spirit. It shines inwardly throughout. Martin must have had the soul of a child to write something this pure. I have seldom come across music that goes so directly to the heart, and in mine it shall long remain. At each Christmas, if not more often, I shall return to this direct, childlike vision of our Savior's coming.

The second lodestar of the liturgical year is Easter, preceded by the Passion. In 1945, Martin was impelled to undertake his setting of the Passion, *Golgotha*, by an encounter with Rembrandt's famous etching, *The Three Crosses*. Like Rembrandt, Martin said he wished to depict "the hour, in the history of the world, when the basic incompatibility between our material world and the world of the spirit was so vividly revealed". He declared his "intention was to make the sacred tragedy come to life again before our very eyes, and above all to portray the divine figure of Christ". As he said, "I endeavored to concentrate all light on the figure of Christ, and to leave every other person in the dark."

Martin took his narrative from all four Gospels and interspersed among the scenes from the Passion excerpts from St. Augustine's *Meditations*. *Golgotha* begins with searing cries of "Père", taken from a passage in the *Confessions*, and then proceeds to Palm Sunday. Martin's choral setting of the Hosannas that greet Christ in Jerusalem is a sublime and ravishing revelation of Christ's true identity. This music will either send chills down your spine or put tears in your eyes, or both. The setting of *St. Augustine's Meditation* number 7 that follows is an exquisite musical meditation of the utmost delicacy and spiritual refinement. In the scene before the Sanhedrin, Martin powerfully contrasts the anger and tumult of the crowd to Christ's serenity. The depiction of the crowd's behavior before Pilate is completely harrowing, as is Pilate's cry of "Ecce homo."

In surprising contrast, Martin gently renders the actual scene of Calvary, taken from St. John's Gospel, as a quiet, grief-stricken prayer, subdued and reverential. The concluding section, the Resurrection, both seraphically and powerfully proclaims victory over death in the majesty of the risen Christ. Here, Martin has created a work of the utmost sublimity, a Passion setting that rises over our own century and that can only be compared to the works of the great master, Bach, in its achievement.

Martin also composed a Requiem Mass, premiered at the Lausanne Cathedral in 1974, the year before he died. In it, he returned to the more chromatic language found in some of his instrumental works. Martin does not provide the soothing reassurance found in the Requiems of Fauré or Duruflé, both of whom omitted the Dies Irae altogether. The chromaticism in Martin's Requiem creates a sense of unease and distress that is entirely appropriate to what he saw as the certain prospect of judgment and the possibility of hell. Death does not waft you into heaven. It brings you to a terrible moment of truth. Martin wished to show death "in all the anguish and suffering, physical and emotional, that it bears". The Dies Irae is three times longer than the next longest section of the work. Unlike the exultant Sanctus in Martin's Mass, the Sanctus in the Requiem expresses anguish. The chromatic edge of anxiety carries through even to the Agnus Dei. This is not neurotic anxiety; it is spiritual realism. The nearly pervasive disquiet is, however, dispelled all the more effectively when the chromatic clouds disperse in the Offertorium, as the sopranos tenderly exclaim the radiance of "Rex gloriae", again in In Paradisum, and in the concluding Lux Aeterna, in which the light triumphantly bursts forth.

In *Golgotha*, Christ's divinity is manifested in his acceptance of his death. In the Requiem, Martin seems to be saying we are most like Christ in accepting our own death. "What I have tried to express here is the clear will to accept death," Martin said, "to make peace with it . . . Equally important, though, is the willingness to behold death in full confidence of the forgiveness to come, in full expectation of true, eternal peace." It is not this peace that Martin attempts to portray but the expression of an "ardent prayer, hoping to attain it by the grace of God". After the Requiem's premiere in Lausanne, Mrs. Martin wrote, "Several people of all kinds came to him with tears in their eyes, saying, 'Thank you, Mr. Martin. You took away from us all fear of death.' After the concert, when he was alone with my daughter, he told her, 'I have achieved my purpose. Now I may die.'"

Martin hoped that his Requiem would bring to its listeners "the same feeling of trust and peace that moved my soul as I worked on it". In it and his other sacred works, Martin succeeded in conveying his profoundly religious inspiration. Whether listeners receive it will in large part depend on what they bring to it. Martin was keenly aware of this dimension when he wrote of how his *Polyptyque*, which was written the last year of his life, might be regarded. He said, "With some people, this music will be able to help them re-create within themselves these pictures of the Passion; for others, they will be pieces, more or less interesting, more or less successful, for solo violin and two string orchestras." *Polyptyque* for violin and two string orchestras, was requested by violinist Yehudi Menuhin, and he considered it the most important work written for him, after the Bartók Violin Concerto. The exceptionally tender second movement *Image de la Chambre haute*, the short and urgent third movement, *Image de Gethsémané*, and the extensive, lyrical solo for violin of the final, *Image de la Glorification*, find Martin's language at his most romantic, without Bach ever receding too far into the background.

For those with ears to hear, Martin's music is like a rock of faith, and its message will reward anyone willing to pay it heed. That message was encapsulated in Martin's last work, completed only ten days before he died: the cantata *Et la Vie l'emporta*. The title roughly translates as, "And Life Won the Day". It did, and will again *toujours*.

Recommended Recordings

Mass for Double Choir (includes Ildebrando Pizzetti's Requiem), James O'Donnell, Westminster Cathedral Choir, Hyperion 67017

Mass for Double Choir (also includes Olivier Messiaen's *Cinq rechants*; *O sacrum convivium*), RIAS-Kammerchor, Daniel Reuss; Harmonia Mundi Musique D'Abord 1951834

Le Mystère de La Nativité; *Pilate*, Ernest Ansermet, Orchestre de la Suisse Romande, Eli Ameling et al., Cascavelle 2006 (OOP). Or: Alois Koch, Lucerne SO et al., Musiques Suisses MGB 6173. This beautifully sung performance is from the 1959 premiere of *Le Mystère*.

Golgotha, Michel Corboz, Sinfonietta de Lausanne, Ensemble Vocal de Lausanne, Cascavelle 3004. Or: Daniel Reuss, Estonian Philharmonic Chamber Choir, Estonian National SO et al., Harmonia Mundi 902056. Or: Marcello Viotti, Munich Radio Orchestra, Bavarian Radio Chorus, et al. Profil Hänssler PH04037. Michel Corboz' is the second recorded performance of this masterpiece, taken from a live concert in 1994.

Requiem, Klaus Knall, Capella Cantorum Konstanz, Collegium Vocale Zurich, MDG 6183. The Jecklin recording of a 1973 live performance of this difficult but courageous work under Frank Martin's own direction is sadly out of print, though used copies are occasionally available. Fortunately Klaus Knall's recording fills the breach beautifully.

In Terra Pax; *The Four Elements*, Matthias Bamert, London PO, Brighton Festival Chorus, Chandos 9465

Maria-Triptychon; Six Monologues from *Jedermann*; Suite from *Der Sturm*, Matthias Bamert, London PO, et al. Chandos 9411

Der Sturm (*The Tempest*), Thierry Fischer, Netherlands Radio PO, et al., Hyperion 67821

Martin's opera *The Tempest* is as outstanding a modern setting of Shakespeare's play as can be heard.

Maria-Triptychon, Polyptyque; *Passacaglia* for Orchestra, Christoph Poppen, German Radio Philharmonic Orchestra, Muriel Cantoreggi, Juliane Banse, ECM 51733930

∿

Bohuslav Martinů: Music with a View

One of the most distinctive voices in 20th-century music was that of Bohuslav Martinů (1890–1959), a composer from a small Bohemian town in Czechoslovakia. Like his predecessor, Leoš Janáček (1854–1928), Martinů was able to fashion an inimitably unique musical language that distinguishes each of his mature compositions and brings his name to mind within the space of a few bars. Like Janáček, Martinů was also a late bloomer. Though a man of innate musicality, Martinů had to search through a number of styles before finding one all his own. Composing some 400 works, he produced prodigiously because he had to; for him, composition was life. He cared little about his works once they were written and was heedless of their fate.

Martinů barely cared for himself. He was poor most of his life and spent many years as a political refugee; his works were banned by the Nazis, and he never owned a home. He was already in his 50s before he received major recognition, and it was not until then that he even attempted the first of the six symphonies that now constitute the heart of his legacy. Nevertheless, by the time of his death from cancer at age 69 in Switzerland, he had left behind a sufficient number of significant works in every genre to establish himself as a major voice of enormous vitality, astounding rhythmic drive, and mysterious beauty. His works expressed everything from the high jinks of the Paris avant-garde in the 1920s to the tragedy of World War II that destroyed his country. In his last years, he attained a free form of expression that was as close to magic as anything written in the 20th century.

In 1890, Martinů was born in the church tower of St. James in Polička. His father was the town's fire watchman, and the church tower was his perch and small apartment. Young Martinů spent his first 12 years with this bird's-eye view of village life. He had to traverse 193 steps if he wished to mingle below. His health was so frail that his father sometimes had to carry him. His formal musical studies started at age 12. His interests and ability in music were so impressive that the villagers took up a collection allowing Martinů to go to the Prague Conservatory for serious study.

Martinů did not fare well in an academic setting. After several terms, he was dismissed in 1910 for "incorrigible negligence". The negligence was not the result of laziness on Martinů's part, for he composed daily, but of his rejection of the conservatory's German-oriented curriculum and of romanticism in general. Martinů's first musical epiphany came in 1908 when he heard a performance of Debussy's *Pelléas et Mélisande*. French impressionism, not German symphonism, represented the future for him. This opinion was confirmed for him by a performance of Albert Roussel's impressionist *Poème de la forêt* (Symphony No. 1), which left a strong mark on the aspiring composer.

Martinů was liberated from Prague when the patient townsfolk of Polička took up another collection—this time to send him to the only musical center for someone seeking to escape German influence and the detritus of romanticism: Paris. There he found others who shared his predilections, such as Darius Milhaud, who spoke for a number of his generation when he said, "My musical culture is determined exclusively by Latin-Mediterranean civilization. . . . Mediterranean music, especially Italian music, has always said a great deal to me; German as good as nothing."

Martinů expressed a similar opinion: "I went to France not to seek to save myself there but to confirm my opinion. What I sought there was neither Debussy nor impressionism nor musical expression, but the true fundamentals of Western culture, which, in my view, harmonize much better with our own national character than a labyrinth of conjectures and problems." The latter part of this remark is a slam at German theory, but some of his statement is a bit disingenuous. Actually, Martinů was quite surprised when, in 1923, he arrived in Paris to find that impressionism was already passé. It had been overtaken by *le jazz hot* and Stravinsky's music, both of which had a major effect on him (as shown in *La Revue de cuisine*; the 1924 Quartet for Clarinet, Horn, Cello, and Side Drum; and *Half-time*). Nonetheless, Martinů sought lessons from Roussel, who had himself left impressionism behind. From him, Martinů drank in the "outstanding qualities of French art that I have always admired: order, clarity, measure, taste, [and] precise, sensitive, direct expression". He might also have added Roussel's motoric rhythms, which influenced him greatly.

Martinů dove headfirst into the Paris musical scene, producing avant-garde works in the latest surrealist fashions. He completely absorbed and perfectly emulated the jazz style, as in the *Jazz Suite*. He then assimilated Stravinsky's influence and turned to neoclassicism. Works from this period, especially chamber pieces, are a marvelous amalgam of Stravinsky (for the spiky rhythms and neoclassicism), Poulenc (for the wit and whimsy), and Czech folk song (for the heartfelt melody). Try the delightful Divertimento for Left-Hand Piano and Orchestra or Serenades 1–3.

Martinů's brand of neoclassicism, like Stravinsky's, was neobaroque. He declared himself a "concerto grosso man". The concerto grosso style relieved Martinů of the developmental problems of symphonic form and any taint of romanticism but also saddled him with its own limitations. He wrote some very brilliant concertos during this period, such as the *Sinfonietta Giocosa* for Piano and Chamber Orchestra, as well as what many consider one of his masterpieces, the Double Concerto, which is charged with apprehension over the gathering storm clouds of World War II.

Yet, the lesser works take on a kind of mechanical hum that can be wearisome, which is all the more ironic since Martinů saw his music as a protest against "the pressures of mechanization" in modern life. The music often proceeds as a succession of skippy knots of rhythm and short, jerky melodies. It sounds motoric, repetitive, and rushed. It sometimes creates the impression of a musical beehive—a bewildering profusion of seemingly individual musical incidents and multiple crosscurrents running simultaneously. Like a beehive, the music is very busy and seems about to collide with itself at any moment, which it sometimes does to great effect. The sheer busyness can be tiresome.

I am less fond of Martinů's dense compositions from this period for the same reasons that I am less than fond of baroque music in general. I easily weary of the endless instrumental figurations and chugging ostinatos. If French writer Colette once likened Bach to "a celestial sewing machine", Martinů can sound like a terrestrial one.

World War II drove Martinů to America, where he flourished. He slowly shed baroque forms and let his inspiration find its own unique shape from the Moravian melodies he used and the extraordinary kaleidoscopic colors he drew from the orchestra. In the mid-1940s, Martinů told his biographer, "From now on, I'm going in for fantasy." To make the point unmistakable, he subtitled his Fourth Piano Concerto *Incantations* and his Sixth Symphony, *Fantaisies symphoniques*. The symphonic flowering of his last decade and a half produced such masterpieces as the six symphonies, *The Parables*; *Toccata e due canzone*; *Les Fresques de Piero della Francesca*; and *Estampes*, all of which qualify as orchestral fantasias. He also composed a magical series of concertos that include the last two of five piano concertos, his last violin and cello concertos, the Concerto for Oboe and Orchestra, and the Rhapsody-Concerto for Viola and Orchestra. His chamber works from this period are also of the highest quality and include the Nonet, Serenade No. 4, Flute Trio, Three Madrigals for Violin and Viola, and the second and third Piano Trio.

It is quite difficult to describe exactly how Martinů's best music works. Not even he knew. Concerning the *Fantaisies symphoniques*, he said: "Something holds it together, I don't know what, but it has a single line and I have expressed something in it—the future will show." Like Janáček's, Martinů's music seems to function by building up large mosaics of fragmentary, repetitive motifs. Short motivic phrases are relentlessly repeated out of sheer excitement or to create tension. Martinů uses accelerating rhythms and rising volume of sound to propel his abbreviated motifs in a scalar ascent, at the top of which a melody erupts and sweeps all before it. Out of the swirling strings and gurgling winds, a broader theme invariably arises. These melodic moments provide both relief from the tense buildups and exhilaration at their resolution.

One perceptive critic noted that "no matter how rhythmic Martinů tries to be, lyricism keeps breaking through." This is an especially keen observation, because rhythm and melody often seem to be at odds with each other in Martinů's music. (No conductor brings this out more brilliantly than Karel Ančerl.) One is tempted to say that rhythm has absolute precedence in Martinů because it is such a prominent feature of his music—especially heavily syncopated rhythms which, at times, seem to be wrestling the melodies to the ground. But his driving rhythms do not whirl about aimlessly, except in bad performances or second-rate works. Almost always, they culminate in melody; melody is the destination to which the rhythm drives the scattered mosaic motifs.

This key operating characteristic of Martinů's music was adumbrated in an amusing early ballet, *The Revolt*, produced in Paris in 1925. In the ballet, for which Martinů himself wrote the libretto, the notes of the musical scale revolt against bad singers, poor piano playing, dance-hall music, and an out-of-tune gramophone. The notes attack and destroy the piano and chase away pupil and teacher. The revolt leads to unemployment in the music world, the suicides of music professors and critics, and Stravinsky's retirement to a desert island. Order and sanity are restored when a girl, dressed in national costume, sings a simple folk song. Much of Martinů's music could have been the object of his own satire. It can initially give the appearance of incoherence, yet ultimately finds its resolution in the beautiful, simple folk song of his homeland.

For refreshment, I turn to his piano concertos. These five works, written from 1925 to 1958, are like a musical splash of cool spring water. They are defined by fancy and delight, curlicues of counterpoint, Martinů's signature syncopated rhythms, and gorgeous melodies. Yes, there is occasional dissonance for spice, but all resolves itself into an almost epiphanic lyricism. There is a minimum of the neobaroque noodling that imparts a mechanical hum to Martinů's lesser works. It is the sense of play, whimsy, and sheer joy that captures me.

For the longest time, there was only one—fortunately wonderful and not yet surpassed—integral recording available. The Supraphon two-CD set bubbles along with Emil Leichner at the piano (he has also ably recorded the complete piano music for the same label on three CDs) and the Czech Philharmonic Orchestra, under conductor Jiří Bělohlávek. As a bonus, the 1938 Concertino for Piano and Orchestra is included. As one would expect from these artists, the performances are completely idiomatic. This music is in the Czech blood. Some performers are wont to punch the syncopated rhythms too hard and make the music freakish. Here the exciting rhythms and lyricism are kept in perfect balance.

The eponymous Martinů Quartet offers a complete traversal of Martinů's seven string quartets on the Naxos label. The first issue in the series contains Quartets 1 and 2, with an even earlier work, *Three Horsemen*. As mentioned earlier, Martinů fell under the influence of the French in his youth. These works are steeped in the sound world of Debussy and Ravel. Add to the mix the quixotic Czech melodies familiar to lovers of the music of Leoš Janáček, and you will know what to expect in these expansive works. The following two CDs contain Quartets 3 to 7. By the time of the Third Quartet, Martinů's style had become less French and more idiosyncratically Czech in respect to the quirky rhythms and Moravian folk-like melodies he employed. In the later quartets, one hears echoes of the extraordinary sound world of Martinů's symphonies, along with his signature chugging ostinatos. I was going to say that Nos. 3, 4, 6, and 7 are especially good, but that would seem prejudicial against poor No. 5, which is perhaps the most distinctive of the lot in its harrowing sorrow. It is certainly far removed from the delightful, almost Haydnesque world of No. 7. In any case, these CDs are self-recommending to anyone with the slightest interest in Martinů. The Martinů Quartet's performances are on the same high level throughout the series.

These very general characterizations can give only the roughest idea of what to expect in this brilliant, mercurial, high-spirited music. In approaching Martinů's huge body of work, one can observe a general rule: the later, the better. The newcomer should start with the symphonies, orchestral works, and chamber compositions from Martinů's last magical period, then, once captivated, work back through his earlier periods, which each contain masterpieces. Because so much of Martinů's music is encased in neobaroque forms, some have felt his work to be aloof and disengaged. After all, Martinů was an antiromantic and the concerto grosso form appealed to him precisely because it expressed "less apparent emotion". Perhaps this is what led Swiss composer Frank Martin to say that Martinů "never came down from that tower" in St. James Church. But he did, all 193 steps, and he gathered all he needed in his years of wandering and exile. Then he went back up again, and from the top, he cast a spell over the whole village.

Recommended Recordings

Recordings of Martinů have exploded over the last 15 years, leaving the intrepid Martinů-explorer with an embarrassment of riches to choose from.

Complete Symphonies, Jiří Bělohlávek, BBC SO, Onyx 4061

Complete Symphonies, Vladimír Válek, Prague RSO, Supraphon 3940

Complete Symphonies, Neeme Järvi, Bamberg SO, Brilliant 8950

Symphonies 5 & 6; *Memorial to Lidice*, Karel Ančerl, Czech PO, Supraphon 3694 (Karel Ančerl Gold Edition, vol. 34)

Orchestral Works & Concertos

Overture, Rhapsody for Large Orchestra; Sinfonia Concertante; Concerto Grosso; *Parables*, Jiří Bělohlávek, Czech PO, Supraphon 3743

Sinfonietta Giocosa; *Sinfonietta la Jolla*; *Toccata e due canzoni*, The Bournemouth Sinfonietta, Thomas Vásáry, Chandos 8859

Complete Piano Concertos, Jiří Bělohlávek, Emil Leichner, Czech PO, Supraphon 1313

Piano Concertos 2–4, Libor Pešek, Rudolf Firkušný, Czech PO, RCA Red Seal 09026-61934-2 (OOP)

Cello Concertos 1 & 2, Concertino, Raphael Wallfisch (cello), Czech PO, Jiří Bělohlávek, Chandos 10547

Violin Concertos 1 & 2, Christopher Hogwood, Bohuslav Matoušek, Czech PO, Hyperion 67674

Concerto for Two Violins and Orchestra; Duo Concertante for Two Violins and Orchestra et al., Christopher Hogwood, Bohuslav Matoušek, Czech PO, Hyperion 67671

Violin Concerto No. 2; Serenade No. 2 for Strings; *Toccata e due canzoni*, Jiří Bělohlávek, Isabelle Faust, Prague Philharmonia, Harmonia Mundi 901951

Field Mass; Double Concerto; *Frescoes of Piero della Francesca*; Charles Mackerras, Czech PO, Prague RSO, Supraphon 3276

Chamber Works

The String Quartets, Martinů Quartet, Naxos 8.553782 (1 & 2), 8.553783 (3 & 6), and 8.553784 (4, 5 & 7). Or: The String Quartets, Panocha Quartet, Supraphon 3917.

Serenades 1–4; Quartet (1924), Ensemble Villa Musica, MDG 304 0774

Oboe Quartet; String Quintet; Piano Quartet No. 1; Viola Sonata No.1, Australian Festival of Chamber Music Players, Naxos 8.553916

Flute Trios; *Promenades*; *Madrigal Sonata*, Feinstein Ensemble, Naxos 8.553459

Piano Trios 2 & 3, The Bekova Sisters, Chandos 9632

Sonatas for Cello and Piano 1–3; *Ariette*; *Sept Arabesques*, Sebastian & Christian Benda, Naxos 8.554502

The Epic of Gilgamesh, Zdeněk Košler, Slovak Philharmonic Choir, Slovak Philharmonic Orchestra et al., Naxos 8.555138

～

William Mathias: Musical Incantations

Mention of Wales often calls to mind the famous line from Robert Bolt's play *A Man for All Seasons*, in which Sir Thomas More says to his perjurious betrayer, Richard Rich, "Why Richard, it profiteth a man nothing to gain the whole world and lose his soul—but for Wales?" Actually, Wales is a rather nice place and, without losing one's soul, one can discover that fact by listening to the music of William Mathias (1934–1992), one of Wales' (and Great Britain's) finest 20th-century composers. For years, I used to scour through London gramophone shops to find records of his work (I bagged a total of nine). In more recent years, his music has found an increasingly generous representation on compact disc, now numbering some 77.

Mathias was born in Wales in 1934 and spent almost his whole life there. A child prodigy, he began piano lessons at age three. He started composing in his fifth year. When he was 12, he wrote a march and school song for Whitland Grammar School that are still in use today. Largely self-taught, Mathias nonetheless studied composition at the Royal Academy of Music with composer Lennox Berkeley and piano with Peter Katin. He then taught for many years at the University of Wales, Bangor, before retiring to concentrate exclusively on composition. Illness felled him at the relatively early age of 57. As his third and last symphony shows, Mathias was in full stride as a composer when he was struck down.

Mathias was a specifically Welsh composer in that his work is steeped in Celtic ethos and myth. His son, Rhiannon, explained, "My father's psyche was fired by the qualities which can be detected in the great poems of Welsh medieval poetry, where, in his words, 'Celtic consciousness [is both] rhetorical and lyrical; on the one hand darkly introspective and, on the other, highly jeweled, dance-like, and rhythmic.'"

Mathias wrote a celebratory, ecstatic kind of music, full of mystery and bardic solemnity. It is splashed in vivid orchestral colors and clothed in shimmering textures, and punctuated, at times, by a barbarous, or jazzy, raucousness (as in the final movement of Symphony No. 2). It combines ritual feeling with uninhibited spontaneity. Melancholic brooding is always interrupted by eruptive fanfares that announce an underlying joy in answer to life's travails. Mathias said, "Music must be one immense act of celebration", and that is what we hear.

Mathias' music is kaleidoscopic, fluent but not facile. Some critics have complained that, in his symphonies, Mathias' discursive lyricism weakens the formal structures. Mathias proved in a number of compositions, most especially in his brilliant series of concertos, that he could write formally pleasing works. But his aim was not to be tidy. He called a number of his compositions "landscapes of the mind", and this title seems a more accurate way to express his goals. "Incantations" would be even better. Mathias wished not so much to write symphonies as to use symphonic resources to conjure a world no less real for being nearly beyond reach. He was one of the few 20th-century composers who could transport a listener to a place that is both past and present, a world charged with mystery, occasionally engulfed in gloom, but finally enlivened by ecstatic joy. Thus his works seem to operate as much by psychological as musical rules. One is never at a loss as to what is being felt or conveyed, which is why even the music's many surprises delight and seem right. The communication is both urgently direct and novel. Mathias' music emanated from a man in the grip of a vision, who was impelled to share it.

If Mathias' music has been critically neglected, it is likely because of its fundamental optimism and its accessibility. It also contains easily ascribable influences, leaving it open to the charge of being derivative. Mathias used a musical language solidly in the vein of Benjamin Britten, Michael Tippett, and Malcolm Arnold. At 50, Mathias acknowledged Messiaen and Tippett as "genuine deep influences". Tippett's influence is especially prominent in the florid lyricism of Mathias' work. Some of Mathias' music could have come out of Tippett's lovely opera, *The Midsummer Marriage*. Mathias' *Invocation and Dance*, for example, is so startlingly similar to some of Tippett's music from that opera that I am left wondering if he were directly quoting Tippett, or whether they both found the same source material in Welsh folk song. Tippett's later development, however, seems to have been derailed, perhaps by the baleful influence of the thought of Karl Jung. Mathias' music sounds like what Tippett could have written had he stayed in his more lyrical mode and not wandered off into knotty hermeticism. One could also add Stravinsky and Bartók as influences on Mathias, but it would not change the fact that Mathias was right to conclude, "Ultimately, I know I have my own voice."

Two pairs of compact discs from Nimbus and Lyrita are indispensable introductions to Mathias' enchanted world. The Nimbus recordings contain his three symphonies, a delicious oboe concerto, and two "landscapes of the mind", entitled *Requiescat* and *Helios*. The Lyrita compact discs feature three of Mathias' finest concertos, for clarinet, harp, and piano, and a group of orchestral works, including the enlivening *Dance Overture*, *Sinfonietta*, two string works, and *Laudi* and *Vistas*, more "landscapes of the mind".

Mathias described his First Symphony, op. 31, as "essentially a work of energy, color, and affirmation". Mathias' description of the qualities of Welsh medieval poetry serves particularly well in capturing the attributes of this work: "brightly jeweled colors contrasting with dark introspection, declamation with tenderness, and intellectual tautness with an almost improvisatory lyricism".

Symphony No. 2, op. 90, *Summer Music*, follows the First Symphony by 17 years, yet shares the same musical language. Its mood, though, is more nocturnal, reflective, and brooding, yet again finally affirmative and deliciously scored, with a raucously jazzy finale.

The Third Symphony was finished just before Mathias died. The first movement begins with a wildly swirling Mussorgskian dance theme, followed by highly rhythmic ostinatos out of Igor Stravinsky's *Rite of Spring*. Whatever the geography of the piece (a Celt on the steppes of Russia?), it is highly arresting and has a gripping coherence and grandeur that even critics of his first two symphonies admitted.

Mathias' concertos display his talent for highly memorable themes and colorful orchestration, but most especially his rhythmic vivacity. It is almost impossible to stay physically still while listening to them. Mathias was a master of the dance, as his *Dance Overture* so irrepressibly demonstrates on the Lyrita compact disc of his orchestral works. The other Lyrita compact disc features three of his best concertos. The Harp Concerto is a joy and one of Mathias' works to which I return most frequently. The scoring is a miracle of delicacy, with single wind and brass only, along with timpani, percussion, and celeste coloring the strings. In it, Mathias deploys several of his best melodies. The result is radiant.

There is also a very fine performance of this work on Koch, coupled with Alberto Ginastera's Harp Concerto. One can also hear how Mathias developed his talent for writing for the harp on a very beautiful Nimbus Records CD, offering his *Sante Fe Suite* for harp and *Im-*

provisations for Harp, along with other 20th-century harp classics from Arnold, Britten, and Fauré.

Mathias' Clarinet Concerto, on the same Lyrita disc, has a haunting lyricism and is inflected with perky, syncopated jazz rhythms. It is a thoroughly winning piece. The Third Piano Concerto is a more percussive, brazen work, which adds a big-city seriousness to its jazzy proceedings. It can also, however, in the turn of a phrase and without missing a beat, reconnect with a lost runic world of the Welsh countryside. As this work demonstrates, Mathias was able to sound thoroughly modern and archaic simultaneously, conflating past and present seamlessly.

There are two excellent compact discs of Mathias' church and choral music: one on Nimbus Records, featuring Christ Church Cathedral Choir, under Stephen Darlington; and the other, entitled *The Doctrine of Wisdom,* on the Gloriae Dei Cantores label, sung by a group of the same name conducted by Elizabeth Patterson. The two discs share only the *Rex Gloriae* in common. Each features a different Mass and different anthems. Mathias' church and choral music is written in a highly declamatory style, sometimes stridently so, but with ample lyrical respites. The relative simplicity of means in these often homophonic works does not allow for the rich allusiveness of Mathias' complex orchestral scores.

The choral pieces are fairly straightforward and clearly expressive. This is not to underestimate their delicacy and tenderness, or their complementary robust exuberance. Some of the anthems may sound simple, but they have a childlike innocence and charm, and effectively serve their purpose with freshness and without a whiff of sanctimony. The impulse to praise is heartfelt. Mathias said, "[T]he concept of light, consciousness, praise (call it what you will) is prominent in my music to a degree unusual in this century. It is also one of the reasons why I am able to integrate music for the church into my work without loss of identity." My choral favorite (on the Nimbus CD) is the rousing *Ave Rex, a Carol Sequence,* op. 45, the Sir Christemas portion of which has become a Christmas favorite in Great Britain. Anyone who enjoys Britten's music of this kind should likewise appreciate Mathias'.

According to music writer Geraint Lewis, Mathias said that "music is the art most completely placed to express the triumph of Christ's victory over death—since it is concerned in essence with the destruction of time." This is a fascinating and seemingly self-contradictory remark, because music is the art most dependent upon time for its existence. How, then, can music destroy time? What Mathias must have meant is that music is singularly able to transport man into *sacred* time, where time stops in the raptness of revelation. In this sense, all of Mathias' music is sacred. It brings you dancing toward that exhilarating final moment that will last forever.

Recommended Recordings

Symphonies 1 & 2; William Mathias, BBC Welsh SO, Nimbus 5260

Symphony No. 3, *Helios*; Oboe Concerto; *Requiescat*, Grant Llewellyn, BBC Welsh SO, Nimbus 5343

Clarinet Concerto; Harp Concerto; Piano Concerto No. 3, New Philharmonia Orchestra, London SO, David Atherton, Lyrita 325

Dance Overture; *Divertimento*; *Invocation and Dance*; *Prélude, Aria, Finale*; *Sinfonietta*; *Laudi*; *Vistas*; London SO, New Philharmonia Orchestra, English CO, and National Youth Orchestra of Wales, David Atherton, Arthur Davison, Lyrita 328

Church and Choral Music: *Missa Aedis Christi*; *Ave Rex*; *Rex Gloriae*, Christ Church Cathedral Choir, Stephen Darlington, Nimbus 5243

Sacred Choral Music: *Doctrine of Wisdom*; *Missa Brevis*; *Rex Gloriae*, Elizabeth Patterson, Gloriae Dei Cantores 026

Sante Fe Suite for Harp; *Improvisations for Harp*; Elinor Bennet, Nimbus 5441

Piano Trio and Sonatas 1 & 2 for Violin and Piano; Michael Davis (violin), other artists, Koch 7326

~

David Matthews: Renewing the Past

In his article "Renewing the Past", English composer David Matthews (b. 1943) declared, "My principles are: that tonality is not outmoded, but a living force; that the vernacular is an essential part of musical language; and that the great forms of the past, such as the Symphony, are still valid." How does a composer renew the past, especially when there has been such a major break with it? I heard part of the answer to my question from Martin Anderson, founder of Toccata Classics, when he handed me a recording of three of Matthews' string quartets. Here, I thought, was someone writing deeply in the grand tradition, but freshly, without any cobwebs.

I arranged to meet Matthews when I next went to London (in 2011). We then had a long conversation about his music. Matthews is the rare kind of intrepid composer who never succumbed to the serial system, despite Pierre Boulez' proclamation of the utter irrelevance of those who did not. His reward was relative obscurity—until now, that is, as a spate of recordings from Toccata Classics, NMC and Dutton are bringing his significant body of work (more than 100 opus numbers) to larger public view. This includes eight symphonies (see the Dutton and NMC labels), 13 string quartets (see the emerging cycle on Toccata Records), and various concerti and vocal works (Dutton and Toccata).

Where does a composer like this come from, and how did he have the nerve and stamina to create so many major works with so little hope of performance or recording? It probably helped that Matthews, along with his composer brother Colin, was an autodidact, which spared him from undergoing the indoctrination in serialism typical of the time. Formally, he studied classics at Nottingham University (which may help account for his literary talent). Then he took music lessons from Anthony Milner and received guidance from Nicholas Maw, an English composer who also fought the tide of the times (listen, for instance, to Maw's neoromantic Violin Concerto). Matthews had the privilege of serving as Benjamin Britten's assistant for three years at Aldeburgh. He and his brother Colin helped Deryk Cooke produce a performable version of Mahler's unfinished 10th Symphony. Matthews was so smitten by Michael Tippett's music that he wrote a book about him, *Michael Tippett, An Introductory Study*.

How does Matthews see his vocation? "I have continued", he explains on his web site, "along a path similar to that taken by Tippett and Britten: one rooted in the Viennese Classics—Beethoven above all —and also in Mahler, Sibelius and the early 20th-century modernists. I have always been a tonal composer, attempting to integrate the musical language of the present with the past, and to explore the rich traditional forms." As we've seen, some of this genealogy was close to personal, and it accounts for the character and sound of his music. If you like the sources upon which Matthews draws, you will most likely like him.

In general, Matthews' work is so steeped in tradition that one must be acquainted with tradition to grasp it fully. I do not mean by this that it is at all anachronistic or nostalgic. It is far too bracing for that. I mean that his self-described "attempt to integrate the present with the past by reestablishing a continuity with those forms from the past which contain the greatest accumulation of historical meaning" requires a level of musical literacy in order to appreciate it. In a salute to Matthews from *Gramophone* magazine on the occasion of his 70th birthday in 2013, writer Geraint Lewis astutely observed of the Matthews string quartets that "this is music about music with no extraneous frills." This is not to say that the music does not work on its own terms—only that those *are* its terms. As Matthews said to me, it helps "to know the tradition so people can see what I am doing new with it". This reminds me of Igor Stravinsky's statement: "To be a good listener, you must acquire a musical culture. . . . You must be familiar with the history and development of music, you must listen. . . . To receive music you have to open your ears and wait for the music; you must believe that it is something you need. . . . To listen is an effort, and just to hear has no merit. A duck hears also."

In other words, if you want to know what is going on at a deeper level, you need a kind of scorecard—in this case, some familiarity with the influences and overt references in Matthews' music. If you don't, you won't know what he intends by playing with them in the way he does. Still, this does not mean that there is nothing to enjoy for the novice listener. Matthews' music is not hermetic, and his mastery of tonal tension and release should grab everyone's attention at the first go. It does mean, however, that the music is so rich and multilayered that it often takes repeated auditions to hear all that is there.

Matthews said that his symphonic style at first emerged from Central European influences, particularly that of Alban Berg. Gradually, his music moved from under Berg's spell and became less angular and more consonant—more engaged with tonal counterpoint. He described his Seventh Symphony as a kind of Sibelian one-movement symphony, also matched with Mahler's Seventh in its use of the tenor horn. This is one of his most attractive, immediately appealing works.

Along with the Seventh, perhaps the most accessible entry into the world of Matthews' music are his tone poems, several of which are gathered on a Chandos CD containing *The Music of Dawn*, a symphonic poem for orchestra that depicts the progression from sunrise to high noon; *Concerto in Azzurro* for cello and orchestra; and *A Vision and a Journey*, a symphonic fantasy, played with wonderful refinement by the BBC Philharmonic under Rumon Gamba, with cellist Guy Johnston. These dazzling works display the extraordinary richness of Matthews' orchestral language. The first two movements of *Dawn* achieve a kind of shimmering stasis, employing sizzle cymbal, caxixi, metal maracas, and rainstick. Before reading Matthews' liner notes, I supposed that he was simulating deep breathing (done far more effectively than the embarrassingly literal use of recorded sounds of heavy breathing in Tippett's Fourth Symphony), punctuated by occasional string pizzicato out of Mahler's Fourth Symphony. Actually, he meant to suggest "the sound of the sea breaking over the pebble beach". Either way, it is mesmerizing. The fourth movement contains invigorating echoes of William Walton's First Symphony. The orchestration by itself is enough to make one wonder if Matthews is a kind of English Villa-Lobos, a question reinforced by the occasional wildness of his music, if not by his style. Overall, the progress from dawn to high noon is pulsing with life in this enchanting "celebration of the morning". The *Azzurro* cello concerto conveys an aching beauty. It begins with a worrying motif sawing away in cello that soon broadens out into a rhapsodic melody. This is a luminous work, with great warmth and considerable tenderness. *A Vision and a Journey* suitably conveys a sense of striving and destination.

Other Matthews tone poems to which I am particularly attracted include *September Music*, with its highly atmospheric, Debussyesque sound world, and with just the right touch of bittersweetness introduced by muted brass; and *Introit*, one of Matthews' loveliest and most introspective works, infused with a soft efflorescence reminiscent of the best of Tippett. It belongs in the company of other British string (with brass) classics.

I can only skip through the incredibly rich symphonies, which require a book by themselves, in order to suggest some stylistic touchstones. Symphony No. 1 is a tour de force, highly kinetic music, with thundering eruptions in the first part, generating at times a huge amount of power. It begins softly, meditatively, developing into a rich string discourse that reflects Tippett, with burbling wind and brass interjections. There's a celebratory feel to it even in the shrieking winds and walloping timpani. Matthews seems to let loose mayhem in parts of this symphony out of sheer exuberance. Some of the rhythms are redolent of Stravinsky, and eight minutes in, we hear what sounds like Villa-Lobos' *Little Train of the Caipira* chugging along the trail; then we return to Tippett. I also heard traces of the Welsh composer William Mathias. This work is an exhilarating, exuberant amalgamation of these influences.

In the Second, one hears a sinuous long-lined melody in the bassoon from a Debussian reverie that is joined by string ostinatos and burbling winds. This is vigorously interrupted by timpani and then brass declamations. The timpani attacks have some of the same visceral thrill as Japanese drumming. In the second movement, there is a touch of influence from the *Peter Grimes* orchestral interludes. The third movement reminds me of Colin McPhee's gamelan music. The close of the Second Symphony is a musical coup de theatre.

In places, Symphony No. 3 sounds uncannily, startlingly like Steve Albert's *RiverRun*. This, of course, can only be an amazing coincidence since both composers finished their respective works in the same year —1983. Albert shared a great deal of Matthews' perspective on music and was also influenced by Mahler and Sibelius; so perhaps it is not so strange that their styles should so closely intersect at one point.

Symphony No. 4 is a playful work, almost a romp, in five movements. Mysterious strings and twittering winds create a crepuscular sound world in the first movement. The second is a breathless, hard-driven Scherzo that seems to race against itself with Stravinskian rhythms. A lovely Andante for strings and first horn is followed by a delicious tango. A closing Adagio segues into an Allegro led by recurrent Haydn-like hunting horn calls. Matthews speaks of "tricks played with the conventions of sonata form" in Haydn's spirit. The symphony does not so much end as simply stop—as if to leave a question mark at the end of the proceedings: Have we caught on to Matthews' musical equivalent to a trompe l'oeil painting?

The start of Symphony No. 5 sounds like an English version of Albert Roussel's Third with the same kind of grinding rhythmic power, but without its grimness. In fact, it is invigorating. The symphony ends with a huge, galumphing procession that swaggers like a force of nature, Matthews' version of Britten's *Spring Symphony*.

There is so much going on in the first movement of Symphony No. 6 that it is hard to keep pace. In the opening I hear Sibelius in the deep double bass background mixed with some English pastoralism (apparently a variation on Vaughan Williams' hymn tune *Down Ampney*), then what sounds like a take on Fafner's music from *Das Rheingold* in the brass, then some Sallinen-like scalar runs in the winds, and, later, more Villa-Lobos. This does not mean that the music is a mishmash of these influences; only that it is very rich in allusions—perhaps not all of them consciously made. I am trying to indicate the sound worlds in which Matthews moves. It certainly keeps you on your toes as a listener and is extremely vivid. Its second movement, Scherzo, is based upon a falling motif—2 notes up, 9 notes down—that is tossed around the orchestra and finally hammered home with some timpani. It is fleet and very engaging. "It's about life really", said Matthews. "There's a lot of struggle and it ends with a temporary resolution; the end is peaceful but there's been a lot of turmoil, especially in the first movement, a lot of different sorts of energy."

Symphony No. 7 puts me in mind of a November 2010 letter, in which Matthews wrote: "The important thing about writing tonal music nowadays is that one must lose self-consciousness about what one is doing. This is difficult, but it mustn't be impossible or we can never recover the confident spirit about tonality which had been lost because of all the attacks on it by Boulez *et cie*." By this I believe he means restoring the naturalness in tonal composition, as against, say, minimalism, which so self-consciously announces, "Here I am breathing again with a pulse in my veins", when it is actually on artificial life-support systems in the emergency room. In any case, Matthews has certainly achieved this in his Seventh Symphony, which is as natural sounding a modern symphony as I have heard. "If there was a symphonic model in my mind it was Sibelius' Seventh", he said. "I knew from the start that my own piece would also be in one movement, and that Sibelius' extraordinarily subtle transitions of tempo from slow to fast and back again would be an ideal to aim for." It begins with a lovely, very long-lined melody that he develops in coherent and convincing ways to its gripping conclusion. He added, "There is a lengthy coda, starting Allegro strepitoso, whose boisterous energy is eventually stabilized in an assertive D-major ending. Because it is probably the most conclusive ending I have ever written, it seems to me like a summing up of all the symphonies I have written during the past 35 years."

In this work it is abundantly clear that Matthews has shaken off whatever self-consciousness a return to tonality and classical forms may entail in this day and age. This music flows freely. As the *Telegraph* put it in its review of the premiere, "What makes Matthews' music lovable is the way it embraces straightforwardly tonal means, with no tricksy post-modern irony or agonised breast-beating."

When I first listened to the Matthews Fourth String Quartet late one night, I was stunned. How is it, I wondered, that music of this quality, written in 1982, is being heard by recording only now in 2010? This is an indictment of the musical establishment, as it is a complete vindication of what Toccata Classics does—and how well it does it. What we hear in Quartets 4, 6, and 10, along with the *Adagio* for String Quartet, is some of the most concentrated, penetrating writing for this medium in the past 30 years or more. It is musical thinking of the highest order and quartet writing in the great tradition of Beethoven, Bartók, Britten, and Tippett, all of whom Matthews mentions as influences. Though he does not list Janáček, I am tempted to add his name because of the elliptical punch and attractive wildness of these works, and Matthews' ability to express so much in so few bars.

These works are full of exquisite moments. Some of the music is searing, much of it dances and sings, and some of it is achingly beautiful and tender. It is all brimming with life. I found the Adagio sostenuto in Quartet No. 4 and the Lontano movement in the Tenth Quartet to be heart-stoppingly beautiful. This is volume 1 in what will be a complete cycle of Matthews' 12 quartets. The Kreutzer Quartet plays this music with staggering conviction and skill. This release exemplifies the mission of Toccata Classics and why such a label is necessary.

The second Toccata release of the string quartets contains Nos. 5 and 12, composed more than 25 years apart and, as Matthews writes in the program notes, "widely contrasted, formally and stylistically". Indeed, that is almost an understatement. In the Fifth, whose three movements are played continuously, the Kreutzer Quartet digs in with such grip and intensity that it almost seems as if they are playing on barbed wire. In its gritty introspection, this quartet is as close as Matthews gets to Shostakovich—from what I have heard so far. There is anguish aplenty —of a particularly piercing quality in the Largo sostenuto, in which a doleful melody is heard over the strumming or pizzicato playing of the other players. This is riveting, tough music.

The Twelfth Quartet (2010) is, according to Matthews, "somewhat modeled on Beethoven's formal plan" of his op. 130 String Quartet, with the *Grosse Fuge*. If you are gun-shy from having heard a catfight passed off as a modern string quartet, start with this work to see exactly how well old forms can be infused with new life, as solidly anchored in the wellsprings of song and dance as real music has always been. While the Fifth sounds very modern in its harmonies, the Twelfth is steeped in classical tonality—to such an extent that Matthews describes the lovely Canto mesto movement, the longest in the quartet, as "my most ambitious attempt to revive classical tonality, with extensive use of modulation". This quartet is much lighter in spirit than the Fifth and has its origins in a serenade. The first movement is filled with marvelous fugal writing. As for dance, Matthews has some fun vamping with a tango in the "Tango" movement, followed by a Haydnesque Menuetto scherzando. Matthews says of the Finale, "Its mood is mostly joyful". Together, these two quartets display the enormous range of expression that Matthews can call forth from the form—from the gritty to the ingratiating. No. 12 joins No. 4 as my two favorites so far in this cycle.

Matthews is as adept at vocal and choral writing as he is with symphonic and chamber music. His *Vespers* has all the hallmarks of a major work. This is a big piece with a broad range of expression. Do not expect something solemn. Like Britten in the *War Requiem*, he interpolates modern texts, in this case three beautiful poems by Rilke, into the liturgical ones. Britten is certainly one of the stylistic touchstones here, as well as Tippett at his finest. This work also has a raucousness, splendor, and sense of wonder similar to that of Vaughan Williams' *Hodie Christus Natus Est*. The Dutton recording of it with the Bach Choir and the Bournemouth Symphony Orchestra, under David Hill, is paired with the Symphony No. 7, with the same orchestra, under John Carewe, both in splendid performances and sound. If you want to approach Matthews through his major works, this might be the place to start.

Here is my provisional assessment of Matthews' music. Against the prevailing trends that have kept his work in semiobscurity, his music emerges as a sign of hope. Matthews has absorbed the vocabulary of modernism without succumbing to it. He turns it to a different purpose—away from the construction of a self-absorbed autonomy and toward something higher than itself. In his article on "Religious Art in the Twenty-First Century", Matthews says, "I would hesitate to call myself a religious composer, yet in the act of composing music I feel I'm asserting a sense of meaning in the universe, in that I'm wanting to find meaningful form and content in contrast to its opposites, whether the nihilistic language of Harrison Birtwistle or the random, chaotic approach of John Cage, both of which I reject."

When I asked Matthews to comment on how the sense of purpose in nature is reflected in his work, he responded,

> To put it rather simply, for me the act of writing music is a testament to a belief that there is some kind of meaning to the universe. I can't take it much further than that, but it seems to me that all is not just random. Music can express that sense of meaning through its structure and also its content. I reject rather strongly any music and indeed any art that seems to express the opposite, that all is meaningless and chaotic. There's a lot of that around. In the natural world one observes a process that is on the one hand mechanical but is also full of wonder, and excites wonder. It is in observing and entering into that spirit of wonder that a lot of the incitement to write music comes.

In his bones, Matthews knows that beauty is a sign of transcendence. His music is a form of semaphore, flagging signals to us through the fog that the light will not be extinguished. In other words, the yearning expressed in Matthews' work is not in vain. It is aimed at more than a possibility—a kind of certain hope for an inexpressible fulfillment of which beauty is the promise. Deny beauty, and you deny the promise. Matthews, no matter how occasionally difficult and at times raucous his music may be, enhances the beauty by struggling for and to it. This is why his work is so rich, so filled with incident and thick with crosscurrents.

Recommended Recordings

The Music of Dawn; *Concerto in Azzurro*; *A Vision and a Journey*, Rumon Gamba, BBC Philharmonic, Chandos 10487 (OOP)

Symphonies 1, 3 & 5, Martyn Brabbins, BBC NO of Wales, Dutton 7222

Symphonies 2 & 6, Jac Van Steen, BBC NO of Wales, Dutton 7234

Cantiga; *September Music*; *Introit*; Symphony No. 4, NMC 084

Symphony No. 7; *Vespers*, David Hill, John Carewe, Bournemouth SO, The Bach Choir, Dutton 7305

Violin Concertos 1 & 2; Oboe Concerto, George Vass, Philippe Graffin, Nicholas Daniel, Bournemouth SO, Dutton 7261

String Quartets 4 & 10, Kreutzer Quartet, Toccata Classics 0058

String Quartets 5 & 12, Kreutzer Quartet, Toccata Classics 0059

Music for Solo Violin (vol. 1), Peter Sheppard Skaerved, Toccata Classics 0152

~

Eric(h) Zeisl and Franz Mittler:
Lost and Found Music

Jens F. Laurson

We will never know exactly how classical music would have sounded in the 20th century, had it not been for the universal calamity of World War II. But we have some clues. Of the several strands of "lost" classical music that became extinct, there is the strain that might be labeled post-Stravinskian: angular, but tonal. This might have developed somewhere along the lines of the music that Walter Braunfels, Boris Blacher, Karl Amadeus Hartmann, or Harald Genzmer composed. There is also a more romantic line of music, very roughly of the type that Richard Strauss was still allowed to compose in the middle of the 20th century, although even a composer of his stature was looked at as a musical dinosaur for writing works like *Capriccio* or the *Four Last Songs*. Erich Korngold, Franz Schmidt, and Joseph Marx come to mind.

A good deal of the harm World War II caused to aesthetics came indirectly. Ideological shifts after 1945—in the West, especially in Germany—seemed to demand a radical departure from everything that had been before. A music in direct contrast to the trends of Soviet realism; a music that resembled absolute freedom and individuality was called for, as was a rejection of all the values that reeked of the old regime. This, it was deemed, could be found in the absolutes of the avant-garde —well intentioned, perhaps, but leading to aesthetic license, not expressive freedom. This exacerbated and finalized classical music's split between the safe and popular repertoire and contemporary music. A very specific type of modernity was so pummeled with subsidies that it no longer needed to be accountable to any public and—as is the nature of subsidies—significantly decreased the chances of all other contemporary classical music to survive on its own merits.

Beyond the perceived, alleged postwar paradigm shift in listening aesthetics there was also the very real threat of physical extermination during the war. Many of the composers who managed to escape a murderous Europe to find shelter in the United States did not fare as well in the new world as did the icons Stravinsky and Schoenberg or the adaptable, seemingly perpetually sunny Korngold. Eric(h) Zeisl and Franz Mittler were two such composers, and their song remains (metaphorically) unsung to this day except for a few *Lieder* that occasionally creep into Austrian song recitals.

Zeisl

Born in Vienna on May 18, 1905, Erich Zeisl decided early on to become a composer—against the express wishes of his café-house running parents, who were musically inclined but not so much to see a proper living to be made in composing. Nonetheless, Zeisl persisted and, at barely 16, published his first songs, which the famous bass Alexander Kipnis included in his repertoire. Refusing to do well in regular school, he got into the Vienna Academy of Music and Performing Arts. The Anschluss—Hitler-Germany's hostile but widely welcomed takeover of Austria—put an end to Zeisl's only just flourishing career in Vienna, and he had to begin an exodus that brought him first to Paris (with the help of Darius Milhaud, who became a life-long friend) and then to New York. Hanns Eisler recommended Zeisl to Schoenberg, and he began working in Hollywood as a film composer for MGM in 1942. Being late to that party, he did not find the success of his friend Korngold, who had established himself in Hollywood long before the war. Instead of winning Academy Awards and composing scores for *Robin Hood* and *Sea Hawk*, Zeisl anonymously contributed to lesser gems such as *Lassie Come Home*, *The Invisible Man's Revenge*, and *Money, Women, and Guns*.

Scholar, producer, and foremost *Entartete Musik* expert Michael Haas describes Eric (who dropped the "h" upon immigration) Zeisl's émigré story as one of raised expectations and dashed hopes, escape from death but loss of soul: "One of Austria's most promising talents in the 1930s —neither an extreme avant-gardist nor a musical reactionary"—Zeisl became an also-ran in his safe haven abroad.

He didn't seem to fit in particularly well and had trouble adapting to the country that would officially become his homeland when he was naturalized in 1945. In a letter from that year he wrote:

> Austria is a country of Johann Strauss and *Wiener Liedern*; that is all what the people here know about our great musical tradition. I have a great fight even for my poor living . . . even Milhaud, Stravinsky, Tansman are struggling. Béla Bartók died in New York of hunger!

Last year I orchestrated a Tchaikovsky operetta which provided living for eight months—but why does Tchaikovsky need to be turned
into an operetta? That's the difference. No composer is important
here.

Also troubling for any resident of Hollywood: Zeisl distinctly disliked
the sun and preferred cloudy, rainy days.

From 1948 to 1950 he was the composer-in-residence at the Brandeis
Camp Institute. From 1947 until his death in 1959 he taught an evening
composition class at Los Angeles City College, a position Stravinsky
recommended Zeisl for. He continued to compose serious music in
those days, including the Piano Concerto, which is a wonderful new
discovery.

Every time I return to the concerto, it becomes more difficult to
believe that this splendid work should have gotten its premiere only
in 2005 for Zeisl's 100th anniversary—by the Saratoga Symphony Orchestra, half a century after its 1951–1952 composition. At the time it
was the only major Zeisl work available on record—a sorry fact that
is slowly changing, with hopeful signs that his music is undergoing a
lasting rediscovery and reevaluation.

The immediate, broad *forte* opening of the concerto has a pleasant
element of monotony and minimalism to it. When the soloist enters together with the orchestra, with rising and falling octaves in both hands,
he or she fills out the space with a murmur of "supplementary" notes
that create busyness amid the stoic, simplistic melody. The wave-like
motion is taken up and modulated by the orchestra's other instruments,
the flute prominent among them. The means might faintly remind of
Brahms, but the result is closer to Ravel.

The second movement, too, has a strangely familiar, gentle air about
it, not per se homophonous with Ravel's Piano Concerto but sympathetic. Liking the latter should be a good indicator as to whether you
also find the former a treat. The third movement moves away from the
simplicity and the niceties. The solo piano introduction is angular and
brooding, followed by a rambunctious and spirited movement that is
hammered out without compromise. But when it relents (Zeisl notes
in the margins: "Broaden!"), there's one more Ravel-throwback, and
this time as obvious as it is brief: The oboe solo introduces a theme
that comes almost unadulterated from Ravel's slow movement. If there
is any significance in that, I do not know; the American connection
(Ravel composed both his piano concertos after the indelible impres-

sions of his American tour in 1928) and the wistful mood alone would seem too slight a reason for that similarity, but there is no reference to Ravel in his correspondence of the time.

The CPO recording of the Piano Concerto also features the ballet music *Pierrot in the Bottle* (1929), which shows Zeisl fusing a relatively advanced harmonic language with a remarkable light-heartedness. It's still much more Strauss' *Til Eulenspiegel* than Schoenberg's *Pierrot Lunaire*, thanks to Zeisl's unshakable Viennese romanticism.

Zeisl, who felt only incidentally Jewish while growing up Austrian, eventually tried to amend for the loss of his Austrian home by embracing Judaism. This led to incidental music for Joseph Roth's play *Job* in Paris, but the venture of creating an opera on that subject faltered after two completed acts. Excerpts from a student production shown in Herbert Krill's documentary film *Eric(h) Zeisl: An Unfinished Life* are unconvincing: not just because of the pitiful execution but also because of less interesting Zeisl-music (however biographically important) set to the hokey and artifice-burdened (however historically significant) morality play of Joseph Roth's. The premiere of the opera, now with acts 3 and 4 finished by Jan Duszyńsky, finally took place at the Bavarian State Opera, after languishing for 55 years. It turns out that in a loving and professional performance it holds several charming highlights in play but, alas, is still not his strongest work.

Of much greater relevance and musical worth is the Requiem Zeisl wrote for his murdered father, who was killed at Treblinka. Not only was it an important and intensely personal statement, it also marked the regained passion for composing for himself, rather than frustratingly churning out music on demand for MGM and Universal-International. Its vigor and passion seem to uncork years of artistic dormancy. Zeisl remarked about the commission of what became the *Requiem Ebraico*: "At that time war in Europe had just ended and I received the first news of the death of my father and many friends. The sadness of my mood went into my composition which became a Requiem, though I had not intended to write one and scarcely would have chosen the 92nd Psalm for it. Yet the completed Requiem thus received a deeper meaning than I could have achieved by planning it that way." The 20-minute work has been given a good number of performances, including by conductors Lawrence Foster, Zubin Mehta, and James Conlon. A fine recording by John Neschling on BIS, the only one currently in print, is very much worth seeking out.

It was on November 28, 1939, when Eric(h) Zeisl arrived in New

York. Just five days later he had his *Little Symphony* broadcast on NBC's
Blue Network with the Radio City Symphony and later repeated upon
popular request. Zeisl's symphony, which he had written three years
earlier, is composed to four pictures of painter Roswitha Bitterlich. It
starts out with jazzy bits, then continues like an accelerated train slipping into a circus-like jollity. After slowing down again, it repeats the
same procedure with different music in increasingly quicker ways for
all of its four pictures. It's an appropriate work to exemplify a happy
start to a happy, if impoverished and all too brief stay in Manhattan
and on Long Island—crowned by the birth of the couple's daughter
Barbara in May of 1940. During Zeisl's New York time he also served
as best man for fellow Viennese exiled composer Franz Mittler.

Mittler

Being linked to the dead-on satirist, disgruntled poet, Nazi-skewering
aphorist, muckraker-playwright, coffeehouse-philosopher Karl Kraus
(roughly something of Austria's H. L. Mencken except that Mencken
never sang Offenbach operettas off-key as a vehicle for biting social criticism), and given his Jewish roots, it was impossible for Franz Mittler
to return to his apartment after Germany annexed Austria. So Franz
Mittler, who was in Amsterdam at the time, went from Holland directly to New York, where he arrived in December, now *Frank* Mittler,
and settled in Washington Heights.

Not the least because he had a talent for languages, Mittler acclima-
tized quickly, and within a year, he found himself a wife in a near-
musical manner: as Mittler exited the Steinway building on 57th Street
in Manhattan he bumped into a young lady. Upon closer inspection,
the young lady turned out to be his fellow student from the Vienna
Conservatory Regina Schilling, who was on her way in—to receive
a piano from a refugee relief agency. Now the foxtrot *Foolish Spring*
that Mittler had dedicated to her five years earlier paid off, and by
December—with Zeisl's bit of officiating help—she was Regina Mittler. On the way to the registrar's office, Zeisl bugged Mittler with repeated questioning as to whether Franz was really sure he wanted to go
through with it, and whether he knew what he was doing, very much
to the increasing annoyance of Mittler's wife-to-be, who sat right next
to them. Reflecting on her parents' marriage, concert pianist, choral
director, and music professor at C.U.N.Y., Diana Mittler-Battipaglia,

coyly-wistfully added to her telling of this anecdote: "Well . . . maybe he was on to something."

A few months after his wedding Mittler accompanied the mezzo-soprano Charlotte Kraus at a recital in the White House that included Mittler's own "Volksweise", one of his most popular songs and a favorite of Bruno Walter. This was an early highlight in his newfound home country, but was marred slightly by the absence of the stately banquet Mittler had hoped for. Instead Mrs. Roosevelt, all austerity, served a few skimpy bites on paper plates.

In 1943 Mittler joined the two-year-old First Piano Quartet (four pianos, mind you!), which arranged and performed small and popular bits and pieces of classical music on the radio, on record, and in concert. That engagement became Mittler's focus for the next 20 years. As part of the foursome he enjoyed national, if ultimately anonymous, fame. They recorded 17 albums for RCA and Decca, appeared together on bills with classical music hall-of-famers Arthur Rubinstein, Jussi Bjoerling, and Gregor Piatigorsky. They received a 1948 Musical America Award, won NBC a Peabody for Outstanding Entertainment in Music in the same year, and appeared on the *Today Show* with Hugh Downs. Their Chopin Favorites were Billboard Classical Chart toppers.

They were also favorites of the Truman family: President Harry Truman found a record of the quartet under his tree, given to him by his daughter. Together they attended the First Piano Quartet performance at D.C.'s Constitution Hall, after which Alice Eversman wrote in the *Evening Star*: "Essentially entertaining in character, the playing of the group is of high artistry. Superbly endowed technically and musically, there is no limit to its virtuosity." *Time* magazine reported on them after their first Carnegie Hall appearance: "All four . . . pianists do the arranging. Each keeps in mind the special talents of the other three. Russian-born Vladimir 'Vee' Padwa . . . is the trill expert. Adam Garner likes to handle special tonal colors; Edward Edson is famed for . . . his 'light delicate touch'. Viennese Frank Mittler . . . quips: 'I do the dramatic pauses!'"

Franz was born on April 14, 1893, the fourth of five children of Josef and Rosalie Mittler. Among that quintet, he showed the greatest musical propensity. He went on to learn the piano, the violin, and the guitar. At nine Mittler played Schubert's *Violin Sonatina* in his first public recital. His little pianist buddy was the youthful, seven-year-old Clara Haskil. When he abandoned the violin in favor of the piano, his instructor was Theodor Leschetizky. Among his composition teachers was Richard Heuberger, who stood for the musical quintessence of Brahms' Vienna.

Mittler enjoyed sojourns at the Cologne Conservatory (1918–1919) and the Theater of the Grand Duchy Gera-Reuss as a conductor. There his full-length ballet *The Golden Goose* premiered, but the score was lost in the turmoil of the second World War, along with a violin concerto, a cello concerto, and his full-length opera *Raffaella*. The latter received only one performance in Duisburg, in 1930, and was never heard again, though a piano/vocal manuscript remains. Mittler returned to Vienna in 1921 and became a sought-after Lieder accompanist—Leo Slezak's partner, among others—and famous for playing all the great song cycles from memory.

The Viennese Mittler was perhaps the greatest spoonerist of his generation. Unfortunately spoonerisms and limericks—based on subtleties of language, accents, and dialects so richly present in that cultural melting pot of prewar Vienna—don't translate. Fortunately Mittler was a genius with languages. He adapted his wit to his adopted language and continued cranking them out, even if not quite as complex as his four-quatrain spoonerism "Arctic Ballade", one of the highlights of his silly-sublime poetic output. The pleasure derived from reading the vast collection of his rhyming gems is great; they are a linguistic window into early 20th-century Viennese history.

It seems to me Isolde's potion mixture
Is too boring for a motion picture

Mittler spoke yet another language, more universal than any of the seven he was fluent in: music. Focusing just on the music might do Mittler-the-polymath discredit, but focusing on the polymath does injustice to the splendid composer. The quantity of his compositions is not enormous compared to the giants—celebrated and forgotten—among 20th-century composers. But among the lot of his 400—mostly minor—works are significant contributions very much worth hearing.

The Brahmsian background of his music education shapes all of Mittler's compositions, which are roughly in the romantic vein of Erich Korngold and Joseph Marx. Early compositions betray his influences: Richard Strauss in the *Four Songs*, op. 6; Schumann in the *Phantasiestück*, op. 5; and Mahler in the soprano-songs *Marienbildchen*, op. 7/1. His 1911 Piano Trio, op. 3, the first and longest published work of Mittler's, was reviewed in *Die Musik* and elicited this response: "A strong talent for melody, a genuine joy in making music seems to speak to me from this very gratifying trio, even if this somewhat Mendelssoh-nian young composer still lacks his own original personality. . . . Especially attractive is the heartfelt melody in the Scherzo; the finale with its Slavic touch is dashing and effective." There are worse things, at 18, than to be called "somewhat Mendelssohnian".

His String Quartet in F was premiered by the Prill Quartet in 1910. Musicologist and critic Richard Specht attested to the 16-year-old composer's "unquestionable talent" and suggested that the composition, "beautifully realized, full of warmth and sensitive expression . . . points toward future personal recognition". In 1935 an astute critic in the *Neues Wiener Abendblatt* wrote that "Mittler's music . . . strives neither for grandeur nor outward excitement, rather it is aphoristic, like small carefully painted pictures rich in atmosphere. His simple, touching melodies, his ingenious ideas and comedy charm the listener." The comedy, the light-heartedness is probably key to understanding Mittler and his work. His *One Finger Polka* was dedicated to Chico Marx' second finger. "Boxing Kangaroo" (from the *Newsreel* Piano Suite) didn't become a classic, but it certainly speaks to the whimsy Mittler had such a knack for. You might describe Mittler as the Francis Poulenc of *Entartete Musik* (Degenerate Music). His settings of poems by Wilhelm Busch—the gory rhyming godfather of the cartoon—are priceless. His newfound home didn't remain uncomposed, either: The *Manhattan Suite* (1947) includes a "Song of the Subway" and "Waltzing in Central Park".

Despite the Brahms-pedigree, Mittler had no time for excessive seriousness. Even the severe form of the string quartet refuses the furrowed brow and gets infused with Mittlerian vivaciousness. The 1909 Quartet No. 1 sounds like an old acquaintance from the first notes on, in a happy, not derivative, sort of familiarity. Mittler also kept his humor when he wrote his Third Quartet between 1915 and 1918, which were not happy years for the continent. Mittler, a lieutenant in the bread-baking division of the Imperial and Royal Army, took the wistful beauty of a disintegrating multiethnic empire as his inspiration, not the carnage around him.

Each movement of this quartet depicts a region of the empire he was stationed in. A "Wolhynian" first movement, a "Serbian Scherzo", and a slow movement titled "Styria" lead to the wild and vividly descriptive "Rapsodia Ungherese". It's all absolutely beautiful, and it easily stands up to other teenage masterworks like Bridge's Sextet, Mendelssohn's Octet, or Korngold's Piano Trio.

Daphne Blumberg, who visited Rome,
Went at Easter to Saint Peter's Dome.
She waved to the Pontiff
A friendly: *Good Yonteff!*
"And Pius waved back", she wrote home.

Not that Mittler was always successful with his compositions. As his daughter wrote on a sticky note that accompanied a private recording of the two unpublished trios: "The last movement of the trio in A minor was so surprisingly bad, we substituted the finale of the G major trio, instead." The rest is good, though, and the other two trios are better still: a Trio in C Major, unpublished (1910) and the above-mentioned Trio in G Major. The Scherzo of the latter was used to fine effect in the 2007 PBS special *Last Stop Kew Gardens*; its distinctive rhythmic cell pops up again in the Scherzo of the Trio in A and in the Allegretto giocoso of the C-major Trio.

For his last six years Franz Mittler escaped the increasingly tedious life of a free-lance musician and a deteriorating marriage, and he moved back to Europe. He lived in Siegsdorf, conveniently near Salzburg, where he taught three summers at the Salzburg Mozarteum. It was the Mozarteum, on the occasion on Mittler's 75th birthday, which honored Mittler with an evening dedicated to his compositions: several Songs and the *Suite in the Ancient Style for Solo Cello*. Franz Mittler, suffering from Parkinson's, died on December 27, 1970, in a Munich nursing home—11 years after his friend Eric(h) had died unexpectedly of a heart attack in Los Angeles.

Recommended Recordings

The works of Zeisl and Mittler have endured silence long enough; they are most deserving of (re)discovery. With major classical artists like the Emerson Quartet, Renée Fleming, and Daniel Hope having picked up at least a Zeisl work here or there, optimism might be legitimate. But there are not yet many recordings available—with many notable lacunae. Zeisl's Symphonic Serenade and Symphony, op. 40 are not available on record and the fine *Arrowhead* Trio (for piano, flute, and harp) is out of print. Happily, of his three sonatas—one each for violin, viola, and cello—only the latter awaits an available recording. Mittler's chamber music is still awaiting competent and well distributed performances. Fortunately more recordings of both composers' compositions are in the works, and with any luck they will find a market of eager ears. Also a fortune is the website of Zeisl's grandson (also Arnold Schoenberg's grandson), E. Randol Schoenberg. Having an eye especially on the musical heritage of the less famous of his composing grandfathers, he created Zeisl.com, where one can search his entire output and listen to excerpts of most works.

Eric(h) Zeisl

Réquiem Ebraico—92nd Psalm, John Neschling, Choir of the São Paulo SO, Naomi Munakata, São Paulo SO, BIS 1650

Piano Concerto in C Major; Suite for Orchestra *Pierrot in der Flasche*, Gottlieb Wallisch (piano), Johannes Wildner (conductor), Vienna RSO, CPO 777 226

Viola in Exile: Viola Sonatas of Eric Zeisl, Karl Weigl, and Hans Gál, Julia Rebekka Adler, Axel Gremmelspacher, Gramola 99026. With its inclusion of Zeisl, Weigl and Gál, this terrific CD does the equivalent of getting a *Surprised by Beauty* Bingo.

Lieder, Wolfgang Holzmair (baritone), Cord Garben (piano), CPO 777 170

Little Symphony; *November* for Chamber Orchestra; Concerto Grosso for Cello and Orchestra, Antonio Lysy (cello), Neal Stulberg (conductor), UCLA Philharmonia, Yarlung 96820

November, Six Sketches for Chamber Orchestra (1940) is an intimate orchestral work based on his piano pieces of the same name. The dramatic Concerto Grosso for Cello and Orchestra (1956) epitomizes Zeisl's mature style from Los Angeles.

Violin Sonata *Brandeis*; *Menuchim's Song* (also includes Copland, Violin Sonata; Ernst Bloch, *Abodah*; Robert Dauber, Serenata), Zina Schiff, Cameron Grant, MSR 1493

Piano Music (including *November* for piano), Eric Le Van (piano), Music & Arts 1271

Komm, süsser Tod (also includes Berg, *Lyric Suite* & Egon Wellesz, *Browning Sonnets*), Renée Fleming, Emerson String Quartet, Decca 478 8399

Franz Mittler

String Quartets 1 & 3, Hugh Wolff Quartett, CPO 777 329 (OOP)

String Quartet; *Four Songs*, Artis Quartett Wien, Wolfgang Holzmair, ORF 4918425

Piano Trio, op. 3; *Character Pieces* for Piano; Lieder & Couplets, Diana Mittler, Anton Miller, Lawrence Zoernig, Wolfgang Holzmair, Preiser 90567 (OOP)

Carl Nielsen: Music *Is* Life

The two giants of 20th-century Nordic music, Danish composer Carl Nielsen and Finnish composer Jean Sibelius, were born in the same year, 1865. Though they sound nothing alike, together they account for my initial love of music. Sibelius' Fifth Symphony and Nielsen's Fourth, both written around 1915, are the two works that revealed to me, in an overwhelming way, what human beings are capable of expressing in sound.

Explaining the differences between the two composers might be helpful in understanding Nielsen, whom Sibelius once told, "I don't reach as high as your ankles." Sibelius' music is a revelation of nature in all of its solitary majesty. Man is the spectator of the awesome drama that is unfolded before him and before which he must tremble, even in his exhilaration. In Nielsen's music, on the other hand, man is very much a participant in the cosmic drama. The revelation is one of the human spirit in contention against, and often triumphant over, terrible and malignant forces that seek to extinguish that spirit.

While, in some of his works, Sibelius deals with mythic figures from the Finnish epic *Kalevala*, there are no people in his music. Nielsen's music concentrates especially on the human to the extent that his Second Symphony is subtitled *The Four Temperaments*, after the four human psychological types. This is a subject Sibelius would never have thought of addressing.

This is not to say that Nielsen neglected nature—think only of his magnificent portrayal of the rising sun in the *Helios Overture*—but simply that he included man as part of it, if not at its center. Man's rhythms are the same as those of nature but not reduced to them. Nielsen wrote, "I have no doubt that the laws of the motions of the sea and air are reflected in every piece of good music of any length and (symphonic) extent." Yet Nielsen was clearly more than a nature poet. Speaking of the Fourth Symphony, he said, "It's all those things that have Will and the Craving for Life that cannot be suppressed that I've wanted to depict. *Not* because I want to reduce my art to the imitation of Nature but [rather] to let it attempt to express what lies behind it." Nielsen thought music was uniquely able to do this because "music is a manifestation of Life, in that it is either completely dead—at that moment when it is not sounding—or completely alive and, therefore, it can exactly express the concept of Life from its most elementary form of utterance to the highest spiritual ecstasy."

Ironically, both Nielsen and Sibelius are often thought of as late-romantics. The opposite is true. In different ways, they both rejected late romanticism and its bathetic sentimentality. Nielsen scathingly criticized its "reckless gorging". He said, "Romanticism's reveling and rioting in its own emotion was detrimental to art. With one hand on its heart and the other gesticulating wildly in the air above its flowing locks, it quite forgot to settle accounts with the craftsman." Such composers, he explained, "begin by expressing moods, feelings, colors, and impressions instead of learning voice-leading, counterpoint, and so on."

Those skills were among the earliest that Nielsen learned and mastered as a youth, first in a poor village where his father taught him the violin and then as a trumpeter in the military band at Odense. During his four-year, teenage military career, he taught himself Bach's *Well Tempered Clavier* and devoured the scores of Mozart, Haydn, and other classical masters. From 1884 to 1886, Nielsen studied at the Copenhagen Conservatory on a scholarship. Afterward, he was engaged as a violinist in the Royal Orchestra, a position he kept until 1905.

All the while, Nielsen was composing. When he was only 17, he persuaded a reluctant visiting composer, Olfert Jespersen, to come to his rooms in Odense to listen to his new Violin Sonata. Having expected the worst from a musical country bumpkin, Jespersen exclaimed that "in this beautiful sonata, there was no Beethoven, no Bach. Rather, it was filled with Mozart's gentleness and grace, which was the sign of the young man's true musical blood." In fact, Nielsen himself claimed, "There is far more to learn in Mozart than in Beethoven." There are certainly places where one hears Mozart's influence in Nielsen's music—for example, in much of his gorgeous wind writing and in the opening movement of the Sixth Symphony—but it is the influence of Beethoven that is most pronounced in Nielsen's symphonic works.

Nielsen's loathing of 19th-century sentimentality must not be confused with any lack of drama or passion in his music. In fact, overwhelming drama is its most distinguishing feature. Nielsen drew this forth from opposing tonalities in very much the same way as did Beethoven when constructing his symphonies. Nielsen wrote, "There must be conflict so that we may have clarity. Perception must be preceded by opposition." Like Beethoven's, Nielsen's symphonies move forward through a series of conflicts based on the clash, and ultimate resolution, of tonalities. Nielsen used the counterpoint he mastered as an engine for generating these conflicts. The orchestra is constantly in motion, asking and answering itself, issuing and meeting challenges. "Without a current, my music is nothing", Nielsen explained.

Nielsen's best symphonies are every bit as engaging as Beethoven's great works, as inexhaustible in their attraction, and as inevitable in their feel. The "alpha and omega" of music, Nielsen said, are "pure, clear, firm, natural intervals and virile, robust, assured, organic rhythm". No matter how harmonically adventurous, Nielsen's works are always classically structured in their tonality and are brought to immensely satisfying conclusions in their "home" keys—even when these are not the keys in which the works begin. Though Nielsen's music seldom sounds anything like Beethoven, these structural features of his work make him Beethoven's true symphonic heir in the first half of the 20th century.

Nielsen's faith in the inexhaustibly expressive nature of tonality made him wary of the atonal experiments in the works of Schoenberg and others, which were rife at the time. He saw no need to abandon tonality or to set dissonance free, though he made ample and powerful use of the latter within a tonal context. He once remarked, "The glutted must be taught to regard a melodic third as a gift from God." Nielsen expressed this traditional disposition in a very beautiful way: "And should our path take us past our fathers' houses, we may one day allow that they were after what we are after, we want what they wanted; only we failed to understand that the simplest is the hardest, the universal the most lasting, the straight the strongest, like the pillars that support the dome."

Nielsen's music became one of the pillars of which he spoke, and the growing number of recordings of his music testify to the increasing appeal of his path (to say nothing of the salutary influence he had on succeeding generations of composers, including the great Danish symphonist Vagn Holmboe, who also did not abandon tonality). Music writer Lewis Rowell gets it exactly right in describing Nielsen's artistic stance as postromantic/premodern.

The main body of Nielsen's work consists of six symphonies; three concertos (for violin, flute, and clarinet); four string quartets; a wind quintet; two operas, *Saul and David* and *Maskarade*, which has taken its place as the Finnish national opera; and several major choral works, as well as a large number of songs. I will briefly remark on the central symphonies, Nos. 3–5, though no one should miss the first two, which are well beyond a beginner's efforts. In fact, the First, written when Nielsen was 27, is one of the finest debuts of any symphonist (indebted as it is, in its orchestral language, to Brahms).

Beginning with his Symphony No. 3, a flow of musical molten lava poured out of Nielsen into three successive symphonic inspirations, which are most likely to carry his name well beyond this century. Nielsen's Third Symphony: *Sinfonia Espansiva*, is a glorious paean to the joy of being alive. If the First Symphony immediately brings Brahms to mind in its orchestral garb, the opening of the Third recalls Beethoven. It charges forth with the most arresting hammer-blow motif since the beginning of Beethoven's Third Symphony. Nielsen aptly describes it as "a gust of energy and life-affirmation blown out into the wide world". It is tremendously exhilarating. The gust of energy is eventually harnessed to a lilting waltz: life is a dance.

In the second movement, Andante pastorale, Nielsen expresses the "idyllic and heavenly in nature". Even more, this music depicts, as Nielsen wrote, "the peaceful mood that one could imagine in Paradise before the Fall of our First Parents, Adam and Eve". Life is also song, and toward the end of the movement, a soprano and baritone radiantly vocalize on the vowel *a*.

The third movement returns us to the world of Beethoven, where an element of struggle is mixed in with idyllic wind writing that contains reminiscences of the earlier waltz. The music generates a powerful sense of striving that is successfully resolved at the very end of the movement. The glorious peroration in the Finale conveys "a general joy about being able to participate in the work of life and the day". This symphony is Nielsen's hymn of thanksgiving.

Nielsen's Symphony No. 4: *The Inextinguishable*, is one of the greatest symphonic dramas ever written, a towering masterpiece that is at the pinnacle of Scandinavian and European musical genius. This is highly expressive, visionary music of apocalyptic power. Nielsen wrote: "In case all the world was devastated . . . then nature would still begin to breed new life again, begin to push forward again. . . . These forces, which are 'inextinguishable', I have tried to represent."

As one can imagine from Nielsen's description, this music relies on a sense of overwhelming forward drive. Its four movements are continuous, evolving tonally and thematically through a number of hazardous encounters with the powers of extinction into the eventual and exhilarating triumph of the "inextinguishable". The elemental, furious struggle between the life and antilife forces takes its ultimate form in the finale, in a battle between two sets of timpani placed at opposite sides of the orchestra that fiercely try to extinguish all else. Amid these tympanic eruptions, the winds shriek and take off like scared flocks of geese. The brass and strings eventually subdue the timpani and harness them to the main, triumphant theme, bringing the work to an exultant, unforgettable conclusion.

Many consider Nielsen's two-movement Fifth Symphony to be his greatest, a judgment from which I demur in favor of the Fourth, though I would not want to be without this magnificent music. The late English Nielsen expert, Robert Simpson, said of the Fifth: "Here is man's conflict, in which his progressive, constructive instincts are at war with other elements (also human) that face him with indifference or downright hostility." The Fifth is, in certain respects, a reprise of the Fourth Symphony. Some of its themes are variations of what is heard in the Fourth, and the story line is familiar: the forces of life gently dawning; the forces of life getting tromped on by the antilife forces; the forces of life fighting back and emerging triumphant. Nielsen follows this scenario a couple of times in the two-part Fifth. At the end of the draft score, he wrote, "Dark, resting forces—Awakened forces". He later explained that it was "something very primitive I wanted to express: the division of dark and light, the battle between evil and good". *The Inextinguishable* is certainly one of the greatest symphonic expressions of this theme, and the Fifth Symphony nearly matches its stature.

However, whatever the similarities, it does distinguish itself from the Fourth with its unconventional shape. Conductor Colin Davis said of this work, "Nielsen is obsessive, almost relentless." This particularly applies to the *Bolero*-like movement in the strings in the first part of the symphony that meets with martial interruptions from a nasty side drum, whose player is instructed by Nielsen to play "in his own tempo, as if he wants at all costs to stop the progress of the orchestra". A struggle for supremacy ensues. However, the impression exists that something extraneous to the music is trying to stop it (unlike the more integral timpani attacks in the Fourth). This makes a dramatic, but not especially musical point, leading to the trenchant insight from music critic Wilfred Mellers: "The famous percussion improvisation in the Fifth Symphony—wherein the side-drum player attempts to destroy the music's evolution—is an externalized presentation of conflict which is exciting once or twice, but less exciting with repeated hearings." Timpani assaults disturb but cannot overcome the development of the triumphant theme. The side drum physically moves toward sound stage right and then, while the rest of the orchestra fights for and achieves a climax almost as magnificent as the one at the end of the Fourth, moves off stage completely, as if exiled from the musical community (in live performance, I find this bit of extra-musical theatricality distracting).

The Adagio in the first movement contains a premonition of victory over the forces of evil in the ascendancy of a gorgeously lyrical theme that overcomes the timpani attack in a breathtakingly sweeping climax, which then trails off in a plangent clarinet solo. Only the faintest echo of the defeated snare drum's rhythm is heard underneath. The second movement bolts forth *in medias res*, as if in the center of a maelstrom, in one of Nielsen's most vigorously developed and exciting pieces of music. The fugal writing in the Presto and the gorgeous Andante in the second part is staggeringly good. He tumultuously reaches for another life-affirming culmination and achieves a triumph of the human spirit. Many have referred to the Fifth as Nielsen's "war symphony". If so, he must have reflected upon the ugly trench warfare of World War I. (I wonder what Shostakovich's reaction was to this work. He must have admired Nielsen's mastery at creating a sense of menace.)

Not all of Nielsen's works are about life and the forces opposed to it. It is clear from *Springtime in Funen*, a work of magical innocence and charm, and other intensely lyrical and gentle music that there was a tremendous tenderness in Nielsen, along with a good deal of fight. In fact, I think Nielsen's fighting spirit was to protect this vulnerable tenderness, which can also be heard in his lyrical Wind Quintet and songs. The listener must explore these works as well to gain a complete picture of this genius.

Unlike Sibelius, Nielsen enjoyed little renown outside of his native country during his lifetime, and toward the end of it, he wondered if he had hit a false chord. In the year of his death, 1931, Nielsen said to his daughter, "I know I've done it as well as I could, but I wonder if it's all any use?" The answer is in his music, which is inextinguishable.

Recommended Recordings

Symphonies and Orchestral Works

Symphony No. 4; *Helios* Overture; Martinon, Chicago SO, RCA Red Seal 76237. Here is Nielsen's visionary music in its greatest performance.

Symphonies 1–6; *Maskarade*, Herbert Blomstedt, San Francisco SO, Decca 478 6469

Symphonies 1–6, Colin Davis, London SO, LSO Live SACDs 0789

Symphonies 1–6; Overtures; Michael Schønwandt, Thomas Dausgaard, Danish National RSO, Danish NSO, Dacapo 8.206002 (3 CDs, 1 SACD, 2 DVDs)

Symphonies 1–6, Ole Schmidt, London SO, Alto 2505

Symphonies 1–6; Violin, Flute, and Clarinet Concertos, Alan Gilbert, New York Philharmonic, Dacapo SACDs 6.200003. The most convincing recordings of the six Nielsen symphonies: Ole Schmidt's raw 1974 recordings, drunk with passion, and Alan Gilbert's gloriously sumptuous, muscular takes, which add a dash of Richard Strauss to Nielsen.

Helios Overture; *Maskarade* Overture; *Pan and Syrinx*, Thomas Dausgaard, Danish NSO, Dacapo 6.220518. This enlivening performance almost won *Gramophone*'s 2007 Recording of the Year.

Violin Concerto; Clarinet Concerto; Flute Concerto, Kees Bakels, Bournemouth SO, Naxos 8.554189

Aladdin, Gennady Rozhdestvensky, Danish National RSO, Chandos 10498. Nielsen wrote music, including songs and choruses, for the 1918 production of the play *Aladdin*. Chandos Classics has fortunately reissued its 1993 recording of the complete score (most recordings only offer a 20-minute suite).

Chamber & Piano Music

Nielsen: The Masterworks, vol. 2, Chamber and Instrumental Music, The Danish String Quartet, Trio Ondine, DiamantEnsemblet et al., Dacapo 8.206003 (2 SACDs, 4 CDs)

Opera

Maskarade, Ulf Schirmer, Danish National RSO and Choir, Decca 460 227 (OOP). Or: Michael Schønwandt, Danish National SO and Choir, Dacapo SACDs. A marvelous musical soufflé depicting the contest between convention and nature.

Francis Poulenc:
Stabat Mater and the Carmelites

The young Francis Poulenc, the witty playboy of French music, specialized in frivolity, spontaneity, and sparkle. A true disciple of Eric Satie, he wrote some delicious ditties and had fun orchestrating some of them for street bands. He dabbled in Dada and other forms of surrealism, from which he derived some ironic humor. Then in the summer of 1936, his best friend and composer colleague, Pierre-Octave Ferroud, accidentally slammed his car into an immovable object in Hungary and died. Upon hearing the news, the 37-year-old Poulenc, long absent from his Catholic faith, figuratively fell to his knees. He recalled his deeply religious father's stories of the power of the miraculous Virgin of Rocamadour, supposedly carved by St. Amadour, the short-statured Zacchaeus of the Gospel. He immediately set out on a pilgrimage to see her in the wild country of the Dordogne. The musical result of this visit was the *Litanies à la Vierge Noire de Rocamadour*, for female chorus and organ, which begin with the invocation "Jesus Christ, hear us."

Thus began one of the most extraordinary musical odysseys of the 20th century. From the pen of this Parisian sophisticate, called by critic Claude Rostand "part monk, part guttersnipe", poured some of the finest devotional music of our time. No irony, no facetiousness, no nonsense syllables—mostly traditional Latin texts set to music with great spiritual purity, with both austerity and tenderness, and, in certain cases, great power. While modern, his idiom is thoroughly tonal, beautifully melodic, occasionally archaic, with dissonance used expressively. Following the *Litanies*, came the Mass in G Major in 1938, the *Quatre Motets pour un temps de pénitence* in 1939 (which Poulenc called "as realistic and tragic as a painting of Mantegna"), the *Stabat Mater* in 1950, and the vibrant *Gloria* of 1959, as well as other works, including the incandescent opera *Dialogues des Carmélites*.

Fortunately, fine recordings of all of these works exist, including one issued by Telarc, featuring the *Stabat Mater* (coupled with the *Stabat Mater* of Karol Szymanowski on Telarc CD-80362) with Robert Shaw and the Atlanta Symphony Orchestra and Chorus. Shaw proved his mettle in Poulenc with a previous recording on Telarc (CD-90236) of the Mass in G Major—now available at budget price. The choral mastery, the marvelously articulated vocal lines, and the fineness of the recording revealed a richness in what can seem a somewhat austere setting of the Mass, though the soprano solo in the Agnus Dei is one of the most sublime and otherworldly moments of any Mass. Surely, this is how angels must sing.

The *Stabat Mater* was occasioned by the death of another of Poulenc's friends, the painter Christian Bérard. Again, Poulenc turned to the Black Virgin of Rocamadour, but this time in a different form. He said, "At first I thought of a Requiem, but that I found too pompous. Then I had the idea of a prayer of intercession, and the heart-rending words of the Stabat seemed to me completely right for confiding the soul of dear Bérard to Our Lady of Rocamadour."

Composed in two months, the half-hour work for solo soprano, mixed chorus, and orchestra is set to the famous medieval Franciscan text, depicting the sufferings of Mary as she stood at the foot of the Cross. The amazing speed with which Poulenc composed it is not only a sign of inspiration; it is also an indication of the music's sense of immediacy and its power to startle, to put the listener in the Passion, directly reacting to the events and to Mary's sufferings. It is as moving and powerful a depiction of its subject—grief, supplication, and, finally, hope—as has been written. It ends in an alternating passionate cry and calm call to be admitted into "paradisi gloria" through Mary's intercession.

Shaw turned in another finely articulated, well-recorded performance with a first-rate chorus. But he is up against some French competition that has caught the pulse and meaning of this masterpiece more completely. At times, Shaw seemed to be admiring the beauty of the *Stabat Mater* without getting inside it and expressing its anguish. This approach worked well with the Mass in G Major because it is a strictly liturgical piece that requires some aesthetic distance. By contrast, Serge Baudo and the National Orchestra and Chorus of Lyon, on an older (1985) Harmonia Mundi recording (905149, OOP), convey a sense of participation in Christ's Passion that is both harrowing and serene. The chorus not only sings, it wails. It cries out. It prays. Also, Shaw did not quite have the orchestral snap that Poulenc requires to put sting and stabbing pain in the music. In short, I can admire the great beauty of Shaw's performance, but I am not moved by it.

You can turn to an even older French performance by Georges Prêtre, the René Duclos Chorus, and the Paris Conservatoire Orchestra on an EMI/Warner reissue, together with the *Stabat Maters* of Rossini, Verdi and Syzmanowski. It has the best soprano of any of them in Régine Crespin, who sings with great finesse and emotion. Prêtre successfully reprised the *Stabat Mater* with another recording of a riveting performance, fully invested with emotional energy, this time with soprano Barbara Hendricks and Choeurs and Orchestre National de France.

Poulenc's operatic masterpiece is *Dialogues des Carmélites*, an opera for those who hate the French Revolution. I am among them. As I discovered during my journeys through France over the past 35 years, the destruction still most present to the modern-day traveler resulted from neither world war, nor from any of the calamities of the 19th century. It dates from the Revolution. During one of my anti-Jacobin pilgrimages through Paris, I came across one of the many poignant sites of loss and remembrance, a church called St. Joseph des Carmes. Until the French Revolution it had been a Carmelite convent. The Jacobins transformed it into a prison. There, in 1792, they slaughtered 114 priests. Voltaire had commanded, *Ecrasez l'infame*. The revolutionaries complied.

Two years later, the prayer police caught a group of Carmelite nuns from Compiègne still secretly practicing their vows. They had been expelled from their convent two years earlier. Declared enemies of the state, the sisters were marched to the scaffold and guillotined on July 17, 1794. Upon this episode, Georges Bernanos, the famous French novelist, based his only screenplay. Sadly, the movie was never made. After his death, however, Bernanos' literary executor fashioned it into a successful play. Poulenc took a version of the text as the libretto for his opera.

Bernanos and Poulenc avoid the melodrama and typical verismo hysterics that normally would be associated with an opera on a subject such as this. They seek neither to sensationalize nor to sentimentalize the events of the Revolution. Those events are depicted only insofar as they impinge on the lives of the nuns and serve only as background to their interior spiritual drama, which is the real subject of the opera. The opera aims at a high level of spiritual realism and achieves it with profound psychological and spiritual complexity. Fear, faith, death, and providence are the subjects of this opera. The story revolves around Blanche de la Force, who, out of her fears of both life and death, enters the convent with an idealized notion of the joys of detachment. The prioress warns her: "What does it avail a nun to be detached from everything if she is not also set free from herself—that is to say, from her own detachment?" Sister Blanche soon witnesses the agonizing death of the prioress, who exclaims: "God has become a shadow. . . . I have been thinking of death each day of my life, and now it does not help me at all." Moments before death, she foresees the desecration of the chapel and cries out, "God has abandoned us!" The shocked Sister Marie, who attends her, keeps the other sisters out of range so they will not be scandalized.

The prioress' difficult death disturbs the community, except for young Sister Constance, who suggests, somewhat blithely, "At 59, is it not high time to die?" Yet it is also Sister Constance who grasps how providential the difficult death may be. She proposes to the puzzled Blanche that the troubled death of the prioress belonged to someone else: "One would say that in giving her this kind of death, our good Lord had made an error; as in a cloakroom they give you one coat for another." She suggests that, because of this, someone who least expects it will be surprised by how easy death is. Constance further upsets Blanche by telling her that they will die young. Blanche spends the rest of the opera resisting this notion. When her own death approaches in the last act, after the nuns have taken the vow of martyrdom, Blanche flees in terror. Only at the last moment, when the guillotine has begun to fall (offstage), does Blanche reappear incredibly calm to take her place by her sisters. They die singing the *Salve Regina*. Blanche joyfully sings the four last verses from the *Veni, Creator Spiritus* as she submits to the blade.

One could easily argue that Blanche's last-minute arrival at the scaffold, composed and ready to die, is, dramaturgically speaking, a deus ex machina. How is it that she suddenly receives the grace for her peaceful, though violent, death? It is not a development we observe. It simply happens. Yet, in this case, the deus ex machina adds to, rather than detracts from, the drama of the work, because it operates on the same plane of grace that is the premise of the whole work. The prioress' deathbed cry that God had abandoned her echoed Christ's cry from the Cross. Yet, mysteriously, Christ's cry was salvific. What of the prioress' ugly death? Did it share in that salvific work? How? The working out of this mystery and the spiritual tensions within it drive the opera. Providentially, the prioress' agonizing death in a peaceful setting makes possible Blanche's peaceful death in an agonized setting.

One could well have wondered whether Poulenc, a master of the song, could have pulled off a full-scale opera like this. Yet it is Poulenc's extraordinary feel for setting words that makes this work such a direct and moving experience. Poulenc's music for this opera also reflects the general attitude expressed in his more explicitly religious works, such as the *Stabat Mater.* He said: "I am religious by deep instinct and by heredity. . . . I am a Catholic. That is my greatest freedom. My conception of religious music is essentially direct, often informal. I try to give an impression of fervor and especially of humility, which to me is the most beautiful aspect of prayer."

This translates into a relatively conservative, though rich operatic style that is part recitative and part lyrical. The opera is set without arias or big numbers. Poulenc does not deploy his full orchestral resources, familiar to those who know the *Stabat Mater* or the *Gloria,* until the very end, at the scaffold scene, when he does so to glorious effect. At whatever volume, the music is charged with the same level of energy as its spiritual subject.

There are six recordings of *Dialogues des Carmélites* available on DVD, but these carry the risk of not liking the production. The music itself is risk-free and can be enjoyed on four recordings on CD. They are excellent. The oldest (in mono), from 1958, is the premiere production under conductor Pierre Dervaux, supervised by the composer. Not surprisingly, it has a special magic. The next, from Virgin Classics (now Erato and OOP), has the advantage of digital sound and a fine French cast under American conductor Kent Nagano. Nagano takes only an extra ten minutes with this two-and-a-half-hour opera. Yet that slight difference tells in the dramatic edge the original performance maintains. Chandos offers a fine recording under Paul Daniels—in English. There's traditional precedence for performing this opera, any opera, in the vernacular, and the advantages are, in this age of original-version eagerness, underestimated. Bertrand De Billy's with the capably playing Vienna Radio Symphony Orchestra is the latest addition and enjoys a great cast. Most of the CD booklets do not bother to inform us that the events of the opera are based on history; the sisters actually did mount the scaffold singing the *Salve Regina* and the *Veni, Creator Spiritus.* The good sisters of Compiègne were beatified by Pope Pius X in 1907.

Recommended Recordings

Dialogues des Carmélites, Pierre Dervaux, Denise Duval, Régine Crespin et al., Orchestra and Chorus of the Paris National Opera, EMI/Warner 48228

Dialogues des Carmélites, Kent Nagano, Dubosc, Van Dam, Virgin Classics/ Erato 59227 (OOP)

Dialogues des Carmélites, Bertrand De Billy, Sally Matthews, Deborah Polaski et al., Vienna RSO, Oehms 931

Stabat Mater; *Sept Répons de Ténèbres*, Daniel Reuss, Carolyn Sampson, Capella Amsterdam, Estonian National SO et al., Harmonia Mundi 902149. Glorious and gently radiant, the recording basks not the least in the easy splendor of Carolyn Sampson, one of the finest, vivacious voices of our time.

Stabat Mater, Georges Prêtre, Régine Crespin, René Duclos Chorus, ORTF National Orchestra, EMI/Warner 972165. A classic account from the LP age and currently available on CD only as part of EMI/Warner's 20-CD Poulenc Cube, a limited edition itself bound to go out of print before long.

Stabat Mater; *Gloria*, Georges Prêtre, Barbara Hendricks, Orchestra National de France, EMI/Warner 749851 (OOP)

Mass; *Quatre Motets pour le temps de Noël*; *Quatre Motets pour un temps de pénitence*; *Quatre petites Prières de Saint François d'Assise*, Robert Shaw, Robert Shaw Festival Singers, Telarc 80236

Mass; *Un Soir de neige*; *Figure humaine*; *Sept Chansons*, Peter Dijkstra, Swedish Radio Choir, Channel Classics 31411. Peter Dijkstra is one of the best choral directors of his generation, and here he whips the Swedish Radio Choir into astounding, exuberant shape in four knockout performances.

Organ Concerto; *Concert champêtre*; Concerto for Two Pianos; Sonata for Two Pianos; Sextet; *Gloria*, various conductors and soloists, including Charles Dutoit, Sergiu Comissiona, Iona Brown, Pascal Rogé, and Jesús Lopez-Cobos, Decca 448270. The Organ Concerto is one of the first works Poulenc wrote after his conversion and a dark masterpiece. The *Concert champêtre* is one of the works that brought the harpsichord back as a concert instrument, and is as graceful as it is charming and coyly humorous: one of the easiest ways to encounter Poulenc for the first time.

～

Günter Raphael: Mute No More

When the history of 20th-century music is written in the next several hundred years, will it bear much resemblance to how we think of it now? I have long suspected that there is a hidden history of classical music during this period that would one day surface. Of course, this is the main contention of and reason for this book. My suspicion has been confirmed by the many musical finds that have slowly surfaced over the years. Certain kinds of music were suppressed because they were too traditional and did not conform to the avant-garde dominance of the concert hall and academy that lasted for a half century. More obviously, music by Jewish composers was suppressed in Nazi Germany because it was considered genetically tainted.

Both reasons for obscurity apply to German composer Günter Raphael (1903–1960). I had not seen a mention of him *anywhere*—and I had been scouring for neglected composers for more than 35 years—until the 50th anniversary of his death, when the CPO label did something magnificent.

With one stroke, it rehabilitated this man's music by releasing a three-CD set with four of his five symphonies, Nos. 2–5, plus his huge Choral Symphony *Of the Great Wisdom*, based on the words of Lao-tzu, and a two-CD set of his works for violin, including the Violin Concerto No. 2. I was staggered to have works of this significance and magnificence drop into my possession as if from nowhere. I would not have known enough to ask for them. For proof of my hidden history thesis, I will from now on now simply point to this music and say: QED.

Before Raphael was unknown, he was, however, fairly well known, if only for a relatively brief time. In the autobiography of German composer Kurt Hessenberg, we get a glimpse at Raphael's earlier renown:

My teacher, the composer Günter Raphael, had at that time, above all of course in Leipzig, a much greater reputation than today. His 1st Symphony had been premiered in 1926, and hence before my time, by Wilhelm Furtwängler at the Gewandhaus with great success. I myself attended, besides a number of orchestral works, chamber music and organ works, the first Leipzig performance of his Requiem at the

Gewandhaus in 1929 under Karl Straube. This important early work
made a deep impression on me. Unforgettable also were the premiere
by the St. Thomas Choir of two works for *a cappella* choir: the 12-
voice Psalm 104 and the 8-voice Motet "Vom jüngsten Gericht", as
well as of the Divertimento for orchestra by the Berlin Philharmonic
under Wilhelm at the Gewandhaus at the beginning of 1933.

Furtwängler also premiered Raphael's Fourth Symphony. Other famous conductors were attracted to Raphael's works, including Sergiu
Celibidache (who conducts the Symphony No. 4 in this collection),
Leopold Stokowski, Hans Schmidt-Isserstedt (who conducts the Fifth),
and Wolfgang Sawallisch. The famous Busch Quartet championed
Raphael's chamber music. He was in the major leagues until the Nazis
came to power and informed him, through Reichsmusikkammer Peter
Raabe, "You are, you know, simply a half-Jew, and in the Third Reich
it is not wished that 'social events' be organized by such a person."
Raphael was thrown off the faculty of the Leipzig College of Music, and
starting in 1939, performances of his music were prohibited. Strangely
enough, the tuberculosis that eventually killed him most likely saved
him from the death camps, as various doctors deliberately kept him out
of reach in sanatoriums and hospitals. Despite his illnesses and precar-
ious existence, Raphael was very productive during and after the war.

   However after 1945, his reputation never recovered to its prewar
eminence—most likely due to the fairly conservative idiom in which
he wrote and the almost total lack of any influence of the avant-garde
on his music. After World War II and the horrors of Nazi genocide,
many artists considered that, since what had recently happened was
inexpressible, the only appropriate thing was to express nothing. And
indeed that was the course chosen by many composers in their increasingly violent and abstract works. Raphael did not choose this path with
the result of his (temporary) irrelevance.

   Raphael wrote in a grand symphonic style rooted in German romanticism, but with a contemporary vigor. In his early symphonies, I hear
echoes of Bruckner, Wagner, and Mahler, but he is not so beholden
that his music sounds derivative. Raphael had a real sense of classical
architecture, melodic flow, and contrapuntal development that keeps
the listener gripped throughout these expansive works. His fugal writing is particularly brilliant. The symphonies are so well constructed
that they bear repeated listening and do not reveal all their secrets at

once. To give some sense of their almost Brucknerian scale, the Second Symphony lasts more than 46 minutes; the Third is 40 minutes long; and the Choral Symphony consumes 72 minutes. None is less than half an hour in length.

These mammoth pieces neither share in the sense of decay nor express the centrifugal forces found in much of the contemporaneous music in the German-speaking world. For Raphael, the center held. Things did not fall apart. This makes his voice nearly unique. His work was constructive in one of the most destructive periods of human history. What inner resources did this man have to write in this way? I have not been able to find out enough about him to begin to answer this question, but I hear in his music a firm spiritual refusal to break the mystic cords with the past. His extraordinary fecundity during his period of enforced silence by the Nazis—what he called his "mute period"—recalled to me the courageous words of Viktor Ullmann, a Jewish composer who did not survive the camps: "We did not simply sit down by the rivers of Babylon and weep, but evinced a desire to produce art that was entirely commensurate without our own will to live."

Symphony No. 2 is an unqualified success. It is an amazing mixture of things. The brass chords in the second movement sound eerily like a premonition of Bernard Herrmann's use of similar ones in *Vertigo*. At its end one hears a slight echo of Richard Strauss. The third movement reverie, marked Molto adagio, is mesmerizingly beautiful and noble, very much like one of Bruckner's extraordinary visions. The pizzicato strings in the Prestissimo could come out of a grotesque Mahler march. The last movement has a Korngold-like opulence. No. 3 is another gem, less beholden to the models of German romanticism mentioned earlier. It is a somewhat leaner, more incisive work, but still on a grand scale. It generates considerable power. I love the way Raphael places his gorgeous string sonorities under some jumpy, anxious motifs in the winds. It makes for wonderful contrasts. In the second movement, one again hears huge orchestral forces deployed contrapuntally, as if Raphael were writing an enormous string quartet. (I cannot wait to hear his six string quartets.) After a sprightly Scherzo, there is more fugal writing leading off the fourth and final movement. The only other early 20th-century composer who could write with this kind of contrapuntal genius in his symphonic works was the great Carl Nielsen.

In the first movement of Symphony No. 4, I hear harmonies similar to those of Swiss composer Frank Martin—but more the sweeter sounds from his oratorios than the more acerbic ones from his orchestral works. In fact, the vocal and choral writing in the Choral Symphony is also redolent of Martin's great works in this medium. Like Martin, Raphael was able to use a version of Schoenberg's 12-tone method without succumbing to its doctrinaire dissonance. Raphael called it "tonal 12-Tone", a strong example of which is the Violin Concerto No. 2, played by his daughter Christine Raphael in the CPO recording. The Fourth may be my favorite of the four symphonies in this set as it is invested with a magical, mysterious atmosphere, and reaches for and achieves a kind of exaltation that lifts the spirit. It is the most optimistic in orientation. It is also the one, for reasons stated below, that cries out for a new recording. In Raphael's Fifth, the opening Allegro is electrifying in its energy and telegraphic intensity. This is perhaps the most modern-sounding of the five works here.

As for performances, the Middle German Radio Symphony Orchestra, under Christoph Alstaedt, beautifully captures Symphony No. 2, recorded in 2007. No. 3, with same orchestra, but this time under conductor Matthias Foremny, gives an alert and completely convincing interpretation, recorded in excellent sound in 2003. The Berlin Philharmonic, under Sergiu Celibidache, provides No. 4 with a visionary performance, but the recording from 1950 has its defects. It sounds as if the tape (or was this made from an old, warped LP?) was stretched in places, occasionally giving the instruments an off-pitch sound. The North German Radio Symphony Orchestra, under Hans Schmidt-Isserstedt, gives No. 5 an intense and exciting interpretation, recorded in somewhat constricted 1960 sound; and the Bavarian Radio Symphony Orchestra and the Bavarian Radio Chorus, under Michael Gielen, give the Choral Symphony an excellent performance, recorded in 1965. These recordings should be the inspiration for one of the world's major orchestras to undertake a new complete cycle of the symphonies.

Toccata Classics has also released a CD of Raphael's music for violin that allows for an even fuller view of this composer. The Sonatina in B Minor is immediately appealing, but I am particularly attracted by the two Sonatas for Solo Violin and the Duo for Two Violins, with their strong echoes of Bach. Raphael's father had converted to Protestantism partly out of his love for Bach, and his son's affection for Bach suffuses this music.

The one thing I am left wondering about is whether, despite the magnificence and melodic beauty of these works, Raphael achieved a style of his own. Because of the more or less traditional means with which he wrote, one is not immediately apparent. Part of the reason is that he may not have striven for a style. But the more I listened, the more clearly one came into focus—tightly wound but hugely expansive music of great depth, structure and vitality, perhaps a cross between Carl Nielsen (had he been a German) and Bruckner. The test will be if I can hear another of his works without knowing it is by him and nail it. All praise to the CPO label for these adventurous and now essential releases that reconfigure the history of 20th-century music. This music is good enough not to need special pleading, but it does help to reveal the dimensions of the Nazi cultural crimes.

Recommended Recordings

Symphonies 2–5, various conductors and orchestras, CPO 777 563. Cobbled together from archival and new recordings made between 1950 and 2007, the sound quality varies, but the performances are never to blame.

Violin Concerto No. 2; Chamber Works for Violin; Jorge Rotter, Christine Raphael, North West German Philharmonic Herford et al., CPO 777 564. The concerto and the 9 chamber works on this disc are performed by violinist Christine Raphael, the composer's daughter.

Chamber Works for Violin, Pauline Reguig, Darius Kaunas, Emilio Peroni, Toccata Classics 0122. This release shares the chamber works with Christine Raphael's disc, but has the advantage of better recordings.

Advent and Christmas Songs, Dresdner Motettenchor, Matthias Jung, Cantate 58019. Beautiful and simple arrangements for a cappella chorus of Advent and Christmas Songs, famous and less well known.

∿

George Rochberg: Recovered Memories

In the 20th century, the battle over the future of music was bitterly fought and not easily won. In a very profound sense, it was a struggle between memory and amnesia. French composer Pierre Boulez spoke for the forces of amnesia: "Once the past has been got out of the way, one need think only of oneself." Others insisted that memory was the foundation of art and identity, as it is of civilization itself. In the end, reality prevailed, as it always does against ideology, whether in politics or art. But this did not happen all by itself.

Though he was at first in their thrall, George Rochberg (1918–2005) helped to break the hold of the amnesiacs. In the United States, the first hammer blows against the musical equivalent of the Berlin Wall were struck in the early 1970s by this turncoat composer. (In an interview in the last part of this book, the composer tells us in his own words how this happened.) Rochberg had been celebrated as the preeminent American practitioner of Arnold Schoenberg's 12-tone method of organized atonality, called serialism, but in a move that shocked the avant-garde, he renounced it. "There is no virtue", he declared, "in starting all over again. The past refuses to be erased. Unlike Boulez, I will not praise amnesia." In personal conversation, Rochberg told me that "there is no movement and there is no repose" in serial music. "You can't internalize it; you can't vocalize it: it can't live in you", he said.

This was not an easy journey for Rochberg. It involved a great deal of thought, passion, and suffering. Rochberg was a member of the Greatest Generation. In World War II, he had been badly wounded while fighting in Patton's Third Army outside Mons, Belgium. He was patched up and thrown back into the front lines. Some years after the war, he stared death in the face again. This time it was the face of his young son, Paul, who was fatally afflicted with cancer. This loss turned Rochberg irreparably against serial music, which, he said, was bankrupted by its inability to express grief, love or hope.

Without any explicitly religious basis for his own beliefs, Rochberg arrived at a hope for eternity in a Socratic way—from experience. As he wrote in the preface to his book *The Aesthetics of Survival*, "Art remains crucial to our sense of ourselves as human and why we insist, against the brute fact of our brief existence, on the survival of our inmost, immaterial essence." So he strove "for authenticity linked to the longing for immortality" and against "the forgetting of being". As he expressed it to me in a letter, he insisted on "memorability, *remembering, remembering, remembering*, without which we know not ourselves or anyone, the past, the evanescent present, [and] face only a blank future." When I quoted to him Schoenberg's remark that he "had been cured of the delusion that the aim of art is beauty", Rochberg said "I have re-embraced the art of beauty but with a madness."

When Rochberg died in 2005, I called his widow, Gene, to express my condolences and ask after the fate of his extraordinary, and at that time unpublished, memoirs. She generously asked if I also knew of David Diamond's passing. I said I had heard, adding, "Two giants are gone." "Well," she said, "to make way for the new." "Yes," I impulsively responded, "but it was George who made that way possible."

James Freeman, a musician and teacher at Swarthmore College, reflected on the liberating impact of Rochberg's conversion:

> If George Rochberg can do something like that, there's nothing that I can't do and get away with it. I don't have to write 12-tone music; I can if I want to. I can write stuff that sounds like Brahms. I can do anything I want. I'm free. And that was an extraordinary feeling in the late 1960s for young composers, I think, many of whom felt really constrained to write serial music.

An angry critic once wrote an article with the title, "Can Modernity Survive George Rochberg?" It turns out it couldn't. That is how important he was. I think that Rochberg was prescient in making the following forecast: "Modernism has done little to satisfy the hunger for the experience of the marvelous, which is timeless and ahistorical. We stand on the threshold of an epoch which has put Modernism behind it. Whatever the art of this new epoch may be capable of, we can ask nothing better of it than to reveal once again, in new ways and images, the realm of the marvelous." It is the whole point of this book to demonstrate that Rochberg's intimation of the future is coming true.

Understand Rochberg's music and you understand the struggle within and against modernity. His was an inside job, which is why he was so resented. We can now listen to Rochberg's journey as he fought his way through to the realization that, as he once told me, "serialism is the denial of memory." In his Third String Quartet, written in 1972, Rochberg recovered the world of tonality. On a two-CD set,

New World Records released recordings of Rochberg's Quartets 3–6, brilliantly performed by the Concord String Quartet. These *Concord Quartets* were very much at the heart of the controversy caused by Rochberg's attempt to "regain contact with the tradition and means of the past". From a composer of what is known as the Second Viennese School (i.e. Schoenberg, Berg, and Webern) came music that could have been written in the First Viennese School by Beethoven or Schubert. These compositions and those that followed them, such as the Violin and Oboe Concertos and the later symphonies, caused an uproar. Rochberg was called a forger, a ventriloquist, a panderer. He took the heat. Anyone who wonders why it is now safe to return to the concert hall should listen to these works, which grapple with the central dilemma of the 20th century and come out on the side of sanity.

Rochberg's recovery of the past was problematic. It had to be. Do you simply pretend that 20th-century music did not exist? How do you reintegrate a nearly lost language? Like T. S. Eliot, Rochberg recalled the past by simply including it, sometimes literally, sometimes stylistically. As he said, the past erupts into the present. Other composers have played with what is called polystylism, the abrupt juxtaposition of 19th- and 20th-century styles, in a way that only highlights the violent break between them. Russian composer Alfred Schnittke specialized in this kind of disjunctive mayhem.

Rochberg was more interested in building bridges over what seemed an impassable chasm. The language in which he attempted this venture was pure Viennese. Rochberg takes you back to the world of Mahler, Franz Schmidt, Schubert, and Beethoven. And then, all of a sudden, you are with Schoenberg, Webern, and Berg. Rochberg keeps rocking back and forth through these four quartets, though he definitely lists toward the First School—to the extent that, in the Sixth Quartet, he even wrote an exquisitely moving set of variations on Pachelbel's famous *Canon in D*. Sometimes, he somehow leans both ways simultaneously. Rochberg obviously tried to exploit the expressive possibilities of both schools. The character of each became explicitly clear in the Quintet for Piano and String Quartet, written soon after the Third String Quartet. This large work is laid out symmetrically, with three movements preceding a piano solo and three following. The outer movements are atonal; the middle movements mix tonal and atonal elements; the inner movements are tonal. Rochberg characterized this structure as "a progression from dark to light, to dark again". The "light" music is quite delightful, particularly the third movement, which sounds like a Schubertian romp, and the fifth, which is a lovely Adagietto. The middle transitional music, especially the sixth movement, is fascinating: the 19th century fighting it out with the 20th.

In listening to his four *Concord Quartets*, two things strike me. One is the nobility of Rochberg's spirit in this endeavor and the other is his total mastery of craft. The nobility comes from the complete lack of irony in the music. Rochberg does not condescend to the past, wink at it, or protect himself from his unabashed use of it. In fact, the painfully beautiful things he expresses through the language of the First Viennese School leave him quite exposed. Rochberg's wholesale revivification of this language and the level of his achievement in utilizing it are astonishing. Whether it is a successful one in Rochberg's own terms, as a healing of the breach between the two, only time will tell.

One magnificent work with which he broke the stranglehold of 12-tone music was his Violin Concerto from 1974. I grew to love this work in its premiere recording with Isaac Stern and the Pittsburgh Symphony Orchestra under Andre Previn. That CD is out of print, and it turns out that Rochberg omitted some 13 minutes of music at Stern's request. Therefore, we now have the restored original version in a stunning performance by violinist Peter Sheppard Skaerved and the Saarbrücken Radio Symphony Orchestra, under Christopher Lyndon-Gee, on Naxos. Aside from the additional store of treasure, this performance seems more sharply etched, with every detail given expressive emphasis. The work has an alluring film-noirish atmosphere.

This is a very big work—every bit as major as the landmark violin concertos of the 19th century. It is full of pain and nostalgia, and aching beauty. At Naxos' budget price, it is almost a disgrace to call a treasure like this a bargain.

Naxos has recorded three of Rochberg's six symphonies, with the Saarbrücken Radio Symphony Orchestra and conductor Christopher Lyndon-Gee. The recording of Nos. 1, 2, and 5 have been highly successful, though, unfortunately, the project was derailed. Since the release of Symphony No. 1 in 2007, there has been no further progress. So, we are still without Symphonies 3, 4, and 6.

However, we can listen to what was going on with Rochberg immediately after World War II, when he composed his Symphony No. 1, an amazingly ambitious and bold work. It is so strong that it helps us to understand why Rochberg could not have been held under the serialist spell for long. There are very few first symphonies that can come close to the scope and tumultuous drive of this more than one-hour-long work. It is extraordinary in every way. It is not easy music; it represents Rochberg's notion of what he called "hard romanticism", which can be harrowing at times and quite dissonant. The opening is riveting. It begins with a highly arresting figure—the sounding of an alarm in several rising notes—followed by pounding staccato chords. The symphony also contains music of great elegiac beauty and poignant reflection. It is dedicated: "To my Mother, in Memoriam".

It is close to unbelievable that the Naxos CD is the first full performance of the score, which was truncated for its premiere in 1958 by Eugene Ormandy. The removal of the second movement is especially puzzling; it has to be some of the finest night music composed outside of Bartók. Why was it removed? The primary influence here, however, is Stravinsky, especially in the last movement, which bristles with *Rite of Spring* rhythms. The influence is expressed in the form of overt homage, not dependence; it is not as if Rochberg does not have ideas of his own. This is a very fecund work, bursting at the seams with intensity, energy, and striking ideas. It is in every sense a harbinger of the greatness Rochberg would achieve in his Fifth Symphony and in other works we have yet to hear, but can now hope to, thanks to Naxos. This series is the best way I can imagine of encountering and understanding the problem of language that engulfed modern classical music, and how it was overcome. It is given a galvanizing performance.

The Second Symphony was the first such American work supposedly written according to the rules of Arnold Schoenberg's 12-tone system. The composer was vastly amused when I told him that I didn't think he obeyed those rules in this work because the themes were too identifiable and there was too much consonance to make it strictly serial. He confessed that he had cheated. Be forewarned, however; this is tough stuff—and even harder "hard romanticism" than the First Symphony. But it is very gripping, and it shows that, if you cheat, even 12-tone music can be powerfully expressive in its own angry kind of way.

If you want to hear what happened symphonically after Rochberg rejected 12-tone music, listen to Naxos' release of his Fifth Symphony. This is still tough music, but it is tonal. It starts with hugely arresting orchestral thunderclaps over frantic ostinatos and staccato rhythms. The past, especially Mahler, does not appear as pastiche, but is fully integrated here. This is a harrowing, tumultuous, magnificent work. If you want to know why the avant-garde became apoplectic over Rochberg's music, listen to the accompanying work, *Transcendental Variations*, a gorgeous string piece derived from the mesmerizingly beautiful Variation movement of Rochberg's ground-breaking Third String Quartet.

Rochberg was also a profound thinker with a poetic gift of expression in his writing, as well as his music. His music speaks for itself, but his writings reveal the depth of his understanding of what he was doing and the reasons for it. As he wrote in the introduction to his brilliant collection of essays, *The Aesthetics of Survival*, he became repulsed by "the sheer mindlessness and unrestrained vanity of egotism that add up to 'the forgetting of being'."

We have another source for Rochberg's thoughts in *Eagle Minds: Selected Correspondence of Istvan Anhalt and George Rochberg, 1961–2005*, published by the Wilfrid Laurier University Press, under the editorship of Alan M. Gillmor. Rochberg maintained his correspondence for a long period with his Canadian composer-friend Anhalt, who did not embrace the same views—which is what makes the conversation so interesting. I have nothing but praise for this endeavor; it is the kind of exchange of which civilization is made.

As the above quotes demonstrate, Rochberg was very eloquent when he composed his thoughts for publication. In his correspondence, we see a more spontaneous kind of expression, but one equally revealing. It shows how early he began questioning the premises of the 12-tone system. Here are a few enticing samples from the more than 400 pages of letters:

1961: I must confess am growing tired of hearing music defined as Varèse defines it as "organized sound". That's like saying that the world is "organized matter" or some such nonsense. Music today is more than sounds and sound manipulation, at least for me. It is a way of reaching the ineffable or exorcising the Devil. . . . Schoenberg has no real value as far as I'm concerned merely as the basis of the 12-tone method.

1965: The end of the 19th century Romantic posture, the vertical man, who thinks he is unique enough to blot out the sun. I for one am utterly fed up with art and artists based on such unholy premises.

1970: Happy to be able to think harmonically and rhythmically as though it were the most natural thing in the world. I passed the stage

of writing tonally from a sense of irony to simply writing it. . . .
My recent listening experience confirms that contemporary music is
a limited palette of essentially neurotic, constricted gestures. All of it
perfectly true—but only of certain kinds of experience—the worst
ones (alienation, trauma, nihilistic-destructive withdrawal, etc.)

1971: I'm presently obsessed with the need to write genuinely tonal
music with all the attendant aspects of melody, accompaniment, etc.
It's like breathing clean air again.

1984: What is fascinating though is how the human mind in this century insists in ever-increasing degrees of intensity in stripping every
possible layer of "natural" meaning from human experience and taking "knowledge" (so-called) even farther and farther away from life
as we experience it to some oxygen-free zone of abstraction. . . . I
see a wild dance going on that most of humanity is partaking in; and
I see the intellectuals distancing themselves as much as possible from
this mad dancing. As music is part of the dance, and a very big part
at that, I prefer to be there myself.

1985: It does not follow that if a work of art symbolically or actually "represents" or tries to represent the terrors of the contemporary world, that it (a) is telling the "truth"; (b) is by virtue of that
effort to tell the truth, a piece of art; (c) is automatically protected
from a justifiable critical view of what it is in itself as at attempt to
make art. . . . For me, while the chaotic horrors of our day are all too
real, I'm not convinced they are "subject matter" for art unless their
rawness is transfigured, transformed through the power of an intense
artistic mind and nature.

I enjoyed these letters in anticipation of the appearance of Rochberg's
memoirs, *Five Lines, Four Spaces*, from the University of Illinois Press.
This book is priceless to anyone wanting to understand what happened
in the 20th-century world of classical music. Rochberg declared, "The
artist's project is to express the fire in the mind, to make, as Robert
Browning said, beautiful things that 'have lain burningly on the Divine
Hand.'" That is what I hear in his passionate music. That is what I
encountered in his person. That is why he became a hero to me, and
why I treasured my all too brief acquaintance with him.

Recommended Recordings

String Quartets 3–6, Concord String Quartet, New World Records 80551

Violin Concerto (Original Version), Peter Sheppard-Skœrved (violin), Saarbrücken RSO, Christopher Lyndon-Gee (conductor), Naxos 8.559129

Symphony No. 5; *Transcendental Variations*; *Black Sounds*, Saarbrücken RSO, Christopher Lyndon-Gee (conductor), Naxos 8.559115

Symphony No. 2; *Imago Mundi*, Saarbrücken RSO, Christopher Lyndon-Gee (conductor), Naxos 8.559182

Symphony No. 1; Saarbrücken RSO, Christopher Lyndon-Gee (conductor), Naxos 8.559214

Rochberg, Symphony No. 2; String Quartet No. 1; *Contra Mortem et Tempus*, Aeolian Quartet, Concord String Quartet, New York Philharmonic, Werner Torkanowsky (conductor), CRI 768

Caprice Variations, Peter Sheppard-Skœrved (violin), Aaron Shorr (piano), Metier 28521

Rochberg et al., *Paganini Celebration* (selection of *Caprice Variations*), Gidon Kremer (violin), DG 415484

Circles of Fire, Evan Hirsch & Sally Pinkas Piano Duo, Naxos 8.559631

Symphony No. 1, Christopher Lyndon-Gee, Saarbrücken RSO, Naxos 8.559114

Symphony No. 2, Christopher Lyndon-Gee, Saarbrücken RSO, Naxos 8.559182

Symphony No. 5, Christopher Lyndon-Gee, Saarbrücken RSO, Naxos 8.559115

Violin Concerto, Christopher Lyndon-Gee, Peter Sheppard Skaerved, Saarbrücken RSO, Naxos 8.559129

Piano Music, vol. 3: *Partita-Variations*; *Nach Bach*; *Sonata-Fantasia*, Sally Pinkas, Naxos 8.559633

~

Albert Roussel: The Freedom of Personal Vision

Why, you are probably wondering, have there been so few, if any, French symphonists? What about Arthur Honegger (1892–1955) and his five symphonies? Sorry—though the French claim him for their own, he was Swiss. Yes, César Franck (1822–1890) wrote one symphony, and Vincent d'Indy (1851–1931) wrote several, but that hardly qualifies them as symphonists (and Franck was Belgian-born). Camille Saint-Saëns (1835–1921) wrote more, but for good reason, only his Third Symphony is played with any frequency. In other words, the French do not have much of a symphonic tradition.

The reason is Germany. The German-speaking world developed and completely dominated the symphony. By itself, that was sufficient cause for the French to avoid it. In fact, the German influence in music was so overwhelming that it left the other musical nations of Europe in a quandary as to what could be distinctively their own (when, with the rise of nationalism in the 19th century, such things became concerns). Preoccupied with not being German, the French fell back on their strong suit: insouciance. The wit and whimsy in the music of composers Erik Satie, Francis Poulenc, and Darius Milhaud are like a big poke in the eye to the prevailing pretensions of German music.

But aside from thumbing their noses, what else could the French do? In addition to disguising their adoption of Italian opera, they composed ballets and, harkening back to French baroque composers such as Rameau and Couperin, wrote charming suites of descriptive music.

More was needed. In addition to the problem of the German symphony, there was the nearly overwhelming influence of Richard Wagner to reckon with. Erik Satie railed against this Wagnerian influence in France by suggesting the French impressionist painters as models for her composers. (See also Koechlin chapter, p. 173.) It is a measure of French musical genius that they were able to do so, as brilliantly exemplified in the works of Debussy and Ravel, the most renowned French musical impressionists.

There was another composer of their ilk who also achieved initial success and fame in the field of musical impressionism but then abandoned it for the very thing at which the French had so miserably failed:

the symphony. Albert Roussel (1869–1937) paid for his audacity with obscurity. His four symphonies are easily the most significant French contribution to the genre in the first half of the 20th century, if not beyond (because the French symphony has not achieved much since then), and he excelled in every other musical form as well. Yet almost every popular classical musical guide passes alphabetically from Rossini to Saint-Saëns without a pause for Roussel.

The neglect is undeserved, but understandable. In fact, Roussel would have understood it, as he claimed that music "will always be destined for very rare listeners". In his case, the listeners may be rare because his music is an amalgam of styles that came together in an original way. Roussel's biographer, Basil Deane, speaks of Roussel's development of the French symphonic tradition as passed "from Franck to d'Indy, although his abrasive final style is far removed in its attitudes from their works". On the other hand, Deane explains, Roussel also "belonged to the succession of French pictorial composers stretching back to the 17th-century harpsichordists, with his ability to translate visual and verbal imagery into precise musical terms". To this stylistic complexity can be added a certain ambiguity in the tone of his expressive message that came from the times through which he lived. Roussel said of his avoidance of musical schools that he "remained somewhat apart in order to have the freedom of personal vision".

So where does that leave us in trying to understand exactly the kind of composer he was? The fact that it is hard to say does not make his music any less an achievement or any less appealing once one abandons the attempt to categorize it. Anyone who loves French music, or classical music, will find a rich store of treasure in this unique master. A four-CD budget box from Naxos of his symphonic and other orchestral music makes this discovery easy and inexpensive. They add to a slowly growing selection of recordings that make a convincing case for Roussel.

Orphaned at an early age, Roussel took to the sea in the French Navy, serving as an officer in the Far East. He loved music so much that he brought a piano on board with him. A naval comrade, who was the brother of a famous opera singer, heard Roussel play one of his own works and promised to show it to an important music director. In one of the most productive white lies in musical history, he told Roussel that the director felt Roussel should devote his life to music (Roussel's friend had not bothered to show the composition to anyone).

Roussel resigned his commission at age 25 and went to Paris to study at the Schola Cantorum for ten years. There he fell under the influence of first Franck and d'Indy, and then, beyond the confines of the Schola, Debussy. Roussel became a professor of counterpoint at the Schola Cantorum and eventually retired to the Norman countryside to devote himself to composition. He was a consummate craftsman who worked carefully and slowly. His output extended to only 59 opus numbers. Their substance and quality compensate for their scarcity.

In his autobiographical notes, Roussel characterized the stylistic periods into which his works conveniently fell. In the first period, from 1893 to 1913, Roussel tells us, with a measure of understatement, that he was "slightly influenced by Debussy". In fact, his early works, caught in the full flower of impressionism, would be unthinkable without Debussy, though they also contain the early fingerprints of Roussel's distinctive style, particularly his vital rhythmic drive and the use of cyclical themes that he had learned from d'Indy.

Roussel's First Symphony, subtitled *The Poem of the Forest*, is actually a glorious suite of four movements depicting the four seasons. Lovers of Debussy and lush harmonies should not miss this impressionist masterpiece. In this period, Roussel also grouped his meltingly lovely Trio in E Flat; the *Divertissement* for wind instruments and piano; the ballet, *The Spider's Feast*; and *Evocations*, a triptych for soloists, choir, and orchestra, written after a visit to India. The exotic *Evocations* is at times an almost hallucinatory recollection of India and its holy Hindu sites. It was an early sign of Roussel's ability to take on major subjects with massive forces that could erupt in almost barbaric power without losing a sense of refinement and control.

The Spider's Feast has an entomological storyline that Roussel anthropomorphized with a magical charm and lightness of touch that immediately vaulted this ballet into the pantheon of France's most popular stage works, where it deserves to remain. Its shimmering textures, brilliant orchestration, and melodic appeal add up to enduring enchantment. Roussel apparently came to resent this work's popularity because he felt it came at the expense of the reputation of his later masterpieces, but that is the danger of writing something this good.

Another fruit of Roussel's oriental wanderings was the opera-ballet *Padmâvatî*, inspired by his visit to the ruins of Chitoor in Rajputan, India, in 1909. There he learned the story of a princess who immolated herself rather than be dishonored by a Mogul conqueror in 1300.

Finished in 1917, *Padmâvatî* is a mesmerizing, gripping masterpiece that shares the exoticism of *Evocations* but adds narrative drive and human passion. It belongs among the French operatic greats of the 20th century and is completely Wagner-free in its influences.

Roussel placed *Padmâvatî* at the beginning of his "transitional period", during which "the style changes, the harmonic sequences become bolder and harsher, [and] the Debussian flavor has completely disappeared." This is certainly true of the Second Symphony, a disturbing, mournful work in which the tonal harmony that could be so deliciously languid and almost lighter than air in the First Symphony, produces, to the extent it is still there, a queasiness in the stomach. Roussel admitted that the symphony "is a fairly hermetic work, whose access is accordingly difficult". The harsher sequences that Roussel speaks of are not there for harmonic spice: they are minatory. Here we also discover the driving ostinato figures that seem about to hammer the music into dulled submission that became typical of his later music. Even the good spirits that develop later in the long first movement seem to have something desperate about them. Clearly this is different music from a changed man. What happened?

The answer is World War I, in which Roussel so honorably served despite bad health. One can only imagine the horrors he witnessed as an ambulance driver and then an artillery officer. He wrote to his wife, "We shall have to begin to live again under a new conception of life; which is not to say that everything that was done before the war will be forgotten, but that everything that will be done after it will have to be different." This explains the difference in the Second Symphony, much in the same way as anticipation of World War II explains the abrupt violence in Vaughan Williams' Fourth Symphony, coming as it did after works of such pastoral calm. The impressionists felt betrayed. Émile Vuillermoz wrote, "Albert Roussel has deserted us."

In his third and final period, starting in 1926, Roussel said he seemed "to have found a definitive style of expression". This style was "more pruned, more distilled, more schematized", allowing him, through neoclassical forms, to write "music which satisfies itself". No more pictorial allusions; no more orientalisms. His works became very direct, concise, astringent, and, at times, abrasive, with rhythmic energy even more predominant than before. This period produced the *Suite in F*, the Concerto for Small Orchestra, the *Sinfonietta* for string orchestra, the great *Bacchus et Ariane* ballet, the String Trio, his only String

Quartet, and the final two symphonies. There are few compositions in the first half of the 20th century that accomplish so much in so little time as these and with such a unique combination of asperity, charm, and vivacity.

Roussel considered the Third Symphony "the best thing I've done". With uncharacteristic immodesty, he said that "from its first performances [it] proved to be one of the most undisputed successes of modern symphonic music." He was right. Is there anything as magnificently propulsive in French music as the Third Symphony, especially in its first movement?

The Third Symphony begins with a jolting ostinato figure that eventually gives way to a five-note theme, "which will reappear, more or less modified, as a main theme or accessory design in the other parts of the symphony". If one listens carefully, one can hear the rhythmic maelstrom of the Third Symphony gestating as far back as *The Spider's Feast*. Poulenc applauded: "It is truly marvelous to combine so much springtime with maturity." Yet there is more here than the manic energy of springtime. Almost recklessly, Roussel repeatedly takes us to the edge and then pulls back. It is not that he is playing a game of musical chicken. He shows us something that, if left to go on, would grind us up. Yet, when that something seems to have us relentlessly in its grip, Roussel transmutes it into music far less threatening, even lyrically touching, and finally triumphant in its human spirit. In a less frantic way, the same thing happens in the Fourth Symphony. This music seems to prove that Roussel was able to overcome the rupture of World War I.

With the Third Symphony, Roussel proved that he could produce a great French symphony that was not beholden to German influences, in the same way that he had shown that he could write a great opera without Wagner. For these feats, he is highly esteemed in France. But there is no reason why his reputation should not be greater in countries oblivious to the concerns that gave rise to these singular achievements. Another interesting thing about Roussel is that he seemed to reach full maturity within each of his three stylistic periods, which makes almost all of his music worth listening to.

Charles Munch largely owned the Third Symphony. He conducted Roussel the way another French conductor, René Leibowitz, conducted Beethoven. He melted the music down to a molten core and spewed the lava in an eruption of tremendous excitement. At the same time, he did not miss any nuances, some of them quite tenderly expressive. Roussel himself congratulated Munch on the "fire, conviction, enthusiastic warmth, and energetic drive" of his rendition. One of Munch's white-hot performances, in only so-so sound from a live performance in 1964, can be heard if one can still find a copy of it at a reasonable price—on an Auvidis Valois CD, along with the Fourth Symphony and the Suite No. 2 from *Bacchus et Ariane*.

The first two complete traversals of the four symphonies, by Marek Janowski with the ORTF Philharmonic Orchestra on RCA Red Seal or Newton Classics, and by Charles Dutoit with the Orchestre de France on Warner/Apex, are worthwhile and available at budget prices. The Munch performances of the last two symphonies, as already stated, are indispensable. A newer, very attractive alternative is Stéphane Denève's Roussel cycle with the Royal Scottish National Orchestra for Naxos, containing the four symphonies and many other indispensable orchestral works in a budget box of four CDs (or individually). It is this cycle that now vies with that of Christoph Eschenbach and the Orchestre de Paris (Ondine, on three separate releases) for top Roussel-Symphony-survey honors.

The Brilliant Classics label has cleverly arranged all of Roussel's chamber music in chronological order on three budget CDs, very well performed by Dutch musicians, that allow the listener to follow Roussel on his fascinating journey.

Roussel's earlier adventure into Hindu modes, *Evocations*, was available on an EMI/Warner Classics CD in a thrilling performance by conductor Michel Plasson and the Toulouse Capitole Orchestra, coupled with the even earlier *Resurrection*, based on Leo Tolstoy's story. EMI/Warner Classics is also responsible for a superb recording of *Padmâvatî*, Roussel's single largest work, and one of his most impressive.

Recommended Recordings

Symphonies 1–4; *Résurrection*; *Bacchus et Ariane*; *Pour une fête de printemps* et al., Stéphane Denève, Royal Scottish NO, Naxos 8.504017 This set must be the best bet for Roussel, certainly when it comes to available recordings in good sound.

Symphonies 1–4, Marek Janowski, Orchestre philharmonique de Radio France, Newton Classics 8802173

Symphonies 1 & 4, Christoph Eschenbach, Orchestre de Paris, Ondine 1092

Symphony No. 2; *Bacchus et Ariane*, Christoph Eschenbach, Orchestre de Paris, Ondine 1065

Symphony No. 3; Le Festin De L'araignée, Christoph Eschenbach, Orchestre de Paris, Ondine 1107

Symphonies 3 & 4; Bacchus et Ariane Suite No.2, Charles Munch, Orchestre national de l'ORTF, Auvidis 4832 (OOP, but available on the Naxos Music Library)

Complete Chamber Music, various artists, Brilliant 8413

Padmâvatî, Michel Plasson, Marilyn Horne, Nicolai Gedda, José van Dam et al., Orchestre du Capitole de Toulouse, EMI/Warner 818672 (OOP). There is the temptation to pick up this opera in a readily available, inexpensive copy on Gala, conducted by the Roussel-championing Jean Martinon and a fine cast. But the 1969 live recording from London, of shaky provenance, is so bad as to make enjoyment unnecessarily difficult.

Evocations; *Résurrection*, Michel Plasson, Nicolai Gedda, José van Dam, Nathalie Stutzmann, Orchestre du Capitole de Toulouse EMI/Warner 65564 (OOP). Evocations seems just to slip out of print, unaccountably. The only other CD it can be found on is a 1978, Grand Prix du Disque−winning Supraphon recording under Zdeněk Košler, and that is equally hard to come by these days.

～

Edmund Rubbra: On the Road to Emmaus

The highest purpose of art is to make the transcendent perceptible. Long after the artistic detritus of the 20th century has been swept away, people still will be listening to the music of English composer Edmund Rubbra (1901–1986) and wondering why we complained about the spiritual aridity of that time. By then, it will have been forgotten that Rubbra's music was buried under this detritus for most of his lifetime and that he never lived to witness its growing popularity. However, Rubbra's contemporary, the great English conductor Sir Adrian Boult, once wrote that while Rubbra conceded nothing to the fashions of the day, "he goes on creating masterpieces, which I am convinced will survive their composer and most of those who are his contemporaries." Boult's prophecy has now come true, as surely it had to, for this composer who strove for and reached the highest aim of art. According to the ArkivMusic website, there are currently some 85 recordings of his music available.

Despite neglect, Rubbra did not lose faith. In fact, he found faith in 1948 when he converted to Roman Catholicism. And he wrote some of the most beautiful, euphonious music of the 20th century. He composed more than 160 works, the main body of which includes eleven symphonies, four string quartets, and four Masses (the *Missa in Honorem Sancti Dominici*, op. 66, owes its origin "purely to an inner compulsion to express my beliefs in music", Rubbra said).

Though writing in a conservative, lyrical vein, Rubbra is not an English pastoralist of what has been derisively called the "cow pat" school of composition—yet another portrayal of bucolic bliss. Nevertheless, he is so strongly grounded in the English polyphonic tradition that some critics have been tempted to call his symphonies "motets for orchestra". In his book *Counterpoint*, Rubbra wrote that the whole of Western music has grown out of melody and, in particular, the interaction of independent melodic lines. Rubbra said that he felt "closest to the English tradition in my orientation to line expressive in itself". Thus, his music features long-lined melodies that unfold organically and that carry the full weight of the musical argument. This kind of compositional approach could work only with a composer possessed of a major melodic gift. This, Rubbra had. He created melodies that "speak". Since everything grows from the emerging melodic lines, his works have great coherence and are easy to follow even at their most contrapuntally complex.

I always have been puzzled at the critical verdict that Rubbra's music has little surface appeal. On the contrary, it captivated me at first hearing and has enthralled me ever since. Rubbra may be compared to Anton Bruckner in terms of religious impulse and a sense of spaciousness, but the sound world is more akin to a combination of Sibelius and 20th-century English composers Gustav Holst and Ralph Vaughan Williams, with both of whom he had studied.

What is clear is that Rubbra's reach is for something that is not simply musical, but sublime. Unlike another great composer, Leoš Janáček, whose music almost fights its way into heaven with a shout, Rubbra is at first meditative, ruminative; then rhapsodic, achingly lyrical; and, finally, exultant, ecstatic, entering heaven in a vision, being lifted into it rather than having to take it by storm. His long, ascending melodic lines weave into enormous, contrapuntal cradles of innocence and beauty, nobility and grace.

Bruckner was accused of writing the same symphony nine times, and the same kind of criticism could be leveled at Rubbra, except in his case it would be 11. (In fact, Rubbra was sometimes called the "English Bruckner" because of his similarly long-lined melodies.) Each work seems to search for the same thing—an effort to get something vitally important absolutely right. Rubbra described how the search commences: "I never know where a piece is going to go next. . . . When I begin, my only concern is with finding a starting point that I can be sure of." The tentative beginnings slowly yield to a sense of purpose that gradually possesses the music and lifts it up. As few composers have, Rubbra achieves a raptness of utterance that is utterly compelling and completely captivating. This is sublime, radiant music. He employs vast melodic lines of great beauty and interweaves them, preferring a polyphonic elaboration of thematic material rather than the more dramatic procedures of sonata-allegro form. Ideas evolve rather than contrast. Rubbra's works are characterized by rigorous organic development and complete cohesion.

For these reasons, Rubbra was ignored as a reactionary. One critic sniffed: "There are symphonists working in England for whom nothing has happened since Brahms." The reactionary label is pasted on

Rubbra either because his music is tonal and polyphonic or because it is religiously inspired. The accusation should have been put more clearly: Rubbra's symphonies contain some of the most broodingly beautiful, ecstatic utterances in British music since Edward Elgar. For transgressing the artistic ethos of ugliness, he was rewarded with obscurity, but it has been dissipating as more and more of his music is made available on recordings. Chandos Records, which played such a significant role in earlier recordings of Rubbra's works, completed the first integral traversal of the complete symphonies with the BBC National Orchestra of Wales under the direction of Richard Hickox. The performances and recordings are triumphs.

In its toughness and high level of energy, Rubbra's bold Symphony No. 1 reminds me of Ralph Vaughan Williams' prewar Symphony No. 4. The work is a bit atypical for Rubbra but shows astounding mastery for a first effort. The highly charged opening movement especially is a knockout. This CD includes yet another premiere, the *Sinfonia Concertante* for piano and orchestra. Except for its hauntingly beautiful and dreamy introduction, the *Sinfonia* is the most romantically extroverted work of Rubbra's I have heard. It lacks the special quality of inwardness that his greatest works have. It sounds like what it is—the experimental product of youth. A release from BBC Radio Classics shows how well Rubbra went on to write for piano and orchestra in his superb Piano Concerto in G, recorded live in 1976 by Malcom Binns with the London Symphony Orchestra under Vernon Handley. Here is that extraordinary raptness of utterance that Rubbra achieved at the height of his powers. What an exultant, rhapsodic, ecstatic work this is. It is accompanied by the heartfelt, broodingly beautiful Soliloquy for Cello and Orchestra and the great Symphony No. 4 (for which, however, Hickox has given a better account on an earlier Chandos release). The performance of the Piano Concerto makes this CD indispensable—but, alas, it is currently unavailable. The Chandos CD also offers the short but exquisite *A Tribute*, which Rubbra wrote in honor of Vaughan Williams' 70th birthday. Richard Hickox and the BBC National Orchestra of Wales meet the highest standards of performance.

One of the Chandos releases pairs Symphonies 2 and 6. The Symphony No. 2 is a lean and tautly argued work that eschews any accompaniment figures to its main melodic lines. In its spareness, it achieves a Sibelian grandeur. It opens with a magnificent, faintly liturgical theme that is developed, as Rubbra puts it, in such away as "to discover how far the interplay of melodic lines could be made to realize the dramatic tension necessary in such a work". The answer is: fully and with great power. (Sir Adrian Boult included a recording of this stunning work in his *Desert Island Discs*.)

The Fifth Symphony, partnered with the Eighth on Chandos, is my favorite Rubbra work. Its opening is straight out of Sibelius. The third movement is one of Rubbra's most rapt and deeply moving. It is hard to draw a breath during it. This is a luminous, grave symphony with an exultant final movement, propelled by fanfare-like phrases in the brass, apparently associated with the word *alleluia* in Rubbra's mind. This could be called an *alleluia* symphony, so long as it is understood that these joyous exclamations come after some very moving, deeply stirring meditations. This composition was written at the time of Rubbra's conversion. Without reading that back into the music, it is not hard to feel a sense of profound spiritual revelation and celebration in it. The Eighth Symphony, subtitled *Hommage à Teilhard de Chardin*, is a gloriously mysterious and optimistic work that heralds the triumph of the spirit.

Symphony No. 6 presents Rubbra at the height of his powers. The Lento opening is hypnotizing. The second movement, Canto, is thought by some to be the single most beautiful movement of Rubbra; it must be the most tender. If the Poco andante section of the last movement isn't prayer in music, I don't know what is; likewise, the concluding Allegro is the musical answer to that prayer.

Also on Chandos are Symphonies 4, 10, and 11. Symphony No. 4 is looser-limbed than Symphony No. 2 and more overtly lyrical, with a mesmerizing ostinato pulsation in long stretches of the first movement. A beguiling Intermezzo follows with a lilting waltz figure. This work ranks with Symphony No. 6 as a masterpiece. It is accompanied by Rubbra's last two symphonies, Nos. 10 and 11. They show no diminution of Rubbra's powers or passion, only greater concentration of thought in their 15-minute durations. They display the kind of concision one finds in Sibelius' last symphonies. In fact, Rubbra said of No. 11 that it is "a culmination of all my symphonies compressed into one movement". These final symphonies prove the total consistency of Rubbra's vision.

Rubbra considered his Ninth Symphony his best work, and his dying wish was that it be recorded. Chandos' release accomplished that. Symphony No. 9 is really a deeply moving Easter oratorio with roots going back to Bach and a text drawn from the Gospels, Catholic Latin hymns, and the poetry of Bernard de Nevers. Rubbra starts his Sinfonia Sacra at the end of the Passion. The first sung words are *Eli, Eli, lama sabachthani,* followed by "It is finished." To portray such a dramatic moment is not only a supreme musical challenge but, if placed at the start, it leaves one with the problem of where to go from there. The answer, of course, is to "The Resurrection", which happens to be the subtitle of the symphony. But musically this is not so easy. Either the death of Christ cannot be depicted with full force, or if it is, everything that follows will seem anticlimactic. Rubbra did not escape this dilemma, but it does not diminish his achievement. The Ninth Symphony contains choral passages of the utmost beauty and nobility, especially the tenor chorus of angels at the empty tomb and the climactic hymn, "Regina Caeli". The extensive narration is exquisitely set for contralto.

Avowedly Rubbra's most personal utterance, this symphony is ironically least like him. While one would easily recognize the hand of a 20th-century English master, the defining individual traits that so immediately identify Rubbra's music are in the background much of the time. Perhaps one can partially account for this by the episodic nature of the text, which would work against Rubbra's usual organic sense. Yet another reason may be that this work is not about Rubbra in a way that his other works are. Rather, it is Rubbra's love for Christ set in music, a musical caress for his Savior, and he therefore keeps himself veiled.

This thought is borne out by Rubbra's depiction of the journey on the road to Emmaus, during which several apostles walked with the risen Christ but did not recognize him. To portray this, Rubbra reverts to an orchestral conversation piece without text. The music is typical Rubbra. This is the one part of the work that could have been lifted out of one of his other symphonies, and I think it is the key to them all. Why does this one movement sound so quintessentially like Rubbra, while so much of the rest does not? British composer Robert Saxton says that Rubbra's "music is, in the deepest sense, a spiritual journey". I knew this but not in so specific a way as the conversation piece reveals.

Rubbra traveled a long road through Eastern religions and other beliefs before reaching Catholicism. In a very real way, he was on his own road to Emmaus, and like the apostles, his "heart burned within him" at the dawning realization that finally brought him to recognize the Lord. Each of Rubbra's works is a step on his road to Emmaus. They are spiritually autobiographical. Each searches, questions, meditates, reaches, and finally discovers; each contains in it an ecstatic moment of divine recognition.

As nearly as any single interpretation can, Hickox' fully captures Rubbra's ecstatic vision. He is totally convincing. Having recorded some of Rubbra's choral music back in the 1970s, Hickox brought his credentials to this symphonic project. He was also personally acquainted with the composer. In an interview, Hickox said, "He's someone I knew quite well and whose music I love. I met him as a child. Then, when I recorded for RCA the Masses that he wrote, he actually came to the sessions. He was always so grateful that anyone did his music, and I will remember the tears pouring down his face. He was a very sweet man." It is we who should be grateful that we can hear these exalted works in such extraordinary performances and recordings.

The Conifer Classics recording of the Concerto for Violin and Orchestra, op. 103, with Tasmin Little and the world-premiere recording of the Concerto for Viola and Orchestra, op. 75, with violist Rivka Golani, both under the sure hand of Vernon Handley with the Royal Philharmonic Orchestra, was deleted but has been reissued as an Archiv CD. Both works are moving and beautifully lyrical. The Viola Concerto is especially tender, a major addition to the limited repertory for this instrument. Naxos also offers the Violin Concerto, coupled with the *Improvisation for Violin & Orchestra*. The Viola Concerto meanwhile has received a marvelous performance on Hyperion with Lawrence Power, Ilan Volkov, and the BBC Scottish Symphony Orchestra. Apart from coupling it with the Walton Viola Concerto, it throws in Rubbra's *Meditation on a Byzantine Hymn*, op. 117, a world premiere on record.

Until Conifer Records released the four string quartets with the Sterling String Quartet, only one recording of a single string quartet had been available. Conifer's recording slipped out of print but was not hard to find used. It has now also been resuscitated and made freshly available by Archiv CD. Fortunately Naxos had filled the temporary gap with two recordings by the Maggini Quartet—one of Quartets 1, 3 and 4, another of the Quartet No. 2 coupled with Rubbra's 20-minute Trio in One Movement, op. 68 and filled out with the beautiful *Amoretti*, op. 43 (five works for tenor and string quartet to sonnets by Edmund Spenser) and the short but haunting *Ave Maria Gratia Plena*.

Marco Polo has given us the rapturous Cello Sonata, but it can also be heard with Jacqueline du Pré (accompanied by her mother, Iris). These are all vital releases.

Three violin sonatas and several works for piano trio are available on Dutton Digital, which has also released a charming CD of Rubbra's complete piano music. Chandos followed up its symphonic cycle with recording premieres of *Song of the Soul* (with text from St. John of the Cross), *Veni Creator Spiritus*, and *Advent Cantata: Natum Maria Virgine*, performed by the Academy of St. Martin in the Fields Chorus and the City of London Sinfonia under Richard Hickox. This CD also contains Rubbra's setting of Gerard Manley Hopkins' poem, "Pied Beauty", called by Rubbra *Inscape*.

The composer Herbert Howells' reaction to Rubbra's music could be fairly replicated by anyone today who is willing to listen: "Now and again there comes a work with the power to make one fall in love with music all over again. In such a mood I found myself when listening to your [Third] Symphony." Simply extend that sentiment to cover any of a substantial number of Rubbra's works, and you will know what to expect.

Recommended Recordings

Symphonies 1–11, BBC NO of Wales, BBC National Chorus of Wales, Richard Hickox (conductor), Chandos 9944–48

Or individually:

Symphonies 2 & 6, Chandos 9481

Symphonies 4, 10, 11, Chandos 9401

Symphonies 5 & 8, Chandos 9714

Symphony No. 9; *The Morning Watch*, Chandos 9441

Violin Concerto: *Improvisation*, Krysia Osostowicz (violin), Ulster Orchestra, Takuo Yuasa (conductor), Naxos 8.557591

Viola Concerto; *Meditation*, Lawrence Power (viola), BBC Scottish Symphony Orchestra, Ilan Volkov (conductor), Hyperion 67586

Chamber Music

Cello Sonata, English Cello Sonatas (plus Moeran & Ireland Sonatas) Raphael Wallfisch (cello), John York (piano), Marco Polo 8.223718

Cello Sonata (plus Elgar and Priaulx Rainier Cello Concertos) Jacqueline & Iris du Pré, BBC Legends 4244

String Quartets 1, 3, 4, Maggini Quartet, Naxos 8.572555

String Quartet No. 2, Piano Trio et al., Maggini Quartet, Charles Daniels (tenor), Martin Roscoe (piano), Naxos 8.572286

Choral

Missa in Honorem Sancti Dominici, op. 66; *Magnificat* and *Nunc Dimittis* in A-flat Major, op. 65; *Tenebrae Motets* (9), op. 72, Gloriae Dei Cantores, Elizabeth Patterson, Gloriae Dei Cantores 024

～

Harald Sæverud: A Norwegian Original

The abundance of first-rate symphonic music produced by Scandinavia in the 20th century is a mysterious secret to most music lovers. Is there life after Jean Sibelius and Carl Nielsen? Try Herman Koppel, Niels Bentzon, Aarre Merikanto, Einar Englund, Klaus Egge, Hilding Rosenberg, Gösta Nystroem, Lars-Erik Larsson or Geirr Tveitt, to say nothing of Vagn Holmboe, Aulis Sallinen, and Einojuhani Rautavaara, whose works are covered elsewhere in these pages. These are certainly among the better known Scandinavian composers of the last 80 years, which is still to say that they are hardly known at all outside Scandinavia itself.

The magnitude of our loss can fortunately be measured by the gain in CD recordings that can almost instantaneously pluck a composer from obscurity and place him center stage. Two Scandinavian labels, Simax and BIS, have done this for Harald Sæverud (1897–1992), one of Norway's finest composers and perhaps its most original.

In an interview with Finnish composer Einojuhani Rautavaara, I suggested Sæverud as an influence on Rautavaara's music. Rautavaara seemed surprised at the mention of Sæverud's name, presumably because of its obscurity, and responded: "Yes, of course. His music has not been around for a long time now, but in the '50s I really studied him and I liked him very, very much. And I think he was quite close to what I wanted to do at that time."

Sæverud's music is now back, and as if in compensation for its neglect, there are two superb partially completed cycles of his nine symphonies, the one from Simax, with Sæverud's hometown Bergen Philharmonic Orchestra directed by Dmitrij Kitajenko, and the other from the BIS label, with the Stavanger Symphony Orchestra, under Alexander Dmitriev. Simax has also released a two-CD set of other orchestral works and concertos, again with the Bergen Philharmonic, but directed by veteran Sæverud conductor Kirsten Andersen.

Sæverud is very famous in Norway, where he is considered, along with his predecessor Edvard Grieg (1843–1907), one of the nation's musical treasures. In fact, Sæverud's famous residence, Siljustøl, situated on 176 acres of unspoiled nature, is only six kilometers from

Grieg's home, Troldhaugen. Aside from geographical proximity, both composers share in the spirit of Norwegian folk music and nature. Grieg brilliantly embellished Norwegian folk tunes. Sæverud created his own. Sæverud excelled in highly elliptical, aphoristic music, some of which is so quirkily peculiar and delightful that it is hard to believe it is not directly quoting folk material. "Allow me to emphasize", Sæverud insisted, "that, while my music has no connection with Norwegian folk songs . . . my melodies have the same origin: the Norwegian landscape and temperament." That temperament, however peculiar to Norway, nonetheless shares in the same ethos expressed by another very individual genius, Czech composer Leoš Janáček, who said that folk song "is the expression of men who know only the culture of God, not an alien, inflicted culture. I believe that a time will come when all art music will spring from a common folk source." It is Sæverud's unique distinction that he is one of those sources. He seemed to possess an inexhaustible spring of highly original melodies, and one need not be Norwegian to delight in them.

Beyond geography and folk sources, however, Sæverud shared little else with Grieg. Grieg was a romantic in spirit and a miniaturist in form. He attempted a symphony as a young man but then abandoned the genre as not his own (writing, "never to be performed" on the manuscript). Adept as he was at miniatures, Sæverud also excelled at larger forms and became Norway's premiere symphonist, numbering nine symphonies to his credit. He was not a romantic in any conventional sense. Some of his music is very lyrical and touching in a childlike way, but it is free of sentimentality.

At the core, Sæverud was far tougher than Grieg, and as one would expect, used a more modern language. Nothing illustrates this more effectively than Sæverud's music for Ibsen's play *Peer Gynt*, which is as gruff as Grieg's earlier music for the same play is sweet. Though Sæverud was thoroughly immersed in nature and thought the intrinsic strength of a theme should alone determine its growth, "just as a flower seed can only become a flower, or an acorn—an oak", he knew that nature is not all flowers and trees. Sæverud's teacher in Berlin once remarked, "There is so much stone in your music." To which, Sæverud responded, "I love stone."

Along with stone, Sæverud's music contains a strange brew of exuberance and melancholy. He speculated that the strong streak of the latter may have originated with his birth in an abandoned churchyard.

"My house was built on its grounds," he explained, "the churchyard was very ancient and in disuse for some time. It is possible that there exists a relation between the morbid churchyard atmosphere and the plaintive sad music which at the time was my entire repertory." In fact, Sæverud entitled his first childhood composition "Death of the Hen". Sæverud displayed his equally prominent sense of humor some years later in an interview. When asked what the death of the hen meant to him as a child, he responded, "I stopped eating eggs."

Sæverud's childhood was also enlivened by a music book brought to him by a cousin that contained cheerful marches and waltzes. He was so impressed by its contents that he determined to make music his life. Perhaps his encounter with this book also accounts for the predominance of dance rhythms in his work, just as his churchyard parturition may have inspired his many chorale-like themes. By the age of 15, Sæverud had composed enough orchestral music to conduct a concert of his own pieces in Bergen. After studying at the Bergen Conservatory for five years, he won a scholarship in 1920 for a further year's study at the Hochschule in Berlin. Sæverud then returned to Bergen to earn his living as a pianist, teacher, and a composer.

He showed his predilections early. Three of his first five opus numbers are symphonies. Having heard Sæverud's First Symphony, the great Danish composer Carl Nielsen wrote to him, "Your composition succeeded in retaining my interest from the first note to the last, a seldom occurrence. . . . I have great expectations for your future career."

Sæverud's future career did not come easily. The folks in Bergen were not entirely pleased with the somewhat aggressive, intense music of this young man, which is hardly surprising considering how provincial musical life in Norway was at the time.

While Sæverud abhorred serialism and other fashionable modernisms, he experimented freely, including with ample amounts of dissonance, to find his own means of expression, which are highly idiosyncratic. The great British conductor Sir John Barbirolli said: "Whether you like the music of Sæverud or not there is no mistaking who wrote it, and this can be said of few composers of the present day." Sæverud's music possesses unmistakable traits. It has its own special weirdness and charm. It is puckish, pungent, defiant, feisty, bold, whimsical, rough-hewn, cranky, fantastic, mischievous, rustic, but sophisticated.

Somewhat like Janáček, without at all sounding like him, Sæverud found a way to anthropomorphize his instruments so that they almost speak. Particularly with wind instruments and the piano, he can say things that are understandable in any language. One particularly poignant example is the *Rondo Amoroso*, which originated in a dialogue between Sæverud and his little son. As Sæverud said, "I was permitted to put down in music the soul of a child." Sæverud also employs repetition to great effect. To show his irritation with something, Sæverud will point a melody at it and repeat it insistently until his point is made, as if he were wagging his finger.

As for his music's development, Sæverud said, "A theme is propagated by generating new versions of the theme itself. One then concentrates on a single part of the theme, allowing it to generate further components, preferably enabling it to grow naturally and systematically as if it were a plant shooting from the earth." There is a free-wheeling, unfettered, almost improvisatory air to the way Sæverud's ideas are developed through variation techniques, which is quite exciting and fascinating. Sæverud uses short motifs somewhat like Janáček and with his same extraordinary rhythmic vitality.

This is an unusual but quite coherent process for holding a symphony together, though it may give an initial impression of aphoristic fracture or haphazard exfoliation, which may account for British critic Robert Layton's judgment that "Sæverud is often not a long-breathed composer." Sæverud is so effective at capturing one's attention in the moment, and at each succeeding moment, that this may seem the case. But he can also deploy long-lined melodies within impressive polyphonic structures that can sustain his occasionally aphoristic utterances over large spans. The music is most imaginatively and piquantly orchestrated, and it possesses a multitude of very affective and expressive melodies. The canvas onto which these components are splashed in bold and original ways is a large one, though woven in a thoroughly accessible and traditionally tonal manner.

Nonetheless, Sæverud found fault with his first three symphonies, and he was still working on a revision of his 44-minute-long Third when he died in 1992. The partially revised Third is available on BIS, and while containing some impressive music, still seems overly discursive.

By the time of the Fourth Symphony, Sæverud had found his footing. The next three symphonies came from the World War II years. They are Sæverud's testament against the Nazi occupation of Norway. Epitomizing the resistance, these works, along with the *Ballad of Revolt*, dedicated to the "great and small heroes of the underground movement", have become part of the fabric of the Norwegian national consciousness. Sæverud said, "I felt that my work must be a personal war within the war with Germany." The *Ballad of Revolt* was prompted, according to English critic Robert Layton, by Sæverud's "fury at the sight of Nazi barracks near Bergen".

The particularly moving and highly concentrated Symphony No. 6, *Sinfonia dolorosa*, was dedicated to Sæverud's friend Dr. Audun Lavik, who was executed by the Germans in 1944. In less than 12 minutes, Sæverud creates, in a nearly monothematic work, an unforgettably powerful lament. Symphony No. 7: *Psalm*, written near the end of the war, has the subtitle "The symphony of adversity, battle, faith and acknowledgment. Father's and mother's symphony". In it, Sæverud returns to the churchyard in which he was born for both consolation and celebration. This one-movement work is built around two chorales (of Sæverud's invention) and is subdivided into five sections: "Hymns"; "Yuletide Variations"; "Stave Church Chimes"; "Fugue"; and "Glorification". It must be emphasized that these works are not polemical tub-thumping or explicit wartime narratives. One need know nothing of their germination to find them musically compelling.

Sæverud's penultimate symphony, No. 8, was dedicated to Minnesota, the home of so many Norwegian immigrants in the United States, where it was premiered to great acclaim. At 40 minutes in length, I find this work, like the Third, too discursive and lacking in memorable melodies. With his Symphony No. 9, however, Sæverud closed out his cycle with another masterpiece, though it was not universally greeted as one at its premiere in 1966. The Poco lento movement is a good example of the fun Sæverud can have with dance rhythms. I have not heard such a delectable treatment of the waltz since the second of Lars-Erik Larsson's *Due Auguri*, as beautiful an apotheosis of the dance as has been written in modern times. The powerful closing movement, marked Moderato ("Tolling Bells in the Mountains"), reprises some of Sæverud's favorite themes and ends in a magnificent climax.

The two Simax two-CD boxes contain nearly five hours of music—19 orchestral works and three concertante works. The newcomer to Sæverud's music should probably begin with volume 2 because it contains so many of Sæverud's most folk-like works, with their touching, completely disarming, and unaffected simplicity. Volume 1 shows the more complicated side of Sæverud and is indispensable for symphony lovers. It offers Symphonies 4, 5, 6, 7, and 8 (three of them recording premieres), along with three other orchestral works. I have heard only two CDs in the BIS cycle, and they are exemplary. The one containing Symphony No. 3 and the Violin Concerto is for the converted, which includes me. The other has the only available recording of Symphony No. 9, making it indispensable. It also offers an excellent rendition of the Piano Concerto (also contained in Simax vol. 2) and the raucous *Fanfare and Hymn*, dedicated to the 900th anniversary of the city of Bergen, but inspired by Sæverud's loathing for the Norwegian tax system, which he equated with slavery.

Recommended Recordings

Symphonies 4–8; *Canto Ostinato*; *Rondo Amoroso*; and *Galdreslatten*, Simax vol. 1 3124

Orchestral Works: *Peer Gynt* Suites 1 and 2; *Romanza* for Violin and Orchestra; Piano Concerto; *Fanfare and Hymn*, Simax vol. 2 3125

Symphony No. 9; Piano Concerto; and *Fanfare and Hymn*, BIS 962

Violin Concerto; Symphony No. 3, BIS 872

∿

Aulis Sallinen: Scandinavian Consolation

Henryk Górecki in Poland, Arvo Pärt in Estonia, Pēteris Vasks in Latvia, Rodion Shchedrin in Russia (at least in his extraordinary work, *The Sealed Angel*) and Giya Kancheli in Ukraine—all are composers who have musically met or are meeting the spiritual needs of their countries mourning over, and recovering from, having been on the ideological rack of the 20th century. One senses in their music the meaning of French writer Andre Malraux' remark, "Either the 21st century will not exist at all or it will be a holy century." But what of the ever-free and prosperous West? Who speaks to the contemporary spiritual needs of the secularized West, where death continues to make its scheduled family visits, and where it has expanded its embrace to millions of the unborn and now to the infirm and the hopeless? How to speak to, much less assuage, that special sense of loss—the emptiness at the heart of plenty?

That one of the answers to this question should come from Scandinavia may well be a surprise since Scandinavia is not known as a hotbed of spirituality, or perhaps even of music (aside from Carl Nielsen and Jean Sibelius in the first half of the century). But like England, the Nordic countries have undergone a major musical renaissance in our time. One of its leaders in Finland is Aulis Sallinen (b. 1935). In 1993–1994, he wrote an extraordinary work, his greatest—*Songs of Life and Death*, for baritone, chorus, and orchestra, "Dedicated to all my Dead, to those whose memory and strength still linger this side of the border". This work speaks to our condition of mortality, the harrowing loss of loved ones, the problem of evil, and how to live in the face of these close-to-incomprehensible experiences, made more so by the contemporary loss of faith.

I confess that I had not expected Sallinen to produce this stunning work. I thought I had detected a coarsening in his later music, if only from its pronounced element of parody and its more extrovert character, especially in his Fifth Symphony.

In the music that first brought him to attention more than 35 years ago, mystery itself seemed to provide the expressive content. For expressive means, Sallinen did not go in for big effects. With long-lined themes and highly atmospheric orchestration favoring chimes, bells, wood blocks, harp, and winds, he slowly, patiently created a subtle sound world that is utterly beguiling and convincingly unique. One can detect in it the fine lineage of Sibelius' nature mysticism. This side of Sallinen can be heard to best advantage on a BIS featuring his beautiful Sinfonia (later designated Symphony No. 1), which begins with a rhapsodic lament of great eloquence, as two solo violas delicately intertwine; *Chorali*, a magical evocation in brass and winds; and the gravely mysterious Sinfonia III (Symphony No. 3). The performances under conductors Okku Kamu and Paavo Berglund, with Finnish Radio Symphony Orchestra and the Helsinki Philharmonic Orchestra, respectively, are enchanted. Also, Naxos has issued an excellent survey CD of Sallinen's Complete Works for String Orchestra, also directed by Kamu. This is some of the finest Finnish music since Sibelius.

In some of his later compositions, there seems to be less a sense of mystery, but bigger gestures, a few of them harsh, and some highly romantic swells to rival the best of John Williams. The big gestures, though as impressive as the music is sometimes beautiful, do not seem to add up to a major statement; they appear to be the atmospherics of a major statement. For instance, the "Dona Nobis Pacem" movement of Symphony No. 4, lovely though it is, cannot quite carry the expressive weight of its title. Sallinen's Symphony No. 5: *Washington Mosaics*, written for Mstislav Rostropovich and the Washington National Symphony Orchestra, is my least favorite of his eight symphonies (though even here I discovered things to like). I found myself missing the sense of mystery and delicacy, the shimmering textures, the allusiveness, and the evocative melodies that initially drew me into Sallinen's melancholic reveries. I got the shards of the mosaic, but not the bigger picture of which they are a part—or perhaps it's just that I didn't like the picture itself.

However, I have been having second thoughts about Sallinen's middle period, provoked by the CPO label's comprehensive survey of his works in what it calls its Aulis Sallinen Edition, produced with Sallinen's oversight. This series has produced crystalline, mesmerizing performances and recordings of, for instance, the marvelously mysterious Symphonies 2 and 4 (which I now find myself far more convinced by), along with the Horn Concerto, with Ari Rasilainen conducting the Norrköping Symphony Orchestra. Perhaps the CD I have enjoyed the most features both early and recent works, the later proving that

Sallinen returned to form. *A Solemn Overture* (King Lear) and the Symphony No. 7 hail from the late 1990s and are coupled with the Symphony No. 1 and *Chorali*. The *Overture* is a bracing, icy, Sibelian work of turmoil and grandeur. The Seventh Symphony is subtitled *Dreams of Gandalf*. The score carries a note that explains that "the symphony does not actually depict the events in the novel [of *The Hobbit*]; rather it is a musical expression of the literary atmosphere and poetry." It is episodic and fanciful. The two early works, suffused with a sense of lament, are brilliant, subtle examples of Nordic nature mysticism. There is more of this side of Sallinen in the lovely *Sunrise Serenade* and in Symphony No. 6: *From a New Zealand Diary*, which evokes his impressions of that country. After 20 some years of listening to these pieces, they are still revealing their treasures to me. The only thing that puzzles me is Sallinen's remark that "there is nothing in common in the music of Sibelius and mine." You could have fooled me. If that is not a Sibelian orchestral swell that begins *A Solemn Overture*, then I have never heard one. Also, one gets an echo of Sibelius at the opening of Symphony No. 7. Sibelius is the obvious reference and starting point in each of these compositions. Sallinen feeds off the same sound world Sibelius created. He does very different things with these sounds (along with some from Prokofiev and Shostakovich)—and in that he is correct— but they are Sibelian, and that is part of their great attraction.

In retrospect, *Songs of Life and Death* is not such a surprise because so much of Sallinen's prior music is some form of lament. Even as a young man in his twenties he was drawn to the subject of death. His 1962 work *Mauermusik*, is, as Sallinen says, "an elegy to the cries for help of a young man condemned to die, cries which echoed in vain from the Berlin Wall to a world which calls itself civilized". His *Four Dream Songs* of 1973 are haunted by death, and in 1977, he composed a cantata, *Dies Irae*. Death is also a frequent visitor in his critically acclaimed operas. Even in music not so directly concerned with the subject of death, such as Sinfonia, the elegiac tone is pronounced.

In the *Songs of Life and Death*, Sallinen has finally written his Requiem, though it is not an explicitly religious work. It speaks of experience and of hope. The experience is death. The hope is love. It is not so much an expression of faith as it is an invitation to belief. The text is provided by a set of eight poems written for Sallinen by Finnish poet Lassi Nummi. Even in English translation the poems are beautiful in their simplicity and purity. Two of them carry liturgical

titles—"Tuba mirum" and "Dies irae", but they otherwise speak to
the world of modern, secular man. While Sallinen and Nummi have a
clear grip on eternity, they invite their listeners into their reflections at
whatever level their listeners can accept. Speaking of where the dead
may be, the penultimate poem says:

> Let your mind be full of love
> if you know where they are
> and even if you do not know if you believe
> and even if you do not have a grain of belief
> if you still hope
> and even if you have lost hope too
> if you still love
> for the greatest of all is love

The work starts with a short reflection on mortality, followed by a
beautifully chanted prayer, "Grant them peace", for both the dead and
the living—including those "whose hearts begin beating at this moment". The work then depicts, in a most extraordinary way, an abortion from the perspective of the child undergoing it in "I, Unborn".
The baritone Jorma Hynninen sings the part of the child, which begins with the hint of a lullaby. Then, as "the seas trembled and the gulf
swallowed me", the music grows agitated. After the abortion, the child
sings, "I have peace", and then tenderly prays for those who took his
life. I have listened to several composers' attempts to write requiems
for the unborn, but have heard nothing to compare to the poignancy
and power of this. It is unique in that it contrasts the strength of the
unborn child with the weakness of those involved in the abortion.
With ineffably moving magnanimity, the aborted child prays, "Give
them peace", for those who "could not / or did not wish / or did not
dare / to stretch themselves, / the arms of the world, / to receive me."

The next poem, "Tuba mirum", is a turbulent jeremiad against man's
pride and a depiction of the destruction it invites. Sallinen and Nummi
then use the forces of nature to introduce the theme of resurrection,
which is invoked in a hushed and exquisitely gentle way with the
promise of spring in "I Can Think You Departed". *Songs of Life and
Death* ends with the invitation to "surrender to life to its uttermost",
for it may even bring you to "endless light?" The deliberate question
mark is there for modern man to ponder.

In his composition diary, Sallinen wrote that he was trying "to seek a form which would match the text's wonderful message: *live a full life . . . when the stars come ever nearer.* The issues dealt with are the ultimate ones: the inseparability of life and death, death's harshness and beauty." He has succeeded with a noble and eloquent score whose vocal lines flow with great natural beauty. The music is at times subtle and tender; at others, angry and powerful. Both wrenching and deeply consoling, *Songs of Life and Death* is a masterpiece. Sallinen composed it with baritone Jorma Hynninen specifically in mind. Hynninen's sublime performance on the Ondine label is artistry at its highest level. Okku Kamu, a longtime champion of Sallinen's music, leads the Opera Festival Chorus and the Helsinki Philharmonic Orchestra in a deeply moving performance.

Socrates argued that eternity must exist because the demands of justice require it. Sallinen and Nummi say that it is love that makes such demands. Love requires eternity. Perhaps their masterpiece can help modern man understand where he is ultimately headed and why.

Recommended Recordings

Songs of Life and Death; *The Iron Suite*, Ondine 844-2

Complete Symphonies, Concertos, Rheinland-Pfalz State PO, Rasilainen, CPO 777640 (5 CDs)

Or individually:

Symphonies 1 & 7; Solemn Overture, CPO 999 918

Symphonies 2 & 4; Horn Concerto, CPO 999 969

Or otherwise:

Sunrise Serenade; Symphonies 1 & 2, BIS 511

Sinfonia; *Chorali*; Sinfonia III; String Quartet No. 3, BIS 41

Complete Works for String Orchestra (including *Sunrise Serenade*); Chamber Music I, II and III, Naxos 8.553747

∼

Ahmed Saygun: The Turkish Bartók

Jens F. Laurson

At the end of the 19th century, many students from Turkey and other Asian countries went to Paris. Many Turks studied at the Sorbonne, for example. At the end of their studies, they received a diploma—but one on which was written: *Bon pour l'orient*—(Good for the East), a qualifier, an asterisk of sorts that meant: we enjoyed taking your money and teaching you, but don't dare consider yourself on a par with Westerners and obviously don't bother applying for a job around here. The condescending phrase has been all but forgotten in France, but in Turkey it still hasn't lost its undignified power.

Turkish composer Ahmed Adnan Saygun (1907–1991) studied in Paris and then returned east to help get his country's classical music scene started. He became the central figure in 20th-century Turkish classical music. He was certainly *bon pour l'orient*. Now, through a number of recent recordings, he is being reimported to the West, and we can happily acknowledge: Saygun is *bon pour l'occident* as well. Indeed, his music enriches us.

An obituary in the *Times* described Saygun as being to Turkey what Sibelius was to Finland, de Falla to Spain, and Bartók to Hungary. As a mere youth, he taught music in primary schools. In 1928 he received a scholarship to study in Paris at the Schola Cantorum, where his teachers included Vincent d'Indy. He returned to Turkey to teach at the School for Music Instructors in Ankara (as a teacher of teachers, influencing Turkish music enduringly). Starting in 1936, Saygun taught at the Conservatory of Istanbul. It was an enlivening time to be there, as Mustafa Kemal Atatürk was bent on building up Turkish civil society in a Western image. He did not neglect music. Atatürk imported musical advisors Paul Hindemith, Dmitri Shostakovich, and David Oistrakh to give classical music a leg up.

It was then that Béla Bartók stepped into Saygun's life. The 26-year younger Saygun accompanied Bartók on his ethnomusicological field trips through Anatolia, where they collected and recorded folk songs.

Afterward Saygun wrote a tome about Bartók's field research in Turkey that became a classic in Turkish musicology. It is this connection, but also the style of his musical output, that earned Saygun the moniker "The Turkish Bartók". It's a fitting title from afar, but as is usually the case with these simplifications, it becomes less suitable upon closer inspection.

In his manual, *Techniques of 20th Century Turkish Music*, Turkish composer, musicologist, and Saygun-expert Alper Maral asks Saygun in an imaginary interview if he is indeed the Turkish Bartók. He has Saygun answer: "More a Turkish Beethoven!" Saygun might not have answered so boldly himself, but he also wasn't too keen on being permanently relegated to a "Turkish Bartók", however flattering or fitting the sobriquet may have been. Nor is it adequate in the sense that the Austro-Hungarian Bartók was really at the end point of a long tradition of classical music. Saygun, meanwhile, was the first great highlight of a brand new Turkish tradition. This modern tradition had been conjured out of air by Sultan Mahmud II when he appointed Giuseppe Donizetti (a.k.a. Donizetti Paşa and elder brother of opera-famous Gaetano) as instructor general of the imperial Ottoman music, in charge of getting the military marching bands into shape. The one notable Turkish composer to have come before Saygun was Cemal Reşit Rey (1904–1985), the eldest of the "Turkish Five", the first Turkish master of polyphony. Unlike Saygun, he was not so much a child of the Turkish Republic, as he was one of the Sultanate-era aristocracy.

Like Bartók, Saygun approached and appropriated basic folk material to forge a new music. He took forms, shapes, melodies, and then composed them in his own way, filling them out—not unlike filling in the colors in a coloring book. But how he did this was different from Bartók. In conversation, Alper Maral elaborated on how Saygun adds his own Anatolian darkness and a deeply felt Anatolian earthiness to his music. That is also something that distinguishes Saygun from Cemal Reşit Rey. The latter was very much an urban composer from a privileged background, Western-educated, and very Istanbul-centric. Saygun on the other hand went to Ankara, knew the country out east, its people, flavors, and colors—and reflects them.

Saygun stylistically crossed the borders (peacefully) into Hungary and Germany to produce highly sophisticated, densely rich music that repays, in fact requires, repeated listening. He was a Turkish Bartók and Hindemith rolled into one, along with his country's indigenous folk influences. The richness of his sources is clearly revealed in his highly distinctive and complex music. Because it reveals the strength of this man's character, his general orientation, and the profundity of his insights into the crisis of modernity, I think it is worth quoting at length from Saygun's artistic credo, written in 1945:

> The twentieth century takes the "ego" to extremes. This century seeks to shatter everything to its very foundations; and its destructive spirit also reverberates in the world of sounds. Local color and "national atmosphere" have undergone a great many changes in the last forty years. In the end, when even artists were seized by the urge to tear everything down, nothing was left of local color or anything else. . . . Only the "stamp of personality" and "ego" remained. . . . It is as if the people of this new era live, not to "integrate" themselves, but to "devaluate." A terrible collapse; a terrible self-abnegation; and—rootlessness.

As you might imagine, Saygun's music is the antithesis of what he denounces, particularly in the fabulous orchestral color he creates. The Cello Concerto on CPO (the Bilkent Symphony Orchestra under Howard Griffiths with cellist Tim Hugh) is particularly appealing in its melodiousness and late-romantic orchestral exoticisms. The accompanying Viola Concerto (with violist Mirjam Tschopp) is also an intriguing work, if not as immediately accessible as the Cello Concerto. It contains an abundance of marvelous, mysterious murmurings.

If the first two issues of the CPO label's traversal of Saygun's five symphonies were taken as the standard, it would have been clear that Turkey was ready to join the European Union years ago. To the extent that this music sounds Turkish, it is clearly from a Western perspective: a Turk looking back at Turkey through Western musical eyes. It is also highly sophisticated, brilliantly orchestrated, and harmonically complex. Not always an easy listen, these works fascinate and are clearly from the hand of a master.

With its release of Saygun's Symphony No. 4, CPO finished its cycle of symphonies, and added a Violin Concerto and folksy Suite. The 1967 Violin Concerto, played by Miriam Tschopp with the Rhineland-Palatinate State Philharmonic under Ari Rasilainen, is in the classical mold of three movements—a dominant first movement with a gorgeous violin and harp duo, a beautiful, mournful cantilena in the second, and a rhythmically bold afterthought of a third movement. It is coupled with the sophisticated Fourth Symphony. The filler, the early Suite for Orchestra, op. 14, is a lesser piece, gently rhythmical, irregularly pulsating, with a sorrowful "Improvisation" as a middle movement, and a final movement, "Horon", that achieves—rare for Saygun—compulsive forward momentum.

CPO also brings us Saygun's other concertos: the two piano concertos are taken on by the same conductor and orchestra with pianist and Saygun-veteran Gülsin Onay. Questions of possibly lacking authenticity can be alleviated by comparing this fine recording to one of Saygun himself conducting the Paris Colonne Orchestra with the 17-year-old Idil Biret, which certainly cannot compete with the CPO release on sheer sonic grounds. Both concertos—the first more lyrical, the second more brooding—can be very vaguely likened to Ravel's, in the sense that you will like the former's if you like the latter's.

In listening to Bartók—especially the string quartets—I hear a motivity that pushes, cudgels the music forward, and presses onwards, like waves. In listening to Saygun's string quartets I don't hear that at all. With Saygun there are little peaks, like those of tents on poles. Saygun doesn't have Bartók's inevitability of forward movement, even his compulsive brutality, but rather an attractive dancing quality.

The Quatuor Danel (also redoubtable champions of Mieczysław Weinberg's quartets) on CPO has given us very fine recordings of the three quartets and the fragments of the unfinished fourth. Scandalously, there are no recordings by Turkish musicians of Saygun's string quartets except for one of the First Quartet, op. 27. That's unfortunate, because there are details, finer points of tricky types of dance, that Saygun references that players not from that culture—however well they play—cannot be expected to know. A bit like Gustav Mahler's music, which has these elements of local flavor that are difficult to replicate or even to hear without a thorough knowledge of the musical culture. But at least with Mahler there's a plethora of examples of how it is done. Alper Maral expounds:

Rhythms like 9/4 time or 7/4 time are standard for Turks. When a German sees that, he starts to count. And while 9/4 time he might have seen in Bach, it's fairly straightforward. It hasn't got the same beat as it would in Turkey. This unwritten and unwritable accents give this music its essence . . . In late Bartók quartets, you will find places where you have to bend the intonation . . . it's not a quarter tone up or down, but it's a bend of the note. And there are lots of places in Saygun where you have to do that, without him having indicated so. You have to know Turkish folk music, even if you are Turkish, in order to do that.

Perhaps Turkey's finest string quartet, the Borusan Quartet, which is centered around an exceptional cellist, will endeavor to show us some of the hidden finer points of this music one day. In the interim, the CPO release is indispensable.

Yunus Emre was a medieval Turkish poet and Islamic mystic, a founder of the Turkish literary tradition. Saygun had already encountered him in his youth, hearing Emre's hymns sung by soldiers in the streets, singing them himself in school, and reading his poems from lithographs. The *Yunus Emre* Oratorio is, certainly for Western ears in search of a grand romantic statement from Saygun, his most important work. In it Saygun fuses Turkish musical traditions with western polyphonic structure. Premiered in Paris in 1947, it was taken up by several Western orchestras and conductors, including Leopold Stokowski, who performed it 1958 in New York before it dropped back into obscurity. It sounds like a logical and attractive extension of the oratorio-line of Bach-Mendelssohn-Liszt, with marvelous sweep and grandeur.

For the longest time, the only available recording on CD was a hard-to-find release on which a Hungarian chorus sings the oratorio in German. Fortunately, this major lacunae in the Saygun discography was filled by a recording of the Osnabrück Symphony Orchestra and Youth Choir, with four Turkish soloists and led by conductor Naci Özgüç on Dreyer Gaido 11796. It jumps to the top of the queue among must-have Saygun recordings.

Recommended Recordings

Yunus Emre, Naci Özgüç (conductor), Osnabrück SO & Youth Choir, Birgül Su Ariç, Aylin Ateş, Aydin Uştuk, Tevfik Rodos, Dreyer Gaido 11796

Cello Concerto; Viola Concerto; Howard Griffiths (conductor), Bilkent Symphony Orchestra, Tim Hugh (cello), Mirjam Tschopp (viola), CPO 777 290

String Quartets 1–4, Quatuor Danel, CPO 999 923

Piano Concertos, Howard Griffiths (conductor), Bilkent SO, Gülsin Onay (piano), CPO 777 289

Symphony No. 4; Violin Concerto, Ari Rasilainen (conductor), Rheinland-Pfalz State PO, Mirjam Tschopp (viola), CPO 777 043

Symphonies 1 & 2, Ari Rasilainen (conductor), Rheinland-Pfalz State PO, CPO 99 819

Symphonies 3 & 5, Ari Rasilainen (conductor), Rheinland-Pfalz State PO, CPO 999 968

Piano Works, Kathryn Woodard (piano), Albany 1168

Piano Works, Zeynep Üçbasaran (piano), Naxos 8 570746

Suite, op. 3; Sonata, op. 20 (plus Béla Bartók, Sonata No. 2, Rhapsody) Tim Vogler (violin), Jascha Nemtsov (piano), Profil Hänssler 9001

Peter Schickele: Schickele Unmixed

If you have heard of American composer Peter Schickele (b. 1939), it is probably because of his musical antics as P. D. Q. Bach or his Public Radio International (PRI) program, *Schickele Mix*, which ran from 1993 to 2007. In either case, these means of acquaintance would probably leave you surprised to know that Schickele is also a serious composer. It surprised me. His broad humor as the unknown Bach has never been to my taste, though his PRI programs were very engaging and one of the best musical education efforts widely available on radio.

The only thing I objected to in *Schickele Mix* was the standard opening announcement, still proudly displayed on the website (www.schickele .com/mix/), that the program is "dedicated to the proposition that all musics are created equal". This is a preposterous proposition. Is all poetry equal? Is a bottle of Thunderbird equal to a Mouton Rothschild? Is "Who Let the Dogs Out?" on the same plane as a Mozart aria? Even though enologically and musically challenged people may prefer the former, I don't think so. And the reasons can be objectively stated.

The assertion that classical music is the greatest music is not based upon my preference or opinion; it is as much a fact as the statement that the noble is higher than the base or the beautiful is prettier than the ugly. Of course, this does not mean you have to like classical music or even prefer it. It does mean, however, that you should be able to acknowledge its inherent superiority. Allow me to offer some analogies.

The great Gothic arches in the central nave of the cathedral at Burgos are a supreme expression of the art of architecture in their seemingly weightless upward thrust, of which the golden arches of McDonald's is the ultimate vulgarization. El Greco's *Annunciation* uses color and form to take the genre of painting beyond itself in a way a billboard advertisement does not. Higher mathematics exists on a higher plane than the simple arithmetic of which I am capable. These are not criticisms, but simple acknowledgments of reality.

I say this because there exists a hierarchy in the nature of reality, including in the world of sound, which is metaphysical. Noise occupies the lowest rung in this hierarchy; it is an undifferentiated mass of sound in which no distinctions exist (see John Cage, p. 81). The lowest kind of music (acid rock?) comes closest to noise. Classical music exists at the highest rung, because it is the apprehension of reality in sound in the most highly differentiated way possible. It is the farthest from noise. There is nothing wrong with entertainment or diversion in popular music, so long as it is not antithetical to higher ends and does not pretend to be something other than it is—as in being *equal*. It's not. (Do not infer from these remarks that I in any way denigrate the wonderful music of, say, Duke Ellington.)

In any case, Schickele's playful abuse of the most famous phrase in the Declaration of Independence is somewhat ameliorated by his next statement quoting Duke Ellington, "If it sounds good, it is good." This reminds me of the kind of thing I used to say to relax nervous yuppies when I was giving wine-appreciation seminars: "Don't worry. It's okay to enjoy the wine you're already drinking; you'll catch on later." Schickele's remarks were in the same spirit, intended to draw in an audience otherwise intimidated by the terrors of classical music.

When I heard Schickele's First String Quartet: *American Dreams*, more than two decades ago, I was thoroughly entranced and actually became angry. I thought, why is this man horsing around with sophomoric musical parodies when he can write music like this? I had not heard a composer so capture the heart of the American musical idiom since Aaron Copland.

The answer is that Schickele has actually composed more than 100 works for symphony orchestra, choral groups, chamber ensemble, voice, movies, and television. In the *New York Times*, music critic John Rockwell wrote that Schickele is playing a "leading role in the ever-more-prominent school of American composers who unselfconsciously blend all levels of American music". Yet Schickele's serious music has only been sparsely available on CD, staring with the RCA Victor recording of the First String Quartet in 1988 (still available from ArkivMusic). Now, there are several more CDs that provide a further opportunity to size up Rockwell's critical appraisal, at least as far as Schickele's chamber music goes.

The Arabesque label released a radiant recording of Schickele's Sextet for Strings, String Quartet No. 2, and the Quintet No. 2 for Piano and Strings, with the Lark Quartet (augmented as necessary). On the Centaur label, the Audubon Quartet, which recorded the RCA CD of Schickele's First Quartet, offers a new rendition of String Quartet

No. 1: *American Dreams*, along with first recordings of Quintet No. 1 for Piano and Strings and String Quartet No. 5: *A Year in the Country*. On Naxos, the Blair Woodwind Quintet offers a substantial five-movement woodwind quintet, titled *A Year in the Catskills*, along with works for smaller groupings.

Rockwell was essentially right—though Schickele is not exactly "unselfconsciously" blending all levels of American music. He is very deliberate about it. Rockwell must have meant that Schickele, given his gift, can do it intuitively, for that is how his music sounds. Square dance and hoedown music, blues-inspired harmonies, boogie-woogie jazz, country waltzes, Appalachian fiddle, and other folk music weave in and out of his works with a kind of quicksilver ease. (There are *no* references to the 20th-century avant-garde music of America or any other country.)

Of his First Quartet, Schickele wrote, "There are several kinds of American music echoed in the quartet, but they are usually transformed or combined or interrupted or given a feeling of distance; hence the subtitle *American Dreams*. The material is almost all original—the only actual quotes occur in the fourth movement—but the influence of the various folk styles pervades the whole work." Much of this statement applies to all of these chamber works. As does the perspicacious remark of a member of the audience who said to him: "Congratulations: You've written a string quartet that doesn't sound European." With Schickele, there is no mistaking the American idiom. (This may have been implanted by his studies with another inimitably American composer, Roy Harris.)

Despite the razzle-dazzle and energetic fun, Schickele's rich-sounding music can be rather simple and direct. Sometimes, it is no more than a single, gorgeous melodic line over a string ostinato or two violins playing single notes to and around each other—sounding each other out, as it were, in a pained embrace as they search for a way to express the heartfelt sorrow of *In Memoriam* or the playful joy of *A Year in the Country*. It is music not from the head but the heart. In this, it has its lineage in Dvořák. (Schickele repeatedly stresses his love for the chamber music of Dvořák, Brahms, and Schumann.)

This is sweet, down-home music, written without condescension. It is the genuine article, with wonderful freedom of expression and depth of feeling. Directly communicative, Schickele's music is about human experience, often with nature—refracted through popular idioms of

American music that are, in their turn, assimilated into classical forms.

The Fifth Quartet is full of playful evocations of nature in the spirit of Vivaldi's *Four Seasons*. The "Birds" movement is expressed by darting strings and birdsong, followed by the humorous "Bugs" movement's pizzicato scurrying. The more reflective movements in all of these works—"Music at Dawn" in Quartet No. 1, the "Prelude and Elegy" in Quartet No. 2, and "Spring Dawn" in Quartet No. 5—are full of sweet heartache and nostalgia. Schickele's Second String Quartet, written in memory of his late brother-in-law, shows a real depth of utterance and is deeply moving. The endearing String Sextet is a tribute to Brahms, at least in form, and the scintillating Second Piano Quintet tips its hat both to Brahms and Schumann.

The Naxos CD of Schickele's works for woodwind quintet is played beautifully by the Blair Woodwind Quintet. The title piece is *A Year in the Catskills*, accompanied by *Dream Dances*, *Diversions*, and other pieces. These are sweet, genial musical musings that percolate pleasantly and sometimes humorously along. Much of it is gentle and reflective, capturing a poignant nostalgia. I am not damning with faint praise. These are works of sheer delight and attractive fancy. There is simply not a mean bone in the body of this music, which spans a 46-year period in his compositional career.

The American Chamber Ensemble offers the *Serenade for Three* for clarinet, violin and piano; the Quartet for clarinet, violin, cello and piano; and the Octet for clarinet, bassoon, French horn, string quartet, and bass on the Elysium label. This music burbles along breezily or softly muses on its graceful melodies. These works are obviously meant to be fun to play and listen to. Schickele does a delightful riff on an early Mozart string divertimento (K. 136) in the third movement of the Octet.

Having immersed myself in these chamber works, I daresay I could now pick out a Schickele work in a blind audition. Such a distinctive style is usually a sign of major talent. Or it could mean that Schickele has limited himself to a group of easily identifiable stock gestures—the riffs, the looping musical swirls, and the chugging bass strings that imitate a locomotive, while the upper registers of the violins sound the whistle—that I hear in nearly every work. One would have to hear more to make a final judgment. Given the enormous enjoyment I have derived from this music, I am eager to do so. Given the wonderfully animated performances on these CDs, I hope that the Lark and Audubon Quartets will team up to give us the rest of Schickele's chamber music.

The recording industry should pay closer attention to this man. Schickele should give the buffoon P.D.Q. Bach a decent burial and concentrate his substantial talents on his serious music. Meanwhile, you should indulge in this high-spirited entertainment. I call it that because it is so immensely enjoyable—popular classical music in the best sense of the term.

Recommended Recordings

Sextet; String Quartet No. 2; *In Memoriam*; and Quintet No. 2 for Piano and Strings, Arabesque 6719

String Quartet No. 1; *American Dreams*; Quintet No. 1 for Piano and Strings; and String Quartet No. 5, Centaur 2502

A Year in the Catskills; Dream Dances; Diversions, Naxos CD 8.559687

Serenade for Three; Quartet; Octet, Elysium 725

Franz Schmidt: Setting the Apocalypse

Some critics think composers should be seismic devices. Music should not only reflect its time but foretell things to come. In fact, it should even help usher in the new age. Thus we are greeted with periodic announcements that a certain composer, misunderstood by his reactionary contemporaries, has finally arrived, since what his work foreshadowed has arrived as well. For example, Gustav Mahler's neurotic, occasionally hysterical music was greeted in the last quarter of the 20th century as a reflection of our own anxiety and neurotic self-obsession (while conveniently omitting Mahler's striving for the eternal).

However, music as Zeitgeist is a recipe for obsolescence. According to this paradigm, the history of art is a series of revolutionary stages, political or otherwise, that open onto an ever-expanding horizon of man's autonomy and freedom. Though despised and neglected in their own time, artists who flout convention erect bold new structures on the rubble of the traditions they demolish. Art is a form of temporal progress that moves man forward by breaking the constraints of the past. But if art serves a primarily temporal function, then after that function is served and history moves on, of what remaining interest is the art? If one's time arrives, will it not also depart? There is the rub. The revolutionary view of art turns out to be a form of temporal provincialism.

Both politically and artistically, the cultural revolution is over, and so should be this view of music as a revolutionary muse. The failure of the revolution has caused great confusion among the intelligentsia, who, at a loss to explain what has happened, have labeled our period "postmodern". Thanks to this confusion, it has become possible to look into the heretofore forbidden cracks of history and see what has been overlooked.

One of those cracks appears between the Second and the Third Reichs, the First and the Second Viennese Schools (in music), and the First and Second World Wars. In those interstices one makes a most interesting find: Franz Schmidt, an Austro-Hungarian composer who lived from 1874 to 1939. His work is finally receiving major attention in a spate of recordings.

The way Austrians talk about him, you would think he was a major composer, only waiting to be rediscovered like Mahler. In fact, it may be the ascendancy of Mahler that has kept Schmidt in the background. Whereas Mahler's music could be fit into the progressive, revolutionary view, Schmidt's could not. In Mahler, one can sense the imminent loss of any sense of scale and control—that music will soon come crashing down in a deflated heap of despair once the hope Mahler tenaciously clung to is removed from it.

Schmidt was born in Pressburg, now called Bratislava. In his *Autobiographical Sketch*, he reports that "music first entered my soul through the Church." His most important music education came from a Franciscan monk, Rev. Felizian Josef Moczik. Trained as a painter, Father Moczik was not a musician by vocation. Schmidt said, "He possessed nonetheless a fundamental knowledge particularly of the theory of music and was an excellent organist, deeply serious about art and religion."

In 1890, Schmidt went to Vienna to study with Anton Bruckner, who was unfortunately too ill to give him more than a few lessons. Schmidt was graduated in cello performance and soon played first chair at the Vienna Opera and the Vienna Philharmonic under Mahler, with whom he had a stormy relationship. Schmidt's First Symphony won Vienna's Beethoven Prize in 1899 and was used by the local critics to denigrate Mahler's symphonic efforts. Schmidt's own appraisal of Mahler's symphonies was not kind; he called them "cheap novels". As head of the opera, Mahler listened to a piano reduction play-through of Schmidt's first opera, the rapturously lyrical *Notre Dame*, but refused to produce it, declaring it, of all things, "deficient in melody". Schmidt terminated his nerve-wracking tenure at the opera in 1914 and devoted the rest of his career to teaching and composition.

Schmidt's music does not look ahead. It can be understood only by looking back. Unlike Mahler or Arnold Schoenberg, Schmidt's exact contemporary, Schmidt stayed within the Viennese tradition of Haydn, Schubert, Brahms, and Bruckner, of which he was probably the last expression. He broke down no walls, forged no new idioms. He understood Schoenberg's radical break with tonality but did not follow him into the Second Viennese School. Yet Schmidt's voice was distinctive. If he was the end of a tradition, he brought it to a close with a burst of autumnal radiance and an outpouring of gorgeous lyricism rivaling that of Richard Strauss.

Schmidt employed an extremely sophisticated and rich harmonic palate that included his trademark use of side-slipping modulations—a technique that induces a momentary state of musical vertigo. Though luxuriating in sensual orchestral sonorities, he retained a sense of form and delicacy, even when deploying huge forces, at which he was expert. He was particularly adept at the variation form, brilliantly displayed in his last three symphonies and in *Variations on a Hussar's Song*, as well as in his organ music.

The terraced dynamics of organ playing are often heard in his spacious string music. His wind and brass writing is particularly inspired. An infectious Viennese lilt can often be detected in his melodic style, along with occasional hints of the waltz. Like his progenitors, Schmidt is grounded in song and dance as the source of music. His flowing lyricism is very late-romantic; his nearly bitonal harmony, early twentieth century; his forms classical and at times baroque. That this amalgam sounds completely natural and even compelling is confirmation of his individual genius.

For all his natural ability and fluency, Schmidt was not prolific. First, his work at the opera and the Vienna Philharmonic interfered, and then, he had to cope with serious health problems. His main production consists of four symphonies, the *Hussar Variations*, two piano concertos, two operas, a good deal of organ music, five major chamber works, and his final work, a massive oratorio called *The Book of the Seven Seals*.

Schmidt said that this oratorio, based on the last book of the New Testament, was his "legacy to the world". By 1933, his work had taken on additional gravity and weight after the death of his daughter, in whose memory he wrote the Fourth Symphony as a threnody. Through his years of heart trouble, Schmidt had lived with the fear of death and must have felt its approach when he undertook this gigantic task in 1935.

As he noted in his introduction to the work, he was the first to attempt such a comprehensive setting of St. John's book of Revelation. Even in abbreviation, setting the Apocalypse to music was a supreme challenge. Schmidt said, "My approach to the work has always been that of a deeply religious man and of an artist. . . . If my musical setting of this unparalleled work, which is as relevant today as it was at its creation eighteen and a half centuries ago, should succeed in bringing the hearer spiritually closer to it, then that will be my greatest reward." *The Book of the Seven Seals* was premiered in 1938, several months after the Anschluss and less than a year before Schmidt's death. It was his greatest triumph.

Like the text itself, *The Book of the Seven Seals* requires close attention.

The subject naturally leads to overwhelming expectations. Working with those expectations, but also against them, Schmidt creates a number of surprises. At the sight of "Him that sat upon the throne", one would expect a musical outburst of Mahlerian proportions. Instead, the Four Beasts sing an exquisite solo vocal quartet: "Holy, holy is God the Almighty." Schmidt draws on the great oratorio tradition going back to Haydn, if not further, but, within classical restraints, adds every element of his individual genius to dramatize the Ultimate. The confidence, ingenuity, and subtlety with which he proceeds through such a huge text in a nearly two-hour work are astounding.

A work on the scale of *The Book of the Seven Seals* is hard to capture on a recording. An Orfeo CD with the Chorus of the Vienna State Opera and the Austrian Radio Symphony Orchestra came close. Though not the heldentenor Schmidt asked for, tenor Peter Schreier sings the role of St. John beautifully in a clear, declamatory style. The other soloists are a mixed bag. On a Sony recording of a 1959 Salzburg performance conducted by Dimitri Mitropoulos, Fritz Wunderlich shows a more dramatic approach to St. John. He gets inside the role and sings with great expressivity. Mitropoulos complements this approach by conducting with more dramatic grip than Lothar Zagrosek on Orfeo. Unfortunately, there is the expected sacrifice of sound quality on the mono Sony. Since Franz Wesler-Möst is one of the few conductors to have gotten Schmidt's Fourth Symphony exactly right, it is no surprise that he excels with this difficult work. His close-to-ideal recording is with the Bavarian Radio Symphony Orchestra and Chorus on two budget-priced EMI/Warner Classics CDs. First of all, he trusts his materials. He finds the right pulse to Schmidt's music and lets it unfold without ever letting it lag. The glorious results have been given one of the most dramatically transparent recordings I have ever heard. The clarity of detail is startling and fully reveals Schmidt's genius. Everything comes together in this stunning performance. To hear the Apocalypse in surround sound, head for Chandos' 2008 SACD recording with Kristjan Järvi, the youngest of the conducting sons of Schmidt veteran Neeme Järvi.

With respect to Schmidt's other works, one might begin with the Second Symphony. Neeme Järvi sweeps all before him with the Chicago Symphony Orchestra in a magnificent reading of this superb work on Chandos (only available in a box set of all four symphonies on four CDs). With Schmidt's beautiful themes, the temptation is to dwell. Järvi does not succumb and reveals much more of the music's dramatic impact than have previous recordings. Listen to the extraordinary way in which Schmidt weaves three unrelated themes together in the first movement in an orchestral tour de force with a shattering climax.

Järvi now has a capable competitor in Naxos' new traversal of Schmidt's four symphonies, all available singly at budget price. In Symphony No. 2, the Malmö Symphony Orchestra, under Vassily Sinaisky, gets inside this sumptuous music and reveals its late-harvest ripeness in all its glory. I love Schmidt because his expression of the overripeness of Viennese culture in the early 20th century is rich but not decadent. He really is the last efflorescence of that extraordinary time before its (audible) decay. One hears that with Sinaisky and the Malmö forces. He may take two minutes longer than Järvi, but he conducts with the marvelous sense of flow so essential for the cumulative impact to register.

The Third Symphony from 1927–1928 is a subtle, finely graded, highly lyrical work of gentle beauty and mystery. The first movement is a mesmerizing treatment of a fairly lengthy tune that is stated, in various forms—some 13 times—without fatigue. The cumulative effect is utterly beguiling and magical, and the movement is passionately powerful in its culmination. Järvi's urgent performance of the Third Symphony on Chandos with the Chicago Symphony Orchestra is slightly handicapped by a distant sound perspective. Vassily Sinaisky and the Malmö Symphony Orchestra bring out the delicacy of the piece in a far more leisurely, relaxed approach in a radiant interpretation, which benefits from a much greater sense of presence in a top-notch recording. Sinaisky's ability to show all the strands in this very rich, sumptuous music is a major plus. The pace is slow (eight minutes slower than Järvi), but the concentration and commitment of the conductor and players carry the day in this extended variation treatment of a very beautiful theme.

The Fourth Symphony, composed by Schmidt as a requiem for his daughter Emma, who had died in childbirth in 1932, is his greatest orchestral work, but has suffered from several recordings with slow tempos. Franz Welser-Möst's EMI/Warner Classics release, at budget price, shows how much the work benefits dramatically from tempos closer to those recommended by the composer. The release includes a beautiful rendition of the *Hussar Variations*. Vassily Sinaisky and the Malmö Symphony Orchestra concluded their cycle for Naxos with a recording of the Fourth, also accompanied by *Variations on a Hussar's Song* (8.572118). Franz Welser-Möst's and the London Philharmonic's performances are more intense and dramatic, but Sinaisky fully captures the glorious sumptuousness of this music. His tempos are broader (by three minutes in the Fourth; by less than two minutes in the *Variations*) but, if you have the patience, the payoff is there. This budget Naxos Schmidt cycle is clearly one of the great bargains.

Another Schmidt treat is the Piano Concerto for piano left hand, commissioned by the famous pianist Paul Wittgenstein, who lost his right arm in World War I. This is a big 45-minute work with a long orchestral introduction replete with Schmidt's signature enharmonic modulations. Schmidt knew the piano almost as well as he knew the cello, and there are lovely lines of delicate tracery throughout the concerto, which shares many of the characteristics of his marvelous symphonies. He again displays his prowess with variation form in the *Concertante Variations on a Theme of Beethoven* for piano left hand and orchestra, which accompanies the Piano Concerto on a CPO CD. The theme is from the Scherzo of Beethoven's "Spring" Sonata, and has more classical charm than romantic drama. Schmidt's treatment of it is delectable in this performance by pianist Markus Becker, with the very fine NDR Radio Philharmonic under Eiji Oue. It is accompanied by Schmidt's Concerto, a gem written for Paul Wittgenstein, on CPO.

Schmidt was as fine a composer of chamber music as he was of symphonies. Try the entrancing Clarinet Quintet in A Major on Marco Polo or the equally fine Piano Quintet in F Major on a Decca disc (coupled with the Bruckner Quintet, played by the Vienna Philharmonia Quintet). On an Orfeo recording, you can get both Quintets in one fell swoop. You can hear the soaring melodies of the opera *Notre Dame*, which contains Schmidt's famous *Intermezzo*, in a very fine performance on Capriccio.

One of the chamber music CDs that I have enjoyed most since its issue in 1996 is the Nimbus Records release of Schmidt's two string quartets, lovingly played by the Franz Schubert Quartet. These are a must, not just for Schmidt fans, but for all lovers of chamber music. They are marvelously rich, sweet, and lyrical, with a touch of sadness and even a whiff of the fin de siècle overripeness (though they were composed in the 1920s). Unlike Bruckner's or Rubbra's essays in the genre, Schmidt's two masterpieces are not symphonies for string quartets. They are completely idiomatic and to scale—the intimate kind of conversation that only four musicians can have. Schmidt regularly played cello in a string quartet for sheer pleasure. His love for and mastery of the form are evident here. So are his musical roots, which go back to Schubert. If music of this kind had to go, it could not have gone out with a more glorious autumnal glow than in these works, given truly beautiful recordings by Nimbus.

These recordings are a good beginning. Let us hope there will be more. Could it be that Franz Schmidt's time has come at last?

Recommended Recordings

The Book of Seven Seals, Vienna Philharmonic, Vienna Singverein Hilde Güden, Ira Malaniuk, Fritz Wunderlich, Walter Berry et al., Dimitri Mitropoulos (conductor), Sony 68442. Or: Christiane Oelze, Cornelia Kallisch, Stig Andersen, René Pape et al., Bavarian Radio Symphony Orchestra, Bavarian Radio Chorus, Franz Welser-Möst (conductor), EMI/Warner 85782. Or: Sandra Trattnigg, Michelle Breedt, Johannes Chum, Robert Holl, et al., Lower Austrian Tonkünstler Orchestra, Vienna Singverein, Kristjan Järvi (conductor), Chandos SACD 5061.

Orchestral Works

Symphonies 1–4, Detroit and Chicago Symphony Orchestras, Neeme Järvi (conductor), Chandos 9568

Symphony No. 1; *Notre Dame* (excerpts), Vassily Sinaisky, Naxos 8.570828

Symphony No. 2; *Fuga Solemnis*, Vassily Sinaisky, Naxos 8.570589

Symphony No. 3; *Chaconne*, Vassily Sinaisky, Naxos 8.572119

Symphony No. 4; *Variations on a Hussar's Song*, Vassily Sinaisky, Naxos 8.572118

Symphony No. 4; *Hussar Variations*, London PO, Franz Welser-Möst (conductor), EMI/Warner 55693

Piano Concerto (left hand), *Concertante Variations* (left hand), Markus Becker (piano), Eiji Oue (conductor), NDR RPO, CPO 777338

Chamber Music

The String Quartets, Franz Schubert String Quartet, Nimbus 5467

Clarinet Quintet, Romance for Piano, Toccata for Piano left hand et al., Aladár Jánoska (Clarinet) et al., Marco Polo 8.223414

Piano Quintet for left hand (plus Korngold Suite for piano left hand and strings) Leon Fleisher (piano), Yo-Yo Ma (cello), Joel Smirnoff (violin) et al., Sony 48253

Piano Quintet (with piano part rewritten for both hands), Vienna Philharmonia Quintet, Decca Eloquence 4762455

Piano Quintet, Clarinet Quintet, Rainer Keuschnig (Piano), Ernst Ottensamer (Clarinet) et al., Orfeo 287921

Notre Dame, James King, Horst Laubenthal, Kurt Moll, Hans Helm Berlin RSO, Berlin RIAS Chamber Chorus, St. Hedwig's Cathedral Choir Christoph Perick (conductor), Capriccio 5181

Othmar Schoeck: From Switzerland with Romance

Jens F. Laurson

From Beethoven's *Eroica* Symphony via Schumann, Brahms, and Wagner, to Richard Strauss and early Arnold Schoenberg, "romantic" is the technically appropriate designation of style. It equally fits an organ symphony by Charles Widor, Chopin's *Études*, a Tchaikovsky opera, or a Rachmaninoff piano concerto. In being so encompassing, it teeters on the brink of meaninglessness, but it remains a ubiquitous term because it *does* have its uses. At the very least it is a broadly common denominator that the reader and the struggling writer share: if the composer died before 1830 and his music is described as "romantic", we know not to expect some postclassical Amadeus-come-lately; if he was born after 1890, and so described, we need not fear strict atonality or aleatoric (chance-based) music.

That's good to keep in mind when describing the music of Swiss Othmar Schoeck—James Joyce's favorite composer—as "romantic". Throughout his lifetime, and certainly after 1945, the idiom of Schoeck (1886–1957) was unacceptably romantic for avant-gardists or too modern for conservatives.

The unequivocally conservative romantic works, with which anyone can be safely encouraged to begin their Schoeck explorations, are usually orchestral, though he is most famous for his some 400 lieder. Schoeck's Violin Concerto is one of the absolutely great underplayed 20th-century violin concertos, along with Ermanno Wolf-Ferrari's. It is also more easily digestible and lyrical than Carl Nielsen's contemporaneous masterpiece. With overt hints of, and quotes from, Beethoven (true to the subtitle *Quasi una Fantasia*), filled with plenty of zip and joy, it is a surprisingly mature and well-rounded masterpiece for a composer who much preferred to write for voice. But he happily made an exception when it came to writing for the violinist femme fatale Stefi Geyer, the dedicatee of this work and the object of his unrequited love.

Pictures of Hungarian Stefi Geyer (1888–1956) show a woman of a certain beauty but with a hard face, despite her youthfully chubby

cheeks. Even late in life, Schoeck described her warmly and recol-
lected her ability to move beautifully and walk elegantly. His infatuation moved him to write his *Album Leaf* for violin and piano, his
Violin Sonata, op. 16, and said concerto for her. The *Album Leaf* she
still premiered, but by the time the first movement of the concerto
was finished in 1911, Stefi had gotten engaged and eventually married
to a Viennese lawyer. That wasn't how Schoeck had planned it, and
he consequently asked his friend Willem de Boer of the Tonhalle Orchestra to give the premiere performance. De Boer turned it into one
of Schoeck's greatest successes. Stefi, whose husband died just a few
years after her marriage, played it eventually and even made the first
recording of the work—in 1947 with Volkmar Andreae conducting the
Tonhalle Orchestra and a greenhorn producer by the name of Walter
Legge.

Moving though her interpretation (Jecklin) is, there are more satisfying modern accounts of the work with violinists Ulf Hoelscher
(Novalis), Bettina Boller (Claves), and most recently Chloë Hanslip
(Hyperion), all of which make a different point about the work's ex-
cellence.

Just a year after Stefi Geyer performed the Violin Concerto, Pierre
Fournier premiered the brand new Schoeck Cello Concerto with the
same orchestra and conductor. It is not as harmonically adventurous
as his prewar works, but is almost as sweet as the Violin Concerto,
and it contains a ravishing slow movement that references the song
cycle *Das stille Leuchten.* There is no struggle between the cello and
the string orchestra, which simply enhances and harmonizes with the
long, singing cello line. This is music to warm yourself by. On the
Claves label, it is accompanied by *Sommernacht (Summer Night),* one
of Schoeck's most popular pieces. Music does not get mellower than
this. There is also a jaunty Horn Concerto, the deliciously languid
Serenade for Oboe, English Horn and Strings, and the charming *Suite for
Strings in A-flat Major.* The *Serenade* has a Ravel-like Spanish flavor to it
—not surprising, considering that the source of its music is Schoeck's
then-popular opera *Don Ranudo.*

Of Schoeck's String Quartets, the older work is slightly more conservative for its time than the younger (they were written 1913 and
1923 respectively), but both are simply gorgeous—the latter by way of
the autumnal glow typical of much of this composer's music and the

former by means of entrancing chromaticism that swerves naturally between the idioms of Dvořák and Zemlinsky or the early, still-romantic Schoenberg.

In the case of Schoeck's *Notturno* (1933), the term "romantic" won't prepare one for what the music actually sounds like. It would mislead. Yet describing this work for string quartet and baritone (a rare combination likely inspired by Schoenberg's 1908 String Quartet, op. 10) as "romantic" is essential to understanding it. *Notturno* is the epitome of extreme, late-romantic music; the squeezing of chromaticism and the stretching of Western music's common harmonic understanding to, and often beyond, the breaking point.

The difference is similar to describing Anton Webern's *Langsamer Satz* as "romantic" (which it certainly, very obviously, is: like *Tristan und Isolde* condensed into 14 minutes of string quartet) and the contemporaneous Alban Berg's Piano Sonata, op. 1 as "romantic" (which it also certainly is, but not at all obviously). What makes the difference between perceiving Berg's sonata as an early exercise in pantonalism and perceiving it as an achingly beautiful, wistful romantic statement saturated with the fleeting airs of Viennese coffeehouse atmosphere is the ability to keep the notes "in the air", and recall them when the notes that give them their proper context finally arrive. It's chromatic, but with incredibly long, intertwined lines. It's like a thoroughly constructed, impressive German sentence the length of two paragraphs in which, to paraphrase Mark Twain, "you won't know the meaning until the writer, who dives into a sentence, emerges on the other side of his Atlantic with his verb in his mouth." If you hold out for the long elusive "verbs" in Berg's sonata, they will then fall into place and make harmonic sense where previously there was only dissonance.

Likewise, we can now gainfully claim that *Notturno* ought to be understood as a romantic work, namely in the sense of Berg's sonata or his *Lyric Suite*. *Notturno*, based on eight poems by Nikolaus Lenau and a short text by Gottfried Keller in five movements, flirts with the outer, atonal, harmonic reaches from a late-romantic vantage point. It must be played with the utmost precision if those long horizontal lines are to be revealed, if the listener is to be able to follow the long, thin strands of music that wind through the score, emerging and submerging. That hyperromanticism can only happen if the players don't count beats, but feel their way from phrase to phrase.

Christian Gerhaher, arguably the finest Lieder-singer of our time, who has recorded the cycle for ECM, has a somber, grave enthusiasm all of his own, but he warms up when talking about *Notturno*:

> Schoeck's music is unbelievably beautiful music, but it's a difficult mix. All in all, it's late-romantic music, but . . . melodically it's atonal. Wrapping your ears around it takes a while; I don't think you can grasp the work upon first hearing. It has immense depth and what is so great about it, looking at the temporal aspect, is how much time these movements get to develop. *Notturno* is an absolute solitaire— there is no comparable work . . . certainly none so immensely rasping and prickly as the *Notturno*.

Notturno, for all its splendid delicacy, is probably Schoeck's most difficult work for a newcomer to appreciate. If many of Schoeck's other vocal works are much more easily digested and conventionally beautiful, they're not the worse for it. Top of the list might be Schoeck's *Elegie*, a morosely delightful 50-minute song cycle for chamber orchestra. A pocket-sized *Four Last Songs* for those with a slightly shorter attention span.

Schoeck had a few famous proponents in his time, among them the late Dietrich Fischer-Dieskau, whose dedication to this wonderful, woefully underrated composer resulted in recordings of many of his songs and song cycles. Fischer-Dieskau was the first to record the boundary-pushing *Notturno*, for example, but also recorded other risky, more conventionally beautiful Schoeck song cycles like *Lebendig Begraben* (*Buried Alive*, 1926, on Gottfried Keller poems and the reason for Joyce's Schoeck-appreciation), *Unter Sternen* (*Beneath Stars*, 1943, on Gottfried Keller poems), *Das Stille Leuchten* (*The Quiet Light Shining*, 1946, on poems by Conrad Ferdinand Meyer), *Das Holde Bescheiden* (*Propitious Modesty*, 1949, on Eduard Mörike poems), and *Nachhall* (*Echo*, 1955, on poems by Nikolaus Lenau). Maybe the loss of Fischer-Dieskau will kindle a series of reissues of these artistically significant recordings, or stimulate new ones—as Schoeck is being rediscovered as an eminently worthy voice in 20th-century music.

Das Stille Leuchten, especially, is a masterpiece in which Schoeck is edging toward the transcendental. With sparse beauty, but also humor and memorable little turns of phrases, he moves toward "Nachtgeräusche" ("Sounds of the Night")—the poem a line of which gives the cycle its name and which ends, in *triple pianissimo*, on these words:

"What can I create in this life / Before I go to the grave / What can I give that might escape death / Perhaps a word, maybe a song / A quiet light shining". Tellingly, though, the last word in this cycle Schoeck reserved for the poem "Jetzt rede Du": "Now you speak! The floor is yours! Laments and jubilation cease—And I will listen." It is an appeal to silence, to things that cannot be spoken of, concluded for another quiet minute alone by the pianist.

Schoeck wrote eight operas, with his 1927 *Penthesilea* of chief importance—a work that is to Schoeck what *Elektra* is to Richard Strauss and that has received increased, much deserved attention from opera houses in the last few years. A sharp and angular, tonal but often aggressive and dissonant work, the one-act opera on Heinrich Kleist's retelling of Amazonian queen Penthesilea's and Achilles' love and death presents Schoeck's harmonically more daring style of the mid '20s and early '30s. In it, Schoeck moves a little more into the direction of Alban Berg, a new discovery of his, and away from his mentor Ferruccio Busoni, who in 1922 lamented, "Schoeck has completely abandoned me. I have not entirely given him up."

In either form of romanticism that he embraced, Schoeck offers a great deal that deserves and will reward attention

Recommended Recordings

Violin Concerto, Chloë Hanslip, Alexander Vedernikov, Orchestra della Svizzera Italiana, Hyperion 67940. Or: Violin Concerto, Bettina Boller, Andreas Delfs, Swiss Youth SO, Claves 509201. Coupled with the near-contemporaneous Glazunov Concerto, Chloë Hanslip's 2013 recording is the most polished and delicate version yet, but the excitement and energy of the Swiss Youth SO under Andreas Delfs and Bettina Boller from 1992 has an undeniable and immediate virtue all of its own. The coupling with Delfs' arrangement of the best of *Penthesilea* as a half-hour suite adds to the attractiveness of the Claves release.

Elegie, Klaus Mertens, Mutare Ensemble, NCA 60186

Das Stille Leuchten, Dietrich Fischer-Dieskau, Hartmut Höll, Claves 508910

Nachhall, Roman Brogli-Sacher, Lübeck PO, Jun Mo Yang, Musicaphon 56931 SACD

Notturno, Christian Gerhaher, Rosamunde Quartet, ECM 001355902

Klaus Mertens, Minguet Quartet, NCA 60133

Stephan Genz, Leipzig String Quartet, MDG 3071815

Cello Concerto; *Sommernacht* (*Summer Night*), Johannes Goritzki, German Chamber Academy Neuss, Claves 8502

Cello Concerto, Cello Sonata, Songs for Cello and Piano, Christian Poltéra (cello), Julius Drake (piano), Malmö SO, Tuomas Ollila-Hannikainen, BIS 1597

Violin Sonatas, Simone Zgraggen (violin), Ulrich Koella (piano), Claves 502503

String Quartet No. 2 (plus Fritz Brun String Quartet No. 3), Amar String Quartet, Musiques Suisses 46238

Penthesilea, Gerd Albrecht, Austrian RSO & Chorus, Helga Dernesch, Jane Marsh, Mechthild Gessendorf, Marjana Lipovšek, et al., Orfeo 364941

~

Dmitri Shostakovich: Beyond Bombast

With Jens F. Laurson

Dmitri Shostakovich (1906–1975) was widely touted as a "Soviet" artist because he was the first significant Russian composer to have been completely educated under the Communist regime. In some sense, Shostakovich may have agreed with this description. Nevertheless, he was in a state of constant tension with the Soviet Union, which alternately celebrated and suppressed his music, depending on how Joseph Stalin was feeling. Stalin first censured Shostakovich's music in 1936, calling the opera *Lady Macbeth of the Mtsensk District* "muddle instead of music". Shostakovich packed a small bag in readiness for the late-night knock at the door that he expected would end in a firing squad or internment in the Gulag. He also abjectly recanted: "I began to speak a language incomprehensible to the people. . . . I know that the party is right. . . . I am deeply grateful for the criticism."

Based on Nicolai Leskov's novella, *Lady Macbeth of the Mtsensk District*, it is a harrowing tale—a "tragedy-satire", according to Shostakovich —in which the suppressed wife of a merchant murders her father-in-law with rat poison after he discovers her with her lover. She then murders her returning husband, is caught by the police, and sent to Siberia, where she commits suicide while drowning the mistress of her unfaithful lover in a lake. And Katerina is the one with whom we are supposed to sympathize.

Shostakovich certainly intended the opera's message for a Soviet audience, which by 1934 was practiced at reading between the lines of historical settings—in this case, 1860s Russia. The huge popularity of this acidic opera during the two years it played before Stalin banned it tells us that Soviet audience understood it.

Shostakovich said he saw Katerina as the "tragic portrayal of the destiny of a talented, smart and outstanding woman, dying in the nightmarish atmosphere of pre-Revolutionary Russia". Change that to: the destiny of a country, Russia, dying in the nightmarish atmosphere of the Soviet Union, and we get closer to what we see and hear. In 1936, it is lucky that the offended Stalin left the opera early and that all he heard was "muddle instead of music", as announced in *Pravda* several days later. Otherwise he might have had Shostakovich killed for this subversive work.

It may be difficult to divine what this piece means outside of the Soviet times in which it was written, but here is a try at decoding it: *Lady Macbeth* is a mordant morality tale of how unhinged passion becomes if it cannot anchor itself in love. We can pretend this opera is about women's liberation or about the stifling of a passionate spirit by the forces of provincial convention, but in any case love is denied at every turn. There is *no* love in *Lady Macbeth*—not between husband and wife, father and son, workers and boss, priest and God, or even between lovers—consider the manic musical parodies of love-making (the famous trombone glissandos), and the hugely ironic Tristanesque music at the beginning of scene 5 sung by an impassioned Katerina to an already disinterested, loutish Sergey.

As a consequence, this loveless society is drenched in alcohol, cupidity, and lasciviousness. Everything is coarsened; everything is false; everything is a lie. This, of course, would be true anywhere where love is so completely absent, but the Soviet Union took a particularly bizarre and surreal turn due to the total lie upon which it was based as to who and what human beings are. When reduced to this level, people become caricatures of themselves. The deprivation of love dehumanizes. It leads to terrible things. This is the cruelty Shostakovich shows. It hurts to watch and sometimes to hear.

This is particularly true of the fourth act, as the prisoners are marched to Siberia, where Katerina suffers her ultimate humiliation and betrayal. This act is searingly well done and leaves some unforgettable images. When Katerina, seized by the realization of her degraded situation, gets physically ill, the opera provides one of its most human and devastating moments. Her illness is a very human reaction of physical revulsion to what had been ingested for most of the preceding three acts, as if life itself—at least, as led like this—is a form of rat poison against which one's system totally rebels. After Katerina's suicide, the prisoners are marched away. They sing a haunting final chorus as they disappear. Surely, the Soviet audiences understood Shostakovich's profoundly moving writing for the convict chorus as the lament of the Gulag.

To save himself after Stalin's condemnation of *Lady Macbeth*, Shostakovich suppressed his more raucous works, such as the Fourth Symphony, and penned the Fifth Symphony as "a Soviet artist's response to just criticism". The symphony was received as a heroic affirmation of the spirit of the Soviet people, and soon afterward Shostakovich was fully rehabilitated with a Stalin Prize for his Piano Quintet. All was well until the next denunciation in 1948. For the rest of his life, Shostakovich kept his bag packed; he was always waiting for the sound of a fist on the door. In 1956, when Shostakovich's friend Flora Litvinova suggested, "And you, too, Dmitri Dmitriyevich, are for the ideas of communism", he answered, "No, communism is impossible." When forced to join the Communist Party in 1960, he is said to have contemplated suicide.

To all appearances Shostakovich conformed and became a good Soviet cultural apparatchik, which included being sent abroad as a musical emissary. The symphonies and choral works dedicated to Lenin and the Revolution dutifully poured forth from his pen. Articles praising the "Great Leader" were signed by Shostakovich. Yet, all was not as it seemed. Even at their best, the symphonies can be enigmatic; at their worst, they inexplicably degenerate into bombast. Some of the heroic symphonies make less than convincing wholes. Their caustic grotesqueries and deliberate banalities, juxtaposed with passages of searing intensity and unrelenting power, can leave the listener reeling and confused. Are the incongruities lapses of judgment or failures of talent? Some of the music seems deliberately disfigured for reasons hard to discern. Why does the meaning of Shostakovich's symphonies seem so elusive?

The answer is that Shostakovich was engaged in secret writing—in the exact way in which political philosopher Leo Strauss defined it, although transposed to the world of music. In *Persecution and the Art of Writing* (1952), Strauss said, "Persecution . . . gives rise to a peculiar technique of writing . . . in which the truth about all crucial things is presented exclusively between the lines. . . . It has all the advantages of public communication without having its greatest disadvantage—capital punishment for the author." To the consternation of many who have interpreted Shostakovich's symphonies programmatically, according to various Communist or "Great Patriotic War" themes, Shostakovich revealed in *Testimony*, his memoirs "as told to Solomon Volkov", that he had been speaking in musical code. The authenticity of *Testimony* has been contested, but Allan B. Ho and Dmitry Feofanov substantiated its claims in their book *Shostakovich Reconsidered* and their follow-up work, *The Shostakovich Wars*. The latter is available online as a download.[1]

For instance, Shostakovich said that the end of the Fifth Symphony is a false apotheosis: "The rejoicing is forced, created under threat. . . . You have to be a complete oaf not to hear that." The Seventh Symphony, subtitled *Leningrad*, was blatantly used for propaganda purposes against the Nazis during World War II. Shostakovich revealed that the Seventh was planned before the war and "consequently cannot be seen as a reaction to Hitler's attack. The 'invasion theme' has nothing to do with the attack. I was thinking of other enemies of humanity when I composed the theme. . . . It's about the Leningrad that Stalin destroyed and that Hitler merely finished off." Of the 10th Symphony, he said, "No one has yet guessed what the symphony is about. It's about Stalin and the Stalin years. The second part, the Scherzo, is a musical portrait of Stalin." Likewise, the 11th Symphony is not about the Revolution in 1905: "It deals with contemporary themes even though it's called '1905'. It's about the people, who have stopped believing because the cup of evil has run over." In the 14th Symphony, Shostakovich said, "I don't protest against death in it. I protest against those butchers who execute people." As for why he said different things to different people at various times (including about his symphonies), Shostakovich gave a reply that, no doubt, Leo Strauss would have enjoyed: "I answer different people differently, because different people deserve different answers." How delicious that he should respond to conductor Yevgeny Mravinsky's question regarding a certain passage in the Eighth Symphony by saying, "The Scherzo in the second movement represents the functionary who has received his exit visa to the West."

Shostakovich's remarks in *Testimony* have the ring of truth: "The majority of my symphonies are tombstones. . . . I'm willing to write a composition for each of the victims, but that's impossible, and that's why I dedicate my music to them all." Here is the real substance of Shostakovich's symphonic message. Yet visits to the graveyard are often difficult, and so is listening to some of Shostakovich's 15 symphonies. That's not to say they are not worth the effort—especially if one looks beyond the most popular ones: Nos. 5, 7, and 10.

Shostakovich's Fourth Symphony is the most Mahlerian of his symphonies: just listen to the opening of the second movement and you

[1] http://www.siue.edu/~aho/ShostakovichWars/SW.pdf

hear Mahler with a Russian accent. At the same time, it contains all the musical seeds that will show up in his future works. First suppressed, then long ignored as inferior, it is—when well performed—not just one of his best but certainly one of his most important symphonies. Shostakovich inexplicably called it a defective, verbose failure, although "with bits that I like", when Kirill Kondrashin gave the belated premiere in 1961, almost 20 years after the wisely canceled premiere.

It's a wild, riveting, sometimes abrasively glorious assault on our senses. A good performance will evoke ghoulish images: the xylophones in the first movement should sound like a horde of drunken skeletons playing ghastly tunes on their exposed ribcages. The climax of the first movement ought to become a thing of thunderous splendor, demented hordes galloping hellward—without any false sense of sophistication: just raw emotion, coagulated blood, vodka, and gunpowder.

There is torment, accusation, and wild-eyed plowing forward, visceral at every turn, and you can positively see a demented orchestra with foam at its mouth plunging fatalistically onward. Beautiful ticktocks lead into the false calm of the third movement's opening—only to proceed to delve deeply into this enervating, beautifully bizarre world that makes the Mahler-influenced first movement seem perfectly normal. The music's thumbscrews tighten at every fresh start after an intermittent lull or (faux-) lyrical passage.

The shrieks, the brutality, the claws, the exhaustion, the climaxes, the pounding, and the relentlessness are harrowing. But most distressing, because of all that preceded it, is the ensuing dreamy delicacy of the ticking-away of the symphony, the final breath and the mourning trumpet that sound like a death knell ringing over a blood-soaked battlefield on a winter dawn. It's a like a comment on a victory everyone knows was a defeat.

Little wonder Shostakovich kept the symphony in the drawer after the *Lady Macbeth* incident. When performed with all that anger, biting, painful sarcasm, and futile energy, the symphony becomes an indictment of whichever regime you currently despise the most. Dmitri Shostakovich could have been interned in any country after such a delivery.

There are many fine recordings, all of which bring different aspects to this work: Rudolf Barshai and the WDR Symphony Orchestra (Alto) the bony rawness, Semyon Bychkov with the same orchestra (Avie

SACD), the brute force; and Valery Gergiev with the Kirov (now Mariinsky) Orchestra (Philips/Decca) the tortuously slow build-up. The recording that brings it all together gloriously is Mariss Jansons' with the Bavarian Radio Symphony Orchestra on EMI/Warner.

Expert Shostakovich-conductor Valery Gergiev, though not known for his light and humorous ways himself, grumbles rightly that to ignore the humor in Shostakovich is to miss the point of his music entirely. That's particularly true for the Ninth Symphony—coy and glittery and frivolously charming, with a brass section that sounds like the Keystone Cops at band camp. Dainty ballerinas and beer hall oompah bands never existed in such harmonious proximity: to undercut so deliberately the mythical status that Beethoven set for his Ninth Symphony already meant making a (musical) statement in and of itself. Doing so in the summer of 1945, following the defeat of Nazi Germany and after announcements in the press had suggested a "Victory Symphony", added a political dimension. Russians were expecting a paean to Stalin, vanquisher of evil and preserver of the people, and what they got instead was the symphonic equivalent of "Ding Dong the Witch Is Dead". In a place and at a time when being apolitical (much less oppositional) was a crime, this was strong stuff.

But it's best to enjoy Shostakovich for musical, not ideological reasons. With all political circumstance out of the way, what remains is one of the most entertaining—indeed best—symphonies there are. Shostakovich channels more Haydn in his Ninth than does Prokofiev in his ostentatious Classical Symphony: more genuine wit and less "I-showed-you-so." In fact, the symphony was so good that Shostakovich was publicly excoriated again and wisely didn't write another until after Stalin's death.

Zdeněk Košler brings out the joyful and buoyant side to the Ninth like few others. An oddity of sorts is its coupling: the Fifth Symphony with Yevgeny Mravinsky, which claims to have been recorded in Prague in May of 1967. It's actually a live performance from Vienna from 11 years later. But, attempted fraud apart, it's a tremendous, raw performance of Shostakovich's most famous symphony, almost aided by the tape distortion. Worth seeking out, even if it is out of print. Yakov Kreizberg's recording of the same symphonies comes not only in state of the art sound but is as thwacking a modern Fifth as has been recorded and never fails the humor of the Ninth.

On January 23, 1974, the 30th anniversary of the break of the German siege of Leningrad and just a little over a year before Shostakovich died, Kirill Kondrashin conducted the Dresden Staatskapelle in Shostakovich's 15th Symphony. The last and latest symphony of the great composer from St. Petersburg was a logical choice for this occasion, but it wouldn't have escaped Kondrashin, or the Dresden audience, that it is a work uniquely unsuited to venerate the Soviet regime. After vocal symphonies 13 and 14, Shostakovich, fatally ill and well aware of it, returned to an almost classical form of the symphony.

Shostakovich spoke of the first movement, Adagietto, as a "toy-shop with plenty of knick-knacks and trinkets—absolutely cheerful". No listener to Kondrashin's or any other recording will get away from the first movement without doubting the composer's own words. If this is a toy shop at all, it's one that sells little tanks, toy guns, and junior's first torture kit. It's a romp with its share of plink and delicate chirping, but this collection of trivialities amid intensity, with crashing marching bands and ballerinas, sounds like a sugarplum-fairy-cum-guerilla fighter. Moments that remind of the Second and Ninth Symphonies are always interrupted by the seemingly random *William Tell* Overture excerpt that all American audiences can identify as the Lone Ranger theme.

It's not impossible that Shostakovich knew the Lone Ranger and his heroic deeds (or his appeal to children, which would go with the toy shop story)—but it's more likely that the Rossini original inspired him. That would be telling enough: a story about a man who is coerced to use his skill (archery, in Tell's case) according to the bidding of a despot—but who then uses it to fight against tyranny. If anything it seems that Shostakovich, in the hospital while composing this movement, had dispensed with subtlety in his political statements.

The strange giddiness of the first movement is immediately subdued by the grave brass chorale that opens the dark second movement. Phases of rest and reply and the cello's lamenting song lead into trombone and violin statements that are everything but "absolutely cheerful". Trombone glissandi (the very ones that enraged Stalin in *Lady Macbeth*) are employed, and eventually the subdued movement wakens and rises slowly to a big orchestral thrashing-about. It's Shostakovich typical of Symphonies 4, 7, 8, and 11—but with an incredible efficiency of means and chamber-like in proportion and scoring.

The friendly little third movement (Allegretto) has Haydnesque moments before the fourth movement takes over with another blatant musical quotation—this time Wagner's "ensuing death" motif from the *Ring*. The yearning opening of *Tristan und Isolde* also appears several times, completing the atmosphere of resignation and departure. Amid many more or less subtle quotations, the finale gathers momentum that leads to a Passacaglia—and then the symphony dithers away in morose mood over ghastly ticktocks of a clock and a last, faint glimmer of percussive hope.

More immediately accessible than many of the above are Shostakovich's 15 string quartets, a large body of fully mature works that were begun after the Fifth Symphony. The quartets are more homogeneous and more easily grasped than the symphonies, perhaps because of the inherently intimate nature of their form, which also precludes their use, or abuse, as de rigueur hymns to the Russian Revolution. (One hapless Soviet minister of culture tried and failed miserably when he once gave orders to organize "a quartet of ten men".) Quartets are protected by their privacy. Also, their messages usually do not have to be decoded.

If Shostakovich's symphonies are tombstones, the 15 quartets are the flowers he lays on the graves. By any measure, this is some of the most extraordinary music written during the 20th century. Of course, it reflects the terrible disorientation of the totalitarian regime in which Shostakovich lived; but no matter how unusual some of his chamber music might sometimes seem, it never loses its reference points in song and dance. This is because Shostakovich's interest is not in abstraction but in expression. The weirdness is not in his means of expression, which are really quite conventional despite the occasional massive doses of dissonance, but in what is expressed—which is hardly strange considering what the man and his country endured. The ghostly dances and songs that pass through Shostakovich's quartets are from a world that Lenin and Stalin attempted to destroy—the world of the human soul, from which emanate the most basic impulses to sing praise and to dance in delight, which is why we still listen.

The stylistic touchstones for the quartets are not, curiously enough, Béla Bartók, Arnold Schoenberg, or Paul Hindemith, the three most influential European composers in the genre at the time. Neither do the principal influences on Shostakovich's symphonies—Mahler and Prokofiev—make their presences felt. Without any intermediaries, the quartets establish their classical lineage directly back to Haydn and Beethoven. This does not mean that they do not contain surprises.

Elements of Russian and Jewish folk song give them a gypsy-like wildness akin to Leoš Janáček's two great quartets. Disorientation does not have any meaning unless there is the anchor of orientation preceding it—giving it context. Using Haydn and Beethoven as touchstones, Shostakovich shows us how disoriented things were in the Soviet Union. While there is exquisite beauty here, much of the music is hair-raising, even frightening. After some string lashings, a wistful melody will float by like a life preserver after a shipwreck. A part of Quartet No. 13 sounds like waves of pain in the brain, a musical migraine. Do not let these descriptions put you off; this is very human music.

Here are some brief comments to convey the character of a few of these extraordinary works. Quartet No. 1 is full of Haydnesque sweetness and light, with liltingly lovely melodies. The Second Quartet is a world apart in its additional depth and gravity. The Third Quartet is the second longest of the 15. It was completed in 1946, after the Ninth Symphony, and is every bit as powerful a composition as the famous Eighth. Its opening Allegro has the same kind of wild, violent swagger and hammered chords as the Allegro from the Eighth, while the ensuing Adagio is beautifully poignant and haunting, surely one of Shostakovich's finest inspirations. The final movement closes with a quiet lament that must be one of the most touching farewells in chamber music.

The Fourth Quartet's opening movement has both a poignant lyricism and wild intensity, followed by a plaintive Andantino. The Seventh Quartet is a brief gem-like work dedicated to the memory of Shostakovich's first wife. The grief lyrically expressed in the first two movements gives way to energetic protests and angry desperation in the extraordinary fugal pages of the third. The piece's concluding movement, an extended assimilation of all the preceding elements, ends with a sense of peaceful resignation, almost a sigh.

The Eighth Quartet, also a mournful work, was supposedly written as a protest against fascism engendered by Shostakovich's memory of war-damaged Dresden. This view, supported by Shostakovich's dedication of the quartet to "the victims of Fascism and War", has led to ridiculous descriptions of the music as depicting the evil drone of hostile bombers and the crackling of gunfire (where the waltz music of the third movement fits into this scenario is anyone's guess). In *Testimony*, Shostakovich explicitly rejected this program: "The Eighth is an autobiographical work" that has nothing to do with "exposing fascism". The piece quotes themes from several of Shostakovich's works and makes use of a musical motto derived from his initials in the German transliteration: D-S-C-H (derived from the German notation of D, E-flat, C, B). The work is weighted at both ends by gentle Largos that convey a feeling of deep sorrow. They frame a ferocious Allegro molto that alternates between stabbing chords and wild, gypsy-like material and an Allegretto based on a strange little waltz. It is extraordinary music, in which Shostakovich takes on the aspect of a Russian Janáček.

Because Shostakovich was a nonbeliever, one can only wonder why in his last quartet, No. 15, he chose to write six uninterrupted Adagios. No one had attempted a string quartet like that since Haydn wrote his exquisite masterpiece *The Seven Last Words of Christ on the Cross*. It is an obvious parallel that Shostakovich must have wished to invite. What can we conclude from the desolation Shostakovich lays before us? Is this the Cross without Christ, or Good Friday without the Resurrection? It might fit things neatly to say so, but the deep mourning that pervades the work is not despair. In this, his last utterance, finished only months before his death, the spirit of song and dance, however muted, still slowly moves. I disagree with those, like violinist Alan George, who claim that the 15th Quartet trails off "into nothingness", a nothingness Shostakovich supposedly embraced. Shostakovich was not a nihilist. Nihilists do not make tombstones and place bouquets on graves. Neither do they thirst for justice. Shostakovich said, "The people who were responsible for these evil deeds will have to answer for them, if only before their descendants. If I didn't believe in that completely, life wouldn't be worth living." Yet, despite all the horrors of the time, it was. His music says so.

Recommended Recordings

Lady Macbeth of Mtsensk, Mstislav Rostropovich, Galina Vishnevskaya, EMI/ Warner 7 49955 2

The 15 String Quartets

Borodin Quartet, Melodiya 10 01077. This set, recorded between 1978 and 1983, has gone through numerous incarnations and brief moments of out-of-printness. Currently it is available, with a bit of looking around, from Melodiya again, in its best remastering and packaging yet. With the Borodin players, one never forgets that there is warm blood running through the veins of this music. Their expressive liberties with rhythms and their tremendous range of nuance bring the music closer to speech.

Mandelring Quartett, Audite 21411 (SACDs). The Mandelring Quartett are Shostakovich-seducers, not Shostakovich-enforcers, and they bring out the sheer beauty of all of Shostakovich's brilliantly harrowing ugliness.

Pacifica Quartet, Cedille 127, 130, 138, 145. The Pacifica Quartet cycle invigorates and enlightens the Shostakovich quartets with couplings of contemporary quartets: Nikolay Myaskovsky's 13th on vol. 1, Prokofiev's 2nd on vol. 2, Mieczysław Weinberg's 6th on vol. 3, and Alfred Schnittke's 3rd on vol. 4.

24 Préludes and Fugues

Keith Jarrett, ECM 437189

Alexander Melnikov, Harmonia Mundi 902019

The *24 Préludes and Fugues* is a marvelous work that eases new ears into Shostakovich's often acerbic style. It is a conversation of Shostakovich with Bach, over 200 years—and what a privilege it is to eavesdrop on that exchange.

Other Works

Piano Trio No. 2, op. 67 (plus Piano Trio No. 1, op. 8 & Aaron Copland's *Vitebsk*) Wanderer Trio, Harmonia Mundi 501825. This work is every bit as moving and haunting as the great Piano Quintet and has been receiving an increasing number of splendid recordings.

Seven Romances on Poems of Alexander Blok for piano trio and soprano.

Symphony No. 4, Mariss Jansons, Bavarian RSO, EMI/Warner 57824

Symphony No. 9 (plus Symphony No. 5), Zdeněk Košler, Czech Philharmonic, Chant du Monde. Or: Yakov Kreizberg, Russian NO, Pentatone SACD 5186096.

Symphony No. 15 (plus Boris Tchaikovsky *Theme and Variations for Orchestra*) Kirill Kondrashin, Dresden Staatskapelle, Profil Hänssler 6065

Jean Sibelius: Finnish Majesty

The reputation of Finnish composer Jean Sibelius (1865–1957) waxed and waned over the course of the last century. In the early part, he was thought by many to be the second most powerful symphonist next to Beethoven, and was certainly the most often performed contemporary composer of that time. In his famous book of 1934, *Music Ho!*, English composer Constant Lambert predicted that Sibelius' was the music of the future, leading the way out of an exhausted tradition while avoiding the sterility of Arnold Schoenberg's dodecaphony. In the aftermath of World War II, however, his reputation began to plummet. He was denounced vitriolically by influential critics such as Virgil Thompson and the Marxist 12-tone disciple Theodor Adorno. Sibelius saw his eclipse coming, and said, "For a time, maybe, little notice will be taken of my works, but I believe that I can hope that they will not be completely forgotten. In every true work of art there is a spark that can never entirely be extinguished."

Sibelius was right. There has been a major Sibelius revival, a good deal of it attributable to the late Sir Colin Davis, who leading the London Symphony Orchestra, completed his third recorded traversal of the complete Sibelius symphonies in 2008. Thirty-five years ago, he recorded them for the first time with the Boston Symphony Orchestra for Philips. His second cycle, also with the London forces, is on RCA Victor (BMG). All are magnificent achievements that prove the durability of Sibelius' spark. Thanks to recordings such as these, as well as those by Thomas Beecham, Leonard Bernstein, Sir Alexander Gibson, Paavo Berglund, Vladimir Ashkenazy, Herbert von Karajan, Osmo Vänskä, and others, Sibelius never really completely receded from view. Although his music may have been absent from concert halls, the popularity of Sibelius recordings shows that audiences loved his music no matter how often critics told them not to.

As Davis' recordings attest, there is more than a spark in Sibelius; there is a conflagration of inspiration. His seven symphonies and many tone poems contain some of the most sublime and visionary utterances in all music. His compositions are perhaps best understood in contrast to those of his great contemporary in Denmark, Carl Nielsen.

Sibelius' music is a revelation of nature in all of its solitary majesty and portentousness. Man is the spectator of the awesome drama that is unfolded before him and before which he must tremble, even in his exhilaration. In Nielsen's music, on the other hand, man is very much a participant in the cosmic drama, and the revelation is one of the human spirit in contention against, and at times triumphant over, terrible and malignant forces that seek to extinguish that spirit.

Apart from the Finnish mythological figures of the *Kalevala* with whom Sibelius deals in his tone poems, there are no people in his music. This not so much limits Sibelius' music as defines it. Imagine one of the breathtaking nature portraits from the Hudson River Valley School of painting that depicts a stupendous mountain range. It matters very much if there are tiny human figures in the foreground of the painting. Such figures may provide a sense of scale, but an audience inside the painting also changes the relationship of what is depicted to the audience outside. They are distracted from the main event. With Sibelius, there are no people interposing themselves between what he portrays and the listener. There is nothing there to distract from the solitary grandeur and mystery of nature. Its impact is direct and over-powering.

Because he composed such stirring tonal music with nature as its subject, Sibelius has often, and I believe mistakenly, been labeled a romantic. He is certainly not one in the conventional sense. The late Glenn Gould described Sibelius' music as "passionate but anti-sensuous". Sibelius is uninterested in letting us know how he feels about the mountain. He wants to show the mountain itself. His music is not autobiographical. The sensibility behind, for example, Richard Strauss' *Ein Heldenleben* (A Hero's Life) is completely foreign to him. So is Mahler's self-indulgence. If anything, Sibelius' music was, in part, a reaction against this kind of late-romanticism. Sibelius' attitude toward nature is worth exploring because it may have something to do with the ups and downs of his reputation.

Sibelius said, "There is music in the whole universe." He believed in the "music of the spheres", the classical Greek idea that the mathematical relationships among the heavenly bodies are the same as those of music. The heavens are literally harmonious. He said, "I believe that there are musical notes and harmonies on all planets." This included planet earth. Sibelius' experience of the world was essentially musical. He was one of those extraordinary individuals gifted with perfect pitch. He not only noted the key and the character in which various birds sang, but experienced the most commonplace, everyday sounds in musical terms. Once, when a repair man was hammering away on the veranda, Sibelius observed, "The man is all the time hitting a *g* that is about a quarter-tone out of tune." Sibelius also experienced colors musically, and often whole visual scenes resolved themselves into musical forms for him. As a young boy, he sat at the piano and tried to play the colors he saw in the parlor carpet. His favorite, a clear green, he said, was "somewhere between *d* and *e* flat". When he first heard the sounds of orchestral instruments, they seemed at once familiar to him. Sibelius never wrote in short score. He heard his music orchestrally; each sound came to him instrumentally—as it were, without intermediaries.

Sibelius saw the larger significance of the musical harmony of the world, and it is the key to the meaning and the power of his music. One day, Sibelius spoke to his personal secretary Santeri Levas about the astonishing sense of law in the universe, and an almost inconceivable harmony that makes every human effort seem tiny and senseless. This realization did not induce in him a sense of futility, but of humility. "That", Sibelius concluded, "is what I call God."

Though Sibelius was not religious in a conventional sense, he was a deep believer. "The essence of man's being", he said, "is his striving after God." He saw art as hieratic and composition as a vocation. In words that could hardly go more directly to the heart of the matter, he said, "It [composition] is brought to life by means of the Logos, the divine in art. That is the only thing that really has significance."

Sibelius tried to make the transcendent perceptible in music. In his diary of 1915, he wrote of his struggle in composing the Fifth Symphony. He said that it was as if "God the Father had thrown down pieces of mosaic out of the heaven's floor and asked me to solve how the picture once looked." He later noted, "I begin to see the mountain that I shall surely ascend. God opens His door for a moment and His orchestra plays the Fifth Symphony." When I first listened to Leonard Bernstein's recording of this work with the New York Philharmonic many years ago, that is what I thought I heard. It changed my life. It lifted me so far outside of myself, I would never be the same. I was staggered. I had not known human beings were capable of such things. Sibelius grasped the harmony of the spheres and played it for us. I wept for joy. I still can hardly contain myself when I listen to this performance on the remastered Sony release of the original 1961 recording.

While Sibelius' remark may seem immodest for a composer to make about his own work, it nonetheless makes clear the goal for which he was reaching. He reflected, "I have always found that the Almighty reveals Himself to me most clearly through my musical understanding, in that wonderful artistic logic that I seldom notice as I compose but can recognize afterward—when the composition is finished." The listener also recognizes that a revelation has taken place and is left in awe of that mysterious communication. In the Fifth Symphony, for example, the feeling of an elemental force overtaking and uplifting one is overpowering. As in many parts of the other symphonies, there are moments in the Fifth when the music no longer sounds as if it is being made by instruments. It comes from another world. Sibelius' music reflects nature in such a way that it becomes an invitation to natural theology.

Modernity, of course, has militated against Sibelius' sensibility. In a *Harper's* article, novelist Annie Dillard, clearly upset at the size of the universe, expressed the deflationary modern view: "We arise from dirt and dwindle to dirt, and the might of the universe is arrayed against us." Some years before her, Sibelius' fellow Scandinavian Ingmar Bergman summed up this view of life by saying: "You were born without purpose, you live without meaning. . . . When you die, you are extinguished." There is music of sorts that goes with this world view: the music of much of the 20th century. Of it, Sibelius exclaimed, "It is inconceivable that ethics are entirely missing in what is written now." He called the results "sound effects" devoid of any inner life. One finds in such music that futility does not lead to humility. Rather, awe is replaced with anguish, anger, and the sound of gnarling. Today, this view has pretty much exhausted itself in artistic terms. How much uglier could art become?

As a result, the curse has been lifted from Sibelius. A January 9, 1998, *Washington Post* review of a National Symphony Orchestra concert gave further proof of this contention. Pulitzer Prize–winning critic Tim Page lambasted the Washington premiere of Wolfgang Rihm's *In-Schrift* as "just one more example of disjunct, angst-ridden, 'Death-of-the-Universe' avant-garde aggression", while he found Sibelius, "written off as an anachronism for several misguided decades, . . . astonishingly fresh and full of mystery, even in a work [the Violin Concerto] that is almost 100 years old".

It appears that Constant Lambert's prediction, long ago dismissed as ridiculous, may have some merit to it. Sibelius was so individual a genius that he left no school behind him. But many more composers than initially suspected have been deeply influenced by him. In the United States, their number includes Roy Harris, Walter Piston, Howard Hanson, and more recently John Adams and Stephen Albert. In Scandinavia and the Baltic region, Kurt Atterberg, Dag Wiren, Uuno Klami, Aulis Sallinen, Einojuhani Rautavaara, and Pēteris Vasks, to name a few, all learned valuable lessons from Sibelius. The great English symphonist Edmund Rubbra would be inconceivable without him.

Sibelius underwent a prolonged compositional silence toward the end of his life (30 years), about which there has been much speculation, and was known for his hefty use of alcohol. Regarding the former, he remarked: "Let no one imagine that composing is easier for an old composer if he takes his art seriously." He is reputed to have destroyed an eighth symphony on which he had long labored. In terms of the latter, why did Sibelius sometimes drink so heavily? I am not trying to excuse it, but understand it. Genius at his level brings one into a close encounter of the divine kind. One does not emerge unscathed or unscorched from this contact. To carry this mark is not only a gift; it is a burden. Having received a premonition of the far country, how can one bear not being there? Alcohol is one inadequate answer—a way of losing oneself. In his art, Sibelius was so successful in taking us with him that I almost cannot listen to, say, the Fifth Symphony without pouring a stiff drink to help with the altitude sickness afterward. How much I want this music to be true! In fact, I know it *is* true—but not here, not yet. If you have never wept for joy at, or been shaken to the roots of your being by, music, here is the music to do it. Should I ever have the privilege of hearing God's orchestra play, I am not sure what I will hear. But if it is Sibelius' Fifth Symphony, I will know where I am.

Recommended Recordings

Fifth Symphony

I've listened to many recordings of the Fifth Symphony (though nowhere near the some 100 that are currently available) and attended a number of live performances. I still hold to the view that the 1961 Leonard Bernstein recording is the greatest.

Symphonies 1 & 5 / *Romance for Strings* (Eugene Ormandy and Leonard Bernstein), Sony Essential Classics (available from ArkivMusic)

Symphonies 5 & 7 (Bernstein), DG 477 9785 and 474 9362

Symphonies 5 & 7; *En Saga* (Davis), Pentatone 5186 177

Symphonies 5 & 6; *The Swan of Tuonela* (Berglund), London PO 0065

Complete Symphonies

Symphonies No. 1–7; Tone Poems; Violin Concerto, Colin Davis, Boston SO, Decca 478 3696 (5 CDs)

Symphonies 1–7, *Kullervo*, Colin Davis, London SO, LSO Live 00191 (4 CDs)

Tone Poems

Naxos has a Sibelius treat from the New Zealand SO under Pietari Inkinen. They offer stirring, crystal-clear performances of a variety of tone poems, including *Night Ride and Sunrise, Kuolema, Pan and Echo*, and Suite from *Belshazzar's Feast* in superb sound (8.570763). For a complete set of the tone poems, one cannot do better than the Chandos two-CD set (241-19) with the Scottish NO under Sir Alexander Gibson.

~

Robert Simpson: A Modern Classic

There is no 20th-century composer I am more predisposed to like than Robert Simpson (1921–1997). I have been in such sympathy with his endeavors that I was actually a member of the Robert Simpson Society, a group in Great Britain that promotes his music. Since the 1980s, Hyperion Records has brought out a steady succession of CD releases containing the main body of Simpson's work, which includes 15 string quartets and 11 symphonies. However, I remain daunted by the titanic challenge of Simpson's music. I have not fully fathomed it. This man's music is so demanding that, beyond the few works that I already have found to be indispensable, it will take some considerable time more for me to assimilate it. Consider this, then, a provisional appreciation.

What predisposed me to Simpson was his music criticism. He was one of the most lucid, insightful music writers of his time. In fact, I did not know that he was a significant composer until after I had read his brilliant books on Anton Bruckner and Carl Nielsen, as well as the two-volume Pelican anthology on the symphony that he edited. Simpson was a person of enormous generosity. He spent his professional career at the BBC promoting the music of others. He discovered the works of Havergal Brian, and it was through Simpson's efforts that all of Brian's 32 symphonies were performed and broadcast by the BBC. Simpson's interest led to Brian's Indian summer, during which he wrote so many of his symphonies in his later years. Simpson was the champion of others who continued in the tonal, classical tradition —Vagn Holmboe, Edmund Rubbra, and the great Scandinavians, Jean Sibelius and Carl Nielsen.

I was overjoyed to hear such an eloquent voice in defense of tonality against Schoenberg and his serial, or 12-tone, system. It is worth quoting at length part of Simpson's introduction to the second volume of *The Symphony*:

> The human sense of tonality has many times been modified, but cannot be abolished. To attempt to abolish it is to cease to be comprehensive, to be narrowly exclusive. If I appreciate the kind of expression Schoenberg achieved (I happen to dislike it) my sense of tonality, though it may be deliberately anaesthetized for the time being, is by

no means abolished. . . . I cannot feel that such music is comprehensive. It is certainly concentrated, but that alone will not make it "symphonic"; if you lose a leg, you have to concentrate in order to move about without it, but however hard you concentrate, you cannot escape the conclusion that it is better to have two legs. . . . With one leg you can hop about, but will find it difficult to invent new dance steps that have more than the temporary appeal of oddity.

Referring to Schoenberg's acolytes, Simpson coined the marvelous phrase, the "coterie of 12-notery".

Ironically, it was Schoenberg's music that set Simpson on his path as one of the premiere tonal symphonists of the 20th century. In fact, Simpson first began composing atonal symphonies according to Schoenberg's system and then destroyed them. He wrote, "It so happens the idea for new treatment of tonality came to me from listening, not to Nielsen or any other composer I love, but to Schoenberg's Piano Concerto. It struck me that in spite of the serial technique the work was fixed to a tonal center, which loomed behind the murk. . . . I didn't want, as Schoenberg did, to deny tonality—I wanted to find a way to make tonal centers react against each other, not make non-tonality react against tonality. . . . So atonality was not for me."

What Simpson defined as his goal was nothing less than music as it was understood to function in the classical period, as opposing tonalities were used by Beethoven and others to propel music forward and unleash torrents of power. Haydn and Beethoven were Simpson's musical idols. Simpson set about exploring the implications of Beethoven's music insofar as tonal architecture, of which Beethoven was the supreme exponent, could be used to generate energy. How could he take Beethoven's discovery further or, to put it another way, how much further could Beethoven's discovery be taken?

Simpson set about to answer these questions in his First Symphony. However, he came in for a rude shock through his first encounter with Carl Nielsen's music, which stunned him into a prolonged silence. Someone had been there before him. In my chapter on Nielsen, I argue that he was Beethoven's true symphonic heir in the first half of the 20th century because, like Beethoven's, his symphonies move forward through a series of conflicts based on the clash, and ultimate resolution, of opposing tonalities. Nielsen used the counterpoint he mastered as an engine for generating these conflicts. As Simpson recovered from his shock, he embraced Nielsen for "the kind of intellectual and spiritual support I needed to help me go my own way". In the First Symphony, that support can be heard almost at the point during its composition when Simpson discovered Nielsen. So profound was Nielsen's impact upon Simpson that one can say that Simpson's exploration of the implications of Beethoven's music was now redefined as being undertaken through the prism of Nielsen's work.

This is one of the things that makes Simpson so fascinating. Though he studied with Herbert Howells, I cannot detect any British influences in his work, except perhaps some musical reminiscences in Simpson's Ninth Symphony of Gustav Holst's "Mars" movement from *The Planets*. Untouched by contemporary musical influences (except Nielsen's), Simpson went directly back to the source for his inspiration. When asked to write commentaries on Beethoven's Razumovsky quartets, Simpson refused and, instead, composed his fascinating Quartets 4–6 as direct commentaries upon them. In this he reminds me of Shostakovich, whose quartets ignored the works of Bartók, Hindemith and Schoenberg, and went straight back to Haydn and Beethoven. In fact, Simpson's Ninth Quartet is an hour-long set of variations on the minuet from Haydn's Symphony No. 47.

Simpson presents us with an extraordinary amalgamation of Beethoven and Nielsen with an almost exclusive concern over the generation of energy through tonal clashes. The Scherzo movement of his Symphony No. 4 is a particularly delicious example of the crosscurrents in his music. Here he combines paraphrases from Beethoven's Ninth, with quotes from Haydn's Symphony No. 76, and melodic surges right out of Nielsen. It is a heady mixture that he pulls off with exhilarating aplomb. In his other symphonies, Simpson does not use exact quotes, but the assimilated influences are still there.

Simpson argued for "thematic and tonal organization" and insisted that "every Symphony should fulfill one of the conditions we demand before praising any new work—that it makes quite clear the rules of its own game." He certainly met his own criteria. The symphonic works are tightly argued, wound like giant steel springs coiled to the breaking point. A process of compression and release is almost always underway. Through repetition, variation, scalar ascents, and accelerating rhythm, Simpson increases the tension over a vast expanse of time until it is discharged in a violent paroxysm of terrifying physical impact. Things then recede in scalar descents and decelerating rhythm. When it works, there is something awesome and breathtaking, if not exhausting, about the journey in both its ascent and descent.

However, there is also something incessant and unrelenting about some of these works. As imposing as the symphonies are, they are sometimes forbidding. Simpson's exertion of "maximum human power" and his effort "to express human force by means of positive musical development" can take his music to extremes that make me wonder about his expressive intentions. Of his Tenth Symphony, Simpson said, "This might be thought of as a 'Sinfonia espansiva,' though not in the same sense as Nielsen's famous work, where the title comes from a particular feeling about human awareness. Here the words could be applied simply to the musical process itself, concerned with a special kind of expansion." Yes, but what is the meaning of this kind of expansion when taken to the lengths that he does? Is it for its own sake or does it have a reference beyond itself in human terms? Many of the CD jacket covers for the symphonies are adorned with striking photos of nebulae and star fields from various galaxies. Through their vast scale and seeming indifference to things human, some of Simpson's symphonies seem as far away as the nebulae, and as cold, though the cosmic drama they capture can be utterly thrilling. Of his Fifth Symphony, Simpson said it deals "with that part of our mind which coldly observes itself no matter what disturbances, mental or physical, occur".

Think of it this way. Imagine Beethoven on the scale of Bruckner, with the predominant tonality emerging, à la Nielsen, only over the space of nearly an hour. Let us also say that there are no long-lined melodies to guide you through this process. As Simpson says of the first part of his Tenth Symphony, the ideas are "short and terse" and "long lines are purposely avoided in view of what is going to happen afterwards." Yes, but how long afterward? To say that a supreme effort of concentration is required by long stretches in these works is an understatement. What they are sometimes missing in all their contrapuntal brilliance is fluidity of line, or melodic flow, principally because of the deliberate subordination of melody to the harmonic tension and tonal conflict upon which he builds his huge structures. Just when you think a piece is about to break into broad melody, it keeps relentlessly hammering away.

Grove's Dictionary of Music and Musicians concludes its article on Simpson by wondering "how many listeners may be able to follow the course of an extended work, appreciating long-term conflicts and key relationships in the ways which Simpson expects." Will I be one of them, beyond the works that have already captured me? Time, and a great deal of concentration, will tell. I already know the effort will be well worth it.

Meanwhile, you will be the poorer if you do not read Simpson and also hear him thinking cosmic thoughts in his music, especially his first four symphonies and almost all the string quartets. I do not mean to imply that his music is overly intellectualized; it is also visceral in its impact, and some of it is easily approachable. His challenge is worth taking up. The first works in both genres are particularly striking and so accomplished that it is hard to believe they could be a beginner's efforts. Start with them to hear what Beethoven might have said had he heard Nielsen and lived in a 20th century without atonality.

Or perhaps you should begin at the end. The Hyperion label brought to a close its magnificent traversal of the 11 symphonies with its issue of Symphony No. 11, coupled with the *Variations on a Theme by Nielsen*. As I indicated, the symphonies can sometimes be intimidating in their vast reach and intergalactic distance from human concerns. Not so the 11th. In it, the stars seem somehow nearer and observed with a kind of spiritual calmness. In contrast to his tightly wound, hugely eruptive earlier symphonies, this work is almost ruminative. I recommend it as one of his more approachable pieces. Of course, Nielsen's influence permeates Simpson's work, so it is especially fascinating to hear what he does with one of Nielsen's themes in a set of variations that display everything from humor, not a frequent element in Simpson's work, drama, and his characteristic skill at contrapuntal writing and projecting orchestral power. It is an excellent introduction to Simpson. The City of London Sinfonia and conductor Matthew Taylor live up to the high standards of the Hyperion Simpson project set by Vernon Handley, the Royal Liverpool Philharmonic Orchestra, the Bournemouth Symphony Orchestra, and the Royal Philharmonic Orchestra in the other symphonies.

Recommended Recordings

String Quartets 1 & 4, Delme String Quartet, Hyperion 66419

Symphonies 1 & 8, Royal Philharmonic, Hyperion 66890

String Quartets 3 & 6, Delme Quartet, Hyperion 66376

Symphonies 2 & 4, Bournemouth SO, Hyperion 66505

Symphonies 3 & 5, Royal Philharmonic, Hyperion 66728

Complete Symphonies 1–11, Hyperion 44191/7

Sergei Taneyev: Forgotten for Looking Westward

This chapter comes close to cheating, as this composer barely breaks into the 20th century, in which he only spent his last 15 years, and there is nothing even faintly modern about him or his music. But without it, you might miss him, and that would be a culture crime—because Sergei Taneyev (1856–1915) wrote some of the finest chamber music I have ever encountered by a composer of whom you have probably never heard. Until I began dabbling in and then fanatically pursuing the works of this Russian composer, I had not heard of him either. If you love the great chamber works of Schubert, Mendelssohn, Dvořák, and Brahms, I challenge you to listen to this music and not be as entranced by it as I have been.

What explains Taneyev's obscurity? His musical conservatism, for one. While his contemporaries Rimsky-Korsakov, Borodin, and Balakirev were looking to the East to form a Russian nationalist school (known as the Five), Taneyev looked to the West. Taneyev's chamber music is more Viennese than Russian, and to the extent it is Slavic, it is closer to Dvořák, whose own antecedents are in Schubert. In fact, a good deal of Taneyev's chamber music inhabits the same elegiac, emotional world as Schubert's. In addition to Schubertian poignancy, it possesses Dvořákian melodic drive and passion, Mendelssohnian charm and fleetness, and a kind of Elgarian nobility. Surely one reason that Taneyev is so neglected is that anyone on the trail of the Viennese lineage would not have sought its continuation in the Russia of this period.

Apart from the disadvantage of not having pursued what is distinctly Russian, Taneyev was secretive about his own works, revealing them only to a favored few beyond his teacher and friend, Piotr Tchaikovsky. Some critics claim Taneyev's renowned self-criticism was based on a kind of pathological self-doubt. That this enormously gifted man could have been so afflicted is one of the great psychological mysteries of the music world (though, considering Bruckner's behavior, one not without precedent). In any case, Taneyev did little to advance his own music, publishing only 36 of his many works and leaving a number uncompleted. Some of them have been unearthed from the archives by the Olympia, MDG, Northern Flowers, and Chandos labels.

It is ironic that Taneyev is little known in the West to which he turned for his inspiration. In Russia, he has a reputation as a major renaissance figure, even though he eschewed the Russian nationalist school. He was a star pupil of the Moscow Conservatory, winning for the first time its gold medal in performance and composition. He was a star performer, playing the solo parts in the premieres of all Tchaikovsky's works for piano and orchestra. He was a star academician, becoming Tchaikovsky's successor as head of the Moscow Conservatory and the author of works that are still considered references today. He was a star teacher. His list of pupils reads like a history of Russian music of the first half of the 20th century: Rachmaninoff, Scriabin, Medtner, Miaskovsky, Glière, and Grechaninov. He was also a mentor of Prokofiev and others. And this covers only his accomplishments in music; he also excelled in philosophy and chess.

Taneyev's academic achievements led Tchaikovsky to say that "he is the best counterpoint master of Russia and I am not even sure that there is his equal in the West." Others thought Taneyev's depth of learning made him more an abstract theoretician than a composer. His working methods added to that impression. As Rimsky Korsakov reported in his autobiography, *My Musical Life*, "Before setting out for the real expounding of a composition, [Taneyev would] precede it with a multitude of sketches and studies: he used to write fugues, canons and various contrapuntal interlacings on the individual themes, phrases and notions of the coming composition, and only after gaining thorough experience in its component parts, did he take up the general plan of the composition." If the process is labored, so must be the results, one might think. What sort of music would one expect of a man who wrote a massive work on *Invertible Counterpoint in the Strict Style*?

In an age of musical exoticism, the cultivation of counterpoint struck Taneyev's contemporaries as fastidious and archaic. As if in rebuttal, Taneyev wrote to Tchaikovsky that despite Mozart's use of double, triple, and reverse counterpoints, "Mozart is one of the most comprehensible and accessible composers and his counterpoint learning often merely helps him be clear. Learning is good only when it leads to naturalness and simplicity." In fact, Taneyev said, "I am attracted by Mozart's elegant and rounded forms, by a freedom and expediency of Bach's part-singing and I am seeking to probe, as far as I can, the secrets of their creativity." Other founts of inspiration were Palestrina, Haydn, and Beethoven. As if to prove how out of step with his times he was, Taneyev concluded in the mid-1890s that "there is nothing more beautiful than Mozart. The consummation of beauty."

Taneyev was, in other words, a classicist in a romantic age. His one opera was the only one in the Russia of its period to be based on a classical source, *The Oresteia*. Though Taneyev did write four symphonies (only one published in his lifetime), the powerful contrapuntal element in his work found its fullest flowering, not surprisingly, in chamber music. In these works, Taneyev's handling of multiple musical lines is more than assured; it is inspired. No matter how laboriously he may have worked over the complex counterpoint in advance, it at no time sounds academic or even premeditated in performance. Though this music is worked out in countless felicitous details, it never strikes one as studied. At the same time, Taneyev's extraordinary sense of structure and grasp of tonal architecture are such that one can return to his music, as one can to Beethoven's, without ever losing the initial sense of satisfaction. In fact, it only grows with repeated hearings.

My first encounter with Taneyev's music was on an old Olympia disc containing his String Quintet, op. 14. The piece is staggeringly good, belonging in the company of the greatest quintets written by his idols. I was dumbfounded that a work of this quality was no longer available. It is a big-boned piece; its third movement alone lasts more than 20 minutes and easily sustains its length.

Next, on another Olympia CD (OOP), I discovered Quartets 8 and 9, which are really unnumbered works from the early 1880s. It turns out that Taneyev wrote nine quartets but saw fit to publish only six of them, leaving these impassioned, brilliant pieces to be forgotten.

Another Olympia CD release features the Krasni Quartet in superb performances of Quartets 1 and 2. My allusions to Schubert are more than borne out by the plaintive nature of these very moving, profound works. This CD seems to be no longer available, but fortunately the Northern Flowers label has issued the complete quartets on five CDs, with the eponymous Taneyev Quartet, which earns its name with these impassioned performances from the late 1970s. It is also great good news that the budget Naxos label has almost completed a new traversal of the quartets with the Carpe Diem String Quartet. It lacks only Nos. 8 and 9. Carpe Diem seems to favor broad tempos, but plays with warmth and affection.

The MDG label has issued a CD with very fine performances of all three String Trios, by the Belcanto Strings. After its premiere performance, the Trio from 1880 remained in a drawer until its publication in 1956, the centenary of Taneyev's birth. More than any others, these three works bear out Taneyev's abiding love of Mozart. They are exquisite. Northern Flowers also offers the Trios, but paired with the Trio for piano, violin and cello, op. 22 on a two-CD set, featuring members of the Taneyev Quartet. Three of the trios are for strings, and one for piano, violin, and cello. The members of the Taneyev Quartet had this music in their blood, and the sound from the late 1960s and late 1980s is perfectly fine. There is only one quibble: it is not complete. The issue omits the unfinished Trio from 1913, Taneyev's last work, which one must go to the MDG Belcanto Strings recording to hear.

My exploration then led me to Taneyev's chamber music with piano, which is as big-boned as his other chamber works, but looser-limbed and less tightly wound within classical forms. His own instrument seems to have inspired Taneyev to more romantic imaginative flights, as can be heard in the Piano Trio, played by the Borodin Trio on Chandos, or the Piano Quintet on Arabesque, with pianist Jerome Lowenthal and other artists. A Centaur CD makes the Piano Quartet, op. 20, available with the Piano Trio. Unfortunately, the best efforts of the Mendelssohn Piano Trio are somewhat hedged in by the boomy acoustic in which this recording was made. I especially love the second movement of the Quartet. It sounds as if someone pinched its main theme for the 1960s popular hit *Blue Moon*.

Northern Flowers has released a two-CD set of the Complete Quintets, two of the three of which are for strings and the other for piano quintet. A supplemented Taneyev Quartet recorded the string quintets in 1980–1981 and the Piano Quintet, with pianist Tamara Fidler, in 1968. The Soviet-era quality of the recordings is perfectly fine. The important thing is that it captures great music-making. The supplemented Taneyev Quartet digs in with verve, grit, and abundant heart.

I aver that the Piano Quintet in G Minor is one of the great piano quintets, as great, I would hazard to say, as Schubert's. Taneyev, a supremely gifted contrapuntist, also wrote with a vigor and passion that are staggering. Because of his learned counterpoint and meticulous craftsmanship, Taneyev got the reputation of being a dry-as-dust academic. This passionate music shows that nothing could be further from the truth. This music seems so much the product of white-hot inspiration that you will find it hard to believe that Taneyev labored as he did in an almost excruciatingly way when he composed. The Russian forces take almost 50 minutes in this work, by far the longest of the three available recorded performances, but it is completely gripping with the sweep, commitment, and tremendous character of their playing. It is close to my favorite version.

However, there is another take on the Piano Quintet, op. 30 (paired with the Piano Trio, op. 22) worth considering. It is played with hair-raising virtuosity by a group of all-stars, led by pianist Mikhail Pletnev. Pletnev et al. may seem a bit emotionally indulgent, but if they are lost in the moment, what moments to be lost in! If they were not digging in so deeply, one might be tempted to call this style of playing self-conscious. But one cannot. There is no affectation here, only affection.

I compared the performance of the Trio to another release of the same work on Dutton Digital, played by the Barbican Piano Trio. In the Allegro, Pletnev's group takes extra time, but they melt the music with their warmth and emotion. I have known this music for several years. I cannot get it out of my mind. These large-scale works (44 minutes for the Quintet and 38 for the Trio) are the music of a great-souled man. If you have a musical bone in your body, you will move to, and be moved by, this music. By all means you must hear Piano Quintet, either on Northern Flowers or Deutsche Grammophon.

Taneyev seemed less sure of himself in his symphonic works, and they did not achieve a status similar to his chamber music, which is probably why he wrote only four symphonies, two of which were left uncompleted (only one published in his lifetime). Still, it is more than worth a listen. Chandos has given us the first pairing of modern recordings of Taneyev's Symphonies 2 and 4, played by the Russian State Symphony Orchestra under Valeri Polyansky. This is majestic music that will leave you wondering why Taneyev never bothered to finish orchestrating the Second and why the Fourth was the only one of his four symphonies to be performed in his lifetime.

Take the stunning first movement of the Second Symphony. It begins with a quiet, gorgeous, long-lined theme that seems as if it is coming out of a dark dream, the beauty of which Polyansky is very adept at displaying. It slowly builds and then segues to a second theme of high energy that sounds as if Beethoven had rewritten Handel's Hallelujah theme. At its climax, it then transforms itself into what could pass, quite improbably, as a passage from one of Elgar's ripest works. There are also grace notes to Tchaikovsky, Wagner, and Mendelssohn in this fascinating piece. Taneyev pulls all this off in a totally integrated fashion. The movement is a brilliant tour de force.

Polyansky captures the sheer beauty and most of the drama, but I must confess that the old Russian disc (no longer available) featuring a performance by the U.S.S.R. Radio Symphony Orchestra, with Vladimir Fedoseyev, aces this one in expressing the last ounce of dramatic tension. Polyansky need bow to no one in his portrayal of the bold Fourth, which begins with a highly arresting three-note staccato theme. Throughout these two symphonies, Taneyev displays his breathtaking contrapuntal mastery.

Naxos allows us to glimpse these works at bargain price with its issue of Symphonies 2 and 4, with Thomas Sanderling and the Novosibirsk Academic Symphony Orchestra. Sanderling broadens the tempos out a bit—he takes seven minutes longer in these two works than Fedoseyev —but the beautiful playing and warmth of his orchestra reveal much. (There are also recordings of Symphonies 1 and 3, but here I think that Taneyev's self-critical stance is justifiably borne out in his decision not to publish them.)

Thomas Sanderling and the Novosibirsk Academic Symphony Orchestra return for rousing performances of Taneyev's *Oresteia* Overture, op. 6. I have always wanted to hear his monumental opera, *Oresteia*, but alas there is no complete recording available. For now, I will settle for the 20-minute *Overture* and music from part 3: the entr'acte before "The Temple of Apollo at Delphi". The very dramatic Overture begins with double basses digging in as deeply as the deepest Russian basses you have ever heard. This is a thrilling, fantastic piece that easily explains Tchaikovsky's high praise of Taneyev's music and increases my eagerness to hear the whole opera. The Novosibirsk Academic Symphony Orchestra plays this music to the hilt. No aficionado of Russian music should miss this.

Toccata Classics released a CD of Taneyev's Piano Concerto (TOCC 0042). The two movements of the concerto, all that Taneyev completed, are the work of a 19-year-old who was discouraged by criticism from Anton Rubinstein and Rimsky-Korsakov. It is nonetheless worth hearing for its display of influences and its signs of early promise. If you are hooked on Taneyev, as I am, you will want to hear this concerto, along with the music for solo piano that accompanies it, ably put forth by pianist Joseph Banowetz and the Russian Philharmonic, under Thomas Sanderling.

Another Naxos release will leave you with no doubt about Taneyev's ability to write beautiful choral music: *John of Damascus*, op. 1, which draws on Russia's sacred music tradition. It is accompanied by the *Suite de Concert* for violin and orchestra, a very engaging and entertaining work. Thomas Sanderling does another superb job, this time with the Russian Philharmonic Orchestra, the Gnesin Academy Chorus, and the very fine soloist, violinist Ilya Kaler.

At the Reading of a Psalm, issued by Pentatone, with the Russian National Orchestra, St. Petersburg State Academic Capella Choir, and the Boys of the Glinka Choral College, under Mikhail Pletnev, is another grand work, comparable to the finest choral writing of Tchaikovsky. Superbly constructed, it shows why Tchaikovsky said that Taneyev's extraordinary grasp of counterpoint was the greatest in Europe. Listen, for example, to the magnificent eight-minute triple fugue that brings the first movement to a close.

If this composer looked westward for his musical orientation, we must listen eastward to hear these extraordinary works.

Recommended Recordings

Complete String Quartets, Northern Flowers

Complete Quintets, Northern Flowers 9944/9945

Complete String Trios, MDG 634 1003-2

Complete Trios, Northern Flowers 9958/59

Piano Quintet; Piano Trio, DG 477 5419

Symphonies 2 & 4, Chandos 9998; Naxos 8.572067

Oresteia Overture and Interlude, Naxos 8.570584

John of Damascus Cantata; *Suite de Concert* for violin and orchestra, Naxos 8.570527

At the Reading of a Psalm, Pentatone 5186 038

∼

Alexander Tcherepnin: From Russia with Love

Growing up in pre-revolutionary Russia, Alexander Tcherepnin (pronounced "cher-up-neen") imbibed music from his composer father, Nicolai, and his mother, an accomplished pianist and singer. "There was plenty of music paper around our home", he recalled in his autobiography. "I observed how my father was writing his scores and tried to do the same while alone." In fact, Nicolai Tcherepnin was quite gifted both as a composer and a conductor. Sergey Diaghilev's *Ballets Russes* started with one of his scores. Nicolai Tcherepnin also taught such distinguished students as Sergei Prokofiev. Regular visitors to the Tcherepnin home included Nikolai Rimsky-Korsakov, Alexandr Konstantinovich Glazunov, and Igor Stravinsky. "So it happened," Tcherepnin wrote, "that I learned how to write music and how to notate my musical ideas before I learned how to write, even before I learned the alphabet."

The end result was that, by his death in 1977, Tcherepnin had produced four symphonies, six piano concertos, 13 ballets, four operas, numerous other orchestral and chamber pieces, and more than 200 piano works. He also produced two sons, Serge and Ivan, who also became composers. If it sounds as if music ran in the blood of the Tcherepnin family, that is exactly how Alexander spoke of it during his life: "Music never stops working in me. It is as if musical sounds are part of my blood circulation. In fact, I cannot separate myself from music. I love it above all, just as I love human beings."

Thanks largely to the Olympia and BIS labels, Tcherepnin's symphonies, piano concertos, and many piano pieces are now available, along with other works, in brilliant performances that show just how vital the surge of music was in his bloodstream. It is not surprising for a composer to whom music was so much a part of life that his compositions are both accessible and exciting. Also, Tcherepnin never seems to have stopped assimilating the musical influences surrounding him. As his surroundings changed dramatically due to the Russian Revolution, World War II, and other vagaries of life, those influences varied considerably, giving his music a highly eclectic sound.

After being grounded in the Russian classics in St. Petersburg,

Tcherepnin was first displaced to Tiflis, Georgia, where his father took over the musical conservatory until the Russian Revolution forced them to flee to Paris. In Georgia, Tcherepnin absorbed the unusual scales used in the folk music of the Caucasus and formalized them into his own nine-tone scale (three tetrachords). In Paris, he became French to the extent that his orchestration became a miracle of transparency and deftness of touch. Paris in the 1920s was the avant-garde musical Mecca, and Tcherepnin joined in the wild experiments of the time, producing in his First Symphony a movement (Vivace) for unpitched percussion alone, which almost caused a riot.

At age 35, Tcherepnin arrived in China on a concert tour. Entranced, he remained for four years and took up teaching and what he called his "folk cure" from his technical experiments. He adopted the Chinese pentatonic scale, which resulted in some lovely musical chinoiserie in his works from this period onward.

The Sino-Japanese War drove Tcherepnin to the United States for a year before he returned to Paris, where he remained for the rest of World War II. In 1949, he moved to Chicago, where he lived for most of his remaining life, teaching at DePaul University. He became an American citizen in 1958. Although Aaron Copland dubbed Tcherepnin "an honorary American composer", there is no discernible American influence in his work. When listening to his music on several occasions, however, I have had the odd thought that Bernard Herrmann might have written something like this, or that George Gershwin, another Russian, already had.

Despite this highly variegated musical itinerary, Tcherepnin remained a Russian composer. His music continued to show the influence of both Stravinsky and, to a lesser degree, Prokofiev. I am also tempted to say that he was influenced by Shostakovich, because that is what I hear in the Second Piano Concerto. But Shostakovich was only 16 when Tcherepnin wrote this work in England. Was Shostakovich, then, influenced by Tcherepnin? Also, strangely enough, in the Third Symphony, I found a stretch of music that sounded uncannily similar to one of the works of Carl Nielsen's student Poul Schierbeck. Schierbeck was actually in Paris the year before Tcherepnin arrived in 1921. Could he have left a musical scent? We do know that Tcherepnin encountered Bohuslav Martinů in Paris as a fellow member of the École de Paris, a group of foreign composers living in France. The influence of Martinů's music is palpable.

If you can imagine a mélange of the above ingredients served up with panache, verve, and high-wire energy, then you will be prepared for the delights Tcherepnin has to offer. His music is strange without being entirely original. Each of its components can be identified as having come from a specific composer or place, but no one else put them together in quite this way. Tcherepnin rationalized his eclecticism by calling himself a "Eurasian composer". His music is exciting and exhilarating, even sometimes impishly humorous, if not finally profound. One critic has called his music "diamond sharp but with heart".

The place to begin exploring Tcherepnin's works is his six piano concertos. Tcherepnin was a virtuoso pianist and enjoyed a stellar career in 36 countries. Many of his concerts consisted only of his own works. This immediately raises the suspicion of vanity productions. I have little patience with compositions that are more about the instrument for which they were written (or the prowess with which they can be played) than they are about music itself. On the evidence of these piano works, however, Tcherepnin did not fall prey to the narcissistic sensationalism of the virtuoso, though much of this music requires virtuoso playing. All of the concertos have substantial musical merit, as well as thrills. They share some of the dynamism of Prokofiev's works in this genre without their mechanical ferocity.

Written "with the exaggeration of youth", according to Tcherepnin, the First Concerto is a romantic workout resembling those of Rimsky-Korsakov or even Rachmaninoff, without the treacle of late-romanticism. The other works share in all of the influences already mentioned, including some exquisitely delicate chinoiserie in the Fourth Concerto, *Fantaisie*. Only the aggressively modernistic Third Concerto takes on an unattractive toughness from what seems to be one of Tcherepnin's experiments in how far he could make dissonance work for him. All of the others are instantly accessible and thoroughly engaging.

The six concertos are available on two different traversals, both of them excellent—one by English pianist Murray McLachlan and the other by Japanese pianist Noriko Ogawa. McLachlan tosses off the bravura passages with ease and plays the softer ones with exquisite delicacy. The only shock comes from the realization that the excellent playing of the sometimes very difficult orchestral music is done by a student orchestra, Chetham's Symphony Orchestra under conductor Julian Clayton. In her energetic and finely articulated performances,

Ogawa is accompanied by the Singapore Symphony Orchestra under Lan Shui. Her recordings are combined on the BIS label with accompanying accounts of Tcherepnin's symphonies, all four of which have been recorded by the Singapore musicians.

The First Symphony is as close as Tcherepnin gets to "bad boy" music. It contains the percussion-only movement and in places seems to be more of an experiment in rhythm than a symphony. The other three works are neoclassical charmers, though that innocent description belies how unusual they are. Symphony No. 3 is especially good despite its indebtedness to Stravinsky's *Petrushka*. These works are orchestrated very colorfully.

Tcherepnin is confident enough in his materials to write sparely, even nakedly, at times. That in itself grabs one's attention. Yet, as he shows in the third movement of Symphony No. 3, he can build a magnificent climax. Throughout these works, Tcherepnin displays a high level of imagination and an ability to surprise, delight, and sometimes mystify. The performance by the Singapore Symphony Orchestra safely puts the few preceding recordings of these works in the shade. The sound is magnificent.

The BIS label has bundled all the symphonies and piano concertos together in a four-CD box at far less cost than buying the individual CDs. On the other hand, the very same set of piano concertos has been reissued at an even lower price on the Brilliant Classics label. A very special CD has been issued by Toccata Classics of Tcherepnin's own performances of his Sonatas 1 and 2 (recorded in 1965), accompanied by other piano works ably performed by Mikhail Shilyaev.

Tcherepnin wrote that "it is the form and not musical language that makes a composition long living. Every musical language becomes outdated sooner or later, but the message expressed by it in adequate form survives." By his own standard, how long will Tcherepnin's scintillating music last? My own guess is that these works are not immortal, but they are immensely enjoyable for the foreseeable future. Try these CDs and judge for yourself.

Recommended Recordings

Complete Symphonies & Piano Concertos, Ogawa, Shui, Singapore SO, BIS

Complete Piano Concertos, Ogawa, Shui, Singapore SO, Brilliant Classics 9232

Piano Concertos 1, 4, & 5, Olympia 440

Piano Concertos 2, 3, & 6, Olympia 439

Symphonies 3 and 4; Piano Concerto No. 6, BIS-1018

Symphonies 1 and 2; Piano Concerto No. 5, BIS-1017

Piano Sonatas 1 & 2; *Four Nostalgic Preludes*; *Moment Musical*, etc., Toccata Classics 0079

Complete Music for Cello and Piano, Chandos 9770

∼

Michael Tippett: A Child of His Time

Twentieth-century music does not get much better than Michael Tippett (1905–1998) in full flower, lending some credence to the claim of his advocates that, in his later years, he was the greatest living British composer. Yet that reputation rested on compositions that came from his first period of work, which featured an extraordinary outpouring of luminous, highly lyrical music of multiple epiphanies. The stream of inspiration from which they came seems to have dried up long before his demise at the age of 93. The works of his mid to late periods were thorny, highly complex, disjunct, and somewhat inscrutable until, at the end, he reverted to his earlier style. Nevertheless, Tippett remains a major figure in Britain's musical renaissance, and many of his works are not to be missed.

When I first encountered Tippett's music several decades ago, I was entranced by its rhythmic vivacity, melodic wealth, and contrapuntal richness. Chords exuberantly leap about trying to find a melody to ride. A profusion of melodic curlicues spin around in their excitement. And pounding propulsive rhythms suddenly break into dance or are suspended for lyrical interludes of flute duets or delicate harp arpeggios. The attraction was immediate, the style of the works inimitable, and the memory they made indelible. I particularly appreciated Tippett in the context of a time that was producing sterile, hermetic music modeled on Arnold Schoenberg's gospel of systematized dissonance. Here was someone writing symphonies, concertos, and fantasias that, while sounding fresh, were deeply rooted in tradition. In short, Tippett was a master of tonal conflict and resolution who reinvigorated the sonata-allegro form. I wanted more. I patiently, anxiously followed Tippett's progress, only to be puzzled by the way in which he seemed to get bogged down in a hermeticism of his own making through which he thought he could confront the most vital issues of the day.

Having learned a great deal more about Tippett since then, I am now amazed that he was able to accomplish what he did. Tippett came to music relatively late. He was raised by his suffragette mother and liberal lawyer father in a household without music. After his first experience of hearing an orchestra perform as a teenager, he announced to his befuddled parents that he was going to be a composer. He studied at the Royal College of Music, but he did not publish anything until he was in his mid-30s. His intellectual pedigree was Trotskyist and, then, pacifist. In 1935, he joined the Communist Party in hopes of converting his brethren to Trotsky's doctrines. He registered as a conscientious objector during World War II and, as a result, spent several months in prison. He was deeply affected by his experience of undergoing Jungian psychoanalysis.

Tippett was rescued from a permanent career as a social agitator by his belated encounter with music, first Beethoven's, then that of the 16th-century English madrigalists, and then Purcell's. This encounter seems to have immunized him from further infatuation with totalitarian ideology, though it did not protect him from the snares of Carl Jung's Manichean world view or endow him with a coherent way of thinking. However, it did embed in him a permanent sense of mission. "Deep within me," he wrote, "I know that part of the artist's job is to renew our sense of the comely and the beautiful." He spoke of his obligation to provide "images of abounding, generous, exuberant beauty". His best music achieves exactly this. Aside from the above-mentioned influences, Igor Stravinsky, particularly in his neoclassic period, had a major impact on Tippett. Among his British contemporaries, the only other one who got as contrapuntally carried away as Tippett was Edmund Rubbra, who also drew upon the same 16th-century heritage.

The first work that brought Tippett to prominence, *A Child of Our Time*, is emblematic of his musical strengths, but also of the weakness of his spiritual perspective that wrought damage further on in his career. The piece, an oratorio, deals with the problem of good and evil. It is based upon a real incident in 1938, when a young Polish Jew, angered at his parents' suffering, assassinated a minor Nazi official in Paris. Nazi retaliation against the Jews in Germany was severe. Hearkening back to Bach and Handel for his foundations, Tippett substituted African American spirituals for the traditional Lutheran chorales. Musically, this works well enough. However, Tippett's attempt to universalize the Jewish plight with the obvious implication that the suffering of black slaves was somehow equivalent was not well received by some Jews, nor was the libretto's morally ambiguous assertion that the young Jewish boy was simply striking at his own darker half in shooting the Nazi diplomat. One must wonder how deeply Tippett saw into the evil of Nazi ideology if he at the same time refused to oppose it by arms.

Also, shooting Nazis turns out to have been an exceptionally good idea, in fact the only one that stopped them from further massacring the innocent.

Key to the Jungian conception of *A Child of Our Time*, and to Tippett's whole world view, is its penultimate text, which is sung by both soloists and chorus: "I would know my shadow and my light, So shall I at last be made whole." Or as Tippett put in his notes, he was concerned with "the possible healing that would come from Man's acceptance of his Shadow in relation to his Light". What might serve as the source of this wholeness? Before closing with another explicitly Christian spiritual, Tippett's text states: "The moving waters renew the earth. It is spring." This vague, pantheistic hope is hardly an adequate answer. What makes the work satisfying is the closing spiritual's invitation to journey to the "promised land" at "Jesus' feet". The only spring that has ever come that could resolve the problem of evil that Tippett raises is that of Christ in his Resurrection. Reconciling the dark with the light is not ultimately a psychological or artistic enterprise; it is a salvific one, undertaken by Christ's "reconciling the world to Himself". This truth has given and still gives inspiration to great artists. Tippett, an agnostic, rejected Christianity as a source, though he poached from it, as in this piece, for his own purposes. He said, "What I *cannot* do is go back into some tradition like Christianity and put something there which prevents that new metaphor being usable at all." That new metaphor was what Tippett thought he could concoct from Jung's psychoanalytical views that would somehow explain things—that is, the opposites of good and evil—at a greater depth than Christianity, Jung's anima and animus, together at last. It did not work, and neither did the confusing mythology he constructed. Some of Tippett's works suffer from the spiritual confusion. While the music he wrote for his opera *The Midsummer Marriage* is magical and gorgeously lyrical, his libretto left the cast in a state of complete confusion over what it was supposed to mean. One critic called it "a chaotic jumble of Western and Eastern mythology and symbolism, part Dr. Who, part *The Magic Flute*, part hippy-dippy, flower-power philosophizing, part Jungian psychology, and part working class transfiguration". In fact, no one has since quite figured it out.

The works from Tippett's golden period include the Concerto for Double String Orchestra, the ravishingly beautiful *Fantasia Concertante on a Theme of Corelli*, the *Fantasia on a Theme of Handel*, the Piano

Concerto, the charming *Suite for the Birthday of Prince Charles*, and the first two of his four symphonies, plus his first several string quartets and, most especially, the radiant *The Midsummer Marriage*, an opera rich in lyricism and magical moments. These are simply not to be missed. Had Tippett done nothing more he would still have earned himself a place in the brilliant constellation of the 20th-century English musical renaissance. After these, however, his works became more astringent and even violent, as in the operas *King Priam* and the *Knot Garden*, the Concerto for Orchestra, and the Third Symphony, which is in an uneasy amalgamation of Beethoven, literally quoted, blues numbers sung by a soprano, and his own highly individual style. In order to show the dislocation in the world, he dislocated his music, while at the same time thinking that his abrasive juxtapositions of unlike things somehow brought them together. This violence burned itself out in the late 1970s, when Tippett seems to have remembered his vocation and announced that he was turning his back "with some pleasure, on the *cruel* world". The result was an Indian summer of some lyrical regeneration that produced the Triple Concerto and the Fourth Symphony, and his last work, *The Rose Lake*, in 1993. Symphony No. 4 does not contain such jarring stylistic juxtapositions; it has internal consistency. Also, along with the compressed power Tippett can generate, it contains strong hints of his old lyricism and ornamental tracery. While harkening back to his earlier lyrical style, these works, except for the last, retained some of the density and toughness from his middle period. I confess to liking them far more now that when I first encountered them.

Tippett was nothing if not ambitious in the issues he tried to deal with, but he did not have the theological framework within which to carry out his vision. Thus, he bogged down in Jungian dualism. Finally, Tippett's works do not adequately deal with the major issues he raised. What is surprising is not so much the disjunct music he wrote, but the abundance of very beautiful music he produced. While Tippett appears to have gotten some fundamental things wrong, he never went completely over the edge. He was always nudged back by his desire for beauty. I would be extremely dismayed if the reservations I have expressed here were to keep anyone from exploring the wealth of wonderful music he composed. I have simply tried to understand why there wasn't more—which is, perhaps, ungrateful of me.

Tippett's music has not suffered from a lack of good recordings, but the original London series of premiere recordings seem to come in and go out of circulation regularly. Any performance conducted by Colin Davis is an automatic recommendation. One can turn to his 1970 recording of *The Midsummer Marriage* at the Royal Opera House for the full glories of this radiant score. The Nimbus label recordings made by the composer himself have been gathered up into a four-CD box, also with contributions by conductors William Boughton and Stephen Darlington. This makes for an excellent bargain introduction, which includes the *Suite in D Major for the Birthday of Prince Charles, Fantasia Concertante on a Theme of Corelli*, and the Concerto for Violin, Viola, and Cello. The Chandos label sponsored its Tippett series with the Bournemouth Symphony Orchestra under conductor Richard Hickox. Luckily, Hickox and his forces give superb interpretations. Also, the clearer Chandos digital recordings reveal a wealth of orchestral detail obscured in the earlier traversal by London. That is an especially important advantage in music as contrapuntally rich as this. There is also a marvelous BBC Symphony Orchestra recording on Teldec, with Andrew Davis, that makes a great introduction to Tippett's best and that includes the irresistible Ritual Dances from *The Midsummer Marriage*.

Recommended Recordings

Various Works, Nimbus 1759 (4 CDs)

Symphony No. 1 & Piano Concerto, Chandos 9333

Symphony No. 2 & *Suite from New Year*, Chandos 9200

A Child of Our Time, Chandos 9123

Piano Concerto; *Praeludium* for brass, bells and percussion; *Fantasia on a Theme of Handel*; *Fantasia Concertante on a Theme of Corelli*, Chandos 9934

The Five String Quartets, ASV 231

Concerto for Double String Orchestra; *Fantasia Concertante on a Theme of Corelli*; Ritual Dances from *The Midsummer Marriage*, Apex 89098

The Midsummer Marriage, Lyrita 2217

∼

George Tsontakis: *Coraggio*

My introduction to George Tsontakis' music came from two of the most profoundly engaging chamber works of the last half century. For a New World Records release of Tsontakis' Quartets 3 and 4, composer George Rochberg, who led American music out of the wilderness of serialism back in the 1970s, wrote the moving liner notes. He quotes Tsontakis saying that his Third Quartet marks a turning away from the world of Tsontakis' Second Quartet, a "severely introverted and intense semitonal (atonal) work". Tsontakis says that the Second "was submerged in the seemingly inescapable malaise of our time", but that the Third, titled *Coraggio* (Courage), "offers a certain exuberance and brightness, an optimism that might be based on our blindness—a momentary lapse into forgetfulness—to what surrounds us, or else perhaps on the tenacious human spirit we have inherited, where even in the worst of times there is a taking of heart and welling up of courage".

In the Third, Tsontakis accepted his "inheritance", meaning the great tradition of music with which modernity broke. Then he went further. I have seldom been as taken by a work as I was when I first heard String Quartet No. 4. In the Fourth, titled *Beneath Thy Tenderness of Heart*, he goes to the core of that tradition and makes the source of courage explicit. As Rochberg wrote, "Tsontakis is not ashamed to be heard praying aloud." The subtitle to this quartet comes from the Russian hymn that opens the work and whose unsung words ask Mary "to deliver us from perils". This music expresses those perils, but also prayer and hard-won deliverance. In his embrace of tonality, Tsontakis has mastered the expressive uses of consonance and dissonance, especially utilizing the later in his powerful portrayal of anguish in the soul. He acknowledges his "reliance on the stability of diatonically triadic harmonies" and his debt "gesturally . . . to the work of the late classical masters". There is no room to give the myriad details of how ingeniously Tsontakis achieves this, but ingenuity is not the point here. This is a great work of spiritual struggle and deep consolation. I have listened to it many times and its richness is inexhaustible. The Fourth Quartet was a prize winner at the Kennedy Center Awards in 1989, which showed that sanity had returned to our prize system. Greatness achieved is now greatness recognized. The American String Quartet gives exhilarating performances of both works, which deserve the accolades of the late music critic Samuel Lipman, who wrote in *New Criterion*, "His quartets give hope that what had seemed impossible is truly possible; beautiful new music can be composed (as it used to be said) from the heart to the heart, even today, and we can begin the urgent process of reclaiming our musical heritage." I think the Fourth is one of the finest and most sublime American works in the genre. Tsontakis' Fifth Quartet is dedicated: "In Memoriam, George Rochberg." How I should like to hear it but, alas, no recording yet.

Yet there is more available. Two releases of his chamber music on Koch contain some half dozen works for piano quartet (Piano Quartet Trilogy) and other chamber combinations (*Heartsounds*). The first CD features *Bagatelles* (Piano Quartet No. 1), an exquisitely touching work, especially in its Solemn movement, which is clearly from the same world as the Third and Fourth Quartets. This piece is immersed in the language of late-classical/early-romantic periods, albeit with some modern harmonies. In fact, Tsontakis says that "these 'Bagatelles' works are about as tonally 'stylized' as I've ever gotten, and even while writing them I felt they were a bit over the top in that way." I don't really care how strongly stylized a piece is in terms of its historical references if it is musically persuasive and coherent. This work is. Tsontakis gets a strong spine in his music from Beethoven and one is evident here. He writes that "snippets and wispy references from Beethoven's late piano 'Bagatelles' inform the tonality and texture of the work, partially in the first and second movements, the latter of which reflects the darker, somber atmospheres of personal loss, but in the cascading finale arises a dance-like perpetual motion."

The Second Piano Quartet begins with what Tsontakis calls "an abstracted jazz progression of sorts". I do not find the stylistic admixture in it as convincing. The second movement tries to return to the world of the *Bagatelles* and is, in parts, very affecting, with real poignancy in its "almost nursery rhyme–like falling figure", but the jazz progression keeps interjecting itself. Why? I take a guess below concerning this feature of Tsontakis' music.

Eclipse, a quartet for clarinet, violin, cello and piano, is another highly imaginative piece, inspired by a lunar eclipse. It has an irresistible, wild, dancing energy in the "Hyperactive" movement. Its other three movements are marked: "Haunting"; "Serene, yet disturbing"; and

"Scherzo: Maniacal". It sounds here as if jazz is melded with Greek folk music or perhaps music from Crete, the locale of Tsontakis' ethnic origins. He does not say so, but I would not be surprised.

Closing the CD is *Bagatelle* for piano, an immediately attractive attempt at what Tsontakis calls "an aquatic liquidity" in the direction of Debussy. He succeeds with this short piano piece.

The second Koch CD contains *Heartsounds*, a searing piece about "romance, disillusionment and hope". It uses the same instrumental configuration as Schubert's *Trout* Quintet (violin, viola, cello, piano, and bass) and is almost as nakedly emotional as Schubert. I especially like the way Tsontakis sets his themes in the different contexts of classical and romantic musical idioms, and lets those idioms reveal what they can about the themes in their particularly distinctive, sometimes haunting ways. For instance, in *Heartsounds* the music seems about to fall apart over its own grief, with obsessive repetitions and, at times, a hallucinatory wildness, if not desperation. To convey this, Tsontakis uses the language of near hysteria from the world of hyperromanticism. The recovery of balance then employs more classical allusions. In this work, Tsontakis is as successful as was Rochberg in resuscitating and expressively employing the past in a completely convincing, powerfully emotive way. This has to be one of his finest works. It certainly keeps pulling me back to itself.

Meditations at Perigree for piano, clarinet, horn, violin, viola, cello and double bass begins with a long, appropriately meditative piano solo. After the other instruments join in, the music reaches another one of the magical Schubertian moments of sadness at which Tsontakis specializes. Then the music launches into what sounds like a honky-tonk version of "Chicago (That Toddlin' Town)". I am not sure what to make of this. It is not a stylistic juxtaposition that convincingly conveys anything to me.

I did not, in other words, find some of these compositions comparable to the Fourth Quartet in the sense of their being as coherently formed. Though much of this music is strikingly good and passionately inspired, it seems too often punctuated by clangorous eruptions that appear, at least to me, as disruptions. On the other hand, Tsontakis is able to construct compact themes of such startling simplicity and memorable quality that he can vary them, put them through a wringer, bounce them upside down, set them to a jazz riff, and still not lose the listener. Rochberg expressed this aspect of Tsontakis' music by saying, "[Tsontakis] has the 'luck' of having concrete musical ideas that the ear can perceive and the mind hold in memory. These ideas tend to be expressed in concentrated, densely packed, nodule-like motives that the composer treats obsessively, and which, as they spread out in time and spin in figurational, centripetal orbits, create structure and gesture." It is extremely satisfying to be taken so far afield and still know where home base is—even though the journey can be more than a bit rough.

Of his orchestral works, I like most the *Four Symphonic Quartets*, named after T. S. Eliot's poem. The raucousness of this music may not attract the average listener. The multiple layers in it struggle against each other, but Tsontakis has his very strong themes emerge from or against the raucousness in thrilling, even magnificent ways. It is not, however, the music with which a newcomer to Tsontakis should begin.

Tsontakis' two violin concertos may be easier to digest, particularly the first one with its appealing second movement. The Second Violin Concerto won the prestigious Grawemeyer Award in 2003. As in a good deal of Tsontakis' music, I find much that is appealing in this work—and here, again, it is particularly the lovely slow movement, titled "Cantilena (Heart)"—and parts that are puzzling. The influence of Messiaen is particularly evident in the Second. In fact, even the title of the first movement "Surges (Among stars)" is Messiaenesque.

Roll magazine's Peter Aaron describes Tsontakis' music this way: "Over time he developed an endlessly entrancing, accessibly modern approach rooted in the romantic impression of Debussy and the proto-serialism of Messiaen but also incorporating influences from before and after the two 20th-century French composers." The music is certainly highly allusive—sometimes like floating islands of melody on a sea of sounds (sometimes it is hard to make out the melody from the welter of sounds) or dream music that only makes sense in a dream. The sounds ripple, sometimes into waves. It is multilayered with currents and undercurrents. The Messiaen-like piano doodling and twinkly triangle sounds create a shimmering kind of clangor.

All of this music reveals a composer who has been or is on a journey. It expresses some great sadness and some great hope. Tsontakis' music seems to be trying to remember something better than the clangor and pain. It gets angry when it does not succeed in fully recovering this memory and then collapses back into tender melancholy. As it approaches the beautiful, it often pulls back as if it cannot really allow itself to do this—too lovely and from a time long gone, something longed for but unattainable. It expresses ambivalence as if it cannot give itself completely. Is that because the search is not over for the thing to which one can give oneself unreservedly?

The deliberately unsettled character of the music conveys as much—that the search is painful, necessary, through dark woods and difficult paths. There are exquisitely touching moments of intimate intensity, a kind of Schubertian quality of suffering and painful illumination. Every once in a while the music seems to lose its balance—or is loss of balance precisely what it means to express? There is a powerful emotional undertow in much of it. The anger is overt and clear. It is the close-to-still moments of deep pain that are the most searing in their hushed intimacy. This is not easy listening, but there is a composer out of the ordinary at work here. This is very searching music, and the search is inside.

The more Tsontakis' music is influenced by Beethoven or Shubert, the more I like it. I also like it when he is channeling Debussy, as in the beguiling *Clair de Lune*. However, the more it is influenced by Messiaen, the less I care for it. The Messiaen-influenced works lose me because Messiaen loses me. That, of course, is not a criticism, but a predilection or, to put it more self-critically, a blind spot of mine. I simply have never fathomed Messiaen's music.

In any event, some of these works, as I hope I have made clear, are indispensable. The releases are listed in order of preference.

Recommended Recordings

Quartets 3 & 4, New World Records 80414

Heartsounds; *Meditations at Perigree*; *Sarabesque*, Koch 7579

Piano Quartet No. 2; *Eclipse*; Bagatelles, Koch 7550

Four Symphonic Quartets, Koch 7384

Violin Concerto No. 2; *Clair de Lune*; *The Past, The Passion*, Koch 7592

Violin Concerto No. 1; *October*; *Mirologhia*, Koch 7680

~

Eduard Tubin: In from the Cold

In the waning days of the Soviet empire, I had the chance to visit Estonia. After a lecture at the University of Tartu, I was invited to dinner by my hosts. As was usual in restaurants in the Soviet Union, the scene was surreal. The faded decor was a bizarre attempt at elegance, the dining room was mostly empty, the waiters looked like goons, and the food was terrible. During our conversation, a middle-aged woman spoke one of the most chilling lines I have ever heard in my life. She said, "You who were born free will never understand us who were born slaves."

Later in the capital, Tallinn, I had a meeting with foreign minister Lennart Meri (later the president of a free Estonia). I asked him about Estonia's most renowned living composer, Arvo Pärt. He was quite struck by the international fame Pärt enjoyed and told me how frequently he was asked about him. In retrospect, I wished I had asked after another of Estonia's musical treasures, a composer whose reputation disappeared about the same time the country did.

There was no Tubin, Eduard, in my handy musical dictionary, or in any other book I had on 20th-century music—until recently. Tubin (1905–1982) slipped down the same memory hole that swallowed his native Estonia after it was occupied by the Soviet Union along with the other Baltic states in 1940. But like Estonia, Tubin's music is back, though the composer unfortunately did not live long enough to see his country liberated. The neglect suffered in Tubin's lifetime has been remedied by Robert von Bahr's extraordinary BIS label and conductor (and countryman) Neeme Järvi, who brought out a complete cycle of Tubin's ten symphonies, accompanied by other orchestral compositions. This extraordinary body of work paints a different picture of Estonia than the one I received at dinner in Tartu. Without over-politicizing Tubin's music, I would say that it is decidedly antislave, free in spirit, and full of anguish over the fate that befell his beloved country.

Tubin studied at the College of Music in Tartu with Estonian composer Heino Eller. In 1944, he fled to Sweden with his family and remained there for the rest of his life. Exile means obscurity for composers who lose both their reputation and creative urge in a foreign land. Tubin, however, remained highly productive in Sweden, though his music took on a grimmer cast away from his homeland. In fact, his symphonies can be neatly divided into two groupings: those written in his native country, Nos. 1 to 4, and those produced in exile, Nos. 5 to 10.

Tubin's early music shares in the nature mysticism and heroic nationalism that characterized the outpouring of Scandinavian music at that time, especially from Sibelius in Finland and Carl Nielsen in Denmark. Both composers are clear influences on Tubin, who otherwise found his own way as a symphonist, creating a distinctive sound that in his later works took on a relentlessness and gritty toughness that no doubt reflected the tragedy of his country. The decidedly darker cast and thicker textures of Tubin's later works may lack the Sibelian breadth, expansive melody, and unforced quality of his earlier pieces, but they gain in extraordinary cohesion and compactness. No matter how dark the shadow of exile may have become, Tubin remained a completely tonal, traditional composer, which may help to explain why his music did not receive more than regional notice—the times being far more propitious for musical revolutionaries.

What BIS' ambitious project revealed was a highly significant symphonist whose stirring works are well worth reviving. The seven BIS releases covering compositions from 1931 to 1973 contain a wide variety of musical expression. (The 10 symphonies are also available in a five-CD BIS box set.) The material runs from simple pastoral treatments of Estonian folk songs to symphonic arguments of real ferocity.

Tubin's First Symphony is very much in the lyrical, highly rhapsodic vein of his other early works, which culminate in the extremely beautiful Fourth. Like Sibelius' First, Tubin's First Symphony is amazingly self-confident and ambitiously large and powerful for a composer's first essay of the symphonic form. Also, like Sibelius' music, its nationalist associations are prominent.

Appropriately enough, its debut took place on the anniversary of the Republic of Estonia, February 4, 1936. Surprisingly, it is a stronger composition than the overly descriptive and somewhat meandering Second Symphony. Neeme Järvi and the Swedish Radio Symphony give it a stunning performance.

Mysteriously subtitled *Legendaire*, Tubin's Second Symphony is full of gorgeous nature painting. It begins softly with some lovely atmospherics that soon give way to a depiction of a stormy sea. In one section, the strings cry out very much as they do in Nielsen's Fourth Symphony. The symphony seems to follow a pattern of storm and abatement. It is pictorially exciting, and there are moments of real beauty, but it is not as convincing symphonically as the First.

Tubin's Third Symphony (1942), like the Second, has a strong pictorial orientation, and it displays a martial character in its heavy use of timpani. It has grand themes, propulsive rhythms, and heroic vistas. The full complement of orchestral resources is deployed in some rousing moments of real sweep and grandeur. The last movement, however, tends toward the grandiose.

Perhaps Tubin's single most beautiful, majestic utterance is the Fourth Symphony, which deserves its appellation, *Sinfonia lirica*. It is frightening to think that this masterpiece was almost lost when the building in which it was housed was bombed by the Soviet Air Force in 1944. The Fourth has both Sibelian breadth and the kind of flowing lyricism found in Scandinavian Wilhelm Peterson-Berger's gorgeous music. It has a completely natural feel to it—that unforced quality missing from some of Tubin's more angst-ridden works. Tubin said that he "wrote the work down fairly quickly", which is not surprising since it seems to spring from a single intense inspiration. For those whose tastes run to the rhapsodic, this exhilarating piece may well become a favorite.

The first product of Tubin's exile is the Symphony No. 5 (1946). It shows that Tubin had cast aside anything inessential to symphonic form. Around the time it was written, he said about his Piano Sonata No. 2 something that applies equally to this work: "It taught me a lesson for life. I learned to concentrate on the essentials and leave out everything else, all that was unnecessary, superfluous, repetitive; each note had to find its right place." The lushness and extravagance of the early works are gone. Less lyrical, stronger symphonically, though not yet dominated by the more abstract rhythmic preoccupations of the Sixth, the Fifth points to the telegraphic concision and obsessive rhythm that would become dominant features of the later works. As for its expressive content, Swedish composer Moses Pergament wrote after its premiere, "There can scarcely be any doubt that this symphony has been conceived and written as a depiction in sound of the Estonian national tragedy, a view in which the drama itself has been painted with the same force and artistic imagination as religiously colored hope for the future and the inspiring prophetic vision of freedom."

Symphony No. 6 (1954) could not come from a more different world than that of Tubin's early works—a nonpictorial one, based primarily upon obsessive rhythm. It has shed any national identity and is practically shorn of lyricism. Its transmogrification of a number of dance rhythms gives it the feeling of a danse macabre. It is a turbulent, relentless work with some horrific timpanic eruptions à la Nielsen. Whereas in Nielsen's Fourth the main theme emerges triumphant from under the percussive rubble, here things conclude in resignation—a serene enough ending, but one born of exhaustion, not resolution. This is a disturbing, not easily assimilated work. Yet it has an eerie, grating power that fascinates. The words of Estonian conductor Olav Roots apply more to the Sixth Symphony than to Tubin's Third, to which they were applied: "The despair, obstinacy, and hate which have overcome a race which longs for its lost independence find musical expression in the symphony." The Swedish Radio Symphony Orchestra premiered the Sixth Symphony in 1955, and its reprise here is extremely potent in execution and stunning in sound.

The Seventh Symphony is clearly part of Tubin's earlier symphonic sound world. The same kind of formal thinking evident in his early symphonies is present here, but in leaner form—less lush and ecstatic, more mature and melancholic, but still quite beautiful and full of longing. It is also without the violence and sense of catastrophe found in the Fifth and Sixth Symphonies.

Tubin's Eighth Symphony (1966) is music of a knottier sort, far more introspective and infused with a sense of tragedy. The whole work is thematically tight. The searing opening movement employs a halting tempo, punctuated by expressive silences that convey a feeling not so much of uncertainty as of deep hurt. The second movement introduces a dancing motto that is driven with great harshness. A variation of it returns in the third movement and is whipped into an infernal whirl that then slowly unwinds. The symphony does not so much end as stop with a held breath. A fascinating and enigmatic work, it receives an excellent performance by Järvi and the Swedish Radio Symphony.

Symphony No. 9 (1969) seems to have escaped the cataclysms that Tubin felt it necessary to express in some of the grimmer works he wrote between it and the composition of Symphony No. 4. While this much briefer and somewhat leaner work has a concision that is quite different from the flowing lyricism of its 1943 predecessor, it also quite clearly inhabits the same tonal and expressive universe. In fact, some may find this a surprisingly traditional composition for 1969, though not unlike similar efforts by contemporary English exponents of tonality. While its two movements are both marked Adagio, there is no lack of propulsion and the melodic interest never flags.

Tubin's last completed symphony, the Tenth (1973), is written in one movement, marked Adagio. It begins somberly in the strings, but recurring horn calls soon attempt to summon the music from its melancholic brooding. These give way to a more energetic and uplifting theme, which is, if not triumphant, at least enlivened by a note of optimism. The two themes alternate effectively, creating a weighty feel for both the inertial pull of melancholy and the great strength needed to overcome it. The spirited theme finally prevails in the Adagio festivo, which builds to the symphony's powerful and magnificent climax, after which comes a long orchestral fade to the end. It would be an overstatement to call Tubin's last symphony elegiac, but it is pervaded by a strong sense of mortality and by the feeling of sadness that comes with the knowledge that triumph is always temporary.

If obtained as a separate issue, the Tenth Symphony is coupled with the *Requiem for Fallen Soldiers*, which was written over a period of almost 30 years (1950–1979). It is an atypical piece for Tubin, and it stands in relation to his work in much the same way that Czech composer Bohuslav Martinů's *Field Mass* (1939) stands in relation to his. Both are nonliturgical works that commemorate national disasters (the loss of independence) in an austere manner, with stripped-down orchestral forces that create sounds characteristic of their respective composers. Bereft of strings, for which he writes so well, Tubin restricts his *Requiem* to organ, piano, drums, timpani, and trumpet, accompanying a male choir and two soloists (contralto and baritone). The text consists of four Estonian poems on death in battle and a mother's lament. A spare and grim atmosphere is effectively conveyed, even if the incessant drumbeat becomes slightly irritating. A bold and beautifully executed trumpet solo at the beginning of the last movement is a striking salute to the dead. Considering Estonia's position during the years in which this work was written, it is understandable that Tubin's *Requiem* does not contain a great deal of consolation or hope.

One can buy the symphonies complete in a BIS box set of five CDs, which may be economical (five CDs for the price of three), but one will miss the accompanying works on the single CD issues. The First Symphony is paired with two much later compositions, the Concerto for Balalaika and Orchestra (1964) and *Music for Strings* (1963). In the concerto, Tubin makes an inviting contrast between the delicate textures of the balalaika—played beautifully by Emanuil Sheynkman—and the orchestral muscle of the vigorous accompaniment. The brief *Music for Strings* is a well-crafted, melancholy piece with an English flavor. Accompanying the Seventh Symphony, the *Sinfonietta on Estonian Motifs* (1940) has the same quality of rapturous romanticism as the Fourth Symphony, which followed it by three years. It is an immensely appealing treatment of Estonian folk music that shimmers like Ravel and delights like the very best works in its genre. The Ostinato section contains a hint of an Estonian *Bolero*, only better, and the beginning of the Finale is imbued with the spirit of English pastoralism. The Concertino for Piano and Orchestra (1945) does not share in the typical Tubin sound. It is a spiky, somewhat neoclassical work, played here with plenty of sparkle and verve by soloist Roland Pontinen. The *Toccata* (1939), which accompanies Symphonies 4 and 9, is a perky, percussive work with the immediate appeal of the showpiece. It also contains the germ of an idea that Tubin seems to have resurrected in Symphony No. 9.

BIS also issued a three CD collection of Tubin's complete piano music. It is an excellent supplement that allows one to hear another side of this important symphonic composer. It is an unexpected side in several respects. First, I would not have automatically assumed that Tubin would be a master miniaturist, yet many of the works to which I have returned most often are his preludes, as well as the folk dances and songs. They are beguiling pieces, with that kind of simple sophistication that wears extremely well and that generates real affection. This very appealing quality is due, no doubt, to Tubin's deep love for the sources in Estonian folk music, from which he drew. Second, the musical idioms of Ravel and Debussy are present in so much of this music that one might almost guess that Tubin was really a French composer who had fallen under the influence of Scriabin. That there is not a hint of this French influence in his symphonies makes this aspect of the piano music a real surprise.

Less unexpected is the ecstatic lyricism, the abundance of memorable melodies, and the rhythmic verve found throughout these works. The early piano pieces—like the early symphonies—are highly romantic and effusive, while the later compositions are leaner and more concise. As pianist Vardo Rumessen, who commissioned the 1976 *Seven Pre-*

ludes, said of them: "We can notice the frugality of expressive means and the strictness of figures, even some asceticism." One can chart Tubin's movement in this direction through the three major pieces in this collection: the Sonata No. 1 (1928); the Sonatina in D Minor (1942); and the Sonata No. 2. As invariably impressive as these works may be, I think I will find myself irresistibly drawn back to the smaller forms in which Tubin exhibits such a great capacity for charm, as in the *Three Pieces for Children*; *Variations on an Estonian Folk Tune*; *Four Folk Songs from My Country*; and the *Suite on Estonian Shepherd Melodies*, among others. Rumessen, who knows all of Tubin's piano music by heart and performed it before the approving composer, plays most beautifully. The sound on this set, as in all these releases, is outstanding.

The unexpected is intriguing and in this case reveals several masterpieces that speak of the beauty of a native land and the sorrow of its loss. Nothing I have heard in Tubin's music could possibly explain, much less justify, its long neglect. Now that the Cold War in music is over, I hope to hear more of these deserving works in our concert halls. Lovers of 20th-century Scandinavian music should be especially interested in these superb releases from BIS, as should anyone wondering why more composers did not continue to write tonal music even after Arnold Schoenberg told them not to.

Recommended Recordings

Complete Symphonies 1–10, BIS 1402/1404

Symphony No. 1 & Balalaika Concerto, BIS 351

Symphonies 2 & 6, BIS 304

Symphonies 3 & 8, BIS 342

Symphonies 4 & 9; and *Toccata*, BIS 227

Symphony No. 5 & *Kratt Ballet Suite*, BIS 306

Symphony No. 7; *Sinfonietta on Estonian Motifs*, BIS 401

Symphony No. 10 & *Requiem for Fallen Soldiers*, BIS 297

Complete Piano Music, BIS 414/416

Geirr Tveitt: The Music in the Waterfall

Before he died, a great music-loving friend of mine, Phil Nicolaides, said that he would regret departing this life because of the wonderful melodies he would never hear. He was wrong. The best melodies are in heaven. This is especially so in the case of the music of Norwegian composer Geirr Tveitt (1908–1981).

Tveitt lived in the Hardanger region of western Norway on a farm that had been in his family for more than six centuries. He was extraordinarily prolific, producing some 400 compositions. July 12, 1970, is a day of infamy in the history of 20th-century music. On that day a fire consumed Tveitt's wooden house and all the musical scores stored in it—more than 300 opuses, most of them unpublished. Since then, people have figuratively been picking through the ashes, trying to reconstruct some of his works. What remains still places him at the forefront of Norwegian music in much the same way as Bartók is in the forefront of Hungarian music. Because Tveitt did not bother with the publication of his works, close to 80 percent of his life's output was lost to this world. However, what remains is so good that one reason I want to get to heaven is to hear the rest of it.

Tveitt's work was completely rooted in the folk music of Hardanger. Like Béla Bartók in Hungary, Tveitt scoured the countryside of his district, notating about 1,000 folk tunes—alas, also lost in the fire. We have some idea of the worth of these treasures because Tveitt adapted 100 of them in an orchestral work, *A Hundred Folktunes from Hardanger*. They were grouped into suites, roughly 15 folk melodies in each. Four of the suites have survived. Another 50 of the tunes were arranged for piano. The BIS label released a splendid recording of the first two suites with the Stavanger Symphony Orchestra under Ole Kristian Ruud. The Naxos label has gone one better by releasing two CDs of the Royal Scottish National Orchestra, under conductor Bjarte Engeset, playing Suites 1 and 4, and Suites 2 and 5 with great élan. In addition, the Marco Polo label has issued two CDs containing 50 folk tunes from Hardanger for piano, played brilliantly by pianist Havard Gimse. In either guise, these works are aphoristic tone poems, or musical haiku, most of them lasting under three minutes, and some only one. The melodies are instantly memorable. Their expressive range is extraordinary, encompassing exquisite tenderness, raucous humor, and a kind of barbarian splendor. They are little lightning flashes of music that illuminate the landscape of life and nature.

The titles of the tunes give some idea of the subject matter of Hardanger folk music: "Consecration of the New Beer", "The Loveliest Song on Earth", "The Hasty Wedding", "Beard on Fire", "Sad Song of an Empty Brandy Keg", "God's Goodness and God's Greatness", "The Lame Fiddler's Hulder-Dance", and "Do You Hear the Falls Singing?" from which Tveitt's biographer, Reidar Storaas, aptly drew the title of his book, *The Song in the Waterfall's Roar*.

The music could hardly be more specific to a location and a particular, provincial culture. So what explains its universal appeal? How can we be so thoroughly delighted by the peasant music of western Norway —or, to be more exact, by music drawing upon it? The reason is that folk music is entirely based on song and dance, which are the original wellsprings of all music. That is what gives Tveitt's music its sense of freshness and innocence, its robustness and vitality, its spontaneity and directness. Both in these vignettes and in his larger works, there is a living, pulsating feeling to Tveitt's music.

Tveitt himself, however, was not a peasant. He was a man of the highest musical and cultural sophistication. He studied in Vienna and Paris with Egon Wellesz, Arthur Honegger, Heitor Villa-Lobos, and Nadia Boulanger, who characterized Tveitt's music as "originality rooted in tradition" and "a breath of fresh Norwegian air". He spoke five European languages fluently and managed to get by in four others, including Arabic and Hindi. He was not a country bumpkin, but he so identified with the region from which he came that he became indistinguishable from it. Tveitt said of himself, "If a leaf grows on a birch tree, it necessarily becomes a birch leaf." He became the song in the roar of the Hardanger waterfalls, or in other words, a source of folk music himself. No one can distinguish between the real Hardanger folk tunes and the ones Tveitt made up. In a hilarious episode in 1951, Tveitt was at the piano in a broadcast studio, ready to play from memory a piece by Edvard Grieg, to be heard all across Europe, when his mind went completely blank. He therefore improvised a Grieg-like piece for the allotted time. No one seemed the wiser for it.

To the Hardanger tunes, Tveitt added a technical sophistication and a sense of orchestral color that can be compared to that of Maurice

Ravel, to whom he dedicated his Second Piano Concerto. While the Hardanger vernacular predominates in Tveitt's music, other Nordic and European influences are also discernible. One can hear them in two other splendid recent releases of his music. Again using the Stavanger Symphony Orchestra and Ole Kristian Ruud, the BIS label has brought out the premiere recordings of two major orchestral works, *Prillar* and the *Sun God Symphony*, which is a compilation of the surviving fragments of his huge ballet, *Baldurs Draumar*.

The BIS release makes clear Tveitt's debts to Ravel not only in his stunning orchestration and impressionistic harmonies, but also in his formal treatment of what are essentially folk music suites. In these larger forms, Tveitt uses a *Bolero*-like scheme of intensification through repetition. The music grows in volume, speed, and rhythmic accent. Tedium is avoided by Tveitt's orchestral virtuosity and improvisatory style. At times, Tveitt's works are also reminiscent of Leoš Janáček in their swirling ostinatos and punchy motifs. As is perhaps inevitable for a Scandinavian composer of his period, Tveitt occasionally falls under the spell of Jean Sibelius, especially in his string and woodwind writing. His work is also reminiscent of another Norwegian musical nationalist, Harald Sæverud. I don't think Norwegian conductor Bjarte Engeset too far off the mark when he writes, "I experience a suspense between lyrical refinement and powerful primitivism in his music, which makes it particularly challenging and rewarding both to perform and to listen to."

The budget Naxos label has issued recordings of Tveitt's Piano Concertos 1 and 5 on one CD, and Piano Concerto No. 4: *Aurora Borealis* with *Variations on a Folk Song from Hardanger* for two pianos and orchestra on another. These are breathtakingly played by Havard Gimse with the Royal Scottish National Orchestra under Bjarte Engeset (Gimse also performs the Hardanger Tunes on the Marco Polo CDs). Naxos has now added to its wonderful recording of Tveitt's Piano Concertos 1 and 5, which I also highly recommend, its own issue of two suites of the Hardanger Tunes, played by the Royal Scottish National Orchestra under Bjarte Engeset.

In the three piano concertos, Sergei Rachmaninoff's influence shows up in Tveitt's propensity to pile chords on top of each other to reach thrilling climaxes. Counterpoised to Rachmaninoff's influence, however, is that of French composer Francis Poulenc. Like Poulenc, Tveitt was utterly unafraid of simplicity. Some of Tveitt's melodies possess a childlike naïveté that goes straight to the heart. The music alternates between orchestral storms and gentle melodies.

There are other recordings of Tveitt's works available on the Norwegian labels Simax and Aurora. These CDs, however, can be hard to find in the United States. With some ingenuity, they can be purchased on the Internet (try Amazon). It is especially worth searching out the highly unusual Harp Concerto No. 2, which begins with a marcia funebre before the harp enters with its soft enchantment. The writing for harp is as fine as anything Ravel or Roussel wrote for the instrument. It is paired with the Suite No. 1 from the Hardanger Tunes and *Nykken* (Water Sprite), subtitled, *A Symphonic Painting for Orchestra*, on Simax. Simax also offers a CD of Tveitt playing his own works in recordings made in the 1940s. The sound quality is execrable. I listen anyway because it is the only way I can hear Tveitt's Piano Concerto No. 3, which Tveitt claimed Brahms played for him in a dream (the score was lost). This CD also features Tveitt playing his Piano Sonata No. 29, the only one to have escaped the fire.

The Aurora label features a modern recording of the Sonata, with Kjell Baekkelund, paired with Tveitt's enlivening Concerto No. 2 for Hardanger Fiddle and Orchestra, a work of irresistible charm and spark. The Hardanger fiddle is a Norwegian folk violin with sympathetic strings and a lot of character. BIS has released both Concertos 1 and 2 for Hardanger Fiddle and Orchestra, with violinist Arve Moen Bergset and the Stavanger Symphony Orchestra conducted by Ole Kristian Ruud. Concerto No. 2 has long been one of my favorite works, but its incarnation on the Aurora label may be hard to find. It is a great treat to have this work easily available, especially with the bonus of the First Concerto, which I had never heard, and the tone poem *Nykken*, which concerns the antics of a water sprite. I find all this irrepressible music irresistible, even when conductor Ruud is a little heavy-handed with his rhythmic tread—as if it were necessary to remind us of the music's folk-dancing roots. But that is a quibble; don't miss this invigorating music. I will say, however, that the Aurora recording of the Bergen Philharmonic Orchestra, under Karsten Andersen, with Sigbjorn Bernhoft Osa playing the Hardanger fiddle, aces the competition in Concerto No. 2 on the BIS label through the extraordinary vivacity of the performance.

All of Tveitt's surviving scores for wind ensemble have been gathered on a Naxos CD, featuring the excellent Royal Norwegian Navy Band under Bjarte Engeset. Three of the relatively short pieces were written for a Norwegian Band Federation competition in 1962. Tveitt took first, second, and third prizes for, respectively, the *Sinfonietta di Soffiatori* (wind instruments), *The Old Mill on the Brook*, and the *Hymn of Freedom*. The opening of *Sinfonia di Soffiatori*, which Tveitt called his third symphony, is the most substantial piece here. It includes double-basses and harp. The disc is filled out with transcriptions of nine selections from *A Hundred Hardanger Tunes*. All of it is infused with Tveitt's signature quirkiness and should be irresistible to wind music aficionados.

The Simax Classics label has given us world premiere recordings of the Tveitt's Quartet for Strings, titled *From a Travel Diary*, a little ballet called the *Household God*, a short Septet for Two Violins, Viola, Cello, Double Bass, Oboe and Horn, and *Midsummer's Eve*, which is also in septet form but with a cor anglais instead of an oboe. The Quartet, in suite form, has eight parts depicting various places in the Mediterranean. This is the best musical postcard in chamber music form that I have heard. Particularly entrancing is Tveitt's depiction of the Mediterranean itself in the opening movement and the "Starry Skies over the Sahara" in the closing one. I was also delighted by his portrayals of Spain in "El Escorial" and "Sevilla", the latter offering what sounded like a Norwegian and a Spaniard dancing together in a conflation of a Sevillana and a Hardanger folk tune. What marvelously idiosyncratic, inspiriting music!

These few CDs, however, only scratch the surface of Tveitt's surviving works, and I hope more will be recorded soon.

But what about Tveitt's other piano sonatas and many concertos, symphonies, ballets, operas, and ballads that perished in the conflagration of 1970? I am afraid I will have to wait to hear them with Phil Nicolaides.

Recommended Recordings

100 Folk Tunes from Hardanger, Suites 1 & 2, BIS 987

A Hundred Hardanger Tunes, Suites 1 & 4, Naxos 8.555078

A Hundred Hardanger Tunes, Suites 2 & 5, Naxos 8.555770

Piano Music: Fifty Folk-Tunes from Hardanger, vols. 1 & 2 (Marco Polo) Naxos 8.225055 & 8.225056

Prillar & Sun God Symphony, BIS 1027

Piano Concertos 1 & 5, Naxos 8.555077

Piano Concerto No. 4; *Variations on a Folk Song from Hardanger*, Naxos 8.555761

Piano Sonata No. 29; Concerto No. 2 for Hardanger Fiddle and Orchestra, Aurora NCD-B 4945

Harp Concerto No. 2; *A Hundred Folk Tunes from Hardanger*, Suite 1, Nos. 1–15; *Nykken* (Water Sprite), Simax 3108

Hardanger Fiddle Concertos 1 & 2; *Nykken* (Water Sprite), BIS 1207

Sinfonia di Soffiatori; *The Old Mill on the Brook*; *Hymn to Freedom*; Selections from *A Hundred Hardanger Tunes*, Naxos 8.572095

Pēteris Vasks and Einojuhani Rautavaara:
Northern Lights

Contemporary composers are increasingly unafraid to write attractive, even beautiful music. Further evidence of this proposition, comes from the lands of northern lights in the works of Latvian composer Pēteris Vasks and Finnish composer Einojuhani Rautavaara.

Vasks writes traditional tonal music of soulful beauty that both laments the suffering of his country and celebrates its enduring spirit. Rautavaara, on the other hand, seems to have wandered through a number of schools of composition, including 12-tone, and emerged as, of all things, a late-20th- and early-21st-century romantic. Each has been favored by CD releases that show them to great advantage. Anyone who thinks modern classical music always sounds either like an explosion in a boiler factory or sonic wallpaper should listen to the music on these CDs.

The son of a Baptist minister, Pēteris Vasks (b. 1946) obtained his vocation from his father: "I've often said that I do the same thing my father did. He was a minister, I am a composer, but we share the desire to reflect the human spiritual dimension and live within it. . . . In my opinion the true mission of music is to talk about spiritual, eternal values that rise above the secular. Similarly in instrumental music, most important is the ethical charge, that you carry this message of faith and love." Because of his pedigree and orientation, he was not favored for a musical education or career in the Soviet Union. Yet discrimination had its advantages. As Vasks said, "We had the tradition of living music at home and in the church." Though he studied at the music conservatory in Riga, he is largely self-taught.

The results are very intriguing: music that is so attractive it is almost embarrassing. His *Cantabile* for strings is the Latvian equivalent of Samuel Barber's hugely popular and moving *Adagio for Strings*. *Cantabile* was written in 1979, not a particularly pleasant time for Latvia. Vasks' goal was "to tell in eight minutes how beautiful and harmonious the world is". Why *so* beautiful? Contrary to the 20th century's predominant aesthetic of ugliness in art to reflect ugliness in life, Vasks felt the urgent need to combat that ugliness. He seems to share the Dostoyevskian belief that "beauty will save the world." Thus the uglier life becomes, the more insistently beautiful his music is. This is not Pollyannaish. The unalloyed beauty he creates springs from a deep spiritual need for it; he chooses it over darkness. Vasks asks, "Is there any point in composing a piece that only mirrors our being one step away from extinction? To my mind, every honest composer searches for a way out of the crises of his times—toward affirmation and faith." Beauty is the language of affirmation and faith.

This language was also Vasks' only weapon in facing Soviet totalitarianism. His Cello Concerto depicts "the persistence of a personality against crude, brutal power; what totalitarian power did to us, how we are to purge ourselves from this manipulation". The introductory "Canto I" depicts "the ideal beauty of the world". The next movement unleashes a frenzied staccato rhythm that attacks the soloist. Vasks says, "Fast music has always been to me a negative sign of evil, aggression, destruction." The massed orchestra tries to crush the cello with a vulgar tune it repeats with ferocity in what sounds like a nightmare at a circus. The cello survives and recovers its lyrical, rhapsodic voice in the last movement, the achingly lovely "Canto II", which Vasks says represents the alternative to what precedes it, as well as "the spiritual steadfastness of my people". Parts of this work remind me of the soprano movement in Górecki's *Symphony of Sorrowful Songs*, but here it is the cello that sings.

Also unabashedly beautiful is Vasks' *String Symphony—Voices*, inspired in part by the last-ditch Soviet clampdown in the Baltic states in 1990. At the very beginning of the first movement, subtitled "Voices of Silence", Vasks creates a most intriguing sound, as if the wind were stirring the orchestra, gently rustling the instruments like they were so many leaves. This is followed by what sounds like a tribute to, if indeed not a quotation from, Arvo Pärt's *Tabula Rasa*. (Vasks remarks interestingly upon the contrast of his music to Pärt's: "I'm a bit different from Arvo Pärt—he's already living in paradise, and his music comes from there. There's no emotion, no drama. My ideal is there, but I am living here, and my compositions deal with the contradiction between the ideal and reality.") The movement is full of twilight murmurings in the strings. "Voices of Life" begins with birdcalls gently rising with the dawn of a new day. For Vasks, birds are emblems of freedom. This movement carries with it a marvelous sense of expectancy. That expectancy is met in the concluding movement, the gravely beautiful "Voices of Conscience". *Voices* is one of the most beautiful string pieces I have heard. It and *Cantabile* strike me as music I have somehow always known without ever having heard it before. I return to these pieces often for that wonderful amalgam of mystery and familiarity. These works should join those of Britten, Vaughan Williams, Barber, and Diamond as among the finest of our time. Of the other compositions on the Conifer CDs, I am particularly taken with the lovely Cor anglais Concerto, with its Sibelian touches, and the heartfelt *Musica dolorosa*. All are movingly performed by the Riga Philharmonic, under conductors Kriss Rusmanis and Jonas Aleksa.

In his Symphonies 2 and 3 (both available separately on the Ondine label, with different pairings), Vasks portrays the tension between the real and the ideal, between harmony and disharmony in the following way: for the real, he veers into Shostakovich territory; while for the ideal, he tends more toward Pärt or Górecki. (I do not mean to suggest that his music is derivative, but wish to give listeners some stylistic signposts. From the variety of his influences, he has forged his own, identifiable style.) Like Shostakovich, Vasks knows how to repeat an obsessive theme to the edge of irritation, increasing its pace and volume, to the breaking point. With brass and timpani, he deploys rat-a-tat motifs to hammer down the individual. He obviously uses these means to portray the grating forces of dehumanization (yet without dehumanizing the listener), before the return of solace in the compensating beauty he amply provides. Some of this is not easy music, but it is hard to put a happy face on the Soviet part of the 20th century —which I mean not only in political, but most especially in spiritual terms.

Tālā gaisma (Distant Light), written for Latvian violinist Gidon Kremer, is Vasks' first work for violin and string orchestra. It is a 30-minute single movement. Vasks achieves a piercing purity of tone reminiscent of Pärt in the early cadenza near the start of the work. Vasks said, "Joy and grief are bound together in this piece, as so often in my work, but in the end hope triumphs." The range and variety of expression in *Tālā gaisma* make it one of Vasks' most attractive and engaging compositions. There are six recordings of it, marking it as Vasks' most popular piece. I am partial to the tremendous concentration that Kremer brings to it in his Teldec recording, but I was bowled over by the performance on an expensive, imported Wergo CD that also contains his two other works for violin and orchestra. It is given an impassioned performance by violinist Alina Pogostkina with Sinfonietta Riga, under conductor Juha Kangas, that grips the listener from the first note to last. It has an exciting live-performance feel to it, even though it isn't. Pogostkina places her staggering virtuosity completely at the service of the expressive content.

The first work on the Wergo is CD *Vox Amoris*, described as a *fantasia per violin ed archi*. According to Vasks, he "started composing the fantasy for violin and orchestra in fall 2008 and finished the score in early spring 2009. What is the message I wanted to announce? It is about the greatest power in the whole world—love. Love is, was and will be as long as we will be. I believe that solo violin and string orchestra is the best combination for a 'love story'." *Vox Amoris* is a tender musical caress. Of which kind of love does it speak? It seems to be the reflection of the state of a soul in love—perhaps of a parent for a child. Its deep tenderness gives that impression. It is not erotic love—it has more selflessness to it. This love is challenged, or rather what it loves is threatened, and it rises to the defense. After the perturbation, the prevailing tenderness returns, and the work closes with passages of the utmost refinement and delicacy. The extended cadenzas are dazzling, as is the wholly committed playing of Alina Pogostkina and the Sinfonietta Riga under Kangas.

The third and shortest work on this recording is *Vientuļais eņģelis* (Lonely Angel), a meditation for violin and string orchestra, also composed for Kremer. It was inspired by a vision. Vasks writes, "I saw an angel, flying over the world; the angel looks at the world's condition with grieving eyes, but an almost imperceptible, loving touch of the angel's wings brings comfort and healing. This piece is my music after the pain." The nearly unbroken violin line is of breathtaking length— a kind of endless singing that suggests something more than human. It expresses a sad serenity. This is one of the indispensable Vasks CDs. If you know the experience of pain and care for the touch of consoling beauty, here it is in abundance.

Einojuhani Rautavaara (b. 1928) studied at the Sibelius Academy in Helsinki and was chosen for a Koussevitzky Foundation scholarship by the great Jan Sibelius himself. In the mid-1950s, he studied with a number of American composers, including Aaron Copland, Roger Sessions, and Vincent Persichetti. The only American influence I detect comes from the way in which Rautavaara deploys massive sheets of string and brass sound—somewhat in the manner of American composer Roy Harris without, however, sounding like him. (In my interview with him, Rautavaara disavowed any direct influence.) Aside from Sibelius, the other apparent Nordic influence is that of the great Norwegian composer Harald Sæverud. Rautavaara captures the same kind of craggy melancholy in the strings and winds that Sæverud was able to express so effectively.

Not only is Rautavaara a self-confessed romantic, he seems to understand what being one means: "The Romantic has no coordinates. In time he is either yesterday or tomorrow, not today. In space he is over there or over there, never here." Perhaps this is why Rautavaara is so hard to pin down stylistically, wandering as he has all over the musical map in his eight symphonies, ten operas (of which *Thomas, Vincent* and *Aleksis Kivi* are the best known), and numerous other works. Yet his most recent work is also neoromantic in style, extremely spacious, leisurely in development, beautifully melodious, and almost lush in a cinematic sense. He has said, "If an artist is not a modernist when he is young, he has no heart. And if he is a modernist when he is old, he has no brain."

Unlike Vasks', Rautavaara's music is not explicitly moral. But it does deal with personal encounters with spiritual phenomena that he calls "angels". Rautavaara does not mean angels in the conventional sense, but as "Jungian archetypes". As befits one influenced by Jung, Rautavaara has written both an *Angel of Dusk* and a counterpoising *Angel of Light*. However, he makes broader angelic allusions to William Blake and Rainer Maria Rilke and explains that his angels stem "from the conviction that other realities exist beyond those we are normally aware of, entirely different forms of consciousness". His apprehension of these inspires his music. "I have a taste for eternity", says Rautavaara.

That taste is expressed in his Symphony No. 7: *Angel of Light*, available on the Ondine label. Rautavaara insists that this highly attractive and sumptuous work should be understood, like his other works, as absolute music and not as program music. Yet he provides the outline of his highly personal encounters with angelic beings in dreams and otherwise, on which the work is based. Can he have it both ways? He does so in the *Angel of Light* with its thematic coherence. But without his explanation of his childhood dreams, I would be puzzled by *Angels and Visitations*, paired on the second of the Ondine CDs with the Violin Concerto. As a recreation of his dream experience, however, it is highly evocative and very effective.

Symphony No. 7 is so attractive on the surface that you might think you hear the whole thing the first time through. In fact, it is so attractive that I was almost ready to dismiss it as a cinematic extravagance. But I kept listening and discovered a hauntingly beautiful piece with more than surface appeal. This work is far less disjunctive in style than Rautavaara's earlier harsher works, in which he employed apparently random eruptions of violence that seemed to arrive from somewhere outside the music (e.g., as in *Angel of Light*'s disc companion, *Annunciations*, from 1977). This work is far more harmonious. It employs an almost constant undulating string ostinato, a grand hymn motif, and builds to several impressive climaxes. It also conveys a sense of vastness and serenity. Listen, for instance, to the meltingly lovely third movement marked Come un sogno (like a dream). Most importantly, the symphony works on its own terms musically; it does not need an angel crutch to hold it up. If it were called "Hymn to the Sea", I would find it equally convincing. That conviction is shaken by only one aspect of the work: its almost cinematic sense. Rautavaara may aim at eternity, but several times, he comes perilously close to ending up at the movies. But what a gorgeous movie!

That Rautavaara did not have far to travel to reach the euphonious world of *Angel of Light* is clear from his Violin Concerto of 1977. While it would not be mistaken for anything but a modern piece, it is solidly within the tradition of even 19th-century concertos, with an entrancingly lyrical line for the violin. Here are more moments of ethereal beauty from this man of angels. Leif Segerstam conducts the Helsinki Philharmonic Orchestra on both of these beautifully recorded CDs. Elmar Oliveira is the superb soloist in the Violin Concerto.

When I asked Rautavaara (see interview, p. 474) if he was going to continue writing in the same kind of neoromantic idiom that produced the gorgeous *Angel of Light*, I received the answer on an Ondine compact disc that features his choral and orchestral work, *On the Last Frontier*, along with his much earlier tone poem *Anadyomene* (Adoration of Aphrodite, 1968), and the Flute Concerto (*Dances with the Winds*, 1975). When I said *Angel of Light* could have been just as aptly named *Hymn to the Sea*, I must have been on to something. *On the Last Frontier* is a sea fantasy, based upon a fantastical text of Edgar Allen Poe about an ill-fated ship.

Rautavaara encountered the text as a child and was haunted by it for six decades until he placed it in this wonderfully billowing, highly evocative and romantic orchestral setting. Both beautiful and terrifying, the last frontier is on the edge of death. Rautavaara seems to be using Poe to invoke one of his dream experiences of angels. In this case, it is a mighty, sea-borne angel of death with "the perfect whiteness of snow". Poe's words could not have been set more magically. They grow out of the music and are carried along to an awesome climax at the end of a slowly building, inexorably growing crescendo, in which a "shrouded figure, far larger than any dweller among men", is revealed. I know of no higher praise than to say that Rautavaara's music marvelously captures the mystery of this stunning encounter.

The other two compositions on this disc are also fascinating, especially *Anadyomene*, in which Rautavaara broke free of serialism, almost against his own will. He wrote, "This music wrenched itself free (and liberated me) from the serial straitjacket and quasi-scientific thinking toward organic music-making." And that is just the way it sounds; here in more than nascent form, is Rautavaara's future development as a romantic. The performances by the Helsinki Philharmonic Orchestra and Finnish Philharmonic Choir under Leif Segerstam, are everything one would wish them to be.

The Ondine label also features two more gorgeous works in answer to my question: the Harp Concerto, with harpist Marielle Nordmann, and Symphony No. 8: *The Journey*, also played by the Helsinki Philharmonic Orchestra under Leif Segerstam. These prove that there is no contemporary composer writing in a more sweepingly romantic, tonally anchored way than Rautavaara. And he is wildly popular for it—a strange but wonderful way for Finland's once-premiere avant-gardist to round out his long and fruitful career. If you were entranced by Rautavaara's *Angel of Light*, you will not be disappointed here. Naxos also has an excellent recording of the Eighth, with the New Zealand Symphony Orchestra under Pietari Inkinen.

Lastly, the Ondine label has issued two other Rautavaara CDs. The first is an exquisite collection of sacred works for mixed chorus, seraphically sung by the Finnish Radio Chamber Choir led by conductor Timo Nuoranne. At the opposite end from Rautavaara's signature big-boned, neoromantic orchestral works, these choral gems, which include *Credo*, *Canticum Mariae Virginis*, *Ave Maria*, and *Magnificat*, are small-scale treasures of a quiet interior life. The other CD features his Piano Concerto No. 3 (*Gift of Dreams*) and the orchestral tone poem *Autumn Gardens*, conducted by Vladimir Ashkenazy, who is also the soloist in the Piano Concerto. Both works are typical of Rautavaara's expansive and sometimes dreamy soundscapes.

Both Vasks and Rautavaara have attempted to reach beyond themselves to express enduring spiritual truths. Is it any surprise that they have chosen beauty as their medium?

Recommended Recordings

Vasks

Cantabile (1979); *Cor anglais Concerto* (1989); *Message* (1982); *Musica dolorosa* (1983); *Lauda* (1986), the Riga PO, conducted by Kriss Rusmanis, Conifer 51236

Concerto for Cello and Orchestra, and String Symphony, *Voices* (Balsis), Riga PO and cellist David Geringas, conducted by Jonas Aleksa, Conifer 51271

Concerto for Violin and String Orchestra, *Distant Light*; *String Symphony*, *Voices*, Kremerata Baltica, Gidon Kremer (violinist and conductor), Teldec 22660

Vox Amoris; Tālā gaisma (Distant Light); *Vientuļais eņģelis* (Lonely Angel), Alina Pogostkina, with Sinfonietta Riga, (conductor) Juha Kangas, Wergo 67502

Symphony No. 2; Violin Concerto, *Distant Light*, Tampere PO, John Storgards, Austral Bosnian Chamber Orchestra, Juha Kangas, John Storgards (violin), Ondine 1005

Symphony No. 3; Cello Concerto, Tampere PO, John Storgards, Marko Ylonen (cello), Ondine 1086

Flute Concerto; Sonata for Flute; *Landscape with Birds*, Naxos 8.572634

Rautavaara

Angel of Light (Symphony No. 7) and *Annunciations*, Helsinki PO, conducted by Leif Segerstam, Ondine 869

Violin Concerto, *Isle of Bliss*, and *Angels and Visitations*, Helsinki PO and violinist Elmar Oliveira, conducted by Leif Segerstam, Ondine 881

On the Last Frontier; Flute Concerto; *Anadyomene*, Ondine 921

Harp Concerto and Symphony No. 8: *The Journey*, Ondine 978

Symphony No. 8; *Manhattan Trilogy*; and *Apotheosis*, Naxos 8.570069

Sacred Works for Mixed Chorus, Ondine 935

Piano Concerto No. 3; *Autumn Gardens*, Ondine 950

Ralph Vaughan Williams: Cheerful Agnosticism

The major figure in the first wave of composers to follow Edward Elgar in Great Britain was Ralph Vaughan Williams (1872–1958). Vaughan Williams came to typify the anomalies and achievements of English 20th-century music. One of his first major successes was *Fantasia on a Theme by Thomas Tallis* for double string orchestra. Vaughan Williams was immersed in English folk song and hymnody. For the *Fantasia*, he took a melody from a group of *Psalm Tunes* composed by Tallis in 1567, which he discovered while editing a new English hymnal. The son of a clergyman, though himself not a believer, Vaughan Williams nevertheless imbued his works with a deep spirituality. He wrote many very moving, explicitly religious works, which only deepens the mystery of their inspiration.

In Vaughan Williams we find the perfect example of the effects of the two-century lapse in the continuity of English music—during which Germans called England *das Land ohne Musik* (the country without music). The Elizabethan influence mixes with that of modernity to produce a sound that, while 20th-century, is hard to place chronologically and is certainly conservative. After the 1910 premiere of the *Fantasia*, the *London Times* wrote, "One is never sure whether one is listening to something very old or very new. The voices of the old church musicians are around one and yet their music is enriched with all that modern art has done, since Debussy, too, is somewhat in the picture. It cannot be assigned to a time or school, but it is full of visions." English critic Peter Pirie pointed out:

> With Debussy the motive for writing diatonic consecutives—which he rarely did—was a conscious archaism, decorative and almost condescending; with Vaughan Williams it was the very stuff of his thought. . . . [Debussy's] excursions into the diatonic modal were time-traveling . . . where the time to which he traveled was actually exotic to him, and selected for that reason. With Vaughan Williams it was the home he had never left.

While Vaughan Williams created a distinctive voice for English music and is perhaps the premiere English musical nationalist, he is also held responsible for ushering in a tide of conservatism from which English composers did not free themselves until the 1960s. His striking individuality has absolutely nothing to do with the avant-garde. Oblivious to and uninterested in the radical musical developments on the Continent, he contented himself with ingeniously adapting the principles derived from folk song to larger orchestral forms. His output was prolific and uneven. He wrote nine symphonies, five of them after he was 70. The unconventional ways in which he put these works together can give them great expressive power, or, in the weaker works, make them sound clumsy as they galumph along.

The intense lyricism, mysticism, and occasional nostalgia in Vaughan Williams' works are part of the giant requiem that English music became for a past that it both mourns and tries to invoke. Vaughan Williams, however, shows a quite unexpected side to his pastoral reveries. He not only mourns the loss of nature, he is angry about it. This anger, quite to the surprise and shock of his audience, erupted in his violent Symphony No. 4 and was heard again in Symphony No. 6 and his ballet *Job*. In some ways, this is Vaughan Williams' strongest, if not most immediately appealing, music. Anger gives his music the sinews that the more meandering pastoral works, despite their charm, sometimes lack.

For quite some time, I was not particularly taken with the symphonies of Vaughan Williams. I always loved the *Serenade to Music, Fantasia on a Theme by Thomas Tallis*, and *The Lark Ascending*, but I questioned Vaughan Williams' stature as a major symphonist. However, I reevaluated my retarded appreciation when the BBC Scottish Symphony Orchestra, under conductor Andrew Manze, presented the Fourth, Fifth, and Sixth Symphonies in a row one evening at Proms in 2012. That may sound like a Vaughan Williams overdose, even for his committed fans, of which there were many present in the full Royal Albert Hall. Not so. I was convinced by it that my neglect has been my loss.

It had been a considerable time since I listened to any Vaughan Williams symphony. This made the impact of the Manze concert all the greater. It was like getting smacked upside the head, brought abruptly out of a daze, not in a painful way, but with the sharp realization of the glories of this music. How can I have not heard these when I first encountered this music many decades ago? Who knows what finally sheds the scales and opens the ears?

Vaughan Williams certainly got a bad rap from some of his fellow countrymen and contemporaneous musicians. Perhaps that helped to put me off. Philip Heseltine, who composed under the name Peter Warlock, supposedly likened Vaughan Williams' *A Pastoral Symphony* (Symphony No. 3) to a cow staring over a fence. Even crueler, Aaron Copland apparently said, "Listening to the Fifth Symphony of Ralph Vaughan Williams is like staring at a cow for forty-five minutes."

Anyone who retains the idea of Vaughan Williams as a member of the "cow pat" school, as composer Elisabeth Lutyens called it, would be quickly disabused of the notion by the wildly eruptive start of the Fourth, which is, if anything, antipastoral and highly minatory. If this is a cow looking over a fence, the fence is electrified and the cow has just been jolted into another pasture. It certainly shocked London audiences with its ferocity at its 1935 premiere.

However, in the Fifth Symphony, Vaughan Williams returned to his more pastoral, violence-free mode in a work of mellowness and extraordinary beauty. The first movement expresses a kind of aching serenity. It's like watching something so beautiful that you remain completely still, but your heart is pounding. The third movement *Romanza* clearly had its inspiration in Sibelius, to whom Vaughan Williams dedicated the work. Gentle string chords cradle the cor anglais solo that evokes Sibelius' *The Swan of Tuonela*—offering perhaps a swan of the Thames? Sibelius must have been pleased.

The Sixth Symphony (1944–1947) is as different from the Fifth, as the Fifth is from the Fourth. The shock of the Sixth is the extent to which Vaughan Williams moved from Sibelius to Shostakovich. The Sixth is infused with Shostakovich's influence with its exaggerated march, the manic episodes, and mechanical repetition. Even the jazz part sounds like one of Shostakovich's parodies. One might be able to pass the Scherzo off as a newly discovered Shostakovich work and get away with it. I don't mean to suggest that the symphony is entirely derivative; it is *echt* Vaughan Williams in its inimitable sound. I simply mean that it is clear that, by 1947, Vaughan Williams had heard Shostakovich loud and clear.

In any case, this is a highly charged, nearly violent work that shows a clear relationship to the spirit of the Fourth. It's no mystery as to why it became known as "The War Symphony", displacing the Fourth from that designation (at least as a premonition of the coming war). It blows away any remaining shreds of the "cow pat" preposterousness regarding Vaughan Williams' music. The Sixth also ends with an extraordinary Epilogue that never rises above *pianissimo*. What Vaughan Williams called "whiffs of themes" float about in the ether. It is eerie music. Some claim it to be a depiction of desolation. It is beautiful and strangely touching.

Of the various versions of Vaughan Williams' symphonies, the ones I listen to most frequently are the RCA recordings by the London Symphony Orchestra, under conductor Andre Previn. They are riveting. RCA offers another complete set of the symphonies, from conductor Leonard Slatkin and the Philharmonia Orchestra, in a ridiculously inexpensive six-CD box set. While I have not heard these, they are well regarded, and I have admired Slatkin in other parts of the English repertory. Last but not least, Decca offers Sir Adrian Boult's first traversal of the symphonies, with the London Philharmonic Orchestra, from the 1950s (in mono sound except for the Eighth and Ninth) in a bargain five-CD set. Vaughan Williams personally supervised these recording sessions (except for the Ninth Symphony—he died the day before), and they are extremely bracing. The mono sound does not insulate the electricity in these exciting performances—it comes straight through.

As mentioned earlier, Vaughan Williams was the agnostic composer of some of the 20th century's most beautiful religious music. He nevertheless showed his affection for Christmas in *Hodie Christus Natus Est*, which is finally available in several excellent versions, most notably by David Wilcocks and by Richard Hickox, both on EMI/Warner. This is a cause for celebration since this music was neglected for some time, and no other 20th-century cantata offers a comparable musical tapestry of the Christmas narrative so full of rapture, jubilation, mystery, merriment, and gravity over its nearly hour-long length. The tremendous vigor of this work belies the 80 to 82 years of age at which Vaughan Williams wrote it and confirms that he maintained his unusual relationship with Christianity to the very end.

According to his wife, Ursula, at some point in his life, Vaughan Williams "drifted into a cheerful agnosticism". As a young man in his 30s, Vaughan Williams had edited the *English Hymnal*. Then, in 1912, he produced the lovely *Fantasia on Christmas Carols* (also included on these CDs). Remaining cheerfully agnostic, he went on to write the exquisite Mass in G—perhaps the loveliest of all 20th-century English Masses—*Dona Nobis Pacem*, *Magnificat*, *Five Mystical Songs*, and other gems. These works show Vaughan Williams at his best because they draw on his roots in English hymnody and folk song. Whatever reservations I had about Vaughan Williams as a symphonist evaporate in this kind of music. *Hodie* demonstrates Vaughan Williams' broad expressive range from touching childlike simplicity to raucous pagan splendor. The gentle narrative is interspersed with hushed magical moments and huge choral and orchestral outbursts that weightily convey that this Child's birth is truly earth-shaking.

Hodie opens with amazing robustness. There is almost a pagan swagger to the music for chorus and orchestra that reminds one of the world into which Christ was born and that the announcement of his birth is being made to *that* world. After the thunderous proclamation from the "Vespers for Christmas Day" that "This day Christ is born", the first of the Gospel narratives from Matthew and Luke begin with a boys' chorus and organ. Their sweet simplicity is followed by an evocation of eerie mystery in the orchestra that accompanies the baritone's rendition of Joseph's dream, in which Joseph is told to accept the Virgin with Child. In that dream, the chorus exults at the prophecy of Emmanuel with the same kind of wild joy as at the opening.

From this point on, Vaughan Williams alternates the Gospel narrative with an eclectic selection of poems. The mezzo-soprano sings an exquisitely serene setting from Milton's "On the Morning of Christ's Nativity". The boys' chorus takes us through Luke from the decree of Caesar Augustus to the manger. The women's chorus reflects ever so quietly and tenderly upon this event in Martin Luther's hymn (translated by Miles Coverdale), that implores of the Child, "Kyrie eleison." Back to Luke, the music for the angel's announcement to the shepherds calls first upon the dream music of Joseph and then breaks out into general jubilation: "Glory to God in the highest." Yet it is jubilation that is grounded in the gravity of the event. It is charged with a profound joy that begins with a kind of giddiness: Can it be true that what was hoped for in the darkness has come to light?

The cantata continues in this fashion, including a poem from Thomas Hardy (another agnostic) and several from the composer's wife, Ursula, that seem to indicate that she, unlike her husband, was a cheerful believer. Her delightful poem "The March of the Three Kings", inspires Vaughan Williams to conjure exotic oriental locales with the kind of barbaric swagger with which he began. At first, the only misstep seems to be the placement and setting of the beginning of the Gospel of John. Vaughan Williams uses this as the beginning of the epilogue, which then continues with more of Milton's "On the Morning of Christ's Nativity". Yet this, too, works. Set to music that combines the opening motif with Joseph's haunting dream theme, John's text compactly recalls all that has transpired. Perhaps Vaughan Williams puts the beginning at the end because the End really is the Beginning.

Richard Hickox pulls out all the stops in his performance with the Choristers of St. Paul's Cathedral and the London Symphony Orchestra and Chorus. Because of my acquaintance with the premiere recording on EMI/Warner with Sir David Wilcocks, who takes an overall gentler approach, it took several hearings to be won over by Hickox' vigor. But his recording is dramatically persuasive, and it powerfully conveys the extraordinary richness of this masterpiece. The choral singing is splendid. Tenor soloist Robert Tear and baritone Stephen Roberts are especially good, and the orchestra moves easily from gossamer strings for gentler touches to glorious blasts of brass in the metaphysical moments. The one thing that the earlier performance has clearly to its advantage is the voice of Janet Baker, to whom the somewhat wobbly mezzo-soprano Elizabeth Gale on the newer recording does not favorably compare.

Add to the merits of *Hodie* the wonderful bonus of the touching *Fantasia on Christmas Carols*, wisely placed on band one before the more substantial work on the Wilcocks CD, and you will have a Merry Christmas with this cheerful agnostic.

I must also mention the three-CD compilation of the film music of Vaughan Williams that Chandos has issued with Rumon Gamba conducting the BBC Philharmonic. Vaughan Williams was nearly 68 years old when he began scoring films, so we have here film music of the highest quality. These scores will also be of special interest to those who are curious about the cross-pollination that occurred between some of them and his later symphonies—for instance, as suggested by the booklet inserts, the music for the *Sinfonia Antarctica* that came from *Scott of the Antarctic*, hints of the Sixth Symphony in the *49th Parallel*, and of the Fifth in *Coastal Command*. In any case, these and the others—*Bitter Springs, The Loves of Joanna Godden, The England of Elizabeth*, and more—are all from the hands of a master. The recordings and performances are superb.

Recommended Recordings

Complete Symphonies, Andre Previn, London SO, RCA 55708 (CDs—now available as MP3s at ArkivMusic)

Complete Symphonies, Leonard Slatkin, Philharmonia Orchestra, RCA 790 2492 (CDs)

Complete Symphonies, Sir Adrian Boult, London PO, Decca 473 2412

Hodie; *Fantasia on Christmas Carols*, David Wilcocks, EMI/Warner 69872 (as an ArkivCD)

Hodie; *Sea Symphony*, Richard Hickox, EMI/Warner 68934

Mass in G Minor, Corydon Singers, Matthew Best (with Howells' Requiem), Helios 55220

Film Music, Chandos 10529 (3)

Heitor Villa-Lobos: Marvelous Mayhem

Charles de Gaulle once said that Brazil is a country of enormous potential—and always will be. The musical analogue of that quip could well be the work of Heitor Villa-Lobos, Brazil's greatest 20th-century composer. Not only did his music portray Brazil as a place of exciting potential, but it promised greatness. Was it ever achieved? Villa-Lobos (1887–1959) was a musical tsunami who left in his wake anywhere from 1,400 to 2,000 works—creative profligacy on a scale not seen since the baroque era. There is something almost childlike in the heedlessness of his musical production.

In 1987, at the time of the centennial of Villa-Lobos' birth, however, there were recordings of only a score of his works available. How could the merits of his achievement possibly be judged on the basis of such a thin slice of his output? That task has become both easier and more difficult due to the profusion of Villa-Lobos recordings that now number in the hundreds (546 CDs on the ArkivMusic web site) and across an ever wider swath of his repertoire. It is easier because there is more to judge; it is more difficult because the picture his works present is considerably more complex than an acquaintance with his few widely popular pieces would lead one to believe.

The general impression from what is now available of his huge body of work is one of marvelous musical mayhem. Pianist Arthur Rubinstein, one of the first to bring Villa-Lobos' work to a wider audience, described his initial encounter with Villa-Lobos during a performance of *Amazonas* in a Rio de Janeiro movie theater. He said of the music, "It was made up of Brazilian rhythms which I easily identified, but they were treated in a completely original way. It sounded confused, formless, but very attractive." It was hard for Rubinstein to discern what was going on because Villa-Lobos' music is a wild amalgamation of Brazilian rhythms, street and folk melodies, baroque and modern musical techniques, and sheer noise. The formlessness that Rubinstein detected was there—at least partially—by design. Villa-Lobos used it to depict nature in a wild inchoate condition, as he experienced it in his youthful explorations of the untamed Brazilian jungle. Nature was sometimes idyllic and serene, sometimes punctuated by outbursts of spasmodic violence, but always teeming with life, including the call of the Araponga bird, the squawking of parrots, the buzzing and whirring of various insects, and other aural exotica. One writer said, "The sensitivity of Villa-Lobos' ear is apparent to those who have experienced the perpetual sound—something between white noise and pandemonium, but always alive—of the rain forest."

Villa-Lobos' father, who died when Heitor was only 12, taught him to play the cello. With his rudimentary education, Villa-Lobos joined the itinerant musicians in the streets and cafés of Rio de Janeiro, occasionally earning enough to help his impoverished mother. He seemed to have a gift for melody and a natural ear for unusual and highly colorful sonorities. Without anyone's permission, he began writing music.

Villa-Lobos was largely self-taught, and the lessons he did take were seldom fruitful. A harmony teacher once tried to tell him how each chord must be resolved. After one chord, Villa-Lobos told him it could be resolved another way. The teacher refused to believe him until the following week, when Villa-Lobos produced a work by Bach that bore out his claim. His teacher responded, "Well, he's another madman like you!" Since Bach was Villa-Lobos' musical god, the compliment could not have been more flattering. It only reinforced his view that the musical academy was not only a waste of time but destructive.

"This is my conservatory", Villa-Lobos once said, pointing to a map of Brazil. Villa-Lobos learned his craft not only by improvising with street and café musicians but by spending several years exploring the interior of Brazil, collecting folk tunes and Indian dance music, and creating outlandish stories for later use in Paris salons. One of the best is that he was captured by cannibals but was able to escape, Orpheus-like, by enchanting the cannibals with his guitar music. Villa-Lobos learned from the musical school of life—his music has dirt under its fingernails.

Aside from the strong Brazilian folkloric streak, the two clearest influences on Villa-Lobos' music are French and Russian. He was exposed to both at Russian Ballet performances, directed by Fokine and Diaghilev, in Rio from 1913 to 1917. At the Russian Ballet, Villa-Lobos first heard the works of Debussy and Stravinsky. The impact of French impressionism can be heard in Villa-Lobos' works of that time, especially his early chamber music, such as the piano trios. Reviewing a Rubinstein performance of Villa-Lobos' *A Próle do Bébé* No. 1, a Rio critic said, "If the program had not told us who the composer was, we might have been tempted to say that here were some unpublished pages of Debussy, written in honor of Brazil."

The influence of Stravinsky is prominent in Villa-Lobos' ballets, such as *Erosão*, *Amazonas*, and *Genesis*, as well as in some of the wilder movements of the *Chôros* and *Bachianas Brasileiras*. Some of Villa-Lobos' music sounds as if he had gotten hold of a giant Stravinsky-machine (of the *Rite of Spring* era) and, without quite knowing what he was doing, began pushing buttons and pulling levers, producing a resounding racket. It is perhaps this hapless, awkward aspect of his work that led to Stravinsky's acerbic remark: "Why is it whenever I hear a bad piece of music it is always by Villa-Lobos?" Despite its obvious influence on him, Villa-Lobos was equally dismissive of Stravinsky's music.

If one were making fun of Villa-Lobos, one might say he sounds at times like a mix of Stravinsky and Xavier Cugat or the *Rite of Spring* danced by Carmen Miranda. The effect, if anything, is original and no less a composer than Olivier Messiaen considered Villa-Lobos a force of nature and the greatest orchestrator of the 20th century. Because of the uneven quality of his huge body of work, one could probably hold all of these views of Villa-Lobos simultaneously. Nonetheless, his best music bursts with life, expressing exuberance, joy, and a wistful melancholy.

No one in Rio knew quite what to make of Villa-Lobos early in his career. Disconcerted by certain gaucheries in his scores that they ascribed to a lack of formal education, his few wealthy patrons shipped him off to France to smooth over the rough edges. Villa-Lobos had an entirely different idea of the purpose of his sabbatical. Upon arrival in Paris, he announced, "I did not come to study with you; I came to show you what I've done." Due to the French love of the exotic, he scored a major success. They were enthralled by his riotous explosions of color and rhythmic drive. The recognition he received in France during this and subsequent stays (from 1923 to 1930) was a springboard for Villa-Lobos' serious consideration as a major talent in Brazil. It is ironic that Brazil, which later embraced him as its quintessential composer, did so only after he gained popularity in another country.

By the time Villa-Lobos returned to Brazil in 1930, he was on his way to becoming a national institution. This became almost literally the case when, under the nationalistic regime of Getúlio Vargas, he became national superintendent of musical education. From that platform, he launched his own pedagogic system to teach the masses choral singing based on Brazilian folk songs. In 1935, in one of several such extraordinary demonstrations, he conducted 30,000 schoolchildren in four-part choral singing in a stadium in Rio.

Even the arduous task of organizing Brazil's musical education system could not staunch the flow of compositions from Villa-Lobos, who said, "My music is natural, like a waterfall." Until his death in 1959, he continued to pour forth works in every genre, producing the 14 famous *Chôros*, nine equally famous *Bachianas Brasileiras* (Villa-Lobos' attempt to demonstrate the natural affinity between Bach's music and Brazilian folk music), 12 long-unknown symphonies, 17 string quartets, numerous other chamber works, many concertos (including five for piano and one for harmonica), operas, ballets, film scores, innumerable piano and guitar works, and songs.

One should begin by listening to Villa-Lobos' most famous works. There are many very successful compilations from both the *Chôros* and the *Bachianas Brasileiras*. These latter nine works, composed over a period of 15 years, are for all kinds of instrumental combinations, including the first for an orchestra of cellos and the very famous and seductive No. 5 for voice and eight cellos. One of the best selections is on an RCA disc from Michael Tilson Thomas and the New World Symphony. It contains exciting renditions of *Bachianas Brasileiras* 4, 5, 7, and 9 and *Chôros* No. 10, with a then young Renée Fleming as the gorgeous soprano voice in No. 5.

Enrique Batiz and the Royal Philharmonic Orchestra have recorded EMI/Warner's *Bachianas Brasileiras* Nos. 1, 5, and 7 (with soprano Barbara Hendricks), a trusty standby that has gone through numerous reissues and re-packagings. The composer himself recorded four Bachianas with Victoria de los Angeles and the ORTF National Orchestra for EMI/Warner in the '50s. The sound is not really satisfactory, but a determined if faded glory comes through.

Still, for anyone committed to Villa-Lobos, the best choice has become the recordings of the Orquesta Sinfônica do Estado de São Paulo (OSESP)—South America's finest orchestra by some margin: the complete *Chôros* and *Bachianas Brasileiras* and then some, on BIS under John Neschling and Roberto Minczuk. The result is lush, colorful expressiveness in state of the art sound. There is also a good budget alternative for the *Bachianas Brasileiras* on Naxos, with the Nashville Symphony Orchestra, under the late Kenneth Schermerhorn, on a three-CD set

A Hyperion/Helios disc is dedicated to Villa-Lobos' instrument, the cello, and features the Pleeth Cello Octet playing, with very invigorating tempos, *Bachianas Brasileiras* Nos. 1 and 5, and a selection of Villa-Lobos' transcriptions of Bach's Préludes and Fugues for a cello orchestra.

These works display Villa-Lobos' exotic evocations of local color but also amply demonstrate that his sensibility was fundamentally romantic. He romanticized the baroque and Bach throughout the *Bachianas Brasileiras*. And no matter what formal designations he gave his compositions, they were essentially suites or fantasias. This is also true of his five piano concertos, available on a budget-priced Decca two-CD set with Cristina Ortiz and the Royal Philharmonic Orchestra, under conductor Miguel Gómez-Martínez. Here Villa-Lobos sounds less like Stravinsky and more like a Brazilian Rachmaninoff. One can also hear the romantic strain in his Cello Concertos that Antonio Menses and the Orquestra Sinfónica de Galicia recorded for Auvidis—and which await reissue. Also out of print, but easy to find, is Robert Bonfiglio's recording of the Harmonica Concerto, which lifts this unusual solo-instrument to inventive heights of beauty and endearing drama, with the New York Chamber Symphony and Gerard Schwarz.

The more raucous side of Villa-Lobos is available on a Marco Polo CD, featuring several ballets—*Genesis, Erosão, Amazonas,* and *Dawn in a Tropical Forest*—bravely played by the Czecho-Slovak Radio Symphony Orchestra under Villa-Lobos specialist Robert Duarte. A very good midpriced recommendation of the boisterous *Chôros* No. 8 and the ballet *Uirapurú* is on Delos, with the Symphony Orchestra of Paraiba under Eleazar de Carvalho. This CD also contains a gorgeous performance of the Fantasia for Cello and Orchestra played by Janos Starker.

Perhaps the least known part of this man's extensive oeuvre are his 12 symphonies. Of course, one must use the term symphony very loosely, as these works are every bit as much fantasias as his other orchestral works. If you are in need of some major orchestral extroversion, go straight to the CPO label's release in its series of complete Heitor Villa-Lobos' symphonies, set down in 1997–2000 by Carl St. Clair and the SWR Radio Symphony Orchestra Stuttgart, with recording premieres of Symphonies 1, 3, 7, 8, 9, 11, and 12. The huge Second Symphony chatters, burbles, and gurgles along in Villa-Lobos' inimitable garrulous style. It may be a gaudy mess but it is marvelously attractive, especially in St. Clair's typically exciting and lucid performance. One might not think that a German orchestra would be a good guide through

Villa-Lobos' musical jungle, but as proven in their excursion through Symphonies 4 and 12, St. Clair and his forces bring clarity, concision, and élan to these inimitably Brazilian works, which is just what they need in performance. The same qualities are evident in the performances of Symphonies 3 and 9; and No. 7 coupled with the Sinfonietta No. 1. If you don't like teeming musical jungles, stay away and just read the guidebooks.

The Koch label beat CPO to the punch with the world premiere recording of Villa-Lobos' Symphony No. 10: *Amerindia*, with the Santa Barbara Orchestra and Choral Society under Gisele Ben-Dor. This is a brave attempt to tame one of the most luxuriant jungle growths Villa-Lobos ever spawned. Symphony No. 10 is a five-part oratorio written for the 400th anniversary of São Paulo, Brazil, in 1952. It employs texts of the Tupi dialect, Portuguese, and Latin in an "allegorical, historical, and religious account of the city". Depending on your tolerance for the exotic, you may dismiss this as an extravagant curiosity or enjoy it as one. It is certainly over the top, even for this musical conjuror.

The São Paulo Orchestra (OSESP) has not only the advantage of idiomatic familiarity, but also that of having access to the partially unpublished scores in their most definitive state. That is already paying dividends in the ongoing cycle of Villa-Lobos symphonies that Naxos is recording under Isaac Karabtchevsky, which shows that, while an uneven body of work, these symphonies are better still than the worthy efforts of CPO.

If anything can change the conventional view of Villa-Lobos, it is his chamber music. I knew there were hidden treasures from having listened to his Quintet for Harp, String Trio, and Flute (1957), which bears a close resemblance to and emerges favorably in comparison with works by Maurice Ravel and Albert Roussel for similar ensembles. (Why isn't this little masterpiece better presented on record?) His *Quinteto em Forma de Chôros* for winds is also a gem. And anyone who thinks of Villa-Lobos as a second-rate Stravinsky of the jungle or an aimless note-spinner has yet to encounter his 17 string quartets. Villa-Lobos was a self-confessed "string quartet addict" and wrote these works throughout his career. It is ironic that, like Shostakovich's quartets, they were among the last part of his work to be recorded, though they contain some of his finest music.

We are beholden to the Danubius Quartet for their pioneering complete cycle for the Marco Polo label and then the Cuarteto Latinoamericano (on Dorian and Brilliant Classics) for further showing off the quality of these works. These compositions demonstrate the quality of Villa-Lobos' musical thinking denuded of the orchestral exotica of his symphonic works. The fertility of invention is extraordinary, especially in the beautifully lyrical and nostalgic slow movements. The quartets are not in conventional sonata form but are more like the "theme and variations" or free-flowing fantasies of Gian Francesco Malipiero in his quartets. The early works show the French impressionist influence, the middle quartets favor the distinctly Brazilian, and the later masterpieces express a spare eloquence all their own. A good starting point is Quartet No. 6: *Quarteto Brasileiro*—and then see if you can resist the rest. It should be apparent that there is more to Villa-Lobos than many suspected.

Recommended Recordings

Alma Brasileira (*Bachianas Brasileiras* 4, 5, 7 & 9; *Chôros* No. 10) Renée Fleming, Michael Tilson Thomas, New World Symphony, RCA Victor Red Seal 68538

Complete Bachianas Brasileiras & Chôros plus Complete Works for Solo Guitar, Anders Miolin (guitar), Cristina Ortiz (piano), John Neschling, Roberto Minczuk, OSESP, BIS 1830

Complete Bachianas Brasileiras, Naxos 8.557460–62

Fantasia for Saxophone, 2 Horns and Strings; Concerto for Guitar; String Quartet No. 6: *Bachianas Brasileiras* 1–3, 5, Various performers, EMI/Warner Classics 94703

Genesis, Erosão, Amazonas, Dawn in a Tropical Forest, Robert Duarte, Czecho-Slovak RSO, Marco Polo 8.223357

Piano Concertos 1–5, Cristina Ortiz, Miguel Gómez-Martinez, Royal PO, Decca Double 430 628-2

Chôros No. 11, Ralf Gothóni (piano), Sakari Oramo, Finnish RSO, Ondine 916

Chôros No. 8 for 2 Pianos and Orchestra; Fantasia for Cello and Orchestra; *Uirapurú*, János Starker (cello), Elizabeth Sawyer & Sonia Muniz (piano), Eleazar de Carvalho, Paraiba SO, Delos 1017

Symphonies 6 & 7 and Symphonies 3 & 4, Isaac Karabtchevsky, OSESP, Naxos 8.573043 and 8.573151

Complete Symphonies, CPO 777 516-2 (7 CDs); Symphonies 3 & 9, CPO 999 712-2

Symphony No. 7 & Sinfonietta No. 1, CPO 999713-2

Symphony No. 10, Koch 3-7488-2 HI

The 17 String Quartets, Cuarteto Latinoamericano, Dorian 90904 (6 CDs) or the bargain label Brilliant Classics (6 CDs)

String Quartets 4, 6, 14, Danubius String Quartet, Marco Polo 8.223391

String Trio & Duos, CPO 999 827-2

The Complete Piano Music, Sonia Rubinsky, Naxos 8.508013. Also available as eight individual volumes

~

Karl Weigl: "The Best of the Viennese Tradition"

Austrian composer Karl Weigl (1881–1949), scion of a prosperous Jewish family, prospered in Vienna. Weigl, who had studied with Alexander Zemlinsky, worked for Gustav Mahler at the Viennese Opera as his rehearsal conductor, an experience Weigl called "the most instructive period of my life". In 1910, he won the coveted Beethoven Prize for his Third String Quartet. In 1922, his eight-part choral work *Hymne* was awarded the prize of the Philadelphia Mendelssohn Club, and in 1924 his symphonic cantata *Weltfeier* won the prize of the City of Vienna. The great conductors and artists of the day played his music—Wilhelm Furtwängler, Bruno Walter, George Szell, Mieczysław Horszowski, the Vienna Philharmonic, and the Busch Quartet. He taught theory and composition at the New Vienna Conservatory and later replaced Hans Gál (see chapter on Gál, p. 115) as lecturer in harmony and counterpoint at the University of Vienna in 1929. His distinguished students included Erich Wolfgang Korngold, Hanns Eisler, Eric Zeisl, and Ernst Bacon. Weigl was not simply a comer; he had arrived.

Some 10 years later, however, he had to flee the Nazi Anschluss. Weigl's renown did not survive his voyage to the United States. He saw it coming. He had penned in his diary in 1937, *Zukunft dunkel* (future bleak). It was; he was practically forgotten, almost permanently. Because, at least until recently, we have inhabited an artistic culture formed by an ideology of progress, we have been loath to consider composers who did not advance in any avant-garde sense, but who chose the derriere-garde, not because they were politically conservative (Weigl was a socialist), but because it didn't occur to them that they had artistically exhausted their tonal means of expression. So Weigl kept using those means right up to the Anschluss, in flight from it, and later in exile. Though he was a refugee, musically speaking Weigl never really left Vienna.

Well before his departure, Weigl had refused to follow his mentor Arnold Schoenberg in his abandonment of tonality. Their close working relationship cooled after Schoenberg embraced his serial system. Rather, Weigl insisted, "As soon as a new form or means of expression is found, any number of fanatics stand up to proclaim the exclusivity of the new art form. . . . One must always repeat the obvious: firstly, conquering new means of expression does not make all former ones obsolete." To prove his point, he went on to write six symphonies, several concertos (for violin, cello, and piano) and eight string quartets.

To his great credit, despite their separate paths, Schoenberg had the generosity to write a letter of recommendation for Weigl in 1938, in which he stated that, "I always considered Dr. Weigl as one of the best composers of the old school; one of those who continued the glittering Viennese tradition. He truly preserves this old culture of musical spirit which represents the best of Viennese tradition." And that is what we hear in abundance in Weigl's Symphony No. 5: *Apocalyptic Symphony*, written in 1945 as a salute to the memory of Franklin Roosevelt. It is steeped in Mahler's spirit and musical idioms, but it also shows his strong kinship with Anton Bruckner and with Weigl's contemporary Franz Schmidt, who had written his own apocalyptic work, *The Book of the Seven Seals*.

Drop the appellation "Apocalyptic" from your expectations in listening to Weigl's symphony, because it is not over the top in the way the title suggests. It is extraordinarily rich and dramatic but within the means of the composers already mentioned. Specific to Weigl are a couple of interesting touches. He begins the symphony with the orchestra tuning up—out from which then blasts a theme from the brass (three trombones and a tuba) on a raised platform—to bring order to the proceedings. I love this touch because, when first exposed to the orchestra as a youth, I thought that the orchestra tuning up was the actual start of the composition I was hearing. Also, Weigl sometimes generates power by compressing his melodies, which then flex themselves to muscle their way out of their confinement. Pressure reaches its release in the rapt Adagio (more than 15 minutes in length) at the heart of the symphony. Brucknerian in its breadth, Mahlerian in its style, this movement contains great music. In its still beauty, it is hard to find a comparison to it other than the sublime Adagietto of Mahler's Fifth Symphony. Weigl did not live long enough to hear it. Leopold Stokowski premiered the work in 1968; gorgeous music like this was his meat. Unfortunately, it was not recorded. I would love to have heard what he did with it. However, Thomas Sanderling and the Berlin Radio Symphony Orchestra sweep us away on a superb BIS recording.

These same artists return in BIS' issue of the Sixth Symphony. The puzzle is that this gorgeous work was ignored for nearly 60 years until the performances that led to this magnificent recording. This rich

40-minute symphony is *echt* Viennese in that it completely inhabits the world from which Weigl had to flee. It sounds like Mahler without the neuroses or a bit like Franz Schmidt in its nobility. Yes, for 1947, it was a bit anachronistic and that, no doubt, is why it lay dormant. Now sleeping beauty has arisen, and you must hear the meltingly lovely Adagio of this masterpiece by a man who clearly earned Schoenberg's appellation as "one of the best composers of the old school".

The Capriccio label has shed light on Weigl's early Viennese years by issuing a CD with his Piano Concerto for left hand and the first of his two Violin Concertos. Lighthearted and generally fanciful, the Piano Concerto was written in 1924 for the one-armed pianist Paul Wittgenstein, who lost his right arm due to a wound in World War I. For some unknown reason, Wittgenstein never performed this attractive work, which was not premiered until 2002 in Vienna by Florian Krumpöck, the pianist on Capriccio's recording with the Norddeutsche Philharmonie Rostock. The long first movement has largely playful interchanges between the soloist and orchestra, culminating in a romantic theme of some nobility. The Adagio bears a more somber mien with some real emotional undertow in the orchestral accompaniment. This short movement moves without break to a closing Rondo allegro that dances away the preceding worries with its breezy high spirits. Weigl was clearly not aiming at the greatness of a major statement with this work, which can be taken for the level of enjoyment and entertainment it offers. In short, it's largely fun music. The solo part shines under Krumpöck's touch, with decent orchestral support under the direction of Manfred Hermann.

The 1928 Violin Concerto, which seems to have been played only once (1930) during Weigl's lifetime, is also a largely playful work, as conservative in style as its piano predecessor, but equally enjoyable with some highly attractive orchestral writing. The Weigl sound world glitters with the instruments serving as so many lights in the night sky. There seems to be an element of phantasy to everything he writes—sometimes of a nearly Mendelssohnian kind. The writing is rich but not overly so. Unlike in Schoenberg's late tonal works, there is no overripeness with the sense of impending decay. Even if old-fashioned, Weigl's work still sounds fresh. There is lightness to its spirit. Violinist David Frühwirth captures most of this, with the support of the same forces as in the Piano Concerto.

For a glimpse of this man's genius in the chamber music domain, listen to the Nimbus Records CD of his String Quartets 1 and 5, played by the Artis Quartett. The First Quartet is almost three-quarters of an hour long and is entirely gripping and lyrically moving. The precocity of Weigl to have written such an accomplished work at age 23 is extraordinary. Schoenberg understood when he wrote to the Rose Quartet: "He [Weigl] has composed a string quartet of extraordinary qualities. . . . I believe this work is, because of its inventiveness and its extraordinarily earnest and well-crafted nature, a decidedly strong example of his talent." These works are of comparable quality to Franz Schmidt's chamber masterpieces and, like them, exhibit no sense of tonal exhaustion.

Weigl's prize-winning String Quartet No. 3 receives a riveting performance by the Artis Quartett, this time on the Orfeo label. The first movement, titled *Innig bewegt* (intimate with movement), is suffused with lilting Viennese charm and warmth—not as if lost in nostalgia but still vibrantly alive. The second movement, *Kraftig bewegt* (powerful with movement), is more forceful with a kind of wild, Gypsy-like dancing. The third movement, *Sehr langsam* (very slow), is the longest of the four and contains some wonderfully eerie, almost spectral writing with the music paring down at times to the beat of one string pulse, as if the heart may stop at any moment. The extraordinary finale, *Stürmisch* (stormy), is a clever and compelling riff on the opening measures of the second movement of Beethoven's Ninth Symphony. Weigl clearly demonstrates their shared language as an unbroken tradition. No wonder it won the Beethoven Prize. This is not musical pastiche but one composer communing with another over the span of a century in a brilliant, thrilling way.

Pablo Casals said, "Karl Weigl's music will not be lost. We will return to it after the storm has passed. We will return to those who have written real music." Well, the storm *has* passed. So, as you will know or learn from listening to these recordings, it is more than time for more Karl Weigl—especially a set of all six symphonies and the complete quartets. A major revival is overdue.

Recommended Recordings

Symphony No. 5: *Apocalyptic* (1945); *Phantastisches* Intermezzo (1921). Rundfunk-Sinfonieorchester Berlin/Thomas Sanderling, BIS CD-1077

Symphony No. 6 (1947); *Old Vienna* (1939), Rundfunk-Sinfonieorchester Berlin/Thomas Sanderling (symphony); Alun Francis (*Old Vienna*), BIS CD-1167

Concerto for Piano (left hand) and Orchestra in E-flat Major

Concerto for Violin and Orchestra in D Major, Norddeutsche Philharmonie Rostock, Manfred Hermann, Capriccio C5232

String Quartet No. 1 (1904); String Quartet No. 5 (1933) Artis Quartett, Nimbus NI 5646

String Quartet No. 3 (1910); Alban Berg, String Quartet, op. 3 & Lyric Suite, Artis Quartett, Orfeo C216 901A

Mieczysław Weinberg: Light in the Dark

When the history of 20th-century music is written in the next several hundred years, will it bear much resemblance to how we think of it now? My encounter with the works of Mieczysław Weinberg (1919–1996) makes me doubt that it will. So much music was ignored or suppressed for aesthetic or political reasons during the 20th century that it will take some time for it to surface and receive a fair hearing. Enterprising record companies, such as Chandos, Naxos, CPO, and Olympia, are in the vanguard of excavating our recent past, and their efforts are already shifting the perspective from which 20th-century music will be judged.

In an extraordinary feat of dedication, Olympia released 16 CDs of Weinberg's music. These discs, many of them Soviet-era recordings of live premiere performances, gave the first substantial representation of Weinberg's enormous output. (Alas, most of them are unfortunately no longer available.) Weinberg composed 26 symphonies (including four chamber symphonies); seven concertos; 17 string quartets; 28 sonatas for piano solo or in combination with violin, viola, cello, double-bass or clarinet; seven operas; several ballets; a large number of song cycles; and incidental music for 65 films; among other works, including a Requiem. One would think the sheer size of his output would command attention. Yet, until fairly recently, Weinberg was absent from every 20th century and contemporary musical reference work I checked and he received a paltry two paragraphs in *Grove's Dictionary of Music and Musicians*, under "Vaynberg". Weinberg's name has variously appeared as: Vainberg, Vaynberg, Vajnberg, Wajnberg, and Weinberg for last names; Moishei, Moishe, Moissei, Moisey (Samuilovich), and Mieczysław for first names. Among the combined 25 possibilities, only one is correct: the Polish Mieczysław Weinberg. What deepens the mystery of this neglect is that a number of his works are masterpieces that belong in any evaluation of 20th-century music. Thanks to the pioneering releases on the Olympia label and a multitude of more recent releases from other labels, a reevaluation has begun.

The story of Weinberg's neglect is a history of the 20th century at its worst, encompassing both the Nazi and the Soviet tyrannies. Weinberg was born in Warsaw, where his father worked as a composer and violinist in a Jewish theater. Mieczysław made his debut in that theater as a pianist at the age of 10. Two years later, he became a pupil at the Warsaw Conservatory. After the Nazi invasion, his entire family was incinerated by the Nazis at the Trawniki camp. He ran the wrong way. As a refugee, Mieczysław fled first to Minsk and then, in advance of the invading Nazi armies, to Tashkent. In 1943, Weinberg sent his First Symphony to Shostakovich, who was so impressed that he arranged to have Weinberg officially invited to Moscow. For the rest of his life, Weinberg remained in Moscow, working as a freelance composer and pianist.

Weinberg was to discover that anti-Semitism was not a Nazi-only specialty. At the 1948 Soviet Composers Union Congress, Andrei Zhandov, Stalin's cultural henchman, attacked "formalism" and "cosmopolitanism", which were code words for Jewish influences. During the meeting, Weinberg received news that his father-in-law, the most famous Jewish actor in the Soviet Union, Solomon Mikhoels, had been murdered (as it was later learned, on direct orders from Stalin). Weinberg, however, who always refused to join the Communist Party, seemed safe and was even praised by the newly elected head of the Composers Union, Tikhon Khrennikov, for depicting "the shining, free working life of the Jewish people in the land of Socialism".

Nonetheless, Weinberg was arrested in January 1953 for "Jewish bourgeois nationalism", on the absurd charge of plotting to set up a Jewish republic in Crimea. This event took place in the midst of the notorious "Doctors' Plot", used by Stalin as a pretext for another anti-Semitic purge. Seven of the nine Kremlin doctors were Jewish. One of them, Miron Vovsi, was the uncle of Weinberg's wife. He was executed. Speaking of Weinberg's arrest, his wife, Natalya, said, "To be arrested in those times meant departure forever." Expecting her own arrest, Natalya arranged for the Shostakoviches to have power of attorney over her seven-year-old daughter so that she would not be sent to an orphanage.

According to Swedish writer Tommy Persson, who personally knew the composer, Weinberg thought he was going to be shot soon after his arrest. In minus 22 degrees, he was taken outside in only his prison garb and shorn of all his hair. He was interrogated and allowed no sleep between 11:00 P.M. and 6:00 A.M. In an act of great courage, Shostakovich sent a letter to the chief of the NKVD (the predecessor to the KGB), Lavrenti Beriya, protesting Weinberg's innocence. But it was only Stalin's death in March of that year that opened the prison gates for Weinberg and many others. To celebrate his release, the Shostakoviches and the Weinbergs held a dinner party at which they burned the power-of-attorney papers.

These events are worth recounting in detail because of the attitude Weinberg took toward them, which is in turn reflected in his music. He seemed to regard his imprisonment with some diffidence. Of the Stalinist peril, he said, "It wasn't a sword of Damocles, because they hardly locked up any composers—well, except me—and they didn't shoot any either. I really can't claim, as other composers do, that I have been persecuted." Weinberg must have possessed an extraordinary spiritual equanimity to say such a thing. His only complaint was that "those in power did nothing to popularize my works." Indeed, the musical establishment largely ignored him.

What sort of music does one write in the face of the horrors of Nazi genocide, World War II, and the Gulag, especially if one has been victimized by all three? In his December 19, 1999, article reflecting on 20th-century music after the war, *New York Times* writer Paul Griffiths opined that "since what had recently happened was inexpressible, the only appropriate course was to express nothing." And indeed that was the course chosen by many composers in their increasingly violent and abstract works. The more repugnant the world, the more abstract the art. The only problem with this approach is that the art it produces is itself repugnant because it is inhuman. Weinberg chose another course. It was neither one of denial, nor one of submission to the Soviet mandate to write happy factory worker music. He said, "Many of my works are related to the theme of war. This, alas, was not my own choice. It was dictated by my fate, by the tragic fate of my relatives. I regard it as my moral duty to write about the war, about the horrors that befell mankind in our century."

Yet Weinberg was able to address these issues with the same spiritual equanimity with which he regarded his imprisonment. Though his music is certainly passionate, he seems to have been able to recollect the most horrible things in tranquility. Since little is known about Weinberg (though there is a biography in preparation), it can only be a guess as to how he was able to do this. In conversation with Tommy Persson, I was told, "Weinberg could always see the bright light in dark circumstances." What was the source of this perspective? Much is revealed in a remark from an interview Weinberg gave after the collapse of the Soviet Union: "I said to myself that God is everywhere. Since my First Symphony, a sort of chorale has been wandering around within me." If "God is everywhere", then there is still something to say. Weinberg found the means to say it in music of great passion, poignancy, power, beauty, and even peace.

Weinberg's musical language may be another reason for his neglect. He frequently sounds exactly like Shostakovich, and that similarity will be the first thing likely to strike any listener. Weinberg embraced the similarity, declaring unabashedly, "I am a pupil of Shostakovich. Although I never took lessons from him, I count myself as his pupil, his flesh and blood." In turn, Shostakovich called Weinberg "one of the most outstanding composers of the present day". Shared stylistic traits are immediately recognizable in the frequent deployment of high string and horn registers, and the sometimes obsessive use of themes. Like Shostakovich, Weinberg wrote open, expansive music of big gestures and extraordinarily long-lined melodies. Both composers were symphonists in the classical tradition who wrote essentially tonal music.

Though ridiculed as "a little Shostakovich", Weinberg actually was sometimes the one influencing Shostakovich, rather than the other way around. Weinberg seems to have been the primary source of the Jewish musical influences in Shostakovich's works, most certainly in Shostakovich's song cycle, *From Jewish Folk Poetry*. And who was influencing whom in 1962–1963, when Shostakovich composed the Thirteenth Symphony (*Babi Yar*), about Nazi atrocities against Soviet Jews, and Weinberg wrote his Sixth Symphony memorializing the execution of Jewish children? So close were the two composers that they observed a steadfast practice of playing for each other each new work as soon as it was finished. Also, each composer, in tribute, liberally quoted the other's works.

However, there are defining differences. Weinberg wrote with irony (and sometimes even humor), but without Shostakovich's sardonic bombast and cutting edge. He held his musical onslaughts more in check. Weinberg's music can be very turbulent and bleak, but the bleakness and turbulence are not unremitting. They are, in fact, relieved by a fundamental optimism in Weinberg's outlook that clearly differentiates him from Shostakovich. The frequent diminuendos with which Weinberg ends his works do not signify resignation or death, but peace. Weinberg wore his heart more on his sleeve; he was more a romantic than was Shostakovich. As a result, his writing is more florid, though his symphonic structures remained more classical. In his later years, Weinberg's music, as evident from his last several chamber symphonies, even increased in lyrical beauty and contemplative value.

The similarities with Shostakovich may also cause one to overlook Weinberg's own significant melodic gift and his extraordinary ability to develop his themes, which cannot be the product of imitation. Weinberg knew how to take a simple idea and build it into a major edifice. There is also the matter of his remarkable fluency. Weinberg's music seems to burst forth from such an abundance of ideas that one can only assume that music was his natural language. Speaking of Weinberg, Russian composer Boris Tishchenko said, "The music seems to flow by itself, without the slightest effort on his part." This fluency, said Tishchenko, allowed Weinberg "to make a 'game' of music making. But even so, this 'game' never becomes simply amusement. In every composition one can hear his pure voice, the voice of the artist, whose main goal is to speak out in defense of life."

In *Grove's*, Boris Schwarz calls Weinberg a "conservative modernist". The reverse would be more accurate. In musical idiom, he was a modern conservative. Besides Shostakovich, other palpable influences are Prokofiev, Stravinsky, and most especially Mahler. Weinberg worked with traditional harmonic and tonal expectations and rarely failed to meet them in satisfying and novel ways. He could sustain a sense of expectancy over long spans of time with vast melodic and contrapuntal structures.

The symphonies are often masterful in their thematic coherence. The whole of Symphony No. 19, for example, is developed out of its gorgeous opening theme over the course of more than half an hour. Although the symphony is subtitled *The Bright May* and has extra-musical associations with the end of the war, it is musically satisfying in the profoundest way. Weinberg's music is also highly variegated, encompassing calliope music, circus marches, Jewish and Moldavian folk song and dance, Shostakovich-like onslaughts, and extremely moving Malherian adagios.

Weinberg's natural musicality is expressed in everything he wrote. He used all the conventional forms—symphony, string quartet, piano sonata, etc., but imbued them with a heartfelt directness and expressive power. If music is a language, one can always hear Weinberg speaking —*cor ad cor*, sometimes of difficult things, but always with an enduring human spirit. Having seen some of the worst things the 20th century had to offer in its totalitarian brutality, Weinberg did not look away, but he also looked up—which makes all the difference.

Chandos has issued recordings of Symphonies 1 and 7, played by the Gothenburg Symphony Orchestra under Thord Svedlund. As far as I can tell, the First Symphony is a recording premiere, while the Seventh Symphony has had only one prior release with its dedicatee, Rudolph Barshai, at the helm of the Moscow Chamber Orchestra. However passionate and superbly played, Barshai's effort was compromised by Soviet recording engineers in somewhat harsh and cavernous 1967 sound. The Chandos Super Audio CD has some of the best orchestral sound I have heard. The richness and detail are superb. Audio-wise, it does not get better than this.

But it is the performance that really matters, and the Gothenburg Symphony Orchestra excels. It is not their first excursion into Weinberg territory. Earlier, Gothenburg and Svedlund gave us one of the very best Weinberg discs featuring four different concertos (two for flute, and one each for cello and clarinet) also on Chandos. The Fantasia for Cello and Orchestra has a drop-dead gorgeous melody, cloaked with a touching nostalgia. When you listen to it, you will wonder how something this beautiful could only recently have received a recording. The one possible excuse is the enormous amount of music this man composed. The two flute concertos on this CD are delightful and sprightly. The Clarinet Concerto was apparently inspired by Carl Nielsen's music and, to its advantage, sounds like it. These four works are among Weinberg's most immediately attractive. The soloists and the orchestra, under Svedlund, are given thoroughly realistic, highly transparent recordings.

The First Symphony is very much under the influence of Shostakovich and especially Prokofiev in the first movement. It was this composition that Weinberg sent to Shostakovich in Moscow. By the Seventh Symphony certainly, no doubt remains that Weinberg was his own man, and his style is immediately recognizable. The Seventh is a fascinating, highly imaginative work for harpsichord and strings that displays Weinberg's trademark mastery of contrapuntal writing, his subtlety in deploying forces, his gripping intensity, and keening lyricism. Svedlund takes three minutes more than Barshai with this music. What he gives up in urgency, he gains in marvelous transparency and range of expression. I was more alarmed by the music under Barshai; I am moved by it under Svedlund. The playing by the Gothenburg members is dazzling. This may now be the single best CD in the Weinberg symphony series.

The Symphony No. 2, for strings alone, written in 1945–1946, should serve as fair warning to those who wish to tie this composer's work to his biography. In the wake of the war's devastation, Weinberg produced a meltingly lovely, thoroughly charming, and relatively untroubled work. Over 40 years later, Weinberg added timpani to strings to produce his Chamber Symphony No. 2, another completely beguiling, classically oriented, if somewhat more weighty work. These are entrancing pieces offered on the Alto label.

The Chandos label also offers the premiere recording of Weinberg's Symphony No. 3, along with a suite from his ballet *The Golden Key*. The Third Symphony is an atypical work for Weinberg in that it shows almost no influence from Shostakovich, carries no angst within it, and is wonderfully melodious and pleasant throughout. Certain sections of it have a kind of almost insouciant breeziness to them, such as often found in the music of Malcolm Arnold. It is brilliantly played by the Gothenburg Symphony Orchestra under Thor Svedlund.

Symphony No. 4 has immense propulsive drive, an engaging telegraphic theme, and wistful Stravinskian interludes. It is coupled with a violin concerto of the first rank, op. 67, charged with breathtaking vitality. Shostakovich said, "I remain very impressed with the Violin Concerto by M. S. Weinberg. . . . It is a fabulous work. And I choose my words advisedly." With its affirmative power and irresistible drive from the first percussion crack of the Allegro molto to the last diminishing violin chord (ushered out by the horns in *triple-pianissimo*), it should become a repertoire piece. Though the Soviet-era recordings by the Moscow Philharmonic Orchestra, conducted by Kirill Kondrashin, with violinist Leonid Kogan for whom it was written (alas, no longer available), leave something to be desired sound-wise, the quality of this music and the outstanding performances are thoroughly winning. If you are not engaged by these works, you need proceed no further. Fortunately, the Chandos label has released an excellent new recording of the Symphony No. 4 by the National Polish Radio Symphony Orchestra under Gabriel Chmura. And also, there is a recording of the Violin Concerto on Naxos, with violinist Ilya Grubert and the Russian Philharmonic Orchestra led by Dmitry Yablonsky.

Of Weinberg's Sixth Symphony, Shostakovich exclaimed, "I wish I could sign my name to this symphony." This is the work through which I first became acquainted with Weinberg on a deleted Jerusalem Records CD, appropriately coupled with Shostakovich's *From Jewish Folk Poetry* (curiously, the two works share the same opus number, op. 79). It begins with a hauntingly beautiful horn theme, which develops and recurs throughout. Several of its movements include a children's choir. Despite its gruesome subject matter, the murder of Jewish children, this ultimately affirmative work is a moving example of Weinberg's ability to recollect in tranquility. Only someone secure in faith and hope could treat this agonizing subject matter in this way. The closing line of the text is: "There will be sunshine again and the violins will sing of peace on earth." Naxos has issued a splendid new recording of Weinberg's Symphony No. 6, with the St. Petersburg State Symphony Orchestra under Vladimir Lande.

The Symphony No. 12, dedicated to the memory of Shostakovich, is a poundingly ferocious and poignant piece. It is magnificent music but not for the faint of heart. The remarkable first movement, close to 20 minutes long, exhibits Weinberg's ability to move seamlessly from angry outbursts to lyrical introspection. This stunning work can be heard on Naxos with Linde et al.

Symphony No. 19: *The Bright May* is music of a man who more than simply survived and who did not return empty-handed from the hell through which he lived. An incredibly long and elegiac melodic line of great beauty begins and almost continuously winds its way through this single-movement masterpiece, which ends in a most poignant way. *May* may be bright, but it is also haunted. Along with the Sixth Symphony, this is perhaps Weinberg's most moving work; he certainly wrote nothing more beautiful.

The Naxos label delivers the premiere recording of Weinberg's Concertino for Violin and String Orchestra, op. 42 (1948). This 20-minute work is an absolute charmer and displays Weinberg's ability to create insinuating or, perhaps I should say, ingratiating melodies. It is accompanied by two fairly forgettable late 19th-century Russian violin concertos by Julius Conus and Anton Arensky. Don't worry—the bittersweet Concertino is worth the price of the disc.

To sample how wonderful Weinberg's chamber music is, go to the Naxos disc featuring cellist Dmitry Yablonsky and pianist Hsin-Ni Liu in the Cello Sonatas 1 and 2, and Solo Cello Sonatas 1 and 3. Two of these four works were written for Mstislav Rostropovich, who compared Weinberg's four Sonatas for Solo Cello with the Cello Suites of Bach. The melancholy First Cello Sonata is redolent of Shostakovich and of comparable quality. It is riveting and deeply moving. Weinberg sings his soul out in the solo cello pieces, which deserve Rostropovich's accolade. The Allegro of the First Solo Cello Sonata is viscerally engaging. Anyone who cares about Russian/Polish music in the 20th century—or simply about great chamber music—should grab this bargain CD.

The Piano Quintet demonstrates Weinberg's prowess with chamber music and almost equals in brilliance and vitality Shostakovich's great Piano Quintet. Weinberg's Piano Quintet and String Quartet No. 8 have been rereleased on Melodiya (Borodin Quartet, with the composer himself at the piano), offering what must be considered a definitive interpretation of the quintet. However, a thoroughly good and gripping modern account from the ARC Ensemble is available from RCA Red Seal, along with the Sonata for Clarinet and Piano.

Weinberg and Shostakovich had a game to see who could write the most quartets. Weinberg won with 17. His cycle is comparable in quality to Shostakovich's, which is saying a great deal because Shostakovich's quartets are his best music. The CPO label has recorded a complete traversal of the quartets with the Quatuor Danel. The first two volumes offer Nos. 4 and 16, and Nos. 7, 11, and 13. Volume 3 contains 6, 8, and 15. This is intimate, very private music, ineffably sad in places and sweet in others. In any case, this is not easy music: the quartets are Weinberg's diary of the soul through times of harrowing sorrow and suffering, including the Stalin years through which he lived. There is a great quality of interiority to this music. It constitutes a significant part of Weinberg's spiritual testament. It can be searing; it can be heartbreaking in its attempts at gaiety, with its sad little dances; it is at all times truthful, with beauty never far away. The Danel Quartet delves deeply into this inwardness and captures its intimacy. If you appreciate the Shostakovich quartets, you must try these.

Volume 4 is every bit as fine as its predecessors. Quartets 5, 9, and 14 contain some ruminative, somewhat subdued, introspective music, but it is never that far from an exposed nerve. The level of the performances and the sonics continue CPO's impeccable standards, as does volume 5, which contains Quartets 1, 3, 10, and the short Capriccio, op. 11, and Aria, op. 9.

CPO has also begun a cycle of Weinberg's Violin Sonatas, volume 1 containing Nos. 4 and 5, and *Three Pieces for Violin and Piano*. Like most of Weinberg's music, there is a marvelous feeling of spontaneity to these works, beautifully captured by violinist Stefan Kirpal and pianist Andreas Kirpal. These pieces lament, sing, and dance. They are, in turns, deeply ruminative and wildly passionate. Toccata Classics has also entered the lists with its volume 1 of the Complete Violin Sonatas, with only one overlapping piece in its first issue. The overlap is with Sonata No. 4, which the Toccata artists, violinist Yuri Kalnits and pianist Michael Csanyi-Wils, play with such searing intensity that it is almost another piece. It is accompanied by Sonata No. 1, the Sonatina for Violin and Piano, op. 46, and the Sonata No. 1 for Violin Solo, op. 82. Kalnits plays the latter with dizzying, breathtaking brilliance, completely at the service of this profound excursion into the cross section of sound and the human soul. You must hear this.

The Neos label has issued a two-CD set of Weinberg's complete Sonatas for Viola Solo and Sonata, op. 28, in a version for viola and piano. These are very spare, concentrated works with minimum surface appeal and a lot of substance. This is music nearing the metaphysical, and violist Julia Rebekka Adler plays it with complete conviction. Not for the newcomer then, but a must for the initiate and for those who wonder what Bach would have done if he had lived in the Soviet Union. Tommy Persson, a longtime friend of Weinberg, responded to this CD with much praise: "I'm simply overwhelmed by [her] very brilliant playing and great understanding of Weinberg's music . . . a most important contribution to the growing Weinberg discography."

Naxos has reissued two Olympia CDs of Weinberg's complete music for solo cello: *Twenty-Four Preludes*, op. 100, and Solo Cello Sonatas 1, 2, 3, and 4, with cellist Josef Feigelson. The touchstone for the sonatas for solo cello is obviously Bach's work in the genre. Weinberg calls upon that tradition and enriches it. These works are even more redolent of Bach than the Viola Sonatas, and have the advantage of the cello's full, burnished sound. They are perhaps more immediately attractive than the solo viola music, but require just as much concentration. I think only great composers try to write music this spare and this deep. These are the world premiere recordings. It would be safe to consider Feigelson's performances as definitive.

In a welcome sign that the years of neglect are over, Claves issued wonderful performances of Chamber Symphonies 1, 3, and 4, with the Chamber Orchestra Kremlin. These works from the last decade of Weinberg's life are serenely beautiful. They have some of the marvelous breeziness of the best 20th-century British neoclassical string music from the likes of Benjamin Britten and others. This CD is a joy.

The lovely *Children's Notebooks* for piano proves that Weinberg was a master miniaturist as well as a great symphonist. His abundant charm and humor are evident here. All of his piano music has been gathered on three CDs, containing a number of world premiere recordings, on the Grand Piano label. The artist is Allison Brewster Franzetti, who plays with a finely shaded, exquisite touch in a broad range of expression. She especially captures the playful pieces and their occasional childlike innocence. She knows how to play the more wistful music as if it were by Eric Satie.

After a life of much pain, Weinberg spent his last several years in bed suffering from Crohn's disease. A month before he died in 1996, he was baptized in the Russian Orthodox Church, one final act by a man who could always see "the bright light in dark circumstances".

Recommended Recordings

Symphonies 1 & 7, Chandos 5078

Symphony No. 3; Suite No. 4 from *The Golden Key*, Chandos 5089

Symphony No. 5 and Sinfonietta No. 1—Chandos 10128

Symphony No. 6; *Rhapsody on Moldavian Themes*, Naxos 8. 572779

Symphony No. 8, *Polish Flowers*, Naxos 8.572873

Symphonies 4 & 6, Moscow PO, conducted by Kirill Kondrashin, Melodiya 1000986

Symphony No. 12 & Flute Concerto, Moscow Chamber Orchestra, under Rudolf Barshai & USSR TV & RSO, under Maxim Shostakovich, Russian Disc Symphonies 14 & 16, Chandos 10334

Symphony No. 19, *The Bright May* and *Banners of Peace*, St. Petersburg State SO, Vladimir Lande, Naxos 8.572752

Symphony No. 4 & Violin Concerto in G Minor, Moscow PO, conducted by Kirill Kondrashin, with Leonid Kogan (violin), Olympia 622

Concerto for Violin, op. 67 (with the Mayaskovsky Violin Concerto), Naxos 8.557194

Russian Violin Concertos (Weinberg Concertino for violin and string orchestra), Naxos 8.572631

Chamber Symphonies 1 & 4, Umea SO, conducted by Thord Svedlund, Alto Musical Concepts 1036

Symphony No. 2 & Chamber Symphony No. 2; Umea SO, conducted by Thord Svedlund, Alto Musical Concepts 1037

Chamber Symphonies 1, 3, & 4, Chamber Orchestra Kremlin, conducted by Misha Rachlevsky, Claves 9811

Fantasia for Cello and Orchestra; Concertos 1 & 2 for Flute and Orchestra; Concerto for Clarinet and String Orchestra, Chandos 5064

Piano Quintet & Quartet No. 12, Borodin String Quartet, with M. Weinberg (piano), Melodiya 1001998

Piano Quintet; Sonata for Clarinet and Piano; *Jewish Songs after Shmuel Halkin*, RCA Red Seal 87769

Cello Sonatas 1 & 2 (with Boris Tchaikovsky's Cello Sonata), Alla Vasilieva (cello) & M. Weinberg (piano), Russian Disc 11 026

Violin Sonatas 1 & 4; Sonatina; Sonata for Solo Violin No. 1, Toccata Classics 0007

Complete Music for Solo Cello, vols. 1 & 2, Naxos 8.572280; 8.572281

Complete Sonatas for Viola Solo, Neos 11008/09

Quartets 1, 3, & 10; *Aria for String Quartet*; *Capriccio for String Quartet*, CPO 777 566

Quartets 4 & 16, CPO 777 313

Quartets 7, 11, & 1, CPO 777 392

Quartets 2, 12, & 17, CPO 777 587

Quartets 6, 8, & 15, CPO 777 393

Quartets 5, 9, & 14, CPO 777 394

Complete Piano Works, vols. 1–3, Grand Piano GP 603; GP 607; GP 610

Recovering the Sacred in Music

The attempted suicide of Western classical music has failed. The patient is recovering, no thanks to the efforts of music's Dr. Kevorkian, Arnold Schoenberg, whose cure, the imposition of a totalitarian atonality, was worse than the disease—the supposed exhaustion of the tonal resources of music. Schoenberg's vaunted mission to "emancipate dissonance" by denying that tonality exists in Nature led to the successive losses of tonality, melody, harmony, and rhythm.

Music went out of the realm of Nature and into abstract, ideological systems. Thus we were given a secondhand or ersatz reality in music that operated according to its own self-invented and independent rules divorced from the very nature of sound. Not surprisingly, these systems, including Schoenberg's 12-tone method of mandatory atonality, broke down. The systematic fragmentation of music was the logical working out of the premise that music is not governed by mathematical relationships and laws that inhere in the structure of a hierarchical and ordered universe, but is wholly constructed by man and therefore essentially without limits or definition.

Sound familiar? All the symptoms of the 20th century's spiritual sickness are present, including the major one diagnosed by Eric Voegelin as "a loss of reality". By the 1950s Schoenberg's doctrines were so entrenched in the academy, the concert hall, and the awards system, that any composer who chose to write tonal music was consigned to oblivion by the musical establishment. One such composer, Robert Muczynski, referred to this period as the "long-term tyranny which has brought contemporary music to its current state of constipation and paralysis".

The tyranny is now gone and tonality is back. But the restoration of reality has not taken place all at once. What began emerging from under the rubble of 12-tone music back in the 1960s was minimalism. In it, tonality returned with a vengeance but was, at first, more like a patient from a trauma ward gradually recovering consciousness. The traumatized patient slowly comes out of a coma, only gradually recovering motor skills, coordination, movement, and coherent speech. The musical movement known as minimalism is the sometimes painfully slow rediscovery of the basic vocabulary of music: rhythm, melody, and harmony. During this convalescence, such minimalists as American composer John Adams have spoken of the crisis through which they passed in explicitly spiritual terms. He said, "I learned in college that tonality died, somewhere around the time that Nietzsche's God died. And, I believed it." His recovery involved a shock: "When you make a dogmatic decision like that early in your life, it takes some kind of powerful experience to undo it." That experience, for Adams and others, has proven to be a spiritual, and sometimes religious, one. In fact, the early excitement over minimalism has been eclipsed by the attention now being paid to the new spirituality in music, sometimes referred to as "mystical minimalism".

If you have heard of the "new spirituality" in music, it is most likely on account of one of these three somewhat unlikely composers who have met with astonishing success over the past several decades: the late Henryk Górecki from Poland, Arvo Pärt from Estonia, and the late John Tavener from England. Though their styles are very unlike, they do share some striking similarities: they, like John Adams, all once composed under the spell of Schoenberg's 12-tone method and were considered in the avant-garde; all subsequently renounced it (as Pärt said, "The sterile democracy between the notes has killed in us every lively feeling"); and all are, or were, devout Christians, two of them having converted to the Russian Orthodox faith, the other having adhered to his Catholic faith throughout his life.

Anyone who has tracked the self-destruction of music over the past half century has to be astonished at the outpouring of such explicitly religious music and at its enormously popular reception. Can the recovery of music be, at least partially, a product of faith, in fact of Christian faith? A short time ago, such a question would have produced snickers in the concert hall, howls in the academy, and guffaws among the critics. In fact, it still might. In a *New York Times* review, a critic condescended to call the works of the three composers nothing but "Feel-Good Mysticism". However, the possibility gains some plausibility when one looks back at the source of the problem in Schoenberg himself and to a mysterious episode that brought what he thought would be his greatest achievement to a creative halt.

Though one of the greatest compositional talents of the 20th century, Schoenberg fell silent before he could finish the opera *Moses und Aron*. It is not as if he ran out of time. The first two acts were finished in the early 1930s. Before he died in 1951 at the age of 76, he had close to 20 years to write the third and final act. He tried four different times to no avail. His failure is particularly ironic because Schoenberg saw himself as the musical Moses of the 20th century. *Moses und Aron* was to be the tablets on which he wrote the new commandments of music. He was saving music with his new system of serialism. But, like the Moses he portrays at the end of the second act, he despaired of ever being able to explain his salvific mission to his people. As Moses falls to the ground, he exclaims: "O word, thou word that I lack."

Schoenberg wandered in and out of his Jewish faith, with a side trip through Lutheranism. He saw no need to be scripturally faithful in his libretto for the opera, so it is all the more curious that he was stymied by what he called "some almost incomprehensible contradictions in the Bible". More specifically, he said, "It is difficult to get over the divergence between 'and thou shalt smite the rock' and 'speak ye unto the rock.' . . . It does go on haunting me." Schoenberg was troubled by the question: Why was Moses, when leading the Jews through the Sinai, punished for striking the rock a second time? The first time Moses struck the rock, water poured forth. The second time, God said to Moses, "Speak to the rock." But Moses impetuously struck it instead. For that, he was banned from ever entering the Promised Land. Why? That unanswered question left Schoenberg with an unfinished opera.

As it turned out, Schoenberg was not the Moses of music. He led his followers into, rather than out of, the desert. However, the silence into which Schoenberg fell before the end of *Moses und Aron* has now been filled. And the music filling it is written by Christian composers who have found the answer to the question that so tortured him. The answer is in the New Testament. The rock could not be struck a second time because, as St. Paul tell us, "The rock was Christ", and Christ can be struck down only once, "once and for all", a sole act sufficient for the salvation of all mankind.

Pärt completely believes, and Górecki and Tavener believed, in the salvific act of Christ, centered their lives upon it, and expressed it in their music. They also shared a preliminary disposition necessary for the reception of this belief. During a trip to Washington, D.C., in the early 1990s, Górecki was asked to comment on the phenomenal success of his *Symphony of Sorrowful Songs*, the Nonesuch recording of which sold more than 800,000 copies. Górecki responded, "Let's be quiet." Perhaps that is the most urgent message of all three composers, "Be quiet." Or perhaps more biblically, "Be still." This stillness is not the empty silence at the end of the second act of *Moses und Aron*. It is a full, gestational silence that allows one, like Moses, to hear the remaining words: "And know that I am God."

This profound sense of silence permeates the works of the three composers. Some of their compositions emerge from the very edge of audibility and remain barely above it, conveying the impression that there is something in the silence that is now being revealed before once again slipping out of range. The deep underlying silence slowly surfaces and lets itself be heard. For those precious moments one hears what the silence has to say. When not used in this way, a grammar of silence is nonetheless employed that punctuates even the more extrovert and vociferous works. Moments of silence stand like sentinels, guarding the inner stillness from the violence of sounds that have not come out of the silence.

Another shared feature of the music of these composers is its sense of stasis. Every critic has noted this feature and some complain about it: "Nothing happens!" Pärt, Górecki, and Tavener do not employ the traditional Western means of musical development. They have found the sonata principle of development that has driven music since the 18th century, and which gives music so much of its sense of forward motion, extraneous for their purpose. Their purpose is contemplation, specifically the contemplation of religious truths. Their music is hieratic. As such, it aims for the intersection of time and timelessness, at which point the transcendent becomes perceptible. As Pärt states, "That is my goal. Time and timelessness are connected." This sense of stasis is conveyed through the use of silence; consistently slow tempos (that make any temporary quickening particularly dramatic); the use of repetition and through the intensification this repetition implies; and a simplicity of means that includes medieval plainsong and organum. (As Pärt says, "It is enough when a single note is beautifully played.")

Repetition can be used as an adornment or a means of meditation, as it was in medieval and Renaissance music. Some of the hymns to Mary that endlessly repeat her name are a form of musical caress. They create a musical cradle in which to hold her name. With these composers, repetition of musical phrases, words, or both is also used as a means of recovery. The repeated invocation is all the more insistent when there is a sense of loss and devastation. In his *Beatus Vir*, Górecki cries out

unconsolingly, almost angrily: "Domine!" Where is God in the midst
of the horror? The almost grating insistence with which "Domine" is
repeated moves from a sense of despair to one of assertion and then
finally to consolation and release. The repetition is exorcistic.

Because of the predominance of these characteristics in the work of
Górecki, Pärt, and Tavener, and their hearkening back to earlier periods of music, they are accused of being reactionary, if not archaic.
However, their work is not a form of cultural nostalgia. Their change
in technique is not an attempt at a new or an old means of expression.
Their technique changed because they have something profound to
express. As Thomas Merton once remarked, the perfection of 12th-
century Cistercian architecture was reached not because the Cistercians
were looking for new techniques, but because they were looking for
God. Górecki, Pärt, and Tavener are looking for God, and they have
found a musical epiphany in the pursuit.

Aside from these shared traits, Górecki, Pärt, and Tavener are quite
unlike in the sounds they create. Curiously, Pärt, the Russian Orthodox Estonian composer, uses Western Latin idioms from the Roman
Catholic Church, while the Western English composer, Tavener, uses
the exotic Russian Orthodox idioms hailing from Byzantium. Górecki,
the Pole, stayed right where he was, in the middle, using earlier modes
of Western liturgical music but staying fairly mainstream. He sounds
the least exotic of the three.

Górecki (1933–2010) was also the toughest of the three composers
and the most modern in his musical vocabulary, though he was considered a conservative reactionary by his erstwhile colleagues in the
European avant-garde. (He said that leading modernist Pierre Boulez
was "unbelievably angry" about his music.) Though at times harsh for
expressive purposes, Górecki's music is never hysterical, like so much
modern music that reflects the horror of the 20th century without the
perspective of faith. He could look at suffering unblinkingly because
Christianity does not reject or deny suffering but subsumes it under
the Cross. At the heart of the most grief-stricken moments of his work,
there is a confidence that can come only from deep belief. When asked
from where he got his courage to resist Communist pressure, Górecki
said, "God gave me a backbone—it's twisted now, but still sturdy. . . .
How good a Catholic I am I do not know; God will judge that, and I
will find out after I die. But faith for me is everything. If I did not have
that kind of support, I could not have passed the obstacles in my life."

Górecki did not shrink from facing the nightmare through which his country and the 20th century have gone. Poland was trampled by both of the destructive ideologies of our time, Nazism and Communism. The moving consolation his works offer comes after real and harrowing grief. (Can someone really refer to this as "Feel-Good Mysticism"?) One can recover from a loss only if one grieves over it, and, yes, expresses anger over it as well. The anger is heard in *Beatus Vir*, as mentioned above. This piece is dedicated to the late Pope John Paul II, who commissioned it when he was still the cardinal archbishop of Kraków. One of the most extraordinary expressions of grief is Górecki's Symphony No. 3 for soprano and orchestra: *Symphony of Sorrowful Songs*. It is a huge, arching, heart-breaking lament, written in 1976. Its three texts are on the theme of grieving motherhood. The first movement, based on Mary's lament at the Cross, is a slow-moving extended canon for strings that unfolds in a moving, impassioned crescendo over the course of nearly half an hour. The central text is a prayer to Mary inscribed by an eighteen-year-old girl on the wall of her cell in the basement of Gestapo headquarters in Zakopane, Poland, September 1944. It includes the admonition: "No Mother, do not weep." Though Górecki drew on Polish folk song, the appeal of this deeply affecting musical requiem can be felt by anyone for whom these themes resonate. This one work gathers up the whole tragedy of Poland in the 20th century and places it before Mary, standing at the Cross.

Another piece written with the same basic architectural structure as the first part of Symphony No. 3 is *Miserere*. Górecki wrote it as a protest over the bludgeoning of members of Solidarity by the militia in 1981, shortly before the declaration of martial law. But, in this work, unlike in *Beatus Vir*, one cannot hear the protest. Its text is: "Domine Deus noster, Miserere nobis." The Lord's name is at first gently, then with growing strength, and finally expectantly invoked for nearly half an hour. The words, "Miserere nobis", are not heard until the final three minutes. Rather than a crescendo, they are presented, to moving effect, diminuendo. Mercy arrives with tender gentleness. *Miserere* is a beautiful work of affirmation and consolation.

Though writing in a thoroughly accessible idiom, Arvo Pärt (b. 1935) is not an "easy listen". His work emerges from deep spiritual discipline and experience, and demands (and gives) as much in return. One will not be washed away in sonorous wafts of highly emotional music—there is no effortless epiphany here. Pärt is the most formally austere of the three, but is also the one with the most ontological sense —he presents a note as if it were being heard for the first time. Even more than the other two, his work is steeped in silence. When he abandoned the modernism of his earlier work, he retreated to a Russian Orthodox monastery for several years of silence. When he emerged, he began writing music of extraordinary purity and simplicity, using medieval and Renaissance techniques. Pärt's music comes out of the fullness of silence. "How can one fill the time with notes worthy of the preceding silence?" he asks. During a rehearsal of his composition *The Beatitudes*, Pärt told the conductor, "The silence must be longer. This music is about the silence. The sounds are there to surround the silence." The puzzled conductor asked Pärt, "Exactly how many beats? What do you do during the silence?" Pärt responded, "You don't *do* anything. You wait. *God* does it."

The closer to the source of silence out of which it comes, the closer his music is to being frightening—or awesome, in the original sense of the word—and heart-breakingly beautiful. Pärt appropriately chose the Gospel of John, the most metaphysical of the Gospels, for the text of his *Passio*. "In the beginning", begins St. John. This feel for ontology, for creation close to its source in the Creator, permeates Pärt's music. It can be heard in instrumental works such as *Fratres* and *Tabula rasa*, or in striking choral compositions, such as the exquisite *Stabat Mater* and the *Miserere*.

Pärt's *Stabat Mater* from 1985 brings us back to the piercing purity of the 13th-century text and to the liturgical roots of the work. Composed for a trio of voices and a trio of violin, viola, and cello, this 24-minute opus, employing medieval and Renaissance techniques, is startlingly simple, intensely concentrated, and devotional. Like all of Pärt's work, it grows out of a respect for silence—in this case, the silence at the foot of the Cross. What sort of music would one make from the foot of the Cross? His answer is both harrowing and profoundly moving. This is not an exercise in musical archaism, but a living testament to faith. It is music to listen to on your knees. (A sublime performance is available with the Hilliard Ensemble on a CD entitled *Arbos*, ECM 1325/831959).

More of Pärt's mesmerizing musical asceticism comes from Harmonia Mundi (HMU 907182) with its release of *De Profundis, Magnificat* and a number of other works covering a span of nearly 20 years (1977–1996). If you are living life in the fast lane, listening to Pärt will be like hitting a brick wall. Everything suddenly stops and becomes very simple. Anyone puzzled by the starkness and seeming severity of his work should know that for Pärt the Word is the priceless jewel that his music sets. It is to the jewel he is calling attention, not its setting, and the necessary precondition for hearing the Word is silence.

This is the reason for Pärt's profound respect for silence and its fullness as the Word emerges from it. Pärt's is music for meditation; it is the sound of prayer. Some might call this a fetish for the archaic; others, a witness to perdurability of true faith. The choral works on this CD may not be the ideal introduction to Pärt (for that go to ECM's *Tabula Rasa* or *Arbos* CDs), but those who know his music will want to have these beautiful performances by Paul Hillier and the Theatre of Voices.

There are two common responses to Pärt's *Passio*: (1) It is boring, ersatz medieval and Renaissance music; why is someone going back to the triad in this day and age? (2) It is a profoundly moving setting of the Passion according to the Gospel of John. Certainly *Passio* is very different from Pärt's *Stabat Mater*, which it is otherwise most like. In *Stabat Mater*, the instrumental music, like a chorus, reacts to the words, dramatizes them and provides a purgation. Pärt foregoes this approach in *Passio*, which is distinctly not dramatic and far more austere. The austerity does not translate into barrenness, but into an intense expression of purity. There is very little in the way of specific dramatic response to this most dramatic Latin text as it literally moves to the crux of Christianity. For example, when the mob in the garden answers Christ's question, "Whom seek ye?" The chorus does not shout his name, but sings it in a most gentle, reverential way. *Passio* clearly is meant as a meditation on the Passion. As such, the words carry more weight. Indeed, one must read this Passion in order to listen to it. It was fashionable not long ago to write vocal music that treated syllables of words independently, oblivious to their meaning. Now the word has returned—or one should say, the Word. With his music, Pärt intends to direct us through the words to the Word. What sustains a work like this? What impels a man like Pärt to write it? Clearly, the answer is faith, for there is no ego in this work. The temptation to focus on the music alone does not present itself. Indeed, if the words mean nothing to you, neither will the music.

However, within the austere means that Pärt has chosen, there are many very moving moments. A simply held note on *veritate* (truth) can be electrifying within the spare musical context, as can also Christ's exclamation: *Sitio* (I thirst). In the ECM recording of *Passio* that Pärt authorized, he seems to have anticipated response (1) above, and did not provide any indexing for the curious to search for "high points"; you will either give up in the beginning or listen to and experience the full 70 minutes. It's all or nothing. Sort of like religion. Newcomers to Pärt are advised to begin their explorations with earlier releases of his music: first try *Tabula Rasa*, then move on to *Arbos* and the *Miserere*, and finally come to *Passio*. It is worth the journey.

John Tavener (1944–2013) once wrote in the spirit of Schoenberg "some severely serial pieces". Later he eschewed such convolutedness and said, "Complexity is the language of evil." His simplicity, though, has an almost theatrical aspect to it. It is more flamboyant, almost voluptuous compared to Pärt, whom Tavener called "the only composer friend" he had. Because of his embrace of Russian Orthodoxy and its oriental musical idioms, his music sounds the most exotic and unfamiliar of the three. But his purpose is as clear. "In everything I do," he stated, "I aspire to the sacred. . . . Music is a form of prayer, a mystery." He wished to express "the importance of immaterial realism, or transcendent beauty". His goal was to recover "one simple memory" from which all art derives: "The constant memory of the Paradise from which we have fallen leads to the Paradise which was promised to the repentant thief." As he said elsewhere, "The gentleness of our sleepy recollections promises something else; that which was once perceived 'as in a glass, darkly' we shall see 'face to face'."

Tavener's music also often begins at the very edge of audibility, rising reverentially from the silence out of which it flows. He called his compositions musical icons. Like icons, they are instilled with a sense of sacred mystery, inner stillness, and timelessness. He often employed the unfamiliar cadences of Orthodox chant with its melismatic arabesques, floating above long drones. Though ethereal, his music conveys a sensuousness absent in Górecki and Pärt. His orchestral writing, even when confined to strings only, as in *The Protecting Veil*, can be very rich. He dramatically portrays visionary moments of epiphany with climaxes that are physical in their impact. The titles of his compositions convey the range of subject matter: *The Last Sleep of the Virgin*; *The Repentant Thief*; *Ikon of Light*; *"We Shall See Him as He Is"*; *Mary of Egypt*; *Canticle of the Mother of God*; *Resurrection*; and *The Protecting Veil*, which commemorates the Virgin's appearance in early 10th-century Constantinople, where, during a Saracen invasion, she drew her protecting veil over the Christians. This latter piece met with enormous success in England.

Devotion shines forth in Tavener's compositions such as *Thunder Entered Her*, whose short text by St. Ephrem the Syrian (c. 306–373) begins, "Thunder entered her / And made no sound." Tavener's *The Lament of the Mother of God* is a striking piece. The ritualized grief of this haunting work is expressed by a soprano voice, representing Mary, and an unaccompanied choir. The beautiful soprano voice floats over the wordless drone of the chorus and ascends step-wise over the span of an octave with the beginning of each stanza, which each time repeats the opening line: "Woe is me, my child." The text of the second stanza reads, "I wish to take my son down from the wood and to hold him in my arms, as once I held him when he was a little child. But alas there is none to give him to me." This is a very affecting work—the Pietà in sound.

Tavener was able to have his *Funeral Canticle* performed at his father's funeral. This 24-minute piece appears with four shorter works on a Tavener Harmonia Mundi release, entitled *Eternity's Sunrise*, performed by the Choir and Orchestra of the Academy of Ancient Music and various soloists, led by director Paul Goodwin. Tavener had complete confidence in beauty and simplicity. The melismatic vocal lines in *Eternity's Sunrise*, a setting of a short poem by William Blake, and *Song of the Angel*, in which the soprano sings only one word, "Alleluia", are soaringly beautiful. They are sung seraphically by soprano Patricia Rozari. *Eternity's Sunrise*, written to mark the academy's 25th anniversary, was Tavener's first work for period instruments, but it does not have a period sound. Tavener's *Funeral Canticle* employs a gently rocking motion in the music that slowly ascends and descends the scale, as if it were cradling one to sleep. It is touching but restrained; it does not call attention to itself. This is ceremonial music, meditative and mesmeric. The text from the Orthodox funeral service conveys the real substance: man's frailty, the hope for salvation, and God's surpassing goodness. As in almost all of Tavener's works, the constant refrain is "Alleluia."

Tavener's *Akathist of Thanksgiving* for chorus and orchestra was composed for the celebration of the millennium of the Russian Orthodox Church in 1988. An *akathist* is a hymn of thanksgiving or supplication used on special occasions. The text of Tavener's work was written in

the late 1940s by Archpriest Gregory Petrov shortly before his death in
a Siberian prison camp. His inspiration came from the dying words of
St. John Chrysostom: "Glory to God for everything." So, shortly before his own death, this priest, surrounded by misery and death, wrote,
"I have often seen your glory / Reflected on faces of the dead! / With
what unearthly beauty and with what joy they shone, / How spiritual,
their features immaterial, / It was a triumph of gladness achieved, of
peace; / In silence they called to you. / At the hour of my end illumine
my soul also, As it cries: Alleluia, alleluia."

It is undoubtedly surprising to a modern, secular sensibility that the
texts for these consoling, spiritual compositions should come not only
from Scripture and liturgy, but from the 20th century's death camps,
both Nazi and Soviet. The late Pope John Paul II was not surprised.
In *Crossing the Threshold of Hope*, he said of the multitude of martyrs
in the 20th century, "They have completed in their death as martyrs
the redemptive sufferings of Christ and, at the same time, they have
become *the foundation of a new world, a new Europe, and a new civilization.*"
Twentieth-century martyrdom as the foundation of a new civilization?
Can this be so, and, if so, how would such a civilization express itself?
Part of the answer is in the music of these three composers. Theirs is
the music of this new civilization. Like the martyrs from whom they
have drawn their inspiration, they have gone against the prevailing grain
of the 20th century for the sake of a greater love.

"O word, thou word that I lack", cried Schoenberg's Moses before
falling to his knees silent. Górecki, Pärt, and Tavener have found the
Word that Schoenberg's Moses lacked, and they have sought new expressive means to communicate it. The new expressive means have
turned out to be the old ones, lost for a period of time in the desert,
but now rediscovered by these three who know that "the rock was
Christ."

That something like this could emerge from under the rubble of
modernity is moving testimony to the human spirit and its enduring
thirst for the eternal. Is this too large a claim to make for these three
composers? Perhaps. But be still, and listen.

~

II

TALKING WITH THE COMPOSERS

Robert Craft on Stravinsky and Schoenberg: The Musical Antipodes of the Twentieth Century

Two composers dominated the music of the 20th century: Igor Stravinsky (1882–1971) and Arnold Schoenberg (1874–1951). Robert Craft (1923–2015) was especially close to the former and knew the latter, whom he called "the one composer who challenged Stravinsky's supremacy in 20th-century music". Craft had a front-row seat on the most important musical developments of our time. More than an observer, he influenced those developments. From 1948 to Stravinsky's death in 1971, Craft served as Stravinsky's musical assistant and confidant. Craft published five volumes of essays, five books of conversations with Stravinsky, and other works. *Stravinsky: Chronicle of a Friendship* documents their years of work together. *An Improbable Life: Memoirs*, published in 2002, was followed by *Down a Path of Wonder: Memoirs of Stravinsky, Schoenberg and Other Cultural Figures* in 2006 and then *Stravinsky: Discoveries and Memories* in 2013. As a conductor, Craft made a series of legendary recordings of both Stravinsky's and Schoenberg's works. He then embarked on a new traversal of the seminal works of both composers, most of which were issued by Koch, which is when this interview took place.

REILLY: Let me begin by simply thanking you. You have certainly played a role in my life. I devoured your books of conversations with Stravinsky when they came out. I absolutely loved them, as I did, of course, *Chronicle of a Friendship*, and your other books. To my mind, they are simply some of the most literate and insightful writings in the field of music.

CRAFT: Oh, that's nice. Thank you.

REILLY: What you are doing is so fascinating. It's as if a conductor in the late 19th century were to say, "Now I'm going to do Wagner's Ring and then the Brahms four symphonies." Yet these two composers were considered the antipodes. You were either in one camp or the other, but not both. And here you are, in an analogous situation, embracing both Stravinsky and Schoenberg and presenting them together. You must be trying to teach us something by doing that.

CRAFT: All I mean to say is that certainly both are worth the attention and the interest. That they are extremely different makes life very difficult for me. I cannot record a Stravinsky session on one day and the next day record Schoenberg. I would have to put weeks in between before I could go from one to the other. It is easy to go back to Stravinsky but very difficult to go from Stravinsky to Schoenberg. There are, of course, innumerable questions of style, of articulation, of attack, and that's where conductors spend most of their time anyway. And also dynamics: there are very few dynamic markings, comparatively in Stravinsky's music to Schoenberg's, because Stravinsky assumes that you know what he would do with these notes.

REILLY: Don't you think that's because the musical pulse in Stravinsky is so much more natural, and Schoenberg is so highly artificial?

CRAFT: Yes. In Schoenberg, it is often actually against the pulse, and the pulse is against the phrase. You get that, too. We recorded *Erwartung*, and he wants this expressionism. There are 400 measures of music. There are 111 tempo changes by metronome alone, and there are some 150 more, which are tempo nuances such as *ritards* and *accelerandos* and *fermatas*. So you don't have a steady pulse, and that's what is wrong with all the performances of it, so far as the score is asking for particulars.

REILLY: Can I ask you about the larger point that the music of Schoenberg and his disciples raises? And that is that this system, which purportedly was necessary because of the exhaustion of tonal resources, really wasn't needed for that reason. It was a reflection of the spiritual collapse of Europe.

CRAFT: Oh, yes, that goes way down. You asked in one of your written questions about Schoenberg guaranteeing a century of the continuation of German music and German musical values. And, of course, that has not happened at all, except it is German in the sense of pathos, of which Stravinsky has none whatsoever. The great moments in Stravinsky are never blowing the roof off, which is exactly what *Le Sacre* does but in a different way. Stravinsky's music is pure, and it is completely controlled; it's always controlled. Schoenberg is always asking for something beyond human possibility, as in the Violin Concerto.

REILLY: Schoenberg is really asking for a reconstruction of reality. One of my favorite sayings of Stravinsky is that "the old original sin was a sin of knowledge; the new original sin is a sin of nonacknowledgment." This is one of the reasons why I find him intellectually and spiritually to be a conservative. I don't know whether you agree with that.

CRAFT: Oh, yes.

REILLY: But I find Schoenberg to be almost an ideologue, because one of the principal features of modern ideology is a loss of reality. And the loss of reality that takes place in his system is, of course, of tonality and of harmonic structure and melody. He claimed that we would be hearing dissonance as if it were consonance. Hearing something as its opposite really requires a kind of metaphysical operation.

CRAFT: Yes, of course. First of all, harmony has been known for centuries. It's out the window with him. There isn't harmony. You are not listening to harmony. Almost every single chord in *Erwartung* has six different pitches and many go up to eight. So the chords have too much in common, the same eight notes, let's say, throughout an entire piece. So you are not moving harmonically at all. Everything that he is doing that is a semblance of movement, of propulsion forward, is done by other means. It is done by emotional extravagance.

REILLY: So there is no forward motion in Schoenberg except through rhetorical devices?

CRAFT: Yes, everything except harmony, except harmonic movement, which is what the music of Beethoven depends on. You never, in any music written, get the sense of movement, of direction, and of the necessity of that direction, as in Beethoven. And here it is the exact opposite. Everything but harmony is what brings you through the piece; you don't quite know. You don't know where the piece is going. It's rare that you have a sense that it can't last forever. You may know the difference between a piece that is going to last five minutes or 25, but never does that sense come from harmonic substance. And that seems to me a large element to pick out of music. There is one person who didn't go along with him on all of this, and that's Alban Berg, who would not give up the two modes, major and minor. When you realize what an immense arsenal of musical power you have in Franz Schubert, how he can go so quickly to the minor and then back to the major. What this means as a resource is endless.

REILLY: In a biography of Oscar Levant, there is a very amusing anecdote. Levant was talking about the string quartet he was writing for Schoenberg. He said, "The constant acerbity which tonally characterized the piece forced me suddenly to rebel. So I inserted two bars of rather agreeable harmony and counterpoint, which didn't germinate from what had preceded them." When Schoenberg saw these two innocent bars, he asked suspiciously, "How did this evolve?" And Levant answered, "Your system doesn't work for me." Schoenberg replied, "That's the beauty of it: It never works."

CRAFT: [*Laughter*] Oh, I think it's marvelous.

REILLY: I was reading this fascinating book by an English philosopher, Roger Scruton, who is also a composer. In *The Aesthetics of Music*, he makes the point that serial music works, to the extent that it does, despite itself, not because of its serial procedures.

CRAFT: That's a way of putting it. I certainly would agree with that. I won't play anything of Schoenberg's that I think I can't get music out of. And there are a lot of pieces that I don't like and probably will not play.

REILLY: For instance?

CRAFT: Well, the Fourth Quartet is to me an absolute abstraction from beginning to end and kind of ugly. For me, the tune in the slow movement for the cello is fairly close to torture. I like the Third Quartet because it bounces along, but there is nothing more to it than that. And the two earlier ones are too dense and too heavy for me. The Schoenberg piece that I love most is *Five Pieces for Orchestra*. It has wonderful colors, and each piece is the right length. It's still tonal music in my view. The recording that came out of *Pierrot Lunaire*, with the *Pelléas*, also makes me think of how much Schoenberg was returning to tonality in *Pierrot Lunaire*.

REILLY: Would you speak to the larger legacy of both of these men? The significance of Schoenberg can't be denied. It looms too large in the century he dominated so much of through his genius. But it seems to have reached a dead end well before now. I think he will be a history-book figure, with the exception of some of the extraordinary pieces, like *Gurrelieder* and maybe *Pelléas*, which will always be played. But what strikes me is that serial music really is a language of irresolution and, therefore, ultimately of angst. It repels people. I think that its influence, after dominating both the academy and the prize system, is over. Whereas with Stravinsky, musicians still love to play him and audiences to hear him. These are the two opposing forces of the century, and one led into a dead end and the other one didn't. Do you think I'm overstating this?

CRAFT: No, I don't. I agree completely. It has come to a dead end. Audiences are just going to walk out. They are not going to listen to it. And I find my own feelings have changed in regard to so many pieces. Once, I recorded the complete works of Anton Webern. I was fascinated by each piece, but with the exception of the early pieces for orchestra, I didn't find anything in them that stayed with me very long. Pieces like the Concerto for Nine Instruments I was interested in when I did it, but strictly for technical reasons. I tried conducting it a couple of years ago, and I couldn't stand it. I thought it was so arid, nothing to it except this rhythmic problem, and everything off the beat. You don't hear any Webern anywhere. Have you ever heard a live performance of a Webern cantata? No. Now in Schoenberg, in *Erwartung*, it seems that he deliberately never writes a close interval. The voice has to sing impossible pitches, and no instrument in the orchestra ever is playing the note that the singer needs or even hinting at it. And I have found there are many octaves in the orchestra (you can't help that with a huge orchestra and the great expanse and range), but they won't be heard as octaves. There is one place where he has the whole orchestra playing octaves, because that's the dramatic high point of the piece. But you don't know what it is about.

REILLY: What do you think of the contemporary music scene, and do you think that Stravinsky's music is still influencing it?

CRAFT: Well, I know it is still influencing it. There are certain composers I can name—for example, Peter Lieberson. His music sounds sometimes like imitations of Stravinsky's, but I don't know enough of it to pronounce on it. I can tell Stravinsky's influence when I work with orchestras, with the Philharmonia, for example. The orchestras immediately come together; they like it. You don't have to say everything; they do it on their own, and they make music out of it. It's a great joy.

REILLY: In respect to Schoenberg's legacy, I read a funny remark Arthur Honegger made more than 50 years ago. Honegger said, "I strongly fear that the 12-tone fad—we already see its decline—may initiate a reaction towards a too simplistic, too rudimentary music. The cure for having swallowed sulfuric acid will be to drink syrup."

CRAFT: Yes, that's a pretty astute forecast.

REILLY: There is the case of the late Italian composer Giacinto Scelsi. He is a sort of cult composer whom the French particularly love. Scelsi immersed himself in the serial system and had a breakdown.

CRAFT: That figures [*laughter*].

REILLY: He was put in an asylum, and he effected his own cure by sitting at a piano and simply striking the same note again and again.

CRAFT: Yes, that's infantile.

REILLY: That is minimalism.

CRAFT: Yes.

REILLY: You said that what you can tolerate in serial music has changed over the years, particularly in respect to Webern. Has anything changed in the way you listen to Stravinsky? Does it speak to you any differently now than when it was fresh for you?

CRAFT: Yes. Forty years ago, I found many things in Stravinsky a little too complex, a little acid, and unnecessarily so. And I don't feel that at all now. Everything seems logical, holds together, and I look forward to all of the music. There is not enough of it played. The very late music should be given at least a chance. It is getting that chance in England, in London. There are young people who prefer that to any other music.

REILLY: Now, you are the person who gets either the credit or the blame—

CRAFT: Both. I get both.

REILLY: For that late music. Can you talk a little about your role in inducing Stravinsky to get what he could out of the 12-tone system?

CRAFT: It's all accidental. There is no ideology there. There is no plan there. It happened because, in 1951, I was conducting this Monday evening concert series in Los Angeles. I was asked to conduct these pieces by Schoenberg, and I did. We did pieces like the *Serenade* and the Septet for the first time on the West Coast. I was very close to Stravinsky, and he came to every rehearsal. He had scores sometimes, and he did get to know these pieces. Of course, some he liked; some he considered strictly theoretical. The Septet suite never went down with him as a satisfying piece of music, though he found its construction fascinating. But a piece like the *Serenade* is Stravinsky music. I mean, it has a lot to do with *Renard*, even *Histoire du Soldat*. The march movements at the beginning and end certainly were inspired by *Histoire du Soldat*. Schoenberg's son-in-law, Felix Kreisler, told me that.

REILLY: That piece also has that kind of rhythmic vivacity that you find in Stravinsky.

CRAFT: Yes. It has that rhythmic life, and it's one of the few pieces that has. But, anyway, that's how Stravinsky got involved with that. And so he experimented a little bit, but it's entirely different. What he does with a series is totally different from Schoenberg and is put to different purposes.

REILLY: You seem to indicate in some of your writings that Stravinsky had reached a creative impasse and that this helped him out of it.

CRAFT: Well, yes. He had finished *The Rake's Progress*, which was his biggest work, and it took him three years. He was a certain age. He was not in great health, and he felt that he had to go in a different direction than what he was doing. But if you trace that path, it's very logical and very simple. He started using a series, but it's not a series in the Schoenberg sense. *In Memoriam Dylan Thomas* is a very moving, profound piece of music. I've seen people holding back tears with that. And that is all done with a series, but it is entirely tonal. It is composed according to tonal harmonic rules, but the combinations are triadic. The most popular of all of his ballets is *Agon*. It begins and ends in C major, but that is not the reason. Of course, *Agon* is half-tonal. There is a mixture that he puts together very ingeniously. It's all traditional Stravinsky music: rhythmic invention everywhere, wonderful dance rhythms, and music that anybody can like. The next piece, *Threni*, is impossible. It is so complex nobody understands it. The *Requiem Canticles* has caught on. It is an established piece. It is always going to be a popular Stravinsky piece. It will stand up with the Mass and the *Symphony of Psalms*. It is light. It is performed much more in Europe than here. In the last part of it, there are supposed to be serial melodies, but these are tonally formed melodies. I don't think Stravinsky could get away from that. In fact, I'm not at all sure that Schoenberg could get away from that entirely, but in the first act of *Moses und Aron*, he certainly does pretty well by getting away from it. I can't listen to that, by the way. For me, that is either way over my head or just not in my ears.

REILLY: It is very interesting as to why Schoenberg didn't finish it. There has been a lot of speculation, but he himself said something about it that no one pays attention to. He came to the impasse because he could not understand why Moses was punished for striking the rock a second time. This question absolutely tormented him.

CRAFT: I'm sure it did because he was deeply into theological problems. But the problem is that he does not take the Bible as is. He has to do his own version—that's with everything. He has written psalms, but he has to write *A Modern Psalm*.

REILLY: That makes it all the more interesting that he allowed this to stop him. He had plenty of time to finish that opera, and he simply couldn't do it. The answer to the dilemma is in a place where it was unavailable to him, because it is explained by St. Paul in the New Testament.

CRAFT: Well, that certainly closes the door on his Moses.

REILLY: In one of your books of conversation, I came across this marvelous statement from Stravinsky: "The stained glass artist of Chartres had few colors, and the stained glass artists of today have hundreds of colors but no Chartres. Not enlarged resources then, but men and what they believe. The so-called crisis of means is interior." It seems to me that there is a great recovery taking place in music today precisely on those grounds that Stravinsky always insisted upon. I have always been so moved by Stravinsky because of his deep appreciation and, indeed, promotion of music as a spiritual communication.

CRAFT: Oh, yes. Music was sacred to him. And Stravinsky is the composer of joy. His music is joyful whether it is *The Symphony of Psalms* or something else.

REILLY: Did you know that, in one of these millennial exercises, *Time* magazine had to pick the composition of the century, and it was *The Symphony of Psalms*.

CRAFT: I didn't know that. I think it might be pretty close to my choice. It is happy music. All of his music is happy music.

Recommended Recordings

Robert Craft specialized in Schoenberg and Stravinsky and recorded most of their works, sometimes many times over. These recordings have travelled from label to label as they respectively folded. A capable conductor knowledgeable of his main foci, many of his recordings are terrific and many above average. The recommendations below are, however, not limited only to Craft's accounts, especially when there are even more impressive alternatives available.

Stravinsky

The Complete Ballets, Soloists, Philharmonia Orchestra, London SO, Robert Craft (conductor), Naxos 8.506009 (6 CDs). Some individual works can be had in better renditions, but as a collection, and with some of the very finest versions of the less-often recorded ballets, it's a bargain Stravinsky box. Most of the discs are available individually, too, the best of which are listed below.

Pulcinella; *Le baiser de la fée* (*The Fairy's Kiss*), Soloists, Philharmonia Orchestra, London SO, Robert Craft (conductor), Naxos 8.506009

Agon; *Apollon Musagète*; *Orpheus*, London SO, Orchestra of St. Luke's, Robert Craft (conductor), Naxos 8.557502

Symphony in C; Symphony in 3 Movements; Octet for Winds; *Dumbarton Oaks Concerto*, Philharmonia Orchestra, 20th Century Classics Ensemble, Orchestra of St. Luke's, Robert Craft (conductor), Naxos 8.557507

Duo Concertant; Sonata for Two Pianos; *Requiem Canticles*, et al., Philharmonia Orchestra, 20th Century Classics Ensemble, Robert Craft (conductor), Naxos 8.557532

Oedipus Rex, *Les Noces*, Mariinsky Orchestra, Valery Gergiev (conductor), Mariinsky Live 510

Le Sacre du Printemps, Leonard Bernstein (conductor), 1958, Sony 546915. The *Rite of Spring* is such a popular work that Sony and Decca have issued entire sets just with that work, with variously six, 10, and 35 different performances. Bernstein's 1958 recording attained a magic touch when Stravinsky reportedly responded to it saying, "Wow!" It still wows many modern listeners, too. Ferenc Fricsay's recording on DG (477 5485) is worth seeking out, as are the modern recordings of James Levine (DG 437531), Pierre Boulez (DG 471741, Decca 478 3728), Valery Gergiev (Philips 468 0352 / Decca 478 3728), and Daniele Gatti (Sony 544255). One of the most exhilarating comes actually in the form of the arrangement for two pianos, performed by

Fazil Say adding three layers of himself on top of another: Fazil Say (pianos), Teldec 381041 / Warner 4699708

Le chant du rossignol, *L'Histoire du soldat* Concert Suite, *Scherzo fantastique* op. 3, *Le roi des étoiles*, Cleveland Orchestra & Chorus, Pierre Boulez (conductor), DG. The *Soldier's History* Concert Suite excludes the narration, which makes this recording particularly attractive to all but those that insist on hearing the text, too. The recordings are marvels of tender precision.

Symphony of Psalms; Mass; *Monumentum pro Gesualdo di Venosa ad CD annum*; *Chorale Variations*, Ghent Collegium Vocale, Royal Flemish Philharmonic, Philippe Herreweghe (conductor), Pentatone SACD 5186349

The Rake's Progress, Bryn Terfel, Ian Bostridge, Deborah York, Anne Sofie von Otter (soloists), Monteverdi Choir, London SO, John Eliot Gardiner (conductor), DG 459648

Schoenberg

Variations for Orchestra op. 31 (plus A. Berg, Lyric Suite Pieces; Three Pieces for Orchestra, A. Webern, Passacaglia for Orchestra), Herbert von Karajan (conductor), Berlin Philharmonic, DG 457760

Transfigured Night op. 4 for String Orchestra; *Pelléas et Mélisande*, Herbert von Karajan (conductor), Berlin Philharmonic, DG 457721

Five Pieces for Orchestra; *Transfigured Night* for String Orchestra; *Three Pieces for Piano*, Daniel Barenboim (conductor, piano), Chicago SO, Teldec 98256 / Apex 2564682429

Five Pieces for Orchestra, Cello Concerto after Monn, Brahms Quartet Orchestration, Fred Sherry (cello), Robert Craft (conductor), Naxos 8.557524. Schoenberg deemed Brahms' Piano Quartet too piano-heavy and went about creating a phenomenally effective orchestration that essentially turns into "Brahms' Fifth Symphony". If you like Brahms and big-boned romantic music, you will love this. The arrangement of Georg Matthias Monn's (1717–1750) Cello Concerto is a rare, early-classical gem, twice removed, romanticized, and reassembled. If you absolutely want to avoid the comparatively difficult *Five Pieces*, you can also look for Robert Craft's early Columbia recording just with Schoenberg-transcriptions reissued on RCA 78746.

Pierrot Lunaire, op. 21; *Ode to Napoleon*, op. 41; *Herzgewächse* op. 20, Christine Schäfer Ensemble InterContemporain, Pierre Boulez (conductor), DG 457630 / DG 001767002

Gurrelieder, Stephen O' Mara, Jennifer Lane, David Wilson-Johnson, Martyn Hill, Ernst Haefliger, Melanie Diener (soloists), Philharmonia Orchestra, Simon Joly Chorus, Robert Craft (conductor), Naxos 8.557518. Amid fierce competition of recordings of this extraordinary musical summation of the romantic era, Craft still holds up nicely. Worthy of consideration, especially for those desirous of audiophile and surround-sound, is Michael Gielen's recording (Hänssler Classic 93198).

Erwartung; Pelléas und Mélisande, op. 5, Anja Silja, Philharmonia Orchestra, Robert Craft (conductor), Naxos 8.557527

Violin Concerto (plus Sibelius Violin Concerto), Hilary Hahn (violin), Swedish RSO, Esa-Pekka Salonen (conductor), DG 001085802. Hilary Hahn manages somehow to make that concerto seem like an extension of the Sibelius with which it is coupled on her disc.

String Quartet No. 3: *Transfigured Night* for String Sextet, Leipzig String Quartet plus Hartmut Rohde (viola), Michael Sanderling (cello), MDG 3070773

Three Pieces for Piano, op. 11; *Six Little Pieces for Piano,* op. 19 (plus Schubert, *Three Pieces*; Allegretto for Piano in C Minor), Thomas Larcher (piano), ECM 465136. Currently out of print but available secondhand is this incongruous and ingenious coupling and intertwining of Schubert's and Schoenberg's *Three Pieces*, providing an ear-opening experience of the pretty coupled with the terse.

For the very daring and curious, the complete Schoenberg of Robert Craft's has been issued on two Naxos sets of five and six CDs respectively, Naxos 8.505223 and 8.506023

Robert Craft achieves a startling transparency of these renditions of Schoenberg's sometimes extremely dense works. Craft lets us know, even in the most difficult parts of, say, the Violin Concerto, what Schoenberg was abstracting from and highlights the musical touchstones throughout these works. Nonetheless, most listeners will find these works hard to bear. The exceptions are the early works, *Transfigured Night* or *Pelleas,* which not only demonstrate Schoenberg's extraordinary musical gifts but show the direction in which he took tonality to the snapping point, before leaving it behind. The same goes for the massive cantata *Gurrelieder,* which sounds like an extreme extension of Mahler's *Das Klagende Lied.* One can hear that snapping point in *Erwartung,* in which Schoenberg brilliantly uses atonality as the language of dissolution to portray the psychological disintegration of a woman who has murdered her lover. If you wish to understand how two roads diverged in the musical world of the 20th century, you should listen to some of these recordings.

David Diamond: America's Greatest Symphonist?

David Diamond (1915–2005) was the last of several generations of great American symphonists who flourished mid-century. This list—beginning with Roy Harris, Howard Hanson, Aaron Copland, and Walter Piston—continued with William Schuman and Diamond himself. Of them all, Diamond created the most substantial body of symphonies, which number 11, in addition to ballets, concertos, a great deal of chamber music (11 string quartets), and an opera. Diamond's declamatory, open-hearted, warm, and generously lyrical music was on the "forbidden list" during the ignominious reign of the 12-tone avant-garde that now seems to have collapsed as completely as did the Soviet Union. Even during his years in the desert, Diamond had the pluck to declare: "I do not believe there is any such thing as atonal music." His credo was that "music that does not nourish you spiritually is not music, only aural sensations."

Thanks to the enterprise of Delos records, Naxos, and other labels and the artistry of conductor Gerard Schwarz, many CDs of Diamond's superb orchestral works and chamber music are now available in stunning recordings, with more, one hopes, on the way. These recordings have helped to vindicate Diamond as one of the greatest American composers of the 20th century. This interview took place several years before Diamond's death.

REILLY: I'll start by saying thank you. Your music has been a source of tremendous joy in my own life. May I ask you about the influences on your work? You knew everyone: Albert Roussel, Maurice Ravel, and Igor Stravinsky, to name a few.

DIAMOND: That was very fortunate, yes. I began in my early years by studying in Europe. You were bound to meet the great people right there in Paris, and then Rochester was a great center for the theater and the arts.

REILLY: In listening to your music, one could pick out certain influences and say, well I hear a little Copland there. Or, when you self-consciously pay homage, as you do in your Concert Piece for Flute and Harp, one can say, I hear Albert Roussel. But in your own mind, which composers had the biggest impact on you when, as a young man, you heard their works?

DIAMOND: Well, strangely enough, it was neither of those composers. The composer who meant the most to me when I was a very young boy was Maurice Ravel, and the music I love the most today is his music. It's a toss-up when I'm bored if I go back to Johann Sebastian Bach, or I take out works of Ravel. They remain as fresh to me as ever. So the combination of Bach's counterpoint and the beauty of his melodic writing is as important to me as Ravel's.

REILLY: That's an interesting background for someone who is thought of as an inimitably American composer.

DIAMOND: Yes, but there again the connection is interesting because Ravel, even before coming to America during that first 1928 trip, had already had a series of 78s of American jazz. And he used to go to that famous nightclub there, it's called the Owl on the Roof. And there he heard a good deal of American jazz. Already in the late 1920s, the G-major Piano Concerto had a lot of jazz influence in it. I guess I was attracted to that, too.

REILLY: You dedicated one of your first big successes, *Psalm*, to André Gide.

DIAMOND: Yes, he was a fairly good pianist, and he began his days playing through some of the preludes from *The Well-Tempered Clavier*, and that impressed me to no end. He had a fine grand piano in his studio, and when I brought the *Psalm* to him, he played through it at once.

REILLY: Did you happen to run into Julien Green with André Gide?

DIAMOND: Oh, I went to visit him very often. I looked him up about 10 years ago. That was an interesting talk that we had because when I was an adolescent I went through his novel called *The Dark Journey*. That novel made a tremendous impression on me. It's a very depressing novel. But I was more or less geared to dark moods and that was exactly the right book for me to read.

REILLY: Let me ask about the inspiration of your own music. I find so much modern music claustrophobic: it constantly collapses in on itself. But your music has such a generous aspect to it. It moves out to fill the space. Even when it's expressing some heartache, it doesn't collapse in on itself. I think that the way your music is so generous in its spirit has to—in some way—be a reflection of your spirit and beliefs in life.

DIAMOND: I'm very happy to hear you say that. I wish all of it really were so. I think it must be so, because others have written about that, but I think it comes from a technical learning of my craft, which had to do particularly with my studies with Roger Sessions and Nadia Boulanger. They always were talking about the long line. You must develop the long line in your music, try to write very long melodies. We would work for hours on constructing a very fine shape to a melodic line. Of course being a violinist helped too, because everything a violinist practices is on the long line. But I think I've always heard in long lines. That means not only melodically, but structurally. Unless you can do that, I don't think you can be a symphonist.

REILLY: I recall a statement of yours made around the time of your 50th birthday that "composers should write music that can uplift the spirits. Music that does not nourish you spiritually is not music, only aural sensation."

DIAMOND: I still think that is true. It is one reason so much of the music that was written during the 1950s and part of the 1960s, music which was basically textural in the sense that the sonorities were the important thing, or patterns of sound, have not lived on. In fact, they've disappeared. Nobody ever listens to them. It's because there is a lack of real musical language which communicates. In other words, there is no melodic substance, and there's no feeling in the sense of emotion, whether it's lighthearted emotion or whether it's dark and profound emotion. All the great music of the past and the great music of the present has that. I admire composers like Paul Hindemith so much because he was very much a composer of his time and you could recognize his work as contemporary music. But he also had great emotion and great craft, and that's why his music lives on. The same for Alban Berg. The same for Prokofiev and Shostakovich. So, when people ask me, are there really great composers in our time? I say certainly, then I rattle off about 20 names, and they're amazed because they never thought of it that way.

REILLY: Well, you know the school of 12-tone composition infected several generations. What I find curious is that the so-called neo-romantics or minimalists of the current generation, whether it be John Adams or Arvo Pärt, all of them began with 12-tone, and all of them rejected it.

DIAMOND: Yes. Eventually they saw through it, just as Schoenberg himself did. I remember about two years before he died, I visited him in Hollywood. He was talking about my Second Symphony. I said, "Maybe I can spend a year working with you in 12-note technique." He said, "You mustn't be interested in that at all. It's not for you, you're a young Bruckner. You don't need that." And then I began reading articles he had written later on in which he felt that, indeed, the 12-note technique was not a technique for everyone.

REILLY: Do you think you are an American Bruckner?

DIAMOND: I can see what people mean sometimes about the symphonies, like the Second Symphony and the Eighth Symphony. They are large-structured and they have very long lines. But I don't think of myself in comparative terms that way. I wish I were a young Bruckner. Right now I feel like Methuselah.

REILLY: It seems that the 12-tone technique or what Robert Simpson, the English composer, called the "coterie of 12-notery", was diagnosed very well by American composer George Rochberg when he turned against it. He said that it involves a spiritual attenuation. It is not simply a change in technique. There is a metaphysical revolution behind it. That's why I found so appealing the statements you've made about how necessary it is for music to nurture one spiritually and that it can't do that without all the components of music.

DIAMOND: Exactly, and if we don't have other human beings to appreciate what we're spending our time on earth doing, then what's the point of composing? I mean, if we are involved in pitches and pitch selection only and color texture only, without melody and without a certain amount of rhythmic energy. There must be radiant melody and urgency of rhythmic impulse. Many composers, even those today, don't have the pulse sense of rhythm. They write repeated ostinati patterns, repeating a series of pitches over and over again, rather than writing a real, what I call, a good Bach bass line.

REILLY: You're talking about the centrality of melody. Have you noticed that even though melody has a kind of innate universal appeal, we have a generation or two that seem to have gone deaf to melody because of the music they're listening to?

DIAMOND: Yes, and I think it's also because they're talentless. There are people who are without talent in terms of what they listen to. They're not really listening to the art of music. They're listening for the sensation of sound. Therefore, all this interest among the young in noisy rock. I don't mind rock when it's sort of quiet, but when there is no substantial melodic writing, then it just disappears in time as it's doing already. I'm glad to read that fewer CDs of rock are being sold. Spiritual listening, of course, is something very special. I think there is such a thing. All we have to do is listen to the great Gregorian chants.

REILLY: You made a comment in 1989 in the *New York Times*, saying about the 12-tone avant-garde that "it was ego, ego plus opportunism."

DIAMOND: Oh, yes. Opportunism and ego. That absolutely is it. Well, can you tell me that's not what Mr. Pierre Boulez is about? You know, I knew him way back when, in Paris, and I knew this was going to be Mr. Self-Promoter, if there ever was one.

REILLY: You ended your comments in the *New York Times* by saying, "I hated all that avant-garde stuff. It was all wrong. They don't write out of love. They write out of the brain. It's all intellectually geared music. I think they know their game is up."

DIAMOND: Oh, yes and that's why I made enemies of all of them. It's only in recent years that they have begun to talk to me.

REILLY: Well, do they know their game is up when you talk to them now?

DIAMOND: Oh, yes. Oh, yes. As a matter of fact, Milton Babbitt and I are such close buddies now, it's very touching. You know, we've been teaching together for a long time. Way back in the '50s he came to visit me in Florence, and he said, "David, you know the kind of music that you write, in a few years there's not going to be any point in doing it because it's all going to be electronic." At that time, he was very much involved in tape. And today, you know, he is allowing a few notes to get into his [12-tone] rows.

REILLY: But this must have affected you. It must have been a terribly difficult time. I'm going to read to you something you said that I got out of an American biographical dictionary of composers published in 1982: "To have felt out of step in one's first years, confirms one's invalidism in these last years. A sad story at best, with just a glimmer of hope before the next catastrophe."

DIAMOND: Oh, yes. I was in a very bad, depressed period when there was no way of getting my music performed. I lived in Italy for close to 16 years, and the entire Italian musical life was dominated by the advanced 12-note avant-garde. Everywhere I submitted music it was turned down because it was considered old-fashioned. It was very hard-going because I loved living in Italy and I got a lot of work written. But the attitude of men like Luigi Dallapiccola and some of the other 12-note composers really, really depressed me to no end. The only sympathetic composer, and a much older person than I, was Gian Francesco Malipiero. I'll never forget when he said to me: "Don't you worry for one moment. Your day is coming. I waited a long time and my day has come and gone. You will have a great, great, public one day." And he had known only up to my Fourth Symphony and the Third String Quartet. So, I was very touched that Malipiero felt that way. But it was not easy to return to America and find the same thing going on here. There was no way of getting anything performed. Only Leonard Bernstein, bless his soul, who played the Eighth Symphony, and Eugene Ormandy, who played the Seventh Symphony, broke that spell. Then I began to be hopeful again because the reviews were exceedingly good and critics began saying, "Wow, so there is a composer who is not writing only this very, very dry 12-note music." So, with the symphony performances in the late '50s and '60s things began to look up.

REILLY: Well, it's nice to see that Malipiero's music is back. He's been vindicated as well.

DIAMOND: Oh, yes. All of his symphonies have been recorded, and they are marvelous works. [Available on Naxos CDs.]

REILLY: Also his string quartets.

DIAMOND: Yes, yes.

REILLY: When I was trying to analyze his marvelous string quartets, I thought, if Janáček had been an Italian and educated by Debussy, this is sort of what you would get.

DIAMOND: I know what you mean. You're not far off.

REILLY: Let me ask you more specifically about your own works. It seems that around the time of the Fifth Symphony your vocabulary changed a bit, not in any extraordinary way, but let's say the music became a little more angular, a little sharper, a little more chromatic. And then, of course, I haven't been able to hear your Ninth and Tenth.

DIAMOND: Oh, that's too bad. I wish you could hear them.

REILLY: But now, of course, I've heard the lovely Adagio from the Eleventh. And that seems to be a return to your earlier language. But what was going on around the time after the Fourth Symphony, during the composition of the Fifth, which had such a prolonged gestation and then a revision? Did this reflect a change in your thought, in your life?

DIAMOND: Oh, definitely a change in my thought. I realized that I could not continue writing strictly diatonic melodic lines. I felt they were beginning to sound like I was repeating myself. As Aaron Copland once said when we were going through the Fourth Symphony, "David, it would be so nice if every now and then there were black notes somewhere." And I said, "You're absolutely right." Now what's interesting is that if you go back to my early 1935–1936 music, the *TOM Suite*, that's very chromatic and at the same time very modal. So, when I began thinking that actually I had written much more chromatic music in my earlier years, I thought now I must bring the two together. And so, I began to introduce more chromaticism into the melodic writing, and therefore, into the harmony as well. But I always wanted to control it so that it never seemed arbitrary. I always felt that there had to be, as Hindemith used to say, a point of reference cadentially. That way you knew where you were going to go and where you were going to stop for awhile, why you came from a certain place and why you were going to another. And I realized that tonality was just that. And I began to concentrate on that. Therefore, the Fifth Symphony has a combination of both. So, it's just an extension. I began to extend what was already there in my earliest years.

REILLY: And the Eleventh Symphony?

DIAMOND: The Eleventh Symphony is the fulfillment of everything. When you hear the entire symphony, you'll see that the slow movement is quite chromatic actually, if you see it in score form. It sustains the interest very well because I go between modality and chromaticism: they work together beautifully in that symphony. The work takes on a kind of grandeur, if I may say so, but that's what I've arrived at. And the Ninth Symphony is more of the same. It's chromatic and diatonic, and has a kind of elegiac quality because it was written in memory of [conductor] Dimitri Mitropoulos. So, I think once the complete Eleventh is out on CD and the Ninth, I think people will be able to see the connection very easily.

REILLY: What about the role of the 11 string quartets? That's a huge body of work.

DIAMOND: Oh, I wish someday somebody would start recording those. I think the story may end up being like Shostakovich's. Nobody really knew anything about his string quartets until after his death. And then suddenly, just about five years after his death, there began these series of recordings of his quartets.

REILLY: I think it's his finest music.

DIAMOND: I think so, too.

REILLY: And how do you place the quartets? In other words, have you composed quartets consistently throughout your compositional life?

DIAMOND: As consistently as the symphonies, yes. Almost every two or three years. And what is peculiar is, I was looking through the dedications. One-half of them are in memory of somebody or dedicated to very close friends for their birthdays. And that tells me something about why they have a kind of elegiac quality, especially the Third, and the Fourth too, the big fugue in the Fourth. It's going to take too much time, money, and preparation to get 11 string quartets recorded. I don't think I'll be around. [The Potomac String Quartet has recorded the complete quartets on the Albany label.]

REILLY: What are you working on now?

DIAMOND: I'm really trying to book the Tenth Symphony, which is the unperformed one, because it is for the opening of the new concert hall in Seattle. And then Mr. Gerard Schwarz will do the recordings of the Ninth and the Seventh, and we're hoping that my opera, *The Noblest Game*, will be done either in Washington, once the new auditorium is finished, or we're still hoping that money can be raised to do it at the New York City Opera.

REILLY: Are you contemplating any new orchestral works?

DIAMOND: No, just trying to finish up orchestrating the opera. I have just finished a new piano quintet, the Second Quintet, for the Howard Hanson Anniversary here in Rochester. I don't know about another symphony. At 82 you can't think the way you did at the age of 50. I know the creative urge is as strong as ever in me, but I don't know whether I'm going to have the physical strength—whether my eyes will hold up, whether my hand will hold up. But if they do hold, there may be another symphony. But I am giving up teaching as of next year, due to ill health. So, I've got to watch it.

REILLY: Which of your pieces would you recommend newcomers go to first?

DIAMOND: I would say the first Delos [now Naxos] CD, the one which has the Fourth and the Second Symphonies. That's a good one.

REILLY: Let me finish by asking what do you think your legacy is? What do you think it will leave people with in respect to what David Diamond did for American music or for music at large?

DIAMOND: Well, a feeling that perhaps the great spiritual values in life don't always have to be religious spiritual values, that they can be the values which the musical art gives us, the great musical art of the past and the present.

REILLY: That's a very interesting comment. Does that mean they're separated from religious values or that it's just grounded in a more pantheistic view of things?

DIAMOND: I think that art has its own specific religious spirituality. It is not a theological spirituality and maybe for that reason it will have a longer survival rate because we're already seeing what is happening to organized religion. Fewer people go to churches now. Catholicism is having big problems. Judaism is having big problems. But what remains very important for me, from the theological standpoint, is that only two great figures hold my spiritual, theological attention. They are, as my father used to call them, Joshua Ben Nazareth, Jesus of Nazareth, and Moses. These two men are going to be always with us in that vast spiritual sense of what their particular contributions were. And once I bring that together with my musical spiritual force, I think that's what the future will be in sustaining my own music.

REILLY: That almost sounds religious to me, Maestro.

DIAMOND: Almost, doesn't it?

Recommended Recordings

All Delos CDs of the symphonies and orchestral works are with the Seattle Symphony or the New York Chamber Symphony, conducted by Gerard Schwarz. Those Delos CDs that have been deleted, except as noted, have been picked up by Naxos, making them even more of a bargain.

Symphony No. 1, Violin Concerto No. 2, and *The Enormous Room*, Naxos 8.559157. Bold, fluid, and rhythmically buoyant, the First Symphony shows Diamond fully formed as a composer at age 25.

Symphonies 2 and 4, Naxos 8.559154. It is hard to overstate the brilliance and beauty of these two works. The Fourth Symphony is especially magnificent —an American classic, a contender for the title of *the* American symphony. It is one of the most stirring, open-hearted, richly melodic symphonies this country has produced. (From where did Diamond conjure the magical opening?)

Symphony No. 3; *Psalm*; and *Kaddish*, Naxos 8.559155. In their Delos incarnation (DE 3101), still available on Amazon, these recordings include the substantial bonus of Diamond's *Music for Shakespeare's Romeo and Juliet*. The finest *Romeo and Juliet* music after Prokofiev, an eloquent and moving *Kaddish* and *Psalm*, and an electrifying Third Symphony make the Delos CD preferable.

Adagio (Third Movement from Symphony No. 11); *Rounds for String Orchestra*, Concert Piece for Orchestra; *Elegy in Memory of Maurice Ravel*; and Concert Piece for Flute and Harp, Delos 3189. The grandly spacious Adagio of the 11th Symphony shows Diamond was still at his creative peak. *Rounds for String Orchestra*, Diamond's most popular piece, is irresistible.

Flute Concerto, The Bohuslav Martinů Orchestra, Charles Anthony Johnson, Albany Troy 308. Diamond's Flute Concerto, written in 1987, is accompanied by other flute works by Antal Dorati, Bernard Rogers and Ernst Krenek. The half-hour concerto is a rich, effervescent work very much in the style of Diamond's early- to mid-period symphonies, with long-lined melodies, punctuated by syncopated rhythms. It is essentially a buoyant, joyous work with shades of bittersweetness in the wistful musings of the flute. Overall, it exudes Diamond's typical generosity of spirit. Flutist Alison Young plays ravishingly.

Suite from the Ballet TOM; *This Sacred Ground*, and Symphony No. 8, Naxos 8.559156. The early ballet is a wonderful Coplandesque score. The symphony is in a later, more angular style.

Quintet in B Minor for Flute, String Trio, and Piano; Concert Piece for Horn and String Trio; Partita for Oboe, Bassoon, and Piano; Chaconne for Violin and Piano; and Woodwind Quintet, the Chicago Chamber Musicians, Cedille

CDR 90000-023. The early works show the urbane French influence in Diamond's training; the *Chaconne* displays his more typical American characteristics; and the later Woodwind Quintet proves that even serial techniques can be used musically. This exhilarating work is brimming with life and rhythmic vivacity

Sonatas for Violin and Piano 1 & 2; Quintet for Clarinet, Two Violas, and Two Cellos; and Preludes and Fugues for Piano, Robert McDuffie (violin), William Black (piano), and others, New World Records 80508-2. Expertly made, American in idiom, rhapsodic, joyful and elegiac, these marvelous works show some of Diamond's range in excellent performances. Although written some 40 years apart, the Sonata No. 1 for Violin and Piano (1943–1946) and the Sonata No. 2 for Cello and Piano (1987) are nonetheless of a piece. The First brims with youthful energy; the Second is slightly more mellow. Both are gorgeous and display the French elegance and clarity that Diamond, like so many American composers, learned at the feet of Nadia Boulanger.

Complete Quartets, Potomac String Quartet

Quartets 1, 5, & 6, Albany Troy 613

String Quartets 3 & 8; Concerto for String Quartet, Albany Troy 504

String Quartets 4 & 7; *Night Music* for Accordion and String Quartet, Albany Troy 727

Quartets 2, 9, & 10, Albany Troy. Thanks to the great dedication and artistry of the Potomac String Quartet—three of whose members belong to the National Symphony Orchestra—and the enterprise of Albany Records, all the quartets were recorded and issued while Diamond was still alive. One may start with the Concerto for String Quartet (1936), String Quartet No. 3 (1946) and String Quartet No. 8 (1964). One could not overstate the elegiac beauty and deeply touching nature of the Third Quartet. Richly contrapuntal, quintessentially American, and directly expressive, these three Diamond works may exhibit changes in style over the three-decade period of their composition, but they also demonstrate a consistency of quality and inspiration that will leave you wondering why we have had to wait so long for a recording project of this kind.

～

Gian Carlo Menotti: Heavenly Muse

Gian Carlo Menotti (1911–2007) passed away at the ripe old age of 95. I met him when he was a spry 90 and had come to Washington, D.C., to direct the 50th-anniversary production of his opera *The Consul* for the Washington Opera Society at the Kennedy Center in January 2001. In the interview, we spoke of matters of the Catholic faith, with which he had struggled, and his mission as a composer. Menotti wrote some of the most popular operas in history, including *The Medium*, *The Telephone*, *The Saint of Bleecker Street*, *The Death of the Bishop of Brindisi*, and the perennial Christmas favorite, *Amahl and the Night Visitors*.

Born in Italy, Menotti received much of his musical education in the United States at the Curtis Institute of Music in Philadelphia. Although enormously popular, his works have been vilified by critics since they are written in a tonal language that draws from the tradition of Puccini and others. Writing of his opera *The Last Savage* in 1964, he said: "To say of a piece that it is harsh, dry, acid and unrelenting is to praise it. While to call it sweet and graceful is to damn it. For better or for worse, in 'The Last Savage' I have dared to do away completely with fashionable dissonance, and in a modest way, I have endeavored to rediscover the nobility of gracefulness and the pleasure of sweetness." In a 1971 letter to the *New York Times*, Menotti responded to the vilification of his works: "I hardly know of another artist who has been more consistently damned by the critics. . . . The insults that most of my operas had to endure through the years would make a booklet as terrifying as *Malleus Maleficarum* [The Witches' Hammer, a medieval guidebook for prosecuting sorcery cases]."

Yet both Menotti and his operas outlived their critics.

Menotti was also the founder of the world-famous music festival held annually in Spoleto, Italy. In the three decades before his death in February 2007, he lived in Lothian, Scotland, with the aid of an Italian cook.

REILLY: *Grove's Dictionary of Music and Musicians* calls you "an American composer of Italian birth". Do you accept that description?

MENOTTI: I could be that, or I also could be an Italian composer of American birth.

REILLY: But you can't be both.

MENOTTI: Except I am still an Italian citizen, but I must say I was born a composer in America. My musical education was here, and certainly, my career was made here.

REILLY: When they discuss influences on you, people mention the music of Puccini, Mussorgsky, sometimes Stravinsky and Debussy. Do you accept these?

MENOTTI: I always feel that a composer is just a human being, and we all have a family. Whether I like it or not, we are influenced by our neighbors, by our family. We're not born out of a shell.

REILLY: Is that your family?

MENOTTI: No, not my family. I've been very much influenced by Schubert. Melodically, I mean. The simplicity of Schubert always moved me to tears. But I did not know Schubert when I came to America because lieder at that time in Italy were almost unknown. There were no lieder recitals in Milan. Only opera, opera, opera.

REILLY: But not Schubert's operas?

MENOTTI: Certainly not those, not even now. I arrived here when I was 16 years old, and for the first time, I heard an American orchestra, the Philadelphia Orchestra with Leopold Stokowski. And that was it; I was thunderstruck. I heard so much music. But when I met Samuel Barber, who had a lovely baritone voice, for the first time, he sang for me Schubert songs, and Schumann and Brahms. Brahms was completely unknown in Italy at that time. He was considered a boring, old-fashioned composer.

REILLY: So German influences on Italian music? It's so interesting to hear you say that because so much of Italian music in the 20th century, certainly in its first half, was a rejection of German influences.

MENOTTI: I was very much influenced by the German school because of my teacher, Rosario Scalero, who was a pupil of Eusebius Mandyczewski [1857–1929], who was a great friend of Brahms. I was so influenced by the sonata form; my teacher believed in it. *The Consul*, if you really think of it, is based on the sonata form: the first movement is the first act, then the second act is the adagio, then there is a scherzo, and then there's the grand finale with the aria. I was very much influenced by the classical form.

REILLY: You are the most frequently performed opera composer of the 20th century. How do you explain this strange phenomenon of critical derogation and condescension, and yet enormous popularity?

MENOTTI: I don't know that my popularity is enormous, but I believe in certain things. For example, I believe—you'll be surprised when I say it —in dissonance. I think that 12-tone and most modern music has killed the importance of dissonance, because if you don't have consonance, how can you have dissonance? The wonderful thing about dissonance is the tension that has to be released. The 12-tones have destroyed this completely. And that's why I love Schubert, because Schubert is very consonant, but then there are times when there's a little bit of dissonance. It becomes so important and so surprising and wonderful. But in Stravinsky and Schoenberg, dissonance doesn't mean anything.

REILLY: It loses its expressive power?

MENOTTI: Absolutely.

REILLY: I think that is tied in with Schoenberg's view of art. He said a very extraordinary thing: "I have been cured of the delusion that beauty is the aim of art." So if beauty is excluded as the purpose of art, what is its purpose?

MENOTTI: If I had known him, I would have asked him, what do you mean by beauty? I say, at least in music, that beauty is a search for the inevitable, that great music is music that can only be that way and no other way. And only God can give you the inevitable. Maybe it is the search for the collective unconscious, but the collective unconscious of what is noblest in man.

REILLY: What about this definition of the purpose of music or art: to make the transcendent perceptible? You seem to be headed in that direction.

MENOTTI: Yes, but the transcendent is what is inevitable.

REILLY: So you accept it at that level?

MENOTTI: Actually, you don't invent anything. You discover something that already exists. I believe what Plato did: we have a vision of an idea, and then you have to try to remember it. James Joyce said, "To create is to remember." Many poets, many writers say that art is the art of remembering. Remembering what? Remembering this fleeting vision that the artist has of an aesthetic truth. Then, you try to remember it.

Some artists are blessed with wonderful memory, like Beethoven and Wagner. Some people may have a vision of this truth, but they cannot remember it. They cannot capture it.

REILLY: Let me ask you about the content of your music. There seems to be a repeated and wonderful tension in your works between sacred and profane love. I was going over the libretto to *The Saint of Bleecker Street*, and I found some fascinating things that define the human soul in the struggle between Annina and her brother, Michele. I wondered if you could comment on this.

MENOTTI: I'm glad that somebody reads my librettos. My last composition is called *Jacob's Prayer*, which is more or less the same thing. It is the fight with the angel, or actually, the Bible doesn't say "angel". A person comes into Jacob's tent and fights with him all night. There is this silent fight between them. Then in the morning, the angel is able to strike Jacob in the leg, and through that wound, he has a vision of God. And I've been struggling with the angel for a long night.

REILLY: And are you looking forward to this "joyous meeting" with God that Annina longs for?

MENOTTI: Well, I don't know if I am going to be wounded or not.

REILLY: In an interview with the *Washington Post* [December 30, 2001], you said, "[My] chief occupation these days is my dialogue with God. I have to face him one of these days, and we have little discussions, private discussions, and that interests me more than composing. I'm trying to get an answer from God." When I read that, you reminded me not of Jacob but of the Book of Job. Maybe God has asked you a question, and He's the one waiting for an answer.

MENOTTI: Yes, I know. He has asked me a few questions. That's the trouble, that's the dialogue, because I don't know what to answer. I have to prepare my answers. We'll see.

REILLY: Some of your answers are in your music, aren't they?

MENOTTI: But you see, I feel very guilty about my music. I think I could have probably composed better music if I hadn't spent so much time with festivals and all the things that have taken so much of my time. I think that to be a great composer, you have to give your whole life to it. You cannot share the love of music with any other kind of love. That's why great composers have also been terrible husbands. You really have to give your whole life to your music. Art is a very jealous mistress to have. She doesn't admit any interference.

REILLY: Your remarks will make a lot of people ashamed of themselves, if they think that you, who have written 25 operas, could have done more. That is extraordinary.

MENOTTI: No, I should have written *better* operas.

REILLY: Let's return to this question of the tension between sacred and profane love in your work.

MENOTTI: Where did you get this? Whom are you speaking to?

REILLY: I made that up myself. I'm speaking to myself.

MENOTTI: I would love to meet this person.

REILLY: I was told you have no particular association with organized religion, but in your works, I find some consistent spiritual, if not religious, themes. In fact, Christopher Keene, in his introduction to the RCA recording of *The Saint of Bleecker Street*, made this interesting comment: "The ambivalent consequences of faith occupy a central position in all Menotti's work: In *The Medium*, Baba is destroyed by the false belief she has engendered and exploited in her clients; in *The Consul*, faith in her husband's cause and the possibility of escape drive Magda down the long road of anguish, madness, and death; faith in Christ heals the crippled Amahl, but it leads the crusading children in *The Death of the Bishop of Brindisi* to enslavement and annihilation." Is this fair?

MENOTTI: Pretty fair. I'm surprised that Keene, who was such a sinner, should have described my metaphysical anguish so well.

REILLY: What about the role of these works in your own life? You have said that *The Consul* was based on an incident you read about in the newspaper of a woman committing suicide when she didn't get a visa to the United States, and *The Medium* on a séance you attended in Salzburg. What about *Amahl* and the healing of your own leg?

MENOTTI: I think that when you write for the theater, willingly or not, you mirror part of your own life.

REILLY: Was your leg healed at a shrine?

MENOTTI: Yes, when I was a little boy. Near Varazze. It's a shrine called Madonna del Monte. I was given benediction, and I walked right away.

REILLY: There was a question and an answer very early in your life from God, then, wasn't there?

MENOTTI: I believe in saints.

REILLY: Did you know Padre Pio [the Italian priest and stigmatic who died in 1968 and was canonized in 2002]?

MENOTTI: I knew Padre Pio. I went to see him. He was an extraordinary man.

REILLY: What was that visit like?

MENOTTI: It was interesting because I was about to write *The Saint of Bleecker Street*, so I wanted to meet a saint. I went to see Padre Pio. He used to say Mass around four in the morning. He didn't want to have people there, but the church was always very crowded. There was a terrible smell of sick people and then the crowd of all these dirty peasants. The first thing I noticed—I went with a friend of mine, a girl from Rome—was that the moment he appeared the air changed. Someone there said, "The odor of sanctity." I turned to my friend and asked, "Do you notice the air? It's changed. It's a strange perfume of violets and disinfectant at the same time." The whole air was clean.

I was waiting at the altar. He wore gloves to hide the stigmata, but then, to say Mass, he had to take the gloves off. He had a little towel to wipe his hands, because blood would come out of them. He said the Mass very, very slowly, and every once in a while he would fall into kind of a trance and stop. Nobody moved. It was a very moving experience. It was a difficult moment of my life.

So then I asked to see him. To my great surprise, because generally it was very difficult to see him, he said to meet him at the convent. I went with my friend. I was scared because she went to see him before me in the cell, and she came out crying. I said, "What happened?" She said, "He just slapped me and told me to get out. He was very rough." Then I went in, and I told him that I didn't quite believe in the Church. And he said, "You must think that I'm an idiot because why do you come to see me then?" I said, "I don't know. I thought I needed you." If he had only embraced me at the moment, probably —I don't know—I would have fallen right back into the arms of the Church. He just talked to me very nicely.

Then, when I left the convent, the padre at the door asked me how it went. I said, "The Mass was really something. I shall never forget it. But meeting him, I was disappointed because he just spoke to me the way any priest would speak: 'God gives you a gift, and you must compose the right music in honor of God', and such." And the man said, "Many people are disappointed when they meet him because he's just a simple peasant. But because of the fact that he talked to you and said he wanted to see you, you'll never forget this meeting. And one day, when you least expect it, he'll help you." He did.

REILLY: He did? How?

MENOTTI: Well, it's something very private.

REILLY: But you have written some music to the glory of God, haven't you?

MENOTTI: Yes, of course. I believe in God.

REILLY: I loved this other statement that you made to the *Washington Post*: "You have to pray to God to give you the gift of inspiration. Brahms, Puccini, Strauss, Mahler, they all say this: it was not I who wrote it; I was only an instrument. If God doesn't help you, you might as well not write music. If God tells you He has left you, then you have to close up shop."

MENOTTI: I believe in that, yes.

REILLY: So God's been helping you all this time.

MENOTTI: Well, that's a compliment you pay me. I think that being helped by God is not enough. You must deserve the gift. Then you must work and know what to do with the gift. There are many musicians and composers who have the gift and don't know how to use it because they are not ready, because they don't work hard enough. God doesn't just give it to you; you have to work for it.

REILLY: So now we're closing with the parable of the talents. God has given you substantial talents, and you're going to return that investment more than twofold, Maestro.

MENOTTI: I'm too old now.

REILLY: No, you've already done it.

Recommended Recordings

Menotti's operas (25) achieved a high degree of popularity, for which he was typically punished with condescension. He was too "old-fashioned". Despite criticism, Menotti never surrendered the role of beauty. We can now hear one of his strongest expressions of it in the appropriately named *Missa: O Pulchritudo*, written in 1979. The *Missa* was actually recorded by the superb William Ferris Chorale at a live concert in St. James Cathedral in Chicago in 1982, but never released until recently. A Chicago label, Cedille, issued it at mid-price (CDR 7001), paired with French composer Louis Vierne's powerful *Messe Solennelle*, op. 16 (1899).

My first reaction was: What kind of cultural prejudice kept this recording on ice for 25 years? This may be the most beautiful thing Menotti wrote. Beauty is its theme.

Menotti replaced the Credo with a passage from St. Augustine's *Confessions* on the experience of beauty: "O Beauty, ever ancient ever new, late have I loved You." I do not think it is too much of a stretch to say that St. Augustine's experience with beauty mirrored Menotti's own.

The *Missa* is inscribed "In honor of the most Sacred Heart of Jesus". In this offering, Menotti deploys his operatic skills with a spiritual fervor that takes the path of beauty to God in a way that nearly overwhelms with its magnificence and passion. The tenor in this performance, John Vorrasi, recounts in the liner notes that he saw Menotti "in the darkened church listening intently. At the climactic moment of the Sanctus (a drum stroke on the phrase 'heaven and earth are full of your glory') he fell forward to his knees, his head bowed down." Vocally gorgeous, the style of the *Missa* is somewhere between Puccini and Poulenc, leaning toward the latter. The performance and recording are superb, as are the production values of the CD booklet, which is adorned with a reproduction of Sassoferrato's lovely 17th-century painting *The Virgin in Prayer*.

Chandos Records is paying major attention to Menotti's oeuvre, not just his well-known operas but also his orchestral works. This is all to the good since the performances emanate from Menotti's own Spoleto Festival and were directed by a marvelous English conductor, the late Richard Hickox. Another Chandos release offers the Concerto for Violin and Orchestra, one of the sweetest, most lyrical works of its sort from the mid-20th century, beautifully played by violinist Jennifer Koh. It is accompanied by premiere recordings of three short cantatas for voice, chorus, and orchestra, all of which reflect Menotti's spiritual concerns. The first two have texts from the writings of St. Teresa of Avila and St. John of the Cross. The third is Menotti's own take on the death of Orpheus. Taken together, these four works reveal sides of Menotti's work with which few are familiar. You will not regret making their acquaintance.

The Consul, Susan Bullock, Louis Otey, Jacalyn Kreitzer et al., Spoleto Festival Orchestra, Richard Hickox (conductor), Chandos 9706. Chandos' recording is live, from a performance from the 1998 Spoleto Festival.

Missa: O Pulchritudo, Cedille CDR 7001

Violin Concerto: *Muero porque no muero*; *The Death of Orpheus*, et al., Chandos 9979

∼

Einojuhani Rautavaara: The Composer of the Angels

Einojuhani Rautavaara (b. 1928) studied at Helsinki University and the Sibelius Academy. In 1955, a Koussevitzky Foundation award allowed Jean Sibelius to choose Rautavaara for a scholarship to study in the United States, which he did at the Juilliard School in New York. Once associated with an extreme form of modernism (he is the only Finnish composer to have written a completely serial symphony), Rautavaara has achieved broad celebrity well beyond Finland and Scandinavia through later works that are almost embarrassingly beautiful. I was able to explore with the composer his extraordinary musical sojourn that has produced eight symphonies, seven operas, 12 concertos, and a multitude of other substantial works.

REILLY: Let's start early in your career, when the great Jean Sibelius picked you as the most promising young Finnish composer. That must have been quite a weight to bear.

RAUTAVAARA: It certainly was. On the other hand, many Finnish composers have felt that they were under his shadow. But I never really felt that way. Sibelius was very important, but I don't think he influenced my music that much. Once, one of my operas was performed in Germany, and the critics there remarked that it was typical Nordic music in that the melodic line is eternal and expressive. This is a typical thing for Nordic composers. Maybe that is true about my music also.

REILLY: Because of the grant Sibelius arranged for you, you were able to study in the United States with Aaron Copland, Vincent Persichetti, and Roger Sessions. I've tried to detect American influences in your music.

RAUTAVAARA: Did you find any?

REILLY: Yes, but not from them. This may strike you as odd, but it's Roy Harris I hear sometimes. You say your Seventh Symphony searches for its own form and finds it. That is very much the way that Roy Harris' symphonies work, too. And the way you deploy these marvelous sheets of string and brass sound are redolent of him, though not in an imitative way or in so direct a way as you hark back to Bruckner in the Third Symphony.

RAUTAVAARA: Somebody has said that before. But it is impossible that Harris would have influenced me because I didn't know his music well enough. It's interesting to hear that again, though.

REILLY: The other influence I hear, particularly in your wind writing in the symphonies, is from Norwegian composer Harald Sæverud. Did his music have any impact on you?

RAUTAVAARA: Yes, of course. His music has not been around for a long time now, but in the 1950s I really studied him, and I liked him very, very much. And I think he was quite close to what I wanted to do at that time.

REILLY: What about other influences? Composer Kalevi Aho talks about the influence of Prokofiev in the second movement of your First Symphony, of Stravinsky in one movement of your Second, and of Bruckner in your Third. Do you accept these descriptions?

RAUTAVAARA: Why not? Those were the masters that I studied very much and whose music I loved very much. Of course, there are signs of this in my way of writing. That's very natural.

REILLY: Speaking of your symphonies, it has been often remarked that your styles are wildly heterogeneous. And you said in an interview, I'm sure somewhat humorously, that you were a little shocked at the differences among them. Kalevi Aho has used Hegel's "thesis and antithesis" to try to explain the large divergences in styles between one symphony and another. In a way, it's typical for a young man to write full-throated, openhearted, romantic music and then, perhaps as he ages, to turn to a more harsh, hermetic, and sometimes dodecaphonic style. It seems that you have reversed this sequence of events. With your later music, you are writing this gorgeous, rich, melodious, romantic music, both in the Seventh Symphony and your String Quintet. That's unusual.

RAUTAVAARA: I think so. The explanation may be that the only way for me to learn things was to write music in the techniques and styles I encountered. When I was young, I thought it was important to follow my time. So I was a modernist. I was an avant-gardist. I was in the Darmstadt movement. And I wrote serialistic works. When I had more or less learned all those techniques, I realized that if you follow your time, you come after it. You are not leading. The only way for me was to write the kind of music that I liked. That was the only criterion possible. I wrote the kind of music I wanted to hear at the moment. For instance, I learned the classical 12-tone technique in my youth, and I wrote several such works. But there was always the problem that harmony was extremely important for me, so important that it was impossible for me to follow the path the avant-garde took in the late 1950s and 1960s. I had to keep harmony. But still, even today, I think that the 12 tempered tones are the vocabulary of the composer in this century, and it's only the question of syntax, of the organization of that vocabulary. My solution has been to seek a synthesis of the modern and of more or less tonal harmony.

REILLY: In this country, many composers were completely under the influence of Schoenberg. However, many of the younger composers such as John Adams, who at one time were totally indoctrinated in serialism, turned against it. George Rochberg was one of the leaders in doing so. What's curious is that in almost every case, there was some profound personal experience in their lives that showed them the inadequacy of the serial technique to express real grief or joy. In Rochberg's case, he lost his son. There was a death in the family of Ellen Zwilich that turned her against it. So it's curious that this inadequacy was discovered through these means. Has anything like that happened to you?

RAUTAVAARA: I can't say I have had similar experiences, but I realized that I was not able to express myself according to the laws of Darmstadt, of serialism.

REILLY: What was it you couldn't express through those means?

RAUTAVAARA: I had an intuition to do it a certain way, and that idea was not possible to handle in terms of serialism. This force of intuition has grown more and more important for me with the years. Many claim that I am mysticizing my composing by saying that I am not the father or mother of my music but a mediator helping it down from somewhere where it already exists.

REILLY: In saying so, you certainly share Sibelius' view of composition.

RAUTAVAARA: I do. What the music tells you to do, you have to do. I taught composition at the Sibelius Academy for about 30 years, and I often said to my students, "Please don't force your music. Listen to your music when it starts to grow, and find out what it wants, because it's so much wiser than you are." Music is very wise, and it has its own will.

REILLY: Sibelius made the marvelous remark about the composition of his Fifth Symphony that "it was as if God the Father had thrown down pieces of mosaic out of the heaven's floor and asked me to solve how the picture once looked."

RAUTAVAARA: That was a very beautiful metaphor, really, and I quite agree with him. In Thomas Mann's wonderful essay on Wagner, he says that it is difficult not to believe that a work has a will of its own, for which its creator is just a tool for its becoming.

REILLY: You have spoken of your taste for eternity.

RAUTAVAARA: Yes, I've always been interested in metaphysical and religious texts and subjects.

REILLY: What is your religious background?

RAUTAVAARA: Evangelic Lutheran, but my most important early experience was in the Monastery of Valamo, which is an Orthodox monastery. When I was 10 years old, I was taken there by my parents. It was 1939, the last summer when it was still possible, because today it belongs to Russia. In the Winter War, Russia occupied it and took it from Finland. But on that island monastery, I had the deepest experience I've ever had. I was so young, and everything was so strange. All the ceremonies, all those bells and icons, the colors and the sounds. It was really a religious experience. It was very important for me.

REILLY: That experience seems to have borne fruit many years later in *Vigilia* [All-Night Vigil in Memory of St. John the Baptist], which is, vocally, extraordinarily beautiful. I wish to quote something that you said about *Vigilia*: It's "a vast mosaic. In the midst stand two figures, St. John the Baptist and the Virgin, Mother of God. They are surrounded by the apostolic congregation and on the periphery—through the mystery of ecumenical unity—by all of Christendom and all of Western culture." That's a stunning statement. To me, that sounds like the mystical body of Christ.

RAUTAVAARA: Yes. I've written so much on different religious and metaphysical subjects. My first work was called *Requiem in Our Time* and then, later, *Canticum Maria Virgines*. I've been asked, are you very religious? And I found an answer in the citation from Friedrich Schleiermacher, the German theologian, from almost 200 years ago. He wrote, "Religiosity is an interest in an inclination to the infinite." And I said, if that is a good definition, if this is really what religion is, then I am religious. I am not very much for churches and denominations. But I am for the infinite, absolutely. And religion, of course, is something we in Western culture cannot separate ourselves from, because I think Western culture, all of it, music and everything, is based on this dichotomy of two opposite forces, Greek philosophy and Christianity. These two are very different, very opposing, very inimical ideologies. They were united in the first millennium and became the core of Western culture. Therefore, Western culture is completely based on Greek philosophy and Christianity. We never escape from them, and because they are such opposing forces, it makes for an interesting culture.

REILLY: Your openness to the infinite is shared in the United States by a number of composers who feel the emptiness of our commercial, consumerist culture and the inherent inadequacy of the modernistic techniques, which you yourself turned from. They feel the need to reconnect with the musical traditions that, as you just said, fundamentally arose from a view that was synthesized from Hellenism and Christianity.

RAUTAVAARA: Yes, somehow this is in the character of our time. My basic conviction is that there are other kinds of realities; or rather I would say other kinds of consciousness, beyond rational concepts and words. I've expressed this in works with "angel" in the title, like *Angels and Visitations, Angel of Light*, and so on. There actually is no word for the concept "angel", but if you want, we can speak of angels. Music is a language where we can tell about those other realities almost with exactness but without words. Therefore, music is much better.

REILLY: So music is the language of angels?

RAUTAVAARA: It's the language of angels, right.

REILLY: You must find it quite ironic that you have been swept up in the contemporary angel craze, since you have been writing pieces like this for several decades.

RAUTAVAARA: It's been somewhat embarrassing that angels have today . . . become so fashionable that the image is banalized. What we see today is the angel of Christian kitsch, a pretty blonde in a nightgown, with the swan wings, and so on. But my musical angels were born in the 1970s when nobody spoke about angels. They were not fashionable at all. *Angels and Visitations* was the first work with "angel" in the title. Those angels were related to the angel from Rainer Maria Rilke, who said every angel is terrifying. It is an archetype for me.

REILLY: You have had experiences, Maestro. Could you tell me whether they were dream experiences or otherwise? Was it a force you experienced, or was it a personal presence?

RAUTAVAARA: Really, it was a dream about an angel; I think it was an angel. I remembered it only in the 1970s, when I was already a grown man. I remembered then that Jacob, in the Bible, meets an angel and wrestles it all the night through. Then, I suddenly remembered that I had this dream when I was only seven or eight years old, a dream that was really a nightmare, coming to me night after night. I was scared because it was a huge, rather formless, gray, and silent being, which came slowly towards me and took me in his arms, and I felt suffocated. I had to fight and wrestle with him. And as I later thought, you are supposed to wrestle with your angel, as Jacob did in the Bible. When I remembered this dream some 40 years later, I understood that it really was a visitation, a revelation. This word *visitation* in English, means "a revelation".

REILLY: A revelation of what?

RAUTAVAARA: Things both positive and negative. And, therefore, those words, angels and visitations, stayed in my mind, repeating like a mantra, until somehow musical energy started to grow around those obstinate words, and I composed *Angels and Visitations* in 1978.

REILLY: Can I ask you about some of the angel pieces? When I listen to your Third Symphony, it's all of a piece. When I listen to the Seventh, I have the same feeling—that I'm entering a world complete in itself. It's unique. Now, in some of your angel evocations, events take place that don't appear to grow out of the music. Some of these events sound catastrophic, random eruptions of violence that seem to arise from somewhere outside of the music and that intrude into it. Have I misread this, or is that what you're trying to express?

RAUTAVAARA: I think that might be *Angels and Visitations*, where there are very opposite, very different, very contrasting things following each other. In the middle of a *cantabile*, there comes a very violent *fortissimo*, and so on. I don't describe anything in that music, but the forces are so opposite, so inimical to each other in a way I simply couldn't help. That's the way they wanted to come to the music.

REILLY: Speaking about your work as a symphonist, you wrote your first several symphonies in relatively quick succession. But after the Fourth Symphony, you didn't write another one for 23 years. Why? Was it because the serialism in the Fourth Symphony brought you to a dead end, temporarily?

RAUTAVAARA: Yes. That is exactly what it was. I went so far, as far as it was possible to go, in this serialistic technique, and that was the Fourth Symphony. Then I realized, "No, this is not my way." I knew after composing it that I didn't want to go on in this direction because I felt like I was becoming a programmer instead of a composer. I was writing a nice, beautiful, more or less mathematical plan, a blueprint for a symphony that just has to be written with notes, and that was not interesting. That wasn't fun anymore. It's not composing; it's something else. So I turned completely away from it.

REILLY: As variegated as your styles have been, hearing the Seventh Symphony, I can now go back and listen to your earlier works and hear wisps of it. I can almost hear the Seventh coming, though not in the sense that I could have ever predicted it. But in the Third Symphony, even in the orchestral parts of the piano concerti, and certainly in some of the cantos, I can hear in gestation the Seventh, which seems to be such a marvelous summing-up of a direction in which you were slowly headed. Is the Seventh a grand summing-up for you?

RAUTAVAARA: Yes, I think every large composition is a summing-up. What you say is very interesting and very true. For example, the Third Symphony is, in a way, a 12-tone work, though nobody believes it. But the 12-tone series is used all through it, and every note comes from the 12-tone series, although there are things in it that are forbidden to the 12-tone technique, like octaves and triads. In the very beginning of that symphony, there is the horn solo. And that horn solo goes through 12 chromatic tones. They are all there. That is the total 12-tone row, but it is a melody, isn't it? Beautiful melody. But to find a synthesis of harmony and modernism, that was my problem. And that is what I have been doing most of my life. I knew that this was the music of my time, but what I wanted to create, what I wanted to hear, was music that was emotional and beautiful.

REILLY: Do you accept the description of yourself as a romantic?

RAUTAVAARA: I think I am. I've given this definition of a romantic: He's one who is not right here but somewhere else.

REILLY: And where is that somewhere else?

RAUTAVAARA: Well, it's either behind or in front of you, coming or gone.

REILLY: Can it also be above you?

RAUTAVAARA: Also that. That's very important, certainly. And he is not right now; he's in the past or in the future, either one.

REILLY: I mentioned "above" because I wanted to close by speaking of your string quintet, *Unknown Heavens*, which is such a beautiful work and very much of a piece with your Seventh Symphony. They're almost matching pieces.

RAUTAVAARA: Yes, they are very close to each other, and there's only one year between them.

REILLY: Some readers will be encountering your music for the first time. Where do you think they should begin?

RAUTAVAARA: Maybe not from the beginning, as I have done, because it takes 70 years, but from the end—that is, from the late works, the Seventh Symphony and the Quintet.

REILLY: Is that where you think you sound most like yourself?

RAUTAVAARA: Yes. At this moment I think so. Of course, you are different. If a composer writes exactly the same thing now as he did when he was 20 years old, then I think he is infantile, isn't he? Something happens with a man in his life. And that must influence his creation, his writing.

Recommended Recordings

The complete symphonies can be had in a budget box or separately, Ondine 1145

Symphonies 1, 2, and 3, Leipzig RSO, Max Pommer (conductor), Ondine 740

The Third Symphony is the most magnificent homage to Bruckner produced in the 20th century.

Seventh Symphony *Angel of Light* and *Annunciations* Organ Concerto Kari Jussila (organ), Helsinki Philharmonic Orchestra, Leif Segerstam (conductor), Ondine 869

The Seventh Symphony is a hauntingly beautiful work that employs almost constant undulating string ostinatos and a grand hymn motif and builds to several impressive climaxes.

Piano Concerto No. 3: *Gift of Dreams*; *Autumn Gardens*, Vladimir Ashkenazy (piano, conductor), Helsinki PO, Ondine 950

Angels and Visitations; Violin Concerto; *Isle of Bliss*, Elmar Oliveira (violin), Helsinki Philharmonic Orchestra, Leif Segerstam, Ondine 881

The preceding three concertos (without the couplings) are also available as part of a budget box of the complete concertos which further includes Rautavaara's *Cantus Arcticus*, his enchanting concerto for orchestra and arctic birdsong on tape. (Ondine 1156)

Vigilia (All-Night Vigil in Memory of St. John the Baptist for Choir and Soloists) Finnish Radio Chamber Choir (Timo Nuoranne), Ondine 910

Also available as part of a budget box of the complete choral works. (Ondine 1186)

Missa a cappella, *Two Vespers* from *Vigilia* (in English), *Ave Maria gratia plena* et al., Latvian Radio Choir, Sigvards Kļava (director), Ondine 1223

String Quintet: *Unknown Heavens*, and String Quartets 1 and 2, Jean Sibelius Quartet, Ondine 909

〜

George Rochberg:
The Recovery of Modern Music

Composer George Rochberg (1918–2005) was the pivot point around which American music took a decisive turn away from Arnold Schoenberg's systematized dissonance, known as 12-tone or serial music, back toward tonality. If it is now safe to return to the concert halls, it is largely because of him. Before turning against 12-tone music in the mid-1960s, Rochberg had been one of its most adept and prestigious practitioners. Thus his "conversion" provoked an outraged reaction from the musical establishment and the avant-garde. However, Rochberg's courage helped to free the next generation of composers from the serial straitjacket to write music that was once again comprehensible to audiences. New World Records has recordings of Rochberg's Quartets 3 through 6, brilliantly performed by the Concord String Quartet. These works, especially the Third Quartet, were very much at the heart of the controversy caused by Rochberg's attempt to "regain contact with the tradition and means of the past". At his home in Pennsylvania, I was able to speak with Rochberg about what is at stake in modern music and about his own extraordinary spiritual and musical journey.

REILLY: What did you find lacking within traditional tonal resources that led you to embrace Schoenberg's 12-tone system in the first place?

ROCHBERG: It suddenly dawned on me that 19th-century romanticism, except for early classical music and the best of baroque, is clearly the best music that human beings have produced to date. I was trying to find a way to say what I had experienced, but transformed in musical terms that meant everything to me, and still to take with me what I had learned from the classics. I was unconscious of this, to tell you the truth. I didn't realize until years after I had launched into that whole experience of the 12 tone that my 12-tone music was utterly different from every other American's, let alone any European's.

REILLY: In what way?

ROCHBERG: Well, it just sounded different. It takes me back to what I started to say. Qualifying 19th-century romanticism, it's a soft romanticism. By soft I mean that one of its deepest sources is a longing for the ideal, a longing for that which can never be—not on this earth. So of course, we invent heavens and gardens of Eden and all kinds of wonderful dream images of the life, which is the total opposite of the one that most human beings through the ages have experienced: harsh, short, brutish. The First World War was the destruction of idealism, the destruction even of nostalgia or of the ability to live a nostalgic inner life—always longing for that which cannot be. After the Second World War was the emergence of hard romanticism, which I realize now is what I was practicing and still do. Hard because you know that the ideal is no longer possible. So you now open your work up to chaos; you open it up to the sharp angularities of dissonance, and you can almost calibrate the degree of dissonance emotionally in a qualifying sense, not a quantitative sense. I think that the best 20th-century music—you could probably include certain Berg, some Schoenberg, only some of it because I think a lot of it is very bad, ugly, ugly.

REILLY: Did the effect of World War II on you play a role in how attractive you found serialism at that time?

ROCHBERG: That's a fair question because there is a relationship. I rarely talk about my experiences in the war. I was preoccupied with just trying to stay alive during the Second World War. I was a second lieutenant in the infantry. I was very bitter about the fact that I was ripped out of my studies at the age of 24. Anyhow, somewhere around the late 1940s, early 1950s, I began to realize that this confrontation with death had been probably the most potent experience in my life up to that point. I had been severely wounded at one stage. I recovered and was sent back to the front. As the years passed, I began to realize that this was really an incredible thing. I once described my feelings during those three years that I was in the Army and particularly the one year that I was in Europe. I experienced what I call "psychic anesthesia", which is a way of protecting yourself against any form of feelings. You are not blotto, but there is probably a two-inch layer of something in your psyche that is holding back immediate impressions. I knew that I had to find a way to hook onto the 20th century. This is very late; I'm now about 30. Up until that point, I'd been struggling with trying to master the tonal and was never happy because you can't be happy with mastering the tonal if your models are what they had to be. I mean, there are no substitutes for Beethoven, Schubert, and Brahms, and all of these monoliths that loom in the sky, right? But I made the effort.

REILLY: I'll tell you what is impelling my question related to World War II: What happened was so cruel and what was seen was so horrifying that the people who experienced it, or even who reflected upon it and hadn't a direct experience of it, fled into abstraction because the more repugnant reality is the more abstract art becomes as an escape from it. Was any of that operating within you when you turned to serialism?

ROCHBERG: No.

REILLY: Because it seems to me that either there is something like that at work, or there is, at an intellectual level, a shared discovery with Schoenberg that somehow the sources of tonality have been exhausted, and we have to go into some bold new frontier.

ROCHBERG: There is a little bit of everything in what you say. As I think back on it, the real reason why I went that way is that I needed to find a language with which I could say what I had experienced, but obviously in a way which was refractive, not brutalized by the nature of the experience itself. That experience itself drew me into the necessity to make damn sure that whatever I composed, if I could manage it, would be as beautiful as I could make it. That was the counter to the horror of all these things which ultimately add up to the noise that human beings produce on this earth.

I can't say very much for the younger generation of European composers. Their abstraction really set in with a vengeance. And they had been through the mill as young kids in their 20s when the war was over. And they are looking around at the ruins of their one-time culture. And they want to revivify it; they want to bring it back but in their way. They want to speak their language. So of course, they embraced the language that was the cutting edge with which you could say all those tough things. But they were not romantic; they were abstract.

REILLY: You began talking about what the serial language allowed you to express—what you felt needed to be expressed in that way. This language was adopted by so many composers, by the academy, by the awards system. It became suffocating. Then there was a wholesale rejection of it led by you.

ROCHBERG: That's what they say.

REILLY: And for good reason. Certainly, you were the most prestigious person to get up and say: No! That was such a dramatic break and thing to do. Having found the means to express what you needed through that serial system, what then turned you against it so decisively?

ROCHBERG: It had reached its limits for myself.

REILLY: And how do you define its limits?

ROCHBERG: I couldn't breathe anymore. I needed air. I was tired of the same round of manipulating the pitches, vertically and horizontally. It wasn't so much that the scales were out of the running; arpeggios were out of the running; octave passages were out of the running; etc.— anything that could possibly smack of the habits of composing 50 years earlier or even contemporaneously the way a Stravinsky or a Bartók would operate. What I finally realized was that there were no cadences, that you can't come to a natural pause, that you can't write a musical comma, colon, semicolon, dash for dramatic, expressive purposes or to enclose a thought.

REILLY: So there is nothing natural about it?

ROCHBERG: There is everything artificial about it. And it doesn't provide you with the unconscious level of feeling that you need to write music, not easily but readily.

REILLY: Composer John Adams said that when he was in college, he "learned that tonality died somewhere around the same time that Nietzsche's god died. And I believed it." Adams was educated in serialism, as most composers at the time were. He said it takes some kind of profound shock to turn you from it. He never talks about what that profound shock was in his own life. Other composers have, like Ellen Taaffe Zwilich. It was her husband's death that turned her around. And you, of course, have referred to your own son Paul's terrible death in 1964.

ROCHBERG: That was the catalyst.

REILLY: Can we talk about how that revealed to you the bankruptcy of serialism and the need to reconnect with the past?

ROCHBERG: It was a shock of a kind that necessitated a new sense of how I had to live the rest of my life. While you are living, you are not living for self-gratification or the satisfaction of appetite. It's like taking on some sort of spiritual or moral obligation to perform at a level which is outside the bounds of the normal human. So, in a way, I can now say calmly, as I think back, that the Third Quartet is really a declaration of that idea in music, though you couldn't necessarily glean it from what it says musically, from what it sounds like. It sounds like a lot of things, even a lot of contradictory things, depending on your point of view. Paul taught me something that I had only experienced myself during the war but not that deeply yet. He confirmed in me all kinds of tendencies that had been there, and I could only give expression to them in my music. If you know my *Contra Mortem et Tempus*, in the space of a couple of weeks, I wrote *Contra Mortem*, followed immediately by the *Music for the Magic Theater*. I wouldn't say I was somnambulistic —that would be very pretty, but a lie—but I was in some sort of a state. This was a few months after Paul's death. These came incredibly easily. They are the beginning of the turn. Then the turn starts speeding up. By 1971, I wrote the *Caprice Variations* for solo violin. That work is a garden of all sorts of possibilities that I am exploring briefly through the variations on Paganini. There are non-tonal things; there are tonal things. That was, musically, the real turning point, not the Third Quartet. Actually, by 1961, I was already experiencing very serious doubts about this thing called 12 tone. What is this thing called atonality? as Cole Porter would ask. And I am beginning to think that there is something wrong here, and you have to work your way out of this labyrinth, this maze, so that you can be free and you can once again sing. I am a natural singer. My 12-tone music also sings in a way that no American 12-tone music sings.

REILLY: You mastered the language of serialism as few composers have. One composer said that all serial music sounds like all other serial music, but not yours.

ROCHBERG: Yes, academic serial music.

REILLY: Also, I don't think you played by the rules.

ROCHBERG: [*Laughter*] What are the rules?

REILLY: The rules are Schoenberg's rules, and you know them very well. But listen to your Second Symphony! There is an astonishing work, which may have a tone row, but it's not a strictly serial work by any stretch of the imagination.

ROCHBERG: What is it masking? What is it hiding?

REILLY: You tell me. Is it hiding anything?

ROCHBERG: Well, what do you hear? I'm just curious. I can tell you some of the reasons why you have found me out.

REILLY: I hear an intense level of energy. I find ample consonance in it. I find identifiable themes. The rhythms are so enlivening, and the orchestration is at a level of breathtaking brilliance—not in the sense that it says, "Look at me", calling attention to itself, but just the level of craft is astonishing. When first listening to the CD, I thought that this is from his serial period and it is going to hurt a little. I put the headphones on, and I couldn't take them off. I was absolutely gripped by the piece and thought, wait a minute; this is not serialism as I know it. He's not playing by the rules here.

ROCHBERG: Well, rules are meant to be broken, which even Schoenberg recognized. The truth of the matter is that the orthodoxy of Schoenberg is not even followed by Alban Berg, who was his friend and close associate. Or Webern. As a matter of fact, Webern is really saying to the old man: You're not tough enough; you're not abstract enough; you're not logical enough. You're too hot. And that has to do with temperament. By the time I wrote that symphony in early 1955, I had discovered something. It didn't matter to me if someone else knew it or not. All these things are esoterica. There was a way of using the hexachord, which Schoenberg invented or discovered, that is really a very sort of natural way of understanding the symmetry of the 12 tones. The idea of the symmetry of the 12 tones led me to understand why music had been what it had been up to that time, completely under the aegis of asymmetry, which is open.

In asymmetry, everything flows; there is enormous energy. The roads are open. The pathways are open, and it's endless really. It's almost arbitrary that the *Eroica Symphony* ends where it does. It could have gone on for 10 more hours, always changing. That's much harder to do with a 12-tone row because it's all circular. Everything is constantly looping back on itself. You might make wide loops so that you get back more slowly, but you're still going around in these looping circles. The crazy thing is that I discovered a row, which gave me the possibility of three inversions, which were natural derivations from the row, which were outlined in their first notes so that the other notes had the same relationship to each other, an augmented triad. This precedes the fact that I discovered later, 10 years later, that that same augmented triad, to which you then add the diminished chord, is the equal distance subdivision of the 12 notes. And now, you are already in the land of the circular. I think that the first note of the first inversion is C sharp; second in order, a major third lower, is A; and the third, a major third lower again, was F. So I decided to use those as what I later came to understand as tonal loci, not keys but places where I could sit for a while and use these relationships. Of course, the row itself was a tune to begin with. It was not some abstract figuration out of which I could do this and that. But sure, I drew all sorts of ideas out of it. In that sense, I followed Schoenberg's lead. All of his rows really start with melodic ideas, good, bad, or indifferent.

REILLY: I have spent the last several weeks listening to your Quartets 3 through 6. And I tried to do a little blind listening by imagining that I didn't know anything about the music—the composer, when it was written, or where. Not knowing anything, what would I think? First of all, I would never think that this was written by an American composer.

ROCHBERG: [*Laughter*]

REILLY: I would say this music was written by a Viennese composer. I would say that this is a composer who is straddling the fault line between the First and Second Viennese Schools. He leans one way, and all of a sudden, you are back in the world of Mahler and Franz Schmidt and Schubert and Beethoven. And then he will just lean the other way and, all of a sudden, you are with Schoenberg, Webern, and Berg. And he keeps leaning back and forth throughout these works. Sometimes, he somehow leans in both ways simultaneously.

ROCHBERG: Oh, I like that.

REILLY: It is also an attempt to stitch that fault line together in some way. So, this is someone of both schools who is trying to reconcile them. Somewhere you are quoted as having spoken of irony in the Third Quartet in your use of either quotations or styles from the First Viennese School. In my blind listening, I don't detect any irony at all. In a letter Mozart wrote in 1781, he says that "passion, whether violent or not, may never be expressed to the point of revulsion. Even in the most frightening situation, music must never offend the ear, but must even then offer enjoyment, in other words, music must always remain music." You reminded me of this because, when I got to the Variation movement in the Third Quartet, I froze. Some commentators say Rochberg is writing like Beethoven. Beethoven was nowhere in my mind because of the kind of sustained stillness you achieve there, a piercing poignancy. I thought I had not heard anything like that since the Adagietto from Mahler's Fifth Symphony. Again, in the Mesto movement in the Fifth Quartet, you express a piercing sorrow that meets every criteria of Mozart. The wholesale revivification of this language and the level of your achievement in utilizing it are astonishing. Your music is saying: Here is what you have forgotten; here are the old masters, not in a museum visit, but as real expressions of these passions, sorrows, and, in some places, joys.

ROCHBERG: I have to say you really understand my music, what I have tried to say. This is all very consciously meant. No irony, no effort to imitate. It's as though I am living this music because it is in me. I know it. In 1972, shortly after I wrote the Third Quartet, I wrote this commentary on Beethoven's op. 102, my *Ricordanza*. Michael Steinberg, the music critic, was in Darmstadt, which was the Mecca of the avant-garde, and he said, "I am going to play a piece for you, and I am not going to tell you when it was written or by whom." So he played the *Ricordanza* and threw it open for discussion. They all agreed it was a 19th-century piece, probably written in the last quarter of the century. It couldn't be Brahms, because it's not Brahms melodically or harmonically. They couldn't identify it. Steinberg said, "Let me enlighten you. This piece was written in America in 1972 by George Rochberg." The place exploded. How dare that man do something like this! This is a traitorous act. It is worse than slumming. It is infamous. It is a disgrace.

REILLY: How about the reaction to your Violin Concerto? We could move that up a couple of decades from the 1870s.

ROCHBERG: I was called everything from forger, to counterfeiter, to panderer, to ventriloquist. It was just a repetition of the reaction to the Third Quartet. On the other hand, others said, this might really be a good work after all; we can't tell yet. I still love the work. I've had a curious response to people's reaction to my tonal music. One of my elder colleagues is reputed to have said, "Why does George want to write beautiful music? We've done that already." Fine.

REILLY: That plays into Schoenberg's famous remark that he was "cured of the delusion that the aim of art is beauty".

ROCHBERG: But I have reembraced the art of beauty but with a madness. Absolutely. That is the only reason to want to write music. The only reason. But what do I mean by what is beautiful? I mean that which is genuinely expressive, even if it hurts. For example, a poet like William Butler Yeats hurts. Whereas I find John Ashbery prosaic, dull—ash cans, concrete on the streets of New York. Nothing rises in me. I am talking about a search for the beautiful. I know that what is really beautiful hurts. Great music is enunciatory, telling us that there are places, things, regions beyond us. It is trying to measure the immeasurable. Music gives us glimpses, glimmers of that immeasurable, and that is why it has to be beautiful.

REILLY: Let me ask you about mixing these two languages, atonality and tonality. In your Quintet for Piano and Strings, I remember the outer movements are atonal and the center tonal. You talked of the progression of going from atonality to the tonal and back as one from darkness to light, and to darkness again. Does this mean you equate atonality with darkness?

ROCHBERG: In a sense, yes. If I were composing right now—I'm not, I'm writing my memoirs—I would probably try to continue where I left off with *Circles of Fire*, which is a kind of grand summation of everything I can conceive of which has a potential beauty, which relates to the past, to my recent past, to my present, and to my potential future.

REILLY: Let me mention to you my larger thesis and see whether you agree with it or not. Schoenberg's diagnosis was that the tonal resources of Western music were exhausted. The anthracite vein had been completely mined; so now, we have to find atomic power or something. Therefore, he comes up with this tone row. What bothers me is that this is a materialistic diagnosis, and the remedy for it is equally materialistic in that it is mechanical. However, the collapse of music in the early part of the 20th century was the result of the spiritual devastation of Europe, not of an exhaustion of tonal resources. Equally, the recovery of tonality in music is a spiritual recovery.

ROCHBERG: I would agree a thousand percent.

REILLY: In fact, I would take it a bit further with Schoenberg. What I discovered in Schoenberg is a Gnostic tendency. His obsession with numerology is one of the tip-offs. He is a Pythagorean in his belief that number is the key to the universe, but not in the ancient classical sense. He was a modern kind of alchemist in the sense that he thought that, through his system, he could manipulate reality and reconstitute it on a metaphysical level. Now that is not a musical enterprise. That is a Gnostic enterprise. Anyone who says you shall hear dissonance as consonance because of my system is engaged in reconstituting reality.

ROCHBERG: I like the way you are putting it. I understand what you are getting at. You are laying it at Schoenberg's feet. But you know Schoenberg was a good friend of the painter Wassily Kandinsky, who incidentally was an anthroposophist. He started out as a theosophist and then wandered off to become a Steinerite [Rudolph Steiner, Austrian spiritualist, 1861–1925]. It fits your idea because all these guys were looking for some spiritual and metaphysical way out of their dilemma. They had diagnosed their problem in a wrong way. People don't often get their own circumstances right. They misread them; they misjudge them. They are not sufficiently grounded in ideas that extend way beyond their present. They lack the substrata, that which is unchangeable, the unalterable. This is the idea of trying to start over again from scratch, which is what Schoenberg essentially did. I think he went way off. There is no virtue in starting all over again. The past refuses to be erased. Unlike Pierre Boulez, I will not praise amnesia. It's always interesting trying to diagnose what hordes of people in an elite do when they look at which way the wind is blowing. They just bought all of this without even studying the consequences or the roots of it.

REILLY: Schoenberg made a very revelatory remark, which takes us back to my notion of him as a Gnostic. He said, "Tonality does not serve; it must be served." In other words, it is something to which you must submit yourself. You must conform yourself to reality; reality does not conform itself to you. His response is "non serviam". I am not going to serve. I am going to establish the new rules which will be served. This is the problem, and I am the solution to it. You will serve me rather than tonality.

ROCHBERG: He did say that the 12-tone system would ensure the primacy of German music for the next century. Now this is a stupid remark. He said, "In the years to come, schoolchildren will be listening to and singing 12-tone melodies." All right fellows, let's sing the opening of the Fourth Quartet!

I had a great experience one time when I was teaching. I walked into class and said to my kids in a seminar on composition, "How many of you know the Schoenberg Fourth Quartet?" Most of the hands went up. I went to the piano and played the D right above middle C and said, "Okay, let's sing the tone row." Five notes later, they petered out. Five notes and *kaput*! I looked at them and said, "How can you claim to know a work like the Fourth Quartet if you can't even sing it yourself, you can't vocalize the pitches of the first violin tune? Start thinking about that. You don't know anything until you can sing it. And that goes for your own music, too."

REILLY: What happens if you can't sing it?

ROCHBERG: Then you're in big trouble. I knew early on that you couldn't make music unless you could perform it yourself. The ideal of adopting an abstract, pseudo-logical technique such as serialism—if you're not a musician what are you going to base it on? The poor kids couldn't remember Schoenberg's tone row! Serialism is the denial of memory. You can't internalize it; you can't vocalize it; it can't live in you. Schoenberg had no understanding of the limitations of human beings and of the ears of musicians. I'll grant the demise of tonality as we knew it, but I won't grant that it was exhausted. What happened is that it went underground. It just transformed itself from within under everyone's noses and ears. They didn't recognize what had really happened, and they assumed it had died. That story is really *The Circles of Fire* [1996–1997]. It's what lies at the heart of *The Circles of Fire*. Music remains what it has always been: a sign that man is capable of transcending the limits and constraints of his material existence.

(For Recommended Recordings, see the Rochberg chapter, p. 281.)

∿

Carl Rütti: Dancing before the Ark

Born in 1949, Rütti grew up in Zug, Switzerland. He has been widely recognized for his compositions in England, whose great choral tradition inspired him at an early age. During several phone conversations and a visit to his home, I was able to explore the deep faith and religiosity that informs his compositions.

REILLY: Your musical education was instrumental, was it not? You studied piano?

RÜTTI: Yes. My instruments were piano and organ.

REILLY: Did you ever seek to study composition formally?

RÜTTI: Yes, I did. But when I showed my music to the music professor, he said that it was silly to compose in a tonal way in this day and age. So there was no need to go to a composition professor.

REILLY: Why did he say it was silly to compose in a tonal way?

RÜTTI: He felt that, after Schoenberg, you could not compose tonal music anymore. But I felt in a tonal way, so I did not think it necessary to study composition theory. I simply studied counterpoint and harmony.

REILLY: I think one of the most frightening things Schoenberg ever said was that he "was cured of the delusion that the artist's aim is to create beauty". What has always surprised me is how many people followed him in that perverse conviction.

RÜTTI: Maybe they were sure that this was the right way. I was never sure that this was the right way. I think beauty is important everywhere.

REILLY: What do you think about contemporary music?

RÜTTI: I think that, after Schoenberg's 12-tone music, one had to go on and on. You couldn't go back anymore. That's why every composer went a bit further. And then, John Cage called the following event the premiere of his newest work: he let a concert piano drop down from a helicopter and smash on the ground. With the destruction of instruments and Cage's noncomposition, in which a pianist sits at the piano for four and a half minutes without playing, you can't go any further. After these events, we were free. That released all the composers of our time. So, there's no more need to go on any further, because the final stage had been reached.

REILLY: So, what do you feel free to do?

RÜTTI: Simply to write the way I want to write.

REILLY: And what is the way you want to write?

RÜTTI: The way I feel. When I start a work, I don't know the way I'm going to write it, but I have a certain vision of the sound and of the structure, and then I try it at the piano.

REILLY: You told me that when you showed a Swiss composer your music, he said it was charmingly naïve. Has that kind of condescension continued, or are you finally getting some respect?

RÜTTI: In Switzerland, it has continued for quite a long time. But in England, I've had another experience.

REILLY: You are a prophet unappreciated in your own land, but they love you in England?

RÜTTI: Yes, that's it, though I'm very much appreciated for my writing for amateur choirs here.

REILLY: How were you drawn to liturgical music?

RÜTTI: I was in high school in Engelberg in a Benedictine monastery school, and there I got a certain sense of liturgy. I'm Catholic, you know. I was singing Gregorian chant in the monastery school as a soprano and, later, as a baritone. We sang almost everything in our Mass. We could sing with organ or a cappella. So I was very used to liturgy.

REILLY: How were you drawn to composition?

RÜTTI: I don't know exactly. I think it really began when I was in England. Before, it was just improvisation. I played in a jazz group. So, I improvised a lot. And then in England, I heard this extraordinarily high standard of choral singing. The voices are like keys. You can play on them like you can play on a piano. And that's why I started to compose for choir first.

REILLY: Do you consider yourself primarily a liturgical composer or a religious composer?

RÜTTI: I would say a religious composer.

REILLY: In other words, the same sort of religious vision infuses all of your work?

RÜTTI: Yes, you can say that.

REILLY: You seem unafraid to address the deepest mysteries of Christianity in your music. And that must take great faith.

RÜTTI: Yes. If I take a commission for a new work, it's always a very strong act of faith, because I have no ability to compose. I just have the hope that I've got the inspiration for it. And probably that's why there's a certain sense of faith in every work.

REILLY: Could you say anything more about the role of faith in your music?

RÜTTI: If you would ask me whether I think God exists or not, I would say it's exactly the same as if you asked me whether I think the sun exists or not. It's so obvious that God has to exist. I see this through my work. When I think that, for about 25 years, I have had one commission after the other, but usually they are grouped for certain instruments or themes, though the commissions come from completely different people. For example, I was recently asked by three different people to write for brass. One is a psalm for brass band and choir, one is a competition piece, and one is a piece for a farmer who sings a very archaic Alpine psalm over his cows and land every evening to bless them for the night. And so, there they are grouped together. I think the real commissioner of my music is God. So I'm always sure that when he asks me to write a piece, He will give me the ideas. And it has worked for all 25 years now.

REILLY: That sense of inspiration is powerfully conveyed in your work. You make the transcendent perceptible. And it's profoundly moving in that very strange combination of something that is so traditional, yet completely fresh. I think it is your unique inspiration and gift to achieve that. What's also curious is the way you have achieved this. I've written quite a bit about Pärt, Tavener, and Górecki, as well as a number of other tonal composers who are your contemporaries. What's interesting about Tavener is that he went to the Orthodox style of music; Pärt, that he has returned to medieval organum and Renaissance styles; and you, yourself, seem steeped in chant and Renaissance polyphony. But at the same time, there would be no mistaking your music as anything other than modern because of the rhythms you use. Tell me about how that evolved in your work, how you became so deeply engaged in the Renaissance style, yet used within it this extraordinarily lively sense of rhythm?

RÜTTI: Maybe the Renaissance style was from my exposure to choral singing in England. When I first heard an English choir, they had this way of singing, especially in Renaissance music. They had to sing a lot of lines and in quite close harmonies. Every voice had to be very pure and without vibrato. And this fascinated me. The work which inspired me most was Scarlatti's *Stabat Mater* for 10 parts. I heard it performed by the BBC Symphony Chorus. For me this was the beginning of writing motets for 10-part voices. In regard to rhythmical music, I was once at a concert in 1975 in Fribourg when Stars of Faith, a gospel group, gave a concert. I was very taken with this music.

REILLY: Now that you have mentioned gospel music, let me say I've read several reviews of your work in the *Gramophone* and in magazines here in the United States. None of them mentioned the first thing I wanted to ask you about your style, and that is: Have you been influenced by Black spirituals?

RÜTTI: Yes, certainly. I remember back in high school I once had this gramophone record of Black liturgy. I think it was American. When the minister gave his sermon, he got more and more excited, and the people in church answered back. Then a piano came in. And the minister was singing the prayers and all the community was answering in a very rhythmical way. This intrigued me.

REILLY: I'm glad to hear you say that because I hear the same kind of uninhibited impulsiveness of Black spirituals in your music. And I was wondering, since you are a Swiss composer, whether I was hallucinating, or whether the influence was really there.

RÜTTI: Yes, of course. As a young boy, I was always interested in the Black music of the United States. And I've tried to improvise at the piano in this way.

REILLY: You certainly have integrated it into Renaissance polyphony in a most exciting way. It's not something one would expect to hear, and it comes with such a rush of excitement. I would say more than that, because what you achieve in your music is a sense of the sacred, particularly in manifestations of innocence, purity, and freshness.

RÜTTI: In the Bible, there is this story about King David when he was carrying the sacred ark to the temple. He danced in front of the ark in such a way that his wife was shocked by it when she saw it. I think this is a very deep meaning of liturgy.

REILLY: What do you mean by that?

RÜTTI: I mean that liturgical music, like the Gloria, has to be very exciting and very rhythmical. That is proved in the Bible by King David dancing in front of the ark. He lost all sense of himself.

REILLY: The first time I heard the Ite Missa Est of your *Missa Angelorum*, and more than just the first time, the hair actually rose on the back of my head. It was extraordinary, thrilling. There, the transcendent is perceptible. But that is the last part of the Mass you wrote. The *Missa Angelorum* is interesting in that you didn't write it all at once.

RÜTTI: Yes, it was my very first commission in Switzerland for boys and male choir. I was asked to write an easy Mass for amateurs. I wrote several parts, but it was too difficult for them. Then, when the BBC Symphony Chorus asked for more music, I gave it to them. I rewrote it in another style especially for the BBC Symphony Chorus. They asked for a Gloria to be added. Finally, at the suggestion of Ian Moore of the Cambridge Voices, I added the Ite Missa Est. I found the Ite Missa Est took on the same spirit as the Gloria.

REILLY: I have never heard an Ite Missa Est such as the one you have written. What was your inspiration for it?

RÜTTI: It was just a thank-you. That's the language I sought in the whole Ite Missa Est.

REILLY: It's like a thank-you from all of Creation.

RÜTTI: Yes.

REILLY: And it starts rather dolefully. It starts in the lower registers and then builds into the higher registers, and then all of sudden all of creation is breaking out in this uninhibited way. The thanks cannot be restrained. It is simply thrilling.

RÜTTI: It has to be.

REILLY: I was listening again last night to your *Nunc Dimittis*, and I couldn't keep a dry eye. I was profoundly moved. That piece is such a gem. You really have captured something very special.

RÜTTI: In the *Nunc Dimittis*, you realize this moment when this old man, Simeon, comes into the temple and sees all his visions are now fulfilled. And he sees this light that he predicted. The English choral sound represents this light. I think the BBC Symphony Chorus recorded it very well.

REILLY: The tenor singing Simeon in that piece, Christopher Hobkirk, did a magnificent job.

RÜTTI: If you only realized that he's the youngest of all of them! You would expect an old man to be singing this. But I think it works out.

REILLY: The voice fits and expresses it so movingly because the soul is always young.

RÜTTI: That's right. The soul is always young.

REILLY: Let's talk more specifically about your other works. I know that the *Missa Angelorum* has been recorded so beautifully by the BBC Symphony Chorus on the ASV label, but you have also written a *Stabat Mater*. Was that your tribute to Scarlatti?

RÜTTI: In a certain way, yes. But there is another reason I wrote this *Stabat Mater*. At a party in London, a lady came to me and told me about her friend's tragedy. This woman's friend had a son who was 17 years old. He fell ill for two weeks and then died. He had been a marvelous cellist. So this girlfriend of hers asked me to write a *Stabat Mater* commemorating this boy, called Adam. I wrote it for solo cello, because he was a cellist, and for mezzo soprano, because his mother was a mezzo soprano soloist singer, and for choirs and string quartet. There is no commercial recording of this yet.

REILLY: I'm also intrigued by your composition on the Song of Songs, which you have turned into the *Songs of Love*, a beautiful anniversary gift for your wife. That's the first time I paid attention to the character of your instrumental writing, because I thought the cello was used so beautifully throughout that piece. The whole composition is glorious.

RÜTTI: Thank you very much. My wife played the cello for some years and we did a lot of music together. That's why I chose the cello for this. I think the cello is a marvelous instrument to express feeling. That is why it worked so well to make the cello the main instrument in the *Stabat Mater*.

REILLY: Another recording is the *Veni Creator Spiritus*. This is an extraordinarily ambitious work for 40 voices in eight choirs. Can you tell us about it?

RÜTTI: I was asked by an English choir that always sings Thomas Tallis' *Spem in Alium* to write a new work to go with the Tallis. I took this risk because, when I was a boy, I thought that to sing 40 parts was simply impossible. But I found out that it really is possible. So I took the chance to write exactly in the same configuration as Tallis: eight choirs of five singers, and for the same group—always three men, two women, times eight. As they were positioned in an octagon, I also had a chance to let their sound turn around me from one place to the other, or to stand in one choir and go through different kinds of sound impressions so that, as a listener, you get the feeling of water playing over you.

REILLY: The recording is beautiful. But I envy you the chance of hearing this live, so that the spatial aspect could have its impact. It must be quite extraordinary.

RÜTTI: It really is. And especially the ending, when the whole church around you is singing in different rhythms. And then immediately, all the baritones come in with the plain chant, "Veni, Creator Spiritus", in long notes. This is very fascinating to listen to.

REILLY: It must have a physical impact.

RÜTTI: It really has. It was performed twice, once in Ely and once in London.

REILLY: Of the five recordings that are available here in the United States, which one would you tell someone coming to your music for the first time to listen to first.

RÜTTI: What would you suggest?

REILLY: That's not fair. I'm afraid I would simply tell them to take it in the order that I discovered your music, which would be, first, the *Missa Angelorum* on the ASV CD, with the *Magnum Mysterium* and the *Nunc Dimittis*. *Verena* is so exotic I might tell them to come to that later, maybe after the *Songs of Love*. The last thing I heard was the *Veni, Creator Spiritus*, which is just magnificent. Now that you've made me answer my own question, what do you think of the answer?

RÜTTI: I think that's a very good answer.

~

With his Requiem, Rütti has made a major contribution to the repertory. Naxos has issued a stunning recording of it with The Bach Choir, the Southern Sinfonia, soprano Olivia Robinson, and baritone Edward Price, under conductor David Hill. Ten years after our first interview, Rütti was kind enough to answer some questions and respond to my impressions of his new piece.

REILLY: This work seems to emphasize the devastating human distress at death, rather than any impending threat of divine retribution that death may bring. You focus on dealing with this deep disquiet and the effort to resolve it to the extent it can be resolved. Is this a fair statement?

RÜTTI: Yes, indeed.

REILLY: Do you consider this work specifically Catholic?

RÜTTI: Yes and no: yes, because the text is in Latin based on the Roman Catholic liturgy. No, as we shall all face the same God after death— Christians, Moslems, Hindus, Buddhists, etc.

REILLY: Except for the vocal solos, which are striking in their simplicity and beauty, there always seems to be more than one thing going on. The choral music expresses one thing, while the orchestra another. The double choir may be doing two different things from the soloists, and then orchestra becomes a fourth person in the proceedings. This makes things very rich expressively.

RÜTTI: The choreographic options of the double choir can enrich the emotional impact on the audience in a live performance. The beginning and the end are a cappella, and a cappella sung on a high standard is the most human and most intimate musical expression for me. In the Kyrie, in the Offertorium, and in parts of the In Paradisum, the orchestra goes naturally with the dramatic development of the singers. In the Sanctus and in the Communio the orchestra has its own function, Sanctus describing the ladder between heaven and earth (Jacob's dream), and Communio symbolizing the archaic river of death. At the beginning of In Paradisum the orchestra illustrates the slow pace in the procession when the coffin is carried from the church to the grave. In Agnus Dei the chamber group of single instruments intensifies the intimate atmosphere of this movement.

REILLY: Also, the work seems to be very tight thematically which, despite the wide range of expression you achieve, keeps the Requiem unified and the experience through which the listener goes continually coherent. One is never musically (or otherwise) lost.

RÜTTI: This was very much my intention.

REILLY: The real anguish seems to begin in the Kyrie, first with the simple but eloquent lament in the solo cello line, then the up rush of orchestral agitation, followed by the stabbing staccato string chords that then serve as an ostinato under the erupting choral cries of Kyrie. This is very powerful dramatically, enhanced by the conflicting rhythms, and never less than thoroughly musical in its means. I have never heard a Kyrie quite like this and think it is an original inspiration. From where did the inspiration for this stunning movement come?

RÜTTI: From the words "Lord have pity on us" (Kyrie Eleison) who have lost a beloved person and who will have to die one day, too. This fact is so existential that praying turns into screaming.

REILLY: And can screaming be prayer?

RÜTTI: Yes, of course: a prayer said in a desperate situation can grow into a scream as it does in the Kyrie after each verse.

REILLY: The lovely Agnus Dei, with only the two soloists and reduced orchestral forces, seems the most private utterance of the whole work. In parts of the Requiem, it is all of creation that participates. Here it is a single person, reflecting and praying. Did you use reduced forces to achieve this sense of intimacy?

RÜTTI: Agnus Dei means the Lamb of God which is sacrificed for us, and the lamb is one of the most innocent animals. The Agnus Dei of my Requiem is dedicated to two dear friends, both soloists of Cambridge Voices who sang most of the solos of my works in the '90s (*Songs of Love, Verena die Quelle, Veni Creator, Alma Redemptoris Mater*, etc.) and who died 2005/2006 much too early.

REILLY: In the Communio, the swirling strings again lift us upward into a peaceful realm. The restatement of the "Requiem aeternam" is now almost blissful. Hope is rewarded. In Paradisum, after the soloists sing the text over the strumming strings, there develops a wild, exultant dance at the mention of "Jerusalem", and during the repeat of "In paradisum", of the kind that implies that all of creation is carried away within it. I think you capture in this wild dance the hope that there is something like this awaiting us on the other side. Tears continue but they are now tears of joy.

RÜTTI: I can't possibly think of more appropriate words to describe this movement . . . After the last note there was, at both premieres (in Winchester and Douai Abbey), an impressively long silence before the audience started clapping, which ended up with a standing ovation. I've been told that this is a rare event for a premiere in the U.K.

REILLY: Would you care to say something about what you personally underwent in writing it? In the Requiem, it seems to me that faith is all the stronger for having survived that greatest, most malicious assault against it—the grave.

RÜTTI: Whenever I write music, I have to be completely involved and have to draw feelings from all my personal experiences. Writing about death was a very special challenge—the Bach Choir hardly dared to ask me for a Requiem—which affected me for more than a year: all my thoughts turned around this issue for quite a while. All the personal memories of my life are woven into this music. Thinking of Mozart and his commissioner for a Requiem, and myself being nearly 60 years old, I had sometimes kind of a queasy feeling. I am grateful how well it turned out.

REILLY: Congratulations. It is a masterpiece.

Recommended Recordings

Sacred Choral Music (includes *Missa Angelorum*, *O Magnum Mysterium*, etc.) BBC Symphony Chorus, Stephen Jackson (director), ASV 954 (out of print but not too hard to track down used on Amazon)

Songs of Love; *O Magnum Mysterium*; *Missa Angelorum*: Gloria, Veronica Henderson, Cambridge Voices, Ian Moore (director), Herald Records 183

Verena, die Quelle; Silja Walter et al., Cambridge Voices, Instrumental, Ian Moore (director), Herald Records 186

Veni Creator Spiritus, Ave Maria, Cambridge Voices, Ian Moore (director), Herald Records 210

Requiem, Olivia Robinson (soprano), Edward Price (baritone), the Bach Choir, Southern Sinfonia, David Hill (conductor) Naxos, 8.572317

~

Appendix:
A Note on Record Recommendations

Jens F. Laurson

Each chapter ends with a list of recordings recommended by the authors. One of the happy signs of the vitality of the music industry is the dramatic increase in available repertoire and different versions in formerly rare repertoire that has occurred since the first edition of *Surprised by Beauty* just 14 years ago.

The lazily repeated death of classical music is malarkey, but it is true that many aspects of the recorded music industry are changing at the same time, at different speeds: the format, the way of recording, the means of distribution, the consumer's listening habits and purchase patterns. Well-stocked retailers of classical music—the kind that would have the recordings we recommend—are all but gone. If you still know of one, enjoy and patronize it. For the rest, there are a slew of options available online. Online retailers of hard copies (often offering downloads as well), such as the behemoth Amazon and the superbly catalogued specialist ArkivMusic.com can't offer the joy of physical browsing, but thus offer nearly anything you could ask for. ArkivMusic's ArkivCD service of producing on-demand, licensed copies (including full liner notes) of out-of-print recordings further allows the collector to opt out of the deletion and reissue cycles of the bigger companies.

Very basic downloading needs are served by iTunes; streaming is covered by Spotify, Rhapsody, and similar services; but their classical selections are organized in slipshod fashion at best, and searches for specific items can be frustrating. The Naxos Music Library is an indispensable tool that caries hundreds of thousands of albums, from EMI/Warner's catalogue down to the most obscure labels, including many of the ones repeatedly recommended in these pages. For an annual fee (or free access through many universities) that entire catalogue is at one's finger tips, wherever one is, given Wi-Fi access or data connection. Combine that with the French service Qobuz, a downloading and streaming service tailored to the audiophile classical music listener that now is also serving an international audience, there is scarcely a recording that isn't available to you in the shake of a lamb's tail, assuming a robust Internet connection.

Still, the CD won't die out for another couple of decades. Not even LPs, enjoying a healthy comeback especially in audiophile circles, ever died out. The CD just won't be the most important medium anymore, and it might not for much longer determine what the natural length of an album is. All the same, we give all the recording information as it pertains to the releases of the physical products. The inveterate music collector or (legal!) downloader will be able to go from there.

The reason we (still) include CD numbers, despite their dwindling usefulness given constant catalogue deletions, reissues, and various ways to interpret and write these numbers, is that in some cases of hard-to-find albums, the CD number will survive in the vestiges of an online catalogue or on a producer's website. When one has to rely on search engines to find music, more information is better than less. Added confusion may arise through the recent sale of EMI/Warner Classics and Virgin Classical to Warner (via Universal): all EMI/Warner Classics productions and reissues will now bear the Warner Classics label, and all Virgin Classical productions and reissues the one of Erato. What used to be labeled Philips, meanwhile, now bears the Decca logo when reissued.

A hint for Amazon searches: searches work best with as little and as pertinent information as possible. When something doesn't show up on Amazon.com, try the same words on Amazon.de (mind the German spelling of transliterated names) or Amazon.co.uk, then take the ASIN code and put it back in the search function on the site where you want to make a purchase. Conforming to stereotype, the German site tends to be better organized, despite fewer users.

As boundaries between in print and out of print blur increasingly, with availability in electronic format, reissues of physical discs, et al., we have included some performances currently out of print if their interpretative quality merited it and if there was a reasonable likelihood of reissue or a healthy second-hand market for it. In those cases we give the essential information of the recordings and their last-known physical manifestation.

Here is a list of useful sites to build your library:

Hard copies dedicated to classical music:

ArkivMusic (arkivmusic.com) Naxos Direct (naxosdirect.com)

Streaming:

Spotify (spotify.com), Rhapsody (rhapsody.com), Amazon Cloud Player (amazon.com/cloudplayer)

Streaming dedicated to classical music:

Naxos Music Library (naxosmusiclibrary.com), Qobuz (qobuz.com), Classics Online HDLL (classicsonlinehd.com)

Downloads:

iTunes, Amazon MP3, HD Tracks (hdtracks.com)

Downloads dedicated to classical music:

The Classical Shop (www.theclassicalshop.net, run by Chandos, Digital Rights Management-free, high quality downloads, theclassicalshop.net), Classics Online (www.classicsonline) is run by Naxos and offers MP3 downloads. ClassicsOnline HD is the lossless/high-resolution version thereof (classicsonlinehd.com). Qobuz (www.qobuz.com) is the most satisfying, highest quality download and streaming experience for classical music, not the least for its excellent and ever improving metadata, but it is not available in the United States of yet.

At Hyperion (hyperion-records.co.uk), you can buy their own and Gimell recordings (often with steep discounts in their "Please, please, buy me" section!), and purchase downloads, including studio master quality.

Some of the most commonly encountered digital file formats:

AAC: lossy, compressed digital audio standard. Potentially higher quality successor to MP3. Includes .m4a, .mp4, .aac and similar files.

ALAC: Apple's lossless, compressed digital music standard.

MP3: lossy, compressed digital audio standard. Classical music should be reduced to no less than 256kbps or variable bitrate settings.

FLAC: lossless, compressed at varying rates, open-source, and easy to tag. The preferred digital format for quality music.

WMA: lossy, compressed Windows Media Audio; a lossless version (WMA Lossless) exists.

WAV: lossless, without compression—the digital file as it is found on a CD.

∽

Abbreviations

BBC British Broadcasting Corporation

CD Compact Disc

DG Deutsche Grammophon, a recording label (music publisher)

LP Long-Playing record

NO National Orchestra

NSO National Symphony Orchestra

OOP out of print

PO Philharmonic Orchestra

RSO Radio Symphony Orchestra

SACD Super Audio CD

SO Symphony Orchestra

An accompanying website for *Surprised by Beauty* has been set up at www.SurprisedByBeauty.org. Access from smartphones or tablets may be completed by scanning this QRcode: